IT WAS NOT A COMPLICATED LOCK ...
Raccoon's magic fingers reached inside with ease
and found the critical element, a simple spring-
loaded bolt. One flick and the bolt was open, the
door unlocked. But there was more, an alarm, and
something . . . a sort of trap. Clever. It might have
worked, too, if Raccoon were not just as clever.

When finally the door swung open, Bandit
waited, watching, listening intently, breathing
deeply of the incense-laden air that came drifting
into the alley. Nothing seemed amiss. It appeared
that he had defeated this clever combination of
security.

Very pleasing, very rewarding . . .

But, if his information was correct, the greater reward awaited him inside.

FADE TO BLACK

DARING ADVENTURES

☐ **SHADOWRUN #9: SHADOWPLAY by Nigel Fandley.** Sly is a veteran who has run more shadows than she cares to remember. Falcon is a kid who thinks he hears the call of magic and the voice of the Great Spirits. Together, they must face deadly confrontation between the world's most powerful corporations—one that could turn to all-out warfare, spilling out of the shadows and onto the streets themselves. (452283—$4.99)

☐ **SHADOWRUN #10: NIGHT'S PAWN by Tom Dowd.** Although Jason Chase was once able to shadowrun with the best, time has dulled his cybernetic edge. Now his past has come back to haunt him—to protect a young girl from the terrorists who want her dead, Chase must rely on his experience and whatever his body has left to give. And he needs everything he's got, as he comes face to face with an old enemy left for dead. (452380—$4.99)

☐ **SHADOWRUN #11: STRIPER ASSASSIN by Nyx Smith.** Death reigns under the full moon on the streets of Philadelphia when the deadly Asian assassin and kick-artist known as Striper descends on the City of Brotherly Love. (452542—$4.99)

☐ **SHADOWRUN #12: LONE WOLF by Nigel Findley.** Rick Larson thinks he knows the score when it comes to Seattle's newest conquerors—the gangs. But when the balance begins to shift unexpectedly, Larson finds himself not only on the wrong side of the fight but on the wrong side of the law as well. (452720—$4.99)

Prices slightly higher in Canada.

Buy them at your local bookstore or use this convenient coupon for ordering.

PENGUIN USA
P.O. Box 999 – Dept. #17109
Bergenfield, New Jersey 07621

Please send me the books I have checked above.
I am enclosing $_____ (please add $2.00 to cover postage and handling).
Send check or money order (no cash or C.O.D.'s) or charge by Mastercard or VISA (with a $15.00 minimum). Prices and numbers are subject to change without notice.

Card #_____ Exp. Date _____
Signature_____
Name_____
Address_____
City _____ State _____ Zip Code _____

For faster service when ordering by credit card call **1-800-253-6476**

Allow a minimum of 4-6 weeks for delivery. This offer is subject to change without notice.

SHADOWRUN

FADE TO BLACK

Nyx Smith

A ROC BOOK

ROC
Published by the Penguin Group
Penguin Books USA Inc., 375 Hudson Street,
New York, New York 10014, U.S.A.
Penguin Books Ltd, 27 Wrights Lane,
London W8 5TZ, England
Penguin Book Australia Ltd, Ringwood,
Victoria, Australia
Penguin Books Canada Ltd, 10 Alcorn Avenue,
Toronto, Ontario, Canada M4V 3B2
Penguin Books (N.Z.) Ltd, 182-190 Wairau Road,
Auckland 10, New Zealand

Penguin Books Ltd, Registered Offices:
Harmondsworth, Middlesex, England

First published by Roc, an imprint of Dutton Signet,
a division of Penguin Books USA Inc.

First Printing, April, 1994
10 9 8 7 6 5 4 3 2 1

Copyright © FASA Corporation, 1994
All rights reserved

Series Editor: Donna Ippolito
Cover: Romas Kukalis
Interior Art: Larry MacDougal

 REGISTERED TRADEMARK—MARCA REGISTRADA

Special thanks to readers Scott Lusby, Ted Swedalla, and Dave Zimmerman, John S. Francavillo and Fern R. Francavillo for productive and unique critiques of the original manuscript; RNC for keeping me honest and more; VD, AP & CR for language tips; JF who knows I'm alive, and TZ who might suspect; RB, SD, KM, FW, JAW and RZ, for, among other things, enthusiasm and support.

And, of course, Oscar, Madeline . . .
and Ginger Ann . . .

Long may you run.

Every sound shall end in silence,
but the silence never dies.

> —Samuel Miller Hageman

Freedom cannot be bought for nothing.

> —Lucius Annaeus Seneca
> (the Younger)

1

At 01:14 hours, everything went dark: the rooftop lounge, the aeropad outside it, every light, beacon, and security system guarding the top of the tower.

Gordon Ito slipped on a pair of light-intensifying shades, checked his watch, and motioned the uniformed security officers out of the rooftop lounge. Only his personal bodyguard remained.

The blackout was on Gordon's order, engineered via a diagnostic program running on the tower's operations mainframes—initialized in error, should anyone ever ask. The blackout had been a pre-condition for the meet about to occur. Gordon did not like the pre-conditions, but he liked far less the reasons that had compelled him to call for the meet.

Recent events now forced him to roll up one of his games, a covert op. The prospect displeased him, all the more so because ending the operation would require special action. All evidence of the op had to be spirited out of the competition's hands, that or eradicated, before any embarrassing disclosures could be made. This would cost Gordon a few more nuyen from his clandestine operating budget, but that meant nothing compared to the risks and the potential for disaster. The games he played always involved high stakes, commensurate risks, and ominous potentialities.

Now, the chopper came into view, a grayish specter cast in silhouette by the radiant illumination of the soaring towers of lower Manhattan. The rhythmic thumping of the craft's rotors resounded softly against the lounge's floor-to-ceiling windows. Gordon recognized the chopper's configuration, that of an A.C. Plutocrat, a big helo with luxury accommodations, usually reserved for the corporate elite.

Carefully, the chopper settled onto the aeropad outside.
"Iku beki desu," said Gordon's bodyguard.

Gordon shook his head. He would attend this meeting
alone, as arranged. He would not need the bodyguard's protection. That much he could be sure of. The person he was
about to meet considered him too valuable a customer—and
perhaps too dangerous a potential enemy—to let anything
unwise occur.

Outside, the whirling rotors slowed. Gordon stepped
forward. Double transparex doors snapped open before
him. As he walked out onto the aeropad toward the waiting chopper, the wind howled and tugged at his tailored
suit. The aeropad sat perched some two hundred and fifty
stories above the street, atop Tower Five of Fuchi Industrial Electronics' monument to economic imperialism.
The wind always raged up here, and it was always cold
and harsh. Gordon knew that better than most.

The door in the flank of the chopper swung open like
a pair of jaws, the lower section descending to provide a
set of steps. A man too tall and lean and gaunt to be anything but an elf descended the steps, his long black duster
flapping in the wind. Approaching Gordon, he extended
the hand-held probe of a weapons detector, checked the
device, then motioned at the Plutocrat with his chin.

"Está bien," the elf said. *"Entré"*

Gordon climbed the steps up into the narrow space directly behind the flight crew. Both pilot and copilot wore
helmets with full, nonreflective visors that masked their
features completely. The pair sat like statues, facing their
controls and the broad forward windshield of the chopper,
never once turning their heads.

The door to the rear cabin swung open. Gordon stepped
through. The elf followed.

The cabin was ostentatiously appointed in black and
red and gold—crushed velvet on the walls, full carpeting,
lush drapes. A pair of men in black mirrorshades and
sharply cut gray suits waited to the left and right of the
door. One was big enough to be an ork bodybuilder; the
other looked Asian and had the build of a sumo wrestler.
Impassive faces, casual postures. Nothing Gordon hadn't
expected. Nothing he'd not seen before.

The woman seated in the captain's-style chair at the
rear of the cabin looked Spanish. She had her sable hair

drawn back sleek and flat from her brow. The gold wire
lead of a datawire hung from her right temple. She wore
black visorshades, a sparkling red jacket adorned with
swirls of black, tight black slacks and gleaming scarlet
boots. Her name was Sarabande. She was *kuromaku*, a
fixer. She motioned casually to the chair facing her from
across a small oval table.

Gordon accepted the offer and sat down.

The subtle thumping of the chopper's rotors grew
louder as the craft ascended, swinging out over lower
Manhattan and across the Hudson, toward the blighted re-
gions of Jersey City and Newark. Gordon glanced at the
drape-covered windows and guessed at the chopper's
movements. He also checked his watch: 01:18 hours. The
upper stories of Tower Five would be back on-line by
now, fully illuminated and operational, while some slag
down in Facility Control would be wondering what the
hell had happened.

"Your business?" Sarabande said.

"On chip."

"Muy bien."

Gordon opened the synth-digit replacing the end of his
left pinkie and drew out an optical chip couched in a
wafer-thin plastic carrier. He held out the chip-carrier.
The elf examined it and passed it to his master. A compact console rose from the center of the table. Sarabande
slotted both carrier and chip into a receiving port.

Several minutes passed.

Gordon waited.

"A very complete dossier," Sarabande said finally.
"The work to be done will require extensive preparation
and will entail a high risk. What price will you pay?"

Gordon replied, "Whatever it takes."

"I will require an immediate advance of three hundred
thousand nuyen."

"I want multi-level back-up and I want the job expe-
dited."

"Five-hundred thousand nuyen."

"And you guarantee completion."

Sarabande showed no reaction. "The work will be attempted by competent parties taking all reasonable steps
to ensure success," she said. "That is your guarantee."

Gordon nodded. It would do.

2

The bar was little more than a counter jammed into an alley between a noodle bar and a booth selling bootleg simchips. The silver-eyed trog behind the counter had a set of snap-blades strapped to his right forearm and a Remington Roomsweeper holstered low on his left hip. He didn't take nothing but certified cred. The tequila he served was synthetic, lousy and cheap. So was the soykaf. For the price of a drink or a kaf, you got to elbow in between the other "clients" and stand there under the awning and watch and wait.

Rico ordered a shot and a kaf, then stood watching the throngs cramming the alley, shuffling by, sometimes near enough to brush his front.

This was Sector 3, Newark metroplex. Free zone. SIN-less territory. No passes, no badges, no restrictions. No System Identification Numbers. No straight suits. The people who lived here couldn't hack it in Manhattan because they had no corporate connection, no background, no SIN. No official anything.

Every slag and slitch had their program for survival. Those who walked the razor knew the rules of the game. Here in Sector 3, if you wanted to live, you carried metal, heavy metal, and you didn't make no secret about it. If you had implanted chrome, you made sure everybody knew it, or at least had reason to suspect it. If somebody met your gaze and held it, you didn't look away for even an instant, because an instant was all it took. This was 2055. There were slags walking the streets who would cut out your heart and feed it back to you before you could know you were dead.

Rico leaned back against the bar, one hand dangling near the butt-grip of the Ares Predator 2 slung from his hip. He kept his eyes moving. He didn't show anything with his face.

Before long, the silver-eyed trog leaned over the bar to say near Rico's ear, "The man's ready, chummer."

Rico nodded.

The alley led onto Ridge Street. Rico joined the jostling, hustling stream of people heading that way: chipheads, gangers, groupie wannabes, day laborers, cheap muscle, anonymous gutterpunks. Every slant of human, ork, elf, troll, whatever. They went dressed in cheap paper uniforms, studded synthleather, gleaming mylar, glistening spandex with chains and ribbons and glowing fiber optics. Face tats and body color. At least a few of these slags were here because they wanted in on the biz. Sector 3 might be impoverished, over-crowded, crime-ridden, the seventh and lowest circle of a decaying urban hell, but it was one of the best markets in the plex. Anything could be had for the right amount of nuyen. And some things could be had for practically nothing at all.

People said this part of the plex used to be lined with little two- and three-story houses, brownstones, tenement apartments. Nice places where nice families lived. Rico doubted it. The traces were few, and most of what people said usually amounted to pure drek, like what comes out the butt-end of a bull.

Sector 3 was all steel and crete now, rising up seven stories with retrofitted pipes and conduits, all of it scorched by the acid of the nightly rains and stained black and brown by soot and all the other garbage in the air. Garish neon signs glared from every direction, the night burned as bright as day. Stores and shops filled the ground floors of the buildings. Booths and stalls flanked the sidewalks. Ad stands lined the curbs, sound tracks reverberating, echoing. The street itself was divided in half by four- and five-story coffin hotels that ran from corner to corner, served by rusted metal gangways. Vehicle traffic was banned. You caught an autocab in the underground, or the subway, or you walked.

Rico paused to look as the staccato stammer of automatic weapons arose suddenly from the general direction of Abington Avenue East. He saw only the mass of people surrounding him, passive, stone-featured faces. He took his lead from the crowd and continued on. The rising shriek of belt-screamers alerted him to the DocWagon

High Threat Response team coming his way, bruising a path through the congested street. The two orks with the team ran interference. Rico shoved into the crowd at his left to get out of the way, then turned the corner onto Treadwell Street.

At mid-block was a four-story brownstone with a porch and steps sided by black metal railing—a remnant of the times long gone, if what people said was so.

On the brownstone's porch waited a pair of razorguys in studded blue synthleather. They were prime cutters, chromed to the max and willing to prove it. Rico knew that for a fact; he could have guessed it at a glance. The cutters held themselves like real gillettes, like they had whatever it might take to meet any challenge from the street. They watched Rico start up the steps with what looked like casual indifference, but as he reached the porch, they stepped into his path—no hesitation, no doubt about what they were doing.

Stop or fight, that was the message.

Sometimes a man had no choice but to fight. This wasn't one of those times. Watching the cutters' eyes, Rico said, "I'm expected."

"We know," one said quietly.

Moments passed. Rico waited. Custom had to be satisfied. Certain things had to be done in certain ways. You didn't just walk up the steps to the man's house and breeze right through the front door. Rico knew all that and had no objections. If nothing else, respect demanded it.

Another prime cutter came to the door, looked out, motioned Rico inside and led him through the house. No one asked to check his weapons or suggested he give them up. Respect worked both ways.

They came to an expansive atrium rising to a translucent roof four stories overhead. Colorful exotic birds flitted around, darting among the limbs of a few tall tress or watching from various perches high up on the walls. The birds alone were probably worth a fortune. The rest was like something you'd only see on the Museum Channel: bushes, flowering shrubs, beds of flowers. A waterfall. A path winding through it all like a stream of pure white liquid marble. Rico's escort paused at the entrance to the garden and motioned him ahead.

The path led to the center of the garden, a circular patio

surrounded by pillars set with busts of slags from ancient
history. Rico recognized two of them—the busts of Alex-
ander the Great and Julius Caesar. The man he was here
to see liked to talk about slags like that sometimes.

The man was known as Mr. Victor. He sat looking at
Rico from the round transparex table at the center of the
patio. He wore his thin black hair drawn back flat against
his head to the nape of his neck, where it blossomed into
the brief bushy extravagance of a ponytail. That was the
only extravagant aspect of his appearance. The rest was
severe, even grim. He wore a suit and tie of jet black, a
crisp white shirt, no jewelry of any kind. Based purely on
his appearance, he might have been an undertaker or a
corporate exec. In truth, he was far more.

He smiled in greeting and waved briefly at the other
transparex chair at the table. Rico nodded and moved to
sit. "How are you, my friend?" Mr. Victor said.

"I'm good."

"One of the best."

Rico shrugged.

"Only the truth, my friend." Mr. Victor smiled faintly,
then snapped his fingers sharply and gestured. The houseboy standing nearby brought a tray of coffee, which he
served in small china cups. Not kaf, not synthetic. The
real thing, its aroma rich and flavorful. Like wine, Rico
thought. Wine from the finest vineyards of France. It
smelled that good. The taste was indescribable.

Mr. Victor waved a hand and the houseboy went away.
"I regret that I had some other business to attend to this
evening," Mr. Victor said. "That is why I could not see
you immediately. Forgive the delay."

"*Seguro,*" Rico said, nodding definitely. "But you
don't owe me no explanations."

"I owe you much," Mr. Victor's expression turned so-
ber, then abruptly filled with disgust. "These slags I saw
before you came . . . they make me ill. They are not men,
you understand? They are like dogs. Eager for any scrap
I will feed them. There is nothing they would not do for
a price."

Quietly Rico said, "They have no honor."

Mr. Victor nodded. "No honor. No morals. No respect.
For themselves or anyone else. One job is the same as the
next. They would kill their own *madras* for enough

nuyen. They call themselves runners. 'Shadowrunners.' "
Mr. Victor turned his head aside and leaned over and
made as if to spit. "They step over the line into darkness,
these dogs. They are criminals. I would not deal with
them except that I have nothing against setting dogs on
other dogs. Criminals against other criminals. I hope you
do no hold that against me, my friend."

"I should judge what you do?" Rico replied. "I don't
think so."

"That is your right. Your right as a man. I respect you.
I respect your opinions. Tell me what you think."

Rico did not have to think long. "I think you got good
reasons for whatever you do. How you deal with criminals is your business. Not mine."

"You hold generous opinions, my friend."

"Maybe. Where it is due."

Mr. Victor sat still a few moments, looking off across
the garden. When he spoke, he kept his voice quiet, private. There was a sadness in his tone. "It's difficult to
find work for a man such as you. There is always work
in the shadows, but some jobs you will not accept. I am
always on the watch for the right kind of work, you know
this. Jobs appropriate not just for you, but for you and
your team of specialists."

Rico nodded.

"You have heard the name L. Kahn?"

"Seguro," Rico said, again nodding. The name L. Kahn
was well known throughout the Newark metroplex. With
that name came many rumors but few verifiable facts.
Rico understood the name to be a Johnson, like a cipher.
A name to be used where real names were never used. The
man behind the name "L. Kahn" was said to have juice,
connections, money. It was said that he had contracted for
some of the biggest jobs ever pulled in the Newark plex.

"I can arrange for you to meet this man."

Rico didn't doubt it. Mr. Victor had juice of his own.
"What's the deal?"

"My friend, I am a businessman," Mr. Victor said. "I
am the man in the middle. I bring prospective clients
together with specialists such as yourself. Whether the
client is a businessman like me or the party offering an
original contract is of no importance to my trade. You see
why I am reminding you of this?"

"You only got some of the details."

"*Si*, a few. L. Kahn asks to be connected with an experienced team possessing a broad range of capabilities. He has said that the contract is for a high-risk job, and that the pay will be commensurate to that risk. I am led to believe that the assignment comes from high places. A success here could add great weight to your reputation."

"What's the run involve?"

"It was described to me as being in the nature of a recovery job. Naturally, I thought you would approve."

"What's being recovered?"

"That is for L. Kahn to say."

"Could be a datasnatch."

"It could be many things, my friend."

"I heard L. Kahn contracted for the Winter Systems job."

"That is only rumor."

"Still . . ."

Winter Systems had contracts for police services in Manhattan, Union City, and other places around the New York-New Jersey megaplex. The Winter Systems *job* had involved the kidnapping and murder of several Winter Systems execs, and, incidentally, a conspiracy that had touched practically every major corp in the megaplex.

The murders were what mattered to Rico. He did not do killing for hire. Neither did he do kidnapping. Neither did anyone in his group. "You trust this slag L. Kahn?"

"Can anyone be trusted, my friend?"

"Some can. Some can't."

Mr. Victor paused for a few moments, then said, "As you well know, there are no guarantees in this life. I would say that L. Kahn can be trusted. More than some, less than others. I have not heard that L. Kahn has ever broken a contract or betrayed a trust. You must decide for yourself, my friend. Merely tell me now whether I should arrange a meet."

Rico thought about it, and nodded, *"Si."*

"Consider it done, my friend."

3

Thorvin didn't much notice the first few bangs and pings against the sides of the van. He was busy. He'd managed to pull the G-6 torque converter out of the drive train of an otherwise ruined Gaz-Willys Nomad. That was like finding gold. The G-6 was built like an anvil, durable as a slab of tempered steel. Finding one amid the wasted, ghost-haunted toxic graveyard of Newark's Sector 13 was a freaking miracle, though it didn't really surprise him. He'd been hunting through the crumbling projects and derelict tenements around the old airport for years. That was how he'd dug up the City of Linden no-parking sign, now hanging in his garage. And who saw any of those standing around anymore? Thorvin knew there were treasures here, minor mechanical marvels, gleaming motes of engineering majesty not apparent, much less comprehensible to the ordinary eye. He just hadn't expected to stumble over, of all things, a G-6 torquer. The prizes to be had in this sector ran heavily on the side of wafer-guided electronics, appliances, household drek.

Something clanged loudly against the side of the van. With that rose a howling that sounded decidedly unnatural.

Thorvin paused and looked up.

When the van starting rocking back and forth like a boat turned crossways to a heaving sea—accompanied by a storm of clanging and banging—he dropped his chrome ratchet and can of lubricant and ran, tool belts clanking, to the front of the van, hopping over toolcases, a stripped-down engine block, an eviscerated Suzuki Aurora, a partly disassembled Kaydee A.C. condenser twinpak, hubcaps, nuts and bolts, an antique C.R.T., and an old General Products multifuel power generator, *like a freaking kangaroo*!

The ghoulies had come a-calling.

Thorvin leaped up into the driver's seat and slapped the black lead from the driver's console into the datajack at the side of his neck. His vision blanked, then returned. The van's external vid-pickups replaced his eyes and ears. The van had become his body.

The ghoulies were there all right, all around him. Pounding on his armor-reinforced, metal-alloy flanks. Using fists, bricks, and metal bars. Skeletal jaws flapping, fingernails like talons, clothes hanging in rags, they looked like rotting corpses just emerged from their worm-infested holes. And Thorvin knew what they wanted. They liked their meat raw. Human was best, decayed and rotting even better, but in a pinch, if enough of them got together, they'd go for anything, even something alive. Even a freaking *dwarf*!

Just the thought of those slimy, decaying monstrosities clawing at his metal-alloy skin sent chills up his rear doors. Back. Whatever.

No effing way they'd get inside.

He had a Magnum V-12 850-horsepower blower-driven petrochem heart. For blood he had Super-98 octane with injected nitrous oxide. He set his power plant to roaring and slammed his tranny into drive. His rear wheels churned, screaming, sending up a billowing storm cloud of smoke, seizing the road and hurling him ahead.

The gleaming red graphic indicators overlaying his external view went wild. Velocity shot toward 200 kph. Engine revs pegged max. Targeting indicators guided by his onboard combat comp streaked left and right, winking and flashing. A raucous symphony of electronic warning tones, beeps, and bleeps filled the back of his head, his real head, somewhere inside . . . not quite forgotten.

Things bounced off his van-body, banged and slammed and then fell away. Building debris, derelict cars, assorted junk, garbage, and other things, not junk or garbage. Things that squished and splatted. Like bodies. There must be *a whole tribe of the freaking zombie cannibals hanging around,* closing in from all sides. That's what he got for treasure-hunting so near the freaking cemeteries.

Suddenly, one stood in the road directly in front of him, a shambling monstrosity with spindly limbs hefting what looked like a freaking shoulder-mounted Panther assault cannon.

Thorvin's own nervous system pegged max.

The M-134 minigun in the pod on his roof popped up and stammered rapid-fire. The ghoulie in the road jerked and spun, then slammed against the crash-grille guarding Thorvin's front end.

An ocean of red-tinted slime splashed across Thorvin's external sensors. Mentally he flinched. The van swerved and pitched, bounding up then slamming down. Things crashed. Fortunately, his all-terrain General Products F-6900 self-healing tires could really take a pounding. He switched on his forward-looking infrared radar and found himself hurtling straight into a building wall.

Panic time.

He cut his wheels right, roared up an alley, smashed through a pair of cyclone fences, and shot out onto a broad open space like a weed-infested parking field.

Bad move.

A half-dozen beat-up, smashed-out petrochem heaps were wheeling around the crumbling, debris-strewn concrete. As many as a dozen motorcycles whizzed back and forth. Every driver and every passenger held some kind of weapon—handguns, rifles, shotguns, SMGs. Thorvin recognized the colors even as the thundering barrage of gunfire assaulted his audio pickups. He'd steered himself right into a freaking *war*! Chiller-thrillers versus a go-gogang, the Toxic Marauders versus the Rahway Blades.

Great. Freaking great.

A cycle came screaming toward him. Bullets pinged and panged rapid-fire off his front grille. Winking red targeting markers homed in on the cycle. Thorvin opened up with his minigun and hurled himself into a skidding, tire-screaming half-circle.

The cycle exploded.

Thorvin fired himself back down the alley. A storm of rocks, bricks, chunks of metal, and other junk crashed against his sides and roof as he roared out onto the street. Ghoulies again. Just freaking great. He set his power plant to whining, and went squealing around the very next corner, almost, but not quite, hopping up onto two wheels.

That was Peerless ADH antishock stabilizers for you.
Nice. Very nice.

"Shank."

What was that? Somebody saying his name? He didn't
know who or why and he didn't really care, anyway. He
ignored it.

"Shank!"

"Dammit, Shank, *wake up*!"

Somebody grabbed his shoulder and started shaking it
hard. He couldn't just ignore it. He guessed who was
probably doing the shaking and realized that ignoring her
would be useless. Evonne was usually okay, chill enough
to live with. But when she got something stuck up her
butt, bad enough to risk waking him up, she could get
him so mad that beating her brains out, or worse, almost
seemed like a good idea.

Luckily for her, he had nothing to prove. Evonne
needed what little brains she had.

The cursing got louder. Hands gripped his arms and began pulling him up, making him sit up. Water splashed
into his face, maybe half a liter. It was kind of refreshing,
really. He rubbed his eyes, stretched his arms and
yawned, and looked around.

The amber-tinted lamp by the bedside cast a glow
through the room that showed Shank all he needed to see.
He was in his bedroom, which was simply furnished,
sheathed in synthfurs and deeply carpeted. Evonne and
her sister Kefee stood beside the bed. Evonne looked angry, Kefee upset. None of that was so unusual that Shank
paid more than passing notice.

What he really noticed, and not for the first time, was
what a hot-looking biff Evonne was—built to last, right
down to her girlish set of fangs. A real turn-on, especially
when she got sleazy, and even more so when she got mad.
Her sister Kefee looked kind of frail, more like a human
biff, not very enticing.

"They're back!" Evonne growled.

Shank ran a hand back over his hair, scratched behind
his right ear. "Who?"

"The *bangers*!" Evonne growled, more forcefully than
before, staring at him like he should just automatically

know what she was talking about. "They're stuffing Chak! Right in the alley!"

Stuffing Chak . . .?

Evonne thrust a hand up and out to her left, toward the alley. Kefee just looked scared and said, "Shank, *please*!"

Right.

Shank shook himself awake. Everybody had obviously decided that the problem, Chak getting stuffed, beaten, or whatever, was something Shank ought to handle. It was probably Evonne's idea. No point in arguing. She was probably right. Shank had kind of inherited Kefee and her kids when Kefee's man got wasted in a Bronx firefight. Chak, her oldest kid, was still pretty young, only nine or ten, and, ork or not, that didn't make him much of a fighter. Not even against ordinary humans. Maybe one-on-one, but not against a whole gang. A gang would call for some serious head-banging.

Shank heaved himself to his feet and headed for the door. The women stepped quickly out of his way—and good thing, too. It looked like he had a fight coming on. This soon after being woken up, he had no trouble getting into the mood.

The passageway outside was jammed, mostly with kids and more women. This week most of the adult males from Shank's hall, the ones any good in a fight, were in the Roselle Park jail, off Raritan Road. Something to do with stuffing a bunch of mafiosi. The maf shoulda learned by now to keep their butts the hell outta Port Sector.

"Coming through," Shank grumbled.

People got outta his way, and those who didn't got bumped. They were all jamming up toward the end of the hall to peer around the corner and up the stairs toward the alley. A helluva lot of good that did. Shank waded through the final meter of bodies, then turned the corner and plodded up the stairs two at a time. The steel trap door at alley-level stood open. Shank trod right on through.

The group was right there, barely three meters away, clearly visible against the dusky gray of a moonless night. Chak looked to be the one on the ground taking all the punches and kicks. None of the gangers seemed to notice as Shank stepped up behind them. That made things pretty fragging easy. He reached out for the nearest two and banged their heads together. They dropped bonelessly to the ground. The other gangers noticed him then. Mostly they just looked at him and stared. And gaped. Very scary. Shank grabbed the nearest one by the arm, jerked him off his feet, swung him around, and then slammed him into the building wall on the right. That one fell, too. Not very tough, these bangers. Not very fast either, all things considered. And not very smart.

One lifted a knife toward Shank's nose, and snarled, "Skin you alive!"

Shank grabbed the wrist behind the knife, then jerked the whole arm into the air, lifting the ganger right off his feet. The slag flailed with his free arm, slapping, punching, and even tried kicking. Shank snorted. What a joke. One punch to the face and the ganger slumped. Shank let him fall.

That left three of the gangers standing. One pulled a gun and pointed it directly at Shank's face, which was really a pretty stupid thing to do. If you wanted to shoot an ork, you aimed someplace that might hurt, not at his rock-hard skull. Shank ducked and reached out and the gun went off. He felt a wave of heat rush past his left ear, but that was it. A second shot went off, but by then Shank had his hand wrapped around the barrel of the gun. Which was all the hold he needed. He jerked the gun free, then grabbed the ganger by his jacket collar.

"Bye-bye," he said, and heaved the slag against a convenient wall, the wall on the left, just to keep things even. The ganger slumped to the ground the same way the others did, like a sack of raw meat.

And that left only two still standing.

That pair began backing away, looking scared. Shank pointed the gun, a Colt Manhunter, something particularly appropriate for an ork to use, and said, "Move again an' you're dead."

The two gangers froze.

By then, Chak was on his feet and looking back and forth like he didn't know what to do, which probably he didn't. The kid's face was streaked with blood and looked kinda swollen, but it'd take more than that to put him out. Never mind who he had for a mother, Chak was husky for his age and he had balls. *Cojones,* some would say. That translated into staying power.

Shank resisted a smile. To tell the truth, he liked the kid. Chak was always asking about his tattoos and the dust-ups he'd been in with the Dragon Regiment and other merc units down in Aztlan and other places. It was hard to resist naked admiration.

"You all right?" Shank asked.

Chak nodded, breathing hard, maybe a little too hard to speak clearly.

"Get a rope and a knife."

"Kay . . ."

Chak nodded and hustled off, but was back in a minute or so. Evonne and her sister and half the crowd from the hallway below followed Chak up the stairs. Shank motioned for the crowd to stay put. He had a gun in his hand and work that needed his attention. He wasn't about to put up with any squawking or unwelcome questions or suggestions. At a wave, Chak brought the knife and rope.

"Tie 'em," Shank told him. "Them two first."

Shank motioned at the pair of gangers still standing. Chak set to work binding their wrists behind their backs, and none too gently. Shank didn't care about that. Those fragging gangers deserved it. That and worse. What worried him was what to do next.

Executing prisoners wasn't his style. He'd had a belly-ful of that down in fragging Azzie-land. He'd once thought he'd seen it all, but that was nothing compared to what butchers the Aztlan troopers could be. He'd have none of that here. What were his options? He could call the cops, but they couldn't give a slot about some minor-ass gang problem, not here in Sector 12. And he couldn't just let the gangers loose. By sundown tomorrow, they'd be hot on the butts of the kids from his hall, and Chak especially. Worse, he'd never hear the end of it. Evonne would see to that. He had to do something along the lines of making a permanent fix.

But what?

Goddamn his thick skull, anyway. If he'd been born any dumber, he'd be dangerous just taking a crap. And some of the slags in his old regiment used to rag him about that, too.

Evonne said, "Shank—"

"Can it."

She did.

Right then, something with about a billion-candlepower's worth of headlights, driving lights, fog lights, off-road lights, and side- and roof-mounted spotlights, pulled into the end of the alley and came rolling straight toward him. Shank realized what was behind all the damn lights just about the time the blinding brilliance of it all forced his eyes shut.

The thing rumbled like a GMC Banshee winding up for an attack run. It was about as close to a real panzer as anyone could get in the Newark plex without the local militia calling out the helicopter gunships. This one had started out as a shorty Landrover, and still resembled a basic stock model, but just about every part had been replaced, upgraded, or refitted. The custom cargo cover on the roof concealed a pair of weapons pods, plus there were gunports all around and other features, custom features.

Rolling to a halt, lights going out, the van became a ghost, dark and grim, blending with the cool gray of the night.

Shank wasn't scared drekless, or even a little, because he'd helped the halfer now hopping out of the van with some of the van's custom installations.

"Hoi, fang face."

"Horn head."

Who said orks and dwarfs couldn't be chummers? Thorvin might be squat and ugly and kinda single-minded at times, but he was as tough as brick and loyal as nightfall. In Shank's book, that made for a first-rate chum.

"What's with the garbage?" Thorvin asked, nodding at the gangers, toolbelt clanking as he strode out in front of the van.

"They're slotting me off."

"That's a freaking surprise. You gonna ice 'em?"

"Thinking about it. What're you doing?"

"Whaddya think? I'm picking you up."

"Oh yeah?"

"We got a meet."

That sounded good. It meant their top gun had finally got them some biz, or at least some kinda offer, and about fragging time, too. Money didn't go far in the plex, never far enough. Especially when you had another slag's wife and kids to worry about. "Where and when?"

"We gotta pick up the man and the deck. Sector 3. Soon as you put on some clothes."

Clothes. Right. "Been over to Sector 13 lately?"

"That's a freaking stupid question."

"Ghouls still hanging there?"

"That's another freaking stupid question."

"Let's dump the garbage there."

Thorvin frowned, looked at the gangers, then back at Shank.

"Load 'em up," he said.

4

The booth was small, just big enough for one person. Brown synthwood paneled the walls. Piper closed the door, then turned and knelt on the cushioned foot of the narrow kneeling bench.

She spent a few moments composing herself, pressed her hair back behind her ears, then slipped the end of a credstick into the chrome-edged port on the side of the bench.

The vidscreen before her came to life. "A New Day" slowly resolved in bold letters at the center of the screen, then faded. The "day" began with a boiling orange-red sun rising out of a pristine sea, waters fresh and sparkling, an ocean teeming with fish and thousands of other forms of life. The sun assumed a golden tint as it rose higher into the crystal-clear blue sky, and hundreds of thousands of birds flew up over the horizon to wheel in enormous flocks across the glittering ocean.

Music, till then only a distant murmur, arose full and majestic, vibrant and alive, celebrating the glory of life in all its multitudinous forms.

The voice of John Donne IX, a direct descendant of the Saint, and leader of the Church of the Whole Earth, arose with the music, beginning with a direct quote from Holy Sonnet Number 10: "One short sleep past, we wake eternally ... and death shall be no more ... Blessed be the Recreator ... the living earth ... and the eternal cycle of life, recycling without end ...

"Amen ..."

In time, the sermon concluded and the music softened. The scenes of a lush and beautiful world continued, sweeping from one view to the next. Piper lowered her eyes and began to speak.

All the world's problems, as she saw it, stemmed from

one thing: greed. People wanted. They were never content with what they had. So titanic corporations sucked resources from the Earth and left only toxic wastes behind. So ordinary people ignored the evidence of their senses, screaming at them from every direction, and worked only to improve their station, their jobs, their material possessions. No one cared about the planet, the poisons in the air, food, and water. Doing anything about that would waste valuable resources, like money, and time, precious time. The power mongers at the top of the food chain had convinced everyone of that. They used the media to exploit people's weaknesses. They saw to it that the common working people would feel too weighed down by the struggle of daily living and the desire to always have *more, more, more*! rather than worry about mere ecology.

People were weak. Few had the means to combat the tyrants of economic politics; fewer still had the will, the strength of spirit. Too many had been crushed and ground into dust by the steel and concrete jackboot of the megacorporations.

Something had to be done. The megacorps had to be stripped of their power and pared down to size. People had to be given back control over their own lives and the life of the world in which they lived—*the very planet all metahumanity depended on for survival* !

Tears streamed down her face as finally Piper shouted, pounding on the arm rests of the kneeling bench with her gloved fists.

It left her feeling cleansed, strengthened, empowered.

She was doing all she could. Almost every night. She only prayed that, in the end, her efforts, combined with that of many hundreds, even thousands, would be enough to save the ravaged Earth.

When she stepped from the booth, the narrow church was nearly deserted. The sunset service had ended some time ago. Only a few stragglers still sat in pews facing the altar and, above it, the enormous vid display of the Whole Earth—white clouds, blue ocean, and brown soil—ringed by the green yin-yang arrows, cycling eternally, representing the cyclical nature of life. Piper brought her fingertips together, forming the Globe with her hands, then bowed and turned to go.

A priest in robes of the four cardinal colors—white,

blue, brown and green—awaited her at the rear of the Church. He was known as Father John, as were all priests of the Whole Earth Church. Piper did not know his real name, but that did not matter. He formed the Globe and bowed as she approached. She did likewise.

"There's a special meeting tonight," Father John said, quietly. "Our brothers ask that you attend."

This came as no surprise.

Practically anyone with any skills at all would be continually in demand somewhere in the Newark plex. Newark had an excess of per diem meat. "Excess people," they were called. The special meeting to which Father John referred would undoubtedly be a meeting of the group known as Ground Wave, the local cell of the Green 4800, an organization of international scope. Ground Wave had need for deckers, ones with the proper perspective. Ones with Piper's degree of experience and skill were needed desperately.

Piper bowed, and said, "I'm sorry, Father. Please excuse me. I cannot attend this evening."

"I trust you've not had a change of heart."

"Of course not." The idea was almost insulting. "I have other obligations."

"What other obligation is there but to the restoration of the Whole Earth?"

That was something Piper could not argue, for Father John would not understand. Life came with many obligations. One might be paramount, but the others could not simply be ignored. She needed money, for instance, if only to eat, if only so she might continue to further the cause. "This is very difficult," Piper said, again bowing. "You're right, of course. I wish I could explain further. It is my fault. Completely my fault. Please excuse me."

Father John hesitated, then nodded. "I presume we may count on you again in the future?"

"Of course." Piper bowed, trying to conceal her expression, her struggle to suppress her annoyance. Father John seemed intent tonight on irking her or on afflicting her with guilt. Of course he could count on her in the future. She'd been working with Ground Wave for more than a year. Piper had more experience with anticorporate activity than anybody in the group.

Unfortunately, she was used to this kind of talk. Used

to people speaking presumptuously and rudely. Used to
people with immensely egocentric personalities. People
with the viewpoint that whatever happened to be right for
them must be right for everyone. She attended frequent
cha-no-yu, the tea ceremony, if only to remind herself
that some people, anyway, were at least basically civilized.

"*Dozo, gomen kudasai,*" Piper said, excusing herself,
bowing and forming the Globe. "I must go now, Father.
Good evening."

Father John bowed and formed the Globe. "Good
night."

The street outside was busy. A veritable river of people
flowed steadily along the sidewalk. Traffic filled the narrow roadway, barely moving at a crawl. Garish neon and
laser adverts in Japanese and a dozen other Asian languages climbed the fronts of buildings as high as nine or
ten stories. Piper made her way up the block and joined
the crowd waiting at the corner with Custer Avenue.

Abruptly, a man wearing the signature red and black
suit jacket of the Honjowara yakuza stepped off the curb
and into the road, blowing a shrill blast on a whistle
while extending his arms out fully to both sides. Traffic
halted. Piper moved with the crowd that flowed out and
across the street. A number of people loudly praised the
Honjowara-*gumi* as they passed the man in the red and
black jacket.

"*Domo arigato,*" the man said politely, bowing in response to each laudatory remark.

Yakuza, Piper knew, might be vicious gangsters, but
they were also very conscious of their public image. The
Honjowara-*gumi* had made this part of Sector 6, Little
Asia, centered around Bergen Street, one of the safest
hoods in the plex. They performed many public services
and would allow no one to abuse their citizens. Gangs
and other criminal elements entered the district at their
peril.

Piper continued up the next block toward Hawthorne,
but only as far as the intricately carved synthwood door
of the Holy Savior Buddhist temple.

As she turned toward that door, another man in red and
black abruptly stepped up beside her, tugged the door

open for her, and bowed, saying, *"Dozo . . . Allow me . . ."*

Piper bowed to the man. *"Domo arigato gozaimasu."*

As she stepped through, the man slipped past her, tugged the inner door open, and bowed, saying, *"Dozo."*

"Domo arigato." Piper bowed and stepped inside.

An acolyte of the temple escorted her to a small chamber where a Buddhist priest waited. For a donation of ten nuyen, the priest led her in a brief prayer ritual and then gave her a quick lecture on the Buddha nature as exemplified by Christ, a lecture she did not really want to hear but felt obligated to endure. She had trouble with Buddhist teachings, even those of the fairly innovative sects of the Newark metroplex. She didn't really believe in any mystical enlightenment—that was her problem. Most people she had encountered in her life seemed all but oblivious to even the most basic truths of their everyday routine. To suppose that even a major event like death would shock them into some form of "enlightened" consciousness required a leap of faith that was beyond her.

Still, this was a part of the sorrow of existence. The teachings of Buddhism and the Whole Earth Church had much in common, most notably the emphases on the cyclical nature of life. Piper felt obliged to seek her own enlightenment even if she did not entirely believe in the concept. Perhaps belief could not truly come until enlightenment was achieved.

When the lecture ended, she went back outside, then through the sliding transparex doors into the Shinto shrine next door. This visit cost her twenty nuyen. Shinto priests were very worldly and always more expensive than their Buddhist counterparts. The priest went through all the usual routines, moaning, chanting, caterwauling, shaking rattles and waving wands, ringing bells and gongs and blowing whistles.

For her money, Piper had evil influences chased away and gained the assurance that the local kami would look favorably upon her. She sometimes found it difficult to believe that any real kami would inhabit a plex like Newark, but even that was easier to accept than the lectures of the Buddhists.

Back on the street again, she walked down to Watson Avenue. Rico waited there.

"You okay, chica?" he said, looking past her right.

"Yes." Piper nodded. "Fine." She slipped a hand onto his shoulder and kissed his cheek. Any greater display of affection would not have been appropriate. Rico preferred to keep his eyes and mind on his surroundings.

"Take care of your duty okay?" he said, glancing down the side street toward Chadwick.

"Yes," Piper said, nodding.

"How's your axe?"

He meant her cyberdeck, not her guitar. Piper didn't have a guitar and, in fact, had little interest in music. Certain of her ancestors had reputedly been great music-lovers, among other things, and that had been enough to turn her off music for good. "I had a roach in the node."

Rico frowned, glancing at her. "What?"

"A geometrically replicating virus."

"Yeah?"

Piper hesitated, gazing at Rico, trying to read his sphinx-like expression, then took a deep breath and said, "Roaches duplicate everything in memory, themselves included, till there's no more room left. This one got into my operating code and . . . it started laying eggs. That's why I kept getting locked out. Memory was jammed. I couldn't power up. I had to jack in with another deck and go over everything with a microscanner."

Rico turned to look up toward Hunterdon Street. "Guess that's why it took so long."

"Well, yes."

Most of a week, in fact. That wasn't long, considering she'd had more than a thousand megapulses worth of onboard code to review, not to mention forty gigapulses of off-line storage. In fact, with only a couple of smartframes to help her, it was a miracle she'd finished any time this year.

"But you got it fixed, right?"

"Yes, it's fine, *jefe*."

Rico nodded, but then three men in red and black jackets emerged from the crowd around them and came to a stop facing them. One bowed, glancing at Rico, then asked Piper in rapid Japanese, "Excuse me, is this person troubling you?"

Piper blinked. The question seemed remarkably presumptuous and offensive until Piper realized that Rico was the only Hispanic-looking person—the only non-Asian, in fact—that she'd seen for blocks. The heavy automatic pistol holstered at his hip didn't do much to help matters. Piper bowed, very briefly, saying in rapid Japanese, "Please excuse me. This is my personal guard, assigned by my employer. Thank you for your concern."

"Ah, I understand." The man bowed. "Excuse us for intruding."

"Please think nothing of it."

The three men moved off. Rico, watching intently, said, "What was all that?"

"Honjowara clan is busy today. We should go."

"No guano."

At the corner they took the stairway to the underground. A narrow corridor flanked by small shops and booths led past the entrances to the Bergen Street subway, rumbling like thunder and rank with oily smells, then on past the entrance to a parking garage, and then on to the truck and taxi lanes near the underground transitway. The familiar, battered gray and black Landrover van waited right there, along with Thorvin and Shank.

They had a meet to get to.

5

At the heart of the beast . . .

Market Street, Sector 1.

The burnt-out ruin of the old county court building stood opposite the shining twelve-story tower occupied by Omni Police Services and associated corporate agencies. Everywhere Rico turned his eyes, the charred, the gutted, and the wasted mingled with the bright and glittery. An addict who'd probably traded his legs, one arm, one eye, and an ear for highs "Better Than Life" lay sprawled on the sidewalk in a simchip-induced coma, while trippers in glinting neo-monochrome and flashing crystal jewels sashayed by. Black limos and gangers riding on whining plastic choppers shared the roadway, roaring past the stripped-down wreck of an old GMC stepvan and other derelicts rusting in the gutters.

Overhead, a helo with winking lights thumped through the hazy, smog-veiled darkness.

Devil take it.

Time to focus, Rico told himself. The rest of the team was in position, and he was as ready as he would ever be. Rico didn't like getting Piper into something like this, didn't even like her being on the street, where anything could happen, but she'd insisted. She demanded to be in the game personally, in the flesh, whenever she might do some good. Rico admired courage like that, especially in a woman. But it didn't stop him worrying.

He wore a long black duster to cover the heavy auto holstered at his hip and the extra magazines on his belt. He drew a black bandanna up from his neck to cover his face as far as the bridge of his nose, flipped up the duster's collars.

The club was just around the corner on the tail-end of Springfield Avenue. Running across the gleaming black

front of the place in subdued gold lettering was the word *Chimpira*. That was Japanese. A joke. Piper had explained that the word came from other words meaning "flimsy gold". Cheap punks. A slick and mean veneer, but take away the clothes and the attitude, and nothing remained. What made it a joke was that all the cheap punks who used the main floor were nothing but a cover.

Trolls guarded the main entrance, and a small crowd of yakuza cutters kept watch on the trolls. The presence of the yak muscle meant that the big boys, the real powers in the Newark plex, the ones who had named the club, must be meeting on the top floor. It also indicated that one or more of the vehicles lining the curbs or the windows in the buildings along the street would be occupied by U.C.A.S. feds: F.B.I., Secret Service, whatever. Surveillance teams. Techs and vidcams. Watching the comings and goings. The feds had been trying for years to get at the heart of the organizations running the plex. It was a losing game.

Rico walked to the black tunnel of the main entrance. The razorguys standing around, including the trolls, all wore something obscuring their faces: shades, scarves, bandannas, a variety of Halloween and theatrical masks, some glowing in the dark. That was the style. You didn't go to Chimpira with a naked face.

In the dark shade of the entrance stood a slag wearing a broad-brimmed hat, black trench, and a mask like a cartoon mummy. The odd pins and devices stuck to the lapels of the slag's trench coat had nothing to do with Chimpira-style, or any other kind of style. Unless it was arcane-style.

Surveillance mage.

As Rico approached, one of the trolls put out a hand nearly the size of a cinder block, and growled, "Whaddya want?"

"Got biz."

"You a cop?"

"Frag that."

"What's the biz?"

"Private."

The mage nodded.

"Twenty cred."

Rico handed over a certified credstick.

The troll motioned him past. "Have a great effin'
night."

Angst-rap thundered through the entrance tunnel. Trids
along both walls advertised pachinko, simsense, whores,
and anything else a body might crave. Money talked,
guano walked. At the end of the tunnel waited a pair of
biffs wearing only skimpy gold chains over their glossy
sable skin. They smiled and cooed hello as Rico stepped
through the sliding black doors into the club's interior.

"Welcome to Chimpira," flashed a laser display. "Visit
our Simchip Suite for the Ultimate in Simmertainment!"

The music only got louder. Lights flickered and
flashed. Fractal displays on the walls sparkled with kalei-
doscopic color. And this was just the front room, like a
lobby. A hexagonal counter occupied the center of the
space. The biffs there had hair of flaring incandescent
light, changing from red to yellow and green and shaped
like short, stubby worms crawling all over their heads.

Five passages like enormous, grotty tubes led from the
room in five different directions. Rico took the one all the
way to the right. The walls of the passage throbbed with
light, like a vein. Scarlet fog flowed around Rico's legs.

At the end of the passage waited a white biff wearing
silvery spandex and fingerless gloves and boots to match.
Silver-studded bands ringed her ankles, waist, wrists, and
neck. Her eyes were like violet pits, infinite; her expression like stone, emotionless. Her hair looked like white
fuzz, shorn practically to the scalp. She had a fine figure,
slim but shapely and obviously well-conditioned. Rico
paid her figure little attention. Too dangerous.

She was called Ravage. Rico had seen her around, had
heard talk about her. She walked the razor: bodyguard,
courier, collection service. She was supposed to be teflon
slick, fast enough to blur. People said she didn't bother
with mere guns because she had all she needed under her
skin. Boosted reflexes, skillwires, cyberspurs, maybe an
implanted pistol. How much damage could this lithe body
actually do? Rico wished he had more than just guesses.

If she had a gun with her tonight it didn't show.

She stood with feet planted and spread wide, her arms
at her sides, her head erect, alert. Violet pits aimed right
at him.

Rico paused about two steps away.

"You solo?" Ravage said.

"Your guess."

"My guess is you're obsolete, old man."

There was nothing in the voice, no malice, not even a shade of menace. It didn't matter. What she said didn't matter. Not from a woman, it didn't. A woman who talked like her didn't merit respect, or anything but a straight estimation of the dangers she might pose. Rico lowered his eyes to the modest prominence of her breasts, then to the juncture of her legs. That was his reply. Ravage didn't seem to notice.

"Road kill," she said.

Rico forced a grin. "Anytime, *muchacha*."

"Soon as I'm free."

She turned her back and started walking like Rico didn't worry her at all. The studded bands around her body caught Rico's eyes. Some of those studs could be optical pickups. Ravage might well have a 360-degree cyberview of the world. Chipped to the max and fluid as a snake. Nothing would surprise him.

She led him onto a low balcony overlooking the club's main floor. Ranged along the right were softly backlit alcoves outlined in glaring neon. Ravage paused at the fifth one down, and Rico got his first look at L. Kahn.

He sat behind an oval table, on a semicircular bench seat that filled the rear of the alcove. The alcove's subdued lighting cast his face and front in shadows, but only until Rico's Jikku Shadowhunter eyes adjusted. Low-light augmentation with glare compensation pulled L. Kahn's sculptured features out of the shade. He looked Amerind, with maybe a touch of Black-Af blood. A thick black wave of hair dangled down over one side of his forehead. Skinny braids hung in front of his ears. He had heavy brows, a substantial nose, and a broad, full-lipped mouth. His medium brown suit looked pure Armanté. The jacket's thin collars rose into massive flanges that curved up and over his shoulders. A cloak curled around his sides, concealing his arms above the elbows.

"Your player," Ravage said.

L. Kahn looked at Rico and gestured toward the right side of the alcove's curving bench. Rico sat there; Ravage moved to sit opposite. L. Kahn tapped the keypad on the table before him, and the pair of nude slitches dancing

around on the tabletop—forty-centimeter-tall laser
displays—abruptly winked out.

"Interesting locale for a meet," L. Kahn said slowly.

Rico replied, "Ain't you been here before?"

"I prefer more secluded climes."

Rico didn't much care. The main fact on his mind was
that job offers sometimes turned out to be setups, traps
laid by people bearing grudges. It paid to be careful.
Chimpira might be on the hairy verge between darkness
and light, but it was safer than some small room off a
back alley. The yaks didn't take kindly to murders on the
premises. Neither did they admit cops. That the slag calling himself L. Kahn had actually shown up tended to indicate that he was who and what he was supposed to be,
rather than some blade out to cap on a contract.

"You got nothing to worry about," Rico said. "You
ain't gonna do nothing but talk and pass cred. I'm taking
the risks and I don't know you from drek."

L. Kahn gazed at him steadily for several moments,
then spoke, his voice a low drawl. "I have contracts to
fulfill. Clients to satisfy. The risk is different in form, but
shared by all. You were recommended to me by a reliable
source. That is why I'm wasting time with you now."

"I'm wasting your time?" Rico said quietly.

"I don't know your name. That implies your name
probably isn't worth knowing."

From a biff like Ravage, it wouldn't have mattered.
From another man, it went too far. L. Kahn's tone made
it much more than a casual remark or a simple statement
of fact. Rico hesitated about two seconds, then leaned
toward L. Kahn and spat in his face.

L. Kahn didn't move a muscle. He didn't have to—
Ravage was already moving. Rico didn't catch the first
stirring, but the next instant he saw her coming closer,
then pitching the table over and out of her way.

Could he get his Predator free of the holster in time?
He had maybe a fraction of a second to decide.

The instincts that come from experience answered the
question for him. If you're going to blast somebody, you
don't bother closing the distance, not in a situation like
this, with everybody at point-blank range. That meant
Ravage wanted it personal. Rico could almost feel the
chrome-steel punch or kick being readied, building up in

the distance somewhere, like an earthquake, closing in fast.

Rico thrust his right arm forward, clenching his fist and bending it at the wrist. Muscle memory did the rest.

Ravage's left hand became a claw, blurring in front of his face, on a collision course. She had razors there, Rico realized, jutting out from under her nails. They would slice through his eyes and cheeks, then maybe return to tear through his throat.

The blurring hand halted barely two centimeters from his face, then hung there, motionless. Ravage might rip his face to shreds, but she would see her guts spill to the floor for the privilege. Rico held the curving chrome blades now jutting from the backside of his forearm just short of the slitch's groin.

Rico grinned up into her face.

"Do it," he rasped.

The violet pits of Ravage's eyes showed nothing, not even a glint of emotion. Her voice was almost mechanical, murmuring, "Road kill."

Rico waited. Instants passed like minutes. Standoff or double killing? Rico had been to this place before. Sometimes it seemed like his whole life was composed of moments like this. His heart hammered, but he had no trouble facing the prospect of his death. Like somebody once said, *A man's fate is a man's fate.* What would be would be. If he died, it would at least be a man's death, an honorable death, giving as good as he got.

A new voice suddenly arose, growling, "The slitch backs off or you're dog meat, chummer."

Out the corner of his eye, Rico saw the large figure now standing where one corner of the alcove met the floor of the balcony. Shank's big hands gripped a massive automatic, an Israeli LD-100. The red blip of the weapon's laser sight shone steadily, unmoving, on the bridge of L. Kahn's nose.

"Ravage," L. Kahn said calmly.

Another long moment passed, then Ravage backed away like a wave slowly retreating from shore. The razors at her fingertips vanished. At near a whisper, she said, "Next time you'll have to be fast, old man."

Rico didn't want to hear about next time. It didn't matter. Whether he could even come close to matching Rav-

age's speed next time they clashed wasn't important. He
could be dead a thousand times over before then. He
could have a heart attack right where he sat just remem-
bering how quickly she'd gotten into his face. If there
ever was a next time, he'd be smart to dust her on sight,
and from as long a range as possible.

L. Kahn dabbed at his face with a brown handkerchief,
and said, "Let us call a draw a draw and get on to biz."

"We still got something to talk about?"

"If we didn't, you would be dead."

"You got a dangerous mouth, my man."

"I can afford it."

Abruptly, a pair of small red blips caught Rico's attention. Waving around and around in circles on his chest. A
third blip ran in circles up and down Shank's side. They
weren't part of the stroboscopic light effects from the
club's main floor. They were targeting sights. Rico ran his
eyes around, vision shifting to infrared to microchip-
enhanced, but he couldn't spot the shooters. Too much
ambient heat, too many bodies on the main floor all moving asynchronously. L. Kahn had pros backing him up.

At least three of them.

Where the frag was Piper? Rico wondered. Was she
safe? He hoped she was under wraps as good as L.
Kahn's shooters.

"Ask your friend to relax," L. Kahn said. "We'll talk."

Rico motioned with his chin. Shank was down on one
knee, using the skimpy railing that guarded the edge of
the balcony to gain what cover he could from L. Kahn's
shooters. With a growl and a sneer, he slid his automatic
under his jacket.

Ravage set the table upright on its pedestal and returned it to its place. She did that one-handed, and the table looked heavy. She smiled as she sat down opposite
Rico. It was just a glimmer of a smile. On her it looked
like a death grin.

"So talk," Rico said.

L. Kahn nodded. "Explications first. My clients are
powerful people. When they make a contract, they expect
it to be fulfilled. And I will see them satisfied. If you take
my money, you will complete the contract in full. When
time is an issue, and for this job, time *is* an issue, I ac-

cept no refunds. You will do the job or face the consequences."

Do the job or die. Almost common enough to be considered standard terms. "You think I'm an amateur?" Rico snarled. "I don't need guano like this. You tell me what the job is and I'll tell you if I'm interested."

L. Kahn seemed unaffected: cool and calm. Rico envied the slag his self-control. Nothing seemed to undo him, even spit in the face. "The job is a bustout."

"I don't do snatches."

"It's a recovery."

"Keep talking."

"The subject to be recovered was in fact snatched. The job is to bring the subject home. This particular subject is highly ranked in a particular field and is therefore of high value. The snatching entity has threatened the subject's spouse, thus forcing the subject to contribute substantially to the snatching entity's various enterprises."

"You're talking about corporate entities."

"Don't ask for specifics unless you're accepting the job."

"Sure. Where's this spouse you mentioned?"

"The spouse remains under the protection of the home entity and will not be a factor in completing the contract. Your only concern will be to recover the subject and deliver the subject unharmed at a specified time and place."

"What's the security threat?"

"It has been assessed as Code Orange."

"A or double-A security."

"Correct."

"So it ain't Fuchi-Town."

"Obviously."

The immense complex that included the five skyraking towers of Fuchi-Town in lower Manhattan had triple-A security, also called Code Red. Fuchi used everything to keep the facility secure: armed guards, electronics, magic. You didn't go up against security like that unless you had a back door or the possibility of making one—and even then it would probably still be a suicide run. "Tell me about your Code Orange."

"Are you accepting the contract?"

"Not without more data."

"You have all the data you need."

"Not to talk money."

"Then you are accepting the contract."

"With conditions. If you don't make the money worth the risk, forget it. If you lie, forget it. If this turns out to be a snatch, forget it. If your subject ain't a willing subject, forget it."

"Have you ever run against Code Orange security?"

Rico cursed, then said, lowly. "Don't insult me again or those shooters won't save you."

"You have many conditions for a man in your line."

"Remember it."

The plex was full of amateurs, children with dangerous toys, who went running off on fool's errands because some stone-faced slag like L. Kahn flashed some nuyen. Rico knew better. You started your fight right here. You stood your ground. If the man didn't like your terms, you walked away. You had two choices in this life. You could live slow or fast. Given the choice, Rico liked it slow, clawing every bit of the way for everything he could get. It was that or nothing.

Moments passed. Rico tried to decide who looked more like a statue: L. Kahn or Ravage. Both seemed cut from the same chunk of stone.

"I will agree to your conditions," L. Kahn said finally, "but I have a condition of my own. You have given me tentative acceptance of the contract. I will tell you more of what you want to know. If any part of what I say reaches the streets, you're dead."

Rico hesitated, then said nothing.

It made no sense that a slag with L. Kahn's rep would keep bringing up points, terms and conditions that any teenage virgin would know. That fact, nagging at Rico, finally inspired insight. He realized he was being worked. L. Kahn apparently knew some things about him, like his sensitivity to personal insults and his difficult-to-manage temper. L. Kahn had been baiting him right from the start, and had intentionally brought him and Ravage into near-lethal collision.

It cast that little death grin of Ravage's in a whole new light. The slitch had known.

L. Kahn was scoping him out. Testing him.

"Keep talking," he growled lowly.

"The facility where the subject is kept makes primary

use of passive electronics," L. Kahn said. "There are multiple back-ups and fail-safes. Guards are armed and of good-to-average caliber. They are stationed at checkpoints, entrances, and exits, but make only perfunctory patrols of the perimeter and facility interior. My assessment indicates that in order to succeed you will need both matrix cover and technical expertise in physical penetration."

"What about magicians?"

Magic was always the wild card. In a world of uncertainties, it was the least predictable element. "There are several mages on premises," L. Kahn said, "but none have been incorporated into the facility's security system."

"Sounds pretty weak."

"There is one more factor. The facility's security posture is monitored. Should there be an active alert caused by intruders, additional security forces will respond to the site. These forces are rated as military-equivalent. They are commando-trained, heavily armed, and come with integral astral support."

"What's the response time?"

"Minutes."

"How many minutes?"

"Lead elements could reach the facility in four or five. Astral support would likely be in the second wave."

"Is that a fact or an estimate?"

"The Sixth World has no facts. Only suppositions."

They soon came to the matter of money, nuyen, the one indisputable fact of living. Rico bargained hard, got more or less what he wanted, and accepted the contract. L. Kahn passed him a chip containing the specifics of the job. The only thing left to do then was to verify L. Kahn's up-front payment in certified credsticks, and plan and execute the run.

"The Chinese have a saying," L. Kahn remarked at the end. "May you live in interesting times. You make for interesting negotiations, Mr. Rico. I'll remember your conditions. You remember mine."

Rico glanced at Ravage and left.

6

"Bird away."

The roof-mounted launcher fired her away from the concrete earth. The rush of acceleration coursed through her titanium-composite airframe. The thrust of her quad turbofan engines, already blazing with power, carried her into the night.

She climbed, engines to max, aiming her nose at the shroud of haze and fumes that hid the stars. Transparent red digits tumbling before her eyes ticked off altitude, energy, and a dozen other transient statistical indicators. Part of her noted those indicators, but only in passing. Mere numbers could never quantify the glory of flight, or the greater truths hidden in the dark. She unfolded her pinions, stretching her wings out full, and banked her engines, cutting power to practically nothing, gliding almost soundlessly into a slow turn that inspired a twinge of pity for all those million souls bound to the earth below.

Now that she was finally aloft, she could breathe. Flying recon drones hardly compared to the quantum rush of driving Federated-Boeing Eagles and Strike Hawks outfitted with military-grade ordnance and full electronics suites, but she could live with the difference. She'd flown her first dumb-boy when she turned fourteen. It was reassuring to note that if she took any triple-A, if she suffered any massive system failure, it wouldn't be her own flesh and blood body that went spiraling at Mach Two into the concrete earth.

For one thing, this CyberSpace Designs Stealth Sniper recce drone couldn't manage anything like supersonic velocity; for another, her flesh and blood body was far below her, still stuck in that frigging wheelchair, inside the command and control vehicle of the Executive Action Brigade.

She could see that vehicle now, through the light-gathering lenses in her belly pod. The heavily modified Ares Roadmaster with the sat dish on top, parked in a shallow gulch, an empty lot, between ferroconcrete huts.

Voices whispered in her ears. "Status on Air One . . ." "Just coming on-line, sir . . ." "Tell that fragging air jockey to get her butt engaged . . ."

Mentally, she could also see the scene inside the Roadmaster C & C. The dim lights, the bank of consoles. Colonel Butler Yates, commander-in-chief of the Executive Action Brigade, pacing back and forth. Major Skip Nolan, the EAB's exec, monitoring communications between the ground teams, checking in with the commo operators, then leaning over her shoulder, she the one real rigger on the team.

Abruptly, Skip's voice murmured into her head, like he was right there with her, gliding through the night. "Get on-station, Bobbie Jo," he said softly. "Colonel's nervous tonight."

She smiled and said, "Affirmative."

The smile was for Skip. She hoped he read it. Everyone else in the world called her B. J., even her own mother, but that was never enough for Skip Nolan. He always wanted more, something special, if only to remind her that there was something special between them. She liked that. It made the whole world seem warmer, nicer, somehow.

As for the Colonel's nervousness, she could only agree. The Brigade had once been one of the foremost mercenary units in the western hemisphere, though under another name. Since the annexation of Mexico by Aztlan and the end of various squabbles in South America, the merc business had gotten very low-key. The Colonel had been forced to dispense with most of the air wing while turning in desperation to the corporate security field. The Brigade's lack of specialists and the Colonel's lack of contacts had made that move chancy. The transition had been rough and it still wasn't clear if the move would pan out.

Bobbie Jo checked her orientation, swung across the black stroke-marks of a dozen streets, then flattened out and slowed to a hover above the confluence of roadways that marked her station.

Hovering in stealth mode ate fuel like fire ate oxygen. Fortunately, she had talked the Colonel into equipping the high-performance Sniper with long-range fuel tanks.

"Air One on station, Colonel . . ."

"It's about time, dammit . . ."

Springfield and Market Streets came together like a great V, slicing through the jumble of buildings and cross-streets at the core of the Newark sprawl. It seemed ironic because that V pointed across the Passaic River to Jersey City and the soaring towers of Manhattan Island. The enclave of power and money. Where everyone wanted to be. Most of the millions in Newark would never get there.

"Status, Air One."

That was Skip, sounding very official. The Colonel must be leaning over her shoulder or breathing hot and hard down Skip's neck. Bobbie Jo focused her downward-looking eyes and went to work, computer-augmenting the best views.

The club stood on Springfield. The front of the place was all dingy and black but for the large gold letters hanging above the main entrance, reading, "Chimpira," whatever that meant. It was supposed to be a hangout for yakuza and other miscreants. Most notably, the miscreants the Brigade had been hired to shadow.

Target indicators winked rapidly in front of her eyes, picking out movement on the ground, computer-directed to single out human-sized targets only. Her view plunged to sidewalk level thirty-seven times in a row for a camera click glance at every face, every moving body, then every two-legged body anywhere near the front of the club. That included the three trolls and eleven Asian norms, all males, immediately in front of the club. None of her real targets were among them. She fired her gathered data back to the C & C. The Colonel would have his status report and the Brigade's new fugitive unit would undoubtedly find some use for the digitized images in her burst transmission.

An hour passed. The Colonel kept demanding more data from Skip, and Skip kept hounding her for more digipics. She circled the club. When the first of the miscreants, the supposed leader, finally appeared, Bobbie Jo fired her alert signal to the C & C.

Target One moving Target One moving . . .

She fired digipics in a continuous stream back to the C & C. Target One exited via the front of the club. Through her computer-enhanced closeups, she saw that he was a Hispanic male of medium height and build and that her images of him matched exactly the digitized pics in her ground-based memory. An Asian female soon followed him out of the club. That was Target Two. Tall and good-looking. Light-skinned for an Asian, but there was no mistaking the slope of her eyes. The two of them met in the alley beside the club and moved to the alley at the rear of the club. There they met Target Three and Target Four: a heavily built ork male and a long-haired dwarf male. Together, they moved through the alleys to King Boulevard and around the corner to Stirling Street. There they entered a gray and black ghost of a van.

Target Alpha moving, all targets onboard . . .

She repeated that.

Brigade comm traffic murmured rapidly in her ears. Ground-based surveillance units were moving into position to follow the van, designated Target Alpha. They didn't have much time. Target Four was a rigger and very hot with wheels. Even as the last of the group climbed into the van and closed the side door, the van was rolling, picking up speed, smoking tires and really moving out.

Bobbie Jo prepared to follow. No need for stealth mode now. Her on-board combat comp set three green target indicators to winking in front of her eyes. Those pointed out the pursuit vehicles. Ground One, Two, and Three, dark mid-sized sedans with stock New Jersey plates. Standard procedure called for one sedan to close with the target vehicle, follow for a short distance and then turn off, while another one closed in.

It didn't work out that way. The van blew the light on Howard and roared up South Orange Avenue. Bobbie Jo's warning was all that kept the pursuit vehicles from being left in the dust. As the cars raced to catch up, the van turned left onto Fourteenth Street and into a gridwork of streets and cross-streets lined with cars and crammed with buildings. The van careened through the grid at breakneck speed, gaining ground with every turn. It broke out onto Springfield Avenue, blew a series of red lights, and in another minute was flying down the entrance ramp to the South Newark Transitway.

Abruptly, Bobbie Jo heard a muted stammer that sounded like autofire weapons, then a voice, distant but urgent, exclaiming, "Ground Three! Ground Three! We're in the middle of a gang bang-up!"

The other two cars were out of the grid and racing up Springfield, but they were nowhere near getting the van into visual range.

"Air One status!" Skip barked.

No choice.

The van was disappearing into the dark of an underground section of the transitway. The pursuit cars would never catch up. Target Alpha was flying. Bobbie Jo punched up her engines and dove, turbofans screaming, to the roof of a tandem-trailered truck just then sluicing down the incline and into the dark of the transitway tunnel.

It was like pitching into an attack run.

One moment she had only the dark haze of the night above her; in the next, she was sandwiched between the roof of the truck's lead trailer and the massive girders supporting the ceiling of the transitway. She had about a half-meter of airspace above her and about the same below. One errant breeze, one minor electronic fluctuation, and the girders above or the truck below would smash her into oblivion.

That scared the hell out of her, only she didn't let herself feel it. She reminded herself that she really wasn't there. Her body was safe. Only the electronic sensorium of the Sniper drone was at risk. But that didn't help.

She kept on, redlining her emotive indexes.

The truck provided cover. The broad roof of the trailer and the glaring lights of the cab would keep her hidden from anyone within easy visual range. She searched ahead with her eyes. Target indicators winked, then she spotted the gray and black ghost-van veering across two lanes and into the gray-lit tunnel of a transitway exit.

Target exiting target exiting . . .

Her target indicator winked rapidly, then blinked out.

She didn't dare follow. The exit tunnel was too confining, and she'd be spotted. The targets were pros, and the van was believed to be equipped with advanced electronics that might very well include short-range antiair radar. Bobbie Jo did what she had to do. She stayed with the tandem-trailered truck for another eight hundred meters. The instant the transitway surfaced again, she punched up full power. The steady whine of her engines rose to a cyclone scream. She arced up and back, soaring over the city, then quickly flipped to bring her belly pod to bear on the ground below.

A dozen target indicators winked in front of her eyes.

She was still scoping them out, sweeping back and forth across the city, hunting the target, when Skip called her back to base.

The Colonel was not happy.

Rico grimaced, clenching his teeth. Barely an hour had passed since he'd accepted the job from L. Kahn and already he didn't like it. The whole thing could be a set-up.

"You sure you saw a drone?"

"Of course I saw it," Thorvin snapped, steering the van around one final corner onto Mott Street. "Any moron with freaking infrared goggles coulda spotted it. I oughta know a freaking Cyber Designs Stealth Sniper Series 53 when I see one. I broke one of the freaking things down about a year ago just to see how it worked. It ain't top of the line, but it ain't half bad either. It's serviceable. All right for standard recon. It just hasn't got anything like the kind of electronics to beat what I got in this van."

"Yes, but whose drone was it?" Piper said. "And who was it eyeing?"

Shank grunted. "Maybe it's just a coincidence."

Rico turned his head to look out the passenger-side window, into the side-view mirror, then at the dark, decaying buildings slowly passing by. Piper's questions struck right at the core of the problem. Rico wished he had answers to match them. He had plenty of guesses, but he didn't like those guesses any more than Shank's suggestion about coincidence.

L. Kahn could have arranged to put up a drone just to send a message that he'd be watching, alert for treachery. It would be a stupid thing to do because Rico would take it as a sign of betrayal, but then L. Kahn didn't necessarily know that Thorvin had the gear to spot the drone.

Any fragging thing was possible. Every one of the four

of them in the van had at least one warrant out for them
somewhere in the U.C.A.S. Cops and feds and practically
every corp in the world all had riggers who could put up
drones. Some of the local security companies used drones
for ordinary surveillance, like night watchmen. And, like
Shank said, it was definitely possible that the drone was
completely unrelated to anything that mattered. There
were dozens of jobs being worked at any one time within
the bounds of the Newark plex. Sometimes you couldn't
turn a corner without stepping into the middle of somebody's dustup. It just seemed too coincidental to *be* coincidental that a drone had shown up overhead just as they
were leaving Chimpira.

On the other hand, Thorvin had lost contact with the
drone once they reached the transitway, and nothing else
had happened to suggest that they were being followed.

"You didn't see no cars following?"

"Not a freaking one."

Still what bothered Rico was the one possibility no one
had mentioned: they might already be blown. The corporate "entity" they were supposed to penetrate to make
their retrieval might already know they'd been hired for
the job. That "entity" might have been watching L. Kahn
and might be hunting for the four of them at this very
moment.

Preemptive op is what corp security slags called it.

They'd be careful, Rico decided. Now more than ever.
They'd get off the street and stay off as much as possible
until the job was done. They'd check out everything two
or three or four times before they started the run. They'd
build in backups on top of backups in case anything went
wrong. If they found even a hint of evidence that L. Kahn
was playing games, they'd handle that, too.

Four a.m., the rain started coming down. Right on
schedule. First it drizzled, then it poured. In less than a
minute it turned into a torrent. The corps controlling
Manhattan seeded the clouds most every night in an attempt to clear the garbage out of the air. Like they said on
TV/3V, the rain brought the garbage down indiscrimi-
nately, on the just and the unjust alike.

Momentarily, the safehouse came along on the right, a
three-story brick building that had been condemned a decade ago, then uncondemned. City records showed it as

turned over to New Jersey Consolidated Power and Light. Piper had made it that way.

The place was crammed in between a two-story factory and a nine-story moving and storage tower. It had two brown metal bay doors large enough to accommodate a semi and no windows at ground-level. The door on the right began rising as they approached. Thorvin had the transmit code. He drove the van across the sidewalk and right inside. The door trundled down behind them.

The ground floor looked like a junkyard, one big room filled with mechanical parts and equipment, a pair of Scorpion motorcycles, a spare van. Thorvin called it his emergency repair shop. What he called it or how he used it mattered far less to Rico than that the rigger should have what he needed to jury-rig repairs when they were on a run.

Rico led the group upstairs. The second floor had bedrooms, a kitchen, and the main room, which doubled as both a living room and conference room. Rico set Shank and Thorvin to clearing up the garbage lying around since God knew when, then handed Piper the datachip from L. Kahn. Piper had her axe. They'd stopped to pick that up. She'd scan the chip, print out a hardcopy, and they could get started with the job.

Piper took the chip, but then slid her arms around Rico's neck and said softly, anxiously, "This one worries me, *jefe*."

Rico exhaled heavily. "We just gotta be careful, chica. I think we're playing with big boys this time. Some damn megacorp."

She nodded. "I'll get to work."

"Good idea."

Rico checked on supplies: food, ammunition, other gear. The devil rats in the basement had been working on the power lines, so he got Thorvin down there to patch things up. When he returned to the second floor, he found Piper sitting on the sofa, axe in her lap. Her eyes rose to meet his.

"Got something?" he asked.

"Surikov," Piper said. "Ansell Surikov. That's who they want us to get."

7

Everybody wanted something.

That's why the crowds stood waiting outside the old stadium beneath the giant TV/3V screen advertising Chromium Retrosocket, coming soon. That's why so many thousands of people jammed the Main Line along Bloomfield Avenue through the western half of Sector 3. And that's why Monk stood in the middle of the traffic lanes, amid a teeming mass of people, with six-story tall coffin hotels on the left and decrepit ferrocrete tenements on the right, all ablaze with flickering, flashing neon signs.

Just a few steps in front of him stood a man on a plastic crate. "What's wrong with society?" the man shouted, waving a sheaf of hardcopy. "Too much coercion! Corporate, government, economic coercion! No one can escape it, not the squatters, not the salarymen, not the execs, not even the SINless! Coercion dooms us all to sterile and empty lives, years with no hope, no goals and no end!

"Neo-anarchism is the only answer! the only way humanity can throw off the chains of oppression! Transcend its degeneracy and rise up out of the mire of the new corporate feudalism!

"We must unite in common cause and seek Pareto optimality!"

Monk frowned.

Pareto what?

A bit further along was a woman shoving a pushcart up the street while she hawked weevo warts, which, when applied with a solution of three percent sodium bicarbonate, would make all men handsome and virile and all women beautiful and fertile.

Weevo warts . . . Monk wondered what those were.

After that came pyramids and crystals, positive and

negative ion generators, a grow-your-own-clone booth, a tarot reader, a palmist, a noodle stand, cheap body organs and cyberware, another noodle stand, soykaf, a Sidewalk Doc, and a group of masked men big enough to be orks, all wearing the black hoods, jumpsuits, gloves, and boots of the Sanitation Department.

"Where's the *stiff*?" one shouted.

Monk tried not to pass judgment. The writer's business was to watch and listen. To learn the patterns of the world and reveal them to others. To do that, he had be like a sponge. He had to soak up everything, remember it, and eventually find ways to explain the seeming randomness of existence to others, regardless of the medium he used.

One of these days, people would read his telebooks or watch his tridplays or experience simsense performances that he had orchestrated, and they would find truth.

And that would be a great day.

He could see it already: "One Day in the Life of the Main Line Mega-market of the Newark Metroplex!"

Or words to that effect.

"By *Monk*!"

He grinned.

What happened then caught him completely by surprise. From somewhere amid the noise of the street, the babble of voices, the reverb of adverts, the rumble of subways and transitways, the roaring of boom boxes and the distant clatter of gunfire, he heard a kind of high-pitched whining sound, but didn't really pay much attention. He didn't think anything of it.

As he turned one way, something hit him from the other direction, first in the leg, then in the hip. The impact itself didn't come as much of a shock. He'd been getting jostled by the crowds for hours, in fact, practically every day of his life. It was what followed that took away his breath.

Whatever had hit him seemed to sweep him right up off his feet. For a second or two Monk felt himself being carried along at near breakneck speed, arched over backward, his arms and legs flying out wide into empty air. Just in passing, he noticed a few things: the blur of a neon sign advertising soykaf; the face of an Asian man, mouth gaping as in astonishment, eyes bulging and staring down at him; a hooded woman battling a pair of gangers over

a handbag; the rear of a fat man's bald head; a rat dashing
across the sidewalk, threading a path through a half a
hundred pairs of feet.

There was that strange whining sound, too.

And a kind of exclamation, like, "Hey!"

Then Monk suddenly realized he was in freefall. He
wasn't quite sure how that had happened. It was really
strange. Like he was just floating in midair. Immune to
gravity. He caught a glimpse of someone smoking a red
cigarette, then spotted a patch of ferrocrete wall, then everything around him was crashing. He was tumbling,
rolling, flipping upside-down, smashing into things. His
body hit the ground. That kind of hurt.

"Are you all right?" somebody called.

Monk wasn't sure about that. He felt kind of funny.
Like he might suffocate and vomit and pass out all at
once. He felt banged up, too. He spent a few moments
just getting back into the habit of breathing. Once he got
that down, he tried opening his eyes and looking around.
The first thing he noticed was the pile of plastic trash
cans around him. The second thing he noticed was someone kneeling next to him. Someone wearing a leopard-
print jacket, pants, and boots. As another moment passed,
Monk realized this someone was female and *looking right
at him*. His eyes widened. He looked at her more closely.
Her hair was frizzled and wild and kept changing colors,
winking from red to orange to gold and back again. She
had bright blue eyes, a pert nose, and lips like Cupid's
bow. She smiled, looking right at him, and showed off
teeth as white as . . . well, anything he had ever seen. She
smelled like a fragrant garden. She was . . . she was . . .

She was *beautiful* . . .

"Hey, you're kinda cute."

"Huh?"

She giggled.

Aches and pains faded to nowhere. Monk stared.
Women never paid much attention to him. Beautiful
women like this one never even seemed to notice he existed. They weren't interested in writers. Didn't consider
them good nesting material. They had their eyes on
salarymen, execs, and the tall towers and big money over
on the other side of the Hudson River.

She lifted a hand to cover her mouth, then helped him sit up. She had slim little hands like a girl.

"You must've been in another world," she said, smiling. "Didn't you hear me beep?"

Monk frowned, wondering what she meant.

"Hey, are you an elf?" Abruptly, she brushed at his spiky hair and leaned over as if to look at the side of his head, maybe at one of his ears. His ears *were* kind of weird. Pointy like.

"Uh . . ."

"My father was a dwarf. Can you believe it?" She looked him in the face again, then smiled and thrust her arms out to her sides as if to invite him to look her over. Monk couldn't help accepting the invitation. She was slim and just plain gorgeous.

"Wuh . . . wiz," he said, breathing hard.

She giggled again, then smiled warmly, right at him. "I'm Minx," she said. "Who're you?"

"Monk," Monk blurted.

"Wiz!" she said, softly. "You know, you remind me of the flower children. They were always in another world. They were these people back in the twenty-hundreds who said we should make love, and mostly just that." She smiled like she thought that was funny. "And they meditated, too. A lot of them wore tie-dyed clothes like you."

"Yeah?"

"Sandals, too."

Monk looked down at the colors splashing across his Fixe Rescue tee, then down the lengths of his faded blue rippers to the black and red sandals on his feet. Flower children? Wasn't that what people called weed-eaters? elves? "I . . ."

"Hmmm?" Minx looked at him inquisitively.

"I think . . . something on the . . . the California Channel . . . about . . . uh . . ." What had she called it? Them . . . "Flower children."

Suddenly, Minx covered her face with both hands and bent forward at the waist. She was laughing, Monk realized, laughing so hard that when she straightened up again she had to wipe at her eyes and gasp for breath. "See!" she said. "See what I mean!"

Monk wondered about that.

"So where do you live anyway?" Minx asked, fluffing

out her hair, then smoothing it back again with delicate movements of her hands. She paused to look at him, and said, "Monk."

"Huh?"

"Wanna go to my place?"

Monk stared, feeling a strange heat rise up the back of his neck and into his face. This couldn't be happening. This beautiful, gorgeous, captivating woman couldn't be talking like that. He must have missed something, misunderstood, misconstrued something she said. But then Minx took hold of his arms and half-pulled him to his feet. She seemed pretty strong for a girl.

And she was small, really tiny. Her head barely reached his chest and he wasn't tall at all. But it only made her seem more gorgeous. When she shook back her hair and looked up at him and smiled and slid her hands up his chest, Monk felt his heart begin to pound. Like it would leap right out of his body.

"You're a lurker," she said. "You watch and listen. I like that."

"Huh?"

She laughed.

Just a few steps away lay a red and black Honda scooter. It matched Monk's sandals. Minx pulled it upright, touched the starter and revved the engine. This is what had bowled him over, Monk realized. The scooter.

"Come on, Monk, you booty," Minx said. "Get on."

Booty?

There was barely enough room. Monk eased himself onto the scooter's seat right behind Minx. There was no way to sit there without touching her, without feeling the soft swell of her hips against the insides of his thighs. The sensation was indescribable and left him feeling short of breath.

Abruptly, Minx looked back, tossing her frizzed-out hair, and pulled his arms around her waist. "Don't be shy," she said. "I'm a girl, you're a boy. Scan it?"

"What?"

"Hang on!"

The scooter whined and they were off, flying out of the alley and up the Main Line. It was a ride Monk would never forget. The scooter weaving wildly back and forth, crowds of people rushing past on either side. Arms and

elbows and other parts of people's bodies banged off
Monk's head, shoulders, and legs. Things began moving
so quickly he couldn't keep track. It became a blur, a
churning sea of people and buildings and the occasional
vehicle, a series of near-misses that defied comprehension. Monk remembered the rat he'd seen threading a
path through hundreds of feet just minutes ago. It was
like that. No one could possibly steer a scooter through
the crowds on the Main Line like Minx was doing, and
yet she was doing it.

A huge black Department of Sanitation truck loomed
up suddenly before them—the scooter was heading
straight for it. In the final seconds, Monk glimpsed a crew
of black-clad men tossing plastic body bags into the back
of the truck.

Monk stared wide-eyed, and shouted.

"Yaaaaaaaaaaahhhhhhhhhhhhhh!"

In the next moment, or what seemed like the next moment, the scooter was in a back alley and purring to a
stop. Minx slipped out of the circle of his arms and stood
up. Monk stood up, too, but his legs were vibrating
like the ground near a subway station. Minx smiled
and chained the scooter to one of the metal struts of the
seven-story coffin hotel rising between the rear of
the buildings.

"Some ride, huh?" she said.

"Yuh," Monk answered. *"Claro."*

"Wizzer." Minx took his hand, then stepped up close.
Monk swallowed. "This is my private place, kay?" she
said quietly. "So don't tell anybody you know."

Monk shook his head.

"You're so booty," Minx said, smoothing a hand like
cool cream across his left cheek.

Booty . . .

Abruptly, she was tugging him by the hand up the
metal stairs and onto the gangway fronting the fourth
story of coffins. Three steps along the gangway, a pair of
ork gangers were tussling, growling, and swearing, arms
and shoulders interlocked. Minx ducked between them
and tugged Monk right along with her.

"Hey!" one of the orks roared. *"Smoothies!"*

Something swept Monk's right foot out from under
him, but Minx dragged him up by the arms and yanked

him ahead at a run. Halfway along the gangway, she stopped, pulled out a credstick, slid the stick into a slot, then pulled open the hatch of a coffin.

"Quick," she said.

"I'll tear ya to bits!" somebody snarled from behind them.

Monk didn't look back. He ducked into the coffin, banging his head on the hatchway. Minx followed, not banging her head, and slammed the hatch shut.

Someone started pounding on the hatch from outside, but Monk hardly noticed. The inside of the coffin was wild, a deluxe cubie, with enough space to actually stand up beside the bed! Storage cabinets ran down the left. Telecom and trideo were set into the wall opposite the hatchway. The low bed, the ceiling, and walls were scarlet red and covered with overlapping twenty-by-twenty five centimeter photos.

The photos caught Monk's eye, snared his attention. They were amazing. He'd never seen anything like them. The first few he looked at, taped on the wall above the bed, looked like shots of . . . traffic accidents. Bodies. Dead people sprawled across dark-stained pavement, hanging out of demolished vehicles. The next few pics he looked at seemed to have been taken inside buildings. These showed bodies, too. Some with missing limbs. Some missing heads. One or two didn't look like bodies at all, not at first, because they were so horribly mutilated they didn't look like anything even remotely human.

"Hey," Minx said.

Monk turned around. Something flashed—light, brilliant white light. Dazzlingly bright. When his eyes finally cleared and he could see again, he found Minx smiling at him, holding up a little camera for him to see.

"Gotcha," she said, smiling.

She had a strange look in her eyes.

8

The little night-glo red-on-white sign on the back alley wall, read, "CyberDok: Top Chrome, Vat Organics, Primo Rates."

Shank touched the buzzer beside the black metal door. Momentarily, a small red bulb on the intercom winked to life while another one lit up on the security camera above the door. The intercom squealed and whistled. "We're closed," said a remodulated voice with clashing harmonics. "Slot off."

"Open the door."

"Shank?"

Shank grunted. People with sec cams ought to look at their monitors.

The door buzzed and slid aside. Thorvin stepped right through, cutting ahead, brushing Shank's hip. That was typical. Shank frowned, then put out one long leg with a slight hooking motion, briefly catching the halfer's ankle. Thorvin tripped, stumbled, caught himself, then turned to look back and snarl, "Watch it, ya freakin' tusker!"

"Eff you," Shank growled.

"Flatline."

Shank grinned and followed Thorvin through the doorway into a small, dimly lit waiting room outfitted with a trio of molded plastic chairs and a plastic trash can. Holographic posters on the wall advertised suborbital and semiballistic flights to exotic locales. That was it for decor.

Shank figured it was enough.

A wall panel slid aside, revealing a doorway, and a smoothie. Her name was Filly. She was big for a female norm, and not bad-looking either. She wore a black and red tee chopped off just below where it mattered, a matching thong, and a pair of black socks. Her smile looked kind of sarcastic. "Dok's into some slag's cerebral cortex," she said. "What's tox?"

"We got a job," Thorvin said.

"Nice for you," Filly replied.

Thorvin grumbled something incoherent. Shank explained, "Rico wants you and Dok in the game."

"Big job?"

Shank nodded. "Heavy opposition. Some corp."

"It's always a corp. What's the pay?"

The pay was an equal share. Everybody always got an equal share because everybody on the job shared an equal risk of getting dead. That was how Rico worked things. Shank wouldn't have it any other way. He told Filly the numbers. For a few days' work, it would be a good piece of change. Assuming nobody got killed.

"Come on," Filly said. She turned to lead them ahead. Shank moved to follow her lead, but again Thorvin scuted in before him. They followed Filly down the hall past Dok's office and examination room to the operating room door. Shank knew the layout; he'd been here before. The building was narrow and deep, and Dok and Filly had the first two floors all to themselves. For just two people, that was a lot of space. Shank guessed the CyberDok business must be okay. Nobody getting really rich, but nobody starving either. In fact, Filly's twisting, swinging butt looked pretty damn well-fed. And well-exercised too, not fat, not skinny, but soft and firm and nicely shaped.

At the end of the hallway, Filly put a finger to the print-scanner on the wall, and the door to the O.R. slid open.

Gleaming chrome cabinets and counters ringed the room. The operating table stood at the center of the floor. The slag lying there on his back was enclosed in a transparent isolation chamber that resembled a contoured coffin. A metal ring surrounded his head like a halo. Maybe a dozen skinny rods of different lengths stuck out of the ring at different angles, and, Shank realized, out of the slag's head.

Dok stood at the head-end of the table dressed in a black and red Jersey Annihilators Urban Brawl tee, shorts, and sandals. His silvery slash-hair and beard made him look like an old man, maybe a little before his time.

"Been scanning the Brawl, Dok?"

Dok looked back over his shoulder and grinned. "I do love to see the body parts fly. Hoi, Shank. Thorvin."

"Dokker," Thorvin said.

"What're you into?" Shank asked.

"A little gray matter," Dok replied. "You might want to keep back a few steps. I'm extracting a cortex bomb."

Dok had his hands encased in a pair of gloves that extended into the isolation chamber. He seemed to be slowly, carefully twisting one of the rods stuck into the slag's head. The monitors at his left elbow showed different views: something that looked like a worm lying in a mass of goo; something that looked like a pin lying in a mass of goo; and various masses of goo, some gray, some red, some yellow, some colored kind of like puke.

Shank edged a bit closer. "Ain't most cortex bombs rigged to blow if you mess with 'em?"

"That's what they tell me."

"What kinda charge?"

"It looks like a Chiba Black. Probably a micro C-9 charge. A few grams of explosive."

"So that's what? A blast radius of about half a meter?"

"Enough to blow this slag's brain to hell."

"Maybe a few of your fingers too, Dok."

"It's a possibility. These're Securemed gloves. Kevlar II-insulated. I probably should have gone deluxe."

On one monitor, something that looked like a pair of pliers slowly drew something that looked like an ant out of a mass of goo on what looked like a strand of spider's webbing.

"What's that?" Shank asked.

"The detonator," Dok replied.

"You had to ask," Thorvin grumbled.

"Rico wants us in on some job," Filly said.

"Is that a fact?" Dok replied. "Good job, is it?"

"Pay's okay," Filly told him.

"We'll be busting some slag outta corp hell," Shank explained. "Least that's how it figures."

"Wage slave making a break for freedom?" Dok asked.

"Naw, the slag got snatched about a year ago. It's an intercorporate thing. The slag's real corp wants him back."

"Does he want to go back?"

"The info we got says the corp that snatched him is using threats against his wife to keep him in line. I don't guess he'd be too happy about that."

"Probably not. Everything else scan okay?"

"Piper checked what she could. You know what this drek is like. It looks chill. About the only thing left to do is go in and meet the slag face to face."

"What if he doesn't want to go?"

"Then I guess we're in deep squat."

Dok looked back again and grinned. "Nothing new about that, is there?"

"Not much," Shank agreed. "You in?"

"I guess I could use the change."

"Got any idea where to find Bandit?"

Dok frowned, then said, "Good fragging question."

Farrah Moffit knew how she looked. Even lying in the dark of the bedroom on the broad expanse of the black satin-wrapped bed, she could see her own image clearly, as if reflected in a mirror.

In a sense, she had become a caricature of herself. Her body had been blown up, filled out, reshaped, and pared down—all with precise surgical attention to every detail—until she resembled less the woman she had once been than a man's lustful fantasy. A holographic dream, a vision of fleshy carnal cravings. There were reasons why that had been done, good reasons, and reasons she more than accepted, but she could never quite get past the idea that all these cosmetic improvements demeaned her. It told others that she probably lacked the native intelligence to get what she wanted without resorting to the lure of her body, that she had probably gone to bed for everything she had ever achieved. Whether that was true or not hardly mattered. The message was clear. She saw it in people's eyes every day. Envy, resentment, contempt ...

A significant sum of nuyen had been spent on her flesh. Practically every part of her body had been modified in some way. Her hair had become a veritable forest, lush and prodigious, tumbling over her shoulders and halfway down her back. Her eyes been given such a lavish growth of lashes they seemed unreal. Her lips, made voluptuous, permanently puckered. Her breasts easily large enough to equip a cow, perhaps two. Round and prominent. And the list went on and on. Even her skin had been changed, given a light golden tan that would never fade.

She could hardly move without being reminded of the changes, without some portion of her body making the differences plain. She supposed that, at heart, she would never be completely satisfied with it all. There was indeed such a thing as *too* voluptuous. Her shape, her figure, her entire *look* was rather outrageous.

The telecom bleeped.

Rather than fumble in the dark and risk bending one of her luxury-length fingernails, permanently implanted, she drew a breath, and said, "Telecom answer. . . . Yes."

The device bleeped again. A moment of quiet passed, then the voice of Ansell Surikov came from the speakers. "Darling?" he said. "Are you all right? The visual's off. You sound—"

"I'm fine," Farrah said lightly, interrupting. She smiled and made her voice soft and expressive. "I've just come out of the bath. I haven't any clothes on."

"Oh, I see," Ansell said, sounding amused.

"Will you be late tonight?" Farrah asked.

"A little while longer. I'm hoping you'll still be up when I get there."

"Aren't I always waiting when you come home?"

"Of course you are." Ansell chuckled. "You must think me a mad fool, darling."

"No more than I, darling."

Ansell said he would be home soon, then wished her good-bye and broke the connection. The telecom bleeped and switched itself off. Farrah lay there in the dark a few moments, gathering her will, her ambition, and energy, then she sat up slowly and shook back her hair.

"Lights."

The lights came on, the onyx lamps scattered around the room creating pinpoints of light that gradually swelled into a fuller illumination. Farrah rose and walked through the connecting door to her wardrobe. The mad fool who had called her on the telecom would be expecting a lush, sensual woman to meet him at the door. If instead he met a naked nymph, one with her proportions, he might have a coronary and drop dead at her feet. And that would be too infuriating to bear.

It still surprised her to consider how easily she had made the transition from mere wage slave to full-fledged corporate prostitute. That was such a dirty word and yet it fit so well. She found that she didn't care, didn't even mind the connotations. She'd grown up in the corporate environment. For the sake of economic reward, she'd traded practically everything she possessed to one corporate unit or other all her life. Now she had included her body as part of the arrangement. Simple as that. The recompense had been more than adequate, enough to turn any ordinary prostitute green and blue with envy. And if her current project worked out, she would have nothing to worry about for a long time to come.

The advance security team arrived to check the apartment for bugs and unauthorized personnel. That was standard procedure. Farrah merely verified that the three-member team had the right corporate affiliation before letting them through the door.

Ansell arrived ten minutes later. His personal escort remained behind in the hall.

Farrah smiled, now wrapped in a neo-monochrome gown of scarlet red glinting with a thousand points of light. The gown emphasized every lavish curve of her figure, baring her arms and shoulders and a striking depth of cleavage. Ansell gazed at her for several long moments, then dispensed with his trench coat, tossing it onto a nearby settee with a grand sweep of his arm.

"You look *ravishing*, my dear," he said, smiling, stepping toward her.

Farrah waited till he laid a hand on her shoulder and leaned close for a kiss; then, from behind her back, she drew out a pair of crystal goblets and a bottle of Bordeaux Superieur, Château Haut Brion . . .

Ansell hesitated, then lifted the bottle and looked at the label. "My dear," he said with a smile, "this is the twenty-nineteen. It's barely coming into its prime."

Farrah inclined one finely drawn brow. "Live a little."

"Dare we?"

Faintly, Farrah nodded, and smiled.

It was the sort of extravagant gesture the man could not resist, Farrah knew. With a wild grin, he took the bottle of vintage wine in hand and declared passionately that, *yes*! they would break the seal this very evening. *At once!*

His darling wife must not be denied. The impulse of the moment would be fulfilled. And one impulse led to others.

The living room glimmered with soft light. Ansell set about opening and decanting the wine. Farrah drew a voluptuous 20-centimeter Montecruz Individuale cigar from the humidor behind the bar, clipped the end, then passed it unlit to Ansell.

"The best of the best," he softly declared.

"Only the beginning," Farrah replied.

"Yes," Ansell replied, smiling archly. "The beginning."

At the touch of one key, the entertainment console initialized a preprogrammed routine. The lighting dimmed. Laser light slowly waxed and waned, filling the room with brooding colors. Music arose, Arabic in flavor. Farrah stepped to the center of the room and began a dance, sinuous as a serpent, supple as warm, flowing honey.

As Ansell laughed and applauded, Farrah reached behind her neck and opened a clasp. His laughter soon changed to cries of delight, for he obviously knew what was to come. Farrah's gown gradually descended into wisps of fabric adorning the lush carpeting around her feet. She continued on, now clad only in the skimpy costume she had worn beneath the gown. In time, she discarded that, too.

The dance led inevitably to the bedroom.

Ansell moaned with pleasure.

9

The lock wasn't complicated. Raccoon's magic fingers reached inside with ease and found the critical element, a simple spring-loaded bolt. One flick and the bolt was open, the door unlocked. But there was more, an alarm, and something . . . a sort of trap. Magic pervaded the frame around the door, not the door itself. Clever. It might have worked, too, if Raccoon weren't just as clever. Disabling the alarm took only moments. Neutralizing the clever spell that would . . . what? Cause sleep. Cause anyone opening the door to fall asleep. Neutralizing that took a few minutes. A very clever spell, indeed. Yes, a spell worthy of Raccoon.

When finally the door swung open, Bandit paused, watching, listening, breathing deeply of the incense-laden air that came drifting into the alley. Nothing seemed amiss. It looked as though he'd defeated this clever combination of security.

Very pleasing, very rewarding . . .

But, if his information was correct, the greater reward awaited him inside.

He stepped through the doorway, nearly silent on plastifoam-soled shoes, and into a room that looked much like any other room. The light-intensifying lenses of his mask showed him a small, crowded space divided into three aisles by tall shelf units, a large workbench, some cabinets, hundreds of various small containers, cartons, and boxes. A storeroom. To his astral perceptions, the place was dark, all but emotionless, dead. It was made of things that were lifeless: plastic, metal, and concrete. Substances torn from the earth and so deprived of life. If not for the radiant life energy flowing weakly through the doorway and the faint glimmer from a potted plant on the workbench, the place would have been pitch-black.

The light-gathering lenses of his mask let him scan the labels on the containers. He saw names like U.C.A.S. Fetish, New Magic, Arcane Instruments, Genuine Focii. Bandit recognized the names and knew that the corporations they named produced nothing of any value. He moved to the door on the other side of the room, slipping through it to enter the talismonger's storefront.

Here was life, glowing, radiating, from various points around the shop. Many of the display cases and shelves were filled with tourist trinkets from the boxes in the back room: drums and rattles, knives, wands, crystals, phony bones, plaster shells. Pretty ornaments to amuse the ignorant. Baubles and toys for children or relatives somewhere in Duluth. Some of the talismans and potions and painted charms were very real, imbued with true power, shining with magical life, but none were of a quality or power that would interest one who followed Raccoon.

Bandit turned to the stairs, the old wooden stairs leading up from the side of the shop to the room on the second floor.

Here was the true hoard: old wooden tables and shelves and antique, glass-fronted cabinets all shining brightly with power. What they said—the derelicts and street urchins and burnt-out magicians he had overheard on street corners—all of it was true. Raccoon could spend many hours here examining the many glowing items, but that would be unwise. Bandit knew what he wanted, and it lay in plain sight, right on the table in front of him.

The Mask of Sassacus, said to confer great powers of influence and persuasion, perhaps bound up with special spells. Bandit hesitated even to touch it, but instinct and desire and the danger of discovery wouldn't let him hesitate for long. Cautiously, he lifted the mask in his fingertips, then held it up to his face to see what change that might make in his vision. He learned nothing for his trouble, but assensed great power. He could almost taste the power. He would carry this mask away and learn its secrets. That would tell him its value.

With great care, he slipped the ornate mask into a pouch slung from his belt. In its place, the spot left empty on the table, he put a small crystal dragon with glinting red eyes. Inside this decorative container was the powdered essence of the reproductive organs of a wyrd mantis, a giant Awakened insect of Europe.

The powder glowed with power, but it had no value to Bandit. His magic would be tainted by anything with the least connection to insects or insect totems. That did not mean that the powder had no value to anyone else. Some might find it a very valuable commodity indeed. Maybe not as valuable as the blood of a dragon, the feather of a phoenix, or the horn of a unicorn, but far more valuable than anything else in this shop. That made it a fair exchange, more than fair, for Raccoon had no need to leave anything. Thievery, as some called it, was part of Raccoon's nature.

The room suddenly filled with light, brilliant light, as from a spotlight. This came from the semi-transparent tubes crossing the ceiling. Bandit felt the light like fire. In one fluid movement, he crouched low to the floor and ducked under the nearest table.

Raccoon guided him well tonight.

Better to hide than to fight.

An old man entered the room. Bandit guessed it was an old man by the pair of spindly legs he espied through the legs of tables between him and the back of the room. He also saw a gun, an old-style revolver, gripped low in a gnarled hand.

"Who's there?" a weak voice rattled. "I know you're here ... Got past my ward ... Sneaky bastard ..."

Bandit pointed a finger and breathed a single word. From the direction in which he pointed came a muted bang and crash, followed by the quick-razor snarl of an alley cat.

"What's this?" the old man murmured. "That old trick. I ain't falling for it."

Bandit grinned. The old man must be a magician, and clever. Clever enough to have set the trap on the alley door. Indeed, as he had said, the cat in the alley illusion was an old, old trick. Raccoon used it often. Most people fell for it.

"Somebody's monkeying around," the old man growled.

Nodding, smiling broadly, Bandit reached into his coat pockets, drew out his hands, then softly blew a long, deep

breath at the old man, simultaneously extending and
opening his hands.

"Huh?" the old man said, "Now what . . . another . . ."

He stood unmoving for several moments, then yawned
loudly. The spindly legs stumbled backward a few steps,
slowly settled onto their knees. Finally, the old man came
fully into view as he bent to the floor, lay down, and fell
asleep.

In a few moments, he was snoring softly and steadily,
his own kind of spell used against him.

Bandit returned to the narrow alley behind the shop.
The night was dark and quiet, marked only by the voices
of the night: the distant rumble of the subway, the passing
of cars on nearby streets, the occasional calls of street
vendors and the talk of passersby. Nothing seemed out of
place.

A brief walk took him across High Street, through
Nishuane Park, jammed with the stalls and booths of
talismongers and occultists, to Harrison Avenue. He felt
like getting some food.

In front of Seven Hexes Pizza, he noticed a gray and
black van. He walked right past it and around the corner
into the deep shadows cast by the tall ferrocrete tenements lining Sutherland. The van followed. As Bandit
stepped into the dark recess of a tenement doorway, the
van glided to a stop at the curb in front of him. The passenger door of the van swung open. A big ork in an
armored black vest and black fatigue pants stepped onto
the sidewalk and joined Bandit in the shadowed doorway.
People called this ork Shank. A dwarf called Thorvin followed along.

"Hoi, Bandit," Shank said.

Thorvin grunted.

Bandit watched these two closely. Their presence here
roused his curiosity. They rarely came looking for him
except when a special opportunity arose. A glance at their
auras revealed only that they seemed calm, untroubled, in
harmony with the plex.

"We got a job," Shank said. "Rico wants you in the
game."

Interesting. Bandit knew this Rico, too. Rico was
clever, in some ways as clever as Raccoon. He had a
woman, an Asian woman, who was perhaps more than

she appeared. Not entirely human, perhaps something other than human. She was clever, too. "The decker," Bandit said quietly. "Is she in?"

Shank frowned, then said, "You mean Piper?"

"Yes." That was the name.

"Sure she's in. She and Rico're planning the run right now. You want in?"

"Likely," Bandit said. "Good money?"

Shank told him about the money. It was good. Bandit didn't really care. Money was useful for buying food and renting hiding places, but that was all. He only asked about money because it was expected. People who didn't want money were not trusted. "The run will take us where? Someplace interesting?"

Shank nodded, slowly. Seeming puzzled. "Yeah. Sure. I bet it'll be real interesting. Heavy security. Some corp facility."

"High-security facility?"

"Ain't that what I just said?"

Shank meant yes. This was very good, indeed. High-security facilities had high security in order to guard valuable things. Things that might be taken, things that might be hoarded. Or sold. Or traded. Or examined for what they might mean. It was difficult to know what might or might not have value with just a first look, so many things had to be taken to a safe place where they might be hidden and examined carefully. Often with magic. Long magic. What the uninitiated called "ritual magic," as if such magic could be done by rote, without thought or inspiration.

"You interested?" Shank asked.

Bandit nodded, just once. "When do we start?"

The night streamed with energy, throbbing, alive. Maurice slowly ascended, then descended, his astral form rising as high as the walls of the surrounding buildings, then settling down to several meters beneath the black concrete of the alley. All appeared in order. The energies of the astral plane flowed smoothly and harmoniously. No malign species of phantom or magically active being seemed to be in the vicinity.

There was of, course, one minor fluctuation, one small disturbance in the flux of astral space, originating from within the warehouse to his right, but this he had expected.

He had come prepared.

He returned to his physical body, his mundane form. This brought him a sense of dissatisfaction, no less than the necessity of leaving his studies tonight in order to "practice" his Art in the sordid world of the mundane. As he regained his sense-awareness of the physical plane, he sat once again in the rear of his Mercedes limousine. The limousine waited, lights out, in an alley off some street in Sector 2, near the airport, the ocean terminals and piers.

"Biffs remain in the car," he said.

The five women sharing the rear of the limo with him grumbled briefly in discord. Much as he might have expected. They were his wives. They attended to the innumerable inconsequential details of daily living, thereby freeing him to pursue his arcane inquiries. They had also produced a number of children, who, in time, would also serve him. They expected to accompany him everywhere, imagining that their service to him earned them various inalienable rights.

On a night like this, when certain undeniable facts of existence invaded the hallowed domain of his research, he would grant no latitude, tolerate no dissension. The biffs would do as he said or else face the consequences. Fortunately for all of them, Daniella, his first wife, had the capacity of understanding to order them all into silence.

Daniella would keep them in line.

With one meticulously manicured finger, Maurice pointed. The door to his right clicked and swung open. The faint shimmering in the air by the limo's ceiling drifted out through the open door. Maurice followed it outside.

The night was cool, the air rank with offensive odors. The ground vibrated faintly as with the distant rumble of machinery or passing subway trains. Maurice tucked his ivory-handled walking stick under his arm and tied the sash of his dark, caped coat. A trivial exertion of will returned him to his astral perceptions. He found his ally, radiant with etheric energy, facing him from just an arm's length away.

The ally, recently summoned, was proving to possess a

peculiar blend of naiveté and eccentricities. Though
bound to Maurice's will, his service, the spirit showed
signs of developing a uniquely willful personality. It preferred to be addressed as a female. With Maurice's permission, it had assumed an astral form like that of a
curvaceous young white woman with long, gold-brown
hair, and wearing a flowing halter-top dress that fell to
mid-calf. It wished to be called "Vera Causa." Maurice
found this troubling.

The spirit spoke to him mind-to-mind, asking, *Your desire, master?*

Guard, Maurice thought.

Yes, master, the spirit replied. *I guard you always. Master is kind and spirits are grateful.*

Indeed.

Returned to his mundane physical perceptions, Maurice
extended his walking stick and moved up the alley. To his
right the big black metal door of a warehouse stood partly
open. He paused to examine both door and doorway,
which appeared to be unguarded, astrally and otherwise.
Master, be cautious, his ally warned. *Danger here. Much
violence.*

That was certainly true.

The open doorway led directly to a landing at the top
of a flight of stairs. A faint luminescence from the radiance of the surrounding city carried in through the doorway to dimly illuminate the landing. The stairs, however,
descended into pitch blackness. Maurice called forth his
magelight with a flick of one finger. The light swelled radiant and full, growing from a mere pinpoint to the size
of a globe mounted atop the head of Maurice's stick.

Lifting the stick out before him, Maurice descended the
stairs. Again, his ally warned of danger, of the violence
that lingered here. Maurice knew the source of this violence. It was the man he had come to see.

The stairs led into a corridor unlit but by Maurice's
magelight. Some distance ahead another door waited
partly open. Maurice paused to examine it, then stepped
through.

That put him in the main chamber, a room two or three
times the size of the average simsense theater. At the distant end burned a single candle. Just beyond the candle's
small flame stood a man stripped to the waist. He had a

mass of wavy blonde hair and a well-muscled, athletically proportioned body. He stood with his feet together, arms at his sides, face turned toward the black of the ceiling hanging closely overhead.

Behind the man, Maurice perceived the huddled form of a woman, nude. Quite dead.

"You come again."

The voice carried quietly throughout the space. It was that of the man. He went by many names, but, as Maurice knew, his real name was Claude Jaeger. His aura was a seething torrent of dark-hued energies. Maurice had encountered homicidal maniacs with clearer auras, but Jaeger was far more dangerous than any lunatic killer. Death clung to him, not like a leech, but as the source of his power.

With a shout, Jaeger suddenly turned and lashed out, perhaps with a kick. The movement was so swift, Maurice could not be certain. A dark shape to Jaeger's right, about the size and shape of a fire door, rang like a bell. Sonics slapped the walls of the surrounding chamber and reverberated. The door, or whatever it was, fell to the floor, clanging loudly, separating into two pieces.

"Does this form of exercise please you?"

Jaeger turned toward Maurice with a face as cold as the concrete underfoot. "It is not exercise," he said. "And, yes, it pleases me greatly." He paused for a moment, then said, "Would you care to try? I have another door."

Maurice considered briefly, then dismissed the thought. Jaeger followed the path of a child, that of a physical adept. His art, as he called it, was devoted to improving his physical power. His exercises included breaking inanimate objects and living bodies such as human beings. The practice of the art eluded explanation for the simple reason that the art itself was absurd. It was eminently practical, no doubt, but had no value beyond the purely mundane. Jaeger himself was like a weapon, effective, but essentially devoid of the desire for truth or for anything more than mere physical stimulation.

"We have work," Maurice said.

"What work?" Jaeger snapped harshly.

Maurice ignored the intemperate tone. He had difficulty enough trying to decide how he might best elaborate, what words would achieve the desired effect. As a general rule, the spoken word displeased him. Speech could be unbearably precarious, intolerably inexact. He much preferred the mathematical precision of the arcane arts, the One True Art. It alone could be trusted.

Quietly, and precisely, he said, "Our client is staging a sensitive operation. We are to back up the back-up, you might say. In case something should go wrong."

Softly, resonantly, Jaeger chuckled. "I would say it in terms very different from those, mage."

Maurice supposed that was so.

10

Unlike the old, three-story brick building on Mott Street, the big GMC stepvan really did belong to the New Jersey Consolidated Light and Power Corporation. It was painted in the corporate colors of blue and yellow, marked with various ID numbers, and loaded with equipment.

New Jersey C.L. & P. had lost track of the stepvan for the moment, Piper had arranged for that. According to her, the corp had one of the worst matrix security systems of all the corps in the Jersey-New York megaplex, but whether that was true or the corp just wasn't up to her standards, Rico didn't know. In the end, it probably didn't matter.

Rico took the passenger-side seat, braced one foot against the dash, and gave Shank a nod. Shank hit the remote that set the big bay door in front of them to trundling up, then drove them toward Doremus Avenue, at the north end of the port, where they picked up the Jersey Turnpike.

It was just after 23:30 hours. The truck lanes were laden with heavy, swift-moving traffic—massive two- and three-trailer tandem rigs, container rigs, Roadmaster articulated and straight trucks, cargo vans and stepvans. Rico turned his head to glance back at the trio on the bench seat to his rear: Bandit, Filly, and Dok. Like him and Shank, they were outfitted with day-glo orange hardhats and vests, all marked for C. L. & P. The five of them were just another repair crew in a sludge-bloated ocean of technicians and crumbling infrastructure. No one would look at them twice.

The highway carried them across the Passaic River and onto the Kearny Peninsula, one of the most heavily industrialized areas in the plex. Rail yards, factories, storage

tanks, and warehouses, all constructed on a mammoth
scale, slid past on either side of the highway. The warning
lights of factory stacks and the flame-stroked steeples of
chemical plants rose high into the orange-phosphorous
glow of the night.

Another bridge and the Hackensack River, then into
Secaucus, another industrial zone, this one sprawling up
the backbone of Jersey and Union Cities, and on up the
Hudson to well beyond the G.W. Bridge.

The backside of Union City was far enough.

Shank turned the stepvan down the ramp to Paterson
Plank Road, then up West Side Avenue.

North of the sewage plant, the road became a broad
boulevard. It was a kind of Executive Row, like a little
slice of Manhattan tucked in between chemical and food
processing plants and the compacted, decaying streets of
Union City's Zone 2, West New York. Broad plazas
glowed with light. Fountains glittered and sparkled. Shining towers rose like polished chrome from the halos about
their foundations to dominate the skyline.

Just past Sixty-ninth Street, Shank slowed the stepvan,
flipped on the amber warning blinkers, and swung the vehicle across the boulevard. He drove the truck, one wheel
at a time, up over the curb and onto the gold-lit plaza set
in front of the imposing headquarters of Shiawase
Compudyne, a division of the Shiawase Corporation of
Kyoto, Japan. There was one very important feature of
Compudyne's North American operations. Rico stepped
from the stepvan to find it right there beside the truck. Set
amid the golden tiles of the plaza was the round black insert of a manhole cover.

Shank tugged the cover up and dragged it aside. Dok
and Filly began setting up the requisite safety-orange
guardrail to surround the open hole and then pulled out
the orange-and-red-striped compressor that would pump
fresh air into the hole. Rico opened a Sony palmtop computer marked for New Jersey C. L. & P., paused to glance
around the plaza, then began tapping the palmtop's keys.

Five minutes passed. Shank climbed down the hole and
into the utility passage under the plaza. Dok and Filly
passed several duffel bags of gear down to him, then began setting up the air compressor. Rico was still tapping

the palmtop's keypad when some slag came out of the Shiawase headquarters building to investigate.

The slag wore a suit and a plastic-laminated ID marked for Shiawase Compudyne security. Rico kept tapping keys on the palmtop till the man stepped up beside him.

"What's tox?" the security officer asked. "There a problem?"

Rico paused to look the slag up and down, then went on tapping the palmtop's keys. "Central office says we got a trickle discharge on a Kay-seven quad feeder. Probably just rats, but we gotta scan it. Might take a couple of hours."

"You got a work order or something?"

"That's top secret," Rico replied. "I could tell you, but then I'd have to waste you."

The guard looked at him sharply. "What?"

No sense of humor. Frowning, Rico looked at the slag again, and said, "Yeah, I got an order. What's it to you?"

"Just doing my job, chummer."

"What job?"

"Shiawase security." The slag pointed at the ID slung from his lapel. "Maybe you're really eco-freaks planning to terror-bomb the place. Gotta scope it out. You scan?"

Rico grinned sarcastically and shook his head. "You freaking guys are all alike." He tapped some keys on the palmtop. "You wanna see my order? Here's my order. You can call that number there if you wanna scan it deep."

"Thanks." The slag looked at the palmtop's display, then pulled an ultrathin cellfone out of his jacket pocket. "This'll just take a sec, chummer."

"Null sheen. I get paid working or talking."

The line rang twice.

"Thank you for calling the repair bureau of New Jersey Consolidated Light and Power. All our customer service representatives are busy. Please hold the line and the next available representative—"

"Repair operations. Jane speaking. May I help you?"

"Yeah, hoi, my name's Mike Kosaka. I'm with the security department of Shiawase Compudyne. I've got one of your crews on my premises. I'd like to verify what they're doing here."

"Whenever repair crews are dispatched, sir, they are issued a work order code. Please ask the crew supervisor for that code."

"Uhh ... hang a sec ... That'd be gee as in gulf, two-four-nine-oh-seven-five."

"One moment, sir."

"Sure."

"... That is a valid work order code, sir. Repair supervisor Ramos and his crew have been dispatched to your location to investigate a suspected line malfunction. This should not involve any interruption of service to your facility. Estimated time for completion is approximately four hours. Have you any other questions, sir?"

"Ah, nope. That'll do it. Thanks."

"Thank you for calling New Jersey Consolidated Light and Power."

"You happy now?" Rico said.

The security officer smiled and nodded. "Thanks for your time."

"I get paid for working or talking," Rico said. The security officer nodded again and turned to go. Rico looked to Dok and Filly, and said, "Let's get that air line going."

Filly plugged the orange-and-red-striped air compressor's power line into the socket on the side of the van, and the compressor sputtered to life.

A smartframe handled the telecom call—a program construct requiring only a modest amount of active memory. The moment the call was complete, the frame switched itself off.

By then, Piper was streaming down the datalines of the Secaucus Local Telecommunications Grid. The planar geography of the matrix here reflected the real-world terrain. System constructs like giant factories and massive towers rose toward the starry dark and the distant nebula of access nodes to the regional grid. Piper noted the hexadecimal addresses passing around her, then cut a hard left to the matrix equivalent of Executive Row.

Constructs like office towers and mansions soared up around her. The one she wanted looked like a small castle crowned with a decahedral globe, the insignia of Kuze Nihon, a multinational conglomerate headquartered in

Tokyo. The castle itself and the computer systems it represented belonged to Maas Intertech, headquartered off West End Avenue in Secaucus.

Piper drove straight at it.

They wouldn't see her coming.

Once the slag in the suit departed, a pair of guards in crisp blue uniforms appeared in front of the paired doors of the main entrance of Shiawase Compudyne. The obvious implication was that Shiawase had decided, for whatever reason, to tighten up security a little, or at least put on a nice show. The guards stood there like soldiers on parade. They didn't bother Rico one bit.

Time to start breaking some laws. Rico didn't care much about the law, because the law worked for the corps and the people who wrote the laws, the ones with money and power. Right was right and wrong was wrong. Any man with morals knew what was right and what was wrong, and, with a little thought, could figure what had to be done about it. Sometimes it took a few busted laws to get things set the way they should be.

Whether the law agreed or disagreed was something for leeches like lawyers to argue about.

Bandit followed the last of the bags of gear into the hole. Dok, meanwhile, had dropped the big orange-and-red-striped hose from the air compressor into the hole, then joined Filly in feeding a line like a heavy-duty extension cord into the hole. The air line and power cord were just stage dressing, making things look right, no less than Rico getting into and out of the stepvan numerous times and tapping the keys of the palmtop.

Five minutes more and Rico put his genuine C. L. & P. hardhat on again and climbed down the metal rungs of the access shaft to the utility passage below.

The passage was almost three meters high, but little more than a meter across. That was just the available space. Cables, pipes, and conduits ran up one wall and down the other, making the ceiling maybe a half-meter lower than it otherwise would have been. Small lighting fixtures ran down the right-hand wall at intervals of about ten meters. These were lit.

At Rico's feet lay several black duffels. He picked up the one marked with a big numeral one and started up the tunnel. Even with the bag of gear, walking was no problem. Trying to run through a space this narrow would be another story, but Rico wasn't planning to do any running.

About a hundred and fifty meters up the tunnel, Shank had hung an IR blackout sheet from the ceiling. No one looking up the tunnel would see beyond that sheet, regardless of vision enhancements. Rico checked while approaching, shifting his Jikku eyes to IR. The sheet's only purpose was to prevent anyone who came down the manhole from immediately detecting what was happening beyond the sheet.

Another hundred meters further on, a second tunnel led off to the left at ninety degrees. Shank waited there at the corner, suited up and ready for action: ballistic mask, flak vest, Colt M22A2 assault rifle slung from his shoulder, Wallacher combat axe and other gear slung from belts and crossed bandoliers.

"Status," Rico said.

"Don't ask me," Shank grumbled. "All he's done is stand there like that."

Dressed in his black trench coat and wearing his sword, Bandit stood about five meters into the side passage. Maybe an arm's length in front of his face the tunnel ended in a brick wall. The pipes and conduits lining the tunnel passed right through the brick barrier.

The plan called for Bandit to use his shaman abilities to scan ahead into the tunnel beyond the brick barrier. Just as a precaution. Once sure the tunnel was clear, they would take down the brick barrier. Rico watched Bandit and wondered. The problem was being able to tell when the shaman was actually doing magic, when he was out of body, and when he was just staring, thinking, maybe working out some problem.

If there was a problem, Rico wanted to know about it now. "Bandit," he said.

Abruptly, Bandit shook his staff. The elaborately decorated head of the staff briefly rattled, then Bandit murmured something soft and low, his voice rising and falling like a song. The song descended into silence. Bandit stood stock-still for several moments, then swung his staff to the horizontal, and held it pointing at the brick barrier.

Nothing much seemed to happen.

Rico waited till Bandit turned back and looked at him, then said, "Ready?"

Bandit replied, "When you are."

The System Access Node had the look of a spacious lobby, enormously broad, fronted by transparent panes, and outlined in computer-simulated representations of sizzling neon.

Across the front of the SAN lobby, a hundred transparent doors slid open and shut as datapaks and message units in the form of green-uniformed messenger icons arrived via the rounded conduits of a hundred datalines.

Inside the lobby, the messenger icons waited on violet-shaded lines pulsing through the floor, leading to the service desk subprocessing unit at the head of the node lobby. White-uniformed control modules slaved to the SPU directing the messenger icons to the chrome-mirrored walls at the left and right of the lobby. The messenger icons moved briskly up the lines, then across the front of the service desk to the sides of the lobby, where they vanished into the mirrored walls.

All very orderly and precise.

Piper stepped forward, following the pulsing violet line in the floor. To the messenger icon directly ahead of her, she said, "Excuse me, please."

The messenger icon looked back over its shoulder, then stepped briskly out of her way, shunting to the violet line to their immediate right. The message icons there adjusted position so as to maintain their proper intervals. Piper advanced. The other messenger icons ahead of her in line looked back and shunted out of her way as well, permitting her to walk directly to the service desk SPU at the head of the node. One of the white-uniformed control modules there watched her approaching and bowed.

Bowing in return, Piper announced, "Priority user requesting interface with Facility Engineering subprocessing unit."

A window framed in gleaming orange opened directly in front of her face. The enormous floating eyeball of a Watcher 7K access IC gazed directly at her. Standard U.M.S. iconology for Intrusion Countermeasures programs, as expected. Her own masking utility was already on-line. She wore the elaborate costume of a traditional Japanese geisha: makeup, hair, kimono, and sandals. Her kimono, a brilliant white, was decorated all over with the decahedral logo of Maas Intertech's parent unit, Kuze Nihon.

The giant eyeball of the Watcher IC retreated into its window. The window closed and vanished.

"Circuit twenty-two oh-five," said the white-uniformed control module behind the service counter, pointing left.

Piper turned and followed another gleaming violet line to the wall of mirrors, then stepped straight into the wall. Firing herself down another dataline and out across the amber-gridded night of the Maas Intertech computer network.

The run was on.

11

Rico motioned at the brick barrier.

Shank stepped forward, edged past Bandit, and attacked the brick with his Wallacher combat axe. The brick and mortar split and crumbled like an old plaster wall in some derelict tenement. After the first few blows, Shank began using his free hand to tug chunks out of the barrier, the pieces bursting into dust between his fingers. The noise level was minimal. Rico gave Bandit an approving nod, but the shaman didn't seem to notice.

Dok and Filly came hurrying along the main passage as Rico was suiting up. Kevlar mask with integral headset, commando-style harness, flak jacket. Predator 2 heavy auto, Ingram 20T submachine gun, both with integral smartlinks.

For tonight's special work, he and the rest of the team also carried Ares Special Service automatics, medium autos with silencers and extended fourteen-round clips. The clips held Armamax gel-stun rounds loaded with special chemical agents. If the impact of the round didn't disable the target, the chem agents would, absorbed directly into the bloodstream through armor, clothing, skin, and damn near anything else. Unconsciousness would result in about three seconds. Sometimes less. People with a dozen armor-piercing slugs in their meat sometimes went on shooting for longer than that, so the delay wasn't really an issue. No more than with any other bullet.

And the mortality issue took precedence, in any event. The Armamax slugs disabled without killing. Rico wasn't into wetwork, murder by another name. He and the rest of the team would switch to hard ammo if and when they had no other choice. When it became kill or be killed.

But only if it came to that.

The objective was to get in and out before anyone even

knew they were there. Smooth as a teflon slide, painless as a razor's slice. Surgically precise. Leave the heavy bang-bang warfare scag to the amateurs out in the streets.

By the time Dok and Filly had their gear set and ready to go, Shank had dug a hole through the brick barrier almost big enough for a troll.

Rico fingered his headset. "Time check."

Piper replied, "Zero-one-zero-three hours."

"Right," Rico said, glancing around at the team. "Lock and load. Namecodes only. Stay alert."

Slides snapped and clicked. Spring-fed ammo clicked into firing chambers. Rico slipped past Bandit and motioned Shank into lead position. They advanced past the ruined barrier, keeping to intervals of about three meters, weapons at ready. Dok and Filly would handle rear-guard. That put Bandit right in the middle, right where he belonged.

This passage was just like the main one, but with one crucial difference. It led directly to the principal utility and engineering building of the Maas Intertech facility. The walls were seeded with vibration and motion sensors. Taking them out was part of Piper's job. She should be in the Maas Intertech computer nexus by now, doing her thing.

If she wasn't, the five of them in this tunnel were meat.

Every system cluster, like every individual system, had weaknesses, and those could be exploited.

Piper's map showed that the interconnected mainframes that composed the Maas Intertech computer cluster had one serious flaw. R & D mainframes were the most vigorously protected, rated at Security Code Red-4. Intrusion Countermeasures guarding the access nodes to these systems would be black, as vicious as IC ever got. The corp knew where its most important assets were located and spared no expense in defending them. The primary security mainframe, however, was merely Code Orange, tough but by no means impenetrable. And the main engineering system, which monitored and controlled the facility's physical devices such as water, light, and heat, was only moderately defended by Code Green security. And that was the cluster's flaw.

Besides controlling heat and light, elevators, automatic

doors, and the like, the primary engineering mainframe
was also responsible for such operations as supplying
power to security monitors and related devices.

The flaw that Piper would exploit.

The sculpted interior of the engineering CPU had the
look of a power station control room or maybe the bridge
of a trideo starship. The heart of the node took the
form of a chief engineer icon seated at an immense, semicircular control console. An array of huge display screens
ranged across the walls facing this console. Data blazing
like electric neon streamed continuously across the wall
displays and the main console displays. From millisecond
to millisecond, the chief engineer icon would reach out
with a stark white hand to adjust some console control or
to enter a brief series of commands via the console key-
board.

As Piper crossed the threshold of the CPU node, a window outlined in brilliant green opened directly in front of
her face. The enormous eye of another Watcher IC access
program faced her squarely. Her masking utility had already changed her iconic appearance. She now wore the
dark gray zipsuit of a Maas Intertech exec. The identity
card clipped to the lapel of her jacket read, in big bold
print, PRIORITY USER, CLEARANCE AA.

The window closed; the Watcher vanished.

Piper stepped up behind the chief engineer icon.

This icon ignored her. Representing the most crucial
decision-making circuits at the core of the CPU, it relied
on Intrusion Countermeasures to defend it from harm. It
lacked both the ability to identify unauthorized intruders
into the node and the capability to do anything about
them.

Piper initialized a custom combat utility. She called it
Power Play. In the consensual hallucination of the matrix,
she drew an enormous, gleaming, chrome automatic pistol with a muzzle the size of her fist and put it against the
back of the chief engineer's head. In another version of
this reality, thirty megapulses of command/override program code infected and interpenetrated the firmware pro-
gramming of the CPU.

The chief engineer icon hesitated, turning its head just
slightly as if to look back at her.

"I'm in charge," she told it.

"Affirmative," the icon replied. "Instructions?"

"Continue normal functions. Do not interfere with any modifications I may make to system operations. Do not initiate any special activities or security alerts without my approval."

"Affirmative."

The chief engineer returned to making adjustments of the various controls. Piper reached out with her free hand and tapped a key on the console. One of the huge display screens on the walls facing the console went black, then blazed with light as the stark white iconic face of the security CPU came into view.

"Identify," the security CPU said.

"Engineering CPU," Piper replied.

"I don't recognize your icon."

"Manual override has been invoked. Authority assistant director Facility Engineering, code seven-seven-nine-four-nine, clearance double-A. Facility engineering is marking power systems microanomalies and is now beginning level-one manual and computer-directed diagnostic checks."

"I understand."

"Be advised that facility technicians will be performing unscheduled maintenance in utility passage One Main at zero-zero-four-five hours, and in other utility passages and service corridors throughout the facility. Disregard all sensor alerts from these locations until further notice. Engineering personnel are on site and will advise when the situation has been corrected."

"Acknowledged."

"End of line."

Piper broke the link with the security CPU, then spent something less than a millisecond shutting down the security sensors in utility passage One Main and other locations critical to Rico and the rest of the penetration team.

It was just a matter of pushing the right virtual keys.

From five thousand feet, the plex looked like a dark ocean of hazy orange, lit by the brilliant red strokes of fire at the top of chemplant stacks and the hundred million glinting, gleaming lights of towers, buildings, and plants.

The Hughes Stallion helo cruised smoothly through the spectral dark. Inside the chopper's command deck Thorvin kept his sensors moving, his throttle back. No need to rush. Not yet.

Direct-vision overlays cut up the terrain below into its discrete parts: Jersey City to the south, Newark to the southwest; Union City, the Hudson River, and Manhattan to the east; the Passaic-Ridgefield sprawl directly to the north. Thorvin noted that in passing. He had plotted a hexagonal course around the Secaucus industrial zone. He watched his course and kept his sensors searching for any suspicious air traffic.

The comm cut into his thoughts; first, a beep, then Rico saying, "Beta . . . time check."

What freaking time was it anyway?

Didn't matter . . .

Thorvin checked his radar and navcomp, initialized the chopper's autopilot, then flipped the main switch on his remote-vehicle multiplex controller.

No more helicopter.

Instead, he had the body of a Sikorsky-Bell Microskimmer, a kind of saucer-shaped drone the size of a trash can lid. Sensors provided a full, 360-degree global view of everything around him, disorienting, but only for a moment.

Dok and Filly were just then lifting him free of the carrypak strapped to Shank's back and setting him down on the floor, which looked like ferrocrete. The penetration team was in one of the underground utility tunnels beneath the Maas Intertech facility. From a few centimeters above the floor, the top of the skimmer's sensor pod, Shank still looked like a dumb trog.

"Beta," Rico said. "Take point."

No problem.

Thorvin wound up his turbofans and slid forward, weaving around the ankles of Shank and Rico and advancing to the end of the passage. Directly ahead was a cavernous labyrinth of massive conduits and equipment rising three stories from the floor, all rumbling like a roadtrain on a quicksilver run.

This was Maas Intertech's power and water hub. Thorvin shot straight for the ceiling, then vectored right for a quick recon. Security cameras had every service aisle and catwalk under surveillance, but that was Piper's problem. Thorvin's problem was the odd dozen technicians moving throughout the hub.

He contacted Rico via direct laserlink to guide the penetration team through the maze.

The cat-and-mouse game couldn't last. There were too many techs and they never seemed to stay in one spot for more than a couple of moments. Sooner or later, one or more of them would turn the wrong way and see the wrong thing. Rico knew it—it was inevitable—but he played the game as long as he could. The longer he and the team went without putting people down, without doing anything that would rouse suspicions, the better their chances of getting out of this alive.

They were moving up a service aisle between conduits at least half a meter in diameter, stacked up two stories on both sides of the aisle, when Thorvin reported, "Contact ahead, passage right, three meters in."

No choice, no alternate routes, no time to wait for the contact to wander away. Rico tapped Shank's shoulder to get his attention, then quickly pointed and gestured to indicate the new threat, somewhere around the corner of the passage coming up on the right. The instant Shank nodded, Rico turned and motioned Bandit forward. A quick whisper and Bandit nodded, then did something with his hand.

About five meters ahead of them, something banged and clanged. That was followed by what sounded like the sharp, shrill shriek of an alley cat.

"What the *frag* was that?" a man exclaimed.

A big slag wearing a gray and blue technician's jumpsuit stepped into the aisle just ahead, first looking up the aisle, then back.

Rico saw the man's eyes widen, but Shank was ready, crouching, Ares Special Service gripped and uplifted in two big blocky hands. The weapon thumped. The technician grunted, lifting a hand toward his ribs, then stumbled and collapsed.

"Larry?" a woman called. "Larry! Oh—!"

A woman in the same style jumpsuit stepped hurriedly into the aisle, bending toward the fallen man. Shank fired again. The woman jerked, falling onto her hands and knees; then, head lolling, slumped to the floor.

Here was one advantage of soft ammo. The two techs would be out for maybe an hour, but nothing about them gave any obvious evidence as to what had happened. No damage to clothes, no apparent signs of injury. Nothing that would necessarily instigate a full-scale security alert. The pair could have passed out drunk. Inside this power and water hub, they could conceivably have contacted some toxic substance or even high-voltage electric and been accidentally stunned or knocked unconscious. Whoever found the fallen techs would probably take a long, hard look at the surrounding pipes and equipment for signs of some technical malfunction. That was good because it would waste time, and one man's loss was another man's gain.

Before this was over, they'd need every millisecond of advantage they could get.

Control of the engineering CPU was just the beginning. By manipulating aspects of the engineering mainframe, Piper could extend her control and manipulate other aspects of the Maas Intertech facility that might impinge on the run.

The chief engineer icon, the critical circuits of the engineering CPU, was now working for her voluntarily. In addition to preforming its usual duties, it was monitoring the progress of the penetration team; it was also disabling security monitors and sensors in an ostensibly random pattern designed not only to safeguard the team and prevent discovery, but also to conceal the team's objective.

Abruptly, a warning tone sounded.

"Medic alert," the chief engineer informed. "Automated signal. Sublevel two, section seven, Advanced Water Purification unit."

"Intercept the signal," Piper said.

"Negative. Signal dispatched via radiolink. Facility MedStat responding, E.T.A. three minutes."

That was too fast, because the site of the alert was too near the penetration team's location. Piper brought up facility maps on the big display screens on the walls. The Maas Intertech emergency medical unit responded from a central suite. They would have to enter the Engineering

Facility through a ground-floor entrance. "Cut power to all north-facing ground-level entranceways and lobbies for the next five minutes. Advise security CPU that we are experiencing scattered power outages related to the anomalies detected earlier. Also, reroute all priority A, double-A, and triple-A engineering terminals to the database management CPU."

"Acknowledged," the chief engineer replied. "Executing. Except I don't have authority to reroute triple-A priority terminals."

"If you had that authority, which key would you use?"

"The big red one there."

Piper reached over and tapped it.

Utility Passage Nine Main led out of the north end of the engineering building and into a series of auxiliary tunnels leading to the engineering sublevel of Residence Quad One, which was composed of four residence towers rising to fourteen stories. The majority of Maas Intertech's corporate citizens and their families lived on-site in this and other quad condoplexes.

The game of avoiding facility technicians ended at the service hatch for Elevator Three West. The hatch swung open as they approached. That was Piper's doing.

The inside of the elevator shaft was about twelve meters square—not a lot of room for five bodies that included a husky ork and a shaman who didn't seem to be paying complete attention—but they'd all been through this drill before.

Secure hatchway. Secure weapons. Secure kevlar-reinforced web-straps to body harness. Crouch low and wait.

They didn't have to wait long.

Cables along both sides of the shaft began to move. A low-pitched humming carried down from above. Rico's microchip-enhanced vision drew the image out of the darkness. The elevator above them was descending, dropping down fast from something like the eighth floor. It didn't stop till it was just centimeters above Rico's head, about half a ton of metal just hanging there, waiting.

They went to work.

This elevator car, like most, had a solid steel floor designed to absorb impact. Cutting a hole through that would take time, minutes they couldn't afford. The run was already twenty minutes old, fifteen from first penetration. By the odds, they didn't have much time left.

A soft electronic tone sounded inside Rico's headset, followed by Piper's voice: "Time is zero-one-two-eight."

That was a warning, and it echoed the warning of Rico's own instincts. It meant that things were happening in the Maas Intertech computers that would inevitably lead to some kind of alert condition. Not right this minute, but soon enough. When it happened, whatever happened, they'd better be on their way out.

The strap now connected to Rico's body harness ended in an industrial-grade suction cup. Rico slapped the cup against the bottom of the elevator, pulled the cup's metal latch and locked it. The cup flattened out against the steel of the elevator. Rico bent his knees till his whole body weight pulled on the cup. It held.

The moment the rest of the team was ready, Rico keyed his headset. "Time check."

"Time is zero-one-two-nine."

The elevator hummed and ascended. The floor of the shaft fell away quickly. Hanging from a single thin strap, having nothing to grab on to if the suction cup or strap gave way helped make it seem that way.

Two stories up, then three. The saucer-shaped drone Thorvin had running followed them right up the shaft, hovering maybe a meter beneath their feet. Rico looked up, but there was nothing to see but the flat steel plate of the elevator. Four stories, five, then six. Almost there. Rico drew his Ares automatic. At his right elbow, Filly did the same.

Seven stories.

"Stand by for landing," Rico said.

The elevator slowed, then stopped, perfectly positioned. They hung directly in front of the doors to the ninth floor. Rico braced his feet against the edge of flooring at the bottom of the doors and lifted the Ares, gripped two-handed. Filly followed suit. A moment passed, then several more. The doors didn't open.

Shank grunted. Impatient.

Maybe half a minute went by, time they couldn't afford to lose. Either Piper was having serious problems in the matrix and couldn't spare the time to pop the doors, or there was another problem. Maybe people in the hallway outside. Maybe security personnel. Maybe an alert had been declared.

The only way to find out without risking more radio traffic was to get—

"A man and a woman," Bandit said. "Up the hall. On the left."

"What're they doing?" Rico asked.

"They're bored."

"Bored like guards standing watch?"

"Maybe."

Rico gave it a minute. They couldn't afford to do anything that might give them away, but neither could they wait. Someone would find the techs they'd put down. Someone would notice an elevator apparently gone out of service. Someone would consider a bunch of seemingly unconnected events, have a sudden flash of intuition, and hit the PANICBUTTON. The longer they waited, the more likely that became. It posed a danger to Piper as well. A decker could die in the matrix. And this was a classic case of how that might come about.

The minute ticked off. Nothing changed. Rico made the unavoidable decision. "Right. We advance. Four, take left, I take right. Two and Three, stand by to jump."

Filly acknowledged.

Rico keyed his headset. "Alpha, pop the doors on my mark. Counting two, one, mark."

The doors slid smoothly apart, revealing the hallway beyond, extending out maybe fifty meters. Standing in front of a doorway about halfway along on the left were a male and a female in loose-fitting gray suits and black mirrorshades.

As Rico brought his Ares into line, his smartlink put a gleaming red triangle over the male's chest. The auto thumped once. Filly's auto thumped at nearly the same instant. The male fell to his knees, then rolled onto his back. The female went down like a bag of rocks.

Thorvin's drone flashed past, humming.

Dok and Shank swung themselves forward, planted their feet on the floor of the hallway, popped their harnesses and then knelt down, training their automatics up the hallway to provide cover.

Once they were set, Rico followed them out, with Filly

close behind. The two of them then turned back to tug
Bandit clear of the elevator shaft. Filly reached out and
popped Bandit's harness. It was a few precious moments,
but that couldn't be helped. Bandit tended to do things in
one of two ways, like an expert or a dunce. Left to himself, he'd probably hang there under the elevator for a
couple of hours before figuring out how to get out and
then actually getting around to doing it.

Rico reminded himself, not for the first time, that the
shaman's strengths far outweighed his weaknesses. And
everybody had weaknesses. It was built-in.

Inside the brilliant cube of the Engineering CPU, a
window outlined in green suddenly opened and the giant
eye of a Watcher program gazed straight into Piper's face.

Things were starting to happen now, all over the Maas
Intertech computer cluster. The power failures she had ordered had been noticed. Programmers and technicians
were trying, without success, to get into the engineering
mainframe. The security CPU had doubtless put the cluster on passive alert. It knew something serious was
wrong, but it didn't know what. It needed more data.

The giant eye gazing into her face was evidence of
that.

Piper drew a balloon from her jacket pocket, stretched
it, blew it up, and tapped it toward the Watcher IC. The
balloon undulated and expanded. The Watcher's eye
drifted aside to avoid it, but couldn't. The balloon
speeded up, enveloped the Watcher, then just held it. The
watcher's eye moved back and forth, but drifted slowly
and steadily upward—inside the balloon—toward the
glaring white ceiling of the node, then just hung there,
immobile.

"Security CPU requesting node-to-node interface," the
chief engineer icon reported.

"Denied," Piper said. "Lock out all external systems."

"Affirmative."

The clock was running down.

12

The door to Condo 9-B shot open just in front of Rico's face. He stepped through and aside, dropping into a crouch. Shank followed. That was just being careful. Bandit reported the condo empty except for the master bedroom.

Two occupants. One male, one female.

Their target had company tonight, and that was no surprise. The corps could be real generous with perks. If Surikov had lacked the means or just the plain luck to find some companionship on his own, the corp would probably provide whatever kind he required. That was how the corps worked. Threaten your spouse if you don't do the job and serve up whores when you did. Whatever got them what they wanted. That was it.

The bedroom door snapped open. Shank went first and Rico followed. A hazy, orange-tinted light surrounded the bed like a veil. Two bodies moved there. Rico's vision overlays showed him the contours of the bodies right through the veil of light and the liquid satin bedsheets. Male on top, female below.

Even as Rico brought his Ares to bear, the female looked right at him, gaped, and put a hand to her throat. Rico saw the movement and guessed what it meant, but there was no way to stop her without risking hitting the man on top of her.

He couldn't risk the shot.

A soft bell-tone sounded. Red strips running up the corners of the room flared red. "A security condition has been initialized," a hushed female voice announced quietly from somewhere near the ceiling. "Remain calm. If this is an actual emergency, do nothing. Security personnel are responding. Do not be alarmed. If you have initialized a security condition in error, please dial one-one-one and identify yourself to the security supervisor."

The slitch on the bed was wearing some kind of PANICBUTTON around her neck. Now she smiled as if self-satisfied. The male looked back over his shoulder, jerked with surprise, and rolled off the female.

"Three," Rico said.

Dok moved to the bed, put a burst injector to the female's leg, and fired. The slitch exclaimed, then went limp. Rico pointed the muzzle of the Ares at the male. "Identify."

The man looked about fifty, distinguished, thinning hair and close-trimmed beard stained with gray. Some extra weight around the middle. Not a big man. Not a small one either. He gasped, drew a couple of panting breaths, stammered, "Surikov ... Ansell Surikov ..." He stole a glance toward the female, eyes wide with uncertainty, fear. "What is this? I insist ..."

The vocal stress analyzer on Rico's commando-style watchband pegged too wildly for a good reading. The slag was really worked up. Rico nodded at Dok, who started making his checks, a quick retina print and DNA scan. The checks weren't foolproof, just the best they could do under the circumstances. The correct patterns had come with L. Kahn's chip dossier. Running the checks took about half a minute.

"We're positive," Dok said.

Rico nodded at Surikov and said, "Who's the Garden?"

Surikov eyebrows jumped. He blurted, "That's my *wife*! How ..."

A Garden of Earthly Delights.

A private thing, Rico knew, between Surikov and his wife. He knew that from the chip dossier provided by L. Kahn.

"How do you know—!"

"We're here to take you home, Dr. Surikov," Rico said, lowering his Ares. "Home to your wife."

Surikov stared at Rico for several long moments, then rubbed a hand over his mouth and made an obvious effort to get hold of himself.

"You wanna go, right?"

Surikov hesitated, then nodded and said, "Just tell me how to proceed."

Rico pulled a pack from his belt, broke it open, and shook it out. A bright orange jumpsuit with built-in plastic shoes, all in Surikov's sizes. "Put this on. Make it fast."

While Surikov was doing that, Dok checked him out again. "Vitals're okay. You on medication?"

"No. Nothing like that."

"Let's do it," Rico said.

Bandit ran his eyes around the living room. The furnishings put forth a character of luxury and fine living, but that was a lie. The walls, drapes, sofas, carpet, the onyx sculptures and semi-holographic pics were all dead, made of plastic and other artificial materials. There was nothing of life here except for the power and water running through the walls, and that was the vague clue to the truth about this room. It was not a fine space for living, as it might appear, but rather a plastic container for corporate slaves, a sort of coffin, really. Just a bit over-sized.

There was nothing of value here, except possibly Surikov. Bandit turned to watch Rico and Dok hustling the scientist up the hall and into the living room. Surikov was worth a lot of money. That might buy valuable things.

Bandit slipped a hand into one of the pockets inside his coat. His fingers found a small silver figurine, like a man made of wicker. Something that might have value for a druid or a witch. It had no value for him and so he placed it on the small platinum-hued table at the end of a sofa. He would leave it in place of Surikov. The little wicker man. A fair exchange.

"Five, move it!" Rico ordered.

Bandit nodded understanding.

Five was his assigned namecode.

Through the apartment to the hallway door, Rico hustled Surikov along at a brisk walk, but the man's physical condition was a problem. He wasn't young and he didn't exercise—that was in the dossier, too. He'd probably survive the stresses of the next few minutes, but anything might happen if he had to get really athletic. The plan was to avoid pushing the slag too hard until there was no other option.

"Time is zero-one-three-four," Piper reported via
radiolink. That meant security forces were responding.
Rico didn't need to be told. The voice still droning from
the ceiling kept him keenly aware of the time trickling
away and the danger, getting more real every second.

As Rico reached the door to the hallway, Thorvin's
saucer-shaped drone shot off toward the end of the hall
opposite the elevators. Shank and Filly dropped into combat crouches. Rico glimpsed the door at the end of the
hall swinging open, and the sudden, dazzling flashes of
the flare-strobes mounted on Thorvin's drone. Rico
turned Surikov toward the elevators. A stun grenade detonated to their rear. Rico hoped it was from the drone.

Elevator Three West now waited in line with the floor,
doors wide open. Rico let Dok hustle Surikov onto the elevator, then turned to look back down the hall.

The drone's strobes were flashing. Another stun grenade banged, and some slag in a uniform staggered back
through the doorway by the stairs. Rico took aim on that
doorway, Shank and Filly came charging up the hall and
past his shoulders. The instant they passed by, he turned
and dove onto the elevator, and the elevator doors slid
shut.

The drone would be left behind to delay and confuse
on-site security forces. It was expendable.

The elevator rose.

Surikov was breathing hard and looking worried. Dok
checked him again and burst-injected something into his
arm. "Stay calm," Dok said. "We've done this before."

"I'm afraid I haven't!" Surikov blurted.

"Time is zero-one-three-six," Piper reported.

That meant trouble. Maas Intertech had security forces
on-site, but they were lightweights. The real trouble
would come from outside. Kuze Nihon maintained a unit
called Daisaka Security, and Daisaka's rapidresponse
teams provided a back-up umbrella for all of Kuze
Nihon's subsidiaries in the Jersey-New York megaplex,
including Maas Intertech. Those teams, commando-
trained and equipped, would be only minutes in arriving.
Rico wanted to be long gone by then.

Daisaka's uniformed forces wore flash that featured the
likeness of the black annis ape, a very territorial creature

who was known to overturn cars before ripping them to pieces.

The elevator slowed to a halt at the fourteenth floor. The doors slid open. A pair of men in light gray security uniforms stood there, right outside the elevator. For an instant the guards just frowned, but then abruptly reached for their sidearms. Shank and Filly's autos thumped simultaneously. Both guards fell.

Rico led the group out of the elevator and cut a sharp left. The door beside the elevator opened onto a narrow stairway that led directly to the roof.

Down out of the hazy orange dark of the night came an olive-green Hughes Stallion chopper running without lights.

They loaded up quick.

13

The room was dark, but Rico's custom Jikku eyes turned the darkness into a dusty gray like twilight. He eased himself out from under the covers, then up off the mattress he and Piper used for a bed. The building on Mott Street wasn't a regular doss, the furnishings nothing more than what they absolutely needed. A simple mattress was good enough to sleep on. A ragged old couch was good enough for sitting. Rico walked over to the couch, then sat down and lit a cheroot. The tea still sitting in a cup on the low table before the couch had gone cold.

Piper's little slim-stemmed pipe lay in the ashtray next to the tea. Rico remembered how strange it had seemed the first time he saw her toting the thing. While running hot wire and other dirty games down in the Carib and South America, he'd seen women toting all kinds of smokers—but a pipe? That was different. Piper said she'd picked up the habit from her mother, but she never talked much about her mother. Rico gathered that her mother was Japanese, and attracted to elves. Piper talked even less about her father, but what little she said usually came with a lot of acid. Rico had guessed that her father was an elf and about as treacherous as any corp. The few times she'd mentioned him, she always ended up talking about corps, and how none could be trusted.

The bedsheet rustled. Piper lifted her head, looking around, then rose onto one elbow. *"Jefe?"* she said softly.

"Go back to sleep, *querida.*"

"What time is it?"

"Almost five."

The time didn't matter. He and Piper weren't on watch for another two hours. They'd gotten clear of the Maas Intertech facility, dumped the helo, and run around a while in Thorvin's van, checking for shadows. No pursuit had appeared. Sometime tonight they'd contact L. Kahn, exchange Ansell Surikov for the rest of their money, and be done with the deal.

"You should rest, *jefe*."

"I'm resting. Go back to sleep."

Runs like these were rough on Piper, Rico knew. She couldn't concentrate only on the matrix. She had to deal with the meat world, too. Security setups, progress of the penetration, coordinate things. Make sure the right elevator was at the right floor at just the right time. Give Thorvin a go, not early, not late, so the chopper and the ride home would be exposed for the least amount of time possible. It was a lot to deal with. A lot of pressure. Probably the worst of it was that no one, least of all Rico, could really know just what she went through, because when she went into the matrix, she went alone.

It humbled him. It made him feel like his skills and abilities weren't really any big deal. Most men were made to fight, to face pressure, conflict. They were born that way. But for a woman to go through what Piper did . . . that was something special.

"We did good," she said softly.

"So far," Rico agreed.

"The kami were with us."

"It ain't over yet."

"What's bothering you, my love?"

"I don't' know." Rico felt restless, uneasy. Instinct said the run had gone too smoothly. No one had gotten as much as a scratch. That rarely happened. The price of a run against a major corp could usually be measured in blood. Had they simply been lucky? Was some surprise still to come? Something that would make up for the easy way things had gone so far . . .

His brain kept reminding him about the team and the plan. The team was experienced and the plan had been a good one, worked out in detail. There had been plenty of weaknesses in the Maas Intertech facility, and the plan had exploited them. On that basis alone, the run should have gone smoothly.

"I don't think I'm gonna sleep till we get rid of this slag," Rico said.

"You're too good a leader."

"I'm responsible."

"You're not a god."

"I'm doing all I can do. That's my *job*."

That was all anyone could expect, no more, no less, and his adamant tone cut Piper short, like he knew it would. They'd had this talk before. Rico had no illusions about his capabilities. He couldn't know how things would turn out. He couldn't see into the future to discover how they were being used—*if* they were being used—or how L. Kahn or somebody else might be planning to betray them. Rico's job was to see that they came outta this alive, the whole team, and Piper especially. That made it hard to sleep or rest, to do anything but worry about what was coming next.

"I'm gonna check around a minute."

"You need rest, *jefe*."

"This won't take long."

A moment to pull on his pants, another to pick up the Predator 2 lying on the table beside the bed. A few more to do what he needed to do. He stepped across the hall to the second bedroom. Surikov was in there, asleep, stretched out on a mattress. He looked okay. Dok said he'd survived the bustout in good shape. A little tired, a little over-excited, but no worse for the wear. Dok and Filly had the room to the right, at the end of the hall. They looked okay, too.

No lights anywhere. That was standard.

Rico moved up the hall to the main room. Shank stood at one of the windows overlooking Mott Street. He held the butt-end of an M22A2 braced against his hip. Thorvin stood at one of the rear windows with an SMG. Bandit sat cross-legged in the middle of the floor.

"How's it scanning?" Rico asked.

"Wiz, boss," Shank answered.

Thorvin grunted and nodded.

Rico paused in front of Bandit. The shaman's eyes were open and staring straight ahead. "Something in the air," Bandit said. "Feels bad."

"Like trouble?" Rico asked.

Bandit looked up at him, and said, "Good bet."

The infrared-enhanced cameras in her belly pod clearly picked out the big ork standing just inside the second-floor window overlooking Mott Street and the smaller dwarfish figure by the window in the rear. For almost an hour, the pair had barely moved except to turn their heads, and that made Bobbie Jo wonder. The average gutterpunk didn't have anywhere near that kind of discipline. Most runners she'd spied on here in Newark and other plexes had the discipline of the typical rock'n roller. They were more interested in breaking out the beer and the whiskey at every opportunity. After a run like the one against Maas Intertech, most would've thrown a party, complete with bootleg chip and recreational psychochems.

A quiet voice, the words, "Good bet . . ." came to her over the radiolink. Probably via the listening post set up in the tenement across from the runners' hideyhole. A laser mike directed at a window. The runners seemed worried about something. Bobbie Jo could understand that.

Skip Nolan's voice quietly arose. "Air One, status."

"No movement," Bobbie Jo replied. "No change."

And no more banter over the radio. It had died out over the last hour or two. The team inside the Command and Control vehicle was tired. So was Skip. She could hear it in his voice. Bobbie Jo was feeling a little worn herself. The runners had slept most of the day prior to their run against Maas Intertech and were sleeping in turns right now. The units of the Executive Action Brigade had been working fourteen-hour shifts since the beginning, since picking up the runners at that yakuza bar, Chimpira. Now only Colonel Yates seemed to have an excess of energy and that was because tailing the runners had changed from a silicon glide into serious biz. The runners had gear they weren't supposed to have. The chopper they'd used to get out of the Maas Intertech facility hadn't been so wiz, just ordinary radar, but the van, that gray and black phantom, *it* had presented problems. The dwarf rigger who did the team's driving and probably most of its repairs had the van outfitted with some kind of wild military-grade sensor gear. Getting the equipment to sleaze it had cost the Executive Action Brigade a few more nuyen than Colonel Yates had been prepared to spend.

Bobbie Jo could still hear the man cursing, cursing everybody, especially the runners and the Brigade's current

client. "If those scummers pull any more crap, we'll ice
'em! We'll ice 'em all!"

Talk like that worried her.

Icing the runners would be murder pure and simple,
and, if nothing else, in direct violation of their orders,
their contract with the client. That would make everything they'd done so far a waste of time and effort.
They'd forfeit their contract and any money they had
coming, and the Brigade's rep would slip a few more
notches. Bobbie Jo didn't think the Brigade could afford
it.

Abruptly, her ground-based combat comp went into active mode. Targeting indicators began winking in front of
her eyes. She felt a shock of surprise strike straight into
her gut as apparently random movements below her suddenly resolved into the semblance of a pattern.

She saw matched sets of vehicles, dark blue sedans
with vans, moving rapidly along the streets that bracketed
Mott Street. If she read their movements correctly, all
those vehicles would arrive at opposite ends of Mott
Street at almost the same instant.

She broadcast her alert signal.

Even as her squeal hit the air, two dark-clad figures appeared on the roofs of buildings facing the runners' Mott
Street hideyhole. Those figures moved toward the front of
the roofs as if to take up sniping positions. Focusing her
lenses and zooming in, Bobbie Jo saw that one of the
figures wore a dark uniform with shoulder flash that included the likeness of a black ape.

What the hell was going on?

Ground teams reported more movements, furtive movements through back alleys, uniformed persons with automatic
weapons taking up positions.

This was crazy. It suddenly looked like a commandostyle
raid was about to hit the runners' hideyhole, right here in the
middle of Newark's Sector 2. It didn't seem possible. Yet
now she heard Skip firing off orders to Brigade units on the
ground, declaring the approaching vehicles hostiles, and then
she saw the big bay door at the front of the runners' hideyhole rolling up.

"Ground Four and Five," Skip said. "Intercept hostiles."

Where Mott Street met Raymond Boulevard, a dark

brown Brigade sedan suddenly shot right onto the roadway, broadsiding one of the hostile sedans, only to be
struck in the tail by the van accompanying that car.

Then, the runner's gray and black van came roaring out
onto Mott street at mid-block, turning toward Fleming.
The hostiles coming up the street from that direction, a
car and a van, abruptly split left and right, skidding sideways and effectively blocking off the roadway. The runners' van didn't even slow down. It slammed against the
sedan's front left side, bounded up onto the sidewalk,
then down again, and went roaring straight at the corner.

Autofire punctuated by the thumping of heavy weapons
was breaking out all over the place.

Thorvin had the power plant to the max as they hit the
street, engine roaring, tires screaming, laying a trail of
smoking black as he turned up the block. He saw the big
sedan and the van coming straight at him, splitting left
and right to block the roadway. No way he was stopping.
The combat subroutine of his onboard computer performed an immediate analysis on the sedan and put a rapidly winking red indicator right where he should hit the
sedan for maximum effect.

It was quite an impact. Nearly shook the datajack right
out of his skull. Cost him an outboard sensor array. But
he had the speed up to eighty kph by then and—freaking
hell—the physics worked! He caught a glimpse of the sedan spinning half a circle as he bounded up over the curb
and tore a path down the sidewalk and straight to the corner. Just a simple matter of mass versus energy, really.

Corner coming up fast.

Skid turn—no other way around it.

Bullets pounded off his skin as the tires gave a banshee
wail and sent him sliding sideways around the corner.

Alarm bells in his ears.

An image leapt into the back of his mind, something
like a jet fighter swooping low over the buildings off to
the left of the intersection. A red schematic flashed in
front of his eyes: A CyberSpace Designs recon drone.

"Bird's with us again!" he snarled.

"Burn it!" Rico barked.

A targeting indicator winked—locking on. Thorvin
popped the M-134 minigun out of his roofpod and opened

up. Three bursts, and the drone went spinning wing-over-wing, down and out of sight.

Bobbie Jo felt the slugs battering her airframe, then the flare of fire from the long-range fuel tanks. Alarm indicators flashed and flickered. The skin over her right wing split and burst into tatters. The concrete ground came swirling toward her.

She screamed. Blackness swallowed her.

14

Another bone-rattling impact and they were clear of the attacking forces converging on Mott Street.

Thorvin had the power plant opened up wide, and the noise was deafening. The roar of the engine rising into a stammering whine that chipped away at the nerves like sustained autofire. Hanging onto his seat with one hand and his Predator 2 with the other, Rico clenched his teeth and stared into the passenger-side rearview mirror. He tried not to think about the people bouncing around in the rear of the van. There wasn't time.

"Splash one drone!" Thorvin bellowed over the scream of the van's engine. "I'm heading for the freaking *you-know-what!*"

Rico nodded. "Do it!"

Surikov cried out from the rear. The slag was scared and rightly so, but he and Dok would have to deal with it. Bandit's warning that someone was about to bust the Mott Street safehouse had come none too soon. The hostiles had moved in on foot and in cars and in vans and had even thrown up a drone. Probably, it was Daisaka Security, the security arm of Maas Intertech's parent corp, Kuze Nihon.

Nobody with organized paramilitary forces brought out the heavy guns just because they felt like partying. There had to be a reason for the attack, and Surikov was the only one that made sense. But the point that bothered Rico most was not who or why, but rather *how* the opposition had gotten to them at Mott Street. How had they been found out?

Two possibilities came to mind. One was that someone might have tailed them to the safehouse, despite Thorvin's declarations to the contrary. Rico didn't think that very likely. Two, Piper might have been traced

through the matrix. She was equally sure that nobody had traced her, but that didn't mean she couldn't be wrong. Rico didn't think much of that possibility either, for the simple reason that where the matrix was concerned, Piper was usually right.

Was there something he'd overlooked? And what in fragging hell could it be? He couldn't believe that anyone on his team had given them up.

One thought came to mind.

He looked at Dok. "Check the slag for a snitch."

"What?" Dok exclaimed. *"Now?"*

"Do I look like I'm *joking*?"

Dok stared for a moment, swaying with the violent motions of the van as it skidded around a corner; then, he bent, broke open his medpack and went to work.

They already knew that Surikov had implants: datajack, chip memory, subprocessing unit. A really advanced skillwire system. Lots of tech drek to expedite and accelerate his scientific research. L. Kahn's chip-dossier had mentioned it. What it suggested to Rico right now was that Surikov might also have been implanted with some kind of electronic microtransmitter, something that Maas Intertech or Daisaka Security could home in on if the slag ever got "lost" or snatched.

Stuff like that wasn't common, but for top execs and ramjamming research slags like Surikov, neither was it unknown. Rico cursed himself for not anticipating the possibility and getting Surikov checked out sooner.

Surikov was lying flat on the floor. Dok bent over him, hanging onto a cargo strap. Two seconds later, the med scanner in Dok's hand began to beep shrilly, and Dok looked up, wide-eyed.

"Come on, Monk! *Hurry!* "

Minx grabbed his hand and tugged, propelling Monk forward, down a flight of stairs leading to a subway station. Only at the bottom of the stairs Minx turned right instead of left, yanked open a metal door marked, PLX-3, AUTH PERS ONLY, and tugged him right through the doorway.

The door slammed shut at his back, then everything went black. Minx tugged him ahead at a run. Their feet echoed against the floor, a smooth, hard floor that seemed basically level, though cluttered with stuff that rustled around his ankles and crunched under his sneaks.

Minx slowed. Something heavy banged and something metallic squealed. A door swung open. They stepped out onto a concrete safety walk that ran along one side of an underground roadway. Monk couldn't recall having ever seen this part of the transitways before. The roadway, only two lanes wide and divided by white dashes, extended off in both directions for a few hundred meters before curving out of sight. The pavement looked really clean. No litter anywhere.

Minx looked back and forth, up and down the roadway, then thrust back her wildly frizzled hair, now glowing red and orange, and grinned.

"This is it," she said.

"What?"

A rumbling arose into a roaring like a race car. A gray and black van came screaming around the curve to the right, blew on by them and disappeared around the curve to the left. Minx frowned.

"Huh?" Monk said.

As the van disappeared, a storm of amber blips began washing across the walls of the transitway, appearing from around the curve to the left. The roar of the van faded away, then swelled. Another truck, a sort of tow truck, came screaming around the curve to the left. This time Minx nodded, glanced at Monk and pulled him ahead, under the railing guarding the safety walk, then down onto the roadway.

The tow truck roared like a semiballistic jet, amber strobes blazing from above the cab and from inside the massive front grille. Monk watched that grille coming closer and closer and closer until it seemed huge, titanic, and it suddenly occurred to him that the truck wasn't slowing down and he was standing right in front of it.

Abruptly, Minx yanked him aside, and the tow truck's tires screamed and white smoke billowed into the air.

"Come *on*!" Minx shouted.

The tow truck screeched to a halt, the door swung open, and Minx all but pulled Monk up the steps and into the cab.

The truck roared ahead. The acceleration was incredible. It thrust Monk against the back of the broad bench seat, holding him there till he could hardly breathe. He glimpsed a pair of black-gloved hands gripping a steering wheel and the front dashboard, blazing with controls— lights, graphic indicators, LED dials and gauges—all winking, gleaming, flaring and flashing incessantly. He stared wide-eyed at the broad white lines of the roadway streaming toward him in a blur. Exocentrical Rumination blasted from speakers all around.

"Who's your friend?" someone shouted. "Real booty!"

There was that word again.

Minx grinned. "This is Monk!" she yelled. "Monk, this is Harry! Harry the Hack, people call her! She's the best hack in the city!"

"Yeah?" Monk shouted, wondering what a "hack" might be.

Minx nodded, smiling.

"Used to drive a cab!" Harry exclaimed. "Never managed to lose the tag!"

Minx sat back, and Monk leaned forward to get a better look at Harry. She had gold-blonde hair drawn back into a thick braid. She also had the perfect, cosmed-generated face of a Maria Mercurial novastar, complete with languid bedroom eyes and a small dark mole a little above and beside voluptuously full ruby lips. She wore a shiny, studded black jacket and black engineer boots. She took a quick drag on a brown Sunset Neon cigarette, then looked across at Monk and grinned.

"What the hell are you looking at!" she shouted.

Monk looked at the dashboard. A TV/3V show was playing on the vid there. "As The E-Mail Turns," rolled across the screen. The first scene showed a glowing neon man in a glowing neon room pushing glowing neon envelopes around on a glowing neon desk, and muttering incoherently. Monk hadn't ever seen this show before. If it made any sense, it escaped him.

Something barked. Monk looked aside to see Minx giving a hug and a kiss to a huge dog with glaring red eyes and vicious white teeth. "We call 'im *Prince*!" Harry shouted.

Prince of Darkness? Monk wondered.

Minx and Harry burst out laughing.

Abruptly, the corridor of the transitway vanished, and they were sluicing through a sea of automobiles and

trucks. The tow truck roared and squealed. Horns blared,
sirens wailed. Monk caught a glimpse of a bus hurtling
straight toward the right side of the tow truck's cab, a
solid wall of cars charging straight toward the tow truck's
nose, and a crowd of people abruptly scattering from all
around the tow truck's front and sides. Buildings, towering buildings, black rain-tarnished retrofitted brick and
ferrocrete buildings spun past in a blur.

Monk felt himself wrenched forward, practically out of
his seat, then thrust against the passenger door, then back
the other way, right across Minx's lap and practically into
the jaws of the giant, red-eyes-glaring Prince of Darkness
dog.

Minx looked down at him and smiled and gently
pressed his hair back from his brow.

"That's the other thing, you booty!" she called over the
deafening roar of the truck. "Whenever you ride with
Harry, you ALWAYS wear YOUR SEAT BELT!"

There was that word again.

Booty.

"HERE WE ARE!" Harry cried.

For a moment, the tow truck seemed to turn sideways.
Tires screamed. Monk, still sprawled across the seat, felt
his feet and lower legs drawn inexorably toward the ceiling. Then the truck stopped suddenly, and he tumbled
onto the floor under the control console.

Minx and Harry burst out laughing.

"Come on, Monk! *Come on!*"

Minx grabbed his hand and tugged him from the cab
and down onto some street somewhere in Sector 2, near
Port Sector. He could smell the rank river, the Passaic
River, that was for sure. Maybe Newark Bay, too. The
street immediately around him, lined with old factory and
tenement buildings, looked like a disaster area.
Cracked-up cars straddled the sidewalks and sat at odd
angles all over the street. Bodies lay all over the place,
too, some of them still moving. Slags in paramilitary armor stood around shouting at one another. Emergency
strobes atop ambulances and Omni police vehicles and
other cars and trucks flickered and flashed brilliantly
against the dusky suffusion of early dawn.

The tow truck growled. Harry had a thick cable

stretched out from the rear of the truck to a big blue sedan sitting on its side.

Minx tugged Monk in another direction, straight toward some heavily armored slag sprawled over the curb. The patch on his shoulder pictured something like a gorilla.

A light flashed, and Monk realized Minx had a camera pointed at the slag's body. She bent down for a close-up. A real close-up shot. So close she nearly had the lens of the camera touching the surface of the pool of blood slowly trickling out from the under the gleaming reflective faceplate of the slag's helmet. And then she moved the camera just a bit aside and lowered her mouth . . . her mouth . . .

"Monk?"

The world began slowly turning around him. He glimpsed Minx smiling quizzically at him and caught sight of Harry grinning and laughing just before the street tilted on end and everything went black.

"You booty . . ."

15

The van glided through the back streets of Rahway, straddling the border of Sector 13. The gloomy dawn resembled twilight. The ancient buildings flanking the road cast dark shadows. Rico knew this part of the sprawl as the Dead Zone. Nobody lived here but ghouls and wandering gangers and the odd slag on the run. There was no power and no water but what people found for themselves. The badges didn't hardly know the place existed, and that was probably good for them, the cops. The fog from some long-ago metaphysical catastrophe rolled forever through the streets. Devil rats, some as big as small dogs, peered from the alleys and out of the windows of abandoned buildings. The only light came from the fires in metal storage drums or seeping down from the sky through a pall of dark clouds.

"Freaking dust devil!" Thorvin growled.

A swirl of fog evolved into a storm of dust and grit rattling against the sides of the van. Rico glimpsed a series of grotesque shapes, faces, contorted bodies only vaguely human, flowing over the windshield and around the van like ghosts, but he knew these were just an artifact of the storm. Metaphysical FX. A token of the Dead Zone. It passed as swiftly as it had come.

"Status," he said.

"Clear," Thorvin growled. "Freaking clear. I got a fouled intake port, but we're freaking clear."

The van rumbled and turned across the road and slowed, descending a steep ramp into a sublevel garage. The garage door trundled down behind them. "Building okay?" Rico asked.

Thorvin nodded. "It's clean."

Rico looked toward Bandit, but didn't bother asking for confirmation. Magicians didn't like using magic in this part of Sector 13. Too much static. That was what Bandit said. Rico took his word for it. "Set the watch," he told Thorvin.

"It's set already," Thorvin grumbled.

From the outside, the building didn't look like much, two stories of crumbling brick with rusty-looking steel shutters over every door and window. The appearance was deceiving, though. The place was a fortress, equipped with sensors, offensive and defensive systems, all capable of independent, computer-directed operation. No one would have to stare out any windows here. The building and its automated systems would stand guard for them.

Rico watched his team pile out of the van. Two hours' sleep hadn't done anybody much good. In any run you reached a point where the adrenaline made you think you could go on forever. But close your eyes and relax for a moment and fatigue washed over you like a floodtide. The abrupt departure from the Mott Street safehouse and the wild ride outta there, like a run through a war zone, hadn't helped.

Predator 2 in hand, Rico led Shank on a quick sweep of the building. The place was clean. The van was clean. Every member of the team was clean. And now Surikov was clean. For sure. Checked and rechecked and declared safe.

Surikov had been the problem. Maas Intertech had implanted a microtransmitter into the back of his neck, then somebody had homed in on that electronic snitch's signal to find him. Guano like that sounded simple enough, but it presented the always image-conscious corps with a potential image problem. Regardless of the truth, the corps liked to avoid being portrayed as oppressive tyrants monitoring and controlling every aspect of people's lives.

That Maas Intertech would take a risk on that score implied that either Surikov was more of a heavy jammer than anyone had admitted so far or else the corps were getting more protective than ever of their assets.

Rico blamed himself for not expecting that. The unexpected was an integral part of the game. You planned for what you could and hoped and prayed that nothing important slipped by or that you could fix it before somebody got wasted.

Dok had removed the transmitter, null sheen. Rico had tossed it into the rear of a pickup back in the transitway.

Now maybe they'd have some room to breathe.

A few hours, anyway.

Thorvin headed into the sublevel utility room to bring auxiliary systems on-line. Rico sent Filly and Shank to the kitchen to get out food and supplies, and Dok and Surikov into the main room, the living room, to lax out. Then he slid an arm around Piper's waist. She met him with a kiss. "I need you to check the newsnets," he said. "Find out what's happening."

"I understand, *jefe*."

No need to explain that she shouldn't do anything that might get her signal traced through the matrix. She understood that this building around them was their bolthole. This was where they ran if they got into trouble. It was never used unless the primary safehouse got blown. Only Thorvin had been here more than a handful of times, and then only to install the security systems and get the place functional.

Piper moved down the hall to the telecom room. Rico checked that the toilet was working, then stepped into the living room. Surikov was collapsed on the sofa, slumped deep into the cushions. He didn't really look bad for a guy his age and weight. A little tired, maybe a little over-wrought. Dok was checking him over. He looked up as Rico lit a cheroot.

"Where are we?" Surikov asked.

There'd probably be no harm in telling Surikov that, but Rico had more to consider than just Surikov. He had to think about tomorrow, all the tomorrows he and his crew might ever have. Surikov was on his way home. No way of knowing what he might say to security people when he got there. No way of knowing who might eventually hear what he had to say. Better to tell him nothing, no more than he absolutely had to know. Today's corporate friend was tomorrow's enemy, and ultimately you had to consider all the corps enemies. Corps and corporates served only one master, the almighty nuyen. That was their only loyalty. "We're safe," Rico said. "All you need to know, *compadre*."

"What . . . what happens now?"

"We sit tight. You relax. You got nothing to worry about."

"I'd feel better knowing something of your plans." Surikov hesitated, looking anxious. "What happens next, I should say. As concerns me."

Rico guessed questions like that were natural. No man liked to feel powerless. If Piper was any standard by which to judge, women didn't like it either. "It's like this," he said. "We make final arrangements to hand you over. Then you go home."

"I take it you're the leader?"

Rico nodded.

"We haven't been introduced."

Rico took a deep drag on his cheroot and slowly blew the smoke out through his lips. "Numero Uno," he said. "Number One. That's what you call me."

"I see." Surikov didn't seem too sure about that. Mostly, he seemed anxious. "I'd like to talk to you about . . . about my going home, as you call it."

"What about it?"

"What 'home' are you referring to?"

The point grated.

It had been no big deal to find out where Surikov used to work before he got snatched by Maas Intertech. Surikov had an international rep in biotech and cybernetics, headware design. Piper hadn't needed to go any further than the public databases to dig out his whole history. He'd been working for a subsidiary of Fuchi I.E. called Multitronics until Maas Intertech decided to recruit him without the option of saying no.

What Rico didn't know for certain, could never know for certain, was where Surikov was really headed. By all indications, he was heading straight back to Fuchi Multitronics. If the run had been intended as a snatch, if Surikov wasn't really "going home," L. Kahn would have been smart enough to tell Rico to go slot, then simply find another team of runners eager for nuyen and not so particular about how they got it.

Rico had taken that as he was working assumption, but it didn't mean he liked making assumptions.

"How much do you know of my background?" Surikov asked abruptly.

"I know where you been. Why?"

"Are you aware that I was kidnapped?"

"Get to the point."

Surikov hesitated, lifting a hand to the back of his neck, the bandage there. Dok had given the slag a local while removing the snitch, so Surikov should be feeling no pain. Maybe the bandage was itching. "I was with Multitronics Labs most of my life," he said. "I grew up under the Fuchi banner, you might say. I'm a company man. I received my baccalaureate at Fuchi University. I hold advanced degrees from several prestigious polytechnic institutions—"

"The point," Rico said.

"My point is that, as you're probably aware, I'm considered something of an authority on intracerebral design, bionetic augmentation. My work is on the cutting edge. To keep that edge, to properly conduct my research, I must have complete freedom."

Rico clenched his teeth. "Yeah?"

"If you're planning to return me to Fuchi Multitronics, you'll be doing me and my work a grave injustice."

A corporate bad-mouthing his own corporation. How many times had Rico heard talk like that? He could count the occasions on one hand. He'd made dozens of runs like this one, and in practically every case the object of the run had been delighted to hear that he or she was going home. The way some of them talked, there was no better place on earth to live than inside the steel fists of giants like Fuchi, Aztechnology, Saeder-Krupp, whatever . . .

But now, anger swelled. Rico spent several moments glaring at Surikov, trying to control his temper, his frustration. He felt the heat rise up the back of his neck and he wanted to snarl, but he forced himself to take a long, deep drag on the cheroot and to blow the smoke out slowly, like he wasn't hardly thinking about getting mad. "I asked you if you wanted to go," Rico said lowly. "Now you're telling me what? You don't wanna go? You wanna go back to Intertech? You wanna go independent?"

"Easy, boss," Dok said quietly.

"I want an answer."

Surikov rubbed at his mouth. His eyes were open a little wider than normal. His face looked a bit red, but the color wasn't anger. Some kind of upset, like he was rattled or flustered. Like a woman. "Let me explain," he said a bit breathlessly. "I realize you've taken great risks. On my behalf. I'm grateful, very grateful. I only wish you could have been fully informed of the problem, as I see it, before you began. You see, the Maas Intertech program for research is nearly as arbitrarily restrictive as Fuchi Multitronics. That's my point. Neither of these corporations are appropriate sponsors for the kind of pure research I'm attempting to do. They've held me as a virtual prisoner. They've used me as just another corporate asset!"

Rico took another long, slow drag of his cheroot. It didn't help. It didn't keep the acid out of his voice. "Maybe you'd like to go to the Carib. Sit under a palm tree. Maybe I should go to Camden or Atlantic City. Play some fragging keno. Wait for the axe to fall."

Surikov looked confused. "I'm sorry, I don't—"

"Mass Intertech belongs to Kuze Nihon. They're almost as big as Fuchi I.E. They're a little slotted off at us right now. You're talking about skanking Fuchi, too. You better have a damn good reason."

Surikov said, "Prometheus Engineering."

Rico had heard the name before. Prometheus was major league. It had a seat on the Corporate Advisory Board that ran Manhattan. It also had a 100-story tower like a DNA spiral on Manhattan's west side, which came with a double-A security from NYPD, Inc. "What about it?" Rico growled.

"Take me to Prometheus," Surikov blurted. "Make any kind of arrangement that suits you and your comrades. Demand some payment. A finder's fee, perhaps. Their director of research should leap at the chance to get me on her staff. She runs a very enlightened program. She understands the importance of basic scientific inquiry. Her researchers have free reign."

"And what about your wife?"

"We could take her too. We would have to, in fact."

Rico nodded slowly, taking another deep drag off his cheroot. Surikov's only problem was that he was insane. "Maybe you'll tell us where we can find your wife. Maybe you'll help us bust her out."

Surikov didn't get the joke.

Dok sat very still, almost motionless.

Rico turned and walked out.

* * *

A quick scan of the virtual bars that served as the bulletin boards and rumor pools of the Newark telecommunications grid, the underground grid, yielded Piper some news.

Hours after their run on Maas Intertech, systems throughout the megaplex were still on active alert.

Half the ramjammers on-line were whooping it up, delighted by the certainty that someone had cut pure ice, pulled off something big. The other half, those with biz to conduct and runs of their own to make, were less than thrilled.

Vaux Hall Pirate News yielded two particularly cogent details: heavily armed Daisaka Security forces were cruising the streets of Newark, and a full description of Thorvin's van, including registration tags, had gone out over the regional law enforcement networks. Piper thought that important news, but not threatening, at least not necessarily.

Newark was not like other towns. Omni Police Services had learned that lesson. Daisaka Security would soon find out for itself, if it didn't already know. Its forces would inevitably discover a whole legion of petty monarchs who considered various sections of the plex to be their private kingdoms. Triad bosses, gangers, yakuza, the maf—none looked kindly on intruders.

Little Asia, Sector 6, was itself a patchwork of competing elements, and the competition often grew fierce. Each element had soldiers to back its claims. All had access to the most menacing of weapons. Daisaka would inevitably find itself facing the prospect of armed conflict, little wars for control, and that was good, for it would keep Daisaka busy.

As for the description of the van . . . Thorvin was downstairs at this very moment repainting the van and changing the registration tags. This particular van had a number of separate identities, all duly integrated into the appropriate state databases.

Piper smiled and jacked out.

The room around her returned, four blank white walls with a Samsung office telecom, an armchair, and the recliner beneath her. The telecom had two lines: a hard line into the local telecommunications grid plus a line to the satellite dish concealed on the roof. Her modified Excalibur cyberdeck lay across her lap.

Rico sat in the armchair, toking on his cheroot and looking dissatisfied. Piper took her slim-stemmed pipe from her belt pouch, packed in some tobacco, and lit up.

"What's the scan?" Rico asked in a voice like a low growl.

Piper gave him a quick summary of what she'd picked up, then said, "You look unhappy, *jefe*."

"We're fragged."

"Why?"

"Surikov doesn't wanna go home."

"Why not?"

"He says he don't like Fuchi Multitronics any more than Maas Intertech. He thinks he'll be more welcome at Prometheus Engineering. Thinks he'll be free to do things his way."

"Corps and freedom are mutually exclusive."

"The slag don't see it that way."

Piper shrugged. "We have our down payment. Our expenses are covered. Let Surikov fend for himself."

"We're responsible."

"No one's responsible for a corporate but other corporates."

"The slag's a scientist."

"That makes him nothing more than a sophisticated form of product designer. He's a suit. We owe him nothing."

"We busted him out, *querida*."

"Yes, and that was a favor."

"A slag like him won't never cut a deal on his own. He's a babe in the fragging woods."

"Then let's give him to L. Kahn and be done with it."

"He doesn't wanna go."

"I don't care what he wants."

People who lived the life defined by the corps deserved the same ruthless brand of indifference the corps accorded the rest of society. The corps had proved that a thousand times over: defiling the Earth, poisoning people, wrecking whole economies, condemning entire nations of people to lives of poverty, disease, and abject misery—whatever suited corporate objectives.

A wise man once said, "Let us drink the blood of the

enemies of humanity." Foremost among those enemies, in Piper's view, were the corps. Not even the treacherous swine of Tir Tairngire equaled the corps, in terms of sheer villainy. Elves at least had some respect for the Earth.

"You're talking like a real killer," Rico said.

"I should weep and sympathize?"

"I know you better than that."

"We'll be shagged if we don't turn Surikov over. Fuchi has long arms. They'll find us and kill us. Or use us as test subjects in their biotech labs."

"There's worse things to die for than a man's freedom."

"*Jefe*, I don't want to die for a damn suit."

"What about honor?"

"I don't want to talk about honor."

"We took a man's life in our hands. You're saying we should just walk away."

"I'm saying we should complete our contract."

"And the hell with honor."

"We agreed to turn Surikov over."

"We didn't agree to a snatch. And that's what we're doing if we make Surikov go back to Fuchi. 'Cause that's where he's probably going if we give him to L. Kahn. We're forcing him against his will."

Piper leaned her head back against the cushions of the recliner. Her lover's code of conduct, his honor, his morals, would get them killed one day. She'd known that for a long time. She accepted it because acceptance was part of love and she could not help loving Rico. She had always hoped to someday subvert him, take some of the self-righteous shine out of his moral code, if only for the sake of survival, but her influence in that regard had been negligible. It was a testament to Rico's wit and savvy and his ability as a leader that they'd been able to stay alive as long as they had, despite his code. "Talk to me, chica."

"I should give up everything for a suit?"

"I ain't asking you to give up anything. If you want out—"

That made her angry. Rico knew better than to talk like that. "Where you go I go," she said sharply. "If you want to get yourself killed, then I'm dead too."

Rico smiled. "You got cojones, *corazón*."

Love talk at a moment like this. It twisted her insides.

It made the hidden truth that only she and Rico knew ride up to the forefront of her thoughts on a tide of foaming emotion. The money she earned from runs like this gave her the means to fight the real fight, the war against the corps, the war to save the Earth before it was totally destroyed. She could face the prospect of death in that cause—had already done so and would do it again, and willingly—but to risk dying for something as despicable as a suit, a man like Surikov, whose life work only made the corps more money, that was almost too much to bear.

Rico came and perched on the arm of the recliner and drew her into his arms. She welcomed his embrace. She admired his courage. She wished she had his strength. Now, she could only think of all the things they would be giving away in trying to accommodate Surikov, and it brought her grief.

Where Surikov found his home was not the only issue. There was another problem that had to be fixed if the man was truly to be free.

Any fool could see that.

16

The rain started at four a.m. By five past the hour, the torrent from the sky became a deluge, crashing onto streets that soon turned into lakes. Rico turned up the collar of his long black duster and walked down Treadwell to the brownstone at mid-block. Five razorguys stood beneath the awning there, three on the porch of the house, two on the sidewalk before it. Two of the cutters held submachine guns barely concealed by their long, dark coats.

Rico was admitted at once, escorted through the house, then into the garden at the center of the house. Mr. Victor waited at the round transparex table in the middle of the garden. Tonight he wore a black smoking jacket and held a long fat cigar in one hand.

With a brief wave, he invited Rico to sit. "How are you, my friend?" he said. "I take it all is not well."

"You take it right," Rico replied.

"Indeed, there are many who would agree," Mr. Victor said. "You have roused the giants from their slumber. The corps have sent their forces into the streets and there is much animosity being worked out, even as we speak. The great father of the Honjowara yakuza is particularly displeased at those who trespass on his territory. Fortunately, the metro police have seen fit to remain strictly neutral, by which I mean uninvolved. I think it is safe to say that by this time tomorrow, the giants will withdraw their forces from the streets. At least, their uniformed forces."

That much was good news. Rico had enough to worry about without having to consider the prospect of shock troops from Daisaka Security. Covert forces he could deal with. Probably.

"Before you say what you are here to say, let me tell you this," Mr. Victor continued. "I have word that several parties are keenly interested in hiring the team that made the run on Maas Intertech. Word is out that the run was very clean, very precise, incurring no loss of life. You have done your reputation a great service. In the future, I will be able to ask a considerably higher price for your services."

"Assuming we're still alive."

"Is that not always the assumption?"

The question was mostly rhetorical. Rico nodded understanding, then waited. Mr. Victor took a long drag on his cigar; then, with a look and gesture of the hand, he invited Rico to speak. "I need somebody to make contact with Prometheus Engineering."

"For what purpose, my friend?"

"Recruitment. I need to know if they got any interest in a certain individual."

"An individual whom you have recently met, perhaps?"

Rico nodded.

"This can be arranged," Mr. Victor said. "However, I feel I must ask what makes you desire such a thing. Have you encountered complications?"

"Serious complications."

Mr. Victor took another long drag on his cigar. "The job has turned out to be other than what it first seemed?"

"I don't know that."

"Perhaps you would care to explain."

Mr. Victor might have no contractual involvement in the job, but that did not mean he had no interest. He had directed Rico to L. Kahn. He had made the first contact. For a man like Mr. Victor, a man of honor, that was enough. That minimal involvement made him at least partly responsible for the job, in as far as it affected Rico and his team.

Rico spoke briefly of the complications. It came down to this: he'd been hired to pass Surikov on to L. Kahn. It looked like Surikov was bound for Fuchi Multitronics, but Prometheus Engineering was where he wanted to go.

"A difficult situation," Mr. Victor remarked. "Naturally, you are not content to simply give your man to L. Kahn."

"I ain't gonna force him into anything. I don't work that way."

"You made this clear to L. Kahn in the beginning."

The meeting back at Chimpira was clear in Rico's memory. "I told him I don't do snatches, and if the subject wasn't willing, the deal was off. He told me he don't accept refunds, that not completing the contract was a killing offense."

"Perhaps this is open to negotiation."

"I doubt it."

"As do I, but there is no percentage in placing you and the lives of your team in further jeopardy until the facts are known. It is conceivable, is it not, that Prometheus Engineering is in fact the party behind the contract? In that event, there is every reason for you to complete the contract as arranged."

"Surikov's wife is supposed to be with Fuchi."

"Even so." Mr. Victor paused, smiling faintly. "You cannot assess the odds, my friend, until you know the facts. If you wish, I will arrange for you to discuss the situation with L. Kahn. Perhaps you can arrive at some mutually satisfactory solution."

Rico had serious doubts that any negotiating would help, but he had too many lives depending on him to refuse the suggestion. "That's a real generous offer," he said. "I owe you."

"On the contrary, my friend," Mr. Victor replied. "I owe you. I owe you a great deal."

The sword was black and it gleamed with the brilliant electron radiance of the matrix. It appeared in Piper's hand as if out of thin air and moved with the mercurial speed of thought.

The gray-armored warrior icon before her lifted its massive battle axe even as her sword slashed through the axe's shaft, and then whirled, finding a chink in the icon's armor and slicing through, piercing the icon, which dissolved into a cloud of fading silvery pixels.

A small, bitter victory over blaster IC. Piper released her sword, allowing it to vanish into the nothingness of inactive memory. The walls of the node around her pulsed red. The system, she knew, was going on active alert. There was no point in even attempting to continue. She'd be lucky just to get out alive.

Now, from further up the corridor, came a pack of killer IC in the form of burning orange wolves. They charged, snarling, fangs flashing. Piper hurled a handful of gleaming black stars at the beasts, then turned and ran.

The race was on. Barrier IC like massive portals—glaring with electron fury—crashed down to block the corridor only milliseconds behind her. If she faltered, if she slowed her pace by even half a step she would be trapped, sealed into the consensual hallucination of the system construct and as good as dead.

She was in the Gauntlet, the maze of nodes and subsystems surrounding the mainframes of Fuchi's Manhattan cluster, which had been designed to protect its most vital elements. The CPUs lay at the cluster's heart, surrounded by data stores, immersed in the sea of subprocessors and slaves that served not only the cluster's data operations but the whole of the Fuchi complex, the Black Towers of Fuchi-town, located in lower Manhattan.

A blazing orange portal slammed down two steps ahead of her. She tugged a small fan from her sleeve, snapped it open and dove, thrusting the open fan out before her.

The portal parted like a ripe banana, splitting down the middle.

Jacking out was not an option. It was too late for that. In the time it would take her flesh and blood fingers to hit the Disconnect key or to wrench the datajack from her temple, she would be caught, traced, and brain-fried by nanosecond-swift IC.

In the next System Access Node waited a red and yellow clown. The icon for a smartframe or perhaps a Fuchi decker. Piper had met the clown icon before. The big sunflower on its chest fired acid IC. The big white custard pie in its hand worked like a trace and burn program. Piper hurled a handful of marbles. In mid-flight, the marbles swelled into silvery globes. As the clown moved to evade, the globes flew into orbit around it, immobilizing the icon with a dazzling storm of red and green program code.

The clown's blazing orange hair stood up on end.

Piper slammed through the node and streaked out across the Manhattan telecommunications grid, free of the Fuchi cluster. The cluster's icon dominated the grid representing lower Manhattan, its form that of an enormous, five-pointed black star, slowly rotating, surmounted by a gigantic tower with five distinct facets, like the facets of a diamond. There was no more dangerous icon in the grid.

She fired herself into the electron-gridded darkness above, seeking the SAN to the regional grid. That led her to the Newark grid and back to where she had begun, and to her original fears and doubts.

Going up against Fuchi, even a subsidiary like Multitronics, was madness. It would make the run against Maas Intertech seem like a stroll through a sunlit meadow. Only a ramjamming neophyte would even consider it, and only because little baby deckers had no conception of the power contained in the Fuchi cluster. They thought sheer enthusiasm, combined with a knack for program code, would see them through anything. It didn't work that way. Piper knew. She had seen with her own electron-surrogate eyes what happened inside the Black Towers. She had heard the screams of deckers who tried to sleaze one too many Watchers or play smoke and mirrors with killer IC one too many times. She had breathed the malodorous fumes from a Mona Lisa jammer hit by so much lethal feedback that the decker's brain began to boil and pour out through her eyes.

If not for Rico, Piper wouldn't even have considered going up against Fuchi. Her lover left her no choice.

They had to do right, never mind that it might get them all killed. It wasn't enough to just turn and walk away, let Surikov do as he would. They had taken "responsibility" for Surikov. They had to see him safely to whatever corporate home he wanted. They had to make contact with the appropriate corporate agent. They had to cut a deal. And even that wasn't enough. They had to get Surikov's wife, too, or the man would remain a pawn of the megacorps.

A man with Rico's convictions didn't belong in the Sixth World. Piper only wished there was some finer place where they could go, a place where doing right wouldn't get them killed.

Fuchi had developed the first desktop cyberdeck, the first neural interface. The corp had all but *written* the matrix out of whole code. Fuchi's advances in intrusion countermeasures had few rivals, and no real equals. Sleazing anything out of its cluster of mainframe computers was going to take miracle work. Surviving the run would require intervention by the gods.

A direct confrontation with the cluster's awesome mainframes would only get her killed. She had to find another way.

She shot herself into Saganville, the heart of the Newark grid. Here, the gleaming white pyramids of system constructs, thousands upon thousands of them, crammed the datalines and rose a thousand levels into the electron night. Amid this megalopolis of constructs, Piper found a particular network address and pushed her signal inside.

Her iconic self stepped into silent darkness. Scents like sulfur and methane wafted past her. A voice, immeasurably deep and resonant, like the voice of a god, demanded, *"WHO ARE YOU?"*

Piper replied, "I am Arielle of Avalon."

"WHAT DO YOU WANT?"

"I want information."

"YOU WON'T GET IT!"

"By hook or by crook, I shall."

"Oh, really? Well, maybe you will. Then again, maybe you *woo-OOOONNNNNNN'T T Tttttt!!!"*

The final word rose suddenly into a cry, then a long, drawn-out scream that faded slowly away. As the scream faded, the voices of a thousand crows arose chattering, rasping, and ranting, raucously laughing.

The darkness before her resolved into a rickety bridge of vines and wooden slats just wide enough for one person to cross alone. The bridge spanned an immense crevasse, infinitely deep and filled with a boiling sea of fire. Piper took hold of the viny guide-ropes at waist-height and began walking across the bridge. Abruptly, the vines parted and the bridge swung downward toward the roaring flames. Piper pulled a knotted cord from around her waist and hurled one end toward the far side of the crevasse. The hook on the end of the cord caught on a rocky prominence. Hand over hand, Piper pulled herself up.

Beyond the cliff-edge of the crevasse was a forest, shining darkly with menace. From the stunted, twisted trees, gnarled like monstrous creatures, hung the skeletal remains of those who had come before her, the persona icons of the doomed. Immense black birds chittered from the tree limbs and pecked at the tattered remains of the skeletons. A hideous smell like corruption hung heavy in the air. A thick grayish fog flowed slowly along the ground. Piper considered how to proceed.

Many paths led into this horrific electron forest. Danger lurked everywhere, in the trunk of a tree, in the stagnant waters of a malignant bubbling pool, in the huge black figures that loomed everywhere in the darkness, in things unseen, rustling softly through the undergrowth. Disease and death seemed to flow through the air and along the ground just as tangibly as the fog.

Piper found her way to a small thatched hut with a single rounded opening. She ducked her head down and stepped inside. The interior of the hut was gloomy. A small fire flickered at the center of the hard-packed floor. Smoke curled through the air. On the far side of the fire sat a dark figure wrapped in a ragged cloak and hood. This, Piper knew, was the icon of a decker known as Azrael. No one knew his real name.

Back in 2029, a virus of unprecedented power had swept through the world's computer systems, scrambling data and frying hardware. To fight the plague, the government of what was then called the United States created a special top-secret group known as Echo Mirage. The team did eventually beat the virus, but few of the special cadre survived with their sanity intact. They were deckers at a time when a direct neural interface produced sensory overload, and, often, incurable psychosis.

Azrael was reputed to be one of the few to survive Echo Mirage. If that was so, if he really had been with the project, he had not survived the ordeal unscathed. No program he wrote was without eccentricities, and he had a maniacal hatred of governments and corps that often seemed to surpass Piper's own.

"What is your quest?" he rasped.

"I seek information."

Azrael laughed and laughed, breathlessly and harsh, as raucously as the crows, then suddenly blurted, "I know this, woman. You said it once already. Am I deaf? Do you think I'm deaf? What is it you really want?"

"Personnel and security data from Fuchi Multitronics."

"You quest the Black Towers?" Azrael laughed again, uproariously, hysterically. He laughed till he wheezed for breath, then he leaned toward the fire, peering at Piper from under the black shadow of his hood. "You will die."

"I think not."

Azrael shouted, "No one has ever penetrated the Black Towers' security processor *and LIVED to TELL the TALE!*"

"That is untrue."

Azrael laughed again, then whispered, "Maybe you're right. Maybe not. Maybe I can help you. Maybe not. How much are you willing to pay?"

"What do you offer?"

"I have secret information, very secret. Many deckers have died trying to sleaze my secrets from me. How many have died? I can't remember. Many more have gone away wounded and bloody. I have unraveled a multitude. I have infected legions. I have dumped whole hordes. My code is great and my vengeance terrible. Terrible! What would you pay for the secret to the Black Towers? Tell me. What would you pay?"

"What do you offer?"

Azrael cackled, then rasped, "An access node that no one living has ever found. Special code that may make the difference between life and lethal feedback, specially attuned to the Black Towers' frequencies and security subroutines. A key, I offer you a key. Do you doubt it? No one has this key but I. Such secrets, such special code. What will you pay? Define your life in cred."

"What is your price?"

The price was high, as Piper had known it must be, and she had little with which to bargain.

They were somewhere in Sector 15. Shank had seen a sign a while ago that read "Scotch Plains", but he wasn't sure if that was a district name or a street name or what. He hadn't seen much besides that sign, a few trucks, some steel and ferrocrete warehouses that looked abandoned, and fences. The fences were usually of the chain-link variety, three or four meters high, and topped by coiling razorwire nasty enough to discourage almost anybody. The only things Shank had seen inside those fences were piles of scrap, mountains of scrap: crete, steel, autos. And a helluva lot of junk.

Abruptly, Thorvin veered the van across three empty

lanes of roadway and slowed them to a halt facing a chain-link gateway.

"What're we stopping here for?"

"Need some parts, you freaking trog."

"What for, halfer?"

"Gotta build something for Rico."

Shank looked again at the gates. The sign there in red and yellow. "That says 'toxic waste.'"

Thorvin snorted. "Don't believe everything you read, fanghead."

"Who says I can read, skankface?"

The gates swung open, the van rolled through.

Into a junkyard like the Grand Canyon.

Clad entirely in non-reflective black, Claude Jaeger moved through the darkness like a darker shade of night, a shadow, a ghost, perhaps a trick of the eye, an illusory image without form or substance, as silent as the night.

The place was in Sector 7, amid the jumble of streets between Stuyvesant and Grove, just over the line from center city. It was called "Meat City". The buildings were old and crammed together, with coffin hotels and cubies filling the side streets. Every kind of scalpel mechanic and medtech had an office or clinic here. Some of the docs were frauds; some dealt exclusively in transplants or contraband chrome. Few were legally licensed. Few cared if a person had any kind of SIN or if the implant a client desired was on the federal government's prohibited list.

This was also where a person came if they just couldn't live with that armor-piercing slug stuck under their ribs or if they wanted to trade body parts for money.

The alleys were lined with chipheads and other derelicts, human refuse, squatting in plastic shelters or just lying on the concrete ground, all short a couple of organs and any number of limbs. Corpses went into the ferrocrete Ditch of the Garden State Parkway. Black-clad sanitation crews swept the Ditch clean every day at dawn and dusk. Claude had good reason to know of that. The art of the physical adept often compelled him to contribute to the carnal chaff disposed of in the Ditch.

Tonight, though, he had other business. A small matter by which he would collect some nuyen. The nature of the business concerned him little, so long as it gave him the chance to express himself through his art.

The little night-glo red-on-white sign on the back alley wall, read, CyberDok: Top Chrome, Vat Organics, Primo Rates ...

This was the clinic and residence of John Dokker, former mercenary, and his friend, Fillecia Antonucci, ex-cop. Both were members of the team hired to bust out Ansell Surikov. That made them important. It might eventually make them dead. Precisely what happened depended on events, Claude knew, and on the wishes of Maurice's client, who had provided the data on John Dokker and the other runners.

Next to the small sign, a black metal door. After a pause, it slid aside, letting Claude step into the dark space beyond. The door slid shut behind him. Momentarily, the tall, gangly form of the mage Maurice came into view, coalescing as if out of the empty dark. "This way," Maurice said, pointing with his walking stick.

Doors opened before them. Claude sensed the magic Maurice used to defeat the mechanisms of locks, but didn't know or care about the spells. Such were the province of technicians.

Two stories up, they entered a room subtly lit like a birthing chamber, crammed with hi-tech equipment, a veritable jungle of cables and tubes, consoles, control panels, and numerous transparex tanks, both large and small, filled with discreetly bubbling fluids.

As Claude stepped forward, he saw clearly what hung inside the fluids of the transparex tanks: a human hand, an eye, a leg, a mass of tissue like blubber. Various internal organs. These would be cultured matrixes, bioclonal secondaries, and a potential source of DNA-matched replacement parts for John Dokker and Fillecia Antonucci, should they ever require replacement parts.

A remarkable achievement for a former mercenary. Claude had never seen a setup like this outside of a corporate lab. He could only guess at what all of it must have cost. It was, however, largely irrelevant as far as tonight's work was concerned.

Maurice tapped the keys of a comp terminal. With a soft gasp of air, a small rectangular port opened in the side of the gleaming metal container standing beside the comp terminal. On the tongue that slid out through the port was a metal disk, briefly awash with swirling vapors. Inside this disk, and the second that soon appeared, would be the original tissue samples from which the clonal matrixes had been grown.

Properly handled, and properly utilized in ritual sorcery, these samples would provide a material link to their original hosts.

And that suggested the point of tonight's business.

17

The meet came down in Sector 4, Newark International Airport. The heaviest security zone in the plex. You couldn't even get into the sector with a weapon unless you met the right guard at the right entrance with the right amount of nuyen. Rico put Filly onto that. She had contacts with the Port Authority cops, and she knew how to talk cop lingua and how to pass the cred.

Thorvin had the driver's seat, Filly the passenger side. Rico had the bench seat in back to himself. Piper, Dok, Shank, and Bandit were waiting back at the Rahway bolthole with Ansell Surikov. Every one of the six of them had agreed to go on with the job as Rico intended. Only Piper and Filly had raised any serious objections, and here was Filly riding shotgun and greasing palms to get them into the airport. Had simple loyalty bought that? Rico could hardly believe it. He had seen so much of the world's treachery that he had trouble believing that such loyalty even existed. Then again, he couldn't think of any other explanation.

It had seemed odd to him that the two women with the crew should be the ones to argue, to object the loudest and clearest to the madness he had in mind. Until he thought about it. Until he realized that most women he had known—even as a kid—seemed somehow more closely tied to life and living than any man could ever hope to be.

The van halted inside the short-term parking lot of the airport's extensive South Terminal complex. Two minutes later a gleaming black Toyota limo pulled up alongside them. "Weapons armed and locked on," Thorvin growled. "Say the word and I'll freaking shred—"

"We're here to deal," Rico said. "Not punch tickets."

The rear door of the limo swung open. Ravage, dressed

tonight in a matte black bodysuit, stepped out first, followed by L. Kahn. Rico tugged open the side door of the van and stepped out to meet them. Filly stayed inside the van, but pushed open her door to show off her weapon, an Ingram 20t submachine gun. That was according to plan. Minimal exposure, ready for a fast breakaway.

The side of the van was barely two meters from the side of the limo. One step put Rico almost within an arm's length of Ravage and L. Kahn. If anyone did the wild thing at that range, people were going to get hurt.

Rico gazed steadily at Ravage. Impenetrable black shades covered the violet pits of her eyes. Rico remembered those eyes very well. Here was a woman with ties only to death.

"I'm impressed," L. Kahn said flatly, his voice a monotone. "Your fixer has influence. Now that you've gotten me here, what have you to say?"

"We got a problem."

"I have no problems whatsoever. You have my package. Your next step is to move that package, as per my instructions."

"Wrong," Rico said. "That ain't the next step."

Ravage's head shifted just slightly, as if she were flicking a glance at L. Kahn from behind her black shades. Rico couldn't help the tension that suddenly shot through his gun arm. His nerves were jumping. L. Kahn remained impassive, icy. He said, "I suggest that you explain."

Rico nodded, slowly, and said, "The man wants assurances. He wants to know where he's going."

"That is irrelevant," L. Kahn replied. "You were informed that this job is a recovery. I'm sure that by now you've confirmed the background history I provided, so you're well aware of where the subject was employed prior to being kidnapped by the competition. Need I say more? Do the math. Have the subject do the math himself and he'll see quite plainly where he's going."

"That ain't good enough. The man wants proof."

"What sort of proof would he like? A banner hung over Manhattan? A notice on the newsnets? This is absurd. You're scamming for more money."

Rico clenched his teeth. "Money's got nothing to do with it, *hombre*. The man wants direct communication with his old boss. He wants the word direct. Proof positive."

L. Kahn's expression seemed to harden. "That is impossible. As you well know."

"That's what the slag wants."

"At our first meeting, you accused me of playing dangerous games. I now say the same to you. The price for the run is fixed. If you bargain any further, you're bargaining for your life. And you will lose the negotiations. That is a promise."

This was going nowhere. Rico saw that clearly. L. Kahn had as much as told him that Surikov was bound for Fuchi Multitronics. But that was as much as he'd get. No one would provide proof. That might serve as incriminating evidence should anything go wrong.

This was the Sixth World. Image was everything.

"The other problem is time," Rico said. "The heat's on. I got the man in a safe place. I don't wanna move him till the sec forces're off the street."

"You find corporate posturing intimidating."

"Maybe you want me to spit on you again."

Ravage tensed visibly.

L. Kahn lifted a hand, as if to hold her in check. To Rico, he said, "I'm prepared to accord you a degree of latitude on the basis of your connections and your reputation. You're now pushing at the limits of my patience. I will admit that the safety of the package is paramount. If you want time, I will grant it. Twelve hours. By the end of that period, the streets should be clear of corporate forces. That is when we will conclude our business. There will be no further delays. Do you understand?"

"I got it, amigo."

"Very good."

L. Kahn got back inside the limo. Rico waited, watching Ravage. The cutter shifted half a step toward him but Rico had his Predator II in hand, the red dot of a targeting sight centered on Ravage's chest before she could finish the movement.

"Be seeing you," she whispered.

Rico bared his teeth in a grin.

The atmosphere inside the Command & Control vehicle was hushed. Colonel Butler Yates stood at the head of the control section in the rear of the vehicle. He had been there almost twenty minutes, silent and glaring, rapping his swagger stick against his leg, as if to remind everyone of his presence.

Doubtless, he also stood there to remind everyone that the Executive Action Brigade could not afford another frag-up. They had lost track of their targets twice already. A third such incident would likely cost them their contract.

Bobbie Jo felt the pressure intensely. She sat facing her console with a face like stone, but no amount of will or attempt at self-control could stop the sweat from trickling under her arms or from making her hands greasy and slick. The loss of the recee drone during the runners' escape from Mott Street had cost the brigade a small fortune, and the emotional cost to her had still not been tallied. The spiraling dive of the drone had brought her back in an instant to a cloudless day over Tampico in what had then been called Mexico. A heat-seeking missile slammed through her tail. What was left of her Federated-Boeing Eagle went ballistic, spiraling down at Mach Two into an Aztlan oil refinery.

Her legs, like her ride, like the whole damn government of Mexico, were broken to bits and burned almost to ashes. She might have gotten new legs but for the damage to her spine and connecting nerves. The price tag for complete reconstructive surgery was almost beyond comprehension.

If she could just stick with the Brigade long enough, two more years, maybe three, she might manage to get the ante together.

She jerked when a hand touched her shoulder.

"Stand by for launch," Skip said, quietly.

Bobbie Jo nodded, wiped her hands on her blue Brigade jumpsuit for the twentieth time, then lifted the wire lead from her console to the datajack in her temple.

Jacking into the sensor feed of a Gaz-Niki GNRD-101 Scorpion struck Bobbie Jo like the thought of flying an Eagle blind. It scared the drek out of her. Suddenly she saw the world from about five centimeters above the ground. She could see left and right and straight ahead, and up, but nothing to her rear unless she turned her body to look. Her body had become articulated, and long and flat, with four sets of spidery legs, two multi-functional manipulator arms that looked a lot like pincers, and a tail, a sort of stinger, with special integral devices. She could hear a Brigade operative whispering, "Ground Nine in position," from somewhere behind her, but most of all she could feel the vibrations running through the ground, the passing near and far of hundreds of vehicles and perhaps thousands and thousands of people, all moving through the South Terminal of Newark International.

Any one of these people could crush her articulated body beneath their heels. The Scorpion was not built to take punishment. It had no weapons and no armor. It was about thirty centimeters long.

Defenseless. Impotent.

"Go, Bobbie Jo," Skip was murmuring into her ears. "Do it."

She scuttled forward, pushing the Scorpion to max. The wheel of a Mitsubishi Runabout seemed to loom up ten stories higher than her head. The chassis of the car, now passing over her, looked like the ceiling of some immense chamber, criss-crossed by massive supports and gigantic conduits and pipes.

The red winking blip of a target indicator kept drawing her ahead, from one car to the next, one row of parked cars to another. She wrenched herself aside when an enormous pair of human feet suddenly slammed to the ground directly ahead of her. She raced back into the shelter beneath a car when a turbocharged Westwind 2000 came bearing down on her at lightning speed. She hesitated only an instant when a gleaming red schematic overlay flashed in front of her sensor view, outlining the mottled black and dull green Landrover van before her.

Two meters more and she was under the runners' van—fast as a devil rat. Her audio pickup snatched voices out of the air, first, the runner's leader, then the fixer L. Kahn, saying, ". . . the streets should be clear of corporate forces. That is when we will conclude our business. There will be no further delays. Do you understand?"

"I got it, amigo."

A beeping sounded rapidly in her ears. Her target indicator soared to the underside of the van. She flicked her segmented tail upward, thrusting up high on her hind legs. The tip of her tail twitched, just once. The dab of

cyanoacrylate glue that spat from her tail stuck to the
chassis of the van and hardened instantaneously. The
micro-miniaturized transponder injected into the glue
would be virtually undetectable until commanded to
awaken.

Then, with a single burst, it would transmit the van's
location to within a centimeter or two.

The sleeper planted, Bobbie Jo scuttled quickly away.

18

"Two, come with me please."

Shank looked up. "Huh?"

"We're taking a ride."

The small group gathered in the bolthole's living room—Shank, Dok, Bandit, and Ansell Surikov—looked at her as if puzzled, but Piper didn't wait for anyone to ask more questions. She had her kevlar-insulated jacket, her deck, and an Ares Model 70 Lite Fire automatic should she need it, and she wasn't going to give herself a moment to back out. She took the stairs to the sublevel garage. A battered Volkswagen Superkombi waited there, the backup vehicle. Taking it out and leaving Dok and Bandit stranded here with Surikov would light Rico's short fuse, but that was too bad. Sometimes Piper also had to do what she had to do. She got into the van and waited. Shank came along in a couple of moments.

"What's tox?" he asked gruffly, cramming himself in behind the wheel.

"We're going to the jackzone."

"Not the fragging Stacks."

Piper nodded.

"Rico ain't gonna like this."

As if she needed to be reminded . . . "Please do not argue with me, Shank."

"You're making a datarun, right?"

"I have no choice."

Programs degraded, code was unraveled, secrets revealed. Fuchi I.E. had a corps of deckers who did little else but scan their cluster of mainframes for intruders, security flaws, and other weaknesses. System integrity specialists, they were called. By this time tomorrow night, the code Piper had gotten from Azrael might be useless. She had to use it now, and she couldn't risk making the

DOOG

run on Fuchi from their bolthole here in Rahway, Sector 13.

Technically, she shouldn't have probed the Fuchi cluster like she had earlier this evening. If she'd been traced, it would have been very bad. She had taken a calculated risk.

Shank started the van and got them through the fog and the dark and the swirling dust storms to Edgar Road. That took them straight into Sector 10, a place people called "the Stacks" because it was the heaviest commercial and industrial concentration in the Newark plex. There were also more telecom lines planted here than anywhere else in the plex, and traffic was intense. For deckers, this was the "jackzone" of choice. A crowded local telecommunications grid might confuse a pursuing corporate decker or some trace and burn IC just long enough for a datarunner to get clear. It also provided multiple opportunities for illegal taps. The few people who actually lived in the Stacks occupied small rooms crammed into the rear of commercial plants or in factory lofts.

Only a fool would live anywhere near the matrix address from which they started a run. That would be like requesting an armed assault from an organization like Daisaka Security.

Shank turned the van down Ripley Place. That was little more than a hundred meters from the New Jersey Transit yards and Port Elizabeth. The rumbling vibrations of trains and the stench from the port were as depressing as the litter-strewn roadway and grimy, decaying buildings running down either side of the street.

Down near the corner with Second Street stood a building with a ground-floor bar called Aulisio's Backroom. Shank parked the van at the curb, then followed Piper inside.

A narrow corridor led toward the back of the building and the dingy little "Backroom," which was filled with the usual collection of scuzboys and punks sporting the usual gutterpunk fashions. The slag behind the bar wore mirrorshades and a turban and only glanced at Piper and her heavily built companion as they moved past the end of the bar and through another door.

Two flights up, Piper put a wire-lead from her deck to the electronic lock on a door. The lock was jacked into a

Sony cyberdeck on the other side of the door. Breaking the Sony's encryption program and the code locking the lock would take a mainframe comp skilled in large-number theory. Her Excalibur inserted an electron key that cycled the lock open in about three milliseconds.

And that was what it was really all about: keys. Another name for information. With information came power. Ignorance brought only misery and death. That was why the world's megacorps took such pains to educate their minions properly, and in the proper corporate creeds. To retain their stranglehold on the Earth's millions, they must keep their iron grip on all the information that mattered.

Piper grunted, and pushed through the door.

The room beyond was small and bare. An old recliner sat near a Fujiki telecom. A sleeping bag and pillow lay along one wall. A garbage can overflowed with waste from a dozen or more Stuffer Shack meals. Piper kept nothing important here because this place was expendable, and necessarily so.

Shank secured the door. Piper took a seat in the recliner and jacked in. She hesitated only a moment before initializing the cyberprog in her deck, just long enough to say, "If anything happens ... tell *jefe* I was thinking of him. Only of him."

Shank grunted. "You sure this is a good idea?"

"There is no option."

Then she was sluicing down the datalines, slipping quietly from grid to grid under the guise of ordinary, low-priority E-mail. Taking the long way to the Manhattan telecommunications grid might cost her a little time, but she preferred to get there discreetly, unobserved, unnoticed. The moment the Black Towers of the Fuchi icon came into sight, she turned aside and entered a small white pyramid, just one of thousands on the Manhattan LTG.

The words "Village Plumbing" flashed in front of her eyes.

Then she was standing in a small electric-white room facing a sculptured dataline. The portal into the open line resembled an enormous skull with gaping jaws. Piper initialized the prog she'd gotten from Azrael. A chartreuse skateboard appeared on the floor before her. The board blazed with the logo: Echo Mirage Express. Her iconic self suddenly exchanged its kimono for boarder gear: helmet, gloves, elbow guards, knee guards, hi-top sneaks. A flashing red and yellow sign appeared before the skull portal to the dataline, reading, "This Way to Fuchi Hell."

She stepped on the board and shot through the skull portal. The skateboard accelerated like a jet, the dataline beyond whipped back and forth like a snake. Sheer velocity tore at her clothes and forced her to lean forward almost horizontally just to keep from being blown off the board.

Abruptly, the dataline ended, the board vanished, her kimono returned, and she was plunging into a gigantic cavern of gray metal shapes and glaring, harsh red light.

Fuchi Hell.

She ripped a cord from around her waist and hurled the weighted end up and around to her rear. The weight caught on something, a pipe. The cord stopped her fall with a jerk. She swung back and banged against a wall of metal, then just hung there, taking in her surroundings. It was like hanging over the abyss, looking into the heart of some industrial monstrosity. The air smelled of molten metal. Enormous furnaces throbbed somewhere far below. Pipes and conduits ran everywhere. Spectral lights flickered and flashed. All the scene needed to complete the hellish image were blazing fires and the moans and cries of tormented souls. Piper could hear those cries in her mind. They were the cries of the millions that corps like Fuchi doomed to miserable lives and wretched deaths.

Hand-over-hand, she pulled herself up, up, up to a gangway sided by a metal railing.

There, she discovered a huge iconic figure in a black hood and long robe with long, full sleeves. The figure arose from the gangway as if from out of a pool of liquid metal. The small red window in the figure's iconic chest winked in alternating sequence, in black, "Mysterious Stranger Smartframe. Beware."

"What do you know of Fuchi Hell?" the figure said.

Very mysterious. Piper resisted a sarcastic sneer, then considered the question, warily. "It's an echo. Like a mirage."

"Reflecting greater realities."

"Apparently."

The Mysterious Stranger Smartframe nodded, and suddenly drew forth a sword more than two meters long, styled like a scimitar, and inscribed with mystical symbols in winking gold. "Follow."

"Lead."

The Stranger turned and led along the gangway, which led to an elevator, which shot up a thousand stories or more in just milliseconds. The elevator doors opened on a gleaming yellow room filled with row upon row of dataterms and dataterm operators extending off into infinity. "The Central Communications Node," said the Stranger. The elevator shot up another thousand stories. The doors opened on another room filled with rows of dataterms and operators, all orange. "The Central Management Information Node," said the Stranger. The elevator shot up further. Another room, this one red. "The Central Security Node."

Piper frowned. "You're showing me some of the most seriously secured nodes in the Fuchi cluster."

The Mysterious Stranger nodded. "You're welcome."

19

"It was *too ... easy ...*," Piper said, not for the first time, emphasizing the words profusely. "I can't help feeling like we're doing exactly what someone wants us to do."

Rico took a long drag off his cheroot, then looked back to the mirror and went on shaving three days' growth of beard from around his heavy mustache. "You're right," he said. "We are doing what somebody wants. His name is Surikov."

"That isn't what I mean."

"We're doing everything we can think of to stay alive. What else can we do? We're locked in."

"This is Fuchi we're talking about."

Rico put the razor down on the sink, then slammed his fist into the mirrored face of the medicine cabinet. That wasn't enough, so he hit it again. He dented the metal cabinet door, he shattered the mirror, he cut the frag out of his hand. But he didn't care about any of that. Right at this moment, he didn't care much about Fuchi or Piper's instinct about her run into the Fuchi cluster. When he looked at Piper it was to see her standing in the bathroom doorway with her eyes pointed at the floor and her face a pinkish color. That he cared about. He'd finally gotten through to her. He'd stood here and listened to all her explanations and now it was his turn to talk.

"You coulda been dusted," he said. "You coulda been traced. You coulda got Shank killed, too. You both coulda been nailed by Daisaka and interrogated, and then we'd all be dead."

"Please excuse me," Piper murmured.

"This is supposed to be a team. I'm supposed to be able to trust you." The thought that he ought to be able to trust her more than anyone else on earth burned him enough to strike another match under his temper. He punched the medicine cabinet again. Hard. Piper's face went deep red, but it wasn't anger. It was shame, embarrassment. Rico had seen the color before. He hated himself for forcing her to it, but he couldn't help it.

"You're right," she said softly. "I betrayed your trust. The shame is mine. All mine. I'm very sorry."

"Dammit, I care about you."

"I'm not worthy."

Rico looked at the shattered mirror, but his anger drained away to nothing. "You shouldn't 'a gone off on your own. You shoulda waited for me. We shoulda had a plan. We shoulda *thought* about it. You *ka!*"

"Yes, I understand. Please forgive me."

Reality was harsh. Maybe Piper was on her own when she went into the matrix. That was irrelevant. If they didn't work as a team, they were dead. The world was too dangerous a place for any one person to see all the angles, even those involving just the matrix. You had to stop and think. You had to get other perspectives, other input. You had to think it through all the way, not once, but twice, and all the while stay aware that there was a larger world that might, maybe just by accident, get directly between you and what you wanted.

Rico took a deep drag off his cheroot, then clenched his teeth and began picking broken bits of mirror out of his hand.

"You got lucky," he said.

"Yes, you're right," Piper agreed.

Twenty minutes later, Piper had no choice but to swallow her shame and get on with biz. She'd been prepared for this: Rico's anger, her own responses. "Inevitable" was the operative term. She had not dared allow time to degrade the prog that had been her key into the Fuchi cluster. That meant no time to plan, as Rico said. No time to consult, no time for considering other options, no time for what might have been a last good-bye. She was quite certain that what had angered Rico the most was that last, no good-bye. It was like a betrayal of love. The semblance of betrayal was only superficial, but that did not mitigate the shame she felt.

They joined the rest of the team in the living room.

Fortunately, no one asked about the loud banging in the bathroom or what might have caused Rico to cut his hand so badly. That would have been unbearable. Piper jacked her deck into the trid, then used the large screen to display the data she had snatched from the Fuchi mainframes. She had background data, building schematics, security procs and assessments, everything they would need to bust Ansell Surikov's wife out of Fuchi's clutches.

The woman's name was Marena Farris, and Fuchi had a complete file on her. She had originally been an analyst with the Fuchi security unit charged with reviewing corporate personnel.

"That's how we first met, in point of fact," Surikov remarked. "Marena conducted my annual review, perhaps three, four years ago. It was rather a foolish affair, actually. How was I getting on with my staff? That sort of thing. We got to talking, and, well . . ."

They were soon married. Surikov claimed that Farris had come to despise Fuchi, its labyrinthine security regulations, the Byzantine corporate structure, and the paranoia all that inspired. Farris took the unusual step of going on indefinite leave so that she would be able to spend time with Surikov whenever he was out of his labs. Piper supposed that if a woman cared enough for a man, she might give up almost anything to better promote their mutual happiness.

Farris lived in a luxury condo tower on Manhattan's Upper East Side. The building was owned by Fuchi, but used primarily by execs and other employees of Fuchi subsidiaries. Security was tight.

No matter. They began developing a plan.

In the dark of the bedroom, Rico capped off a bottle of Nutrimax tonic water and leaned back against the headboard of the bed. With his Jikku eyes, he watched Piper grope around at the side of the bed, then slip carefully under the covers. Her face was a grayish mask. She turned her back to lie on her side.

Rico reached out to smooth a hand over her hair.

"You're still angry with me," she said softly.

"Maybe," Rico admitted. "But tomorrow we might be dead meat."

"Yes . . . you're right. Please excuse me."

A moment passed, then she turned toward him and snuggled in against his side, laying her head on his chest. Rico ran his hand over her hair some more. It was smooth and soft like silk. "I don't wanna lose you," he said. "That's why I got so burned."

"You were right," Piper whispered. "I was wrong. I'm so ashamed."

"It couldn't be helped."

"*Jefe*, I don't know . . ."

It wasn't worth worrying about, not now. "L. Kahn ain't gonna be too happy when we give him the news."

"That is true."

"I don't know about this one, chica. I didn't like it from the start. Maybe it's like you said. We're just doing what somebody wants."

"We can think about that tomorrow."

"Sure. Tomorrow."

The van rushed down the transitway, shifting lanes, veering from side to side, bypassing other traffic. Rico glanced to his rear for about the fourth or fifth time, finding it hard to keep his mind where it oughta be.

Piper shared the rear bench with Shank, but she didn't seem any more aware of him than anyone or anything else. She had her axe in her lap, her head down-turned. Her long, curling black hair had slid in front of her shoulders, obscuring her face. She was past yesterday's trouble, the embarrassment he'd caused. Probably, she was praying. Talking to the kami again. Rico wished that didn't make him so uneasy. There had been a time, before he met Piper, when no one he knew paid any heed to gods till death was right around the corner, staring them in the face.

He'd known Piper for almost five years now and he still wasn't used to her praying.

Getting old. Obsolete? Maybe he'd been born that way. A couple of centuries too late. Into a world where honor meant nothing and a man's pride could be measured by the caliber of his gun. He figured he had some life left in him, regardless. Never mind what that slitch Ravage said.

"This gonna be a charity job, bossman?" Shank said gruffly. "Or we gonna get paid?"

"We'll get paid," Rico replied, lowly.

Shank and the team would get all they were due, and not just their share of the up-front money, even if Rico had to reach into his own pockets. Right now, the money was the least of his concerns.

Staying alive, at least a step ahead of the opposition, was the number one priority. After that came money. Somewhere in between staying alive and getting paid came his personal resolve to do what had to be done, find Surikov a new home, get the slag's wife busted out so that neither of them would be trapped in the ferrocrete fist of their corporate overlords. Rico just thanked his luck that he had a team he could rely on. Otherwise, everything went to scag, right out the window.

The transitway surfaced into Sector 10.

Time to get serious.

20

The slag in the elaborate red uniform frowned in puzzlement as Filly and Rico got out of the big blue and white sedan and moved across the sidewalk toward him. Filly didn't know his name, but she sized him up at a glance. Doorman. Very decorative but probably not a threat to anybody. Maybe a little basic training in security procedures, such as how to call for help when something bad came down.

Filly motioned at him with her chin. "Security super."

"Right inside," the doorman replied, waving a thumb at the transparex-fronted lobby of Forty East Seventy-third.

"What's the name?"

"Rasheen. Mo."

"Thanks."

The doorman smiled and nodded and put his key to the lock that set the double transparex doors to the lobby sliding open. Filly stepped on inside, Rico at her right. She took the lead because she knew the drill. She'd spent nine years on patrol with Winter Systems in the Bronx. She knew the procs, the lingua, and most importantly the attitude—casual, matter-of-fact, like she had every right to do whatever the hell she was doing and there was no fragging question about it.

The lobby was big and open, a dunkfield worth of carpeting, small gardens in the corners. A broad, semicircular counter sat at the rear of the space. The slag seated behind it wore the dark gray uniform of Fargo Security. He smiled and stood up as Filly and Rico approached. From his position at the security desk, the guard could have no trouble seeing the sedan at curbside, marked for the NYPD, Inc., or the matching uniforms worn by Rico and Filly.

"Hoi, chummers," the guard said, still smiling.

"You Rasheen?" Filly inquired.

"Yes, that is right. I am called Mo. Is there something for which I can help you officers?"

"Got a little problem," Rico said, as Filly walked around to the rear of the security counter.

"I am very sorry to be hearing that," Rasheen said, glancing back and forth. "How can I be helping you, please?"

The rear of the security counter was one big console equipped with monitor screens, two keyboards, and a suite of other controls. Those controls had complete override authority for the street doors to the lobby and the lobby doors to the elevators. No one got through the lobby unless the guard here tapped the appropriate key. Piper could commandeer the console from the matrix, but that wouldn't stop Rasheen here from calling a security alert.

Every guard on site carried a radio. Rasheen had a portable right on his console. Also, Fuchi internal security had assigned a special detail to watch over Surikov's wife up on the thirty-fifth floor. That detail would go on full alert if they caught even a whisper of strange things happening. One radio call about a malfunctioning security console would do it.

Filly stepped up beside Rasheen, and said, "Turn and face the wall."

"We got a warrant," Rico said.

Rasheen went wide-eyed. "I am begging your pardon—"

"Do it *NOW*!" Filly ordered.

"Please explaining to me—!"

Filly grabbed Rasheen's arm and twisted it. That made him turn to face the wall or lose the arm. Rasheen turned. Rico came around and relieved Rasheen of his sidearm and various defensive weapons. Filly forced Rasheen down to his knees and applied handcuffs.

"You must be erroneously arresting me!"

"I don't think so."

"Please letting me call my director!"

Rasheen would not be calling anybody.

The building at Forty East Seventy-third Street on Manhattan's Upper East Side was called the Crystal Blossom Condominiums. The mainframe running the build-

ing's utilities and monitoring security functions was a
Fuchi machine, but had only the most tenuous of connections with the machines installed in the Black Towers of
Fuchi-Town. It was operated by the Manhattan Property Management Corporation, a Fuchi subsidiary. Code
Orange security. That was tough, but not nearly as tough
as the Black Towers' Code Red cluster.

The System Access Node to the Crystal Blossom mainframe looked like the anteroom to a bank vault. The
iconic room was gray, the vault door gold. This was
standard matrix imagery and it indicated little or nothing
about the security status of the system beyond.

Piper entered the node with her masking utility on-line.
The guards in their sky blue Fuchi blazers didn't react at
all to her presence. From inside her jacket, Piper drew out
a huge magnifying glass and examined the guards' program code. The guards—mere access IC—still did not react. Piper drew out a pair of glowing red and green
lollipops the size of tennis rackets, each winking with the
legend, in orange, ENTRY REQUEST. She held the pops
out to the guards, and now they noticed her. They looked
at the lollipops and accepted them. And began licking
them.

They would continue licking forever—caught in a virtual loop.

Piper drew out a pouch, marked Movable Holes. The
hole she selected took the form of a slim black disk
whose diameter was about equal to the height of her
iconic self. She slapped the disk against the vault door.
READY began winking in neon red at the center of the
disk. She stepped through—through the hole, through the
vault door—and into the dataline beyond.

She had the entire Crystal Blossom system under her
command in something just under a millisecond. It was
more than just "too easy."

Kami save them. It seemed impossible.

The doorman started tapping on the transparex doors
out front and lifted his hands as if to ask what was going
on. The doors wouldn't respond to his key. That would be
Piper's doing.

One of the elevators dinged, and a uniformed guard
came walking into the lobby. He was dark-skinned like

Rasheen and the look on his face immediately turned to shocked surprise.

"What is happening here?" he asked, voice lilting wildly up and down.

Rasheen blurted something in some foreign lingua.

The newcomer stopped, looking back and forth. "Why have you arresting my brother?"

"Come're," Filly said.

"Answer please!"

Something from the security console started bleeping. Filly let Rico worry about that. She stepped toward the newcomer, Rasheen's "brother." She laid a hand on the butt of her sidearm. Any normal corporate would take that as a hint and act accordingly. "Don't give us any trouble," she said adamantly. "Put your hands on the wall and shut up."

"You're not arresting me!"

The slag went for his gun.

Filly lunged forward, seized the guard's gun arm, and pounded a shock glove-covered fist into his face. That quickly, she had a full-scale brawl on her hands. The shock-glove treatment didn't seem to affect the fragger. She twisted his arm and slammed him back against the lobby's rear wall. The slag managed to tug his gun free of its holster. Rico stepped up on her left and rammed a fist into the guard's mid-section just as the gun detonated.

All this just to keep up appearances, the likeness of a legitimate arrest by police, to keep that special detail up on thirty-eight unawares.

The roar of the gun affected Filly like the peel of a siren. She felt the adrenaline surge even as Rico staggered back, turning half a circle. She went animal. She pummeled the guard. She slammed his elbow back against the lobby wall to maybe numb the gun arm, and then tugged the pistol out of his hand. She rode him down to the floor on his chest, dragged his arms behind his back, and applied a pair of cuffs.

Panting for breath.

Looking for Rico.

The bossman stood leaning against the rear of the security counter. He shook his head as if to clear it. A dark

spot was forming around the tear in the thigh of his right
pants leg.

Fragging great.

When the elevator doors slid open, Bandit had the spell
waiting, held in the palm of his hand. He saw the lengthy
corridor stretched out ahead of him and the two men in
dark suits standing near a door on the right. Bandit
opened his hand. A noise like an alley cat shrieking arose
quick and raw from the distant end of the corridor. The
suits looked, and a pair of thumps sounded from Bandit's
left and right. The thumps were from Shank and Dok's
automatics. The bullets they fired were not lethal, but the
pair of suits up the corridor slumped to the floor anyway.

Not dead. Just unconscious.

Shank and Dok hustled up the corridor. Bandit followed
along at his own cautious pace. He saw nothing of any interest in the corridor. Shank motioned for him to hurry.

The door marked 35-8 slid open. Shank and Dok hustled inside, automatics thumping again. Bandit followed.
A small, richly decorated foyer led into a luxurious living
room. Another suit lay sprawled on the floor of the foyer.
Bandit followed Shank and Dok into the living room,
running his eyes around, taking in the wealthy furnishings: paintings, drapes, vases, bonsai, crystal goblets, deluxe trideo with simsense. All very deceptive. A mundane
could probably live here for years and never realize that
he or she was actually living in a crete and plastic coffin,
all but cut off from the essential energies of the universe.

A quiet exclamation came from another room.

Nothing to worry about.

Bandit considered the situation, then took a small, vel-
vety pouch from his duster pocket and laid it on an end
table. The pouch contained the extracted essence of a
number of herbs and roots used in ritual magic by mages.
Bandit had once thought that the combined essences
might prove valuable for him, but the expectation had
turned out to be false. Useful perhaps for a mage, not for
a shaman.

It would make for a fair exchange.

Steinberg was staring at some bowl game on the trid.
Tsugaru looked sound asleep, sprawled on the sofa. Steva

Karris glanced at her wrist chrono for the fifth time this hour and mentally began ticking off the seconds.

There was nothing more boring than sitting watch on some corporate property, especially one that never went out, never left her assigned corporate quarters, for chrissakes. Steva didn't know the woman's name, didn't even know if she had a name. It was like playing nightwatch for some out-of-the-way corporate facility of dubious interest to anyone. A big yawn. That wasn't to say that she wouldn't do her damnedest to protect Fuchi corporate property. She'd just be a little more excited about it if she had some idea that she'd been posted to a job that made a difference.

Her wrist chrono dinged. She looked up as Devoe came up the hall from the bathroom. "You're on."

"So soon?"

Steva nodded toward the foyer. Devoe knew better than to argue. He straightened his suit and headed out.

Abruptly, he was back, whispering urgently, "Alert! Alert! Status five! Code Red!"

Karris grabbed her Ingram SMG and lunged for the foyer, the others close behind.

Dok had met some wildly sculptured biffs in his time, but this one was the most outrageous he'd seen outside a Tomikon bordello. She was built for sex. Every curve shouted it.

Her name was Marena Farris. She was Ansell Surikov's wife. When the lights came on, she was lying there on her back on the broad black expanse of the bed. She wore some kind of sheer, silky nightgown that covered her to the ankles, but didn't hide a thing, not the rounded prominences of her breasts or even the broad, dark patches surrounding her nipples. Not even the part lower down, beneath her waist. Discreetly veiled in hair as fine as the whitish-blonde masses surrounding her face.

She lifted her head. A soft exclamation slipped from her lips. She sat up, one hand rising as if to defend her eyes from the lights.

"We're busting you out," Shank announced.

Farris gasped and blurted, "What?"

The woman was obviously overawed. Who wouldn't

be? Dok thought. Awakened from a sound sleep by the sudden glare of the bedroom lights? met by a pair of slags in full battle gear? Dok smiled and said, "We're taking you to your husband. He's safe, okay? Don't wor—"

It was too much.

Abruptly, Farris' eyes rolled upward and she fell back on the bed, limp. Dok hurried over and broke out his medikit. Farris' vitals were running strong, remarkably strong for someone in a dead faint, but not so strong that any kind of incident seemed imminent.

Shank grunted. "You carry her."

"Someone'll bust my skull," Dok said, grinning.

"Do it anyway."

"Hai, commander."

"Eff you. Hurry up."

Dok put one knee on the bed and gathered the woman into his arms. She was no lightweight, but then the best-looking ones never were. No doubt his chummer Shank would agree. He only wished that he'd gone for the stage two muscle replacement at that clinic in Johannesburg, the one with the specialist direct from Chiba City.

Then again . . .

Maybe not.

As Shank led back through the condo toward the corridor, Piper's voice came to him over his headset. "Time is oh-two-twenty-four," she said. "Condition Two."

That wasn't good.

Condition Two: Somebody injured. It had to be Rico or Filly, or Piper woulda called Condition Three, and that woulda been panic time because it woulda meant that Thorvin and their ride outta here wouldn't be on schedule—or might not be coming at all. Shank stole a glance back over his shoulder. Dok had caught Piper's warning, judging by the look on his face. Shank gave the old mercenary signal for double-time, pumping his fist. Almost in sync, the two of them leaned forward into a quick jog.

In the living room, Shank stopped, incredulous. Bandit was standing there looking around like a reviewer from *Modern Condo*. Shank cursed. "You're supposed to be watching the corridor!"

The shaman just looked at him, his face as blank as a

wall. They'd gone over this part of the plan a dozen times, and Bandit still didn't get it. Shank felt a sudden surge of anger. Slotting sonovabitch. Frag it anyway. No time for jacking around. Someone was blooded—they had to *move*!

He hustled through the foyer to the corridor door, then immediately jerked himself back into the foyer and clear of the doorway. A female voice carried in clear and loud from outside. "Fuchi security! Throw your weapons into the corridor! Come out with your hands up!"

Shank glanced at Dok, standing right there beside him, and said, "We could be in trouble."

Dok smiled. "Glad you noticed."

It was always difficult to keep in mind what the others wanted. They designed complicated plans with ends he sometimes found obscure. Bandit ran with Rico and the others because the runs often proved interesting in various ways, but he was not used to concerning himself with others' desires. He had his own way of seeing the world. He knew that few shared his view of things. He understood that most looked at life in ways that were either flawed or illusory.

Why should he watch the corridor? He had seen it once already. There was nothing there of interest. There was always the chance that something might occur there that might pose a danger, but he had never encountered a danger that he could not escape.

The problem, of course, was that the others lacked his ability.

Quickly now, he hurried after Shank and Dok. He heard someone shout about Fuchi security. Shank seemed uncertain, unsure of what was happening or what to do. "We could be in trouble," he said.

"Glad you noticed," Dok replied.

Bandit projected astrally, sized up the situation in the corridor, then stepped to the doorway, announcing loudly, "I surrender. Don't shoot. I'm coming out."

"Keep your hands UP!" a voice shouted.

Shank growled, but Bandit ignored that. One step more took him through the doorway and into the corridor. The two suits who had been out there before were still lying unconscious nearby. Four other suits had appeared. They were scattered about to the right of the doorway, crouching low like animals in anonymous gray skins, ready to pounce. Bandit supposed they were professionals. They certainly looked like they knew what they were doing. They all held guns. Submachine guns, in fact.

"FACE DOWN ON THE FLOOR!" one shouted.

Bandit nodded, merely to sign understanding. He also murmured words of power, the song of a spell, one of the first he had ever learned. The spell mounted and ignited the instant he finished pronouncing the final word. The suits' arms all suddenly leapt upward. The guns they held jerked free of their hands and sailed back over their shoulders. Snatched away by Raccoon's clever paw. The guns clattered to the floor some distance to the suits' rear. The suits, in that instant, seemed too astonished to do more than exclaim and look around. Bandit's second spell triggered automatically. The suits' pants jerked downward to around their ankles. Another of Raccoon's wily tricks. The guards jerked and swayed and stumbled around, now shouting in alarm, hobbled by their own pants.

Bandit turned and looked back.

Shank and Dok both opened fire from the doorway. The guards all staggered and fell.

They were just knocked unconscious.

Shank grabbed Marena Farris by the shoulders. Dok looked at him in wonder, then took a new hold around the woman's hips. Together, they ran for the elevators. The elevator doors slid open barely two steps ahead of them.

Rico and Filly were already there, guns drawn. Rico's pants leg was wet from about the middle of his thigh to almost the knee. "Got a bleeder!" Filly announced.

Bandit got on. The elevator went up.

Dok bent to look at Rico's leg.

"Time is oh-two-twenty-seven," Piper informed over Shank's headset.

Farrah Moffit heard the helicopter and had a fair idea of what was going on, but she decided to do nothing about it.

It seemed like the only sensible course. She was keenly aware of both her deficiencies and her strengths, and she was no combat specialist. With only minimal training in self-defense, she lacked both the physical stamina and the instincts to meet a man or even a woman head-on in any kind of physical contest. She had only an elementary knowledge of firearms. She would be a fool to offer anything more than the most token of passive resistance.

In the meantime, she gathered information, what little she could discern with her head hanging, her hair fallen across her face, her eyes closed, her body limp.

Her supposed rescuers had apparently disposed of the special security detail assigned to watch her, and had done so in rapid order. That made them highly dangerous. But not insuperable. She knew at least one of them was wounded. One was an ork. She'd seen him in the bedroom, along with an Anglo male with grayish, razor-cut hair. And there was at least one female with the group.

Farrah remembered being carried at a run, presumably down the corridor from her condominium, and then the sound of the elevator doors opening. The timing seemed a little too precise to be mere coincidence. Perhaps it wasn't sheer coincidence. Perhaps these runners had matrix support.

As the whoop-whoop-whoop from the helicopter rotors ascended in speed and volume, she wondered where these people were taking her, and then all at once the truth struck home.

She couldn't believe it.

21

Dok had the bullet out even before the chopper finished crossing the Hudson River, the wound patched and dressed by the time they set down in the blighted wastes of Sector 13. One thing Dok knew was how to be fast. Rico was thankful for that.

"The tranq should keep the edge off the pain," Dok said. "It's a local. You might need something more to get to sleep."

Rico grimaced, and nodded. The fire in his right thigh had subsided into a dull ache, kind of like a bone bruise, menacing, but nowhere near as harsh. He could live with it. He didn't have much choice. Gun in hand, he limped across the nine or ten meters from the chopper to Thorvin's van, then waited for the rest of the crew to pile in. Marena Farris was awake and walking but acting more unconscious than not. She was clean, no implanted microtransmitters, no snitches—at least none that Dok could detect. The fact that they were all still alive and had made a clean break from the extraction site seemed to confirm that Farris was indeed as clean as Rico thought.

Now, Dok and Filly wrapped Farris in an orange duster and together half-carried her into the van. Filly was sticking like glue to Dok. Probably a good idea.

Thorvin drove them to Sector 10 where they picked up Piper. She was good, null sheen. Then they took the long drive through the transitways up to the northern tip of the Newark plex, just across the line from the Passaic sprawl.

The bolthole in Rahway had served its purpose, providing emergency backup and a chance for them to regroup. Rico did not want the place found out. Time now to change locations.

Thorvin parked the van in a dingy alley between the backsides of two sets of three-story rowhouses in Sector 20, a district called North Caldwell. Rico knew it as a working-class ghetto, home to wage slaves and the less violence-prone of the SINless who dominated the Newark plex. It was also the site of their new safehouse. Shank had arranged for the squat through his contacts with the ork underground. It was a shambles, and it stank, but it would serve.

They were lucky to be alive, lucky the run had gone more or less as planned, lucky to have eluded the air patrols over Manhattan, lucky that no pursuit had developed. And that wasn't all, Rico reminded himself. He was lucky the bullet that hit his leg hadn't cracked a bone or torn any major arteries. Luck like that was rare enough to make him wonder about God, not only the Christian God, but other gods as well.

Looking forward to a few nights or weeks spent in a squalid whore of a safehouse was nothing to complain about.

Surikov was there and waiting. So were the pair of cutters on loan from Mr. Victor, assigned to stand guard. Rico paid them off and headed upstairs for a shower. He had no real interest in watching Surikov's reunion with his wife, and Shank could set the watch.

He'd barely gotten his shirt off before the bathroom door swung inward and Piper slipped inside. She didn't say nothing at first. She came right to him, slid her arms around him, and put her head to his shoulder. He knew what this was about, and here in the confines of the bathroom, away from watchful eyes and people he had to lead, he didn't mind it at all. It was good to see she cared, good to feel it, know it. Rico's father used to say that a man without a woman was hardly a man at all. It took a woman's tenderness and caring for a man to really appreciate what being a man was all about. Without the kind of softness a woman could give, men turned into animals.

At a whisper, she said, "Are you sure you're all right?"

Despite everything, his leg, the situation, Rico smiled into her hair, giving her a kiss there. "I ain't complaining."

"You lost so much blood."

"Not that much. What happened in the matrix?"

"Too easy, *jefe*." Now she looked up at him, her expression worried. "The Crystal Blossom mainframe is

Code Orange security, but the IC never came near me. I took complete control of the system."

"Maybe you're just good at your work."

"No one's that good. Or not many. And no one goes against Code Orange without at least tickling the IC. Not unless someone on the inside wants it to happen that way."

Serious guano. Piper wasn't popping off theories just to hear herself talk. If she said that someone must've set up the system to give her easy access, Rico felt obliged to consider the possibility. "Who would want it that way?"

"I don't know, *jefe.*"

It didn't scan. No one had any reason to help them bust out Marena Farris. Fuchi and Maas Intertech had every reason to work against them. Both would be losers if Surikov got what he wanted. Prometheus Engineering might conceivably have reason to help, but Prometheus couldn't be involved, not yet, because Mr. Victor was only just making contact.

So, who did that leave as possible players?

One thought came to mind. "What about your contact?" Rico said. "The slag who got you the key into the Fuchi computers? Maybe he was on the inside."

Piper shook her head. "He'd have no reason to help me now. Our deal began and ended with the Fuchi cluster. The Crystal Blossom mainframe isn't a part of that cluster, *jefe.*"

"Maybe L. Kahn did something."

"But he wouldn't help us now," Piper said softly. "Even if he had known what we would do."

Rico nodded. Pain and fatigue had him brain-fuzzed. If anything, L. Kahn would be opposed to the bust-out of Marena Farris because once Farris was free, Surikov could forget Fuchi and join any corp he wanted.

"You should sleep, *amante,*" Piper said.

Her Spanish always came out awkward, like she had to force her tongue to work in ways it really couldn't handle, but the effort warmed him. Rico drew her head to his shoulder and kissed her, and took a breath to speak, but got no further.

From somewhere below came a sound like the thump of a silenced weapon, then a crash like a lamp being smashed, then shouts, Shank's resonant voice among them.

Piper jerked back out of the way as Rico turned and threw himself at the doorway. He grabbed up his gun in passing, not the Ares Special Service, the heavy Predator II, loaded with hard ammo. Any problem that had come to meet them here in the safe house would take hard ammo to put down.

The Predator's smartlink came on line at once. The targeting indicator whipped down the hall to the stairs as Rico darted through the bathroom doorway, dropping into a combat crouch, the heavy auto leveled in a two-handed grip.

Nobody there. The problem was still one floor down.

When he reached the living room, he found Surikov sitting on the dilapidated sofa. Blood streamed down the left side of his head to his neck. Marena Farris stood squirming against the opposite wall, straining up on her toes, rasping, straining for breath. Shank had one big hand wrapped around her throat. Dok's face was red like it would pop. Thorvin and Shank together seemed to be trying to keep Dok from getting at Farris, like he wanted to kill her.

"Fragging slitch! I'LL KILL YOU!"

Filly stood at the center of the room cursing furiously and dabbing with her hand at her cheek, which showed some blood, like from a cut. She was the only one in sight with a gun in her hand.

"The slitch grabbed my piece!" she said, forced to shout to be heard over Dok's near-incoherent cursing.

Rico couldn't fragging believe it.

Any of it.

He threw an arm around Dok's neck, dragged him back bodily, and flung him down hard, then put the muzzle of the Predator in Dok's face and shouted, *"I'LL DO YOU!"*

Everybody stopped dead.

And it stayed like that for a while, everybody hanging, waiting, watching. Rico had a rein on his temper, but it was a short one and they all knew it, including Dok. Rico waited till Dok's wide-eyed look of surprise and fury faded a little, then slowly straightened up.

Certain things had to be said, and they could only be said in his father's tongue. Never mind that only Shank and Dok had any understanding of Spanish that approached real fluency. The words had to come out. It was that or start shooting.

He let them have it.

"Fragging amateurs," he growled, once he found his way back to English. "You wanna get us all killed? What the frag! *What the frag!*"

"Easy, bossman," Shank said quietly.

Rico let that pass.

It was too much, the sheer sequence of events, never mind the motivations. Never mind the how-come and the why.

Shank ran it down for him, anyway.

Apparently without warning, Marena Farris had clawed at Filly's face, then grabbed Filly's automatic, then fired it at Surikov. Farris hadn't seemed to know how to handle a pistol, so it was probably pure luck that she'd hit Surikov at all. While Shank was getting the gun away from her, Dok suddenly went off like a jet, which was the only part that made any sense.

Dok would boff anything with two legs and tits, but Filly was his special lady. The only one who really mattered. Man or woman, it made no difference—anybody who fragged with Filly was going to have to answer to Dok. Rico could respect that, but not now. In the here and now it was amateur drek and they couldn't afford it.

"Who's on watch?" he said sharply.

"I got the rear," Thorvin said, turning and walking out of the room. Rico turned and found Piper halfway down the stairs, just standing there watching, wide-eyed with shock.

"Take the front, chica."

Piper moved to the windows at the front of the room and slipped behind the heavy drapes without a moment's hesitation. Rico looked down at Dok.

"You got a patient."

Dok closed his eyes for a moment, like maybe he was holding back another fit of fury, then banged a hand to the floor before getting up and stepping over to Filly. Her little cut didn't look like a problem, nothing compared to Surikov's wound, but Rico said nothing. Going head to head with Dok over his lady would earn him nothing but trouble. You could only push people so far.

"You're okay otherwise?"

"Don't baby me, dammit."

Filly was in a fine mood herself. She had reason, Rico figured. Her frag-up could've gotten somebody killed. If she'd been doing her job, Marena Farris would never have gotten her gun.

Rule Number One: Never lower your guard.

Rule Number Two: See rule one.

Rico turned to Shank. "Put her upstairs. Watch 'er."

Shank nodded. "Right."

Marena Farris said nothing. She was too busy trying to breathe. When Shank let go of her neck, she slumped toward the floor like she had noodles for bones. Shank grabbed her left upper arm, pulled her back onto her feet, and half-carried her up the stairs. Rico would get to her shortly.

First things first.

Dok was checking Surikov by then. Head wounds always bled like pigs. Rico had seen enough of them to know. The blood sometimes ran so heavy all over a person's face you couldn't tell a man from a woman. This one didn't look too bad. Dok soon confirmed his guess. "The shot glanced off," Dok said tersely. "Took some scalp with it. You'll live."

"It feels like a hammer," Surikov said at near a whisper.

"I got something for that."

"I want him awake," Rico said.

Dok hesitated, then said, "No problem."

Rico's leg was throbbing. It was probably more his own flaring of temper than anything else. Blood pressure, some drek like that. He found himself a chair and sat down facing Surikov. Dok stood up and said, "Look, boss . . ."

"Don't say nothing," Rico growled. "You know the score."

"If that slitch—"

"You do what you have to do. Just remember the score comes out even in the end. And you ain't gonna get me killed."

"Dok," Filly said. "Just chill."

"I'm not gonna let—!"

"We both fragged up! Let it go!"

Dok let it go. For the moment, anyway. Rico looked at Surikov. For a slag who'd just been shot in the head, he didn't look too bad. A little pale, a little shook up, a little bloody. A few moments passed, then Surikov met his gaze.

"What's your story?" Rico said.

"Excuse me?"

"What the frag's going on?"

"I don't . . . I don't have any idea." Surikov looked astonished.

"Your wife just tried to dust you." Rico looked at Dok. "She is his wife, right?"

Dok didn't answer.

"You checked her, right?"

Doc still said nothing, but the answer was obvious.

"You didn't verify her identity."

Filly cursed.

"Fragging Fuchi security was right there!" Dok exclaimed. "We didn't have time. We just grabbed her and ran."

"Do it now."

Dok turned and headed upstairs.

Rico had few doubts about what had happened, or what was happening here now. His team's weaknesses were showing.

The truth was that even an old pro like Dok could get sloppy, stupid. The kind of body Marena Farris owned would make a lot of slags get stupid, and Dok was one of them. Filly knew it, and Rico knew it. That was why Filly had cursed. That was also why she'd stayed so close to Dok ever since they'd left Manhattan tonight. Given the right opportunity, Dok couldn't keep his pants on to save his life. He had a half a dozen little pieces of fun scattered all over the plex, not to mention the new ones he was always finding. Filly put up with it because she knew she was number one and she knew what that meant to Dok. Rico put up with it because it usually wasn't a problem, wasn't usually any of his freaking biz. It only mattered now because people were slotting up and that could get them all killed.

Being under pressure was no excuse. It was irrelevant. Shank and Dok were pros. They were paid to handle the pressure and paid to do it right.

The only thing more dangerous than busting out Surikov's wife would be coming away with the wrong woman. Busting out a willing corporate defector was one thing. The kidnapping of a loyal employee . . . that could start a fragging war.

Rico gazed steadily at Surikov, waiting, trying to scope the slag out.

Everything was about Surikov. His reaction to Marena Farris grabbing a gun and trying to waste him mattered more than any explanations Farris might have to give. Rico wondered if the slag had some special agenda that he hadn't mentioned yet. Rico hadn't forgotten what he'd seen that night at Maas Intertech when he and the team busted Surikov out. The man had been on top of a woman and going at her like he owned her. Maybe that woman had been nothing more than a corporate joygirl. Maybe not. Maybe Surikov had Dok's kind of problem with women. Maybe not. Maybe the only reason Surikov had wanted his wife busted out was so he could settle a score with her. Who knows? Maybe the only reason Marena Farris was still alive was because Surikov hadn't grabbed a gun first.

Paranoia was catching.

Dok returned. "It's a match," he said. "Ninety-eight percent certainty. She's Marena Farris." He paused a moment, then said, "Boss, I'm sorry. It won't happen again."

Right. "You're on watch in two hours. Take a bedroom."

Dok and Filly headed upstairs.

Rico looked over at Surikov. The slag leaned his head back against the sofa and closed his eyes. "I can't believe it," he said finally. "I can't believe that's truly Marena. She would never . . . She's not a violent woman."

Piper had provided comparative data for both a retina print and DNA scan from straight outta the Fuchi security files. "Ninety-eight percent certainty," Rico said. "It don't get much more certain than that."

"They must have done something to her."

"Yeah? Maybe she hates your guts."

Surikov's eyes flared wide. For a moment, he seemed about to roar with anger, but then the emotion faded. He stared at the ceiling, and shook his head very slightly. "No," he said. "You don't know Marena. The real Marena. I can imagine what you must think, based on her looks. But she's a very loving woman. She's devoted to me. I can see it in her eyes. That's how I know this woman who just tried to shoot me isn't her. She doesn't have Marena's eyes. Good God, *what have they done to her*!"

The emotion in Surikov's voice built slowly and steadily to that final exclamation. Rico wasn't sure what to make of it. No question that a corp like Fuchi could do practically anything to a person if they wanted to spend the money. Could they install some kind of implant to override a person's brain and turn them into a one-shot killer? Rico had heard of it being done. Hell, the right mage with the right batch of spells could make a person do almost anything and leave him thinking it was his own idea. That much he had direct from Bandit.

Speaking of which . . .

Where the frag was Bandit?

22

Shank guided Marena Farris to the door at the end of the second-floor hallway, then into the room there. She seemed weak, dazed. Bandit followed them in. Shank guided the woman to the bed, made her sit, then looked at the shaman.

"I'll watch her," Bandit said.

"Rico told me to do it."

Bandit lifted the Mask of Sassacus up before his own face and whispered words of power. The past few days had given him some time to further examine the mask and to experiment with it. He had harmonized its power with his own.

Aloud, he told Shank, "You must be hungry. Why not get something to eat?"

Shank grunted, nodded. "Yeah, you got a point. Thanks, chummer."

"Do not think of it."

"Think of what?"

"Just kidding."

Shank paused a moment, looked at Bandit, then grinned ferociously and left. Bandit considered the mask, then noticed Marena Farris slowly turning to face him. She would not see the mask. It was cloaked. Only Bandit could see it.

Marena Farris appeared emotionally upset. She moved her hands about her face, covering her mouth, her eyes, wiping at her brow, her cheeks. She spent several moments pressing her hair back from her face. Her eyes looked red, her face flushed.

"Care for a cigarette?" Bandit asked.

Marena Farris shook her head.

Bandit shrugged and took a cig from his open pack, then ignited it with a lighter from his duster pocket. He

didn't actually draw the smoke into his lungs; only into his mouth, then blew it out. He was a practiced smoker. He practiced the habit because people seemed to become more at ease when they saw him doing something so mundane. That was his only reason for smoking. To appear somewhat mundane.

He smoked Millennium Reds. One of the most common brands available. They could be gotten anywhere.

Between one drag and the next, he gazed at Marena Farris as she appeared on the astral plane. She looked back at him, though only on the physical plane, it seemed.

"You have an interesting aura."

Marena Farris smiled a polite kind of smile. Not very enthusiastic. Not very interested. Perhaps a bit pained. Was it an attempt at deception or a reflection of her true feelings? On the astral plane, she was a storm of color, a boiling cauldron of light, of life energy. In Bandit's experience, such a tumultuous aura reflected tumultuous emotions or thoughts, sometimes both. The intensity and diverse coloring of the aura said more about the individual, their strength, their will, the force of their life.

"What's going to happen to me?" Marena Farris said.

Bandit wondered how she meant that. Did she mean now? tomorrow? next year? Did she wonder what would happen to her when her body grew too worn and decayed to support her biological existence? "I wonder," Bandit replied, pausing to take another drag of the cig. "You're much older than you seem."

She gasped softly, then.

As in surprise.

"What . . . what do you mean?" she asked quietly.

"What do you think?" Bandit replied.

"Well, yes," she said, slowly. "Yes, you're right. It's true. I am. Older than I look. Why . . . do you ask? Why am I telling you this?"

"You'd like to tell me more."

"Yes, I would." She stopped and smiled again and nodded. Then frowned. "I don't understand."

"There's nothing to understand."

"Yes, yes, there is. I'm sure of it."

"You just like talking to me."

"Yes, I do. But there's more. You're . . ."

"No."

"You are." Her expression grew pained. She gasped for breath as if running a race. "You're ... doing things to me. Stop it. Stop it, *please*! It *hurts* ..."

Incredible.

Bandit lowered the mask. Marena Farris dropped her head to her breast. Her hair tumbled down around her face, concealing her features completely. But not her aura. Bandit looked at that again just to see how it had changed, but it was difficult to read. Certain aspects of it were puzzling, out of sync, conflicting with the whole. Conflicting with aspects of her aura that seemed to imply that she had a great latent potential for magic. Great enough that she might have made a powerful mage, had she begun the study early enough.

Then again, her potential was not entirely latent. She had some very minor raw ability. Unrefined, untrained. A sensitivity to spells of influence, a sort of natural resistance, and great strength of will.

Bandit wondered if she might not be one of those people, successful people, powerful people, who are often credited with great personal charisma, charm, influence, and a thousand other traits that mundanes found so difficult to describe.

Magic by other names.

It would be interesting to spend more time with Marena Farris. Bandit could see the value in it clearly. If nothing else, her own natural resistance would help him reveal the true depth of power possessed by the Mask of Sassacus.

The bedroom door swung inward.

Rico entered. "Looking for you," he said. "Have a seat, I wanna talk to our guest."

Bandit found himself a chair.

Heading into this, Rico tried to keep an open mind.

Marena Farris lifted her head and met his eyes. She looked distraught enough to cry, scared, too. It made her seem more human.

Her Fuchi file said she was forty-three, but she didn't look anywhere near that age. Maybe twenty-five. She had the kind of looks that leapt out and demanded a man's attention, no question about it. Her face was pure exec, cool and sophisticated, flawless. Her figure was beyond belief. She had all the makings of a primo slut or prostitute, the kind of woman who got whatever she wanted, regardless of what it took. She'd started at Fuchi as a corporate joygirl, a sort of combination hooker and geisha, but had broken out of that mold in just a few short years. The corp had educated her, boosted her up the ladder.

Rico noticed how the light from the room's only lamp gleamed on the moist skin beneath Marena Farris' eyes, and he decided how to proceed. An honorable man would plumb his own depths searching for mercy. Understanding. Compassion. But Rico couldn't afford it.

"What's your story?"

She hesitated, blinked like she didn't understand, then looked at him steadily and said, "Please don't kill me."

Rico clenched his teeth. "Gimme a reason."

"I'm worth more alive."

What the hell was she talking about? Rico struggled to keep his face deadpan, concealing his surprise. Did she think she'd been kidnapped? That someone intended to kill her? Rico thought he ought to explain, only he didn't wanna explain, not till he got the truth out of her. "You always say hello to a slag by trying to waste him?"

"What else could I do?" Farris seemed to get choked up. Her voice wavered. Tears spilled from her eyes. She moaned, looking around like she wanted to find some way out. "You had me, you brought me straight to him. He obviously hired you for that." She paused a moment, hand at her brow. Her fingers trembled visibly. "I can't believe this is happening. Isn't there anything I can say? I'll give you any amount of money, twice whatever he paid you, if you'll get me out of here."

Rico hated playing games like this, especially with a woman, especially with one who looked like she expected to be killed at any moment. It made him feel dirty—like slime. It didn't really matter that she was a suit, a corporate. She was still a woman. If so much wasn't at stake . . . Rico clenched his teeth. "You got money?"

The question nailed her attention. Her eyes went wide. She nodded. Adamantly. "Yes. I have a lot of money. I don't . . . I don't care how much you want. Just let me go. Please let me go."

"Later," Rico said. "We'll talk about money later. I wanna know some things first."

She nodded, looking like she'd willingly tell him anything. Rico wondered whether to believe it.

"How'd you figure it out?" Rico said. "What we got in mind."

Farris lowered her face to her hand, stared at the bed. She seemed about to cry again. "I've known for some time that Ansell loathes me. He can be very vengeful. That's why he volunteered—"

"Volunteered? For what?"

Farris looked at him again. "You don't really need to know that. It's proprietary."

Rico stepped toward the bed. "I'll tell you about proprietary. I almost got my cojones blown off coming after you. So you're gonna tell me what you know. Everything."

"Please ... I took an oath."

A real corporate thing to say.

Rico sat down on the edge of the bed facing her. A new rise of fear showed plainly in her eyes, yet something in the way she held her head, the angle of her chin, seemed almost like a challenge. Defiant. That changed when the razorspurs slid out of the rear of Rico's arm and snicked softly into position. Farris' eyes caught the movement. She looked, then looked again. When Rico lifted his forearm, moving those blades toward her throat, she stiffened, lifted her hands to her face, and leaned away.

Another moment and she was squirming.

She gasped. *"Please!"*

When she started shaking. Rico drew back. She was hard to read, and harder to figure. One big contradiction from start to finish. She could peddle that body of hers in any bar in the sprawl without even trying, yet she seemed sharp, maybe sharp enough to go anywhere, right to the top. She didn't seem like the type to be physically brave, and yet this same woman had just grabbed a gun and tried to blow away her own husband. What the hell kind of sense did that make? None. None whatsoever. Surikov didn't seem to understand it. Rico sure didn't.

"Consider yourself threatened," he said. "Now talk."

Farris was more than just a few moments calming down. If it was an act, it was a fragging good one. Every move flush, a seamless performance. Right down to the way she pursed her lips, as if forcing herself to at least *seem* in control of herself, when really she was shaking. Rico wasn't sure if he believed her act or not.

"You said your husband volunteered. Volunteered for what?"

"A special program," Farris said in a voice that seemed weak with emotion. "He didn't have to do it. He did it to get away from me. To spite me."

"Spite you why?"

"Because things didn't work out."

"What things?"

She hesitated and swallowed visibly. "Our relationship," she said. "Our marriage."

Rico figured that much had to be true. If it hadn't been true, it was now. Unless Surikov didn't mind almost getting wasted by his wife. "Tell me about this special program. You said your husband volunteered."

"It's a secret."

"You wanna get hurt?"

She lowered her head, shook it, and said, "It was a program to infiltrate Fuchi competitors. Security services have been doing that ... doing it forever. The problem is ... your average security operative lacks the qualifications to get at the data you really want. The agent typically ends up on the competition's security staff or else posted in some security function to an executive, with only very limited access to proprietary material. The Fuchi program changed all that. We developed an interdisciplinary scheme for training scientists and researchers to work as security operatives, and to work effectively. That's basically what it was about."

"Keep talking."

Something crossed her face, maybe dismay. "The program was very involved," she said softly, almost moaning. "It was five years in the making. I was part of it from the beginning. Ansell resented the hours I logged. He's very possessive. He wanted me to be with him whenever he was free from his work. My work didn't matter to him. I tried working from our condo and ultimately went on leave, but by then it was too late. He resented me, resented everything about me, and that resentment turned vile. It turned into hatred."

"So he volunteered for your program."

"It was ... it was a way to use my own work against

me. He felt that I had betrayed him. This was his revenge. Knowing how it would make me feel."

Rico wondered how much of this was true. Farris' file said that she had worked on some special project for going on five years. More than that, he didn't know. A lot of what Marena Farris was telling him wouldn't likely appear in any files. "Surikov's a big deal biotechnician. You're telling me Fuchi put this slag, this asset, into some experimental program and sent him straight to the enemy. I don't buy it."

"Ansell's qualifications made him perfect for the role. That was the point of the program, to get astute people into the competition's camp, people who would know what they were seeing, who could report in specific detail on how competition research was developing." She hesitated a moment, wiped her eyes. "Yes. Ansell Surikov is a highly qualified scientist with an enviable reputation. Fuchi has many highly qualified scientists with good reputations. None of them are irreplaceable."

"Where'd they send him?"

"Kuze Nihon. A subsidiary, Maas Intertech. That's located in New Jersey."

"How long you been on leave?"

"About . . . about three years."

Her Fuchi file agreed. "Why do you rate your own personal security team?"

Farris hesitated, "I . . . I was never told why. In the beginning, I assumed it was because I had always been loyal to the corporation. I'm still an asset, even if I am on leave. I haven't resigned."

"What makes you an asset?"

"I'm a psychologist."

Her Fuchi file verified that. Fuchi had sent Farris to several universities in the U.C.A.S., and she'd earned a degree in psychology. It had seemed odd to Rico that a corp would spend money like that on a corporate hooker, but apparently it wasn't as strange as he thought. Piper said that a lot of the megacorps used their more sophisticated joygirls and joyboys a lot like shrinks. Some even worked as spies for corporate security.

That whole train of thought made Rico wonder if he was sitting next to something as potentially nasty as a trapdoor spider. Farris looked and acted upset, and yet the things she was saying told him that the brain behind her dark brown eyes was alive and working just fine. Did she really believe that her husband had hired help to murder her? That much didn't make much sense.

"Psychologists at Fuchi get personal security teams?"

"I suppose I'm a special case. Certain people hinted that threats had been made against Fuchi, against security personnel in particular. I accepted that. Later, as I put my life back together, I began to wonder if perhaps the threat had something to do with Ansell. Perhaps he had been found out. Perhaps Kuze Nihon was using threats against me to make Ansell work for them."

"Why would he care?"

"You would have to know Ansell to understand that."

"Try me."

She seemed puzzled for a moment. Whether puzzled by the demand or puzzled that it should be made, Rico couldn't tell. She said, "Ansell doesn't respond well to coercion. He's out of his element here, so you've probably found him easy to deal with. In the corporate environment, where he's at home, he's highly independent of mind and intensely aware of his own personal purview. He believes he should be allowed to pursue his work utterly without supervision or constraint. He views even the slightest intervention by management as a complete usurpation of his rights as a scientist. That same egocentric perspective dominates his personal life as well. A threat against his wife would be no less a threat against him as a man. It wouldn't matter if he cared whether his wife lived or died. What would matter is his power to control what happened."

"If anybody's gonna ice you, it'll be him."

"That would be his view. Highly simplified."

"How does he go from spiting you to wanting to kill you?"

"Presumably, Maas Intertech realized he was an infiltrator and began using him as such, limiting his access, feeding him false data to pass along to Fuchi. They would naturally put restrictions on his research and he would resent this. Probably, he would blame me, for if I had not encouraged his spite, he would not have gotten into a situation like that. It's all my fault, you see."

"So he'd come after you for revenge."

"Isn't it obvious?"

"You make him sound like a psycho."

"Then I haven't been clear." Farris paused, wiped at her eyes some more. "Perhaps I should explain that the desire for personal power is a defining factor in many men, just as the desire to form cooperative relationships is a factor in many women's development and personalities. Ansell is as rational a man as you might ever meet. He functions very effectively in the corporate milieu. His personal power is extremely important to him, but he's not inflexible, not compulsive, in the clinical sense. At times, he deliberately exaggerates his need for control, as a ruse he uses merely to achieve a degree of control that he'll be comfortable with, knowing all the while that certain of his demands will be refused."

"Rational men don't dust their wives."

"If you really believe that, you've been misinformed."

"Yeah?"

"Rational people sometimes do irrational things. I'm explaining myself to you at length when I should probably be saying as little as possible."

"You been threatened."

"Yes, I know." She pressed a few curling strands of hair back from the side of her face. Her fingers gave a tremble so slight Rico almost missed it. "Fear may be a rational response to danger, but it does not necessarily motivate rational behavior." She paused again and swallowed. "I want to cooperate fully because I'd rather you were my ally than someone I should fear. I try to avoid classic behaviors like that, and yet I find that I can't. Right now, it's practically a compulsion."

"Right now" bothered Rico a good deal less than what might be somewhere ahead of him.

Marena Farris was going to be trouble.

Hell, she was already trouble.

"Was she lying?" Rico asked softly when they came out of the room onto the second floor hallway.

Bandit nodded and said, "Yes. She lied."

"About everything?"

"No."

Rico wanted to know more, specifically when Marena Farris had lied and when she had told the truth. Bandit wondered how to answer. Spells of detection, especially those involved with detecting truth and lies, were not like spells for casting mana bolts and fireballs, which either worked or didn't work as the caster intended. Spells for assensing truth most often yielded mixed results, perhaps because most people spoke in a mixture of truth and falsehood.

There was also the question of whether such spells assensed the objective truth or merely the truth as the target of the spell knew it. Had Marena Farris lied in certain respects or simply recited lies she had mistakenly accepted as truth?

"What did she lie about?" Rico asked.

Bandit replied, "Take your best guess." He was no multiphased lie detector, and he disliked trying to function as one.

Rico grimaced, seeming displeased.

"Your wife says you volunteered for the program."

Surikov frowned, looked unhappy, even angry. "Volunteered? I did nothing of the kind. I was *ordered to* enter the program! I had no choice whatsoever."

"They musta had some kind of hold on you."

"A hold? Of course they had a *hold!* If I'd refused them, I'd have ended up in the Antarctic somewhere, running computer-directed tests on plankton."

Surikov looked and sounded like he would have considered that a real tragedy, and Rico could believe it. He'd heard this kind of talk before. People like Surikov grew up on the inside of the corporate infrastructure. They didn't know any better. When the Master Suit gave orders, nobody disobeyed. You did what the bosses told you or you suffered the consequences. Even a slag with serious ego problems wouldn't want any black marks on his record because that would be bad for his career. And corporates didn't seem to see much difference between the words "life" and "career."

If one went down the toilet, the other followed.

"You said you were snatched outta Fuchi Multitronics."

"Is there a difference? I was given no options. Whether I was kidnapped or thrust out upon my path, I had no choice. I was badly used. The morality of it is identical."

There was a difference, though. Fuchi might try to retrieve Surikov in either case, but this was not just "either" case. In this particular case, which was the only "case" that really mattered, L. Kahn had claimed that the client wanted to retrieve the subject of a kidnapping, and if that was a lie—as Surikov and his wife both claimed—then Rico had every right to call off the deal with L. Kahn.

Suddenly, his course seemed surprisingly clear.

If he got out of this alive, he'd have to make some kinda statement, a statement about fixers who lied. Something L. Kahn would not like. Something people would hear about.

"You got two options," Rico said. "You go where your husband's going, or you wait till I'm ready to let you go."

Marena Farris watched him from the bed in the second-floor bedroom with eyes that got really big and round and an expression that seemed as expectant as it was fearful. "Does that mean . . . you *will* let me go?"

"Not till I'm ready."

"But you will let me go, eventually?"

"When the time's right."

Farris slumped a little, lifting a hand to her face, closing her eyes. "It's so hard to believe you won't just kill me," she said in an undertone. "But that's what you're saying, isn't it? You're not going to kill me?"

Rico clenched his teeth. "I don't do murder."

Farris gasped. She did that a couple of times, head down, hand still over her face. Maybe she was crying. Soon, she lifted her head and wiped at her eyes. "Where is Ansell going?"

"It ain't settled yet."

"You're not taking him back to Fuchi, are you?"

Rico wondered if he should tell her. His first instinct was to say nothing. She didn't need to know. It did make him wonder, though. She'd just tried to kill the slag and now she wanted to know what was happening with his life?

Before he could decide what to say, Farris said, "You should bring him back to Fuchi."

"Why?"

"It's the best environment for a man like Ansell. It really is. I'm not saying that just because I happen to work there. Fuchi's research facilities are the best, and the research program is tailored for scientists of Ansell's ability. I don't really think he'll be happy anywhere else."

"That's his problem," Rico said. "His decision. Your decision I already laid out for you. Which is it?"

"If you aren't taking Ansell to Fuchi, I'd rather you just let me go. Someplace safe. Near a telecom."

Right.

"She ain't going with you."

"She isn't? Why not?"

"Because that's her decision."

Surikov frowned, then looked at Rico expectantly. "You've got the guns," he said, quietly. "You could force her."

Rico clenched his teeth. "I don't think so."

"I could make it worth your while."

"Forget you even thought it."

"What about Marena Farris?"

Rico looked up as Piper pulled another soyburger out of the wave and turned to the micro-sized kitchen table. You'd think that in an ork safehouse, the kitchen would be the biggest part of the house. Not so. Rico finished chewing on a mouthful of burger, and said. "We're gonna hang on to Farris a while."

"How come, boss?" Shank asked.

Rico watched the ork devour a burger in one bite. "Because we don't have to let her go yet."

"And if Fuchi comes, we'll have a hostage."

Rico didn't like that word, didn't like hearing Piper say it. Taking a hostage had never been part of his plan. He wanted to let Farris go, right now. And he would, except . . .

"Corporates use everybody." Piper said, delivering more food to the table. "It's only right that we should use them. They should know the terror and violence that ordinary people live with every day. They should know what it's like to live in constant fear of death. What it's like to be considered valueless."

"Nobody's gonna lay a hand on her."

"Fuchi won't know that. That's the point, *jefe*."

The real point was subtler. Rico felt sure of what had to come next, but he had doubts, serious doubts, about Surikov and Farris, and especially about Farris.

No one spoke chiptruth—no way, no how. Everybody lied to at least some degree. The question was did he have as much of the truth as needed to go ahead? Rico had the feeling he was missing some essential part of the puzzle, some basic truth that would make everything crystal clear if only he had the sense to see it. Maybe it was just paranoia. He had no choice but to proceed with making a deal with Prometheus for Surikov; it was that or sit on his butt, and yet he couldn't help wondering if something Surikov or Farris might be holding back would cast everything, the whole situation, in a brand new light.

Let Farris go? Sure, he'd let her go, just as soon as he knew that nothing she knew could hurt him or the team or the deal for Surikov. That would cost her time and inconvenience and maybe a whole lot more, but she owed Surikov that, that much at the very least. In another situation, she'd be heading into court on charges of attempted murder. Here, she was getting off easy, no matter what happened.

"This run's turning into a freaking nightmare," Thorvin growled. "I don't trust either one of the freaking fraggers, Surikov or Farris."

"Shut up and eat," Shank remarked.

"Eff you, ya freaking trog."

"Short an' squat."

"Anybody wants out," Rico said, "say it now. We're gonna be up to our necks in guano before this is done."

"Ain't we already?" Shank said.

"No one wants out," Piper said. "We're with you, *jefe*. You know that."

"Yeah," Shank said, with a nod. "Sure."

Rico looked at Thorvin. The rigger hesitated, about to take a bite of soyburger, then looked at Rico out the corner of his eyes. "Miss a chance to kick some corporate butt?" he muttered. "You must be freaking dreaming, ya freakin' . . ."

Rico nodded.

Point made.

23

The brownstone on Treadwell looked like an armed camp. Six cutters stood on and around the steps leading up to the front door. Three of them held submachine guns in the open. Three more stood inside the entranceway, two armed with assault rifles, the third with a light machine gun.

Things were getting real all over.

As always Mr. Victor waited at the center of the house, in the garden. He invited Rico to sit. The houseboy brought coffee.

"I have many more inquiries for the services of your team," Mr. Victor said. "I have intimated that you might be available in the near future, and at prices exceeding twice your usual rates. I have been answered only with enthusiasm. Let me know the moment you are prepared for more work. I will have a job for you that very day."

"*Gracias,*" Rico said. "That's good to know."

"You do not seem pleased, my friend."

"I got problems."

"As do we all," Mr. Victor replied. "We live in troubled times. How may I help you?"

Rico said, "The job for L. Kahn is as good as a snatch. Surikov and his wife both tell me that he went to Maas Intertech as an infiltrator. A spy. That ain't how L. Kahn told it. He said Maas Intertech stole Surikov away. So either he was lying or his client was lying. Either way, the deal's off."

Mr. Victor's expression turned grave. "There will be repercussions," he said. "I regret that under the circumstances I am not able to intervene on your behalf."

"You didn't contract for the job," Rico replied. "It ain't your problem. I just want you to understand why I'm doing what I'm doing."

"Of course," Mr. Victor said. "I understand completely. You know which is the honorable path, my friend. The man of honor takes responsibility for his own acts. He faces the consequences for what he must do. However, there must be some way in which I can aid you. Be candid."

"You could talk to Prometheus Engineering."

"In what regard?"

"That's where Surikov wants to go. He likes their style, some guano like that. Surikov's supposed to be a real hot property. Some hotjack scientist. I figure we could get a finder's fee."

"Call it a delivery charge."

"*Si*. Whatever."

Mr. Victor seemed to consider briefly, then said, "Perhaps I can do you this service. Let me see what I can arrange. Excuse me for a few moments."

"*Sí. Gracias.*"

"*De nada.*"

Rico got up and walked around the perimeter of the garden. He made a point of gazing mostly at the ground or up at the tree limbs and birds overhead, anywhere but toward the table at the center of the garden. Mr. Victor wanted to do his biz in private. Rico had no problem with that. None whatsoever.

Maybe twenty minutes passed before a servant came to lead Rico back to the table. Mr. Victor invited him to sit with a brief gesture. "As it happens," Mr. Victor said, "I have a contact in a position to negotiate on behalf of Prometheus. They are interested in obtaining your man. He is known to them by reputation. They are also interested in his wife."

"She don't wanna go to Prometheus."

"I understand. I merely held out the possibility of the wife being part of the deal. It is no matter. Your fee will approximate what you would have gotten if you had finished the job for L. Kahn."

"You know that? what I agreed to?"

"My friend, it is my biz to know such things."

Rico nodded. If he had hesitated a moment to think, he could have saved himself a question. Mr. Victor had contacts, lots of them, practically everywhere it sometimes seemed.

Had anyone else spoken like this, alluding to privileged info of this type, Rico might have pulled a gun, forcing a confrontation from which there would be no turning back. Mr. Victor he could trust. Mr. Victor understood honor and knew when to speak and when to keep his mouth shut.

"This price is acceptable to you?" Mr. Victor asked.

Rico nodded. "Absolutely."

The portable telecom on the table bleeped. Mr. Victor picked up the handset, telling Rico, "*Un momento, por favor.*"

Rico began to get up, but Mr. Victor motioned for him to remain seated. The phone call lasted maybe half a minute, then Mr. Victor broke the connection and said, "All is arranged. Pickup will be this evening. Your man must pass a DNA and retina scan prior to transfer. Payment will be made in certified credsticks. I trust that is also acceptable?"

Mr. Victor was only asking as a courtesy. It wasn't necessary. Rico nodded. "*Muchas gracias.*"

"*De nada.* My friend, once this job is done, you will come and see me and I will have a real job for you. *Mucho dinero.* Your are into the big time, now. Serious nuyen. Congratulations."

"There's one other thing I need."

"And what would that be?"

"A meet with L. Kahn. It has to be by telecom."

"That is easily arranged." Mr. Victor replied. "Allow me to ask what matter you will discuss."

Rico put it on the line.

By the time Ravage was finished, Willy Hogan had several cracked ribs, two broken arms, a broken leg and his face was practically unrecognizable, battered and drenched in blood. Hogan's wife and child shrieked from the bedroom doorway. The others crowding this tenement apartment in Sector 11, a mix of orks and norms, waited motionless, silent.

This was Hogan's payment for taking nuyen and providing no information for it.

L. Kahn watched without really watching. He had other matters on his mind. Hogan, a former Fed, a supposedly skilled technician, had been just one of the many ways in which L. Kahn had arranged to keep tabs on the team hired to extract Ansell Surikov from Maas Intertech. The client had ordered multiple backup, and L. Kahn had delivered, yet every one of those backups had met failures of varying degrees.

The mission assigned to the backups was simple: track the runners who had Surikov, be prepared to move in if anything went wrong. How difficult could that be? L. Kahn had little patience for incompetents or self-styled experts like Willy Hogan. Even less when he was feeling pressure from above. He had ambitions. He would not be scammed by the many jokers and con artists running around the Newark plex.

Ravage finished her task, leaving Hogan sprawled in his own blood, just barely alive. L. Kahn turned and found his way back to his black Toyota Elite limousine. Ravage climbed in after him. Once inside the car, she tapped the intercom and told the chauffeur, "Drive."

They were soon down the great ditch of the Garden State Parkway and into the tunnels of the Westfield transitway. L. Kahn looked at the boy lounging on the seat beside him. His name was Jared. He wore a bluish synthleather bodysuit. He was cruel and cunning but malleable. And very attractive.

Unfortunately, the phone picked that moment to bleep.

L. Kahn directed his eyes to the limo's center console. The telecom screen there opened a window to display the image from an incoming call. A second window displayed the code of the originating phone, and the location—Sector 9, proximate to the border with the Passaic metroplex and immediately adjacent to Sector 20. The so-called "Executive Action Brigade" had finally located the runners in Sector 20.

L. Kahn reached out and tapped the telecom key to accept the call. When he saw the dark-skinned Hispanic face that appeared on the screen, he forced himself to remain calm.

"Mr. Rico" this one liked to be called.

"You lied," Rico said.

L. Kahn felt a twinge of anger and puzzlement, but suppressed it. Half-truths and lies were an integral part of the biz. Even a rank amateur should know that. What mattered most was the money, money and power. What inspired this razorguy Rico to cloak everything he said in pretentious moral language, L. Kahn did not understand. "You will make delivery tonight," L. Kahn said simply. "Twenty-three hundred hours. Sector 17."

"Wrong."

"You refuse to make delivery?"

"Like I told you at the start, I don't do snatches. I'm no dog you can just order around, amigo. We know who your client is and the man don't wanna go. Your money's on its way back to you. The deal's off."

"Turn the subject over to me and I will forget you said that."

"Not today, amigo."

"Your lives will be forfeit."

"We was born that way."

The image on the screen froze and held as the disconnect icon appeared. L. Kahn maintained his composure for a few moments longer, then cursed. That face glaring out of the screen, it was too much to endure. He should have known that pretentious slot Rico would be trouble. A shadowrunner with ethics.

Who could believe it?

L. Kahn leaned back in his seat, growled with frustration, then smashed his boot heel through the telecom display screen.

The order came at 19:40 hours.

Ten minutes later, Skip Nolan stood in the dingy, litter-strewn alley behind the street of ghetto rowhouses in Sector 20, North Caldwell. Like the four men and two women of Team A, he wore the armored assault uniform of the Executive Action Brigade.

The Team B leader signaled ready. Team B would take the front and upstairs portions of the narrow rowhouse where the runners had holed up. Team A would take the rear and basement areas. Somewhere up above, in the night, Bobbie Jo had the whole block under surveillance. No one had entered or left the house for hours. Ground-based surveillance teams had seen lights going off and on and curtains moving and figures silhouetted against window shades. The house was hot, making infrared analysis difficult, but no one had any fears that the runners might have slipped away again. A vibration detector dropped onto the roof of the house had picked up people moving around inside, and a laser snooper had picked up conversation off one of the windows. And on top of all that, the runners' van was parked right behind the house.

The runners were there, no question about it; and now, according to orders, they were going to be taken down.

Skip didn't know why the Brigade should suddenly go from a surveillance role to an interdiction role, but he wasn't planning to worry about it. That wasn't his job. Taking down runners in the Newark metroplex wasn't so different from scoring smugglers along the C.A.S.-Pueblo border or supporting a coup in Guatemala. The world was full of conflicting interests. When forces clashed, somebody lived and somebody died, and maybe once in a while the right people got what they deserved.

He keyed the mike of the headset worn under his helmet. "Team A, Team B . . . let's rock."

Two men swung a portable ram, smashing the rear door of the rowhouse right out of the frame. As the door went down, a third trooper flung a stun and smoke grenade that went off with a bang. Squad One rushed into the kitchen, weapons tracking from side to side, then called "clear" and moved on. Another grenade banged from the front of the house. Skip followed Squad One through the swirling smoke as far as the stairs to the basement and there pointed Squad Two up the hall toward the front of the house.

Another grenade detonated upstairs. Squad One called out that the basement was clear. Skip started toward the front of the house, but already he felt the uncertainty gnawing at the pit of his stomach. One room after another came up clear. Still no weapons fire, no report of confrontations, no sign of the runners. In another moment or two, the Team B leader would call the second floor clear and then Skip would know that the worst had happened yet again. The place was empty. The only bodies present belonged to the E.A.B.

How the hell had those fraggers gotten away?

"Bitches stay in the car."

None of the women complained, and that was well. The call regarding the change in the runners' status had come at an untimely moment in Maurice's studies. The last thing he wanted to do was waste time traipsing around the metroplex after a group of recalcitrant runners, but unfortunately he had no choice.

Gathering his coat around him and hefting his walking stick, Maurice stepped from his Mercedes limo. The night was cool and quiet, but rife with a tension that hinted at things to come. Claude Jaeger stepped up beside him. Maurice looked at the faint shimmering in the air before him and shifted to his astral senses.

Vera Causa stood facing him. She smiled and turned to indicate the house directly behind her, saying mind-to-mind, *This dwelling gives a fine view, master.*

Maurice looked at Jaeger. "Clear this house."

"Is that an order?" Jaeger replied.

"Consider it a recommendation."

Jaeger nodded and walked over to the rowhouse's front door. The woman who answered the door fell without a sound, then Jaeger proceeded to neutralize the rest of the occupants. Maurice moved through the house to the kitchen. Through the transparex panes of the rear door, he could see the dark, litter-strewn alley behind the house and the mundane forces now gathering.

Vera Causa indicated the rowhouse directly opposite. That was the runners' safehouse. The runners' van waited there. Finding the house and the van had not been difficult. A spirit such as Vera Causa moved with the speed of the astral. She could pursue a supersonic jet halfway around the globe. The forces of the Executive Action Brigade had literally led his ally here.

Taking refuge in the wastes of Sector 13 had provided the runners with more safety than they knew. Vera Causa had refused to enter the area, despite Maurice's command to follow them from their meeting with L. Kahn at Newark International. Maurice himself found that blighted region discomfiting to approach on any but a purely mundane level. It had therefore been necessary to forego any direct action. Continuing to monitor the Brigade had led them here to Sector 20 and the district of North Caldwell.

Maurice watched with interest as the dark armored figures wearing the flash of the Brigade gathered at the rear of the house and prepared to force entry.

The runners had a shaman, called "Bandit." Despite

Maurice's best efforts, he had been unable to learn much
about this shaman. Many people in the plex seemed to
know his name, but few admitted to anything beyond a
basic physical description and facile rumors. An astral
glance at Bandit's aura and the foci he carried, such as
Maurice had caught at the airport, might lead one to conclude that Bandit had little true ability in the Art, and
even less in terms of true power.

That was obviously an inaccurate perception, Maurice
now saw. The rowhouse occupied by the runners was protected by a powerful ward, a lattice of blue-green energy
that throbbed in brilliant counterpoint to the rhythms of
the natural energies pulsing and flowing through the night
in this part of the plex. Any magician could cast a ward,
but only one of considerable ability could cast a ward as
strong as the one now burning before him.

This indicated to Maurice that the shaman must be
masking his aura, and to do that he must be a powerful
magician, an initiate, in fact.

This changed things considerably. It made Bandit a potentially dangerous opponent, and it urged Maurice to
caution. The ward could certainly be defeated, but that
would likely cost Maurice energy, and he had not come
prepared to begin any sort of conflict at anything less
than his full measure of vitality. The appearance of this
unexpectedly powerful ward warned him to wait and
watch.

The Brigade's troopers stormed the house, smashing
down the rowhouse's rear door and entering like soldiers.
The ward of course had no effect on their entrance, providing only a barrier against spells and astral surveillance. No form of sorcerous traps appeared to be keyed to
it.

They seem confused, master, Vera Causa remarked.

They?

The soldiers.

An insightful observation, Maurice thought, for a spirit
so recently conjured. Vera Causa's rapid progress along
the learning curve gave him cause to wonder yet again.

The raid of the safehouse soon ended. The runners
were not found. Maurice projected onto the astral and
moved into the alley to watch and listen to troopers there.
They appeared disturbed.

The runners, it seemed, had not been observed since they had entered their safehouse. They had gone inside and stayed there. They had not departed via their van or any other vehicle. They had not climbed out through the roof and made their way across the rooftops to another location. How, then, had they escaped? Maurice circled the safehouse, stepping through the walls of the adjoining rowhouses and out to the street in front of the safehouse, then around and back to the alley. The building walls adjoining the safehouse were intact, so the runners had not simply broken into an adjoining structure and slipped away. Only one direction remained in which they could have gone, and that was down.

Maurice descended into the earth, and here he found the answer to the Brigade troopers' questions.

The runners included an ork, and that implied some connection to the ork underground—and that could mean many things. The Newark sprawl had a population of orks the equal of any city in the urban Northeast, perhaps the whole of North America, and they were always busy. Maurice had information indicating that many had begun going underground shortly after the Awakening, the better to escape the oppression of fanatical humans. Their subterranean constructions had since become quite extensive. Some sections of the city were honeycombed with tunnels and passages that appeared on no official schematics. And the orks had dug deep in many places. Deeper than any rational human would care to descend.

The deeper one went, the greater the sense of claustrophobia the tunnels bred. It posed a threat to sanity that Maurice did not care to challenge. And tonight there was no need.

A tunnel passed directly beneath the safehouse, a mere few meters below ground level. It appeared to be an old tunnel, braced by wooden beams. In places the walls were crumbling into mounds of sawdust and earth. The runners had doubtless used this tunnel to escape the perimeter set up by the Brigade.

Maurice considered. He doubted that the runners would remain in these tunnels long. Their leader would not allow it. To do so would be to invite forces like the Executive Action Brigade down into the tunnels, and that would put others, innocents, such as orks, at risk. The runners would therefore surface as swiftly as possible and seek other accommodations, a new safehouse, before continuing on their course.

The Executive Action Brigade was obviously at a loss. Their technological methods had failed. It would, therefore, be Maurice's task to find the runners' new safehouse. Fortunately, he had the means to do so.

He returned to his waiting limo.

The heavy metal grille of the storm drain was set into the ferrocrete of the gutter, but it also had an opening set into the curb like a shallow arch.

That arch gave a good view of the fronts of the rowhouses opposite, but only to someone jacked into a Mitsuhama control deck and using the sensors of a modified Sikorsky-Bell microskimmer for eyes. That someone was Thorvin—*who else?* The moment he saw the pair of dark blue vans turning the corner down by Hamilton, he fired a signal to Filly.

"Show-*time!*"

Her signal to get the hell out.

The vans came rushing up the block and squealed to a sudden halt in front of the safehouse. To say Thorvin had been expecting this would be a freaking understatement. He'd been expecting exactly this kind of a commando-style raid ever since he'd discovered the microelectronic bug some piece of scag had glued to the underside of the van. A nasty little piece of silicon that bug was. The sneaky kind. A real snitch. Virtually undetectable until it was activated, at which point it fired a microburst location signal.

The minute that snitch came on-line, the van's detection system went wild, and the rest was history.

Getting out had been a problem. They couldn't just leave. They'd needed someplace to go to and not just anywhere would do. They had a flabby scientist and a weak-limbed corporate biff to chaperone around. And the moment Rico told L. Kahn to eat squat, the whole world would come down on top of them. Including their backup on the job, or whoever had been tailing them. Move in to grab Surikov and Farris and ace the team. That's why corps hired backups. And that's why Rico had decided on the trick. Keep everyone concentrating on the house in

Sector 20's North Caldwell for as long as possible, and meanwhile get Surikov and Farris to safer precincts, which they'd done last night.

The van behind the house was an integral part of the trick. It was a decoy, of course, a virtual twin of Thorvin's super-charged vehicle, though only from the outside. Thorvin had thought Rico must be frizzed when he ordered up a twin of the Rover, but what the frag? That's what bosses were supposed to do. Plan ahead. Prepare for the unexpected. Even if it meant looking brain-numb. This particular part of the plan hadn't cost much. A day of hunting around through the sprawl's scrapyards, some welding and paint, and he had put together a look-alike, right down to the registration tags. The decoy's engine barely had enough power to drag the body more than a block at a time, but then motivating power didn't matter.

The rest of the trick was easy. Leave someone in the safehouse to move around, turn lights off and on, talk to themselves. Act like a crowd of people. Shank and Filly volunteered. They'd be moving now to the trapdoor in the basement, which led into the tunnel under the house. If Shank and Filly had any sense, they'd be moving extra-fast, because the commandos out front were already out of their vans and applying a portable ram to the safehouse's front door.

Thorvin watched the commandos go through the safehouse door. A close-up view got him a look at the flash on their uniforms. No black annis patches here. Nothing even hinting of Daisaka Security. The logo of the freaking Executive Action Brigade appeared on every left shoulder, every one that Thorvin could see. That was interesting. Thorvin had heard of the E.A.B. They'd recently been involved in clearing gangers outta certain parts of Sector 17 where certain corps had condoplexes. The E.A.B. made decent commandos, but they weren't exactly specialists at being subtle.

Why would anyone hire the effing E.A.B. for backup on a job like this? Thorvin wondered while descending to the concrete conduit that shuttled rainwater down the length of the block. It joined up with the sewer line running along Hamilton Drive. Before long, Shank and Filly came up the shaft from the tunnel below.

Thorvin keyed his mike. "How'd it go?"

"Smooth as effing ice," Shank replied.

"So why would anyone hire the freaking E.A.B. to tail us on a job like this?"

"Why the hell not?" Filly replied. "They come cheap."

24

The first shots came at ten p.m.

Victor Guevara was sitting in the garden at the center of his house. He happened to be glancing at his watch just as the first shots sounded.

It began with a long clattering burst of an automatic weapon, followed immediately by a fusillade of single shots and bursts. Several panes in the french doors looking into the garden from the front of the house abruptly burst into fragments. At the same moment the idle chirpings and whistles from the birds in the garden rose suddenly into a cacophony of caws and shrieks.

For an instant, Victor felt caught off-guard, but he was not surprised. He tensed and looked up, then willed himself to retain his composure.

The nights had grown very dark of late, and a man in his position had certain vulnerabilities. A civilized man recognized that, accepted it, and took what precautions he could. In anticipation of dire events, he had sent Christiana, his wife of twenty-three years, along with Dionne and Ivana, his daughters, and his son-in-law and two grandchildren to spend some time with trusted relations in Boston, where they would be safe. Though his personal inclinations might forbid him from fleeing trouble, honor demanded he take every conceivable step to ensure the safety of his family. And this he had done.

Now came several shouts, and louder peals, the screams of the dying. Victor would pay excessive premiums for insurance after this, not only for himself but for his employees, but he did not consider this, not for more than a fleeting instant. What he thought about were the spouses and families of those dying to protect him. It would eventually fall to him to say certain words and make certain gestures to those who survived the dead, in a futile attempt to somehow ease their losses. He would do this because it was his responsibility as a man. Because, again, honor demanded it. Only dogs and other animals could turn away from their dead as if they were nothing more than mounds of rotting garbage. Victor might be many things, some better than others, but he was no dog. Of this he had no doubt.

Even in his youth, during his days in Sector 19, the violent districts of Roseland and Pleasantdale, he had been like this. Ambition came first, but nothing came before honor, self-respect, and his beliefs about his rights and obligations as a man.

He had joined gangs and had led gangs. In time, he'd achieved a position with a local syndicate known as Rueda, the Wheel, and from there had gone on to forge his own network of contacts and agents. Everywhere he went, he always spoke to people politely, with respect. Always, he dealt with others as a man of honor. He did not lie and he did not cheat. He endeavored to give a fair value for any moneys spent. Fulfilling his ambitions had not been difficult. People were only too willing to be persuaded of his ability as a negotiator and intermediary. They knew they could rely on his discretion. They knew his word stood for something. Amid the routine betrayals and vicious treacheries of the Sixth World, his word had become as valuable as platinum.

No longer did he carry any weapons. The days of blood and thunder had passed for him. It seemed to Victor that if he could not survive based on the alliances he had made, the work of more than half a lifetime, then perhaps he deserved to die, or perhaps if was fate's inexorable ruling.

The *Japonéses* had a saying: *A man's fate is a man's fate.* If so, he would meet his fate willingly.

So it was that when Victor heard a crash from above, and a squad dressed as commandos descended through the roof of his garden on rappelling lines, he remained seated calmly at his table, sipping his coffee and awaiting what would be.

The battle for his house was soon at an end.

A number of dark-clad, helmeted figures surrounded him with weapons at the ready. The initials E.A.B. showed on the left breasts of their upper-body armor. Victor knew what this stood for and could guess who had sent these troopers to his house.

He could also guess why they had been sent.

One distinctive figure emerged from the front of the house. She wore a silvery bodysuit and black-studded bands. Her eyes were like violet holes, empty, as emotionless as her face. Victor knew this woman by name and by reputation. Some years ago, when she was new and unknown, he had given her a number of jobs, her first professional contracts. She had since risen through the ranks of the Newark underworld. She now commanded a certain respect from even the most powerful of the crimelords ruling the metroplex.

"*Cómo está*, Ravage," Victor said.

Ravage paused beside his round table, watching him, perhaps surveying him for weapons. She held a Scorpion machine pistol pointed at his face. Likely, she did not understand how he could sit here, calmly sipping his coffee, and therefore she suspected some as yet unnoticed threat.

Victor would show her no fear. Pride alone demanded that. Ravage had become just another animal. She had put morals and ethics aside to do whatever a client might desire. This added untold quantities to her merchantability, and spoke clearly of her character, or lack of it. Victor saw little difference between the Ravage standing before him now and a common whore. She had packaged herself as a product for others to rent.

No honor. None whatsoever.

"Someone wants to talk to you," Ravage said.

Victor nodded once, and said, "*Sí.* I know"

From the large unpaned window of his office 230 stories above lower Manhattan, Gordon Ito watched the lights of the city gleaming against the night. He lit a Platinum Select cigarette. He recalled that his current mistress had said something about having dinner tonight. Too late for that now. He checked his watch to confirm it. No great loss.

He returned to the high-backed chair behind his desk, looked across the room at his bodyguard, and pointed toward the door to the outer offices. The guard bowed formally, then turned and left.

An optic key in the touch-sensitive top of his onyx

desk brought a telecom screen rising up out of the desktop. Gordon tapped a few more optical keys. Call-protection software designed to scan the phone lines for taps and other forms of eavesdropping came on-line automatically each time Gordon made a call, unless for some reason he chose to cancel such security measures.

The Fuchi logo appeared briefly on the telecom screen. This was replaced by a straight-on view of an oriental woman wearing a Fuchi corporate blazer.

"Mr. Ito," the woman said.

"Ms. Yin," Gordon replied.

The digital clock on Gordon's display ticked off five seconds. This pause was standard protocol. Yin said, "One moment, please."

The Fuchi logo returned, but subtly modified, veiled by a black triangle. This represented Special Administration, and, hence, Gordon's own department as well.

As far as most Fuchi employees knew, the S.A. did not exist. It appeared on no corporate schematics delineating lines of authority, and it received its funds from diverse sources, funneled through obscure bank accounts. Gordon suspected that not even the board back in Tokyo knew of its existence, with the exception of Richard Villiers, Chief Executive Officer, and Villiers' number two man, Miles Lanier. Villiers had set up the S.A. and charged it with counterintelligence and other covert functions.

"Mr. Ito."

"Mr. Xiao."

"*Konichiwa.*"

"*Konichiwa.*"

The veiled Fuchi logo remained on the screen, but the voice belonged to Xiao, Gordon's boss and chief of Special Administration. A small icon appeared on Gordon's screen—voiceprint confirmed. Xiao never allowed his image to cross telecom lines, not even protected internal lines. A little touch of paranoia. Gordon understood that Xiao looked Korean, trim and spare, with close-cropped black hair. "Your calling time is convenient," Xiao said. "I have just finishing eating."

That was no coincidence. The hour was approaching midnight. Xiao usually woke in the late afternoon and worked through the night. Gordon's informant had predicted that Xiao would be awake now and just concluding his evening meal. There was no more propitious time to call than as Xiao concluded a meal. He apparently had a penchant for fine food. Gordon had a psychoanalyst working on that one, as well as other traits that had come to Gordon's attention.

"What brings you to my screen tonight, Gordon? Is it business? The Farris business?"

Gordon held back a curse. The bastard already knew. Xiao had informants of his own, and at least one of them was in Gordon's own outer office. Gordon would have the informant removed, except that it was sometimes useful to see Xiao misinformed, indirectly, discreetly. "I take it you've heard about the abduction at Crystal Blossom."

"Most certainly I have heard," Xiao replied. "I run the most efficient clandestine service in the corporate overworld. I have the most efficient chief of operations in the human sphere. Would you not agree, Gordon?"

Xiao's voice was, as always, emotionless, monotone. Gordon suppressed his immediate reaction to the implications of Xiao's words, and admitted, "I could have called you sooner. But I wanted more data before I laid things out for you."

"Your obsession with completeness is gratifying."

"It has plusses."

"Has Fuchi Internal Security become involved?"

"Negative." IntSec was totally in the dark, as it should be. Technically, IntSec and the S.A. were on the same team, but Xiao didn't see it that way. Neither did Gordon. The two organizations were as different as spies and security guards.

"Have you identified the criminals who abducted Marena Farris?"

"The data's on my comp. Partial ID's. My tech teams pulled a lot of trace evidence from the scene. We're cross-referencing with police databases. I suspect a local group."

"Is it the same group that ran on Maas Intertech?"

"Do I have to answer that?"

"You may instead tell me what you intend to do about Farris."

"Why does she interest you so much?"

"A loyal corporate employee abducted from a Fuchi facility? Must I answer that, Gordon?"

Gordon resisted a pained smile. Xiao made a good sparring partner. Sometimes, too good. Xiao would be the last man on Earth to miss the implications of Marena Farris' abduction. On the most superficial level, it gave some indication that Gordon's arrangements to roll up a special op, arrangements made through the *kuromaku* Sarabande, had gone wrong. Xiao would not be pleased with that. Xiao had personally ordered that the special op be rolled up. Xiao had also personally ordered that Marena Farris be "set aside," held and protected, when the special op first began.

"I wouldn't worry about it," Gordon said. "I ordered multiple backup."

"There is an image issue here."

"You're worried about image?"

That didn't ring right. Xiao's concern with image usually began and ended with Special Administration. Gordon concluded that Xiao was lying. The question was, why?

Xiao said, "I have recently had communications regarding the Fuchi image. Communications from lofty quarters. It is not a matter of total insignificance. Therefore, I have decided that you should do nothing further. Leave Farris to me. I will attend to the matter of her abduction personally."

"My pleasure," Gordon replied.

The display screen went blank. Xiao was never one for extended good-byes. Gordon lit another Platinum Select and sat back in his chair, wondering what the hell the fragger was up to.

It had to be something special.

Aubrey ran his eyes over the driver's curvilinear console, met the driver's expressionless glance, then turned to the door at the rear of the driver's compartment. The door opened for Aubrey at a touch of the thumb-lock. He stepped through.

The main passenger cabin had the look of a luxurious lounge: drapes, carpeting, glinting marbleized furniture, subdued gold lighting. To the right stood Zoge, a former *sumotori;* to the left, Rollo, an ork. Both were massively constructed. As Aubrey paused to look at them, they each gave a quick nod.

Aubrey moved to the door at the rear of the cabin. The thumb-lock let him through. The rear cabin was private and small, a very compact and ornate bedroom.

On the bed lay a dark-skinned biff recently come from Las Paz, Bolivia. Her name was Bela. Her Spanish was practically incomprehensible and she knew nothing of life in the sprawl, but what she did know she knew very well. She had heavy black hair and wore only a contented smile and a small gold cross on a delicate chain slung around her neck. She turned onto her back and parted her knees so that Aubrey could see what she had between her thighs.

Aubrey saw nothing he hadn't seen before in any number of different configurations. He sneered. Bela replied with the haughtiest of smiles. Then the door to the microscopic lavatory stall on the right opened and Sarabande stepped out, tossing back her lustrous sable hair. "Ready?" she said.

"*Sí,*" Aubrey replied.

"Very good."

Aubrey watched as Bela went to work, brushing Sarabande's hair, weaving it into a braid, fetching clothes, and kneeling to fit shoes onto Sarabande's feet. The slitch actually paused to kiss Sarabande's right ankle and to murmur words of endearment. Sarabande didn't seem to notice. Sarabande had eclectic tastes, but she was easily bored, especially when biz awaited.

Aubrey smiled savagely. Bela would soon be gone, perhaps in a matter of days.

Sarabande finished dressing. Aubrey preceded her into the main cabin, then headed up front to the driver's compartment.

The bus sat idling in the north parking field of the Governor Florio Rest Area, located along the Jersey Turnpike just south of Carteret and the Newark sprawl. A black Toyota limousine pulled in and parked nearby. Aubrey watched on the driver's console displays as an unlikely pair emerged from the limo and came toward the bus. They walked side by side: Ravage in her signature silver bodysuit and L. Kahn in his usual medium brown Armanté suit with cloak. One was a pro, a serious threat. The other was a sham. Expendable.

They paused alongside the bus. L. Kahn glanced at

Ravage, who, after a quick glance around, lifted a hand and knocked.

Aubrey let them wait a few moments, then moved down the steps as the driver opened the door. Ravage watched closely, well within striking range—barely an arm's length away—as Aubrey waved the probe of a Bailey Aardwolf magnetic anomaly and chemical detector past L. Kahn's front. The multiphase device discovered nothing indicative of weapons, propellants, or explosives.

Aubrey nodded at the bus. "*Bueno. Entré.*"

L. Kahn stepped past. Aubrey watched Ravage. The razorchick watched her client mount the steps of the bus. Her thoughts were obvious. Her client was leaving her zone of control. She did not like that.

"*Hasta la vista,*" Aubrey said quietly.

Ravage looked at him, then turned and walked away. She would have to follow in L. Kahn's limousine. No one entered Sarabande's presence with guards or with weapons of any kind.

Once Ravage was out of striking range, Aubrey turned and also climbed the steps. The driver immediately closed the doors and got the bus moving. Aubrey waited until the bus rolled out onto the highway, then thumbed the lock to the inside door and followed L. Kahn into the main passenger cabin.

Tonight, Sarabande wore gold visorshades with mirrored lenses, a gold jacket adorned with swirling silver, a red blouse and matching slacks and boots. The boots shone as brightly as chrome. Dressed in her business armor, the woman revealed almost nothing of her innately sensual nature. She sat behind a small round table in the left-rear corner of the cabin. Occupying the center of the table was a compact compdeck. A gleaming red cable ran from the deck to Sarabande's right temple.

For going on a full minute, she did not move, did not even seem to breathe. Aubrey could not tell if she was in the face of her computer or merely making L. Kahn wait.

Without prelude, she said, "You arranged the attack on Victor Guevara?"

L. Kahn hesitated briefly, then said, "Yes. That's correct."

A moment passed. "You questioned him."

"Yes."

"What did he tell you?"

L. Kahn hesitated again. "This is my personal—"

"I asked you a *question.*"

Aubrey tensed involuntarily. The subtle emphasis that suddenly entered Sarabande's voice cut the air like a scalpel, fine and precise and utterly ruthless. The effect of that edge on L. Kahn was plain to see. He stopped in mid-sentence and stiffened. Moments passed, then he said uncertainly, "Guevara claims to have no knowledge of the runners' present location or their intentions. Yet, the runners' leader has been in constant contact with him. I'm not finished with him yet."

"Then he is still alive."

"Yes. I have him in a safe place."

"That is fortunate."

Sarabande lifted one hand casually to her temple, as if adjusting her datajack. This was her signal. Aubrey stepped forward, whipped a braided garrote around the neck of L. Kahn and tugged it tight. L. Kahn rasped and staggered. He began to struggle, but Rollo and Zoge immediately stepped in, placing themselves between L. Kahn and Sarabande. One slammed a massive fist into L. Kahn's face; the other drove a fist into his midsection. L. Kahn's head snapped aside, blood and saliva spraying from nose and mouth. He grunted loudly and sank to his knees, gagging. Aubrey removed the garrote, put one foot to L. Kahn's back and shoved.

L. Kahn sprawled onto the floor at Sarabande's feet. That was suitable. What this man apparently did not know was that Victor Guevara had been one of Sarabande's local agents for many years. A very reliable agent. Guevara had brought Sarabande many useful contacts and a great deal of nuyen. Sarabande did not like such persons being troubled, interfered with in any manner.

Aubrey stepped over and lowered his foot onto the back of L. Kahn's neck, forcing the slag's face flat with the floor.

Sarabande recrossed her legs, and said quietly, "You have been played for the fool that you are. While the runners were bargaining with you for more time, they were plotting the abduction of the subject's wife. They now have both these persons. They obviously have no intention of turning the subject over to my client. I am very displeased."

L. Kahn grunted, moaned. "They broke . . . contract."

"Indeed."

Sarabande signaled again. Aubrey drew back a step. Rollo and Zoge moved in, dragged L. Kahn up off the floor and onto his feet. Aubrey delivered three precisely aimed and executed hand strikes directed at specific points of L. Kahn's upper body, then turned and whirled, slamming the heel of his boot across L. Kahn's face.

The man sagged as if made of mud. Blood streamed from his nose and mouth. Rollo and Zoge turned him on his knees to face Sarabande. Aubrey grabbed a fistful of hair and yanked L. Kahn's head up straight.

"When you are given instructions, you follow them to the final decimal," Sarabande said. "You do not decide on your own to mount private adventures. You are one little fly in my web. You do what you are told. Nothing less, nothing more. You will release Victor Guevara at once. You will then sanitize this entire operation. Is that clear?"

L. Kahn seemed to have barely the strength left to nod, much less speak.

Sarabande signaled.

Rollo and Zoge dragged L. Kahn around to face Aubrey. The meeting was over. It was time for one final warning. Aubrey drew a knife from his pocket. The black monocule-edged blade snapped out of the handle and into position with a soft click. Aubrey grabbed hold of L. Kahn's hair to steady his head, then put the tip of the blade inside L. Kahn's left nostril.

"Remember," Aubrey said. "Do what you're told."

L. Kahn grunted, and Aubrey tugged the knife free.

It was a very, very clean cut.

25

"I'm hungry."

"Come're."

Lying on his back on the bare mattress, Monk turned his head to the right and wondered what Minx meant. It was way too dark to see, but he could feel her lying right up against his side, her head resting lightly on his arm midway between his shoulder and elbow. He could feel the warm weight of her luscious, lithe body weighing against his side all the way down to his ankle. He could feel the soft, gentle pressure of her body grow subtler, then fuller, each time she took a breath.

Come're?

Where ... ?

Then, he felt her moving, maybe rising onto one elbow, lowering herself onto his chest. The feel of her body descending onto his inspired him to a not-so-subtle excitement. They had just made love like that, her on top, he on the bottom. He guessed she wanted to do it again. With her, he'd do it forever.

"Monk?" she said softly, her face just a breath away, her hair showering down all around them. "Do you like me?"

"Uh-huh."

"Would you like to be with me always?"

"Sure."

"I'm glad." Her lips brushed his cheek. "You're so booty. And it doesn't always work right unless you want it."

"Huh?"

"Breathe with me, silly. That'll make you."

"Make me wha ... ?"

Her mouth closed over his. She exhaled, long and deeply. So long and so deeply that when it came time for

him to breathe, he simply inhaled her air, her breath. They did that a couple of times. It was wild and kind of sexy and the excitement it inspired in him made Monk want to go on breathing like that forever. It made him want other things, too. He began running his hands up and down her sides and over her slender back, down over her behind, then up and over the back of her head and through her lavish hair.

They got it together, their separate parts. Minx began shifting back and forth, making it work. She kept her mouth on his throughout. The harder and faster they moved, the harder they breathed, passing the same breath back and forth, back and forth.

By the time it ended, Monk felt dizzy—dizzy with excitement, and dizzy with something that seemed like love.

The room actually seemed to be spinning, turning around and around and tilting wildly back and forth. The darkness took on a reddish glow, as if the sun were returning from night to twilight, and then to the last fiery radiance of sunset. Minx laughed and her laughter echoed. She smiled and her eyes seemed to gleam a fiery red. Her whole body had a crimson hue. Everything did.

Grinning, Minx leaned down into his face, till their noses touched, and she crooned, "I made you."

"Made you, made you," her voice echoed.

"Huh . . . ?" Monk said.

"Huh . . . ? huh . . . ?" his voice echoed.

"Come on! come on! come on!" Minx said. *"Let's go! let's go! let's go!"*

"Go where? go where? go where?"

Minx laughed and laughed and laughed. She tugged him up by his arms. The floor tilted downward, then upward, then back and forth and up and down. Minx grabbed him around the waist and tugged him forward, pitching forward down the slope of the floor, then staggering up, up the slope of the floor. A cacophony of raucous voices and uproarious laughter echoed and resounded. Leering, red-hued faces streamed toward him from out of nowhere, only to vanish right in front of his nose. Minx forced him to run headlong down a flight of stairs, then dragged him stumbling up and down a long, red-hued passage.

"Hurry! hurry! hurry!" Minx said. *"Monk! Monk! Monk! It's time! it's time! it's time!"*

A metal door slammed open above them.

Minx dragged him up, up and out through the door, then down more stairs and onto the broad, red-hued pavement of a four-lane transitway.

Suddenly, everything seemed normal, just red, except for the fact that the transitway was empty of traffic.

Monk looked to his left and saw a MediVan with flashing strobes and glaring headlights bearing down on him from maybe two meters away. He opened his mouth to scream, but didn't quite make it. Someone jerked him back off his feet—right off the ground—and set him down again a good two or three meters away from where he had been, but now facing in the opposite direction.

Something shrieked shrilly.

"Monk, *quick!*"

The MediVan door was open. Minx all but shoved him through, up the step and onto the seat. The driver looked human but skeletally thin, like death. The two orks in the rear had huge, savage tusks. When they smiled, their eyes gleamed a fiery red.

Minx shoved onto the seat beside him.

Tires screamed, the MediVan roared ahead.

"Hear about the wreck on the skyway?" shouted one of the orks in the rear. "Guy jumped the divider, hit seven cars, decapitated fifteen people before his tires ever touched the ground! Slammed into an oxygen tanker and incinerated himself and a buncha other cars! They still don't know what he was driving!"

Minx bent almost double with laughter.

The MediVan shot down a narrow tunnel and into the burning red glow of the night. A man crossing the street directly in front of them dove toward the sidewalk. His briefcase bounced on the MediVan's front hood, then struck the front windshield and split wide open. Hardcopy and comp disks whipped across the windshield and vanished. The MediVan's siren began whooping and wailing.

"Boner!" the driver shouted.

He grinned, eyes glaring red.

Monk looked at Minx as she grabbed his head and tugged him into a kiss, her breath gushing into his mouth hot and wet, her hand thrusting down and squeezing his groin.

"So booty!" she cried.

The night filled with flashing stroboscopic lights of red and near-red. The MediVan screamed to a halt. Minx thrust a reddish MediVan jacket around the back of Monk's shoulders, pulled one on herself, and tugged him out of the van.

Cars and bodies littered the roadway. Gunfire stammered and roared. "This one!" Minx exclaimed, tugging Monk around in a circle. She thrust him right at the sprawled body of a woman, a very large woman in clinging reddish clothes. "Now! Do it now!"

"What . . . ?"

She thrust him down, his head to the woman's, his mouth to the woman's mouth, and then with two fingers clamped his nostrils shut. Monk grunted in surprise, abruptly exhaling—just once.

Maybe that was the wrong thing to do.

"No, Monk! No!" Minx exclaimed. "Not like that!"

Abruptly, the woman jerked and stiffened beneath him and her eyes flared open wide, glaring a fiery scarlet-red.

"Oh, *drek!*" Minx cried.

The woman began clawing Monk's face. She moaned louder and louder, like a creature risen from the grave and bent on exacting a terrible vengeance.

"*FIEND!*" Mink shrieked.

Monk stared, wide-eyed, till suddenly Minx was tugging him back, right onto his feet.

"TOO LATE! RUN, MONK, RUN!"

They ran. They ran across the width of the street—dodging around smashed cars, jumping over bodies—and in through a doorway and up a flight of stairs. Monk glanced back only once. The woman he had breathed into was up on her feet and staggering around. She grabbed some slag in reddish camos and tore his eyes right out of his head.

Monk opened his mouth and screamed.

The slag screamed, too.

A door slammed open. Monk pitched forward through the doorway. The door slammed again to his rear as he tumbled to the floor, onto his back. In some little, one-room apartment.

Panting, gasping, thrusting back her hair and groaning, "Oh godddddd . . . ," Minx knelt down beside him and laid her head on his chest. "That was the wrong thing to do, you little booty," Minx said, catching her breath. "She must've been dead already."

Monk gaped, panting. "Dead?"

Abruptly, Minx's hands were moving gently all over his face, and she gazed down at him with a red-hued look of genuine affection. "Oh, Monkie . . . *are you tired?*" she crooned. "You must *feel* tired. Like you're drained or something."

Now that she mentioned it . . .

"Come're," she murmured. She pressed her mouth down over his, and exhaled. Monk felt his whole body tingle with excitement. When she did it again, breathed into his mouth again, he inhaled deeply. It was sexy and wild and it made him feel like, like . . . Like sex. Better than sex.

Later, when they were lying nude in each other's arms, Minx whispered, "Are you still hungry?"

Monk thought about that. "I'm not sure."

Minx smiled and snuggled close. "You're so booty."

"You're all red," Monk said. "Everything's red."

Minx giggled. "Of course."

26

The door from the alley led into a narrow hallway that ended at a squarish room crowded with artifacts: chairs, a couch, kitchen appliances, trideo, simsense gear, bookdisks, chips, several cyberdecks, and what looked like the scattered components for several more cyberdecks. Bandit had no particular interest in any of this. He investigated further. A small room off to the left turned out to be a lavatory. A third room looked like a bedroom.

The character of the bedroom stood out. Life glimmered here, though faintly. The spiritual essence of the world seemed to matter here. This room must be investigated further.

Bandit returned to his body.

"Okay?" Rico asked from the front of the van.

"Yes," Bandit said. "Interesting."

"You didn't see anything dangerous?"

"Not likely."

Back from his brief trip onto the astral, Bandit sat cross-legged in the rear of Thorvin's van, amid a clutter of tools and spare parts. He waited while Rico gave instructions to the rest of the group. This deep into Sector 6, Little Asia, they were probably safe, thanks to Piper's connections, but they would take no unnecessary chances. Dok and Filly would stay on guard here in the van. Everyone else would take a squat, go into the small apartment Bandit had scouted and shack out.

Bandit followed Rico and Piper, Shank, Thorvin, Surikov, and Marena Farris out of the van, across the alley, and into the cluttered apartment.

"You sure this is okay?" Rico said.

"I'm sure," Piper replied. "The slag who lived here caught big-time feedback. The rent's paid till the end of the month."

"Who's the slag?"

"Someone I know from the trons."

Farris and Surikov took seats at opposite ends of the couch. Shank paused, watching them. Bandit stepped into the bedroom.

The air smelled of incense. The walls had been painted to look like a forest. A few plants, dried and nearly withered, sat in colored pots. Figurines and shiny trinkets decorated the chest of drawers, the bureau, and the small table in one corner, along with a few animal pelts and bones, vials of crystals, and a small drum. A pair of sleeping bags lay on the floor under a veil of mosquito netting. Beneath the pillows at the head-end of the sleeping bags lay a small cache of drugs, feel-good stuff, illegal, and a book, *The Shamanic Tradition,* by Arthur Garrett, Department of Occult Studies, U.C.L.A.

None of this had any real value. Bandit flipped through the book by Garrett, just curious, then dropped it onto the sleeping bags. The character of the room suggested a medicine lodge, where a shaman might do long magic, but that impression was apparently a lie.

The book by Garrett as much as proved it.

Fluffy stuff, very philosophical.

The real surprise came from the closet. Bandit assensed something there, something hinting of power. He found an open black plastic case that was just under a meter long. Inside was a flute, a big one, apparently carved out of wood and ornamented with shamanic symbols. Bandit ran his fingers lightly over the wood. On the astral plane the flute was a living entity—visible and real—alive. Softly radiant with energy. Like a focus, a weak one, only recently made.

Odd . . .

The flute seemed to call to him, as if from across a great distance, faintly, so faintly, like some part of himself that he had forgotten long ago.

He wondered . . .

He considered the sword hanging from his belt. He had carried it a long time. When he was younger and less skilled in the ways of Raccoon, he had sometimes needed the sword to defend himself, but he had not used it in ve~rs. He would probably never use it again. He had
e to understand that such violence as a sword might

do was not compatible with the ways of Raccoon. Maybe it was time he gave up this part of himself completely. Maybe he should leave the sword in exchange for this flute, which somehow seemed representative of an older part of himself, his life, his being, and a part more important now.

No question it would be a fair exchange.

"You're making a mistake," Farris said.

"Naturally, you would say that," Surikov replied.

"This won't work out as you think."

"Why should that bother you?"

"Ansell, you know I have only your best interests in mind. I still care about what happens to you."

"I should believe that? After all that's happened?"

"Yes, yes, you should. I was wrong, I know that now. I'm sorry. I was afraid, deathly afraid. I know that's no excuse, but can you really hold it against me? What would you have thought in my position? I'd been taken from my room in the middle of the night by people I didn't even know. People with guns. I knew you were angry with me. I knew you blamed me. What else could I have thought?"

"You really thought I wanted you killed?"

"I know that's not very rational. I wasn't thinking very rationally at the time. Maybe I wasn't thinking at all. I don't know. I'm just afraid that you're making the same mistake, that you aren't thinking. You feel you've been betrayed, not just by me. You're full of anger. Maybe you feel that going to Prometheus Engineering will be a kind of revenge . . ."

Surikov shook his head. "That's not it at all."

"Darling, how can you be so sure? You've been with Fuchi all your life. I know you haven't always gotten everything you wanted, but you were happy. For a time, you were very happy. If you could just put aside your anger, you'd see that you weren't happy at Maas Intertech for the same reasons that you won't be happy at Prometheus Engineering."

"So I should return with you to Fuchi? You must be mad."

Shank grunted and took a seat on the floor, then leaned back against the wall beside the hallway leading in from the alley door. Marena Farris didn't miss much. Ever since trying to waste Surikov, the exotic-looking biff had spent every available minute trying to persuade the slag to go back to Fuchi. She had a one-track mind, and she was smart. No matter what Surikov said, she found some way to twist it around and turn it into a reason why Surikov should return to the Black Towers. This far along, it was starting to grate. Shank had heard enough of Fuchi already.

He leaned his head back and closed his eyes. He'd been slightly more than a day without any sleep. No big deal. He'd gone a lot longer than that in Bogotá and Panama City, some years ago. The smart soldier knew to grab a few zees any time he had the chance.

Not enough furniture to go around, but Shank didn't mind the floor. A carpeted floor was a lot better than a bug-infested hole in the ground . . .

Now if Marena Farris would just shut up . . .

The worst of it was that their situation would probably improve if Farris got things her way. Thorvin had spotted the Executive Action Brigade coming after their asses in North Caldwell, Sector 20, and Rico suspected that the E.A.B. had been hired as their backup and that Fuchi had done the hiring, maybe through L. Kahn. If Fuchi got what they wanted, they might be content to let bygones go by, call off the backup, and forget it.

If not . . . Well . . .

There'd be plenty of time to catch up on sleep when it ended, whichever way things ended.

"I want you to stay with Farris."

Piper ran her hands up over Rico's chest to his shoulders, then leaned her head against his chin, his neck. "What if something goes wrong?" she said, softly. "You might need help."

"You're a decker. Not a cutter."

"I can shoot."

"If things go that wrong, one more gun won't make any difference. And I need you to watch Farris anyway."

"She's not going anywhere."

"That's the point. She's our responsibility."

Of course he would feel that way. Piper decided not to
e. She knew less about guns and fighting and had less

experience with either than anyone on the team. That made her the obvious choice to keep watch on Marena Farris.

Rico and the rest of the team were ready within an hour, suited up, weapons checked, and heading out to the van. Rico put a pair of cuffs on Marena Farris' wrists and another pair on her ankles. "That's so you don't get into any trouble," he explained.

"Please don't go through with this," Farris said. "This meet. It won't work."

Rico hesitated a moment, then said, "It's already done."

Piper followed him to the alley door, there for one last embrace. "Be careful, *jefe*," she murmured.

"Always," Rico replied.

Once he had gone, Piper had nothing to do but sit in one of the armchairs and wait and worry. She held an Ares Special Service, but doubted she would need it. In all likelihood, no one would be coming to rescue Marena Farris, and Farris didn't seem like the type to try and break free on her own. This only emphasized Piper's feelings of uselessness. Tonight's meet had no need for a decker. She could jack in and monitor police activity, but the police, as usual, would probably prove to be irrelevant. She could try and infiltrate the Prometheus mainframes, in case Prometheus tried a double-cross, but the chances of her learning about that from the matrix seemed close to nil. Corps kept records on almost every aspect of existence, but documents on any illegal or quasi-legal operations were likely to be hidden away in Code Red datastores, or in some node isolated from the corporation's mainframes.

About the only thing she could do was pray, ask the kami to be kind. Before she could decide where to start, Marena Farris said, "I know you must mistrust me, but I want you to know that I'm grateful for the way you've treated me."

Piper felt a twinge or irritation. It was hard to look at Farris and not feel something like that. The woman appeared every bit the swank corporate whore, sophisticated and yet slutty. Impossibly over-developed. "I don't need your gratitude."

"I've often heard stories that make runners seem like

wanton criminals," Farris said. "I know that some are brutal killers. That's obviously not the case with you and your people."

"Why are you talking like we've done you some big favor?"

"I'm still alive, aren't I?"

"What does that matter to me?"

"It could matter a great deal, depending on how things go."

"What things?"

"The meeting tonight with Prometheus."

"What do you know about it?"

"Probably more than you suspect." Farris paused to shake back her hair, then met Piper's gaze with an intimate look, an expression that pleaded to bridge the distance between them. Piper did not believe that look, not for an instant. Nor did she believe the sudden change in Farris' voice, which grew shockingly soft. "It's easy enough to see what you think of me. I know you probably don't trust me. That's why I haven't said much concerning what I know. I'm not just some little psychologist or some cosmed-sculptured biff. I've had access to some very proprietary data. I'm worth a lot more alive than dead."

Piper sneered. "No one's planning to kill you."

"Your man told me that already."

"Then it's true."

"He's a good man."

"The best."

"Good people are hard to find. Their beliefs put them at a disadvantage. They have to be very good at what they do, and they have to be well-informed, or bad things happen."

"Why are you telling me this? *Corporate*."

Farris hesitated, smiling, but managed to make the smile look reluctant, almost painful. "You're right," she said. "I am a corporate woman. Through and through. But if this meeting with Prometheus doesn't go right, I want you to remember that I warned you. I warned your man."

"So?"

f I were you, I'd be afraid."

er briefly considered the gun held casually in her

hands, then looked at Farris, and said, "Why should I be afraid?"

"How much do you really know about Prometheus Engineering?"

"You tell me. What should I know?"

"You may not know enough. That's my point."

Piper lifted the gun and pointed it at Farris. The Ares was loaded with soft ammo, but Farris could not know that. Like most guns, the Ares could fire either soft or hard ammunition. "I want you to tell me everything you think I should know. Everything that's pertinent."

An anxious look came over Farris' face. Her lips faintly quivered. She swallowed, and said tentatively, "Are you going to shoot me if I don't?"

Farris described herself as a "corporate woman." She was employed by one of the most unprincipled despoilers of the Earth that humanity had yet created. Answering her question took hardly any thought at all. "Give me an excuse."

"Your man won't like that."

"My man doesn't like many of the things I do. That's my problem. Your problem is what happens between now and when he comes back."

"Yes," Farris replied, "I can see that."

"Good. Now talk."

Farris talked.

In the van, Shank looked at the flute, frowned and said, "Hoi, Bandit. Where's your sword?"

Bandit said, simply, "It's not my sword anymore."

"Huh?" Shank said. "What'd you mean?"

Bandit replied, "It's not my sword anymore."

Shank wondered about that.

27

The Willow Brook Mall lay just across the Passaic River, putting it just beyond the border where Sector 20 of the Newark plex met the western extent of the Patterson-Passaic sprawl.

The mall had three strategic aspects: it attracted slags from the plex as well as burbies from the corporate outlands; it straddled the confluence of several transitways and limited-access highways; and its parking fields went on forever.

At two a.m., Field 17D in the northwest quad was deserted but for a few scattered sedans and one black Toyota Elite limousine. Rico scanned the limo from a distance, checking the registration tags. Elites were as common as water, even in the Newark plex, but this wasn't L. Kahn's limo. Same model, different year.

"Think we'll make it?" Shank asked.

The time for worrying was over. "Ask me later."

"Nice answer, boss."

Shank put the Renault-Fiat Eurovan in gear and drove ahead. The rest of the team was in Thorvin's van, parked a safe distance away. They would stay out of sight, parked among other vehicles, until certain preliminaries had been satisfied.

Rico keyed his headset, and said, "We're moving."

Thorvin acknowledged.

Shank steered the Eurovan into field 17D and brought them to a halt about two spaces away from the waiting Elite. A few moments passed, then the rear door of the limo opened and a suit got out. He didn't look like nothing special, average height and build, medium age, dark gray suit and gloves to go with it. Standard corporate e. The style made the slag a real Johnson, anonymous, perfect front man for a corp. You might see him a thousand times a day on the street, but you'd never remember him because nothing about him was at all memorable.

A second suit appeared, standing up on the far side of the limo. This was no Johnson. Rather, it was the suit's security man, a prime cutter.

Rico got out and met the suit midway between the van and the limo, pausing about two steps away, near enough that they'd both be in trouble if anybody got stupid. They looked each other over. The suit motioned very briefly with one hand, glancing toward Rico's hip. He spoke with a voice as bland as his looks. "Mall security might spot that shooter of yours."

"We ain't gonna be here that long."

The suit nodded vaguely. "You have the merchandise, I presume?"

"You got the juice?"

The suit slowly drew open one side of his suit jacket, revealing the heavy automatic holstered under his shoulder as well as the plastipak of certified credsticks in his inside breast pocket. "The price as agreed in certified sticks."

"I wanna check 'em."

"First I see what I'm buying."

"You see, but you don't touch until I check the sticks."

The suit nodded, letting his jacket swing closed, and said simply, "Agreed."

Minor points, but even minors points counted here. In this game, nobody trusted nobody and even a little slip could push the panic button and bring out the shooters. Rico didn't mind letting the slag see Surikov. He could "see" him from five or ten meters away. He'd be unlikely to try anything, if he had anything in mind, till the range narrowed a bit. Step by step, slow and careful—that was the game plan, the accepted procedure.

Rico keyed his headset. "Ready."

Thorvin acknowledged.

Momentarily, the van came rolling up. Thorvin stopped it, according to plan, on the far side of the Renault-Fiat Eurovan from where Rico stood with the suit. When Filly and Dok emerged with Surikov, they stepped out in front of the Eurovan just far enough to show Surikov's face.

"You're very careful," the suit remarked.

"It pays," Rico replied.

"Once you've checked the credsticks, I want a DNA and retina scan."

"My man checks your equipment."

"That's fine."

Checking the suit's credsticks didn't take long. Rico had a portable verifier on his belt, not a stock model. Piper and Thorvin had put the unit together. Piper said the unit's integral chipware would detect phony bank encoding to a very high degree of certainty. That was good enough for Rico. He slotted the sticks one by one into the unit, waited for a pair of soft beeps, then passed them back to the suit. The sticks passed inspection.

Another slag emerged from the Toyota Elite. The suit introduced him as a technical aide. The aide showed Rico the pair of scanners he intended to use on Surikov. Rico motioned Dok over. Dok checked the scanners with gear of his own.

"Standard equipment," he concluded.

"Your man goes with my man," Rico said to the suit, "checks the merchandise, reports to you, then we make the swap."

"Agreed."

The final check took about a minute. The aide returned and gave the suit a nod. "Bring me the merchandise and then you get the sticks," the suit said.

"Right."

Here was the moment that counted. Rico took a quick look around. The suit's cutter hadn't changed position. The parking field around them looked clear. Thorvin wasn't giving any alerts based on readings from his own equipment or anything Bandit had to say. The assumption, then, was that everything looked chill. Rico motioned for Dok and Filly to bring Surikov forward. Their steps, scuffing against the pavement, seemed really loud. They moved slowly, at a measured pace. Seconds stretched out long.

"That's close enough," the suit said, lifting a hand toward Surikov, palm out. Then the slag's forearm jerked and something like a shotgun roared, and Rico realized sleazebag had a cybergun implanted in his arm.

hat explained the gloves. The glove on the right hand

covered the firing port. The glove vanished with the roar
of the eyber gun and a flaring red tongue of fire.

As the roar began to fade, Rico had the Predator from
his hip holster gripped in his hand and coming up, coming on-line, and putting a red targeting indicator on the
suit's face.

In the background, on the far side of the limo, the suit's
cutter was moving.

This time, Rico realized, the game was for keeps.

Bandit discerned nothing of any interest on or around
the parking field or for a kilometer or more in any direction. The spells he used uncovered no imminent threats,
no enemies. The only thing that really seemed to merit
his attention was the suit's limousine.

In astral space, the distance between Thorvin's van and
the limo was negligible. Bandit crossed it in practically
no time at all. Getting further than that was another matter. The limo at first seemed like an ordinary car, but that
wasn't quite true. Something about it was wrong, out of
character for a car. Several minutes of probing brought
Bandit an answer. The limo was protected by a powerful
ward. He hadn't realized this before because the ward
was masked, hidden, deliberately concealed. This was
very unusual. Concealing a ward was difficult. It suggested to him that someone or something of great value
must be inside the limo. Unraveling the ward would be a
worthy challenge.

Before he could finish, however, he assensed the violence erupting around him on the physical plane, and
gained a sudden insight as to the reason for the limo's astral ward.

He returned to his physical body, looked toward
Thorvin, and said, "I think there's a mage in that car."

"What *CAR?*" Thorvin shouted over the roar of gunfire.

"The limousine."

The blast of the cybergun caught Dok completely off-
guard. He saw the suit lift a hand palm-out, then that
hand disappeared behind a flaring of fiery red. The blast
assaulted his ears. He caught himself in mid-stride, saw

Rico's gun coming up and felt Surikov falling, pulling
him off-balance.

Dok tightened his hold on Surikov's arm, but it was
pointless. The man dropped like meat, collapsing onto his
back. Dok staggered, then caught his balance, looking
down in time to see the results of the suit's single shot
unfolding. The blast from the cybergun had shredded
Surikov's neck. He was dead or close to it. Dok began
bending toward the man and opened his mouth to shout,
but too late. It happened too fast. Surikov's eyes quivered
like gelatin, then began boiling. A dark, viscous fluid began trickling from his ears. Steam swirled. The man's
face began collapsing in on itself. Dok knew exactly what
was happening. He'd seen effects like this before. Not every cortex bomb was designed for explosive force. Some
were rigged with white phosphorous or burn-gel. They
might be keyed to life signs, or to a remote, and they left
nothing behind but a puddle of simmering goop.

Filly shouted into his face.

Autofire erupted.

The Predator hammered the night like a cannon. The
suit staggered backward, head snapping back, blood
splashing his chest. Rico turned and hurled himself into a
dive.

Heavy weapons thundered. Rico recognized the rapid-
fire stammering of the minigun atop Thorvin's van and
the higher-pitched bursts of Shank's M22A2 assault rifle.
There was also a quick, clattering burst that might have
been from an SMG. Rico thought of the suit's cutter.
Probably him.

He tucked and rolled and came up running. All he had
to do now was make it to Thorvin's van without getting
his cojones shot off. Slot in and run.

One minute everything was calm and peaceable-like. In
the next, Surikov was down and Rico was blasting away
with that heavy auto of his, and targeting indicators were
popping up all over the place and heavy autofire was
coming in from every direction.

*   much for any advance warning!*

er trust a freaking shaman for anything!

rvin revved his supercharger and spun the weapons

pods up top. Hostiles were coming up right out of the ground, like from manhole covers and storm drains. He set his minigun to stammering and fired a broad pattern of minigrenades, smoke and concussion both. What really worried him was the pair of bogies just now appearing on his radar overlay.

"PAIR OF BIRDS INCOMING!" he roared.

Make my freaking night.

Bandit stepped out through the open side door of the van and took a quick look around.

Just beyond the Eurovan that Rico and Shank had brought along was the suit's shiny black limousine. Bandit couldn't see the suit anymore. The slag had fallen, and Bandit had an idea he might be dead. Raccoon did not care much for killing or for any kind of fighting, but this was probably an exceptional situation. Things did not look good.

A few steps in front of him, between him and the Eurovan, Shank was shooting away on full auto.

Then the mana shifted. It had nothing to do with Shank. Bandit sensed what was coming before he had any real right to know. He lowered his head a little and leaned toward his left to peer around the front end of the Eurovan. From there, he saw something move on the far side of the suit's limo. The mage was emerging, standing up, using the limousine for cover. A dark hood cast his features in shadow, but not his aura. Bandit's eyes widened as he saw the pulsating power in the mage's astral form. They widened still further as he assensed the power of the spell the mage was drawing together.

This was very bad.

Swirling energy coalesced and condensed, growing more intense, more menacing. The world seemed to slip toward blackness as the mana mounted rapidly toward a climax. Bandit wondered what would happen when that climax finally came, but decided against waiting to find out. He had a very, very strong feeling that he would not like the effects of the mage's spell one bit.

Rather than wait, he murmured two words and pointed. From his finger shot a slender stream of energy that blended with the forces gathering around the mage. Momentarily, the mage hesitated and wiped at his eyes. Then he coughed, and then he was growling and clasping his hands to his face as he hacked and coughed and rasped for breath. The stench of the vapors that now swirled around him would spread quickly. The nauseating odors took effect at once.

The mage abruptly bent over and vomited.

Bandit nodded. Another lesson learned. Powerful, complex spells had their uses. Raccoon preferred to keep things simple wherever possible. Here, simple made complex irrelevant. Or almost irrelevant. For another moment, the energies the mage had conjured continued to gather, uncontrolled, building toward a new climax, a chaotic release of immense power.

This could be bad.

Really bad.

A crackling detonation rushed across the night sky, growing in strength and volume until suddenly it erupted and a searing bolt of pure white energy struck down out of the night. Dok felt more than saw it. The hairs running up his spine to his neck stood on end. A tremendous blast shook the ground. A roaring explosion followed. A blinding white light flared. For an instant, it was like watching a nuke explosion on trid. Out of the corners of his eyes, Dok glimpsed what he thought was the suit's Toyota limo leaping off the ground, disintegrating into whirling, razor-edged bits of shrapnel.

Somewhere between that first immense blast and the roaring explosion that followed, Dok felt Filly bump into his side, and suddenly she was falling right in front of his feet.

Caught in mid-stride, halfway around the front end of the Eurovan, Dok pitched forward and plunged to the pavement. He heard Shank bawling, "COVERRRRR!" He heard that roaring explosion and caught a glimpse of the disintegrating limo. He thought for sure that Filly must've stumbled. Or maybe she'd heard that first ground-shaking blast and just instinctively went prone.

Shrapnel or bullets or maybe both slammed against Dok's ballistic-insulated chest and shoulder and arm as he scrambled around on his hands and knees to get back to Filly. She was bleeding. There was blood in the hair at the back of her head, and she wasn't moving. Suddenly the worst seemed like a possibility, but Dok knew, God how he knew, that it would be just like Filly to take a hit, even a bad one, without ever making a sound. She was one tough woman.

He seized her from under the shoulders, began dragging her toward the van. No time—*no time for first aid now!* He had to get her into the van—*into the van and then do whatever he had to do!* Patch her up good. Keep her alive till they got to a clinic somewhere, *if it was really that bad!*

It was hard to breathe, so hard . . .

Suddenly, Rico was there, grabbing Filly around the hips and helping to heft her in through the van's side door.

No time to lose.

None at all.

28

They were most of the night shaking their pursuit and checking and rechecking that they were clear.

The few things Bandit said about the mage who had been at the meet made the slag sound like some incredible master of the arcane arts. Like the guy could've laid waste to the whole parking field, everything in it, and half the Willow Brook Mall if he'd only had the time to get the magic together. Maybe the way things ended pointed out the advantage of learning your stuff on the street, instead of in some high-tower occult academy. On the street, you learned that you were either quick or dead. That was one thing about Bandit. As much as he sometimes seemed to be living in some other world, he knew how to be quick, and he knew when quick meant everything.

Good instincts, Rico thought.

What else could you call it?

Thorvin sent the van flying down the transitways. They crisscrossed the plex and doubled back too many times to keep track. Rico found it hard, impossible, to keep track because he couldn't believe how the meet had ended. It made no fragging sense.

There was also the action in the rear of the van.

Dok worked on Filly for more than an hour, long after it became obvious to Rico that what little Dok could do with the gear on hand just wouldn't cut it. Maybe if he'd had a full surgical kit with respirators and all the drek like in the average emergency ward, maybe then something too good to believe might have happened. The way things were, with all their asses on the line, they had to get clear, and everything else took second place.

Filly never moved. She didn't breathe. She didn't show the least sign of life. Whatever had hit the back of her

head had penetrated bone. It had probably been over in an instant, before she could feel the pain, before she even knew what hit her.

If it was gonna happen, that was the way it oughta happen. That was how Rico wanted to go. Here one moment, gone the next. A death with some dignity.

That didn't help Dok.

"She lived how she wanted, amigo," Rico finally said. "She was true to herself and true to you. She was real. She had to be there. She wouldn't've let you go alone. No *effing* way, compadre."

Shank grunted, nodded agreement, and told Dok, "We're with you, bro."

Dok turned his head toward the ceiling and closed his eyes and said nothing. Clamped his eyes tightly shut and clenched his teeth together till the muscles in his jaw were twitching. Trying hard to keep things inside. Rico knew what that was like. He also knew it was no use. Some feelings were just too powerful.

It was almost dawn when they got to Little Asia. Thorvin turned the van down the narrow alley to their latest bolthole and parked. No sign of pursuit or surveillance. Rico got out, looked around. The van's side door slid open and Bandit stepped out, also looking around. Inside the rear of the van, Dok sat staring at Filly's body. "Come on, bro," Shank said.

"I wanna be alone," Dok said harshly.

"Come on, chummer."

"Leave me *alone!*"

"Dok," Rico said, letting an edge slip into his voice, "you're still bleeding. Shank's bleeding. We're all bleeding. You come inside, take care of biz. You want time then, you got it."

The speech seemed to work, but the minute Dok stepped out of the van he started cursing. Getting mad, crazy with fury. His words rose into snarls like an animal might make. He turned and began slamming his fists into the side of the van. Then he rammed his head into the metal. Once wasn't enough. He couldn't stop. Probably, he wanted Filly so bad he'd do anything, take any risk, go up against anybody, kill anybody, to get her back. He couldn't just quietly accept the truth. He had to do something.

A woman was always a woman, even just lying in bed asleep. It wasn't like that for most men, and, Rico knew, it wasn't like that for Dok. He was a soldier as much as he was a doc. He was a former mercenary. Just saving lives was never enough. He had to prove himself as a man. He had to do things. Crazy, dangerous things like shadowrunning, even if it got him killed. It was more than just machismo. It was pride and self-esteem and an essential part of his identity. He had to do something about Filly, even if anything he could do would be futile. Even if it was just pounding himself bloody against the side of a van.

Rico watched for maybe three seconds, then grabbed Dok by the arm, jerked him around and thrust him back bodily against the van. Dok struggled, pounding at Rico's shoulders and shouting, but Rico kept shoving, pinning him against the metal. Shank helped. Grief ultimately beat out fury, and that grief was too much to contain.

A man strong enough to love, really love, opened himself to the possibility of pain. A man who could do that didn't give a damn who knew how much it hurt or how the pain showed.

The flood subsided abruptly. Dok sagged, his eyes going wide, his face turning pale. Rico caught him up hard, gripping him around the body.

"I'm hit," Dok murmured. "Christ . . ."

Rico said nothing.

Shank helped carry Dok inside.

The moment Piper heard the rumble of the van, she snatched up her automatic and hurried up the hall to the alleyway door. A brief glance through the peephole confirmed her suspicions. She pulled the door open, then stood and watched as Dok climbed out of the van, as he cursed and shouted, and, finally, as Rico and Shank carried him toward the door. Glancing back and forth, she felt only confusion until she saw the reddish stains on Rico's cheek and hands, and then the lower legs of someone lying just inside the open sidedoor of the van. On those legs was a pair of dark hi-top boots. Filly's boots. Piper looked at the blood staining Dok's jacket and the rips in Shank's armored vest and the scratches on his arms and knew right then that the meet had gone very badly.

It took her a moment to put it all together: Dok's rage, Filly's boots. No sign of Ansell Surikov.

The slotting corporates had fragged them again. Now someone was dead, *another good person was dead,* and more were wounded. Piper couldn't just stand there and watch the wounded bleed. The anger and the frustration that came welling up from inside demanded that she respond. It was her duty.

She turned and hurried back down the hall. From her knapsack, she took a clip containing hard ammo, twelve armor-piercing rounds. At the touch of a switch the clip full of soft ammo dropped from her Ares Special Service. She thrust the new clip in, pulled on the slide, and released it. One soft round popped out and fell to the floor. A hard round took its place.

She stepped into the bedroom.

Farris lay there on the floor, on her side, arms cuffed behind her back. The little trickle of blood from the corner of her mouth was nothing compared to what she deserved, and what she was going to get. Those who served the megacorps were no better than the nefarious scum who ruled over the corporate hierarchy. They were the enemies of every moral person, of all metahumanity. They deserved no mercy. For their crimes against the Earth and every future generation, they deserved to die. They deserved to rot in hell.

"*Kuso-jitsugyōka,*" Piper snarled.

Farris looked at her, gaping, and then shrieked.

Piper pointed the auto at Farris' face and squeezed down on the trigger, but them something brushed her side and bumped her back. A huge hand swept along the outside of her arm, encompassed her forearm and tugged it upward, lifting her right off her feet.

"You fragging bent?" Shank growled.

He tugged the gun from her hand.

Dangling above the floor, Piper cursed at him wrathfully in Japanese.

Then Rico was there in the doorway, looking from her to Farris and back again. Piper stopped, stopped struggling, stopped cursing. Contained herself. Completely.

Shank lowered her to the floor. She rubbed her aching arm and glanced at Rico, but could not meet his eyes.

"What's this?" Rico said.

Piper shook her head, said nothing.

"*What the frag's going on?*"

"It was necessary."

Rico glared and curtly motioned her out of the room.

As Piper stepped into the main room, Dok looked up from the couch, met her eyes and said, "Filly punched out."

Piper couldn't help but be moved by the emotion in his face and voice. Despite her most immediate difficulty. Despite Rico's anger. She had known Filly for several years, almost as long as she had known Dok. She regarded them as friends. She knew how close the couple had been. "I'm sorry," she said softly. "Very sorry. I'll pray for her. Pray that the kami are kind to her spirit."

Dok nodded, looked away.

In that moment, Thorvin came into the room, hopping forward on one leg. Blood was dripping from the engineer's boot on his left foot. He paused and leaned against the wall. "Freaking slug came *right through the door!*" he growled. "Musta found a gap in the freaking armor."

Suddenly everything seemed to be going wrong.

They must have offended the kami.

She most of all.

Dok was hit, but no worse than anybody else—of them that survived the meet. They'd all been blooded, all except Bandit, who had the devil's own luck.

Getting Dok to tend the wounded took some work. He kept staring into space like he was in a trance or something. He kept forgetting the names of things he needed out of his kit. He made such a mess of one bandage he tried putting around Shank's arm that he had to pull it off and start over. He wasn't all there. Rico could understand that, but he also understood that none of them could afford an infected wound or the loss of any more blood than they had already shed.

Once the team was patched, Rico drew Dok into the bedroom to check on Marena Farris. She was on one of the sleeping rolls, sitting up and free of the cuffs. She looked anxious, upset. Rico didn't blame her. He'd be upset too if somebody pointed a gun in his face.

Dok checked her out. One side of her mouth was a little puffy. Nothing to worry about. Nothing for Dok or Farris to worry about.

Rico remembered the trickle of red he'd seen coursing down from the corner of her mouth. She hadn't got that lying on the floor. She'd been in the other room when the team left for the meet and her hands had been cuffed in front, not behind her back. The obvious conclusion was that, for whatever reason, Piper had gotten a little rough.

If Rico hadn't seen her pointing an Ares at Farris' face literally as he came through the door, he probably wouldn't have believed it.

But for the swelling by the mouth, Farris' stylishly contoured face was otherwise unmarked. The worst Piper could've done was slap her, maybe slap her a couple of good ones. That wasn't the point, though. The point had to do with what was right and what was wrong, what he could let pass and what he couldn't tolerate. He had serious problems with any woman getting beaten or abused, especially one like Farris, who obviously presented no real physical threat to anyone. The fact that another woman had done the beating made no difference. The fact that Farris had been cuffed and totally helpless only made the matter worse.

It made him want to throw up.

Once Dok stepped out of the room, Rico said, "What happened here won't happen again. You can take that for a promise."

Farris nodded, looking troubled. "What happens now? To me, I mean."

"That ain't decided."

Farris hesitated, then said, "Have you spoken to your woman?"

"What woman?"

"The Asian woman. I don't know your names."

"Who said she's my woman?"

Farris seemed disturbed by the edge that slipped into Rico's voice. "I'm sorry," she said in a hushed voice. "I just assumed . . ."

"Don't assume nothing."

"Yes, of course. Excuse me. But you should still speak to her. There are things you should know. We talked."

"We'll get to that later."

"There's something you have to tell me?"

Rico nodded. "The meet didn't go too good."

"How is Ansell?"

"He didn't make it."

"You mean he's dead?"

Rico nodded again.

Farris looked more than just saddened by the news. How much more Rico couldn't tell. Farris lowered her head. She wiped at her eyes. "Could I be alone, please?" she said. "This is . . . I'm afraid I'm getting rather upset . . ."

"If you want anything, just ask."

She shook her head, her hair falling forward, shielding her face.

Rico left her and went into the front room where he found Piper waiting. The look on her face was getting familiar: embarrassment, shame. Rico nodded toward the alley door. She preceded him up the hall and out into the alley. Rico spent a moment glancing around, checking that the alley was clear, then turned to Piper and said, "You wanna tell me what you thought you were doing in there?"

"It would be very difficult," Piper replied, looking everywhere but at him.

"Do it anyway."

She took a while getting to it. "I wasn't really thinking," she said in a whisper. "I saw that the meet had gone bad, *jefe*. I saw you were wounded. I saw Filly lying there in the van. I realized she was dead. I felt I had to do something. I felt it was my duty."

"Murdering Marena Farris."

"She is a corporate. Corporates are our enemies."

"Yeah? Let's talk about duty. You had a duty to me to watch out for Farris. You had a duty to the team."

Piper's face turned a dark shade of red.

She covered it with her hands.

"Please . . . ," she moaned.

Rico turned and walked away a few steps, then lit a cheroot. It was that or bust a gut, or get violent. The frustration was almost too much. The way he felt now, Piper seemed like a complete stranger, a total mystery, a disaster waiting to happen, a slight against his honor that he didn't even want to consider. She was as gentle as a dove in bed. How the hell could she attempt cold-blooded murder? Did her hatred of corps run that deep?

Maybe the old saying was true.

Never trust an elf . . .

In a voice that wavered with emotion, Piper said, "I am shamed. It is my way, *jefe*. I have always been shamed. From the moment of my conception. I am *kawaruhito*. You cannot imagine . . . In Japan, all metahumans are vile. Reviled. They are hated. I was sent to Jigoku-To-Shi. That is Hell City. That is its name, *jefe*. It is a horrible place. I escaped. I found a way to Seattle, UCAS. I had heard of the promised land. The land of promise. Tir Tairngire. But they would not let me in. My own people. Elves like me. Like my father, they rejected me. So I am doubly shamed."

Rico had never heard this story before, not these particular details. Piper didn't talk much about herself. And Rico didn't expect a self-effacing Japanese and word-wary decker to give away any more than she might need, certainly no more than she wanted. He'd always been willing to accept whatever she chose to give and just forget the rest. He struggled to do that now. He struggled to see what this excerpt from her life story had to do with almost murdering somebody. Was shame the key point? Had she suffered so much of it that a little more didn't matter? He knew well enough that she wouldn't stand here and ask forgiveness because she'd had a rough life. *Please feel sorry for me and forget what I did* . . . Piper would never say that, not intentionally, anyway. Piper wanted nobody's pity.

"Shame is my fate, *jefe*. It is all I am capable of. I have failed you twice on this run, and that is my shame. And I will fail you again, no matter what I do. Or how hard I try." She hesitated, then blurted, "You should leave me. For your own good. You should have nothing to do with me."

Rico clenched his teeth. He didn't believe in "fate." Luck, maybe, but that was different.

Piper had been acting under impulse, he decided. The shock of seeing Filly dead, the heat of the moment. Everybody got that way sometimes, and these hadn't been a great couple of days. The run had become an abortion. They were all feeling the pressure, and pressure had a way of bending people outta shape.

It all came down to one point, though. The same point that had been there from the start. "I don't work with killers," Rico said lowly. "Murderers. I won't live with one neither. Work like that, wetwork, it's for scum. The garbage you see in the gutters. That's your choice. You decide what's gonna be."

Piper started breathing hard before he got halfway done. He barely got out his last word before she said in an anguished voice, "I choose you, *jefe*. I choose you ..." Her breath caught and she grunted, almost crying. "I just ... I'm just afraid ... the corps, corporates ... *they're going to kill us this time!*"

It was a distinct possibility. But it changed nothing.

Rico drew Piper into his arms and held her. They weren't dead yet, and Rico wasn't about to give up. Too many lives, too much at stake. His job was to find a way outta this mess they'd somehow come to own. Quitting wouldn't work. Neither would lying down and dying. "Just don't gimme any more problems, chica," he said. "I got enough already. *Comprende?*"

Piper nodded, face buried in his shoulder. "*Hai. Wakarimasu, jefe,*" she said. "I understand."

29

The room was small and squarish, the decorations rather crude and the furnishings threadbare. The walls had been painted to look like a forest. A few dying plants slumped here and there in colored pots. The air smelled of incense. The pair of sleeping bags on the floor provided the only place to sit.

Farrah Moffit ran her eyes around the room one more time, just to prove to herself again that she had no way to escape.

Even if she could get out of this room, she would need to find a working telecom, then manage to stay alive and free long enough to be picked up. The odds on that seemed long. She had seen and heard enough to guess that she was somewhere in the New York-New Jersey megaplex, but where exactly she did not know. Queens, the Bronx, Westchester—they all looked the same to her. One great mass of grimy ferrocrete. Outside Manhattan, she was lost.

Certain smells in the alley had made her think of Manhattan's Chinatown, but that probably meant nothing. A great many Asians lived in the urban Northeast. Practically every metroplex in the region had some sort of Asian enclave, some quite large.

The runners who held her captive had done a very good job of keeping her in the dark.

If only she could believe the leader's promises that she would not be harmed. Her time with Fuchi had cured her of any such naiveté. She would be kept alive for as long as that served the runner's purposes; then, in all likelihood, she would be killed. She had never previously dealt with shadowrunners herself, but she had heard enough and read enough and seen enough on trideo to be acquainted with the breed. Most were glorified gangers, criminals by another name, and quite vicious. They would not allow her to live for the simple reason that she could point them out in a police line-up, should police become involved, and she could testify to their crimes, should matters ever reach a court. They would not leave her behind. They would not simply let her go. Eventually someone, probably that Asian girl, the decker, would come into this room, put a gun to her head and pull the trigger.

If only she knew more of what was happening. What she would give for just a few minutes in front of a trid.

She felt so isolated, so alone.

This, of course, was part of the runners' strategy. They wanted to keep her in a state of mental uncertainty and emotional turmoil, this to persuade her of the value of cooperating fully, of being compliant. Submissive. Weak. An elementary stratagem, a common technique for interrogations. The leader kept assuring her she would be safe, while other members of the group threatened her with violence, and, in one case at least, made good on the threat. A neat little twist deliberately designed to add to her fears and her confusion.

To her chagrin, it was all working very nicely, though only to a limited extent.

Certain inescapable facts kept coming to mind. As a hostage held for ransom, she would be as good as dead. Fuchi did not pay ransom. That was the corp's stated official policy, and it held true for all but the highest corporate officials. The entire draconian apparatus in charge of Fuchi security worried little about humanitarian values or the sanctity of human life. For someone in her position, a fairly low-raking member of the corp's Special Administration, Fuchi would be more likely to send in a corporate assault team, kill everyone, sacrificing certain corporate assets rather than submit to extortion.

That put her life in her own hands exclusively, and that frightened her. Pleading would do no good. Deceptions would get her only so far, and might get her killed before she was due.

No, Farris realized, she wouldn't get out of this alive unless she offered the runners something, something substantial, something that she alone of all their contacts had to offer them.

Deciding what that was did not take long.

* * *

The food Dok and Piper brought was not bad. It was mostly fish and rice, warm and easy to eat and quickly finished. Bandit liked his food that way.

Once done, he picked up the flute, surveyed it astrally, ran his fingertips over the polished wood. It appeared to have been made by a highly skilled craftsman. It had no flaws that he could detect. As soon as he had the time, he would return to his special place, his place of long magic, and bind the instrument's energies to his own. He would enhance its power, too.

Now, he lifted the flute to his mouth and played a few tentative notes. He did not know how to play a flute, but he would learn. He stopped when he noticed the others in the room—Rico, Shank, Dok, and Piper—all looking at him.

"When did you get so musical?" Shank grumbled.

Bandit thought about that, and said, "Ask me later."

"Sure. Maybe next year."

Bandit nodded. A year from now would be fine.

"If we're still alive."

"If we aren't, how would you ask?"

Shank stared at him a few moments, frowning. Apparently, he had no answer. That was good. It assured Bandit that Shank had not suddenly become so "magical" that he could speak from beyond the grave.

Orks should stick to weapons and combat and leave questions concerning magic to others.

"What?" Piper said, looking confused.

Rico stood, and said, looking at Bandit, "I'm gonna question our guest. I want you to watch her for lies."

Of course.

Reluctantly, Bandit followed Rico into the bedroom, where he had found the flute. The woman was in there now, the one with the unusual aura. Latent magical ability. Marena Farris.

Rico closed the door.

Marena Farris looked like she'd been crying: red eyes, shiny brow and cheeks. A few wet-looking curls of hair stuck to her cheeks. She looked at him with an expression that seemed to mix grief and fear into something intensely vulnerable.

It would've been easy, too easy, to walk over, crouch down, talk to her soft and low and try to reassure her. Any woman in Farris' position probably deserved no less. Just for being a woman caught in a bad situation. Yet Rico forced himself to plant his feet in front of the door, then crossed his arms and looked at Farris long and hard, like he'd be taking no drek from anybody. He had more to consider than just this woman's feelings. "Okay," he said, "you got my attention. What'd you know about all this?"

"Did you talk—"

"We talked," Rico said, interrupting. He had heard what Piper had to say about her talk with Farris. "Now I wanna hear it direct."

Farris wiped at her eyes, then looked at him and said, "Where shall I start?"

"How do you know about Prometheus?"

"It was part of my job as a member of Special Administration—"

"Of what?"

Piper had mentioned this, but Rico wanted to hear more. Farris elaborated. She made the Fuchi "Special Administration" sound like a corp within a corp, a special network designed to monitor practically every phase of the corporation's business. Part of Farris' job, apparently, was to covertly stick her nose into different Fuchi departments' business.

"Get back to Prometheus."

Farris nodded. "Fuchi has done extensive psycho-profiling of all its primary competitors. There's an entire department devoted to competition research. I participated peripherally in several studies, including a recent study of Prometheus."

"Convenient."

"It was essential. I served as liaison between the infiltrator program and competition research. We weren't about to choose the target for our infiltrator by random selection. We viewed our first insertion as a sort of beta test-model. We wanted to ensure that whoever we sent would enter an environment where he or she would have a high chance of success."

"You said the meet with Prometheus wouldn't work out. Why?"

A wary, almost fearful look entered Farris' eyes. Rico wouldn't be surprised if she was aware that Surikov wasn't the only one who had died at the meet with Prometheus. She had to know that others had been wounded. Rico, for one, had a bandage on his left arm that couldn't be missed.

Farris hesitated, then said, "When was the last time you heard of Prometheus accepting someone from a competing corporation?"

"I'll ask the questions."

Farris flushed. "Excuse me," she said. She spent a few moments regaining her composure, that or figuring out what to say next. Rico wondered how much of the wary, fearful act was real. Bandit offered no clue. Not yet anyway. "Well ... my point," Farris said, "is that Prometheus has a very strong intra-corporate program. They develop their personnel resources from within. They've taken a few special individuals who desired to change corporate affiliations, but those were exceptional people, primarily mages with very arcane specialties."

Rico could accept that, as far as it went. Magicians were special. They weren't half as common as most people seemed to think. Ones with Bandit's ability were damn rare.

"Typically," Farris continued, "the corporate mindset views a change of affiliation as a sort of betrayal. Would you trust someone who betrayed their corp? Trust them with proprietary data? Your edge against the competition? Corps guard their secrets very closely. They scrutinize personnel recruited from other corps scrupulously. Prometheus more than most."

Rico nodded. Never trust a traitor. He'd heard that before. "Why'd they kill your husband?"

"Because," Farris said, seeming stung, "they'd rather deprive a competitor of the value of an Ansell Surikov than risk recruiting a potential traitor. Another corp's loss is their gain. That's how Prometheus sees it."

"And that's how you knew the meet wouldn't go right."

"That was my assumption."

"So why didn't you say something?"

"Would you have believed me?"

"Does it matter?"

"Of course it matters. Everything I do influences what you think of me and that matters quite a lot." Abruptly, Farris seemed on the verge of tears. Her eyes got moist and her lower lip quivered. "If I had said they might try to kill you, and they didn't, if your meet had gone as planned, you'd see me as a schemer. You'd think I had some hidden agenda, that I had tried to deceive you." Her breath caught. "It may not seem very brave, but I want to get out of this alive. I'm horrified over what's happened, over Ansell's death, but nothing scares me more than the power you have over me. I'll do anything I have to do . . . to get through this."

Some slags would take a statement like that and run and never stop, especially with it coming from someone who looked like Farris. Some slags would use any situation to take advantage of a woman. Not Rico's style. Not even on his worst day. "One of my people might still be alive if I'd known what you know about Prometheus."

Farris' expression grew anguished. "I'm *sorry*," she said. "It's hard to know what to do. If I had it to do over, I would take my chances and tell you. I was afraid. I'm still afraid."

"You got reason."

Farris seemed to shudder. "Yes, I know," she said quietly, almost in a whisper. "I know I have reason to fear you. That's why we must talk. I have something that you might want."

"Like what?"

"Ansell Surikov."

30

"Surikov is dead."

"No. He's not."

Farris looked scared, but she spoke in the dead-calm tone that people used when they know exactly what they're saying, and know that they're right.

Rico looked at the stress analyzer on his wrist. If Farris was lying, she was damn good at it.

A long silence followed. Farris' eyes never wavered, despite her fearful expression. Mentally, Rico ran down the short list of possible explanations. Farris could be lying. She could be nuts. Desperate enough to say anything or too far gone to notice. Even if Surikov had been revived, magically resuscitated, or his apparent death only some magician's illusion, Farris would have no way of knowing that.

Rico could think of only one other explanation and it wasn't a good one. Possibly, just possibly, he and his team had been not only double-crossed, but reamed right from the start. Tricked somehow. He didn't see how. "Surikov's not dead?"

"No." Farris shook her head.

"Then who was the slag we busted out of Maas Intertech?"

"Michael Travis. One of Ansell's research assistants."

It didn't seem likely. "No way," Rico growled. "No fragging way. We had retina scans. We had fragging DNA scans."

"Yes, but how did you confirm those scans?" Farris asked softly. "Based on data obtained from Fuchi?"

"I'll ask the questions."

Farris just watched him a moment. The fear in her expression seemed to mix with sadness, maybe regret. "Not even Fuchi datafiles are immutable," she said. "The infiltrator program anticipated the possibility that certain relevant datafiles such as personnel files might be surreptitiously accessed. These files were altered. Datasets were exchanged. Michael Travis' retinal and DNA patterns were inserted into Ansell's files. The real Ansell Surikov, his codes and patterns, are now part of the datafiles that originally belonged to Michael Travis."

Rico said nothing. He guessed that what Farris was saying was possible, but she made it sound too easy. There was more to changing identities than just a swap of data in computer files. "Surikov's face is all over the datanets. He's been at conferences. He's been on trideo. People know what he looks like."

"Yes, that's true," Farris agreed, as softly as before. "And that is one reason why Michael Travis was chosen. He and Ansell have similar physical parameters. Similar physiques. Only a modest amount of cosmed surgery was necessary to complete the likeness."

Rico shook his head, tempted to sneer. "You can't cut a slag into a disguise like that. You can't make him a duplicate of somebody else. It's been tried. Surgery leaves scars. You can't cover up the traces. Not all of them."

"You're correct," Farris said. "Ordinarily, any surgery would be detected by a close medical examination. Precluding an attempt at deception. In this case, however, it was possible to disguise the cosmetic alterations as necessary surgical reconstructions." Farris hesitated a moment, then said, quieter than before, "Ansell has always been something of a bacchanalian. And rather indiscriminate. It was a simple matter to modify his files to show an episode with Gray's Syndrome."

Rico grimaced. "That's real convenient."

"Efficacious. And therefore essential."

Gray's Syndrome was one of several virulent, sexually transmitted diseases that had arisen over the last five or ten years. People said it had come with the Awakening. Elves seemed to be particularly prone, but no one was immune. Gray's was nasty, though usually not fatal, given the right medical care. It corrupted a person's appearance. Made him or her look old and sick and deformed. And it happened fast, in just days. By the time a person realized he had it, his hair could be falling out and his teeth turning black and jutting out of his mouth like the fangs of an ork. The pain was said to be horrendous. Some people were transformed practically overnight. Some people, those who couldn't afford surgical corrections, killed themselves rather than go through life looking like some simsense-inspired horror. Some people just went insane.

Rico supposed it would take a lot of surgery to restore a man from an episode with Gray's. That much cutting might well be used to cover the surgery needed to turn some slag into a near-duplicate of Ansell Surikov.

Clever.

"Okay," Rico said. "Say you made this slag Travis look like Surikov. He passes the scans. That doesn't make him Surikov."

"That is where headware comes in."

"Yeah?"

Farris nodded. "The base implantation involved some highly advanced bionetics to boost the cerebral functions. This provided a framework for implanting a new form of semi-organic skillsoft, the bionetic equivalent of personafix BTL, encoded with Ansell Surikov's persona matrix."

"Meaning what?"

"Meaning that Michael Travis not only looked and acted like Ansell Surikov, he believed that he *was* Ansell Surikov."

"And nobody at Maas Intertech noticed that this slag Travis had all this drek inside his head."

"Ansell Surikov has numerous cerebral implants. Most scientists do. Michael Travis' implants were simply designed to conceal their personafix functions." A look like surprise passed over Farris' features. "Even I couldn't tell them apart. And I've had more experience with Ansell than merely as a psychologist."

"Which one are you married to?"

"Ansell. The original Ansell."

"So if Surikov was really Travis, why'd you try to kill 'im?"

Farris' expression turned sad, hurt. "I've already explained that. Everything I told you about Ansell applied to Michael Travis. Almost everything. Michael volunteered for the infiltrator program. He did it to spite me. We'd been having an affair. It didn't work out. I only referred to him as Ansell Surikov because, in effect, he *was*

Ansell, functioning as Ansell. I believed that he had hired you to kill me. Ansell is quite capable of that, given adequate motivation, and Michael Travis' implanted persona overrides made him just as capable. I thought that my only chance for surviving would be to kill him first."

Rico almost didn't give a damn. He could see he wasn't going to catch Farris in any kind of lie. She had all the angles of her story worked out, whether this was chiptruth or pure fantasy. What worried him was the chance that her story was actually true, what that implied about all he had done, and what he ought to do next. "So if it's this slag Travis who got iced, where's the real Surikov?"

"That's what you and I must talk about."

"We're talking about it right now."

Farris dropped her eyes and shook her head. "We're talking about the past. I want to talk about the future."

"What future?"

"Ansell's future," Farris said. "And your future. And mine."

"I ain't got no future."

"Perhaps you do." she said quietly. "It's conceivable that I could give it back to you."

Rico watched Marena Farris intently. She looked about as uncertain and uneasy as ever, but now he didn't trust it, not nearly as much as before. A minute ago she'd been just a frightened woman telling a story he could either believe or dismiss. Now she talked like a person with a plan and Rico didn't like it. Farris was too smart—and too damn good-looking. She looked too much like the conniving blonde biff in every action-adventure flick he'd ever seen. Biffs like that always had something up their sleeve to match what they had inside their shirts or pants. The words that came out of their mouths always made things perfectly logical, even if those words were sure to get you killed.

Farris' lower lip quivered. "I can help you," she said. "I'm not just a psychologist."

Hadn't she already said something like that to Piper? *I'm more than I seem* ... Rico accepted that without question. "I know what you are," he said. "Get to the point."

"Of course," Farris said quietly. "The point is this.

Ansell isn't happy where he is. Fuchi Multitronics has put very tight limits on his work. He would like to go somewhere else, to another corp. If you were to help him get there, this other corp would reward you generously."

Rico sneered. "You're dreaming, chica."

"No," Farris said, shaking her head. "No, I'd already begun negotiating on Ansell's behalf before you carried me away. Only a few days have elapsed. I could finish the deal by telecom. You could come away from this with a lot more money than you've got now, and I could probably arrange to get at least one group of people off your back. I could make that a condition of the deal."

"You're talking about Maas Intertech."

"I believe you've had some experience with Daisaka Security? The Asian woman mentioned that. Daisaka is linked to Maas Intertech through the parent entity, Kuze Nihon. I could arrange for them to be turned off."

"I slotted off Fuchi once this month by busting you out. I figure that's enough of a problem to live with."

"Yes," Farris said, nodding. "You've struck a blow against Fuchi corporate pride. They want you, but they can only hunt for you in so many ways, and the SINless are hard to find. But it isn't just Fuchi. Daisaka wants you, too. Isn't that so? And the more people looking for you, the greater the chance that someone will find you. I'm offering you the opportunity to drastically reduce the numbers of your opponents and to make some money that you might very well need in the days and weeks ahead."

"I should trust you to cut a deal?"

"Yes, you should," Farris said. "I have the most compelling reasons possible for dealing in good faith. I want to live."

"You know people at Maas Intertech?"

Farris didn't answer. She just stared at him. A couple of moments of that and suddenly Rico felt like he was facing the blank stare of a fixer, revealing nothing. It was almost scary. Who the hell was this biff really? Why did it seem like she knew more about things than any one person had a right to know? Surikov, Travis, the infiltrator program, details about Fuchi competitors ... It made Rico wonder if she knew even more than she was saying.

Her gaze was like a promise, telling him that she had contacts, contacts that could make a deal, a deal that anyone in their right mind would grab at, if only to better the chances of getting out of this mess alive.

Rico didn't want to believe it.

A voice whispered softly at Bandit's left ear, saying, *"Master, look."*

Bandit shifted to his astral perceptions.

The bedroom now glowed softly with the radiance of life, the astral forms of Rico and Marena Farris, Bandit's own, and one other, a spirit. The spirit took the form of a large raccoon, but one that walked erect. It hovered behind Bandit's left shoulder as if to hide from the other astral forms in the room.

This particular sort of spirit was known as a watcher. It was a simple spirit capable of simple tasks. Bandit had assigned it to watch the astral terrain in the vicinity of the apartment.

"You've noticed something?" Bandit asked.

The watcher nodded vigorously, and extended a paw toward the wall at the rear of the room. Bandit looked at the wall, but saw nothing of interest. *"Come swiftly, master,"* the watcher said. *"Come and look! You said if I noticed anything strange . . . Well, this is very strange indeed!"*

Bandit shifted to the astral plane, leaving flesh and bone behind. He wondered what the watcher had noticed. Still sitting cross-legged, he rose from the floor, turned and followed the watcher through the rear wall of the room and into the alley behind the building.

The night pulsed softly with primal energies. The auras of hundreds of people glowed dimly through the rear windows of buildings lining the alley. Other subtler gleamings of life showed here and there along the length of the alley—the auras of a rat, several weeds, birds pecking at a sprawling pile of garbage. Bandit took all of this in at a glance, and, seeing nothing of value, turned his attention elsewhere. Something else, something far more significant, demanded his attention. It tugged at his magician's sense with sudden violence—and held it.

Through the alley leading to the next block came tendrils of mana: drifting, flowing. Curling slowly forward like sinuous snakes, radiant with power. Rising, falling. Flowing up and down. Curving in and out. As the tendrils neared the back alley, they began turning outward, fanning out left and right, as if to proceed in both directions up and down the back alley; but then they curved back again as if returning to a single course.

Here was magic in the making, a long magic. Nothing else could bind the mana into such form or send it much beyond the limit of sight. Could this appearance be mere coincidence? Bandit doubted it. Long magic built up slowly, over the course of hours. It was a far more exacting magic than the manabolts and fireballs that fledgling magicians tossed off on the spur of the moment or amid the chaos of a gun battle. The leading tendrils of the spell seemed to be coming toward the building where Rico and the others had taken refuge. Even now those tendrils were crossing the back alley, slowly, sinuously snaking their way toward the wall, through which Bandit had emerged.

A group of armed razorguys passing through the alleyways might have been a coincidence. There were hundreds, possibly thousands of razorguys in the plex and they all had to live somewhere. Magic and magicians were far less common. Uncommon enough to be rare.

What was the point of this sending? Bandit spent a short while considering this, assensing the spell being cast. It appeared to be a spell of detection, one designed to find a particular individual. What individual, he could not tell. Did this have something to do with Rico and the team, Ansell Surikov, or Marena Farris? Bandit wondered.

On occasions in the past, Bandit had in fact observed the sendings of other magicians, sendings that had nothing to do with him or anyone he knew or anything he was doing, but he could count those occasions on the fingers of one hand.

Always, it was best to be careful.

He returned to his physical body. Rico was crouched right in front of him, gazing at him steadily, questioningly. Bandit considered that questioning gaze, then said, "Trouble's coming."

"What trouble?" Rico asked, grimacing.

Bandit replied, "How bad do you want to know?"

Through the rear windows of the van, Shank watched the Asian slag turn in off the street and come hustling up the alley, walking fast, almost breaking into a run. He didn't look like trouble, but his haste made Shank wonder. He was dressed like a cook: greasy white apron, shirt, pants, sneakers. If he had any weapons, they were under his hide and crammed in pretty tight. He was skinny to the point of skeletal. He might've just climbed out of a grave.

"What's this freaking piece of drek?" Thorvin said.

Shank grunted, wondering, tightening his hold on his compact Colt M22A2.

The slag kept on coming, hustled up alongside the van, then turned to the door of the apartment the team was using as a bolthole. He pounded on the door with a fist. Shank stepped out through the rear door of the van, stepped around the rear corner of the van, took one step further and put the muzzle of the Colt at the back of the slag's head.

"Be real careful," he growled, his voice low and menacing.

The slag froze, except to slowly turn his head. That head barely came up as far as the middle of Shank's chest. From what Shank could see, the slag looked surprised enough to be terrified, eyes open wide.

Abruptly, the door to the apartment swung inward and Piper stepped into view. Shank put a hand around the back of the slag's neck, about to push him inside, just into the hallway, to scope him out, but then the slag was looking at Piper and nodding and bowing the way Asians do, and Piper was bowing, too.

"*Okyaku sáma ga kite imásu!*" the slag said. He spoke quickly and quietly, seeming excited. Shank wondered what the fragger was saying.

Piper's eyes went wide. "*Dóo yuu ími désu ka!*" she said, breathlessly.

"*Shookáijoo o mótte inákereba narimasén ka!*"

"*Ara ma! Osore irimasu! Dónata desu ka!*"

"*Nan-no shirushi ga yoroshii desu ka!*"

They went on like that for a few moments more.

Shank looked up and down the alley. Nobody passing the street-end of the alley seemed in any particular hurry, no more than usual for this part of town. On the street itself, a sanitation truck rumbled by, workers in black masks, gloves and jumpsuits mounted on the truck's steps. For a night in Little Asia, for any part of the Newark sprawl, things seemed pretty quiet.

"*Hai! Wakaramasu! Domo arigato gozaimasu!*" Piper said.

"*Do itashimashite!*" the slag said.

Shank lowered his weapon.

Piper bowed and the slag bowed, too. They both bowed again. The slag hurried back toward the street. Shank looked at Piper. She looked at him and said quickly, in English, "Shank, we must go. Get ready to run."

"Null sheen," Shank replied. "Run where?"

Piper stared at him wide-eyed, then suddenly shook her head and hurried back down the hall to the apartment. Shank shrugged.

Behind him, the van rumbled to life.

31

"A deal has been made, *jefe*," Piper said rapidly. "Daisaka has approached the oyabun himself. Kobun of Honjowara yakuza and agents of Daisaka Security are sweeping the district together. It is said they make discreet inquiries, but that is just cover. They will find us unless we leave here."

Rico grimaced. "How much time we got?"

"We must go now. Right now."

Piper didn't need to give any extra emphasis to her words. Rico could see the emphasis in her eyes. She was scared, and probably with good reason. "Somebody sold us out?"

"Not how you are thinking."

"One of your contacts."

Piper shook her head. "Perhaps Honjowara-*sama* has used us to obtain something he wants from Daisaka. That is most likely. But we have been warned, *jefe*. Warned to get away. We have been used as pawns. That is not the same as betrayal."

Maybe, maybe not. It sounded like the kind of deal that a slag like the oyabun could make with impunity. Rico was in no position to argue about it. What the fragging *sama* wanted from Daisaka was none of his business. An honorable man might have told Daisaka Security to go slot, but Rico decided to be glad for small favors. Without the oyabun's token consent, they'd never have been able to lay low in this part of the plex; and without the warning that had come to them now ... they might've wound up dead.

"Let's flash."

They gathered their gear. Bandit threw a few handfuls of some sparkling stuff all around the front room of the apartment and sang something too soft to make out. Rico didn't know what it was for and didn't waste time asking. They headed out to the alley. Dok and Piper got Marena Farris into the van. Rico tugged the side door closed and got into the passenger seat and then they were rolling, turning toward the nearest transitway.

"What's our terminus?" Thorvin said.

A fragging good question, Rico thought. This run was pushing their limits. They'd used all the presets, contacts, and hideyholes they'd had lined up in advance. They'd stepped beyond the last step of the plan. They could head for the fortified bolthole in Sector 13, but Rico wanted to save that till they had autofire burning their butts and nowhere else to turn.

They stopped in Sector 11, just across the border from Little Asia. Thorvin parked the van in the big parking garage two stories below the Hillside New Jersey Transit station. Rico put a credstick into a public telecom, stabbed the Vid Off key, and tapped in a special number.

Momentarily, Mr. Victor's voice came through the handset to Rico's ear. "How are you, my friend?"

"The meet went wrong," Rico said. "The man's trash. The client wasted the merchandise. We had to fight our way out."

Brief silence. "I am sorry to hear that. I am shocked, though I have had certain difficulties myself. We live in dangerous times. Tell me, how did your problems arise?"

"How do they usually arise?"

Another silence. "What will you do?"

Revenge was out of the question, for the moment. Staying alive was the immediate problem, that and what to do with Marena Farris and her proposal. Rico considered mentioning that proposal to Mr. Victor, but decided against it. Mr. Victor's arrangements hadn't been working out so good lately. Rico still trusted him, but right now it seemed enough to trust him with something simple. "We need a new hole."

"Perhaps I can help you with that, my friend."

Mr. Victor knew a slag who knew an address. Mr. Victor would arrange a meet. Rico clenched his teeth, but said that was chill. Mr. Victor then said, "You should know that your former employer has put out the word. Nuyen is offered for information on your whereabouts."

Rico hesitated. "You serious?"

"Quite serious."

Incredible.

Mr. Victor had to be referring to L. Kahn, and that was incredible because fixers didn't usually put out rewards, not directly. That was like L. Kahn admitting to the world that somebody had stuck it to him, and fixers didn't like to admit that. Fixers tended to be acutely conscious of their image, no less than corps. What it suggested to Rico was that L. Kahn must be feeling pressure. Maybe from Fuchi. The suits at Fuchi wouldn't be too happy about their merchandise getting dusted. And they wouldn't be too happy about the disappearance of an employee named Marena Farris either.

Rico returned to the van, gave Thorvin directions. He could feel Farris staring at him from the rear of the van. That stare was a question waiting for an answer.

The guano was getting deep. Daisaka Security, the Executive Action Brigade, yaks, informants. Maas Intertech, Prometheus, Fuchi. On top of all that was Bandit's latest warning. The shaman hadn't been too clear, but it sounded like somebody had been coming at them magically in the minutes just before they fled the bolthole in Little Asia. How the frag did that fit in? From the original chipfile for the run on Maas Intertech, Rico knew that Daisaka had magicians on-line, but was that his explanation? And did it matter?

And now Marena Farris had a proposition, one that could get at least part of the opposition off their backs.

Rico wondered if he really had any choice.

The problem with corps was that they had the resources to buy just about any kind of contact or informant that might suit their purposes: cops, hustlers, gangs, whole city blocks, entire governments. You couldn't evade power like that forever. Something had to give. Either the corp eventually decided you weren't worth the effort or the nuyen anymore, or it got you, grabbed you by the cojones and made you dance however it wanted, then dropped you down the nearest garbage chute.

Rico and the rest of the team could try and lay low, but that would take money, hard nuyen. They all had some, but how much would they need? Enough to sit for months, a year, two years? They'd have to change IDs, maybe alter their looks. Dok could handle some of the

surgical mods, but that was just the beginning. Piper
would need new programs and hardware just to stay up to
date. Rico himself would need some cybernetic mods to
keep his bodyware from falling behind the leading edge
of tech. They'd all need things: Dok, Shank, Thorvin. It
was a question of how they would get what they needed.
The reality was hard.

You didn't get bucks for front-line cyberware playing
doorman for some bar or collecting on gambling debts. It
took big bucks—and big bucks meant taking big risks.
Smuggling contraband. Stealing major paydata. Breaking
some slag out of a corporate contract that was the moral
equal of slavery.

It came down to two choices. Dying was the easy way
out. Simply send Marena Farris back to Fuchi, then sit
around and wait for the corps to come and scrag them.
The hard way meant going along with what Marena
Farris was proposing, check it out, investigate. Then, if
everything looked chill, do it. That might get them just as
dead, but Rico could see no other way that they could
ever get enough nuyen together at one place and one time
to make a difference.

And time was running down.

His wives waited silently, as wives should, seated
around him in the rear of the Mercedes limo as he whispered sorcerous words and wove the spell into existence.
A handful of sparkling motes appeared in the air before
him and gradually swelled into a pulsating, coruscating
cloud. Daniella lowered a window. Maurice pointed. The
cloud drifted out and across the alley to the door of the
runners' apartment. It spread across the door and sifted
through the door's substance, passing into the spaces beyond.

In a matter of seconds, it would expand to fill the three
small rooms of the apartment, stunning unconscious everyone it touched.

A second spell turned the alley door into dust.

Maurice nodded. Clad all in black, Claude Jaeger
turned and darted through the empty doorway and disappeared into the apartment. He would swiftly dispatch the
runners and anyone else he found there. And then their
contract would be complete. The knowledge and talent of

a skilled magician would be forever lost, and that would indeed be a loss, but it could not be helped. The runners had gone rogue, and L. Kahn had ordered they be exterminated. But the more important point was that, with tonight's work done, Maurice would finally be free to return to his studies. He had wasted too many days working magic on the world instead of pursuing knowledge, truth. He was impatient to be done.

Momentarily Jaeger returned to the doorway. He cast a mouthful of sputum to the concrete floor of the alley. "Mages," he said, with a sneer. "You fragged up."

Impossible.

And yet . . .

Shifting to his astral senses, Maurice looked at his ally, Vera Causa. At his command, she had scouted the apartment astrally and confirmed that the runners were present. But for that, she had said nothing since their arrival here in Little Asia. She said nothing now. She did not even look at him. Was it possible she had erred?

"Guard," he told her.

"Yes, master," she replied. *"Of course."*

There was an acid quality to that reply which Maurice did not like. He considered whether this bound spirit might be escaping his control. A difficult matter to decide.

He snapped his fingers and pointed. Daniella thrust open the door on his right and preceded him outside. He did not object when she and the other slitches followed him into the apartment. Daniella had a certain limited ability in the arts, and the others also had certain skills that might prove useful.

To the mundane eye, the apartment looked deserted. It was cluttered with furniture, kitchen appliances, trideos, bookdisks, and what looked like the scattered components from several cyberdecks. Pillows and blankets, discarded fast-food containers, and other anonymous litter also lay strewn about. The former occupants seemed to have departed swiftly. And yet appearances deceived. On the astral level, the runners appeared to be lingering still. Amid the pulsing fluctuations of the life energy coursing irregularly about the room glowed not one but seven auras, or what appeared to be seven human and metahuman auras.

It was as if the runners had gone but had somehow managed to leave their auras behind.

Maurice had never seen anything quite like it.

Plainly now, he assensed that these "auras" were merely a spell, a clever manipulation of mana, drawn from the surrounding etheric energies. What amazed him was the fact that he had been unable to detect this deception while working the ritual spell that had brought him here to these rooms. He had been duped. Led to believe that John Dokker and the rest of the runners were still present.

How, he wondered, could such a perfect mirage have been assembled? Until now, he had imagined his ritual spell of detection to be inexorable, long and slow, but certain to succeed. Obviously, such was not the case. He felt persuaded by the desire to learn more of this deluding spell. He must investigate the intricacies of a work that conjured such perfect fantasies.

Concentrating his astral perceptions, he moved nearer the false auras. In that very instant, the spell unraveled, as if it had expected the touch of his mind, as if it wished to keep its secrets. Mana flashed, bursting outward in all directions, blazing, rejoining the pulsing streams of the world.

Maurice felt a swift pang of grief, then soft despair.

As he returned to his mundane perceptions, he heard a crash like that of a trash can being knocked over, resounding outside in the alley, then the sudden savage snarl of a cat.

Jaeger turned and darted toward the alleyway.

The moment struck Maurice. The snarl of the cat stirred his memory. He tilted his head back, nodding, closing his eyes, and softly laughed. It had become a night for tricks, new and old. The snarling cat in the alley. What manner of shaman could use such a juvenile trick and yet could manipulate magic of a complexity as to conjure illusory auras?

"Husband," Daniella said. "Scan this."

Maurice opened his eyes, then followed his first wife into what appeared to be a bedroom. Lying on a bureau was an item that at first glance resembled a common monofilament sword, an artifact manufactured and distributed throughout the plex in the thousands by Ares

Macrotechnology and other corps. On the astral plane, however, the sword's significance was obvious. It's aura had the character of a living thing that lived no more. The sword had once been imbued with power, as a focus for spells. The memory of those spells lingered still. Maurice doubted he would be able to determine much about the spells, but that was a secondary consideration.

The vibrations of the person who had carried the sword also lingered. That was what made the sword significant. Plainly, it had been left behind by the runners' shaman, perhaps in exchange for something he had taken. That was the shaman's way, the most persistent of the rumors Maurice had heard. When Bandit took a thing, he left another in exchange. Maurice could hardly believe his luck, or the shaman's stupidity.

The sword would serve as a material link, and thus, through ritual magic, would lead Maurice directly to the shaman, thence the runners, regardless of where they had gone.

And this time Maurice would bow to no clever illusions.

32

The Chapel of the Eternal Light was just over the border from Little Asia in Sector 7. For five hundred nuyen, they laid out Filly's body in a room with perfumed air, quiet music, and molded plastic flowers, no questions asked. That included a five-minute trideo funeral service, cremation, and an urn for the ashes.

Rico paid the tab, despite Dok's protests. It was his responsibility. He was the leader. It was his failure to properly prepare for the meet with Prometheus that had cost Filly her life. Compared to the moral weight of that fact, five hundred nuyen was nothing.

They all knew the risks. Death was part of the game. For the sake of the survivors, Rico was trying hard not to think about the price of his failures or the chance that he might slot up again. If you wanted any chance at surviving, you did what you had to do and saved all the grief, self-doubts, and questions till the run was over and people were safe in bed.

When the pre-recorded serviced ended, Piper said, "I want people to remember, when gray death sets me free, I was a person who had many friends, and many friends had me." She paused a moment, then added, "Filly had many friends. And we her friends have her still. In our hearts. We will always have her there."

Another surprise. Rico puzzled. The words seemed somehow too openly compassionate for a reticent Japanese, and too Christian for a fanatical Buddhist-Ecologist. Maybe it was gender. Maybe it took a woman to speak with that much compassion, to get past her own habits and beliefs long enough to say what ought to be said. Rico wondered where the first few rhyming lines had come from. They sounded like something from a poem, but Piper had never shown any interest in poetry.

Wasn't anything what it seemed anymore?

Dok cursed and cried, then clenched his teeth and turned and walked away. Rico didn't think any less of Dok for any of that. He was only showing his strength.

An hour later, they met Mr. Victor's contact amid the stacks and factories of Sector 10. The slag pointed them to an unoccupied warehouse not far from Port Sector.

The place was five stories tall, about as wide as a tractor-trailer, jammed between a truck terminal and some kind of foundry. The air smelled like burnt metal.

Beyond the big bay door was a loading bay, an open area, narrow but long, with a loading platform at the rear. Beyond the platform was a short hall sided by several small rooms: an office, a bathroom, and what looked like a lounge. Plastic-molded furniture and cushioned benches. Semi-nude holopics of celebs like Maria Mercurial and Taffy Lee and the *Sayonara Baby* joygirls decorated the walls. A scattering of trash, narc caps, BTL carriers, and rat shit littered the floor.

"Now I know we're in deep," Shank grumbled.

A curt reply leapt to Rico's lips, but he held it back. Shank was right. Maybe they'd never enjoyed luxury accommodations while on a run, but they'd usually managed to find something you could call decent. Places where you had no second thoughts about using the furniture or maybe taking off your clothes for a shower. Taking refuge in a rat-infested squat in one of the filthiest parts of the plex didn't say much for how things were going. A glance at the bathroom confirmed it.

They supped on Nathan's Finest with rice and noodles. Rico watch Marena Farris dab at her mouth with a paper napkin. He'd have to make a decision about the woman: use her or lose her. Accept her proposal or let her go.

"Let's hear your proposition again," he said.

Farris hesitated, looking at Rico as if uncertain. Piper threw him a sharp glance.

Dok scowled. "What proposal?"

"Huh?" Shank added.

Farris told her story. The slag they'd busted out of Maas Intertech hadn't been Surikov, just a double named Michael Travis. The real Surikov was still with Fuchi Multitronics and not particularly happy about it. Farris had begun negotiating a transfer to another corp on the

real Surikov's behalf just prior to being lifted. If Rico and
the team would help her complete the transfer, she'd see
to it that they were taken care of, paid cash nuyen, and
forgotten by Daisaka Security.

"I wouldn't trust the fragging slitch."

The words could've been Piper's, but they came from
Dok, hard and raw. Rico sat back and lit a cheroot. Shank
said, "Nobody's asking you to trust 'er."

"No, of course not." Dok grinned acidly. "Just risk our
lives!"

"We could use the money."

"Even if she's telling the truth, she can't guarantee
Daisaka stays off our butts."

"There ain't no guarantees about nothing, chummer."

"And," Thorvin said, "we could still use the money."

"Money won't buy back your life, friend."

"Can't see living long without it, either."

Dok looked at Rico, and said, "You can't be thinking
of going ahead with this?"

"No?" Rico said.

"It's *insane!*"

"No more than any other run."

In a way, Rico supposed, maybe they owed it to the
slag who'd died in the parking field of the Willow Brook
Mall, and to Filly. Both those people had lost their lives
because of corporate treachery. Doing right by Farris and
the real Surikov—assuming he *was* the real Surikov—
would be a form of vengeance. Maybe the only kind of
vengeance they could hope to exact. Somewhere down
the road they might be able to cost Fuchi and the other
corps a few percentage points on the exchange and lose
them some money, crash their computers or spread nasty
rumors about their financial health. For the moment,
though, scoping out Farris' offer was the only chance for
vengeance they had. A forced transfer of corporate assets.
It wouldn't hurt a corp the size of Fuchi much, but it
would still hurt.

"You in or out?" Rico said.

Dok stared, briefly. "You're saying the decision's already made?"

"The decision is we scan the scene, check what we
can, make plans, do it right. If everything's chill, then we
go."

"We could be walking into a trap!"

Rico took a long drag on his cheroot before speaking "Look around you," he said. "The trap's already set."

"Yeah," Shank said. "An' it's closing fast."

The grime-smeared window beside the loading bay door gave a fair view of the street out front. Rico stood watch, if for no other reason than he couldn't sleep. Too much on his mind. He wasn't there in the gloom of the loading bay more than half an hour before Piper appeared on the platform at the rear of the bay.

"Jefe . . . ?"

"Here, chica."

For someone with ordinary eyes, the bay was nearly black. Piper groped her way down off the loading dock and across the bay. Rico caught her searching hand and drew her over to the side of the window. She hugged herself to his flank.

"We should just walk away, *jefe,"* she said softly.

Rico murmured, "You know I can't do that."

"Why?"

He recounted the reasons for her, but the truth of it went beyond questions of money and survival. It went beyond any debts real or imagined to those who had died. It came down to something very simple: Marena Farris. Maybe the woman had plans to get away from Fuchi, but the fact was that she hadn't been ready to leave when they lifted her; so, in effect, she'd been snatched. Kidnapped. And now they'd had her too long to just send her back. Fuchi security would likely assume that she'd been tampered with, that they were getting some kind of trojan horse—maybe a spy or saboteur—in place of a loyal employee. She'd be questioned, analyzed, watched every minute of the day and night. She might never be trusted again. Piper would probably say it didn't matter, the woman was a fragging corporate, an enemy. Rico didn't see it that way. Farris might be a corporate and maybe she had secret agendas, but she was still a woman, and still a human being. That warranted some consideration. To Rico, it meant she had the right to walk her own path, and to get set back on that path if somebody tugged her in a direction she didn't choose herself.

Making that happen would take some doing, and Rico

wished he could really trust what Farris told him. He
hoped she was playing straight, or straight enough that
any discrepancies didn't matter.

"Maybe we should go away somewhere after we finish
with this," he said.

Piper clenched him tightly around the waist, moaning,
"I don't care what we do as long as we get out of this
alive."

"We'll make it."

For all their sakes, Rico hoped he was right.

33

At just after three a.m., Marena Farris' aura changed subtly, indicating she had finally fallen asleep, curled up on one of the cushioned benches in the lounge.

By four a.m., she seemed to be sleeping deeply. Everyone else in the lounge was sleeping, too.

Bandit waited a bit longer, then began.

His fingers found the medallion under his shirt. He used this because the medallion held power. The spell he began gathering, for all its subtlety, demanded great power.

He lifted his free hand slightly, just slightly, just enough to point his fingertips toward Marena Farris; then, he began mouthing the words, powerful words, never to be spoken aloud. This was one of his most intricate spells, designed and developed over the course of years. Each word must be spoken in a very specific manner, and must be spoken silently so that their secrets should remain forever secret.

Slowly, the mana gathered, first around his slightly uplifted hand, then flowing together into a narrow stream that flowed slowly, slowly, slowly across the etheric plane. Slowly arcing over Marena Farris' slumbering aura. Slowly surrounding her aura. Interpenetrating. Then curling, turning, joining. Gradually weaving a web. Gradually forming a connection.

Sleep, the magic softly directed. *Sleep till you are told to awaken . . .*

From out of the depths of mind came a sound, a soft gentle sound, a sound of concord and harmony and willing acquiescence. Slowly it arose and slowly it coalesced, assuming form and substance, evolving into a word, a word like, *Yessssss . . .*

At the proper moment, with his free hand, Bandit lifted

the Mask of Sassacus. *We are one . . . one mind, one spirit . . .*

Yessss . . .

Your trust in me is complete . . .

Yessss . . .

You have confided everything to me . . . you have entrusted me with all your secrets great and small . . . sharing your secrets with me brings you great pleasure, great warmth . . . you desire to tell me everything . . . you wish to share everything with me . . .

Yesss . . . it is so . . .

There is something you wish to tell me now . . .

Yesss . . .

Who is the man you call Ansell Surikov?

He is Ansell . . . my husband . . .

There is something you wish him to do . . .

Yesss . . . it is true . . .

Tell me . . .

I . . . wish him to go to a new place . . . a new . . . organization . . .

Tell me why . . .

It will profit us both . . .

Are you keeping secrets from the runners?

Yes . . . they do not know my name . . .

What is your name?

Fa . . . Farrah Moffit . . .

Why is this name important?

If they knew it, they would not trust me . . .

Hours later, when the woman Marena Farris, Farrah Moffit, awoke, she slowly sat up, pressed back her hair, then turned her head and looked right at him, looked at him and stared.

She knew.

Bandit pondered how that could be.

"Would you trust a traitor?"

In the subdued light of the dilapidated warehouse office, Rico turned in the swivel chair to face the door. To his left, Piper sat in an armchair with her axe across her lap and a datacable jacked into her head. In the shadows of the doorway before him stood Bandit, fingering his new flute.

Rico pointed with his chin. "Say again?"

"Would you trust a traitor?"

"Close the door."

Bandit stepped forward, swung the door shut.

"Who we talking about?" Rico asked.

"The woman. Marena Farris."

"She's a traitor?"

"That's what she thinks."

"A traitor to who?"

"Perhaps Fuchi Multitronics."

"She told you that?"

A few moments passed. Bandit looked down at the flute in his hands. His expression, as usual, was unreadable. What he was thinking was anybody's guess. "I ascertained certain things. She is afraid for her life. She wishes Ansell Surikov to join a new organization. She fears you will not trust her. She views herself as a traitor. Some of what you know of her is false. She has not always worked for Fuchi Multitronics. Her name is not Marena Farris."

What the frag? Rico forced himself to keep cool, lean back in his chair. "What's her real name?"

"Farrah Moffit."

Rico searched his memory. The name meant nothing to him. "Who is she?"

"A former employee of Prometheus Engineering. Sent to Fuchi as a mole. Ten years ago a Fuchi joygirl named Marena Farris was quietly killed. Farrah Moffit took her place. She insinuated herself into the Special Administration and used this position to learn Fuchi secrets and transmit them to Prometheus. She believes she is now under suspicion. She did not willingly go on leave. She is afraid to return to Prometheus because she has transmitted no data since put on leave. She fears they may kill her. She believes that moving to Maas Intertech is her only way out."

Rico rubbed at his brow. Maybe a hundred or so questions should have come to mind by now. Maybe he was too tired to think that hard. Maybe the run was wearing him down. Only one thought came to mind. "Why Intertech? Why would they trust her any more than anybody else?"

"Her contact is in a position of power. They met some years ago. If she could bring him someone of value, someone like Surikov, to Intertech, her contact will see she gets what she wants."

"What does she want?"

"She wants to counsel children."

"What?"

"She is a psychologist. She is disaffected with corporate intrigues. She wants to counsel children, perhaps have a child of her own. She wants out of the game."

"You believe that? All of it?"

"I believe she believes it."

Nothing was ever certain. "Who's her contact at Maas Intertech?"

Bandit gazed steadily at Rico a few moments, then said, "I didn't ask."

Rico clenched his teeth, drew a deep breath, then let it go.

What mattered most? That was the question that kept coming back to Rico's mind.

The problem with this run was that too many factors kept getting involved. You could get frizzed just thinking about it, just trying to keep all the details straight in your mind, just trying to work out everyone's angles.

All the scag about who Farrah Moffit really was and where she came from probably made no difference. Maybe she was just caught in the middle, stuck somewhere she didn't want to be, the victim of megacorps, no less than Rico and his team. Maybe she just wanted a way out. Rico realized at length that there was no way he could know for sure and that thinking about it so much was a waste of precious time.

You had to focus on the key points. What really mattered. What seemed to matter most.

Was the Ansell Surikov who Farrah Moffit kept talking about really the real Ansell Surikov? Rico tried to figure a way to answer that question for sure, then stopped himself. What was the point? His objective now was to get Farrah Moffit back on track. What difference did it make what she called this slag she wanted to get away from Fuchi, as long as the slag wanted to go.

Only three questions really seemed crucial: was Farrah Moffit's contact at Maas Intertech for real? could she cut the deal she promised? and did Ansell Surikov, or whoever, really want to leave Fuchi?

First . . .

Piper opened her eyes. The display screen of the telecom on the wall beside her flickered and came to life. "Security at the Crystal Blossom Condominiums has been tightened, *jefe*, but the telecom lines are unaffected. I have a clean line direct to the apartment where we lifted Marena Farris."

"You mean Moffit."

"Yes, excuse me." Piper rolled her eyes, looking a little exasperated. "Where we lifted *Farrah Moffit.*"

Rico stepped down the hall to the lounge. Dok sat there—cleaning his Ingram SMG—opposite Farrah Moffit. Both he and Moffit looked up as Rico entered. Moffit looked about as anxious and forlorn as anyone Rico had ever seen. He guessed that was only natural. "Who's your contact at Maas Intertech?" said Rico, without preamble.

A timid look came into Moffit's eyes. "Must I . . . Must I give him a name?" she said hesitantly.

Dok cursed softly. Moffit glanced at him anxiously. Rico said, "We ain't going nowhere till you scan. Till we scan what you got. Till everything checks out. *Comprende?*"

Moffit seemed to resign herself to it. She nodded, just faintly, then said softly. "His name is Osborne. That could be a corporate pseudonym. I don't know. He's the Vice President for Internal Policy and Review. He controls a kind of internal intelligence section, along with various resource units such as personnel."

"How do we make contact?"

"We've established a protocol."

"Let's hear it."

The proc wasn't very complex. When Moffit wanted to contact Osborne, she called his office via a public telecom, ID'ing herself as a personal friend. If Osborne wasn't available, Moffit left a particular message and called back later. If Osborne wanted to contact her, he followed much the same routine. The only sophisticated part was that they used portable voice-translation gear to prevent their voice prints from ever being matched to their corporate personnel files.

Rico motioned Moffit to her feet. "Let's make a call."

Moffit seemed willing. Rico ushered her up the hall to the warehouse office and sat her down facing the telecom screen. He gave Piper the nod; she closed her eyes. The telecom screen flashed blue with the unit calling window of the local telecommunications grid. The words VIS PICKUP OFF appeared in the upper-right corner. The code for the telecom being called appeared in large numerals at center screen.

Moffit caught her breath, and looked up and around at Rico, her eyes wide with surprise. "That's my condo's call code."

"First we talk to Surikov."

Moffit's eyes flared enormous. "No!" she exclaimed. "They'll pick up the call! They'll realize we're—!"

"Can it."

A slag who could have been Surikov's twin appeared on the screen. Rico looked closely but couldn't see any difference between this Surikov and the one who'd died at the Willow Brook Mall, Michael Travis. Surikov opened his mouth as if to speak, then glanced downward. PRIVACY ON winked on and off at the bottom of the screen. Surikov compressed his lips, then reached to the side and drew a telecom handset up to his ear.

"Yes?" he said. "Who's this?"

"Dr. Surikov," Rico said.

Surikov nodded, now looking a bit impatient. "Yes, yes," he said. "Your vid's off. Who am I speaking to?"

Another message from Piper winked on the telecom screen: LINE SAFE.

One final check had been made. Surikov's telecom was clean, right down to the handset at his ear. "You don't know me," Rico said. "I'm calling about something you wanna know about. Be careful what you say and how you react. This line's clean, but your apartment may be monitored."

Surikov frowned puzzledly, maybe irritated. "I'm afraid I don't—"

Rico gave Moffit's shoulder a nudge. She jerked her head up and around to look at him, then looked back to Surikov when Rico motioned at the screen. She seemed nervous as hell, desperate. Definitely off-guard. As Rico intended.

The question was: how would she handle herself?

Moffit abruptly shifted in her seat, sitting up straight. Her fingers shook. She gasped. "Darling ... darling, don't say anything, *don't say my name!*"

That last came out in a rush. Surikov opened his mouth as if to interrupt, but then stopped.

"You'll give us away," Moffit continued, only pausing to gasp again. "Someone may be listening. Listening to what you say. Please don't say anything for a moment. I know this is hard. Just say ... say yes if you recognize my voice."

Surikov was gazing intently out of the telecom screen. Rico couldn't be sure if the slag was angry, incredulous, or both. "Do I—" he said, abruptly cutting himself off. "Well, of course. Of course I do."

"Darling, please be careful," Moffit said. "Be very very careful. I'll explain everything that's happened as soon as we're together. Right now I need you to help me. Think carefully. Do you know what I mean when I refer to our special project?"

Surikov frowned, now seeming puzzled. "Well," he said, "yes. Certainly." He waved one hand vaguely. "What else could you mean?"

Moffit nodded. Her eyes seemed riveted to the telecom screen. Her gaze seemed even more intense than Surikov's. "This is why I'm calling," she said. "This is what I'm working on. Our special project. I'm with people who are going to help. After we're done with this call, you must act as if nothing unusual's happened. Do you understand, darling?"

"Yes, obviously." Irritation rose suddenly into Surikov's face, but in an instant faded to nothing. He nodded. "Yes, yes, I understand. I'm just, well ... I didn't expect this."

"I understand, darling. Please listen. The people I'm with are very, very careful. They want confirmation from you that you're willing to go along with our project. You must say something to convince them, but you must assume someone's listening to you at your end."

Moments passed. Surikov pressed his hand back over his brow and his thinning hair. His eyes widened briefly, like a man struggling with the incomprehensible. Twice he opened his mouth as if to speak, then said nothing.

"Well," he said finally, "I don't know quite how to say this. I just want to be reunited with my wife. Everything else is rather secondary. It's been, very difficult . . . difficult to concentrate on my work. I'm so used to her being here. I know she loves me very much, and she wants what's best for me. What more can I say? I trust her implicitly. She wants what I want. I want what she wants. Do you see?"

Farrah Moffit turned her head and met Rico's eyes. She looked scared, expectant, and hopeful all at the same time. Rico looked at the man on the screen, then back at Moffit, watched her a moment, then nodded. "Say bye. We'll be in touch."

Moffit said that, and then a few other things that only helped persuade Rico that the relationship between her and Surikov was real, or real enough that it didn't matter.

The slag wanted what Moffit wanted.

Likely, that was what he'd be getting.

34

Twenty minutes in the lavatory did slightly more for her psyche than for her looks. More than half that time Farrah spent seated on the toilet, face in her hands, eyes closed, struggling to regain her composure, and to reinforce it.

The ploy by the runners' leader had caught her off-guard. She had walked into that little room at the top of the hall expecting to face Osborne, only to be confronted by Ansell. It had forced her to shift mind-sets very abruptly, in little more than a moment. With a man like Osborne, she could afford to be every bit the corporate woman, cool to the point of ruthless. In fact, she had to be like that. With Ansell, she couldn't afford to be anything less than the stereotypical woman, as defined by Ansell's own views. Approaching the man in the wrong manner would have invited disaster. Failing to impress upon him the dangers of the situation would have invited so much greater a disaster. It had forced her to think very quickly, to make leaps of intuition she felt only half-able to make. It left her in a state—heart pounding, body shaking—practically on the verge of fainting. She needed time alone to recover, and to prepare for what was coming.

She felt as if things were beginning to rush past her too swiftly, slipping out of control. She told herself that wasn't so. Her plan was coming together. She would make it work.

She had to.

Before the grime-streaked mirror over the lavatory sink, she did what little she could to improve her appearance. There wasn't much. She had no supplies. She was lucky the runners had seen fit to provide her with a change of underwear. She washed her face, then combed her hair and tied it behind her head. Fortunately, the subdued tones permanently bonded to her face, lips, brows, and lashes simulated the most basic effects of makeup. The resulting look was neat enough, though anyone who knew her would see the difference at once. She looked somewhat less polished than her usual self. Unfinished. A woman would certainly spot that. But would a man like Osborne notice?

"I'll make you a promise," said a quiet voice.

Farrah turned to face the man standing in the doorway. The latest one to act as her guard. His graying, razorcut hair and three-day growth of beard made him appear the oldest of the runners. He was also the one who had seemed most acutely distressed after the runners' meeting with Prometheus. The woman who had died at that meeting had apparently been his woman.

"If you cross us," he said, lowly, "you'll never see home again."

Farrah believed it. For all this man's apparent skill at first aid, he carried himself like someone used to confrontations, physical violence. Farrah did not doubt that he could kill her if so moved, without difficulty, without remorse. It was a frightening realization. Her days lately had been fraught with such realizations.

"You scan?" the man insisted.

"I won't cross you," Farrah replied, somewhere finding the capacity to speak in a voice that did not waiver. "I want to get out of this alive. I want to get back to my husband."

To Farrah, those seemed like persuasive proofs, but she saw at once that she had slipped and slipped badly. The man's expression turned venomous, his mouth twisting into a vicious sneer. "That's it," he snarled, motioning with his gun. "Move it."

She did, stepping again into the hall, expecting something, she wasn't sure what—a blow at the back of the head, a shove at the very least. Nothing like that happened and she immediately saw why. The runners' leader waited, watching from the top of the hall. The leader's expression was hard, but she saw none of the fury that had lit his features on previous occasions. Farrah suspected that she might have at least a slim chance of survival as long as she did nothing to provoke that fury.

At a motion of his head, she moved past the leader and

into the little room outfitted like an office. A shabby office. The Asian woman was jacked into her deck. Here was another variable that kept Farrah's nerves on edge and twitching. The Asian despised all corporates, everything to do with corporations and corporate living. She seemed to want all corporates dead. Farrah hadn't the slightest doubt that this one might kill her too, given the right opportunity, given the right "excuse."

The leader closed the door, then turned to Farrah, saying, "We play this like you're making all the arrangements. You'll be against a black background. The man won't see nothing but you."

Farrah nodded. "I understand."

"Remember what I told you."

"I will." The man had given her precise instructions on the details of the agreement she was to complete. Farrah closed her eyes and told herself again that she would somehow make this work. She had no choice. Everything depended on it.

"You set?"

"Yes. I'm ready."

The telecom calling screen appeared on the wall display. That was swiftly replaced by the willow and lotus logo of Maas Intertech. Then came the face of a very young and very attractive Asian woman. "Mr. Osborne's office. May I help you?"

Farrah smiled. "May I speak to him, please."

The woman also smiled, apparently in recognition. "Oh, yes. One moment, please."

"Thank you."

"You're quite welcome."

The corporate logo returned, then Osborne appeared. He was not a good-looking man. His face resembled putty that had been sculpted into rough, square lines, then baked to a stony texture. He wore his hair samurai-style, shaven above the brow, drawn back behind his head. Prominent eyebrows threw his eyes into shadow. Of his clothes, only a plain, collarless white linen shirt, buttoned at the neck, showed on the screen. A small, dark, circular pin that kept winking with the light clung to the shirt's right breast.

"Nice of you to call," Osborne said. "I understand that you've been lifted."

Osborne did not seem pleased at all, but Farrah had no difficulty guessing why. If he had heard some rumor of her abduction, he would be presuming, at the very least, that their previous negotiations were now void. That would mean the loss of certain opportunities. She would have to correct that presumption, bring him up to date. "The situation has changed."

"Yes. I'm aware of that, I'm also aware that a certain person died at the Willow Brook Mall. I'm not sure if I should be thanking you or cursing you for that. Do we have anything else to discuss?"

"Quite a lot, in fact."

"I'm listening."

"My basic offer to you is unchanged. However, I now have the capability to recruit the person myself and deliver him to you at a suitable time and place."

"And just how has this happened?"

"It happened. The result is this. I'm willing to concede certain of the extras we discussed, the ones you found most problematic, in exchange for certain consideration."

Osborne said nothing for several moments. Doubtless, he was pondering what she might want in place of any extras she had previously demanded. All such "bonuses" were not created equal. Simple monetary value was not always a deciding factor. "I'm still listening."

"The main points relate to my recruitment team. They want a cash award for their efforts."

"That sounds workable. What other points?"

"As a result of other recruitments they've handled, they are currently receiving a great deal of unwelcome attention. They would like that to stop."

For a moment, Osborne seemed on the verge of asking what all this had to do with him. Osborne was not so slow of wit as to actually put that question into words. "You're not saying what I think you're saying?"

Farrah nodded. Once.

Osborne paused to light a cigarette, then said, "Daisaka Security is looking for your recruitment team?"

"That's correct."

"You know what I'm thinking? That you engineered the disappearance of a certain person from my corp's facility. Why would you do that?"

"I would not."

"No? I think it's an interesting concept. For several reasons. It takes a big gun out of our R & D effort and makes your boy all the more valuable. It also saves me the trouble of explaining how an impostor got into our program. The more I think about it, the more I like the idea."

"Then you should be grateful."

"Maybe I am. Maybe I'm taking this as a warning." He paused and gazed at her pointedly. "But that doesn't change certain facts. You want our agreement documented and certified, correct? Like any full and proper recruitment. Unfortunately, I have no authority over Kuze Nihon's security arm or any other organization beyond the purview of Maas Intertech."

Farrah smiled, pointedly. "You're too modest."

"Simply a realist."

"But you do have influence."

Osborne took a swift drag from his cig. "I might agree to quietly exert myself in certain quarters, but I will not agree to provide any substantive evidence of this aspect of our agreement. You'll have to take my word for it."

"These people we're dealing with are not fools, Osborne."

"That fact has been made poignantly obvious."

"Let's speak of facts. The fact is that this team and I together are providing you with an unparalleled opportunity."

"That's for me to judge."

Farrah had no doubt that Osborne knew what she meant and that he also agreed. The runners' lifting of Michael Travis had shown Maas Intertech's security unit to be at least rather lax and possibly incompetent. Heads would be rolling by now, the entire security framework under intense review. If Osborne could suddenly present Ansell Surikov to the board of directors, he would, by comparison, seem a hero. The fact that an impostor had been working under their very noses need never be mentioned. The death of Michael Travis could be explained away in any number of ways, if that death had even become generally known. "You must have your eye on the CEO's office."

"I have my eye on a lot of things," Osborne said very quietly. "I'm open to discussing your new terms because

I want your boy. I'm sure you've reached that conclusion. If I have to use my influence, as you call it, I will. I'll do what I have to do. It's even conceivable that I might have a job or two of my own for this team of yours, and therefore a reason to make efforts on their behalf. But don't try to push under my skin. I get unreasonable when people do that."

Farrah suppressed a shiver. One thing she definitely did not want was to encourage a man like Osborne to get unreasonable. That could prove fatal. "You have my sincere apology."

Osborne did not seem overly moved. "I suggest we talk money. How absurd a fee does your team expect?"

For an organization with the resources of Maas Intertech, it wasn't a great deal of money and Osborne didn't even blink at mention of the sum.

They completed their negotiations in short order.

35

That slag Osborne had said it. Rico wondered about it. Could Farrah Moffit have been the one who'd set up the original run against Maas Intertech? She handled herself real slick on the telecom, cool and corporate. Yet, to Rico it didn't seem likely. She was a fragging psychologist. She'd gotten her start at Fuchi as a fragging joygirl. She turned doe-eyed and timid the minute anybody raised their voice. It didn't matter, but it did make him wonder.

Rico rubbed at his eyes and suppressed a yawn. It seemed like days, weeks, since he'd last slept a damn.

"What now?" Moffit asked quietly.

Rico grimaced. "Now you go back to the lounge."

He and the team had some plans to make.

"Master," the voice whispered. *"Wake up."*

Bandit woke, shifted senses, and opened his eyes to the astral counterpart of the lounge. The auras of Dok and Farrah Moffit glowed from opposite sides of the narrow room. Between them hovered the Raccoon-like form of a watcher.

"Something strange, master," the watcher said. *"You said . . ."*

"Yes."

Bandit motivated his astral self, sat up, crossed his legs and ascended, moving forward. The watcher led up the hall, through the door to the warehouse loading bay, across the bay, then through the large bay door and outside.

As Bandit passed through the astral form of the bay door, he entered the glare of directed mana, a spell, like turning to face the sun. Instinctively, he tugged himself back, back into the dim radiance of the loading bay. As he did that, he threw up a shield, a spell of his own, surrounding his astral body in a sphere of guardian power.

Then—nothing. No mana bolts streamed through the dormant aura of the bay door to strike his shield. No monstrous spirits appeared to confront him. Just what had he encountered? He descended into the ground, moved forward a ways, then came up through the buildings on the far side of the street. He saw an old, fat man seated on a toilet and smoking a fat cigar, but other than that . . . nothing.

The night sky shone with the reflected radiance of the Earth's energy. The air rumbled with the workings of nearby factories. Cars and trucks moved along the streets.

The magic that had glared in his face was gone. It had touched him and disappeared. What was it? What could it mean?

Trouble, for sure.

They took the meet in Jersey City, on Pacific, right near the railroad yards. Meets at very high-profile localities like malls hadn't gone too good in the recent past, so this one was taking place in the litter-strewn parking lot of the local Quik Shop store.

At three a.m., the lot was deserted.

Rico looked around from the passenger seat of the van. The surrounding neighborhood was grunge, three- and four-story grimy brick and cracked, crumbling sidewalks. It was like Newark's worst, only the cops still worked here and they never went easy. Jersey City had its own private corporation and that corp had its own cops. They were a mob like all the other mobs, only they had the law behind them. They specialized in street justice. Make the wrong move and you ended up sprawled in some dark corner with a hole through the back of your head.

Not a good place for pyrotechnics. The Jersey City cops rode in armored cars and command vehicles and had assault teams on twenty-four-hour alert. If things got real hot, they called out the fragging panzer. Or one of their gunships.

At a quarter past the hour, a crimson Toyota Ambassador pulled into the lot. It was marked for Paladin Cabs. That meant body armor, run-flat tires, and gun ports.

Tonight it also meant a bodyguard.

The guard looked like a gutterpunk in razor-sharp threads. He came out of the rear of the cab in a dark gray suit, glanced toward the street, stood up, glanced toward the street, closed the door of the cab, and turned to face Thorvin's van. Then he shot another glance toward the street. Rico recognized the habit. It was something you developed after seeing too many people sliced and diced to bloody ribbons in the thrasher parts of the sprawl.

A pro would keep his eyes moving, but he'd be discreet about it. This said something about the slag inside the cab. Osborne might be a dangerous man, but he'd never walked the razor himself. If he had, he wouldn't have a clown like this for a guard.

At Rico's signal, Shank tugged open the side door of the van and then waited, crouching, watching the clown and cradling his M22A2. Rico gave the clown a few moments to adjust to that, then pushed open the passenger door and stepped outside.

Osborne came over to face him. With a quick look up and down, he said, "You did a fine job on my security."

Rico nodded. "You got sticks?"

Osborne drew a synthleather wallet from his jacket pocket, folded it open, and handed it over. Rico checked the credsticks with the reader on his belt. They checked out.

"We'll set the delivery once we got the merchandise."

"When do you go?"

"Soon."

"Make it so. I've got a lot riding on this deal. Do it fast enough and we'll have things to discuss in the future."

"Sure, amigo. Slot and run."

Osborne nodded, got back in his cab, and left. Rico glanced up at the night sky, then returned to the van.

The nightly rain would be coming soon.

Too soon.

36

"Time is oh-two forty-five hours."

Rico acknowledged that over his headset. The message came from Piper and it meant she had done everything she had to do inside the Crystal Blossom condo's mainframe computer.

Rico keyed his headset. "Go."

The helo veered abruptly, vectoring left and up as the doors siding the main compartment slid open. Rico wound the thick, slik-coated drop-rope around his left forearm and popped the safety line affixed to his commando harness. Shank nodded from the door opposite.

Abruptly, they were coming up over the edge of the roof of the Crystal Blossom condoplex.

"*Now!*" Thorvin said.

Rico stepped out into empty air.

The timing was precise. The helo slowed just as he slid to the end of the drop-rope. He hit the roof's flat, gritty surface with both feet, tumbled once and came up onto his knees, scanning the rooftop with his Ares Special Service in hand. Shank landed an instant behind him. The helo arced away so as not to attract attention, dwindling into the night and the infinitude of buildings and glaring lights sprawling across Manhattan.

The roof was clear. Rico rose and jogged over to the building's southern face. Shank followed. They pulled black climbing ropes from their harnesses and thrust K-2 autopitons against the low ferrocrete wall rising like a rim from around the edge of the roof. The cryomag tips of the K-2s burned holes straight into the crete. Secondary probes then extended outward from the pitons' main shaft, embedding the devices in the crete.

That took about five seconds. They spent another three

or four connecting the ropes to the pitons, then to the I.M.I. power winches on the front of their harnesses.

"Set," Shank growled.

"Go."

The winches were programmed. From the roof, fifty stories above the ground, they fell about eleven stories straight down, then the winches cut in. Harnesses jerked and pulled. They slowed, jogging feet-first off the face of the building. They came to a halt before the wall of mirrored macroplast panes guarding the living room of Condo 35-8. This was where they'd picked up Farrah Moffit and where they would now find Ansell Surikov.

They applied flashtape to the mirrored windows. One quick flash seared a large hole through the panes.

They swung inside.

The heart of the Crystal Blossom condoplex mainframe used standard CPU matrix iconology: a white room walled by control panels. At 02:44:58:21:19 or so, Piper attached a black-box program icon to the Master Logic Panel icon, then transmitted her ready signal to Rico.

"Time is oh-two forty-five hours."

A while passed, then a warning signal from the engineering subprocessor advised of a breached external wall panel in Residence 35-8. The black box on the main console piped that signal, changing it, shunting it to the building diagnostic subprocessor, initializing a Level 1 diagnostic search of engineering subsystems.

Momentarily, another warning came, and another diagnostic search began.

The loop was complete.

"Alert! Alert!"

Hearing that, Skip Nolan looked down the row of comm operators facing the spectrally lit consoles lining the Executive Action Brigade's command vehicle. One console was showing its red alert light on top. Op Three was working the console rapidly.

Fingering his headset, Skip stepped up behind the Op. Window One on the console's main display showed a broad expanse of city populated by soaring towers gleaming brightly in the night.

"We've got a hit," said an excited voice. A burst of

static interrupted the signal. The transmit display on the console ID'd the speaker as part of Ground Eleven, the surveillance team assigned to monitor a tower on Manhattan's Upper East Side.

"Ground Eleven, report," said Op Three.

The surveillance agent's voice returned in mid-sentence. "—just skimmed the roof. We make it a Hughes Stallion, possibly armed. We've got some activity—"

More static.

"—scanning two unknowns rappelling down the south face."

Window Three on the console's main display abruptly zoomed in on the Crystal Blossom condoplex. Two dark, human-sized figures seemed to be clinging to the building's mirrored surface, maybe thirty, thirty-five stories above street-level. Something flashed, and a black squarish patch appeared in the building's mirrored skin. The two figures disappeared into the black patch.

Skip suppressed a curse.

He'd been all but incredulous when Colonel Yates ordered a surveillance team to monitor the exterior of the condoplex. What the hell did this building have to do with their mission? The brigade didn't have resources to waste like this. Their targets were somewhere in Newark, not Manhattan. They'd scraped up enough street-level intelligence to be reasonably sure of that. All the colonel would say was that he had special intelligence, not through regular channels.

Now it looked as if someone were making a run on the condoplex. Skip jacked into the console, replayed the vid, and zoomed in tight on the two dark figures hanging at the side of the building. Computer analysis found a ninety-seven percent correspondence between the figures on the wall and datastore references on two of the runners who'd participated in the run against Maas Intertech.

That was a match.

The colonel's long shot appeared to be paying off.

Skip looked up the line of consoles to the crippled body in a wheelchair. Bobbie Jo, her mind and spirit, were linked to an underpowered backup drone drifting slowly over eastern Newark, futilely, it now seemed. She was too far from the action to make any difference, way too far away. The drone was too slow, and Bobbie Jo was getting too timid. She'd be lucky if Colonel Yates didn't cancel her contract. The colonel didn't believe in on-the-job therapy.

If only she could have found the will to pilot one of the brigade's assault choppers ... Things might've worked out better for her.

But—no time for that now.

He jacked into his command console. "Alert, alert. Cap One, you are go. Stand by for target designation on channel three."

A monotone voice replied, "Acknowledged. Lifting off."

From the background came the rapid thump-thump-thumping of rotorcraft.

When the lights came on, Surikov lay on the bed with his legs hanging over the side like he'd been sitting there a while, then just leaned back and fell asleep. He wore a black robe. He looked about fifty, sophisticated, with thinning hair and a close-trimmed beard turning gray. Extra weight around the middle. Not a big man. Not a small one either. A liquor bottle lay close to hand.

Rico tossed the bottle back toward the center of the bed and tried shaking Surikov awake. When that didn't work, he took the opportunity to press Dok's DNA scanner against Surikov's arm. The check took about thirty seconds and came back positive. ID confirmed. Again. He tugged Surikov up into a sitting position and cuffed him.

Surikov grunted, moved his head, gradually starting to come around. He smelled like booze. "What ... ?" he mumbled. "Who's there? What's going on?"

"We're taking you to the Garden."

"A garden of delight," Surikov said, smiling stupidly. "That's my wife."

"We're taking you home."

Surikov stared for several long moments, then rubbed a hand over his mouth and made an obvious effort to get hold of himself. "How ... Tell me ... how do we proceed?"

No fragging guano.

The runners had called him Cannibal.
With her head lowered and hair hanging around her

face, Farrah watched the runner watching her, trying to look as if she were doing anything but paying him any attention.

He made her nervous.

According to what she'd overheard, the runners had brought this Cannibal in specifically to stay with her, to serve both as guard and jailer. The ork runner had referred to Cannibal as a "hired gun." He looked like that. Like the kind of person who would do whatever someone asked, as long as the pay was satisfactory. Red and black slash-tats made his face a vicious mask. His teeth were filed to points and colored jet-black. He wore some unusual dark metallic armor on his upper body, and a small grayish skull dangled from his left ear. He carried a compact rifle—possibly a submachine gun—a pair of pistols, a rather short-looking sword, and numerous knives.

Farrah wished the runners had trusted her enough to leave her by herself. She would rather they'd left her here in handcuffs and manacles than leave her unfettered with this scuzpunk for a guard.

Cannibal leaned against the wall opposite and watched her. Some unknown quanta of time slipped past. Cannibal pushed away from the wall and turned and walked slowly out of the warehouse lounge. His footsteps moved up the hall. The door to that space beyond, the loading area, squealed and then banged. Silence descended, but lingered only moments.

Too soon, the door squealed and banged again and Cannibal returned. He leaned against the wall again, facing her, cradling that rifle in his arms. He grinned.

"Do I make you nervous?"

How to reply to the sociopathic personality? Farrah tried to decide. She could not expect him to observe any of the ordinary social conventions. Almost any response at all would only encourage him. An outright challenge, looks or words of defiance, might well incite him to violence. Better, it seemed, for her to do nothing, say nothing, make no response whatsoever. Better to appear completely cowed, in hopes of providing little or no provocation.

"I could do you in a second," he said. "I could do you in a way we'd both enjoy. One time I did this biff in bed.

First we bopped, then I took her heart out. I could do you like that. One minute, you're in heaven. The next ...."

Farrah suppressed the tremor that rose up through her insides. If he came near her ... if left no choice but to try to save herself, she would have one chance and one chance only.

If would be do or die.

37

No alarms, no shouts . . .

So far so good.

Rico watched Surikov pull on the hi-visibility orange jumpsuit with built-in plastic shoes intended to ID him as a noncombatant, then helped him get into a commando-style harness. Surikov moved slow and fumbled a lot, like he was still feeling whatever he'd been drinking, and like he'd drunk too much.

Rico hustled him out to the living room, the slag stumbling and tripping in the dark. Rico kept him upright and forced him ahead, then keyed his headset. "Time check."

Piper replied, "Time is oh-two forty-eight hours."

Maybe another minute went by. Rico kept his eyes moving, glancing toward Shank and the entry to the condo. He kept expecting to hear shouts, shots, detonations, a Fuchi security team blasting into the place and spraying the room with autofire. What he got instead was the thumping of a helo. As the sound drew near, a blackish blur shot through the hole in the exterior window panels, smashed across the top of the wetbar, shattering bottles and glasses, then thudded against a wall.

The blur was a stickihook, a macroplast weight with an adhesive skin and a loop connected to a rope. Shank rapidly freed the rope from the hook and brought it over. The rope had three ends, each with a mountaineer's heavy metal clasp. Rico snapped one clasp onto Surikov's harness and one onto his own. Shank took the third.

Surikov seemed to wake up then. He pointed toward the hole in the window panels, saying adamantly, "We are *not* going out through that—"

Right.

Rico put a medjector to Surikov's right arm and fired.

The slag blinked and jerked his arm away, then got woozy-looking, like he might slump to the floor.

"Time check."

"Time is oh-two fifty hours."

Shank helped get Surikov over to the hole in the window panels. The rope connected to their harnesses grew taut.

One quick look and they went together through the hole.

The roof of the foundry gave easy access to a window on the warehouse's fourth floor. Claude Jaeger waited several moments, watching. The window, easily visible from the street below, slowly settled into a gummy, glutinous mass oozing over the window sill like mucus.

The mage got that much right, at least.

Claude hopped through the empty frame, landed lightly on his feet and sank into a crouch. This floor of the warehouse smelled of resin and paint. Piles of antique furniture, some apparently made of actual wood, divided the space into long, narrow aisles. Claude found his way to the stairs. Two flights down, he paused before a metal fire door and listened.

Footsteps approached, softly echoing—the calm, measured footsteps of a sentry, one wholly unaware of any intrusions onto his turf. Claude drew back and flattened himself against the wall to the left of the doorway. In a moment, the door banged and swung inward, right past Claude's nose. The sentry followed through. In that instant, Claude saw the sentry's face from only a few steps away. The man's eyes gazed straight ahead, into the greater darkness of the stairwell.

Claude's fist shot forward and back, and the sentry collapsed. The satisfying feel of snapping bone and crunching cartilage lingered. Claude smiled, then dragged the sentry's body fully into the stairwell.

One down, one to go.

When the rest of the runners returned to this hideyhole, they would find only death. By then, Claude would be waiting in ambush.

He moved cautiously through the doorway and into a large space, the truck-loading bay located at the front of the building. He stood on a loading dock at the rear of that bay. The extra-large door to a freight elevator stood immediately to his left. Beyond that an ordinary-sized door. This led into a narrow hall, past an office, a lavatory, then into a smallish room outfitted like a ramshackle lounge.

The woman there, seated on a cushioned bench, looked like she belonged with the slitches in the holopics on the walls around her: enormous hair, jutting breasts, a face both sublime and whorish. As Claude entered, she lifted her head and drew back fearfully, eyes wide and round. She gasped and blurted, "Who are you?"

Claude smiled and continued toward her. "Your friends sent me to get you out of here."

"What?" She looked at him as if astonished.

But when he reached for her, astonishment turned to animal fear. She jerked aside and began rising to her feet. Claude seized her elbow and flung her down onto the bench. Her head tilted back and her jaw dropped open and something like a blackish length of spaghetti or string shot out from under her tongue. Claude felt the tap against his chest and saw the string whip back into the woman's mouth, vanishing before he could really grasp what was happening.

Cybersnake. Narcoject delivery system. The burning spike of pain that suddenly pierced his chest suggested hypercyanide, but then he felt his heart hammering like it would burst and realized his eyes had gone out of focus.

What was it? Atropine? Working this quickly? He felt his legs give way and suddenly found himself lying on the floor on his back, staring blindly at the ceiling.

How had that happened? What was going on? Why was he so hot, burning up? He couldn't breathe. It felt like he had a metal strap ringing his neck and another around his chest, crushing him. He tried to force air into his lungs, but the pain was overwhelming.

Angels. He heard angels singing . . .

Surikov was wide-eyed and looking around as the towers swung by, but then the winch above their heads pulled them up beside the door in the helo's flank. Dok reached out, and in another moment Rico, Shank, and Surikov were all inside.

Dok hooked a safety line onto Surikov. Rico popped

the line off his own harness and moved forward to the
copilot's seat. The helo banked and picked up speed, vectoring down a long chasm of steel and crete towers.

"Three birds!" Thorvin shouted. "Coming in on freaking intercept!"

Rico shouted back. "Port Authority cops?"

The Port Authority had jurisdiction over Manhattan air
space and regularly put patrols in the air. Thorvin shook
his head. "I don't think so!"

Who the hell could it be? Rico wondered. Piper'd had
the Crystal Blossom tower locked down solid. They'd
been in and out in just minutes. Who could even know
they'd been there, much less have helos in the air and
coming down on them this fast? "Can ya lose 'em?"

"Do I HAVE A FREAKING *CHOICE*?"

"Master," the voice whispered.

Bandit closed his eyes to the tilting, vibrating world of
the helicopter's interior and looked to the astral plane.
The raccoon-like form of the watcher crouched before
him.

"*You must come,*" it said.

Bandit considered that.

Very risky.

Claude Jaeger dead? Killed by a woman? There was no
doubting the witness of his astral senses, yet Maurice
struggled with the concept, astounded. The physical adept
had often seemed sufficiently formidable to be virtually
indestructible. He should have known, Maurice thought.
Time disproved all such lies.

Now he would have to finish the job himself.

Disgruntled, he left his biffs in the Mercedes and
crossed the street to the narrow front of the warehouse.
The smaller of the two doors clicked and opened at a
word. He stepped into the long, narrow, rectangular space
of a loading area, then mounted the loading dock at the
rear and continued on through another door, down the
hall and into what looked like a lounge. The woman was
there, huddled on a cushioned bench and quietly sobbing,
her face and head completely hidden under a disheveled
mass of shiny whitish-blonde hair. Jaeger lay dead on the

floor, on his back, a look of inexpressible bliss monopolizing his features.

"*Master,*" said Vera Causa, his ally, murmuring into his ear. "*Beware . . .*"

Maurice shifted to his astral perceptions in time to see the radiant figure emerging from the wall at the back of the lounge.

The shaman . . .

The slags in the pursuing helos were pros. Thorvin's evasive maneuvers didn't throw them. Neither did the halfer's E.C.W. They came in high and low, and Rico had no choice but to point Thorvin toward the Hudson River. They'd have to sprint for the Jersey side, hoping Thorvin could find the speed to get them clear of their pursuit.

As they passed out over the dark expanse of water, the first slugs clattered against the helo's hull. One penetrated the airframe to gouge Shank in the upper right thigh, another fractured the window at Rico's side, spitting a jagged sliver of transparex across his cheek. The wound wasn't deep and the blood loss was minimal, but it didn't improve his mood any.

He looked to the rear and saw Bandit sitting crosslegged, unmoving, eyes closed, flute lying across his lap.

No help coming from that quarter.

"They're GAINING!" Thorvin shouted.

"Push it!"

"I'm freaking pushing, ALL RIGHT?"

Bandit paused at the rear of the lounge. He had seen the corpse in the stairwell and now he saw the body on the floor here in this room. Things were happening. It seemed that Rico's concern for Farrah Moffit's safety had been more than justified. Bandit only wondered how two men had come to be dead, while Moffit still lived.

A tall, thin man stood at the head of the lounge, just in front of the door to the hallway. His aura now grew radiant, revealing truths. The man was a magician, and he was using his astral senses. That meant he was probably looking at Bandit, seeing him. That didn't bother Bandit much. What bothered him was what he saw standing beside the man.

The spirit had a female form. It looked from Bandit to

the other magician and back again several times. Was this a conjured spirit or an ally? Either way, it boded no good.

Two against one.

Bad odds.

Bandit felt inclined toward just leaving. The equivalent of one step back and he would be on the other side of a physical wall and all but immune to spellcasting. There was a problem with that, though. Farrah Moffit was important. Rico had made a point of impressing that on everyone. If Bandit simply stepped out, she would be at the mercy of this magician.

"I regret this," the magician said. *"Have you any last words?"*

Bandit nodded. *"Goodfellow."*

The spirit so named emerged from the wall at the rear of the lounge and paused at Bandit's left. It took the form of a human, but slim, short, and bearded, and wearing peculiar clothing with ruffles and lacy trim. It looked at Bandit for a moment, then across the astral terrain to the other magician, then, with a flourish, bowed, extending one arm with the hand palm up.

The floor rumbled and quaked and split open. The magician opposite shouted and fell through the hole, down and out of sight.

Goodfellow bowed again and vanished.

The other magician's spirit leaned over to gaze into the hole, then looked at Bandit and smiled. "You should go away," it said, "before my master wakes up."

Bandit could see the wisdom in that.

Manifesting on the physical plane, he moved over to face Farrah Moffit. She sat on a cushioned bench with her back pressed to the wall and her legs drawn up before her body. Her eyes were wide and round and she held one hand thrust back against her mouth. She looked terrified. She went on staring at the hole in the floor till Bandit moved directly into her line of sight, then her eyes widened further as her gaze met his.

"Come with me if you want to live."

Moffit gasped, then slowly nodded her head.

The LZ became a killing zone.

They had no choice but to put down. It was that or wait to get shot out of the air. The pursuing helos didn't hes-

itate to fire even as they passed over heavily populated
sections of the Newark metroplex. Populated, sure, but by
who? Nobody that mattered.

Thorvin's hideaway for the helo was in the ruins of
Sector 13, an old abandoned airport near the wastes of
some long-forgotten cemetery. Chain-link fencing topped
by coils of razor-wire surrounded one of the smaller
hangars. Thorvin put the helo down inside the fencing,
and the other helos closed in.

Bullets hammered against the airframe. Thorvin turned
the helo parallel to the front of the hangar to provide
cover. One of the hangar doors slid open and Thorvin's
van came rolling out, guided by remote. The weapons
pod on top opened up and began blazing. By then, Rico
could see that the other helos were dropping uniformed
troops to the ground.

Bandit was still in a trance. Shank grabbed him up and
Rico grabbed Surikov and they broke for the van.

It was a straight run—from the side of the helo to the
side of the van—no more than about five meters.

The troops moving in cut loose with a storm of
autofire.

Abruptly, Dok veered left and out beyond the front end
of the helo, shouting and blazing away with his Ingram.
It was a suicide move. The instant he saw it happening,
Rico thrust Surikov toward the van and lunged across the
ferrocrete. But not even his enhanced reaction time and
speed could get him going fast enough. His ears were full
of the stammering of autofire weapons and Dok's shouts
of vengeance and wrath, and none of it mattered. None of
it made any difference.

Dok rammed a fresh clip from his belt into the Ingram,
then his head snapped back and he plunged to the ground.
Rico didn't hesitate.

As he moved beyond the front of the helo, slugs
pounded into his chest. The impacts stole his breath. He
staggered and fell to one knee. It didn't feel like the bullets had penetrated his armored jacket, but it hurt. Mother
of God, how it hurt. He forced himself forward, grabbed
Dok beneath the shoulders and started dragging him back
toward the van. More slugs slammed into his chest and
shoulders. Another moment and he'd probably be dead,
laid out as limp as Dok, but then Shank was there, grab-

bing Dok around the chest, lifting him off the ground and
shoving Rico toward the van.

They had only one chance left. They had to dive like
devil rats into the transitways before armor-piercing slugs
or a wire-guided missile took them out. They had to go
where the helos couldn't reach them. It was up to Thorvin
now.

And it didn't get any closer than this.

Farrah Moffit huddled in the corner formed by the rear
of the dumpster and the wall of the alley. Bandit hovered,
sitting cross-legged, just far enough above the ground to
see over the dumpster to the street. Hours had passed and
that was bad. If he didn't get back to his body soon . . .

Moffit broke down again. She had a strange way of
crying, like a series of violent coughs, one rolling swiftly
into the next. The upset seemed genuine. Her first episode had started when he asked her what had happened to
the slag called Cannibal and to the other man, the one lying dead in the lounge with Moffit. She seemed deeply
disturbed. Perhaps she had led a sheltered life in her corporate towers, insulated from the realities of the plex. At
least she didn't make too much noise.

Some more time passed, then a rumbling arose, then
Thorvin's van pulled into the end of the alley.

Rico got out and looked around.

"They're here," Bandit said.

Farrah Moffit rose and went to the van and all but fell
sobbing into Surikov's arms.

Bandit rejoined his waiting body.

Dok looked dead.

38

It didn't end till they did the final check on Surikov.

The slag had a snitch, a microtransmitter implanted at the back of his neck, just like the other Surikov, Michael Travis, who they'd busted outta Maas Intertech. Farrah Moffit had told them to expect that. All the senior research staff at Fuchi had them, she said. She herself didn't rate high enough for that.

Getting the snitch out took some work. Rico had some experience with emergency med, but Shank had more so he did the job. Dok's equipment did most of the actual cutting. By the time Shank was finished, Surikov was pale and faint, but Dok's gear indicated that he'd get over it.

They lost their pursuers. They picked up Farrah Moffit, and Bandit too. A second Bandit. A Bandit that looked like a ghost. A Bandit that hovered, floated over the ground, and finally disappeared into the body of the Bandit that had been with them from the beginning. It was eerie and would have been freaky only Rico had seen things like this before.

Astral projection, it was called.

They headed for the bolthole in Rahway, Sector 13. It seemed called for. They were shot to piss, the rain had come and gone, and they all needed some sleep.

One last piece of work: they called Osborne to set up the exchange of Surikov and Moffit for nuyen. The meet was set for that night.

When Rico finally lay down, it was almost noon. He seemed to fall asleep in just moments. Piper shed her clothes in the dark, then carefully lay down beside him, shifting in against his side, lowering her head lightly to his shoulder. She lay there with him throughout the afternoon, moving little, resolved to let him sleep.

She could not, would not allow herself to sleep. These final few hours before their meet with Maas Intertech might be their last time together, intimately, as man and woman. She tried to savor every moment, the feel of his body, his musky aroma, his warmth, the soft sound of his breath. She called to mind everything she had ever admired about him. She struggled against the tears that welled time and again into her eyes. She prayed silently to the kami for deliverance, but had no real doubt about how the night would end.

Life provided few pleasures, and scant love. Too soon it was all over. She struggled against regret and bitter sorrow.

She had known all along how it would end, this run, everything. Fate would not be denied. The corps had all the power. Maas Intertech, through its parent organization Kuze Nihon, had virtually unlimited resources. The complete operational forces of Daisaka Security might be waiting for them tonight when they arrived at the meet. What chance did they have against such an army? They would be crushed like worms beneath the feet of giants.

She only wished she'd met Rico sooner, that she'd spent more time at his side. He was the only man she had ever really loved. There would be no life without him.

One thought brought a fleeting token of contentment. If she died tonight, she would die not for Ansell Surikov or Farrah Moffit. She would die not to further the battle against the oppressive megacorps, and not to save the planet. Rather, she would die for *jefe,* for her lover. She would die defending all that he believed in and all he considered good. She would die for him, and for him alone.

Nothing else seemed to have any meaning now.

The argument started as dusk descended into darkness. Shank looked at Thorvin, and Thorvin shrugged.

"I don't believe it either," Thorvin said.

It began with Piper declaring, loudly, somewhere down the hall from the main room, that she would accompany the rest of the team to the meet with Maas Intertech. She could do nothing in the matrix. At the meet, she could at least carry a gun. Rico told her curtly she wasn't going. She protested. He cursed. They both started to shout.

It was the first time Shank had ever heard Piper yell.

By nine p.m., they were standing in a room with plastic flowers, perfumed air, and quiet music at the Chapel of the Eternal Light in Sector 7. For five hundred nuyen, they got the same deal for Dok that they had gotten for Filly. Only this time, when the pre-recorded trideo service ended, nobody had anything to say. Dok had said it all himself when he ran like a wild man out onto the tarmac, shooting his SMG. It was about Filly and revenge and doing what you had to do, damn the consequences. Damn even death.

After the service, a slag in a neat black suit came with an urn full of ashes. Rico thrust a fistful of the ashes into Surikov's pants pockets.

"Don't ever forget," he said. "What you're getting didn't come free."

Surikov paled, and said, "No. No, indeed."

The meet came down in Sector 9 amid the gang-ravaged projects of Owens Park. The street was just one block long. Piles of building debris, the empty shells of gutted autos, and every kind of junk and garbage lined the street. Plastic sheeting and thin macroplast panels covered the windows of the buildings, all abandoned but for squatters and derelicts.

Heavy clouds lingered overhead, backlit by the moon and reflecting a strange, almost unearthly light.

Nobody seemed to be around.

At just past midnight, a pair of white, short-frame Toyota limos turned the corner and came slowly up the block. They stopped across from the van, near the opposite curb. Rico waited and watched. Thorvin had a drone in the air, keeping everything under surveillance. Bandit was in a trance, watching astrally. No warnings from either of them. Maybe Osborne was straight.

Maybe things would work out.

The rear door of the lead limo swung open. The slag who stepped out was nothing like the punk-like clown Osborne had brought to the first meet. This one was a real cutter, cool and corporate, easy in his movements, watchful and wary without showing more than he had to.

Shank stepped out of the van, showing his iron. Rico followed, then moved out as far as the middle of the street. Osborne met him there. Thunder rumbled in the distance, and the air felt unusually warm and humid.

"Sticks?" Rico said.

Osborne handed him a synthleather wallet containing seven certified credsticks, which checked out on the reader on Rico's belt. Rico handed the wallet back, then keyed his headset.

The side door on the van slid open, giving Osborne a plain view of Surikov and Moffit. Piper was in the van with them. Rico hoped she had the sense to stay clear, stay under cover. She knew how meets like this worked, but he feared she wouldn't do what she should.

"My tech's in the other car," Osborne said.

Rico nodded.

Osborne waved, and a slag in a dark blue suit came forward. After Dok's diagnostic analyzer declared the tech's DNA and retina scanner safe, Rico nodded toward the van. The tech went over to scan Surikov. Rico kept his eyes on Osborne and the cutter, but neither looked suspicious or like they had anything more on their minds than the careful biz of "buying product," or "recruitment."

The clouds overhead seemed to be coming lower. A few curling tendrils of fog drifted along the street. No warnings from Thorvin or Bandit, though.

The tech returned from the van. Nodded.

Osborne motioned him back to the second limo, then looked at Rico and said, "Anytime you're ready."

"You're satisfied the product's real."

"As real as it gets."

Rico keyed his headset. As Surikov and Moffit came walking out to the middle of the street, Osborne handed over the credsticks. "Thank you," Moffit said, looking at Rico.

She even made it sound sincere.

Rico backed away, then turned quickly and climbed into the van. Shank followed and slammed the side door. The van rumbled and rolled ahead, accelerating quickly.

Surikov and Moffit and the pair of white limos disappeared into the gathering fog.

Then, the van rounded a corner, and Bandit said, "Trouble."

There was no distinguishing fog from clouds. The van slid into a sea of whirling, billowing white. Thorvin shouted curses.

Abruptly, something came straight at them. Rico had just enough time to see it was a helo flying right on the deck, barely two meters above the pavement. It seemed almost near enough to touch. The only detail he noticed was the black annis logo on the forward slope of the helo's nose.

Something exploded. Maybe a rocket. Rico saw fire. The world roared and crashed and tumbled and when it finally came to a halt, he could barely see anything for all the smoke. Blood was running into his mouth, he felt a tightness in his left side, and if he breathed too deeply it hurt like hell. The van seemed to be lying on its roof, windows cracked and smashed. Rico struggled to stand, but something hanging above him kept getting in his way, and then he realized Piper was right beside him, gasping, grunting with pain, suddenly coughing.

He found her shoulders. Her grunts rose into shrill cries as he pulled her up. Smoke filled his eyes. It was turning from gray to black. Where the hell was the door? any door . . .

Something crashed. Shank shouted. They stumbled out onto the street. Smoke mixed with fog. Burning debris littered the roadway for as far around as Rico could see.

The shooting started, a full company's worth of weapons blasting away on autofire.

"WHERE'S THORVIN?" Shank hollered.

The ground roared at their backs with the fury of another explosion. The shock wave all but knocked Rico off his feet. Rico staggered and caught himself, but Piper stumbled and fell to her knees. Rico tugged her back up, but she wouldn't stand, wouldn't stay on her feet. That was when he saw the bloody mass of hair at the side of her head and the dark stains on the back of her jacket.

"She's FINISHED!" Shank bellowed.

Shank yanked Rico forward, and Piper slipped out of his hands, falling like a sack, a sack of meat. Rico tried to stop, but Shank kept pulling him and then half a dozen rounds slammed into his shoulders and back and he nearly passed out.

This was it, he realized. The end. There was no cover anywhere. It seemed like a thousand machine guns were stammering from all around. He tried to pull the Predator 2 from the holster on his hip, but he couldn't get a firm enough grip to tug the weapon free.

He stumbled over chunks of debris, piles of trash, with Shank shoving him forward and shouting, "Keep MOV-ING!"

When finally Rico stopped and looked around, he stood in an alley and Shank wasn't around. The alleyway was deserted. He staggered forward a few steps, then turned and started back. All he could think of was leaving Piper sprawled like a bag of meat on some street in no-man's land without anyone to mourn her passing.

What the frag . . .

What the frag was wrong with him?

His legs gave out. He hit the ground hard. He felt so tired, so weak. He couldn't keep his eyes open. He laid his head against the cool, gritty concrete and exhaled deeply.

Fade to black.

39

Minx hesitated and looked away, a faint smile curving the corner of her lips. When she did that, Monk now knew, she was listening to radio calls or maybe getting a telecom call over her implanted headware. She had once been a sort of messenger. Now, she mostly took calls from friends.

The *change* didn't affect that, the implants. After the *change* you couldn't get stuff like that put in, for various reasons that Minx hadn't yet explained, but anything you had before the *change* went on working just like before.

Which was good, Monk thought.

Now, Minx looked at him and smiled.

"It's time," she said.

"Uh-huh."

They ran—ran and ran—down stairs, down a long tunnel, more stairs, through a door, then onto the elevated walkway beside the lanes of a transitway. They had to run because they had what Minx called "only a small window of opportunity." That meant they had to be fast. They had to be "on time."

The red-hued darkness didn't slow them down. Monk could see just fine. Better than in full daylight, in fact.

A huge stepvan with flaring strobes and flashing lights came screaming around the corner of the transitway and screeched to a halt right in front of them. The passenger door banged open. Minx tugged on Monk's hand and they scrambled inside.

The truck roared and raced ahead. The slag at the wheel in the Omni Police Services uniform looked at them and grinned. His eyes glared a fiery red. He laughed. Minx covered her mouth and swayed with silent laughter. Monk couldn't resist a grin, though he wasn't exactly sure just what he was grinning about.

Minx had this sort of private joke between her and her friends that wasn't entirely clear. Monk guessed it had something to do with what they were, or what they had become, or the *change*, or something, but he hadn't quite figured it out.

Minx didn't seem to mind.

"You're so booty," she told him. "You'll scan it. Just give it time."

The stepvan roared out onto some ground-level street, and everything got hazy and foggy. The haze and denser patches of fog all looked kind of reddish. Everything did.

Abruptly, they came to a halt in what looked like the middle of a war zone. Police cruisers everywhere, flashing strobes, slags in uniforms, slags with guns. Minx grabbed Monk's hand and pulled him from the stepvan. There was a body on the pavement just a few meters away. The body of an Asian woman.

Minx smiled and nodded, urging him with her eyes, her whole expression, to go ahead.

Monk knelt down. The Asian woman might have looked dead, just at a glance, 'cause there was a lot of blood, but she wasn't really dead, not quite yet. The subtle radiance of the living lingered about her body. It was hard to see, and Monk had only just recently begun to notice this kind of thing, but now that he knew what to look for, now that Minx had pointed it out, he could see it and see it clearly, as long as he took a moment to look.

He leaned down and put his mouth over the woman's mouth, then slowly inhaled. He kept inhaling till he felt a tingling suffuse his whole body. With that tingling came a pleasure even better than sex, at least in his limited experience. It was more than just physical pleasure. It made him feel full, strong, powerful, almost indomitable. If he let his imagination run wild, a danger Minx had warned him about, he could almost see himself possessing such great power that almost anything . . .

Minx squeezed his shoulder, and bent to kiss him. They exchanged breaths, exhaling into each other's mouths, then inhaling that sweet, sweet breath.

"Now it's my turn," she said softly, smiling.

Monk nodded. "Sure."

There were other bodies waiting.

* * *

They were at Chimpira when the call came in L. Kahn
took it via the telecom at his booth. Ravage, sitting beside
him, heard the entire exchange. An informant reported
that the runners who had been hired to bust Ansell
Surikov out of Maas Intertech had just been ambushed up
in Sector 9. Police were at the scene, but the informant
believed the runners to be dead.

L. Kahn broke the connection, sat still for a moment,
then softly cursed. "I hired backup in depth and what
happens? Daisaka Security gets them with a gunship.
There's no justice. No justice at all."

Ravage agreed, and reached over and picked up L. Kahn's
drink, drew it to her mouth and had a sip. L. Kahn frowned
and looked at her. It was his unhappy frown. Intolerant.

"I've had enough problems lately," he said. "Don't test
my patience."

"I get these impulses," Ravage replied.

"You'll have to learn—"

If he had more to say, he didn't get it out. Ravage
splashed the drink into his face. As he began reacting to
that, she slashed her hand across his throat. The razors
protruding from under her synthimplanted nails tore
through flesh like a knife through air. No significant resistance.

As the first blood came pumping, pulsing, spraying out
through the wounds, she reversed direction, making a fist
and slamming it back into L. Kahn's face, shattering bone
and gristle and driving his head against the back of the
booth. The man bled, banged backward, and slumped in
little more than an instant.

Then Ravage hopped up and away, before any of the
blood and gore could stain her clinging silver-hued bodysuit.

The pair of orks L. Kahn had hired as extra guards
turned to look, then just looked at her and waited. These
particular orks had no illusions about their place in the
Newark underworld. They understood that when orders
came from above, the good soldier simply nodded and
obeyed. In this case, they had accepted nuyen from her,
from her new employer, before nodding and pledging
obedience. With a quick gesture she indicated that they
should take charge of the body.

"Toss it in the Ditch."

Sanitation would cart it away.

On her way out of the club, Ravage stopped at a telecom and dialed the number her new boss had given her. The boss' helper answered, a dark-skinned elf. He looked a question at her.

"It's done," she told him.

"Muy bien," the elf replied.

That finished her biz for the night.

The sunlight seeping through the dark, grime-smeared window swelled and faded away. Days were passing, but Rico hardly noticed. He lay on a bare mattress on the floor of a squalid room in an abandoned building. He had a bottle by his side and some food. He had bandages wrapped around his chest and covering more cuts and gouges than he had interest in counting. Some fleeting instinct for survival had compelled him to find a street doc and go to the safest refuge he knew.

When he finally woke up in that alley, he'd gone back for Piper, but by then the streets were deserted, the bodies gone. Even the wreck of the van had been removed. It took the heart out of him. Maybe it had cost him his soul.

Little things came to mind now, how Piper used to smile or laugh, the way she cast her eyes down when something embarrassed her. For all the razor-edged skill she'd had as a decker, she had been and would always be in his memory a reticent Japanese, a soft-spoken, loving, and loyal woman, more beautiful than any he had ever known. It occurred to him that this crumbling building wasn't far from where they had first met. This very apartment was where they had first made love. The place hadn't been such a wreck those few years ago. It had been tired and worn, but safe. Quiet.

How many months had they lived here? He couldn't remember. He'd been surprised to find the building still standing.

It was all he had left. He hadn't been smart enough to save anyone. He'd let them be used by the megacorps. Sure, they got Farrah Moffit together with the real Surikov and had turned the pair over to Maas Intertech, but so what?

What did it matter now?

In the night he smashed the bottle and brought the jagged end to his neck, and held it there a couple of minutes. He felt the jagged knife-edge of glass grazing his skin, but he knew that this was futile. He didn't have the strength to do it. He didn't care enough to end it. He lowered his arm and let the broken bottle roll away. It was over. He was already dead. He would just lie here till the final fragments faded into the night.

Hours passed. He became aware of some soft sounds, faraway creaks and squeaks. He thought of rats and devil rats and the other creatures that inhabited the darker corners of the plex, and then the door to the room slowly swung inward.

A pair of dark figures appeared in the doorway, silhouetted by the deeper black of the hall. One looked small and seemed curved like a female. The other one had the heavy build of a big male, big enough even for an ork.

"I knew I would find you here."

What the frag . . . The voice was Piper's. Slowly, Rico sat up, shifting his Jikku eyes to low-light to better scan the doorway. To his astonishment, he saw Piper standing there, and Shank. They looked battered and bloody, but they were standing there alive. Rico struggled to speak. He couldn't manage anything coherent. He couldn't believe what he was seeing.

"One short sleep past and we recycle endlessly, *jefe*," Piper said softly. "And I'm going to prove it to you, my love, but first you must let me kiss you."

She shifted closer, smiling warmly.

Her eyes glowed a fiery red.

40

The chopper settled lightly onto the aeropad atop Fuchi Tower Five. By then, Gordon Ito was up, out of his seat and waiting at the front of the passenger compartment. His deputy director, executive aid, and exec sec all scurried to shut down notebook comps and close briefcases. His personal bodyguard simply rose and moved to stand beside him.

The moment the hatch was open, the steps lowered, Gordon strode down to the aeropad and across to the rooftop lounge. He moved briskly, but did not rush. He had something he wanted to attend to immediately, but that did not call for haste. Nothing could, in Gordon's view. Haste made waste, and in his position, hasty decisions and actions most often promised to result in disaster.

The elevator delivered him twenty stories down to his office suite. Moments later, he stepped into his private office. The tea lady delivered tea. Gordon lit a Platinum Select cigarette, then took up his tea and spent three minutes staring out the wall of windows behind his desk, considering how to proceed.

The decision made, he returned to his desk and brought up the telecom. In another moment the Fuchi logo, veiled by a black triangle, filled the screen. "Mr. Ito."

"Mr. Xiao."

"*Konichiwa.*"

"*Konichiwa.*"

"What brings you to my screen this evening, Gordon?"

"I've just had some intelligence handed to me. I thought you might find it interesting. I'm told that Ansell Surikov and Marena Farris have been recruited by Maas Intertech."

"Yes, I'm aware of that, Gordon."

"Were you planning to do anything about it?"

"I think not."

Gordon forced himself to pause a moment. Xiao's reaction was too complacent even for a man who demonstrated practically no emotion. Something had to be up. "You took the lead on this. You specifically ordered me to lay off Farris and Surikov. Now they're both with Intertech. That's going to improve Kuze Nihon's position in at least one or two key technological areas. And you don't want to do anything about it?"

"It is not necessary, Gordon."

"I'll remind you that Surikov is a leading light in biotechnical research."

"Maas Intertech does not have Surikov."

Gordon sat back in his chair, took a drag on his cigarette, and considered. His intelligence couldn't be wrong; it came straight from the source. That meant Xiao had to be wrong, or lying—or did it? "Then who do they have?"

"They are back to square one, Gordon."

Gordon hesitated an instant, then said, "You sonovabitch."

"Yes," Xiao replied. "I fear I've done it to them again."

Xiao had set them up—Maas Intertech, everyone. Gordon included. "How did you do it? Obviously, you fabricated another impostor. But you didn't do it the way I did it. You'd never use someone else's trick."

Two moments of silence, then the display screen blanked, the connection broken.

Bastard.

Epilogue

Raccoon was clever.

His paws were cunning hands. He could break open any trap and escape any danger, whether in forest or city, mountain or subterranean tunnel. But that did not make him perfect, not hardly. Or untouchable. Or fearless. Or certain of his own motives. Not as far as Bandit could see.

He had managed to avoid injury when the van turned over. He had managed to avoid being shot by any of the dozens of guns which had raked the street with bullets. He hadn't, however, quite managed to avoid being singed by the fiery explosion that had turned the van into a smoky inferno. Neither had he wasted any time removing himself from that fog-laden street of death.

His ways were Raccoon's ways, and Raccoon did not fight when so obviously outnumbered. It did not seem sensible to Bandit that anyone in such a situation would stand and fight, or do anything except run.

Or was he kidding himself?

It was not often that such troubling thoughts followed him to his medicine lodge. This was his private place, his alone place. Here, in this tenement basement, he had gathered the trinkets and fetishes and ritual materials of the ways of magic. Here, in this dark little room, he had survived the ordeal that had given him his first true taste of the deeper truths of metamagic. The problems of the outside world, the mundane world, seemed strange and alien in this place, as if they did not belong.

Now, he looked down at the flute lying in his lap, then lifted it to his mouth and slowly, quietly, began to play. He didn't worry about playing any particular song or certain special notes. He let the music flow from within. He let something other than his rational mind decide how the song should sound.

In a while, be became aware that he was no longer alone. The Old Man had come again.

Bandit turned to find him sitting cross-legged right behind him. The Old Man looked vaguely Asian, but his thin gray hair flowed down over his shoulders and everything he wore appeared made of natural leather, brown leather, tan, like native people used to wear long before the Awakening, with necklaces and beads and bones. Bandit turned to sit facing him. They watched each other for a long time.

Was this Raccoon in some human guise or merely a spirit that had chosen to serve as his guide? Bandit wondered. The Old Man's voice was as dry as sand and as creaky as old wooden boards. Yet there was a power, vibrant and strong, beneath the scratchy, sometimes wavering old voice.

"So," the Old Man said. "What do you want? You called me. You must want something."

"I don't know," Bandit said, frowning. "I'm troubled."

The Old Man shrugged very slightly. "I have no answers. I'm just an old man."

"You're wise."

"Sure, that's what you think, I'm old and wise. I must have all the answers." The Old Man nodded, faintly. "Maybe you're wrong. If I ever had any answers, I probably forgot them. A long time ago. Before you were even born."

"There must be something you can tell me."

Another silence passed, then the Old Man said, "I could tell you a lot of things. Old people can talk for hours. A long time ago I heard two people talking. I think they came from across a great ocean. One kept asking questions and the other one kept trying to answer. How many fish are there in the pond? one asked. The other one didn't know. He tried to guess. What he didn't seem to understand was that there was no answer. Maybe there aren't any answers at all, except the ones you find for yourself."

"What about truth?"

The Old Man shrugged again. "Truth is one of those things. Everyone sees it their own way. You're a shaman.

You should know that better than anyone. Ask twenty magicians the truth about magic. How many answers do you get?"

"At least twenty."

"I could tell you a lot of things, if I could remember, but what would it mean? What things mean to you is what counts. What are your answers? What do they say about you? Where do they lead you? What kind of shaman does that make you? Things like that. How do you like my answer so far?"

"I'm not sure."

"That's probably good. I'm an old man. I've had time to work things out. You're still pretty young. You should have questions. Things you're not sure about. I've made my peace with mother planet. You haven't. Maybe you haven't even started yet."

"I don't know what you mean."

The Old Man frowned. "Maybe you've been spending too much time in the city. I guess you haven't paid much attention. That's understandable. It can be hard to think in the city. What I mean is the planet's our mother. It's simple enough. You understand. You just haven't thought about it much. Everything comes from the Earth. Without her we're just so many unlikely ideas floating around in empty space. Without the Earth, we're all dead."

"Maybe I should attune myself with the Earth. With nature."

"You tell me. You're a shaman. You've attuned yourself with spell foci so you could do better magic. What about nature? What about the Earth?"

"How do I do this?"

"You're a shaman. You tell me."

"Maybe I should go to the wilderness."

"If you think so. The wilderness is part of the Earth. I don't think anybody can argue that." The Old Man paused, then said, "Maybe I'm not being clear. All I'm saying is that maybe you know the city so well that you've forgotten something. Something important."

Bandit considered. "The city is part of nature, too."

"I don't think anybody can argue that."

"Is that what you meant to tell me?"

"I guess that's part of it."

"What am I missing?"

"What good would it do to tell you what I think? I could be wrong. If I said the wrong thing, or if you took it wrong, you might waste a lot of time chasing after bad ideas. Why should I have that on my conscience? You're the one asking all the questions. You think you're missing something. What do you think you're missing?"

"It could be anything."

"You're right. If that's what you think. Maybe that's your answer. Me, I'm thinking of something specific. I'll give you a hint. You decide if it means anything."

"Okay."

"What's in the city?"

"People."

"What about them?"

Bandit frowned and exhaled heavily, and looked at his flute. The flute gave him his answer. It forced him to see it. "People are part of nature, too."

"I don't think anybody can argue that."

"Maybe I've been around so many people for so long I forgot about that. There's a lot of people in the city. It's easy to tune them out. Maybe I wanted to tune them out. Maybe I had to tune them out to concentrate on the magic. To learn. To grow."

"Maybe that's your answer."

"Maybe I should tune people in."

"It's an idea," the Old Man agreed. "The one thing I'm sure about is that people are part of the world just like every other living thing. I don't see how you can be in tune with nature without being in tune with people too. It's okay to go to the wilderness. Go wherever you want. Nature is everywhere. It infuses everything, surrounds everything. Just don't forget about people. You know what I mean. It's obvious."

Bandit nodded.

"If you want to know nature, you have to experience nature, not just the parts of the world you like. You have to hear the cry of the hawk as it dives down to kill a mouse. You have to hear the roar of the tigress when one of her cubs comes up missing. You have to listen to the murmuring of the mountain stream, the hiss of the snake, the death-cry of the prairie dog, the croaking of the frog, the rustle of leaves, the whisper of the wind. You have to hear the voice of the Earth, no matter what form it takes.

Maybe every form it takes. And I guess you have to listen to people, too. They're part of the Earth."

Bandit nodded. "You're right."

"I'm an old man. I just listen to things you say and tell you my opinion, I could be all wrong. What you think is what matters."

"I think I must attune myself to people."

"Then that's your answer."

An answer, yes, but not the whole answer. Bandit thought about that a while, then said, "I wish I could have done more. I wish ... I wish I could have helped my friends."

"Your friends the runners."

Bandit nodded.

"Sometimes you don't know you've got friends till they're gone."

"I'm not sure what's happened to them."

A long silence passed, then the Old Man said, "Sometimes people get a bad hand. Sometimes the odds are too great. You did what you could. When the time came, you saved yourself. Probably that's all you could have done. Maybe that's all you should have done. The shaman's path can be hard to know. I guess you still have things to learn."

Bandit nodded.

"Maybe you just have to put this behind you."

"I feel ... regret. Maybe remorse."

The Old Man stretched out his arms and yawned. "Then you must be human. Every human being wishes that he or she could have done some things differently. It's like a law. Part of nature. Part of what you are. You try to learn from your mistakes. If you're smart, you'll do better next time."

Bandit nodded.

"I need some sleep."

"Will we talk again?"

"Sure. Just play that flute. I think you've been looking for it a long time. Maybe you didn't realize. Just play the song and I'll come. You know which song."

Bandit thought about that, then nodded.

"Just remember I sleep a lot. Old men get cranky when they miss their sleep. You understand."

"I guess."

"Remember this, too. The world wasn't built in a day. It took a long time to get this far and it still isn't finished. It never will be finished. When something's finished, it's dead. But even then, it isn't finished. Nothing ever really is. Sometimes it just looks that way."

"Life is a journey. Not a series of destinations."

"There's your answer. See you later."

Bandit hesitated, gazing into the empty darkness at the rear of his lodge. Then he spoke softly, gently, saying, "Sleep well."

"What is it about you that makes me feel as I do?" Inca demanded.

Roan smiled at the spark of challenge in her eyes. "What do you mean? Do I make you feel bad? Uncomfortable?"

"No...I *like* being close to you."

He saw her eyes fill with confusion for a moment over her admission. He knew Inca was a virgin and, more than ever, he realized just how innocent she was.

"You make me feel safe in my world," she continued. "And in my world there is no safety. How can that be?"

Roan's heart soared. She trusted him. He needed—wanted—that trust. Just as much as he wanted her....

LINDSAY McKENNA

MORGAN'S MERCENARIES
HEART of the WARRIOR

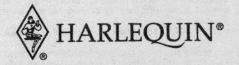

HARLEQUIN®

TORONTO • NEW YORK • LONDON
AMSTERDAM • PARIS • SYDNEY • HAMBURG
STOCKHOLM • ATHENS • TOKYO • MILAN • MADRID
PRAGUE • WARSAW • BUDAPEST • AUCKLAND

ISBN 0-373-47058-4

MORGAN'S MERCENARIES: HEART OF THE WARRIOR

www.eHarlequin.com

Printed in U.S.A.

A homeopathic educator, **Lindsay McKenna** teaches at the Desert Institute of Classical Homeopathy in Phoenix, Arizona. When she isn't teaching alternative medicine, she is writing books about love. She feels love is the single greatest healer in the world and hopes that her books touch her readers on those levels. Coming from an Eastern Cherokee medicine family, Lindsay has taught ceremony and healing ways from the time she was nine years old. She creates flower and gem essences in accordance with nature and remains closely in touch with her Native American roots and upbringing.

To Karen David, a real, live warrioress and
healer. And a good role model for the rest of us!

Chapter 1

"No...!"

Roan Storm Walker's cry reverberated around the small, dark log cabin. Outside, the rain dripped monotonously off the steep, rusty tin roof. Breathing harshly, Roan pressed his hands to his face, dug his fingers frantically into his skull as he felt his heart pounding relentlessly in his chest. His flesh was beaded with sweat. Lips tightly compressed to halt another scream, another cry of grief and loss, he groaned instead, like a wounded cougar.

Lifting his head, Roan turned the dampened pillow over and dropped back down onto the small, creaking bed. He had to sleep. *Great Spirit, let me sleep.* Shutting his eyes tightly, his black lashes thick and spiky against his copper-colored skin, he released a ragged sigh.

Sarah...how he missed her. Brave, confident, foolhardy Sarah. It had been two years and he still missed her. How badly he wanted to touch her firm, warm shoulder or to smell that jasmine scent that always lingered tantalizingly in the strands of her short red hair. Gone...everything was gone. Swept from his life like litter before some invisible broom. Sarah, his wife, was dead, and his heart had died, too, on that fateful day. Even now, as he lay listening to the rain splattering against the roof of his cabin high in the Montana Rockies, he felt the force of his aching grief. The waves of agony moved through him like waves crashing in from the ocean and spilling their foamy, bubbling essence on the hard, golden sand.

Unconsciously, he rubbed his fingers across the blue stone hanging around his neck—his medicine piece. He'd worn the amulet continually since his mother, a Lakota medicine woman, gave it to him—before her death many years ago. Composed of two cougar claws representing the cougar spirit that was his protector, and two small golden eagle feathers, it hung from a thick, black, sweat-stained leather thong around his neck. The center of the medicine piece was an opalescent blue stone, roughly fashioned in a trapezoid shape. The bezel around the stone was of beaten brass that had long ago turned dark with age. No one knew what the stone was, or where it came from. He'd never seen another one like it in all his travels. His mother had told him it came from their ancestors, passed on to the medicine person in each succeeding generation of the family. He always touched this piece when he was feeling bad. In a way, it was like sending a prayer to his mother and her line of ancestors for help with the heavy emotions he wrestled with. Roan never took off his medicine piece; it was as much a part of him as his heart beating in his chest.

He closed his eyes once more. He was good at forcing

himself to go back to sleep. His mother, a Lakota Yuwipi medicine woman, had taught him how to lucid dream. He could walk out of one harsh reality into the more amorphous world beyond the veil of normal human reach. More than likely he was able to do this because he had the genes of that long line of medicine people coursing richly through his bloodstream. His father was an Anglo, a white man—a physics teacher. Between both parents, Roan found it easy to surrender over to a power higher than himself, give himself back to the night owl's wings of sleep, which almost instantly embraced him again.

As he moved from the pain of the past, which continued to dog his heels like a relentless hound on the scent of the cougar spirit that protected him, his grief began to recede. In lucid dream and sleep, he could escape the sadness that was etched in his heart. This time, as he slipped into sleep, Walker heard the distant growl of thunder. Yes, a Wakan Wakinyan, a mighty thunder being who created the storms that roved across the Rockies, was now stalking his humble cabin hidden deep in the thick Douglas firs on a Montana slope.

A slight, one-cornered smile curved Roan's mouth as he felt his mood lightening, like a feather caught in a breeze and being wafted gently into the invisible realm of the Great Spirit. Yes, in dreaming there was safety. In dreaming there was relief from the pain of living in human form. Roan expected to see Sarah again, as he always did whenever this shift in his consciousness occurred. The Lakota called the state dreaming "beneath the wings of the owl," referring to the bird they considered the eagle of the night. Within the wings of this night protector, the world of dreams unfolded to those who knew how to access this realm. Reaching this altered state had been taught to Roan at a very young age and he had found it an incredible gift, a means of healing himself, really, over the last twenty-eight years of his life.

Sarah? He looked for his red-haired Sarah, those flashing Celtic blue eyes of hers, and that twisted Irish grin across her full, soft lips. Where was she? Always, she would meet him while in the embrace of the owl. Full of anticipation, he spied a glowing light coming out of the darkness toward him. Yes, it had to be Sarah. As he waited impatiently within the darkness, the golden, sunny light grew ever closer, larger, pulsating with brilliant life of its own.

His cougar spirit's senses told him this wasn't Sarah. Then who? Even as he felt his disappointment, something strange happened. His cougar, a female spirit guardian with huge, sun-gold eyes, appeared out of the darkness to stand in front of him. He could see that her attention was focused fully on the throbbing, vital orb of light drawing closer. Walker felt no fear, simply curiosity, despite the fact that it was unlike Anna, his cougar spirit guide, to appear like this unless there was danger to him. Yet he felt no danger.

The mists surrounding the oblong light reminded him of thickly moving mist on a foggy morning at the lake below his cabin, where he often fished for a breakfast trout. Anna gave a low growl. Roan's heart rate picked up. The golden oval of light halted no more than six feet away from him. Slowly, it began to congeal into a body, two very long legs, slender arms, a head and...

Walker felt his heart thundering in his chest. His cougar guardian was on full alert now, her tail stiff, the hackles on her neck ruffled and the fur raised all the way down her lean, supple spine. Roan was mesmerized as he watched the person—a woman?—appear. What the hell? He wasn't sure what or who he was looking at.

Huge, willow-green eyes with large black pupils stared fiercely back at him.

Swallowing hard, Walker felt every cell in his body respond to this unknown woman who now stood before him. Although the golden light had faded to a degree, so he could see her clearly, it still shone around her form like rays of brilliant sunlight. She warily watched him as the tension built and silence strung tautly between them.

This was no ordinary human being. Walker sensed her incredible power. Few humans he'd ever known had an aura of energy like hers. It was so brilliant that he felt like squinting or raising his hand to shield his eyes from the glow. Her eyes drew him. They were magnetic, commanding, fierce, vulnerable and magical all at the same time.

He tried to shift his consciousness; it was impossible. She held him fully within her powerful presence. She was tall, at least six feet. Her skin was a golden color. What she wore confounded him. She was dressed in army camouflage fatigues and black, shiny military jump boots. On her proud torso she wore an olive-green, sleeveless T-shirt crisscrossed with two bandoliers containing bullets. Slung across her left shoulder was a rifle. Around her slender waist was a web belt with a black leather holster and pistol, several grenades and a wicked looking K-bar knife. Down her back, resting between her shoulder blades, hung a huge leather sheath, knicked and scarred, that held a machete with a pearl handle. She was obviously a warrior. An Amazon. A soldier used to fighting.

Roan could see and sense all these things about her. Despite her dynamic presence, the threat she presented in the armament she wore, the way her hand curled around the thick leather strap that bit into her shoulder as it held the rifle in place, she was beautiful. Roan could not tear his gaze from her full, square face, those high, proud cheekbones. From her narrowing, willow-green eyes, that fine thin nose that flared like the nostrils of a wary wild horse, or those compressed, full lips.

Her hair was thick and black and hung in one long braid over her right shoulder and down between her breasts, which were hidden by the bandoliers of ammunition. There was such pride and absolute confidence in her stance, in the way her shoulders were thrown back. As she lifted her chin imperiously, Roan wanted to simply absorb the sight of her and the feeling of that incredible energy swirling around her. He wondered if she was a figment of his imagination, a hybrid between Sarah and some kind of superhuman woman.

The instant he thought that, her eyes snapped with rage and utter indignation.

"Do not waste precious energy and time on such speculations!" she growled at him. "You were born into a medicine family. You know better!" She jabbed a finger at the amulet he wore around his neck. "You carry the stone of the Jaguar Clan. You are one of us! I am Inca. I am asking for your help, Roan Storm Walker. Well, will you give it? I do not beg. This will be the only time I stand before you. Answer me quickly, for many will die without you here by my side to fight the fight of your life and mine. I am in a death spiral dance. I invite you into it.''

Walker felt her outrage at the very thought that he might say no to her request. *Inca.* A mysterious name. The name of a woman from…where? Perhaps from the Inca empire in Peru? Her accent was thick, reminding him of Spanish. He touched the blue stone that lay at the base of his throat. It felt hot, and throbbing sensations moved through his fingertips. The amulet he wore was powerful; his mother had told him so, and Roan had often experienced strange phenomena regarding it. But he'd never before felt the level of energy that was emanating from it now. He glanced down and saw a strange turquoise-white-and-gold light pulsating around it, like a beacon.

''Where do you come from, Inca?'' he demanded in an equally fierce voice. He was not afraid of her, but he respected her power. Where he came from, women were equal to any man.

''I come from the south, Storm Walker. The stone you wear around your neck tells me of your heritage. The spirits of your ancestors led me to you. You are needed in my country. Time is short. Many lives are at stake. My guardian says you are the one.'' The woman's green gaze grew demanding. ''Are you? the *one?*''

''I don't know. How can I help you?''

''You will know that when you see me the second time.''

He searched her shadowed features. She had the face of an Indian, all right—most probably of Incan heritage if she was from the south. Her stance was uncompromising. This woman feared nothing and no one. So why was she approaching him? He looked around, feeling another, invisible presence near her.

"Your guardian?" he asked.

A sour smile twisted her mouth and she gazed down at his gold cougar, which stood guard. "Watch," she commanded. "I run out of patience with you."

In moments the golden light enveloped Inca once more. Roan watched with fascination as the woman disappeared within spiraling bands that moved like a slow-motion tornado around her. But what walked out of the light moments later made him gasp. It was a huge stocky, black-and-gold male jaguar.

Roan vaguely heard Anna growl. In response the male jaguar hissed and showed his long, curved fangs. His golden eyes were huge, with large, shining black pupils. As the animal stalked around them, his tail whipping impatiently from side to side, his thick body strong and sensuous as he moved, Walker watched in awe. Anna remained on alert at his side, but did not attack the slowly circling jaguar.

The coat on the cat was a bright gold color, patterned with black crescent moons. To Roan, the massive jaguar seemed formidable, invulnerable. His mind churned with more questions than answers. A woman who turned into a male jaguar? She was a shape-shifter—a medicine person from South America who had the power to change shape from human to animal, and then back into human form at will. That in itself was a feat that few could manage successfully. He recalled that his mother, who worked with the Yaqui Indians of Mexico, had possessed shape-shifting abilities herself. One never knew, seeing a bird, a reptile or a four-footed, if it was in fact human or not.

Walker had been taught never to kill anything that approached him in such a bold, fearless manner.

As he watched the male jaguar make one complete circle, Roan was wildly aware of the throbbing power around the animal...around this mysterious woman called Inca. As he stared, he felt an intense, searing telepathic message being impressed upon him, body and soul.

I cannot control the tides of the ocean. I cannot change the course of the winds. I cannot control what is free and yearns to roam. I can only bend and surrender to a higher power through my heart, which rules me. I bend to the will of the Great Goddess, and to the Jaguar Clan. I ask you to willingly, with pure heart and single-minded purpose, to work with me. My people need your help. I ask in their name...

To Walker's surprise, he felt hot, scalding tears stinging his eyes. The impassioned plea made him blink rapidly. Tears! Of all things! He hadn't cried since...since Sarah had died so unexpectedly and tragically. Trying to halt the tumult of feelings radiating through his chest and around his heart, he watched the jaguar through blurred vision. What the hell was going on? This was no lucid dream. This was some kind of phenomenal, otherworldly meeting of the highest, purest kind. He'd heard his mother speak in hushed tones of those times when the gods and goddesses of her people would come to her in her dreams. She had often described rare meetings just like the one he was having now.

Was Inca really a human being? A shape-shifting medicine woman? A shaman who lived in South America? What was the Jaguar Clan? All questions and no answers. The stone at his throat seemed like it was burning a hole in his flesh. He felt it with his fingertips; it was scalding hot. This was the first time it had ever activated to this extent. His mother had said that the stone possessed powers beyond anyone's imagination, and that at the right time, he would be introduced to them. Rubbing his throat region, he understood this was no ordinary meeting. This had something to do with the stone's origin and purpose.

The jaguar stopped. He stared up at Roan with those huge eyes that were now thin crescents of gold on a field of black.

Walker felt the inquiry of the massive jaguar. His heart was beating hard in his chest, adrenaline pumping violently through him. Fight or flight? Run or stay and face combat? She was a warrior for something. What? Who? *Who does she represent? The light or the dark?* Walker knew she wasn't of the darkness. No. Everything within him shouted that she was of the light, working on the side of goodness. Yet she was a combat soldier. A modern-day Amazon.

Roan felt his cougar rub against his thigh, and he draped his fingers across the female animal's skull. She was purring and watching the jaguar with interest. Looking down, Roan saw Anna was once again relaxed, no longer on guard or in her protective stance. *That* was his answer.

Lifting his head, Walker looked over at the male jaguar. "Yes, I'll come. I'll be there for your people."

Within seconds, the jaguar disappeared into the cloud of brilliant, swirling light. And in the blink of an eye, the light was also gone. *She* was gone. Inca...

The drip, drip, drip of the rain off the tin roof slowly eased Walker out of his altered state. This time, as he

opened his eyes, the grayness of dawn through the thick
fir trees caught his attention. Twisting his head to one
side, he looked groggily at the clock on the bedstand:
0600. It was time to get up, make a quick breakfast, drive
down the mountain to Philipsburg, fifty miles away, and
meet with his boss, Morgan Trayhern, leader of the super
secret government group known as Perseus. A messenger
had been sent up the mountain two days ago to tell him
to be at the Perseus office in the small mining town at
0900 for a meeting with him and Major Mike Houston.

As Roan swung his naked body upward and tossed off
the sheet, his feet hitting the cool pine floor, he sighed.
Hands curling around the edges of the mattress, he sat
there in the grayish light of dawn and wondered who the
hell Inca was. This lucid dream was no dream at all, he
was sure. He'd never had an experience like this before.
The stone against his upper chest still burned and
throbbed. Rubbing the area, he slowly rose to his full six
foot six inches of height, then padded effortlessly toward
the couch, where a pair of clean jeans, a long-sleeved
white Western-style shirt, socks and underwear were
draped. *First, make the coffee, then get dressed.* He piv-
oted to the right and made his way to the small, dimly lit
kitchen. Without coffee, no day ever went right for him.
He grinned a little at that thought, although his mind, and
his heart, were centered on Inca. Who was she? What had
he agreed to? First, he had to see what Morgan Trayhern
and Major Mike Houston had up their sleeves. Roan knew
Houston had worked down in South America for a decade,
and he might be the right person to share this experience
with. Maybe…

* * *

"What the hell are we supposed to do?" Morgan Trayhern growled at Mike Houston from his place behind the huge dark maple desk in his office.

Army Special Forces Major Mike Houston turned slowly away from the window where he stood and faced his boss. "Inca *must* lead that Brazilian contingent into the Amazon basin or Colonel Jaime Marcellino and company will be destroyed by the drug lords. Without her, they're dead," he said flatly. Then his eyes snapped with humor. "They just don't know it yet, that's all."

Rubbing his square jaw, Morgan dropped the opened file labeled Inca on his desk. "Damn...she's a lone wolf."

"More like a lone jaguar."

"What?" Disgruntled, Morgan gave Mike a dark look.

"Jaguars," Mike said in a calm tone, "always hunt alone. The only time they get together is to mate, and after that, they split. The cubs are raised by the mother only."

Glaring down at the colored photo of a woman in a sleeveless, olive-green T-shirt, bandoliers across her shoulders, a rifle across her knees as she sat on a moss-covered log, Morgan shook his head. "You vaguely mention in your report that Inca's a member of the Jaguar Clan."

"Well," Mike hedged, "kind of..."

"What is that? A secret paramilitary organization down in Brazil?"

Mike maintained a dour look on his face. He unwound from his at-ease position and slowly crossed the room. "You could say that, but they don't work with governments, exactly. Not formally..." Mike wasn't about to get into the metaphysical attributes of the clan with Morgan.

He tiptoed around it with his boss because Mike felt Morgan would not believe him about the clan's mysterious abilities.

"But you're insisting that Inca work with the Brazilian government on this plan of ours to coordinate the capture of major drug lords in several South American countries."

"Morgan, the Amazon basin is a big place." Mike stabbed his finger at the file on the desk as he halted in front of his boss. "Inca was born near Manaus. She knows the Amazon like the back of her hand. The major drug activity is in the Juma and Yanomami Indian reservation around Manaus. You can't put army troops into something like this without experts who know the terrain intimately. Only one person, someone who's been waging a nonstop war against the drug lords in that area, knows it—Inca."

With a heavy shake of his head, Morgan muttered, "She's barely a child! She's only twenty-five years old!"

Mike smiled a little. "Inca is hardly a child. I've known her since she saved my life when she was eighteen years old."

"She's so young."

Mike nodded, the smile on his mouth dissolving. "Listen to me. In a few minutes you've got to go into that war room with emissaries from those South American countries that are capable of raising coca to produce cocaine, and sell them on this idea. Inca has a reputation—not a good one, I'll grant you—but she gets the job done. It ain't pretty, Morgan. She's a Green Warrior. That's slang for a tree hugger or environmentalist. Down there in Brazil, that carries a lot of weight with the Indian people. She's their protector. They worship her. They would go to hell and back for her if she asked it of them. If that

Brazilian army is going to make this mission a success they need the support of the locals. And if Inca is there, leading the troops, the Indians will fight and die at her side on behalf of the Brazilian government. Without her, they'll turn a deaf ear to the government's needs.''

"I read in your report that they call her the jaguar goddess.''

Raising one eyebrow, Houston said, "Those that love her call her that.''

"And her enemies?''

"A Green Warrior—'' Houston grimaced ''—or worse. I think you ought to prepare yourself for Colonel Marcellino's reaction to her. He won't have anything good to say when he hears we're going to pair him up with Inca.''

Studying Houston, Morgan slowly closed the file and stood up. "Mike, I'm counting on you to help carry the day in there. You're my South American expert. You've been fighting drug lords in all those countries, especially in Peru and Brazil. No one knows that turf better than you.''

"That's why Inca is so important to this operation,'' he said as he walked with Morgan toward an inner door that led to an elevator to the top secret, underground war room. "She knows the turf even better than I do.''

Morgan halted at the door. He rearranged the red silk tie at the throat of his white shirt. Buttoning up his pin-stripe suit, he sighed. "Did you ever find anyone in our merc database who could work—or would want to work—with the infamous Inca?''

Grinning a little, Houston said, "Yeah, I think I did. Roan Storm Walker. He's got Native American blood in him. Inca will respect him for that, at least.''

Morgan raised his brows. "Translated, that means she won't just outright flatten him like she does every other male who gets into her line of fire?"

Chuckling, Mike put his hand on Morgan's broad shoulder. The silver at the temples of his boss's black hair was getting more and more pronounced, making Mike realize that running Perseus, a worldwide mercenary operation, would put gray hairs on just about anyone. "She'll respect him."

"What does that mean? She'll ask questions first and shoot later?"

"You could say that, yes."

"Great," Morgan muttered. "And Walker's in the war room already?"

"Yes. I told him to stay in the shadows and keep a low profile. I don't want him agreeing to this mission you've laid out for him without him realizing he has to work directly with Colonel Marcellino. And—" Mike scowled, looking even more worried "—he needs to understand that the ongoing war between Marcellino and Inca will put him between a rock and a hard place."

Snorting, Morgan opened the door, heading for the elevator that would take them three stories down into the earth. "Sounds like I need a damned diplomat between the colonel and Inca, not a merc. Roan's always taken oddball assignments, though. Things I could never talk anyone else into taking—and he's always pulled them off."

"Good," Mike murmured, hope in his voice as he followed Morgan into the elevator, "because Walker is gonna need that kind of attitude to survive."

"Survive who?" Morgan demanded, "Marcellino or Inca?"

The doors whooshed closed. Mike wrapped his arms around his chest as his stomach tightened with tension. The elevator plummeted rapidly toward their destination. "Both," he said grimly. "There won't be any love lost between Marcellino and Inca, believe me. They're like a dog and cat embroiled in a fight to the death. Only this time it's a dog and a jaguar...."

elbows, his well-worn jean's and a pair of dusty, scarred cowboy boots, he knew he stuck out like a sore thumb in this assemblage, members of which were now scrutinizing him closely. Let them. Roan really couldn't care less. At twenty-eight he was already a widower, and the dark looks of some colonels and generals were nothing in comparison to what he'd already endured.

"Gentlemen, this is Roan Storm Walker," Morgan began. "He's an ex-Recon Marine. I've asked him to sit in on this important briefing because he will be working directly with the Brazilian detachment."

Roan noticed a tall, thin man in a dark green Brazilian Army uniform snap a cold, measuring look in his direction. The name card in front of him read Marcellino, Jaime, Colonel, Brazil. The man had hard, black, unforgiving eyes that reminded Roan of obsidian, an ebony rock, similar to glass in its chemical makeup, which was created out of the belching fire of a violent volcano. Instinctively Roan felt the controlled and contained violence around the Brazilian colonel. It showed in his thinned mouth and his long, angular features that hinted of an aristocratic heritage. Everything about the good colonel spoke of his formal training; he had that military rigidity and look of expectation that said his orders would be carried out to the letter once he gave them.

Maybe it was the intelligence Roan saw in Marcellino's restless, probing eyes that made him feel a tad better about the man. Roan knew he would have to work with him, and his instincts warned him that Marcellino was a soldier with a helluva lotta baggage that he was dragging around with him like an old friend. People like that made Roan antsy because they tended to take their misery and un-

Chapter 2

What in the hell am I doing here with all this fruit salad?
Roan wondered as he slowly eased his bulk down into a
chair in the shadows of the huge, rectangular room. Fruit
salad was military slang for the ribbons personnel wore
on their uniforms. Ribbons that spoke of various cam-
paigns and wars that they served in, and medals they'd
earned when they'd survived them. His own time in the
Marine Corps as a Recon came back to him as he scanned
the assembled group of ten men. Roan recognized two of
them: Morgan Trayhern, who sat at the head of the large,
oval table in a dapper gray pinstripe suit, and Major Mike
Houston, who was a U.S. Army advisor to the Peruvian
military. Roan amended his observation. Mike was retired.
Now he was working for Perseus and for Morgan.

Roan was the only other person besides Morgan and
Mike wearing civilian attire. In his white cotton Western
shirt, the sleeves rolled up haphazardly to just below his

conscious rage out on others without ever realizing it. And Roan wouldn't join in that kind of dance with anyone. It was one of the reasons why he'd quit the Marine Corps; the games, the politics choked him, and he withered within the world of the military. His gut told him Marcellino was a man who excelled at those bonds of politics.

Clearing his throat, Morgan buttonholed everyone seated around the oval table. One by one he introduced each man present. Roan noted there was either a colonel or a general from each of the South American countries represented at the table. In front of him was a file folder marked Top Secret. Roan resisted opening it up before being asked to. When Morgan got to his corner, Roan lowered his eyes and looked down at the well-polished table.

"I've already introduced Roan Storm Walker, but let me give you some of his background. As I mentioned, he was a Recon Marine for six years. A trained paramedic on his team, he saw action in Desert Storm. His team was responsible for doing a lot of damage over in Iraq. His specialty is jungle and desert warfare situations. He holds a degree in psychology. He speaks five languages fluently—Spanish, German, French and Portuguese, plus his own Native American language, of the Lakota Sioux nation. He will be working with Colonel Jaime Marcellino, from Brazil. But more on that later."

Roan was glad once the spotlight moved away from him. He didn't like being out front. People out front got shot at and hit. He had learned to be a shadow, because shadows could quietly steal away to live and fight another day. As he sat there, vaguely listening to the other introductions, Roan admitted to himself that the fight had gone out of him. When Sarah died two years ago, his life had been shattered. He had no more desire to take on the world. With her his reason for living had died. If it hadn't been for Morgan nudging him to get back into the stream of life, he'd probably have drunk himself to death in his cabin up in the mountains.

Morgan would visit him about once a month, toss a small mercenary job with little danger to it his way, to keep Roan from hitting the bottle in his despair. Trayhern was astute about people, about their grief and how it affected them. Roan knew a lot about grief now. He knew what loss was. The worst kind. He tried to imagine a loss that would be greater than losing a wife or husband, and figured that would probably be losing a child. It was lucky, he supposed morbidly, that he and Sarah never had children. But in truth he wished that they had. Sarah would live on through that child, and Roan wouldn't feel as devastated or alone as he did now. But that was a selfish thought, he knew.

Still, he felt that losing a loved one, whether spouse or child, was the hardest thing in the world to endure. How could one do it and survive? As a psychologist, he knew the profound scarring that took place on the psyche. He knew firsthand the terrible, wrenching grief of losing a woman he loved as well as life itself. And Roan swore he'd never, ever fall in love again, because he could not afford to go through that again. Not ever. His spirit would not survive it.

"Gentlemen, I'm turning this briefing over to Major Mike Houston. You all know him well. He was a U.S. Army advisor up until very recently." Morgan allowed a hint of a smile on his face. "Mike is now working for

Perseus, my organization. He is our South American specialist. One of the reasons you have been handpicked to represent your country is because you have all worked with him in some capacity or another. Major Houston is a known quantity to you. You know he's good at his word, that he knows the terrain and the problems with the drug trade in South America. You know he can be trusted.'' Morgan turned to Mike. ''Major Houston?''

Mike nodded and stood up. He, too, was in civilian attire—a pair of tan trousers, a white cotton shirt and a dark brown blazer. When he turned on the overhead, a map of Brazil flashed on the screen in front of the group.

''The government of Brazil has asked this administration for help in ridding the Amazon basin of two very powerful drug lords—the Valentino Brothers.'' Mike moved to the front and flicked on his laser pen. A small red dot appeared on the map. ''We know from intelligence sources in the basin that the brothers have at least six areas of operation. Their business consists of growing and manufacturing cocaine. They have factories, huge ones, that are positioned in narrow, steep and well-guarded valleys deep in the interior of the rain forest.

''The Valentino Brothers capture Indians from the surrounding areas and basically enslave them, turn them into forced laborers. If the Indians don't work, they are shot in the head. If they try to escape, they are killed. What few have escaped and lived to tell us about their captivity, relate being fed very little food while working sixteen hours a day, seven days a week. If they don't work fast enough, the overseer whips them. There is no medical help for them. No help at all.''

Mike looked out at the shadowy faces turned raptly

toward him. "All of you know I'm part Quechua Indian, from Peru. I have a personal stake in this large, ongoing mission. We have drug lords enslaving Indians in every country in South America in order to produce large quantities of cocaine for world distribution. If the Indians do not do the work, they are murdered. The captured women are raped. After working all day they become unwilling pawns to the drug dealers at night. Children who are captured are forced to work the same hours as an adult. They suffer the same fate as an adult." His mouth became set. "Clearly, we need to make a statement to these drug lords. The head honchos aren't stupid. They use the rain forests and jungles to hide in. Even our satellite tracking cannot find them under the dense canopy. What we need, in each country, is someone who knows the territory where these factories are located, to act as a guide, to bring the army forces in to destroy them."

Mike grimaced. "This is no easy task. The Amazon basin is huge and the military must march in on foot. The only way units can be resupplied is by helicopter. When they get farther in, helicopters are out of range—they can't reach them without refueling—so we must rely on cargo plane airdrops. The troops' medical needs aren't going to be met. If there is an emergency, a sick or wounded soldier will have to be carried out to a place where a helicopter can pick him up and transport him back to the nearest hospital. As you all are aware, I'm sure, there are a lot of deadly things out in the Amazon. Piranhas in the rivers, channels and pools. Bushmaster snakes that will literally chase you until they sink their fangs into you. Mosquitoes carrying malaria, yellow fever and dengue. There's always the threat of unknown hemorrhagic viruses, victims of which can bleed out before we can get them proper medical help. There are insects that with one bite can kill you in as little as forty-eight hours if you are without medical intervention.''

Mike paused, then moved on. ''Colonel Jaime Marcellino has been chosen to lead the Brazilian Army contingent, a company of their best soldiers—roughly one hundred and eighty men. He is their rain forest specialist. He has knowledge of the problems inherit in that environment.''

Jaime bowed slightly to Houston.

Mike went on. ''We all agree that Colonel Marcellino's experiment with a company of men in Brazil will teach us a lot about how to organize military attacks against drug strongholds in other countries. What we learn from his mission will help all of you in preparation for yours. He will be our guinea pig, so to speak. Mistakes made there we will learn from. What works will be passed on in an after-action report to all of you.''

Moving toward the front of the room, Mike tapped the map projected on the huge screen. ''We have it on good authority where six factories, in six different valleys, are located. We have a guide who will lead the colonel's company to the nearest one, which is about ten hours southeast of Manaus, up in a mountainous region known as Sector 5. The colonel's company will disembark at Manaus, motor down the Amazon and, at a predestined spot, off-load and meet their guide. The guide will then take them through a lot of grueling hilly and swampy terrain to reach the valley where the factory is located. Once there, Colonel Marcellino will deploy his troops for a strategic attack on the facility.'' Mike shrugged. ''It is our hope that the

Indians who are captive will be freed. We don't want them killed in the cross fire. The Valentino Brothers have heavily fortified operations. Their drug soldiers are men who live in the rain forest and know it intimately. They will be a constant threat.''

Jaime held up a long, narrow hand with closely clipped carefully manicured nails. ''Major Houston, I am sure my men will be able to take this factory. Do not look so worried.'' He smiled slightly.

''Colonel, I wish I could share your optimism,'' Mike said heavily. ''I don't question your willingness and passion for this mission. But it's going to be hard. No army in South America has tried such a thing before. There's bound to be a steep learning curve on this.''

''We are prepared,'' Marcellino answered in his soothing well-modulated tone. He looked at Morgan. ''My men are trained for rain forest warfare.''

Morgan nodded. ''We realize that, Colonel. That's why you're being asked to lead this mission. Even though your men have trained for it, that doesn't mean they've actually undertaken missions in the basin, however. There's a big difference between training and real-time experience.''

Jaime nodded. ''Of course, Mr. Trayhern. I'm confident we can do this.''

Mike Houston cleared his throat. ''For this mission, we are sending Roan Storm Walker with you, Colonel. He'll be your advisor, your translator, and will work directly between you and the guide. He will answer only to you and to Morgan Trayhern at Perseus, which has the backing of this administration to undertake this plan of attack. Even though Storm Walker has no military designation, his judgment will be equal to your own.'' Houston drilled

Marcellino with an incisive look. "Do you understand that?"

Jaime shrugged thin, sharp shoulders beneath a uniform resplendent with shining brass buttons and thick, gold braid and epaulets. On his chest were at least twenty ribbons. "Yes, yes, of course. I will order my officers to acknowledge that he has full authority to override their decisions in the field." Frowning, he turned and looked down the table at Storm Walker. "However, he must check with me first before any action is taken."

"Of course," Mike assured him. "Roan knows chain of command. He recognizes you as the ultimate authority over your men."

Nodding, Jaime raised his thin, graying brows. "And what of this guide? What is his status with me?"

Mike sent a brief, flickering glance in Morgan's direction and kept his voice low and deep as he answered. "The guide knows the terrain, Colonel. You should listen to the advice given to you. This is a person who has lived in the basin all her life. Storm Walker will be her liaison with you, and she'll be your point man—woman—on this mission. You'd best heed whatever advice she gives you because she knows the territory. She's had a number of skirmishes with the Valentino Brothers and has every reason for wanting them out of the basin."

Curious, Jaime straightened, his hand resting lightly on the table. "Excuse me, Major. Am I hearing you correctly? You said 'she'? I thought our guide would be a man. What woman has knowledge of the basin?" He laughed briefly and waved his hand. "Women stay at home and have our children. They are wives and mothers—that is all. No, you must have meant 'he.' *Sim?*"

Mike girded himself internally. He flashed a look of warning in Roan's direction. Now the muck was going to hit the fan. "No," he began slowly, "I meant *she.* This is a woman who was born and raised in the basin. She knows at least fifteen Indian languages, knows the territory like the back of her hand. No one is better suited for this assignment than she is. Roan Storm Walker will interface directly with her, Colonel. You will not have to if you don't want to."

Though he frowned, Jaime said laughingly, "And why would I not want to meet this woman and hear her words directly? If she is Indian and knows Portuguese, there should not be a language problem, eh?"

Biting down on his lower lip for a moment, Mike said quietly, "She is known as the jaguar goddess, Colonel. Her real name is Inca." He saw the colonel's eyes widen enormously, as if he'd just been hit in the chest with an artillery shell. Before the Brazilian could protest, Mike added quickly, "We know the past history between Inca and yourself. That is why Roan Storm Walker is going along. He'll relay any information or opinions from Inca to you. We know you won't want to interface with her directly due to…circumstances…."

Marcellino uttered a sharp cry of surprise. He shot up so quickly that his chair tipped over. His voice was ragged with utter disbelief. "No! No! A thousand times no!" He swung toward Morgan, who sat tensely.

"You cannot do this! I will not allow it! She's a ruthless killer! She murdered my eldest son, Rafael, in cold blood!" He slammed his fist down on the table, causing the wood to vibrate. "I will not permit this godless woman anywhere near me or my troops!" His voice cracked. Tears came to his eyes, though he instantly forced them back. "I lost my eldest son to that murdering, thieving traitor! She's a sorceress! She kills without rhyme or reason."

Choking, he suddenly realized how much of his military bearing he'd lost in front of his fellow officers. His face turned a dull red. He opened his hands and held them up. "I apologize," he whispered unsteadily. "Many of you do not know me, know of my background. My eldest son, the light of my life...the son who was to carry on my name, who was to marry and someday give me grandchildren...was senselessly and brutally murdered by this woman named Inca. She is wanted in Brazil for thirteen murders. Thirteen," he growled. Straightening up, his heart pounding, he again apologized. "I had no idea you would suggest her," he told Morgan in a hoarse tone.

Morgan slowly rose and offered a hand in peace to him. "Please, Colonel, come and sit down."

An aide scrambled from near the door to pick up the colonel's fallen chair and place it upright so that he could sit down. Hands shaking, Jaime pulled the chair, which was on rollers, beneath him. "I am sorry for my outburst. I am not sorry what I said about this sorceress." Sitting down, he glared across the table at Morgan and Mike Houston. "You know of her. You know she's a murderer. How can you ask me to tolerate the sight of her, much less work with her, when she has the blood of my son on her hands?" His voice cracked. "How?"

Houston looked to his boss. This was Morgan's battle to win, not his. Sitting down, he watched Morgan's face carefully as he rose to his full height to address the emotionally distraught colonel.

"Jaime..." Morgan began softly, opening his hand in a pleading gesture, "I have four children. I almost lost my oldest son, Jason, in a kidnapping and I know of your grief. I'm deeply sorry for your loss. I truly am." Morgan cleared his throat and glanced down at Mike who sat looking grim. "I have it on good authority that Inca did *not* kill your son Rafael. She said she was on the other side of the basin when he and his squad surprised a drug-running operation in a village. Inca denies killing your son. The person in this room who knows her well is Mike Houston. Mike, do you have anything to add to this, to help the colonel realize that Rafael was not murdered by Inca?"

Mike leaned forward, his gaze fixed on Jaime's grief-filled face. The colonel had lost his hard military expression, and his dark eyes were wild with suffering and barely checked rage. Mike knew that in most Latin American countries, the firstborn male child was the darling of the family. In the patriarchal cultures in South America, to lose the eldest son was, to the father of that family, to lose everything. The eldest was doted upon, raised from infancy to take over the family business, the family responsibilities, and carry on their long heritage. Mike knew the people in Jaime's social strata were highly educated. Jaime himself, descended from Portuguese aristocracy of the 1700s, had a proud lineage that few others in Brazil possessed. Rafael had been trained, coaxed, nurtured and lovingly molded according to this prominent family's expectations. Mike knew even as he spoke just how devastating the loss was for the colonel.

"Colonel Marcellino. Inca is my blood sister." He held up his hand and pointed to a small scar on the palm of his hand. "I met her when she was eighteen years old. She saved my life, quite literally. She almost died in the process. The Inca I know is not a murderer. She is a member of the Jaguar Clan of Peru, a group that teaches their people to defend, never attack. If someone fires on Inca, or someone attacks her, she will defend herself. But she will never fire first. She will not ever needlessly take a life."

Marcellino glared across the table at him. "Do not paint a pretty picture of this murdering sorceress. The men in Rafael's squad saw her. They saw her put a rifle to her shoulder and shoot my son cold-bloodedly in the head!"

"Listen to me," Mike rasped. "Inca was two hundred miles away from the place where your son was killed. She was with an old Catholic priest, Father Titus, at an Indian mission on the Amazon River. I can prove it." Mike pulled out a paper from the open file in front of him. "Here, this is an affidavit signed by the priest. Please, look at it. Read it."

Belligerently, Jaime jerked the paper from Mike's hand. He saw the sweat stains on the document and the barely legible signature of the old priest. Throwing it back, he barked, "This proves nothing!"

Mike placed the paper back into the file. Keeping his voice low and quashing his feelings, he said, "No one in your son's squad survived the attack by the drug lord and his men. I saw the report on it, Colonel. All you have is one person's word—a man who was later captured and who is suspected of working with the same local drug lord who indicted Inca. He said Inca was there. You have a drug runner's word. Are you going to believe him? He has every reason to lie to you on this. He wants to save his hide and do only a little bit of prison time and get released. How convenient to lay the blame at Inca's feet. Especially since she wasn't there to defend herself.'' Houston tapped the file beneath his hand. ''I know Father Titus personally. The old priest is almost ninety. He's lived in the basin and has helped the Indians at his mission for nearly seventy of those years. At one time he helped raise Inca, who was orphaned.''

''Then all the more reason for the old priest to lie!'' Jaime retorted. ''No! I do not believe you. The blood of thirteen men lays on Inca's head. There is a huge reward, worth six million cruzeiros, or one million dollars, U.S., for her capture, dead or alive, in Brazil. If I see her, I will kill her myself. Personally. And with pleasure. My son's life will finally be avenged.''

Roan shifted slightly in his chair. The atmosphere in the room was cold and hostile. Not one man moved; all eyes were riveted on the colonel and Mike Houston. Roan saw the hatred in the colonel's face, heard the venom that dripped from every stilted English word he spoke. The colonel's black eyes were a quagmire of grief and rage. Part of Roan's heart went out to the man. Jaime had made the worst sacrifice of all; he'd lost a beloved child. Well, Roan had something in common with the colonel—he'd lost someone he'd loved deeply, too. But who was Inca? The woman he'd seen in his dream earlier? She sounded like a hellion of the first order. Warrioress, madwoman— who knew? Roan looked to Mike Houston, who was laboring to get the colonel to see reason.

''Inca's only responsibility is as a Green Warrior for Mother Earth,'' Mike said quietly. ''She has taken a vow to protect the Amazon Basin from encroachment and destruction by anyone. Twelve of these so-called murders were really self-defense situations. Plus, the twelve men who are dead are all drug dealers. Inca does not deny killing them, but she didn't fire first. She shot back only to save herself and other innocent lives.'' Mike held out a thick folder toward Jaime. ''Here is the proof, colonel. I haven't understood yet why the government of Brazil has not absolved Inca of those trumped up charges. I'd think Brazil would be happy to see those men gone.'' He laid the file down. ''But I don't want to get off track here. You can read her sworn statements on each charge when you want.''

''It is well known she hates white men!'' Marcellino snapped, his anger flaring.

''Not all,'' Mike countered. ''She's my blood sister by ceremony. She respects men and women alike. Now, if someone wants to destroy, rip up, start cutting down timber, hurt the Indians or make them into slaves, then Inca will be there to stop him. She will try many ways to stop the destruction, but murdering a person is not one of them. And as I said, she will fire in defense, she will never fire the first shot.''

''And I suppose,'' Marcellino rattled angrily, ''that the thirteen men she killed fired on her *first?*''

''That's exactly what happened in twelve cases,'' Houston said gravely. ''Your son is the thirteenth to her count, he shouldn't have been added. Members of the Jaguar Clan can be kicked out of it by firing first or attacking first. She can only defend herself. So twelve men fired *first* on her, Colonel. And she shot back. And she didn't miss.''

''She murdered my son! He's one of the thirteen.''

"Inca was not there. She did not shoot your son."

Morgan appealed to Marcellino. "Colonel, would you, as an officer, lead your entire company of men into an unknown area without proper help and guidance?"

"Of course not!"

"Inca knows the basin better than anyone," Morgan said soothingly. He lifted a hand toward Roan at the end of the table. "This man will be standing between you and Inca. You won't have to face her. You won't have to see that much of her. He's your liaison. Your spokesman, if you will. Inca can lead you and your men safely to this valley in the mountains. I know much is being asked of you, and that is why Roan is here—to assist and help you as much as he can. Anything she tells him, Roan will relay on to you or your officers. I realize the pain of your loss, and we tried to come up with a plan that would somehow protect you and her both during this mission."

"I will kill her if I see her."

"No," Morgan said, his voice hard and uncompromising, "you won't. If you really want to take this mission, you will promise to leave her alone."

"And you will not order one of your men to shoot her, either," Houston growled. "Any attempt on Inca's life, and she'll leave you and your company wherever you are. And if you're in the middle of the rain forest, Colonel, without a guide, you'll be in jeopardy."

"Then I will hire an Indian guide to lead us."

Houston shook his head. "There isn't an Indian willing to lead you into the area, Colonel. If the drug lords find out that they did, they'd move into their village and murder everyone in retribution."

Jaime tried to take a breath. It hurt to breathe. His heart

was wild with grief. Rafael had been murdered two years ago, but it felt like only yesterday. Rubbing his chest savagely, Jaime snarled, "You cannot ask this of me. You cannot."

Morgan moved around the table and faced him squarely. "Colonel, if I thought for a heartbeat that Inca had killed your son, I would not have asked you to head this mission. Nor would I have asked Inca to be your guide. I believe Mike Houston. I've never met her, I only know of her reputation in Brazil. I know that if a person becomes a legend, many times the truth gets tattered and distorted. I believe the old priest's affidavit. He has no reason to lie to protect her. Priests don't lie about something like this. I've also read her sworn statements on each charge. I believe she's innocent in such charges." Morgan eased his bulk down on the table next to Marcellino's chair.

"Colonel, you are a man of consummate honor. Your family's heritage stretches back to the kings and queens of Portugal. You were the only person we wanted for this mission. You are a brave and resourceful man. You are someone who is good at his word. Your love of your country has been obvious in the twenty years you've served in her military. You are one of the most decorated men in your country." Morgan held the officer's dark gaze. "I believe, Colonel, that if you will give me your word that you will not harm Inca for the duration of the mission, that you can be trusted. Look beyond her. Look at what you will accomplish for all the people of Brazil. You will be a hero."

Morgan raised his hand and swept it toward the rest of the men sitting around the table. "And think of the glory you will receive, the recognition, for going in first to strike a blow for freedom from these drug runners. Your name will be on the lips of people around the globe. Is that not a credit to your son? Could this mission be undertaken in his name? In his memory?''

Morgan saw Marcellino sink back into the chair. He knew the officer's ego and pride were tremendous. And typical of South American aristocracy, fame and power would appeal strongly to the colonel. Morgan was hoping it would break the logjam on this mission. He tried to sit there appearing at ease, even though his gut was knotted while he waited for the man's answer.

Roan watched the proceedings with rapt attention. So, he was to be a bridge, a liaison between this wild woman from Amazonia and the colonel who wanted to kill her in the name of his lost son. Roan realized the immensity of his mission. Was this woman, Inca, sane? Was she manageable? Would she respect him enough to stay out of Marcellino's way so they could successfully complete the assigned task? Roan wasn't sure, and he had a helluva lot of questions to ask Houston when the time was right.

All eyes were on Marcellino as he sat back, deep in thought over Morgan's softly spoken words. No one moved. The Brazilian finally looked at Houston. ''What makes you think she will work with Storm Walker?''

''He's Indian like she is. Inca respects Indians.''

''He's a man.'' Marcellino's voice dripped with sarcasm.

''Inca doesn't hate men. She respects men who have honor, who have morals and who aren't destroying Mother Earth. Roan, here, comes from a similar background. He'll be able to understand her, and vice versa. I believe it is a good match, and I believe Inca will get along well with him.''

''And what if she doesn't?''

''Then,'' Mike said, ''the mission is off. Morgan and I realize your loss, Colonel. We've worked hard to put the right people in key positions to help you get through this mission successfully. If Roan can't forge the bond of trust we need with Inca, in order to work with you, then this mission is scrubbed.''

Nodding, Marcellino glared up at Morgan. ''If it had been anyone but you asking this of me, I would tell him to burn in hell.''

Relief shuddered through Morgan, though he kept his face expressionless. Reaching out, he placed his hand on the colonel's proud shoulder. ''Jaime, I share your grief and your loss. But I'm convinced Inca is innocent of your son's death. She is the only person we know who can give you success on your mission. I know I'm asking a lot from you in begging you to rise above personal hurt, grief and rage, and look at the larger picture. You can be the deliverer of hundreds of people. The name Marcellino will be revered in many Indian villages because you had the courage to come and eradicate the drug lords from the basin. I know you can do this. And I don't deny it will be difficult...''

The colonel slumped slightly. He felt Morgan's grip on his shoulder, heard the sincerity in his rumbling voice. ''Very well,'' he whispered raggedly, ''you have my word, Morgan. I will reluctantly work with Inca. But only through this man.'' He pointed at Roan. ''I don't know what I'll do if I see her. I want to kill her—I won't deny it. He had best make sure that she never meets me face-to-face...."

Morgan nodded and swallowed hard. "I know Roan will do everything in his power to convey that message to Inca. She will be your scout, your point person, so the chances of seeing her are pretty slim. But I'll make sure he tells her that. I have no wish to hurt you any more than you've already been hurt by your son's loss."

Eyes misting, Jaime forced back tears. He looked up at Morgan. "And do you know the terrible twist in all of this?"

"No, what?"

"My youngest son, Julian, who is a lieutenant, will be leading one of the squads under my command on this mission."

Morgan closed his eyes for a moment. When he opened them, he rasped, "Colonel, your son is safe. Inca is not going after him—or any of your men. She is on *your* side of this fight."

"This time," Marcellino said bitterly. "And for how long? She is infamous for turning on people when it suits her whims and wiles."

"Roan will see that things go smoothly," Morgan promised heavily, shooting him a glance down the table.

Roan waited patiently until the room cleared of all but him, Morgan and Mike. When the door shut, he slowly unwound from his chair.

"I didn't realize what I'd be doing."

Mike nodded. "I'm sorry I couldn't brief you before-hand, Roan."

Morgan moved toward the end of the table, where Roan

stood. "More importantly, do you *want* to take this assignment?"

With a shrug, Roan said, "I wasn't doing much of anything else."

Morgan nodded and wiped his perspiring brow with a white linen handkerchief, then returned it to his back pocket. "I've never met Inca. Mike has. I think you should direct your questions to him. In the meantime, I'm going to join the officers at a banquet we've set up in their honor in the dining room. See me there when you're done here?"

Roan nodded, then waited expectantly as the door closed behind Morgan. Silence settled over them, and Roan discovered Mike Houston's expression became more readable once they were alone. Roan opened his hand.

"Well? Is she a killer or a saint in disguise?

Grinning, Mike said, "Not a killer and not a saint."

"What then?"

"A twenty-five-year-old woman who was orphaned at birth, and who is responsible for protecting the Indian people of the Amazon."

"Why her?"

"She's a member of the Jaguar Clan," Mike said, sitting down and relaxing. "You're Native American. You have your societies up here in the north. Down in South America, they're known as clans. One and the same."

"Okay," Roan said, "like a hunters' society? Or a warriors' society?"

"Yes, specialists. Which is why the societies were created—to honor those who had skills in a specific area of need for their community. The welfare and continuing survival of their families and way of life depends on it.''

"So, the Jaguar Clan is...what?''

"What kind of society?'' Mike sighed. "A highly complex one. It's not easy to define. Your mother, I understand, was a Yuwipi medicine woman of the Lakota people. She was also known as a shape-shifter?''

Roan nodded. "That's right.''

"The Jaguar Clan is a group of people from around the world who possess jaguar medicine. They come from all walks of life. Their calling is to learn about their jaguar medicine—what it is and what it is capable of doing. It is basically a healers' clan. That is why Inca would never fire first. That is why she defends well, but never attacks. Her calling is one of healing—in her case, to help heal Mother Earth. She does this by being a Green Warrior in Brazil, where she was born.''

"The colonel called her a sorceress.''

"Inca has many different powers. She is not your normal young woman,'' Mike warned him. "Combine that with her passion for protecting the people of the Amazon, the mission she is charged with, and her confidence and high intelligence, and you have a powerful woman on your hands. She doesn't suffer fools lightly or gladly. She speaks her mind.'' Mike grinned. "I love her like a sister, Roan. I don't have a problem with her strength, her moxie or her vow of healing Mother Earth and protecting the weak from drug runners. Most men do. I figured you wouldn't because, originally, Native American nations were all matriarchal, and most still have a healthy respect for what women have brought to the table.''

"Right, I do.''

"Good. Hold that perspective. Inca can be hardheaded, she's a visionary, and she can scare the living hell out of you with some of her skills. They call her the jaguar goddess in the basin because people have seen her heal those who were dying."

"And do you trust Marcellino not to try and kill her?"

"No," Mike said slowly, "and that is why you'll have to be there like a rock wall between them. You'll need to watch out for Inca getting shot in the back by him or one of his men. You're going to be in a helluva fix between two warring parties. Inca has a real dislike for the military. According to her, they're soft. They don't train hard. They don't listen to the locals who know the land because they are so damned arrogant and think they know everything, when in reality they know nothing."

"So I'm a diplomat and a bodyguard on this trip."

"Yes. You're at the fulcrum point, Roan. It's a messy place to be. I don't envy you." He smiled a little. "If my wife and child didn't need me, and vice versa, I'd be taking on this mission myself. Morgan wanted someone without family to take it, because the level of risk, the chance of dying, is high. And I know you understand that."

Nodding, Roan ran his long index finger across the highly polished surface of the conference table enjoying the feel of the warm wood. "Is Inca capable of killing me?"

Chuckling, Mike said, "Oh, she can have some thunderstorm-and-lightning temper tantrums when you don't agree with her, or things don't go the way she wants them to, but hurt you? No. She wouldn't do that. If anything, she'll probably see you as one more person under her umbrella of protection.''

''Will she listen to me, though? When it counts?''

Shrugging, Mike said, ''If you gain her respect and trust, the answer is yes. But you don't have much time to do either.''

''Where am I to meet her? Hopefully, it will be without Marcellino and his company.''

''On the riverfront, near Manaus, where the two great rivers combine to create the Amazon.''

''How will you get in touch with her?''

Houston gave him a lazy smile. ''I'll touch base with her in my dream state.''

Roan stood there for a second absorbing Houston's statement. ''You're a member of the Jaguar Clan, too?''

''Yes, I am.''

Roan nodded. He vividly recalled the experience he'd had earlier—the dream of the woman with willow-green eyes. ''What color are Inca's eyes?'' he asked.

Mike gave him a probing look. He opened his mouth to inquire why Roan was asking such a question, and then decided against it. ''Green.''

''What shade?''

''Ever seen a willow tree in the spring just after the leaves have popped out?''

''Many times.''

''That color of green. A very beautiful, unique color. That's the color of Inca's eyes.''

''I thought so….'' Roan said, his own eyes narrowing thoughtfully as he realized he and Inca might have already met….

Chapter 3

Inca was lonely. Frowning, she shifted on the large stack of wooden crates where she sat, her booted feet dangling and barely touching the dry red soil of the Amazon's bank. Her fine, delicately arched brows knitted as she studied the ground. In Peru, they called the earth *Pachamama,* or Mother Earth. Stretching slightly, she gently patted the surface with the sole of her military boot. The dirt was Mother Earth's skin, and in her own way, Inca was giving her real and only mother a gentle pat of love.

Sighing, she looked around at the humid mid-afternoon haze that hung above the wide, muddy river. The sun was behind the ever-present hazy clouds that hugged the land like a lover. Making a strangled sound, Inca admitted sourly to herself she didn't know what it was to feel like a lover. The only thing she knew of romantic love was what she'd read about it from the great poets while growing up under Father Titus's tutelage.

Did she want a lover? Was that why she was feeling lonely? Ordinarily, Inca didn't have to deal with such an odd assortment of unusual emotions. She was so busy that she could block out the tender feelers that wound through the heart like a vine, and ignore them completely. Not today. No, she had to rendezvous with this man that her blood brother, Michael Houston, had asked her to meet. Not only that, but she had to work with him! Michael had visited her in the dream state several nights earlier and had carefully gone over everything with her. In the end, he'd left it up to Inca as to whether or not she would work as a guide for Colonel Marcellino—the man who wanted to kill her.

Her lips, full and soft, moved into a grimace. Always alert, with her invisible jaguar spirit guide always on guard, she felt no danger nearby. Her rifle was leaning against the crates, which were stacked and ready to take down the Amazon, part of the supplies Colonel Marcellino would utilize once they met up with him and his company downriver.

She was about to take on a mission, so why was she feeling so alone? So lonely? Rubbing her chest, the olive-green, sleeveless tank top soaked with her perspiration from the high humidity and temperature, Inca lifted her stubborn chin.

She had a mild curiosity about this man called Roan Storm Walker. For one thing, he possessed an interesting name. The fact that he was part Indian made her feel better about this upcoming mission. Indians shared a common blood, a common heritage here in South America. Inca wondered if the blood that pumped through Walker's veins was similar to hers, to the Indians who called the Amazon basin home. She hoped so.

Her hair, wrapped in one thick, long braid, hung limply across her right shoulder with tendrils curling about her face. Inca looked up expectantly toward the asphalt road to Manaus. From the wooden wharves around her, tugs and scows ceaselessly took cargo up and down the Amazon. Right now, at midday, it was siesta time, and no one was in the wharf area, which was lined with rickety wooden docks that stuck fifty or so feet off the red soil bank into the turbid, muddy Amazon. Everyone was asleep now, and that was good. For Inca, it meant less chance of being attacked. She was always mindful of the bounty on her head. Wanted dead or alive by the Brazilian government, she rarely came this close to any city. Only because she was to meet this man, at Michael's request, had she left her rain forest home, where she was relatively safe.

Bored by sitting so long, Inca lifted her right arm and unsnapped one of the small pouches from the dark green nylon web belt she always wore around her slender waist. On the other side hung a large canteen filled with water and a knife in a black leather sheath. On the right, next to the pouch, was a black leather holster with a pistol in it. In her business, in her life, she was at war all the time. And even though she possessed the skills of the Jaguar Clan, good old guns, pistols and knives were part and parcel of her trade as well.

Easing a plastic bag out of the pouch, Inca gently opened it. Inside was a color photo of Michael and Ann Houston. In Ann's arms was six-month-old Catherine. Inca hungrily studied the photo, its edges frayed and well worn from being lovingly looked at so many times, in moments of quiet. She was godmother to Catherine Inca Houston. She finally had a family. Pain throbbed briefly through her heart. Abandoned at birth, unwanted, Inca had bits and pieces of memories of being passed from village to village, from one jaguar priestess to another. In the first sixteen years of her life, she'd had many mothers and fathers. Why had her real parents abandoned her? Had she cried a lot? Been a bad baby? What had she done to be discarded? Looking at the photo of Catherine, who was a chubby-cheeked, wide-eyed, happy little tyke, Inca wondered if she'd been ugly at birth, and if that was why her parents had left her out in the rain forest to die of starvation.

The pain of abandonment was always with her. Wiping her damp fingers on the material of the brown-green-and-tan military fatigues she wore, she skimmed the photo lightly with her index finger. She must have been ugly and noisy for her mother and father to throw her away. Eyes blurring with the tears of old pain, Inca absorbed the smiling faces of Michael and Ann. Oh, how happy they were! When Inca saw Mike and Ann together she got some idea of what real love was. She'd been privileged to be around these two courageous people. She'd seen them hold hands, give each other soft, tender looks, and had even seen them kissing heatedly once, when she'd unexpectedly showed up at their camp.

He's coming.

Instantly, Inca placed the photo back into the protective plastic covering and into the pouch at her side, snapping it shut. Her guardian, a normally invisible male jaguar called Topazio, had sent her a mental warning that the man known as Storm Walker was arriving shortly. Standing, Inca felt her heart pound a little in anticipation. Michael had assured her that she would get along with Roan. Inca rarely got along with anyone, so when her blood brother had said that she had eyed him skeptically. Her role in the world was acting as a catalyst, and few people liked a catalyst throwing chaos into their lives. Inca could count on one hand the people who genuinely liked her.

The slight rise of the hill above her blocked her view, so she couldn't see the approach of the taxi that would drop this stranger off in her care. Michael had given her a physical description of him, saying that Roan was tall with black hair, blue eyes and a build like a swimmer. Mike had described his face as square with some lines in it, as if he'd been carved out of the rocks of the Andes. Inca had smiled at that. To say that Roan's face was rough-hewn like the craggy, towering mountains that formed the backbone of South America was an interesting metaphor. She was curious to see if this man indeed had a rugged face.

Inca felt the brush of Topazio against her left thigh. It was a reassuring touch, much like a housecat that brushed lovingly against its owner. He sat down and waited patiently. As Inca stared into the distance, the midday heat made curtains where heat waves undulated in a mirage at the top of the hill.

Anticipation arced through her when she saw the yellow-and-black taxi roar over the crest of the hill on the two-lane, poorly marked road. She worried about the driver recognizing her. Although there were only a few rough sketches of her posted, artists for the government of Brazil had rendered her likeness closely enough for

someone to identify her. Once Storm Walker got out of
the cab, it would mean a fast exit on the tug. Inca would
have to wake the captain, Ernesto, who was asleep in the
shade of the boat, haphazardly docked at the nearby
wharf, and get him to load the crates on board pronto.

The taxi was blowing blue smoke from its exhaust pipe
as it rolled down the long hill toward Inca. Eyes narrowing, she saw the shape of a large man in the back seat.
She wrapped her arms against her chest and tensely
waited. Her rifle was nearby in case things went sour. Inca
trusted no one except Mike Houston and his wife, Rafe
Antonio, a backwoodsman who worked with her to protect the Indians, Grandmother Alaria and Father Titus.
That was all. Otherwise, she suspected everyone of wanting her head on a platter. Inca's distrust of people had
proved itself out consistently. She had no reason to trust
the cab driver or this stranger entering her life.

The cab screeched to a halt, the brakes old and worn.
Inca watched as a man, a very tall, well-built man,
emerged from the back of the vehicle. As he straightened
up, Inca's heartbeat soared. He looked directly at her
across the distance that separated them. Her lips parted.
She felt the intense heat of his cursory inspection of her.
The meeting of their eyes was brief, and yet it branded
her. Because she was clairvoyant, her senses were honed
to an excruciatingly high degree. She could read someone
else's thoughts if she put her mind to it. But rather than
making the effort to mind read, she kept her sensitivity to
others wide open, like an all-terrain radar system, in order
to pick up feelings, sensations and nuances from anyone
approaching. Her intuition, which was keenly honed,
worked to protect her and keep her safe.

As the man leaned over to pay the driver, Inca felt a warm sheet of energy wrapping around her. Startled, she shook off the feeling. What was that? Guardedly, she realized it had come from *him*. The stranger. Storm Walker. A frisson of panic moved through her gut. What was this? Inca afraid? Oh, yes, fear lived in her, alive and thriving. Fear was always with her. But Inca didn't let fear stop her from doing what had to be done. After all, being a member of the Jaguar Clan, she had to walk through whatever fears she had and move on to accomplish her purpose. Fear was not a reason to quit.

The cab turned around and roared back up the hill. Inca watched as the man leaned down and captured two canvas bags—his luggage—and then straightened up to face her. Five hundred feet separated them. Her guard was up. She felt Topazio get to his feet, his nose to the air, as if checking out the stranger.

The man was tall, much taller than Inca had expected. He was probably around six foot five or six. To her, he was like a giant. She was six foot in height, and few men in the Amazon stood as tall as she did. Automatically, Inca lifted her strong chin, met his assessing cobalt-colored eyes and stood her ground. His face was broad, with the hooked nose of an eagle, and his mouth generous, with many lines around it as well as the corners of his eyes. His hair was black with blue highlights, close-cropped to his head—typical of the military style, she supposed. He wasn't wearing military clothing, however, just a threadbare pair of jean's, waterproof hiking boots and a dark maroon polo shirt that showed off his barrel chest to distinct advantage. This was not the lazy, *norteamericano* that Inca was used to seeing. No, this man was hard-

bodied from strenuous work. The muscles in his upper
arms were thick, the cords of his forearms distinct. His
hands were large, the fingers long and large knuckled.
There was a tight, coiled energy around him as he moved
slowly toward her, their gazes locked together. Inca dug
mercilessly into his eyes, studied the huge, black pupils
to find his weaknesses, for that was what she had to do
in order to survive—find an enemy's weakness and use it
against him.

She reminded herself that this man was not her enemy,
but her radarlike assessment of him was something she
just did naturally. She liked how he moved with a boneless kind of grace. Clairvoyantly, Inca saw a female cougar walking near his left side, looking at her to size *her*
up! Smiling to herself, Inca wondered if this man was a
medicine person. Michael had said he was Lakota, and
that his mother was a medicine woman of great power
and fame. His face was rough-hewn, just as her blood
brother had described. Storm Walker was not a handsome
man. No, he looked as if his large, square face had been
carved from the granite of the Andes. She spotted a scar
on his left cheek, and another on the right side of his
forehead. His brows were thick and slightly arched and
emphasized his large, intelligent eyes as they held hers.
Few men could hold Inca's stare. But he did—with ease.

Her pulse elevated as he stopped, dropped the luggage
and straightened. When his hardened mouth softened tem-
porarily and the corners hooked upward, her heart
pounded. Her response to him unnerved Inca, for she'd
never responded to a man this way before. The sensations
were new to her, confounding her and making her feel
slightly breathless as a result. When he extended his large,

callused hand toward her, and Inca saw a wand of white sage in it, she relaxed slightly. Among her people, when one clan or nation visited another, sacred sage, ceremonially wrapped, was always given as a token of respect before any words of greeting were spoken.

Just this simple acknowledgment by him, the sacred sage extended in his hand, made Inca feel a deep sense of relief. Only Indians knew this protocol. Something wonderful flittered through Inca's heart as she reached out and took the gift. If the sage was accepted, it was a sign of mutual respect between the two parties, and talk could begin. She waited. The dried sage's fragrance drifted to her flaring nostrils. It was a strong, medicinelike scent, one that made her want to inhale deeply.

"I'm Roan Storm Walker," he said in a quiet tone. "I've been sent here by Mike Houston."

"I am called Inca," she said, her voice husky. He was powerful, and Inca wanted to back away from him to assess the situation more closely. Ordinarily, men she encountered were not this powerful. "I was not expecting a medicine person. I do not have a gift of our sacred sage to give you in return."

Roan nodded. "It's not a problem. Don't worry about it." His pulse was racing. He wondered if she could hear his heart beating like a thundering drum in his chest. Roan had realized for certain as he got out of the cab that Inca was the same woman who had entered his vision state that morning at his cabin. It was definitely her. Did she remember talking to him? Asking him to come down here to help her? If she did, she gave no hint to him. He decided not to ask, for it would be considered disrespectful.

She was incredibly beautiful in his eyes. There was a

wildness to her—a raw, primal power as she stood confidently before him dressed in her military attire. Even though she wore jungle fatigues, black GI boots, a web belt around her waist and an olive drab T-shirt, she could not hide her femininity from him in the least. She wore no bra, and her small breasts were upturned and proud against the damp shirt that provocatively outlined them, despite the bandoliers of ammunition crisscrossing her chest. Her face was oval, with a strong chin, high cheekbones and slightly tilted eyes. The color of her eyes made him hold his breath for a moment. Just as Mike Houston had said, they were a delicious willow-green color, with huge, black pupils. Her black lashes were thick and full, and emphasized her incredible eyes like a dark frame. Her hair was black with a slightly reddish tint when the sun peeked out between the sluggishly moving clouds and shined on it. The tendrils curling around her face gave Inca an air of vulnerability in spite of her formidable presence. He rocked internally from the power that surrounded her.

Roan had spotted the rifle leaning up against the crates, and he sensed her distrust of him. He saw it in the guarded look of her eyes. Her mouth was full and soft, yet, as she turned her attention to him, he watched it thin and compress. Mike was right: he'd have to earn her trust, inch by inch. Did he have the necessary time to do it? To protect her? To work as a liaison between her and Marcellino's troops?

"Why do you worry about me?" Inca growled. She turned and put the sage into a small, coarsely woven sack that sat on top of the crates. "I would worry more for you."

Frowning, Roan wondered if she'd read his mind. Mike had warned him that she had many clairvoyant talents. He watched as she shouldered the rifle, butt up, the muzzle pointed toward the ground. Any good soldier out in a rain forest or jungle situation would do that. Water down the barrel of one's weapon would create rust. Clearly Inca was a professional soldier.

"Come," she ordered as she strode quickly to the dock.

"*Olá!* Hello. Ernesto! Get up!" Inca called in Portuguese to the tug captain. The middle-aged, balding man roused himself from his siesta on the deck of his tug.

"Eh?"

Inca waved toward the crates. "Come, load our things. We must go, pronto."

Scrambling to his feet, the captain nodded and quickly rubbed his eyes. His face was round, and he hadn't shaved in days. Dressed only in a pair of khaki cutoffs that had seen better days, he leaped to the wharf.

Inca turned to Storm Walker, who stood waiting and watching. "We need to get these crates on board. Why don't you stow your gear on the tug and help him?"

"Of course." Roan moved past her and made his way from wharf to tug. The boat was old, unpainted, and the deck splintered from lack of sanding and paint to protect it from the relentless heat and humidity of Amazonia. Dropping his luggage at the bow, he watched as Inca moved to the stern of the tug. Her face was guarded and she was looking around, as if sensing something. He briefly saw the crescent-shaped moon on her left shoulder though it was mostly hidden beneath the tank top she wore. Mike Houston had warned him ahead of time that the thin crescent of gold and black fur was a sign her membership in the Jaguar Clan.

Inca barely gave notice to the two men placing the supplies on board. Topazio was restless, an indication that there was a disturbance in the energy of the immediate area. A warning that there was trouble coming.

"Hurry!" she snapped in Portuguese. And then Inca switched to her English, which was not that good. "Hurry."

"I speak Portuguese," Roan stated as he hefted a crate on board.

Grunting, Inca kept her gaze on the hill. Nothing moved in the humid, hot heat of the afternoon. Everything was still. Too still for her liking. She moved restlessly and shifted her position from the end of the wharf to where the asphalt crumbled and stopped. Someone was coming. And it wasn't a good feeling.

Roan looked up. He saw Inca standing almost rigidly, facing the hill and watching. What was up? He almost mouthed the query, but instead hurried from the tug to the shore to retrieve the last wooden crate. The tug captain started up the rusty old engine. Black-and-blue smoke belched from behind the vessel, the engine sputtered, coughed like a hacking person with advanced emphysema, and then caught and roared noisily to life.

"Inca?" Roan called as he placed the crate on the deck.

His voice carried sluggishly through the silence of the damp afternoon air. The hair on his neck stood on end. *Damn!* Leaping off the tug and running along the dock, Roan ordered the captain to cast off. He had just gotten to the end when he saw two cars, a white one and a black one, careening down off the hill toward them. His breath jammed in his throat. He could see rifles hanging out the open windows of both vehicles.

"Inca!"

Inca heard Storm Walker's warning, but she was already on top of the situation. In one smooth movement, she released her rifle and flipped it up, her hand gripping the trigger housing area and moving the barrel upward. She saw the guns stuck out of the windows. She felt the hatred of the men behind them. Turning on her heel, she sprinted toward the tug. It was going to be close!

To her surprise, she saw Storm Walker running toward her, his hand outstretched as if to grab her. Shaken by his protective gesture, she waved him away.

"You have no weapons!" she cried as she ran up to him. "Get back to the tug!"

Roan turned on his heel. He heard the screech of brakes. The first shots shattered the humid stillness. Bits of red dirt spurted into the air very near his feet. *Damn!* More shouts in Portuguese erupted behind them. Inca was following swiftly behind him. He didn't want her to get shot. Slowing, he reached out and shoved her in front of him. He would be the wall between her and the attackers. Who the hell were they, anyway? Digging the toes of his boots into the red dirt, Roan sprinted for the wharf. Already the tug was easing away from the dock. The captain's eyes were huge. He wanted out of here. Pronto!

More gunfire erupted. Inca cursed softly beneath her breath. She halted at the end of the wharf and shouldered her rifle. With cool precision, with wood exploding all around her, she squeezed off five shots in succession. She saw Storm Walker leap to the tug, which was sliding past her. Turning, she jumped from the wharf onto the deck

of the vessel herself. It was a long jump, almost five feet.
Landing on her hands and knees, she felt Roan's large
hands on her arm drawing her upward. He was pushing
her behind the cockpit of the tug in order to protect her.

Growling at him, she jerked her arm free. "Release
me!" she snarled, and then ran to the side of the cockpit
closest to the riverbank. The men were tumbling out of
the cars—six of them. They were heavily armed. Inca
dropped to one knee, drew the leather sling around her
arm and steadied the butt of the rifle against her shoulder
and cheek. She got the first man in the crosshairs and
squeezed off a shot. She watched as the bullet struck him
in the knee. He screamed, threw up his weapon and fell
to the earth, writhing in pain.

Rifle fire rained heavily around them. The captain was
swearing in Portuguese as he labored hard to get the
tug turned around and heading out to the middle of the
mile-wide river. Pieces of wood exploded and flew like
splinters of shrapnel everywhere. He ducked behind the
housing of the cockpit, one shaking hand on the old, dilapidated wooden wheel.

Crouching, Roan moved up alongside Inca. He reached
out. "Let me borrow your pistol," he rasped, and leaned
over her to unsnap the holster at her side.

Inca nodded and kept her concentration on the enemy.
Ordinarily, she'd never let anyone use her weapons, but
Roan was different. There was no time for talk. He took
her black Beretta, eased away from her and steadied his
gun arm on top of the cockpit. She heard the slow pop at
each squeeze of the trigger. Two more men fell. He was
a good shot.

Those left on the shore fell on their bellies, thrust their

weapons out in front of them and continued to send a hail of fire into the tug. They made poor targets, and Inca worked to wound, not kill them. It wasn't in her nature to kill. It never had been. To wound them was to put them out of commission, and that was all she strove to do. Wood erupted next to her. She felt the red-hot pain of a thick splinter entering her upper arm. Instantly, the area went numb. Disregarding her slight injury, Inca continued to squeeze off careful shots.

Finally the tug was out of range. Inca was the first to stop firing. She sat down, her back against the cockpit, the rifle across her lap as she pulled another clip from her web belt and jammed it into the rifle. Looking up, she saw Storm Walker's glistening features as he stopped firing. This man was a cool-headed warrior. Michael had been right about him being a benefit to her, and not a chain around her neck. That was good. His face was immobile, his eyes thundercloud dark as he glanced down to see how she was doing.

"You're hurt...."

Roan's words feathered across Inca. She glanced down at her left arm. There was a bright red trail of blood down her left biceps dripping slowly off her elbow onto the deck.

Without thinking, Roan stepped across her, knelt down and placed his hand near the wound. A large splinter of wood, almost two inches long and a quarter inch in diameter, was sticking out of her upper arm. Her flesh was smooth and damp as he ran his fingers upward to probe the extent and seriousness of her wound.

"Do not touch me!" Inca jerked away from him. Her

nostrils flared. "No man touches me without my permission."

Shocked by her violent response, Roan instantly released her. He sat back on his heels. The anger in her eyes was very real. "I'm a paramedic.... I'm trained—"

"You do not presume anything with me, *norte-americano,*" she spat. Scrambling to her knees, Inca made sure there was at least six feet between them. He was too close to her and she felt panic. Why? His touch had been gentle, almost tender. Why had she behaved so snottily toward him? She saw the worry in his eyes, the way his mouth was drawn in with anxiousness.

Holding up his hands in a sign of peace, Roan rasped, "You're right. I presumed. And I apologize." He saw the mixture of outrage, defiance and something else in her narrowed eyes in that moment. When he'd first touched her, he'd seen her eyes go wide with astonishment. And then, seconds later, he saw something else—something so heart-wrenchingly sad that it had blown his heart wide open. And within a fraction of a second, the windows to her soul had closed and he saw righteous fury replace that mysterious emotion in her eyes.

Shaken by his concern and care for her, Inca got to her feet, despite the fact that she felt some pain in the region of the wound. They were a mile away from the dock now, the little tug chugging valiantly along on the currents. For now, they were safe. Placing the rifle on top of the cockpit, she turned her attention to the captain.

"Captain, I need a clean cloth and some good water."

The grizzled old man nodded from the cockpit. "In there, *senhorinha.*" He pointed down the ladder that led below.

"Do you want some help removing that splinter?" Roan was behind her, but a respectful distance away. As Inca turned she was forced to look up at him. He was sweating profusely now, the underarms and center of his polo shirt dampened. His eyes were not guarded, but alive with genuine concern—for her. Inca was so unused to anyone caring about her—her pain, her needs—that she felt confused by his offer.

"No, I will take care of it in my own way." She spun around and headed down the stairs.

Great, Roan, you just screwed up with her. He stood there on the deck, the humid air riffling around him, cooling him as he placed his hands on his narrow hips. Looking back toward shore, he saw the men leaving. Who were they? Who had sent them? Was Marcellino behind this? No one knew Roan's itinerary except the good colonel. Worried about Inca, Roan stood there and compressed his lips. He'd forgotten Native American protocol with her. In his experience and training, Indians did not like to be touched by strangers. It was considered invasive. A sign of disrespect. Only after a long time, when respect and trust were developed, would touching be permitted.

Running his fingers through his short hair, Roan realized that he had to think in those terms with her. He was too used to being in the Anglo world, and in order to gain her trust, he must go back to the customs he'd grown up with in his own nation—the Native American way of doing things.

Still, he couldn't get the feel of her skin beneath his fingers out of his mind or heart. Inca was firm and tightly muscled. She was in superb athletic condition. There wasn't an ounce of spare flesh on her tall, slender frame.

Not many women were in such great shape, except, perhaps, some in the military. Rubbing his chin, he moved back to the cockpit.

Ernesto was mopping his forehead, a worried look in his eyes. He obviously hadn't expected such an attack, and his hands still shook in the aftermath. He offered Roan a bottle of water. Roan took it and thanked him. Tipping his head back, he drank deeply.

Inca reemerged at that moment. She saw Roan, his head tipped back, his Adam's apple bobbing with each gulp he took. Again, fear rippled through her as she made her way up the stairs. A soft breeze cooled her sweaty flesh as she moved topside. Wanting to keep distance between them, she took another bottle of water that Ernesto proffered to her. She thanked him and drank deeply of it.

Roan finished off the water. He'd felt Inca's return. The sense of her power, of her being nearby, was clear to him. As he put the plastic bottle back into the box near the wheel, he glanced up at her. His mouth dropped open. And then he snapped it shut. Roan straightened. He stared at her—not a polite thing to do, but he couldn't help himself.

The injury on her upper left arm was now completely healed. No trace of swelling, no trace of blood marred her beautiful skin. As she capped the bottle of water and gave him a glaring look, he shifted his gaze. What had happened to her wound? It looked as if she hadn't even been injured. But she *had* been and Roan knew it. The captain, too, was staring with a look of disbelief on his face. He was afraid of Inca, so he quickly averted his eyes and stuck to the task of guiding the tug.

Roan had a *lot* of questions. But asking questions was

a sign of disrespect, too. If Inca wanted to tell him what she'd done to heal herself, she would in her own good time. Mike Houston had told him that she was a healer. Well, Roan had just gotten a firsthand glimpse of her powerful talents.

"How far do we go downriver?" Inca demanded of him. Despite the tone she used, she was enjoying his company. Normally, men managed to irritate her with their arrogant male attitude, but he did not. Most men could not think like a woman; they were out to lunch instinctually and jammed their feelings so far down inside themselves that they were out of touch completely. Inca found the company of women far preferable. But Roan was different. She could see the remnants of his worry and concern over her wounding. He didn't try to hide or fix a mask on his feelings, she was discovering. The only other man she knew who was similar was her blood brother, Michael. Inca liked to know where a person stood with her, and when that person showed his feelings, whether they were for or against her, Inca appreciated it.

Roan smiled a one-cornered smile. At least she was still talking to him. He saw the frosty look in her eyes, the way she held herself, as if afraid he was going to touch her again. Remaining where he was, he said, "Let me get the map out of my luggage." He brightened a little. "And there's a gift in there for you from Mike and Ann, too. I think things have calmed down enough that we can sit and talk over the mission while you open it."

Inca nodded. "Very well. We will sit on the shady side of the boat, here." She pointed to the starboard side of the tug. Suddenly, she found herself wanting to talk to Roan. Why did he have the name he did? How had he earned it? She watched as he moved to the bow of the tug to retrieve his luggage.

Settling her back against the splintery wall of the cockpit, Inca waited for him. Roan placed the canvas bag, which was tubular in shape, between them and slowly sat down, his legs crossed beneath him. As he unzipped the bag, she watched his deft, sure movements and recalled his touch.

Men did not realize their touch was stronger and therefore potentially hurtful to a woman or a child. Mentally, she corrected herself. Not all men hurt women, but she'd seen too much of it in South America, and it angered her to her soul. No one had the right to hurt someone frailer or weaker.

"Here," Roan said, digging out a foil-wrapped gift tied with red ribbon. "Mike said this was special for you." And he grinned.

Inca scowled as she took the gift. She made sure their fingers did not touch this time. Oh, she wanted to touch Roan again, but a large part of her was afraid of it, afraid of what other wild, unbidden reactions would be released in her body because of it.

"Thank you."

Well, at least Inca could be civil when she wanted to be, Roan thought, laughing to himself. He was discovering it was all about respecting boundaries with her. He watched covertly, pretending to search for the map, as she tore enthusiastically into the foil wrapping. She was like a child, her face alight with eagerness, her eyes wide with expectation. The wrapping and ribbon fluttered around her.

"Oh!"

Roan grinned as she held up smoked salmon encased in protective foil. "Mike said you had a love of salmon."

For the first time, Inca smiled. She held up the precious gift and studied it intently. "My blood brother knows my weaknesses."

"I doubt you have many," Roan said dryly, and caught her surprised look. Just as quickly, she jerked her gaze away from him.

"Do not be blinded by the legend that follows me. I have many weaknesses," she corrected him throatily. Laying the package in her lap, she took out her knife and quickly slit it open. The orange smoked fish lay before her like a feast. Her fingers hovered over it. She glanced at him. "Do you want some?"

"No, thank you. You go ahead, though, and enjoy it." Roan was pleased with her willingness to share. Among his people, it was always protocol to offer food first to those around you, and lastly, help yourself.

She stared at him through hooded eyes. "Are you sure?" How could he resist smoked salmon?

She was reading his mind. He could feel her there in his head, like a gentle wind on a summer day. For whatever reason, Roan felt no sense of intrusion, no need to protect his thoughts from her. He grinned belatedly as he pulled the map from the plastic case. "I'm sure. The salmon is your gift. Mike and Ann said you love it. I don't want to take a single bite of it away from you. Salmon's a little tough to come by down here," he joked, "and where I come from, there's plenty of it. So, no, you go ahead and enjoy."

Inca studied him. He was a generous and unselfish person. Not only that, he was sensitive and thoughtful to others' needs. Her heart warmed to him strongly. Few men had such honorable traits. "Very well." She got to her feet and went over to the tug captain. Roan watched with interest. Ernesto, his chest sunken, his flesh burned almost tobacco brown by the equatorial sun, reached eagerly for part of the salmon. He took only a little, and thanked Inca profusely for her generosity. She nodded, smiled, and then came and sat back down. Lifting a flake of the meat to her lips, she closed her eyes, rested her head against the cockpit wall and slid it into her mouth.

Roan felt Inca's undiluted pleasure over each morsel of the salmon. In no time, the fish was gone and only the foil package remained on her lap. There was a satiated look in her eyes as she stuck each of her fingers in her mouth to savor the taste of salmon there.

Sighing, Inca lifted her head and looked directly at him. "Your name. It has meaning, yes?"

Shocked at her friendly tone, Roan was taken aback. Maybe his manners had earned him further access to her. He hoped so. Clearing his throat, he said, "Yes, it does."

"Among our people, names carry energy and skills." Inca lifted her hand. "I was named Inca by a jaguar priestess who found me when I was one year old and living with a mother jaguar and her two cubs. She had been given a dream the night before as to where to find me. She kept me for one year and then took me to another village, where another priestess cared for me. When I was five years old I learned that my name meant I was tied to the Inca nation of Peru. Each year, I was passed to another priest or priestess in another village. At each stop, I was taught what each one knew. Each had different skills and talents. I learned English from one. I learned reading from another. Math from another. When I was ten, I was sent to Peru, up to Machu Picchu, to study with an Andean priest name Juan Nunez del Prado. He lived in Aqua Caliente and ran a hostel there for tourists. We would take the bus up to the temples of Machu Picchu and he would teach me many things. He told me the whole story, of what my name meant, and what it was possible to do with such a name." She lifted her hand in a graceful motion. "What my name means, what my destiny is, is secret and known only to me and him. To speak of it is wrong."

Roan understood. "Yes, we have a similar belief, but about our vision quest, not about our name. I honor your sacredness, having such a beautiful name." Roan saw her fine, thin brows knit. "With such an impressive history behind your name, I think you were destined for fame. For doing something special for Mother Earth and all her relations. The Incas were in power for a thousand years, and their base of operation was Cuzco, which is near Machu Picchu. In that time, they built an empire stretching the whole breadth and length of South America." Roan smiled at her. He saw that each time he met her gaze or shared a smile with her, she appeared uneasy. He wondered why. "From what I understand from Mike, you have a name here in Amazonia that stretches the length and breadth of it, too."

"I have lived up to my name and I continue to live the destiny of it every day," she agreed. Eyeing him, her head tilting slightly, Inca asked, "Have you lived up to yours?"

Inca would never directly ask why he had been given his name, and Roan smiled to himself. She wanted to know about him, and he was more than willing to share in order to get her trust. They didn't have much time to create that bond.

"My family's name is Storm Walker. A long time ago, when my great-great-grandfather rode the plains as a Lakota medicine man, he acquired storm medicine. He had been struck by lightning while riding his horse. The horse died, and as he lay there on the plain afterward, he had a powerful vision. He woke up hours later with the name Storm Walker. He was a great healer. People said lightning would leap from his fingers when he touched someone to heal them of their ills or wounds."

"Yes?" Inca leaned forward raptly. She liked his low, modulated tone. She knew he spoke quietly so that the captain could not overhear their conversation, for what they spoke of was sacred.

"One member of each succeeding generation on my mother's side of the family inherited this gift of lightning medicine. When our people were put on a reservation, the white men forced us to adopt a first and last name. So we chose Storm Walker in honor of my great-great-grandfather."

"And what of Roan? What is a roan? It is a name I have never heard before."

He quelled his immediate reaction to her sudden warm and animated look. Her face was alive with curiosity, her eyes wide and beautiful. Roan had one helluva time keeping his hands to himself. He wanted to see Inca like this all the time. This was the real her, he understood instinctively. Not the tough, don't-you-dare-touch-me warrior woman, although that was part and parcel of her, too. When there wasn't danger around, she was wide-open, vulnerable and childlike. It was innocence, he realized humbly. And the Great Spirit knew, he wanted to treat that part of her with the greatest of care.

"Roan is the color of a horse," he explained. "Out on the plains, my people rode horses. Horses come in many colors, and a roan has red and white hairs all mixed together in its coat." He smiled a little and held her burning gaze. "My mother was Lakota. A red-skinned woman. My father was a white man, a teacher who has white skin. When I was born, my mother had this vision of a roan horse, whose skin is half red and half white, running down a lane beneath a thunderstorm, with lightning bolts dancing all around it. She decided to call me Roan because I was part Indian and part white. Red and white."

Inca stared at him. She saw the vulnerable man in him. He was not afraid of her, nor was he afraid to be who he was in front of her. That impressed her. It made her heart feel warm and good, too, which was something she'd never experienced before. "That is why you are not darker than you are," she said, pointing to his skin.

"I got my mother's nose, high cheekbones, black hair and most of her skin coloring. I got my father's blue eyes."

"Your heart, your spirit, though, belongs to your mother's red-skinned people."

"Yes," Roan agreed softly.

"Are you glad of this?"

"Yes."

"And did you inherit the gift of healing?"

Roan laughed a little and held up his hands. "No, I'm afraid it didn't rub off on me, much to my mother's unhappiness."

Shrugging, Inca said, "Do not be so sure, Roan Storm Walker. Do not be so sure...."

Chapter 4

Roan had excused himself and went to the opposite side of the tug from where she stood. Once he felt sure they were safely motoring down the Amazon, the shooters nowhere in sight. His adrenaline had finally ebbed after the firefight. He'd noticed her hands were shaking for a little while afterward, too. It was nice to know she was human. It was also nice to know she was one cool-headed customer in a crisis. Not too many people that he knew, men or women, would have been so efficient and clear thinking in that rain of hot lead.

Absently, he touched the medicine piece at his throat and found the blue stone was so hot it felt like it was burning his skin. It wasn't, but the energy emanating from it made it feel that way. The stone always throbbed, hot and burning, anytime he was in danger. Roan knew without a doubt, from a lot of past experience, that the mysterious blue stone was a powerful talisman. There had been so many times in the past when it had heated up and warned him of forthcoming danger. One of his biggest mistakes had been not listening to his intuition the day his wife, Sarah, had gone climbing and died. On that morning, before she left, Roan had had a powerful urge to take off his amulet and place it around her slender neck. He knew she would have accepted the gift, but he'd never, ever entertained the thought of giving the stone to anyone. It had been ingrained by his mother and the tradition of his mother's tribe that the medicine piece should remain with one person until near the time he or she was to die, and then be passed on to the next deserving recipient. Still, the urge to give Sarah the stone had been overpowering, but he'd fought it because of his ancestral tradition. He told himself that it was wrong to take the stone off and give it away prematurely. Sadly, he now knew why his cougar guardian had urged him through his intuition to give Sarah the necklace to wear that day. It *might* have saved her life. He would never know. Rubbing his chest, Roan frowned, the guilt eating at him even to this day.

When he'd grabbed a cab at the airport to head to the dock, the blue stone had begun to throb with heat and energy. Roan had thought the stone was warning him about Inca, but he'd been wrong. She wasn't the one to fear; it was the gang that followed him to the dock that had brought danger.

He wanted to ask Inca a hundred questions now that things were calming down, but he knew Indian protocol, so he had to forego his personal, selfish desire to get nosy. Still, being in her company was like being surrounded by an incredible light of joy and freedom.

Moving to the other side of the tug, he dug deeply into

his canvas carry-on bag. Because he was Indian, and because it was only proper to introduce himself to the spirits
of this new land, Roan pulled out a large, rainbow-colored
abalone shell, a stick of sacred white sage and a red-tailed
hawk feather fan. Native Americans did not presume that
the spirits of the water, land or air would automatically
welcome them into their midst. A simple ceremony of
lighting sage and asking for acceptance was traditional.

Once the flame was doused, Roan placed the smoldering smudge stick in the shell. Picking it up, he faced the
north direction, the place where Tatanka, the great white
buffalo spirit, resided. Leaning down until the shell was
near his feet, Roan used the fan to gently waft the thick,
purling smoke upward around his body. The smoke was
purifying and signaled his sincerity in honoring the spirits
of this land. Fanning the smoke about his head, he then
placed the shell back on the deck. Sitting down, his back
against the cockpit, Roan closed his eyes and prayed. He
mentally asked permission to be allowed to walk this land,
to be welcomed to it.

As he said his prayers, his arms resting comfortably on
his drawn-up knees, Roan felt a burst of joy wash over
him. He smiled a little in thanks. That was the spirits of
the river, the land and air welcoming him to their territory.
He knew the sign well and was relieved. Roan didn't want
to go anywhere he wasn't welcomed by the local spirits.
It would have been a bad choice, and bad things would
have befallen him as a result.

Opening his eyes, he dug into his tobacco bag, which
he always carried on a loop on his belt. The beaded bag,
made out of tanned elk hide and decorated with a pink
flower against a blue background, was very old. It had

been his mother's tobacco bag. Digging into it, he held the proffered gift of thanks upward to the sky, and then to the four directions, to Mother Earth, before bringing it to his heart and giving thanks. Then, opening his hand, he threw the fragrant tobacco outward. He watched the dark brown flakes fly through the air and hit the muddy water, then quickly disappeared.

To his surprise, four river dolphins, sleek and dark, leaped within ten feet of the tug, splashing the peeling wood of the deck. Stunned, Roan watched the playful foursome race alongside the tug.

"The river spirit has taken your prayers and gifts to heart," Inca said in a low, serious voice as she approached him from the left.

Surprised, Roan tried to hide his pleasure that she was coming to speak to him. He would never gain her trust if he kept going to her and plying her with endless questions; she'd slam the door to herself tighter than Fort Knox.

The dolphins leaped again, their high-pitched cries mingling with the sound of the foaming, bubbling water. They arced high and splashed back into the river.

Roan smiled a little. "Helluva welcome. I didn't expect it."

Inca stopped and gazed at him critically. He looked relaxed, his large, scarred hands resting on his narrow hips. His profile was Indian; there was no question. Only the lightness of his copper skin revealed his other heritage, through his father. "The dolphin people don't often give such a welcome to strangers to their land, to their river," she murmured. She saw and felt his amazement and gratitude. Maybe Michael was right after all: Roan stood apart from all other men she'd known before. He was more like a Jaguar Clan member, knitted into the fabric of Mother Earth and all her relations. Roan understood that all things were connected, that they were not separate and never had been. Her heart lifted with hope. It was a strange, wonderful feeling, and automatically, Inca touched that region of her chest. She studied the medicine piece that hung around his thickly corded neck. With her clairvoyant vision she could see the power emanating from around that beautiful sky-blue stone he wore.

"You said your mother was a healer, yes?"

Roan nodded and squatted down. "Yes, she was." He saw that the smudge of sage had burned out. Tossing it into the river as an added gift, he took the abalone shell and placed it back into his bag.

"And did she heal by laying her hands on others, as we do in the Jaguar Clan?"

Roan wrapped the feather fan gently back into the red cotton cloth and placed it back into the bag as well, and then zipped it shut. He craned his neck upward and met her half-closed eyes. There was a thoughtful look on Inca's face now. She was so incredibly beautiful. Did she know how attractive she was? Instantly, he saw her brows dip. Was she reading his mind again? Frustrated, Roan figured she was, as he eased to his full height once again.

"My mother was a Yuwipi medicine woman. Her assistants would tie her wrists behind her back and tie up her ankles and then roll her up into a rug and tie the rug up as well. The lights would be doused, the singers and drummers would begin. The ceremony takes hours, usually starting at nightfall and ending at dawn. My mother, with the help of her spirit guides, was released from her bonds. She then prayed for the person whom the ceremony was for. Usually, that person was there in the room. There could be five, ten or fifty people sitting in that room, taking part in the ceremony. Lights would dance through the place. Horns would sound. The spirits brushed the attending people with their paws, their wings or tails. All prayers from everyone were directed to the person who was ill.''

Inca nodded. "A powerful ceremony. And did the person get well?"

He smiled a little and put his hands in the pockets of his jeans. "They always did when my mother conducted the ceremony. She was very famous. People came to her from around the world." He glanced at Inca's shoulder, where the splinter had wounded her. "And your clan heals with touch?"

Inca nodded. "You could say that."

"And healing is your calling? Your vision?"

"It is my life," she said simply. Lifting her hand, she watched as the dolphins sped away from the tug, finished with their play. "I took a medicine vow when I became a woman at age twelve. The jaguar priestess who was training me at that time inducted me into the service of our mother, the earth. She then prepared me to go to the clan's village for training, which began at age sixteen."

Roan shook his head. "It sounds like you were passed around a lot, from person to person. Did you ever find out who your parents were?" Instantly, he saw her close up. Her eyes grew opaque with pain and her lips compressed. Roan mentally kicked himself. He'd asked the wrong damn question. "Forget it," he said quickly. "You don't have to answer. That's too personal...."

Touched by his sensitivity, Inca found herself opening up at his roughly spoken words. She saw so much in his large eyes, in those glinting black pupils. Normally, if someone broached a question regarding her past, she'd shut down, get angry and stalk off. Not this time. Inca couldn't explain why her heart felt warm in her breast, or why her pulse quickened when he gave her that special, tender look. Always, she felt that blanket of security and warmth automatically surround her when Roan met and held her gaze. She was unsure of how to react, for she'd never met a man quite like this before. She wanted to be wary of him, to remain on guard, but his demeanor, and the fact that he was Indian like her, made her feel safe. Safe! No one had ever given her that sense before.

"No, I will answer your question." Inca sat down and leaned against the bulkhead. The last of the shakiness that always inhabited her after a confrontation left her. Being with Roan was soothing to her hard-wired nervous system, which was always on high alert. She crossed her legs, her hands resting on her thighs. Roan did the same, keeping a good six feet of space between them. Inca sighed. There was always something soothing about the gentle rocking of a boat in the arms of the Amazon River. "At times like this, I feel like a babe in my mother's arms," she confided throatily. "The rocking motion...somewhere in my memory, a long time ago, I recall being rocked in the arms of a woman. I remember fragments of a song she sang to me."

"One of the priestesses?"

"No." Inca picked at a frayed thread of the fabric on her knee. "I remember part of the song. I have gone back and asked each woman who helped to raise me if she sang it, and none of them did. I know it was my real mother...."

Roan heard the pain in her low voice. He saw her brows dip, and her gaze move to her long, slender, scarred hands. "I was abandoned in the rain forest to die. As I told you before, a mother jaguar found me. I was told that she picked me up in her mouth and carried me back to where she hid her two cubs. When the first jaguar priestess found me, I was a year old and suckling from the mother jaguar. I have some memories of that time. A few...but good ones. I remember being warm and hearing her purr moving like a vibrating drum through my body. Her milk was sweet and good. The woman who found me was from a nearby village. In a dream, she was told where to go look for me. When she arrived, the mother jaguar got up and left me."

Inca smiled softly. "I do not want you to think that the people who raised me from that time on did not love me. They did. Each of them is like a mother and father to me—at least, those who are still alive, and there are not many now...."

"You were on a medicine path, there is no doubt," Roan said.

"Yes." Inca brightened. "It is good to talk to someone who understands my journey."

"My mother set me on a path to become a medicine man, but I'm afraid I disappointed her." Roan laughed a little and held up his hands for a moment. "I didn't have her gift."

"Humph. You have a spirit cougar, a female, who is at your side. Medicine people always have powerful spirit guides. Perhaps you will wait until middle age to pick up your medicine and practice it. That is common down here in Amazonia. Most men and women do not even begin their training until their mid-forties.''

''You were trained from birth, which means you brought in a lot of power and skills with you,'' Roan said. He saw Inca smile sadly.

''There are days when I wish...'' Her voice trailed off. Shaking her head, she muttered, ''To be hunted like an animal, with a price on my head...to be hated, feared and misunderstood.'' She glanced over at him. ''At least the Indians of the basin understand. They know of my vow, know I am here to help protect them. The white men who want to destroy our rain forests want my life. The gold miners would kill me if they saw me. The *gaucqueros,* the gem hunters, would do the same. Anyone who wants to rape our land, to take without giving to it something equal in return, wants me dead.''

Roan felt her sadness. Quietly, he said, ''It must be a heavy burden to carry. I hope you have friends with whom you can share your burdens and dreams.''

Rubbing her brow, Inca whispered, ''I am all but thrown out of the Jaguar Clan. Grandfather Adaire has sentenced me and told me never to return to the village where all clan members train. I—I miss going there. Grandmother Alaria...well, I love her as I've loved no one else among those who have raised me. She is so kind, so gentle, all the things I am not.... I am like a rough-cut emerald compared to her. She is so old that no one knows how old she is. I miss talking to her. I miss the time we spent together.''

''Then you're an outcast?'' Roan saw the incredible pain in every feature of Inca's face. In some part of his heart, he knew she was opening up to him in a way that she rarely did with anyone. The energy between them was tenuous…fragile, just like her. He found himself wanting to slide his arm across her proud shoulders, draw her into his arms and simply hold her. Hold her and comfort her against the awful weight of pain she carried. In that moment, she was more a hurting child to him than a warrior woman.

"No, not exactly an outcast… Oh, to be sure, some members have been cast permanently out of the clan." She gave him a pained, one-cornered smile, and then quickly looked away. "My sentence is an ongoing one. Grandfather Adaire says I am walking on the dark side with some choices I have made. And until I can walk in the light all the time, I am not allowed to return to the village as a full member of it."

Roan frowned. "Light and dark? Familiar words and themes to me." He opened his hands. "Where I come from, in our belief system, light does not exist without darkness, and vice versa. You can't have one without the other. And no human being is ever all one or the other." He glanced over at her. "Are they expecting you *not* to be human? Not to make mistakes?"

She laughed abruptly. "The Jaguar Clan is an honorable part of the Sisterhood of Light. There are rules that cannot be broken…and I broke one of them. It was a very serious thing. Life-and-death serious." Inca frowned and tugged at the frayed thread on her knee until it broke off in her fingers.

"Mike Houston said you saved his life," Roan said. He ached to reach out to her now. There were tears swimming in her eyes, although Inca's head was bowed and slightly turned away from his in an effort to hide them from him. In her softened tone he could hear the wrenching heartache she carried. She moved her hands restlessly.

"That is why I was asked to leave my own kind, my home…. Michael was dying. I knew it. And yes, I broke the rule and went into the light where the souls of all humans who are dying go. I pulled him back from the Threshold. I gave my life, my energy, my heart and love, and drew him back. If not for Grandmother Alaria, who revived me because I was practically dead after saving Michael, I would not be here today."

"So, you saved a life? And Grandfather Adaire kicked you out of the clan for that?" Roan had a hard time understanding why.

"Do not be judgmental of Grandfather Adaire. He was only following the code of the clan. You see, we are trained in the art of life and death. Because we have the power, that means we must walk with it in strict accordance to the laws of the universe. I broke one of those laws. Michael had made his choice to die of his wound. I had been caring for him for a week, and for the first time in my life, I felt as if I had met my real brother. Oh, he was not, but that was the bond we had from the moment we met. It was wonderful…." She sighed unhappily. "I saw him slipping away daily. My heart cried. I cried alone, where no one could see me. I knew he would die. I did not want it to happen. I knew I had the power to stop it. And I knew it was wrong to intervene." Inca smiled sadly as she looked at the shore, which was a half a mile away on either side of the chugging tug.

"I wanted a brother just like Michael. I'd been searching so long for a family—I was so starved to have one—

that I did it. I broke the law. And I did it knowingly." Gravely, Inca turned her head and met his dark blue eyes. "And that is why I was asked to leave. What I did was a 'dark side' decision. It was selfish and self-serving."

Roan choked as she finished the story. He felt anger over it. "Didn't Grandfather Adaire realize that, because you were abandoned, family would mean so much more to you than it would to others?"

She hitched one shoulder upward and looked out at the muddy river. "That is an excuse. It is not acceptable to the clan. I broke a law. It does not matter *why* I broke it."

"Seems a little one-sided and unfair to me," he groused.

"Well," Inca said with a laugh, "my saving Michael's life, in the long term, had its positive side. He asked to become my blood brother. And when he fell in love with Dr. Ann, and she had his baby, Catherine, I became a godmother to their child." The tears in her eyes burned. Inca looked away. She wanted to wipe them away, but she didn't want Roan to know of her tears. No one ever saw her cry. No one. Choking on the tears, she rasped, "I have a family now. Michael and Ann love me. They accept me despite who I am, despite what I do for a living." She sniffed and reached for a pouch on her right side. "Look...here...let me show you baby Catherine...."

Roan watched Inca eagerly fumble in the pouch. The joy mirrored in her face was like sunlight. She valiantly tried to force the tears out of her glimmering willow-green eyes as she handed him a frayed color photo.

"This is Mike and his family," he said.

"Yes," Inca replied, and she leaned forward, her shoulder nearly touching his as she pointed at the baby held between them. "And this is Catherine...I call her Cat. She has a male jaguar spirit guide already! That is very special. She is special. Ann and Michael know it, too. Little Cat is my goddaughter."

The pride was unmistakable in Inca's passionate voice. It took everything for Roan not to respond to her excitement. She was so close he could smell her. There was a wonderful, fragrant scent to Inca. It reminded him of the bright pink Oriental lilies that grew behind his cabin, where Sarah had planted them. Looking up, he smiled into Inca's glimmering eyes as he handed her the photo.

"You should be proud of Catherine. She's lucky to have you as a godmother. Very lucky."

A sweet frisson of joy threaded through Inca's heart at his huskily spoken words. When she met and held his dark blue gaze, Inca's heart flew open. It caught her by surprise. A little breathless, she quickly put the photo back into the protective plastic and snapped the pouch shut.

"In my mind," she said, "what I did to save Michael's life was not wrong. It hurts to think I can never go home, but now my home is with him and his family, instead."

The sweet bitterness of Inca's past moved Roan deeply. "I don't know how you handle it all," he admitted. "I'd be lost without my family, my parents.... I don't know what it's like to be an orphan."

"Hard."

He nodded and saw that she was frowning. "I can't even begin to imagine...."

Inca found herself wanting to talk more to Roan. "You are a strange man."

He grinned. "Oh?"

"I find myself jabbering to you, making my life an open book to you. Father Titus was such a talker. He would tell me everything of what lay in his heart and feelings. Being Indian, we are normally quiet and reserved about such things. But not him. He made me laugh many times. I always thought he was a strange old man with his bird's nest of white hair."

"He was vulnerable and open with you."

Sobering, Inca nodded, "Yes, he was…and still is, even though I do not visit him as often as I would like because my duties are elsewhere."

"So…" Roan murmured, "am I like Father Titus?"

"No, I am! I blather on to you. As if I have known you lifetimes. I bare my soul to you, my heart—and I do not ever do that with anyone."

Wanting to reach out and touch her hand, Roan resisted. Instead he rasped, "Inca, your heart, your soul, are safe with me. Always and forever."

Regarding him gravely, Inca felt his words. She was afraid of him for some unknown reason, and yet, at the same time, drawn to him just as a moth is driven to dive into the open flame of a campfire. "You are of two worlds, Roan Storm Walker. One foot stands in the white man's world, the other in the Indian world. Yet you are not a two-heart. Your heart belongs to Mother Earth and all her relations."

"Judge me by my actions," he cautioned her. "Not my skin color."

Inca gazed at him raptly, before she suddenly felt the pull of the jaguar's warning.

Danger!

"Something is wrong." Inca was on her feet in an instant. When her spirit guide jaguar gave her such a warning, her life was in danger. "Get up!" she ordered Roan. Running around the stern of the tug, Inca grabbed her rifle.

Roan struggled to his feet. The soft, vulnerable Inca was gone in a heartbeat. Shaken by her sudden change, he stared at her. Secondarily, he felt the stinging, burning heat of the blue stone at the base of his neck throbbing in warning—only he hadn't felt it until now because he was so taken with Inca.

"What's wrong? What is it?"

"My guardian has warned me. We are in danger."

Before Roan could say another word, he heard the heavy, whapping sounds of a helicopter approaching them at high speed. He turned on his heel. Coming up the river, directly at them, was an olive-green, unmarked helicopter. It flew low, maybe fifty feet off the water's surface. His eyes widened. This was no tourist helicopter like the one he'd seen plying the skies of Manaus earlier. No, this was a helicopter, heavily armed with machine guns and rockets. The lethal look of the dark, swiftly moving aircraft made his heart rate soar with fear.

"Captain Ernesto!" Roan called. Before he could say anything, the blazing, winking lights on the guns carried by the military helicopter roared to life. Roan cursed. He saw two rows of bullets walking toward them like soldiers marching in parallel lines. The tug was right in the middle of the two rows.

"*Jump,* Ernesto!" Roan roared.

Inca positioned herself against the cockpit. She aimed her rifle at the charging helicopter. The first bullets hit the tug, which shuddered like a wounded bull. Wood splinters exploded. Crashing, whining sounds filled the air. The thick thump, thump, thump of the blades blasted against her ears. Still she held her ground. Aiming carefully, she squeezed off a series of shots. To her dismay, she watched them hit the helicopter and ricochet off.

"Inca! Jump!"

At the urgency of his tone, she jerked a look toward Roan. Before she could say anything, he grabbed her by the arm and threw her into the water.

Choking, Inca went under. She was heavily weighted down with the bandoliers of ammunition she always carried. Panicked, she gripped her rifle. Wild, zinging, whining bullets screamed past her as she floundered, trying to kick her way back up to the surface. Impossible! She had to remain cool. She had to think. Think! If she could not focus, if she could not concentrate, she would drown and she knew it.

Kicking strongly, her booted feet also weighing her down, Inca felt the current grab her. The water was murky and opaque. She could see nothing. Bubbles streamed out her open mouth as she lunged toward the surface.

Where was Inca? Roan looked around as he treaded water. The helicopter was blasting the tug to bits. Ernesto had not gotten off in time. Roan suspected the man did not know how to swim, so he'd stayed with his tug. Jerking at his boots, Roan quickly got rid of them. Inca? Where was she? He saw some bubbles coming to the surface six feet away from him. Taking a deep breath, he dove, knowing she was in trouble. She was too weighted down by the ammo she wore and she'd drown. Damn! Striking out in long, hard strokes, he followed the line of bubbles. There! He saw Inca, a vague shape in the dim, murky water.

Lunging forward, his hand outstretched, Roan gripped her flailing arm. Jerking her hard, he shoved her up past him to the surface.

Inca shot up out of the water, gasping for air, but still holding on to her rifle. Roan surfaced next to her and immediately wound his arm around her waist.

"Get rid of the boots!" he yelled, and he took the rifle from her.

Struggling, Inca did as he ordered. She saw the tug in the distance, a blazing wreck. The helicopter was mercilessly pummeling it with bullets.

"Now the ammo!"

"No!" she cried. "Not the ammo!"

"You'll drown!"

"No, I will not." Inca flailed and pushed his hand away. "Swim for shore," she gasped.

Roan wasn't going to argue. He kept the rifle and slung it over his shoulder. They struck out together. The Amazon River might look smooth on the surface, but the currents were hell. He kept his eye on the chopper.

"It's turning!" he yelled at Inca, who was ten feet ahead of him. "It's coming for us! Dive!"

Inca saw the military helicopter turning, its lethal guns trained on them. She heard Roan's order. Taking a huge breath into her lungs, she dived deeply and quickly. It was easy with the extra weight of the ammo around her upper body. At least twenty bullets zinged around her. Roan? What about him?

Worried, Inca halted her dive and turned around. Roan? Where was he? She could hear the helicopter's shattering sound just above them, the reverberation pulsating all around her. It was hovering over the water, very near to where she treaded. Roan was wounded! She felt it. No!

Anxiety shattered Inca. She kicked out violently and moved in the direction she knew Roan to be, even though she could not see him. The helicopter moved away, the dark shadow leaving the area. Concentrating, her lungs bursting for air, Inca kicked hard and struck out strongly. Roan? Where was he? How badly was he shot?

Her heart beat in triple time. Inca didn't want to lose Roan. She'd just found him! He was so much like her blood brother, Michael. Men like Roan were so rare. And she wanted—no, demanded of Mother Earth—that he be saved. She was lonely, and he filled that lonely space within her.

Yes, it was selfish, but she didn't care. Inca struck out savagely. She felt Roan nearby now. Well, selfishness had landed her in hot water with the clan before. Inca knew she was being tested again, but she didn't care if she failed this test, too. She would not let Roan die!

Blood and muddy water moved by her in thin, crimson and brown strips. She saw a shadow up ahead, striking toward the surface. Roan! Inca followed and, with her hand, pushed him upward. She could see blood oozing around his lower leg. He must have taken a bullet to the calf. Was his leg broken? Could he swim?

Unsure, Inca moved up, slid her arm around his massive torso and urged him upward.

They broke water together, like two bobbins coming to the surface. Water leaked into her eyes. She shook her head to clear them. The helicopter was moving back down the river, leaving them. Relief shuddered through Inca.

"Roan! Roan, are you all right?" She held on to him as he twisted around. His lips were drawn back from his clenched teeth. His face was frozen with pain.

"My leg…" he gasped, floundering.

"Can you use it to swim?" Inca cried. Their bodies touched and glided together. She kicked strongly to keep his head above water.

"Yeah…not broke. Just hurts like hell… And the blood. We've got piranhas in this water…."

Inca tugged at his arm. "Do not worry about them. Just head toward that shore. Hurry!" Mentally, Inca sent out her guardian and told him to keep the bloodthirsty little piranha schools at bay. Once they got the scent of blood in the water, fifty to a hundred of them would attack and shred both of them in a matter of minutes. That was not how Inca wanted to die. Nor did she want the man who relied heavily on her now to die, either.

"Kick! Kick your good leg," she ordered. "I will help you…."

It seemed like hours to Roan before they made it to the sandy red shore. Gasping for breath, he crawled halfway out of the water before his strength gave out. He was weakened from the loss of blood. Looking over his shoulder, he could see his bloody pant leg.

Inca hurried out of the water, threw off her ammo belts and ran back to him. She urged him to roll onto his back, and then hooked her hands beneath his arms. Grunting and huffing, she managed to haul him completely out of the water and onto the bank. Positioning him beneath some overhanging trees, she stopped for a moment, panting heavily. Dropping to her knees, she took out her knife and quickly slit open his pant leg to reveal the extent of his wound.

"H-how bad is it?" Roan gasped. He quelled the urge to sit up and grip the wounded leg. He felt Inca's hands moving quickly across his lower extremity, checking it out.

"Bad…" she murmured.

Roan forced himself to sit up. The bullet had torn through the fleshy, muscled part of his lower leg. Fortunately, it had missed the bones. Unfortunately, the wound was still spurting blood.

"An artery's been cut. Put pressure on it," he muttered. Dizzy, he fell back, and felt blackness encroaching on his vision. His gaze was pinned on Inca. Her hair was wet and stuck to the sides of her face. Her expression was intense, her eyes narrowed as she reached out and placed her hand across the jagged wound.

"Close your eyes," she snapped. "Do nothing but rest. Clear you mind. I will help you."

He didn't have much choice in the matter. Her hand, the moment it touched his feverish leg, was hot. Hot like a branding iron. Her fingers closed across his leg, strong and calming. Groaning, he stopped struggling and lay beneath the shade of the overhanging trees, breathing hard. His heart was pounding violently in his chest. Sounds meshed and collided. He was dumping. His blood pressure was going through the floor and he knew it. *Damn.* He was going to die. Darkness closed over his opened eyes. Yes, he would die.

Just as he drifted off into unconsciousness, Roan saw something startling. He saw Inca kneeling over him, her hand gripping his leg, and the blood spurting violently between her fingers. He saw the tight concentration on her face, her eyes gleaming as she focused all her attention on his wound. Roan saw darkness begin to form above her head. It appeared to be a jaguar materializing. Was he seeing things? Was he out of his mind? Was the loss of blood pressure making him delirious? Roan gasped repeatedly and fought to remain conscious. The head and shoulders of a jaguar appeared above Inca. And then it slid, much like a glove onto a hand, down across her head and shoulders. Blinking rapidly, Roan saw a jaguar where Inca had once been. Sweat ran into his eyes. Then he saw Inca, and not the jaguar.

Simultaneously, he felt raw, radiating heat in his lower leg. He cried out, the burning sensation so intense that it made the pain he'd felt before feel minor in comparison. Automatically, his hand shot out, but he was weak and he fell back. In the next instant, he spiraled into a darkness so deep that he knew he was dying and whirling toward the rainbow bridge where a spirit went after death.

Chapter 5

Roan awoke slowly. The howl of monkeys impinged on his consciousness first. Secondly, he heard the raucous screech of parrots as they shrieked at one another in a nearby rubber tree. And then—he was fatigued and it was an effort to sense much of anything—he felt warmth against his back. At first he thought it was Sarah snuggled up beside him, because she would always lay with her back against his in the chill of the early morning hours. The sensation in his heart expanded. No, he wasn't imagining this; it was real. Very real.

As he pried his eyes open, the events of the night before came tumbling back to him in bits and pieces until he put it all together. He'd been shot…he'd been bleeding heavily and he distinctly remembered dumping and preparing himself to die.

Wait… Inca…

His eyes opened fully. Roan pushed himself up on his

elbow and twisted to look over his shoulder. In the gray dawn light, a vague yellowish-white glow illuminating to the cottony clouds suspended over the rain forest, he saw Inca. She was curled up on her side, one arm beneath her head, the other hand wrapped protectively around the barrel of the rifle that paralleled her body.

He'd been dying. Inca had leaned over him and placed her strong, firm hand over the spurting, bloody wound on his leg. He glanced down to see the pant leg torn up to his knee, revealing his dark, hairy calf. Sitting up and frowning, Roan slid his fingers along the area that had been chewed up by the bullet. Nothing. There was no sign of a wound. And he was alive.

"I'll be damned."

Twisting to look over his shoulder again, he stared hard at Inca. She had healed him with her mystical powers. Now he recalled the burning heat of her hand on his flesh. He'd thought he was getting third-degree burns. He'd fainted from loss of blood. Scowling, he touched his brow. Yes, he was feeling tired, but not as weak as yesterday, when he'd lost at least a couple pints of blood.

Looking down at her, Roan's heart expanded wildly. In sleep, Inca looked vulnerable and approachable. Her hair, once in a thick braid, was now loose and free about her shoulders and face. Black tendrils softened the angularity of her cheeks. Her thick, ebony lashes rested on her golden skin. His gaze moved to her lips, which were softly parted in sleep. Instantly, his body tightened with desire.

Grinning haphazardly, Roan forced himself to sit up and look around. Running his fingers through his sand-encrusted hair, he realized he needed to clean himself up. Testing the leg, he was surprised to discover it felt fine, as if nothing had happened to it. A flock of scarlet ibis, with long, scimitarlike beaks, flew over them. Their squawks awakened Inca. He watched, somewhat saddened because he'd wanted more time to simply absorb her wild, ephemeral beauty into his heart.

As Inca opened her eyes, she met the penetrating blue gaze of Roan Storm Walker. Lying on the sandy bank, the warmth of it keeping her from being chilled in the dawn hour, Inca felt her chest expanding like an orchid opening. The look in the man's eyes was like a tender, burning flame devouring her. She was most vulnerable upon awakening. Normally, Inca would shove herself out of this mode quickly and efficiently. Nearby, Topazio lay and yawned widely. There was no danger or her spirit guardian would have growled and jolted her out of her wonderful sleep.

Inca drowned in the cobalt blue of Roan's large eyes. She saw a soft hint of a smile tugging at his mouth. What a wonderful mouth he had! She had never considered men beautiful, or bothered to look at them in that light before. With Roan, gazing at him was a sensuous pleasure, like eating a luscious, juicy fruit.

Inca found herself wanting to reach out and slide her fingers along his flat lower lip and explore the texture of him. She wanted to absorb that lazy smile of welcome. Simultaneously, she felt that incredible warmth of an invisible blanket embracing her once more. This time she didn't fight it. This time, she absorbed it and knew it came from Roan to her—as a gift. Inca accepted his gift in her sleep-ridden state. Nothing had ever felt so good to her. It made her feel secure and cared for. That particular feeling was so new to her that it jolted her even more awake.

Her eyes widened slightly as she considered the feelings that wrapped gently around her like a lover's arms.

Always, it was Inca who cared for others, who protected them, and not the other way around. The last time she'd had this feeling of care and protection was as a child growing up. After being asked to leave the village of the Jaguar Clan at age eighteen, she'd never felt it again. Not until now, and this sensation was different, better. She felt like a thirsty jaguar absorbing every bit of it.

As she studied Roan's shadowed features, the soft dawn light revealing the harsh lines around his mouth, the deeply embedded wrinkles at the corners of his eyes, she realized he laughed a lot. Father Titus had similar lines in similar places on his round, pudgy face, and he was always laughing and finding pleasure in the world around him, despite the fact that he was as poor as the Indians he cared for.

"You laugh a lot," she murmured drowsily, continuing to lie on her back observing him.

Roan's smile broadened boyishly, then faded. "I used to. I lost the ability to find much to laugh about two years ago."

Placing one arm behind her head, she gazed up at the soft, grayish-yellow clouds that hung silently above them, barely touching the canopy of the rain forest. "Why did you stop laughing two years ago?"

Roan lost his smile completely. He felt the tenuous intimacy strung between them, and realized he was starving for such intimacy. He'd had it once before and he missed it so very much. Now it was a gift growing between himself and Inca, and Roan was humbled by it.

"Two years ago, my wife, Sarah, died in a climbing

accident.'' Roan felt old pain moving through his chest. He pulled his knees upward and wrapped his arms around them. He looked out at the silently flowing Amazon that stretched endlessly in front of him.

"You'd have liked Sarah," he told Inca in a low, intimate tone. "She had red hair, cut short. She was an artist who drew the most incredible flowers and landscapes. She was a hellion. She knew no boundaries except the ones she wanted to create for herself. She was a world-class mountain climber. And she laughed at danger...." Roan closed his eyes. Why was he telling Inca all of this? It had sat in his heart like an undigested stone, rubbing and grinding on almost a daily basis. Yet, by him speaking to Inca, it was as if that stone was finally dissolving away and not hurting him as much.

"She was a warrior woman."

Nodding, Roan answered, "Yes. In all ways. She was a part of nature. More animal than human at times." He smiled fondly in remembrance. "We lived in a small cabin up in the Rocky Mountains in Montana. Hurt birds and animals would show up on our porch, and Sarah would care for them, feed them, tend their injuries, and when they were well enough, she'd free them. She'd always cry...." He shook his head and smiled gently. "Sarah was so attuned to nature, to life, to her own heart. One moment she'd be laughing and rolling on the floor with me, and the next, she'd read a newspaper or magazine and begin to cry over something sad she'd read."

Inca digested his hoarsely spoken words. She realized he was allowing her entrance into the deepest part of his heart. She had no experience with such things, but she sensed that she needed to be careful. Just as she offered comfort when she held a sick baby in her arms for healing, Roan needed that comfort from her right now. Pushing her fingers through her hair, Inca whispered, "How did she die?"

"On the Fourth of July, a holiday in our country. She was climbing a tough mountain made of granite to get ready for her big climb on El Capitan a week after that. She had friends that climbed that mountain every year. But this time Sarah was alone. I knew where she was, and what time she was to come home...." Roan felt his gut knotting. "I was out back of the cabin, fixing my truck, when I felt her fall. I could hear her scream in my head...and I knew..."

Wincing, Inca said, "You were in touch with her spirit. People who touch one another's hearts have this direct way of talking to one another."

Roan nodded. "Yes, we had some telepathy between us."

"What did you do then?"

"I jumped in the truck and drove like a madman to the rock wall where she'd been climbing." His voice turned ragged. "I found her dead at the bottom. She'd died instantly of a skull fracture." And if he'd given her his medicine piece to wear, she might still be alive today. But he didn't voice his guilt over that issue.

"A clean death."

"Yes," Roan said, understanding Inca's words. "At least she didn't feel any pain. She was gone in a heartbeat. I'm glad she didn't suffer."

Wryly, Inca looked up at him. He was suffering and she wanted to reach out and console him. Shocked by that, she curled up her fingers. "But you have been suffering."

"Sure. When you love someone like I loved her... well..."

Inca sat up. Her hair fell around her back, shoulders and arms, the ebony strands reaching well below her breasts. She opened her hands. "I do not know what love is. I have seen it between Michael and Ann. I have seen a mother's love of her child, a father's love of his children."

Giving her a look of shock, Roan tried to hide his reaction. "But...you're twenty-five years old. Isn't there someone in your life—a man—you love?"

Scowling, she skimmed the hair through her fingers and separated it into three long swatches. Expertly, she began to braid it, her fingers flying through the silky length. "Love? No, I do not know love like that."

Trying not to stare at her like an idiot, Roan quickly put some facts together about Inca. "Don't your clan members ever marry among themselves?"

Shrugging impatiently, Inca said, "Almost always. Only we understand each other's special skills and talents. People outside the clan are afraid of us. They are afraid of what they do not understand about us. Sometimes, a jaguar clan member will marry outside of it. Michael married Ann. There is no law as to who you marry. Of course, we would like the blessing of the elders."

"And does the person marrying a member of the Jaguar Clan know about his or her special skills?"

"Eventually, perhaps. And sometimes, no. It just depends. I know that Ann knows everything about Michael and his skills. She accepts them because she loves him." Inca took a thin strip of leather, tied off the end of her braid and tossed it across her shoulder. She saw the amazement on Roan's features. Why was he so surprised she did not have a lover? Did he not realize that in her business she had no time for such things? Life and death situations took precedence over selfish pleasures such as love…or so she told herself.

"Does Ann have problems coping with Michael's unusual abilities?"

Inca smiled. "I think so, but she tries very hard to accept what she does not understand about metaphysics. And their daughter has her father's skills, as well. Clan blood is carried on, generation after generation. One day my godchild, little Catherine, will be going up to the village for years of training." She smiled, satisfaction in her tone. "Until then, I get to see her from time to time, whenever I am near Mike and Ann's house."

Inca's family. It was all she had, really. Roan was beginning to understand her loneliness, the lack of a man in her life who could love her, care for her and give her safe harbor from a world that wanted her dead at any cost. Frowning, he rubbed his face, the feeling of his beard spiky against his fingers.

"Do you have any children by Sarah?"

The question caught him off guard. Roan eased his hands from his face and met her inquiring gaze. "No… and I wish I did, now."

"She did not want children?"

"We both wanted them. We'd been married only two years and wanted to wait a couple more before we settled down to having a family."

Inca rose slowly to her feet. She wriggled her bare toes in the red sand. "That is very sad. My heart goes out to you. Sarah was a warrior. She died loving what she loved to do, and in that there is great honor.'' Inca looked up at the clouds that now had a golden cast because the sun was going to rise shortly. ''But it was her time to pass over. She had accomplished all that she set out to do in this lifetime.'' Giving Roan a dark look, she added, ''We all have a time when we will die. When whatever we wanted to accomplish is complete. And when that happens, we leave. We walk over the Threshold to the other worlds.''

He slowly got to his feet. He felt a little weak, but not bad, considering what had almost happened. ''Speaking of dying...I owe you my life, Inca. Thanks.'' He stuck out his hand to shake hers. ''My mother could heal by touching a person, too, so I'm no stranger to what you did.''

Inca stared at his hand and then slowly lifted hers. She slid her slender fingers into his roughened ones. Trying to tell herself she did not enjoy making such contact with this tall, stalwart warrior, she avoided the sincerity of his burning blue gaze and whispered unsteadily, ''I did nothing. My spirit guide did it. You should thank him, not me.''

Roan closed his fingers gently over Inca's proffered hand. Her fingers were strong and yet, even as she gripped his hand, he felt her softness, her womanliness just waiting like a ripe peach to be lovingly chosen by the right man—a man who would honor her as an incredible woman and human being. He found himself wanting to be that man. The thought shook him deeply as he watched her hang her head and avoid his gaze. In some ways, she was so childlike, her innocence blinding him and making his heart open when he'd thought it impossible that anything could make him feel like this again.

"Thank *you* and thank your guide," he murmured, and released her hand. He saw relief in her features as she snatched it back. Inca wasn't used to being touched. At least, not by a man who had heartfelt intentions toward her.

"It was not your time to die," Inca said briskly. She looked down at his bare feet. "Ernesto died in the attack," Inca said sadly. "He was a good friend and helped me often."

Roan frowned. "I'm sorry, Inca."

Nodding, her throat tight with grief, she whispered, "I will pray for him." Lifting her head, she said, "We must go. There is much to do. I know where to get shoes for both of us. I always hide gear at different villages in the Basin in case I need replacements." She frowned, dropped her hands on her hips and looked up the Amazon to where they'd nearly gotten killed the day before. "Who attacked us? Marcellino? He hates me. He blames me for his son's death when I had nothing to do with him dying."

Brushing off the seat of his pants, Roan said, "Marcellino gave his word he wouldn't try and kill you. Could it be drug runners?"

A wry smile cut across her face as she hoisted the bandoliers back into place on her shoulders. "That is always possible. Drug lords hate me. For once, the country's government and they agree on one thing." She slung the rifle across her shoulder and gave him an imperious look. "They agree that I need to be dead."

"They'll have to come through me, first."

His voice was a dark growl. Shocked, Inca realized

Roan meant it. She saw his brows draw down, his eyes narrow. And she felt his protection wrapping around her. Laughing with embarrassment, Inca said, "You are the first man who has said that to me. Usually, it is the other way around—I protect men, women and children. They do not protect me."

"Even you need a safe harbor, some quiet, some down time," Roan reminded her. He looked around and then back at her. She had an odd look on her expressive features—one of pleasure mixed with shock. It was about time she got used to the fact that a man could care for her. Even though Roan honored her abilities, he knew that no human being was impervious to all the world's hurts. Sarah had taught him that. Inca was a woman. A beautiful, naive and innocent woman. And with each passing moment, Roan found himself wanting more and more to draw her into his arms and protect her from a world gone mad around her. She was too beautiful, too alive to die at the hands of some drug lord or crazed government soldier who wanted the considerable bounty on her head. No, as long as he was here, he'd make damn sure she was protected.

"Your feet," Inca said, pointing to them. "You lost your boots in the river. Where we need to go, you cannot travel. Your feet are soft." She held up one of her feet and pointed to the thick calluses on the bottom. "I can make it to the village, but you cannot."

"What if I cut off my pants to here—" he gestured with his index finger "—and wrap the cloth around them? Could I make it then?"

"Yes." Inca moved to the trees along the shore. She took out her knife and cut several long, thin, flexible vines from around one tree. She held them out to him. "Here, use my knife, and tie the cloth with these onto your feet."

Thanking her, Roan took her knife and the vines. In no time, his feet were protectively wrapped in the material. As he stood up and tried his new "shoes," she laughed deeply.

"My people will gawk at you when you enter their village. They will wonder what kind of strange man wears material on his feet."

Chuckling, Roan said, "Let them laugh. I'll laugh with them. How far is this village where you have supplies?"

Shrugging, Inca said, "By my pace, it is an hour from here." She eyed him. "But I do not think you will keep up with me, so it may take longer."

Grinning, Roan said, "Let's see, shall we?"

"Stop here," Inca said, and held up her hand. They halted near the edge of the rain forest. Before them was a Yanomami village of around fifty people. The huts were round in shape and thatched with dried palm leaves. In the center of the village were cooking pots hung on metal tripods. The men and women wore little clothing. Around their necks were seed and bead necklaces. Some wore feather necklaces from brilliant and colorful parrots. Their black hair was sleek and straight, cut in a bowl fashion around their heads. All the women wore brightly colored material around their waists, their upper bodies naked, save for the necklace adornments. Naked children of all ages were playing among the huts. Babies either sat on the yellow-and-red packed dirt, or hung on their mother's back as she worked over a cooking pot, stirring it with a stick.

Inca quickly divested herself of her bandoliers of ammunition, her knife and rifle. She laid them carefully beneath some bushes so that they were well hidden from prying eyes. She saw the question on Roan's face.

"I never enter any village with my weapons. I come in peace to my people. They see enough warfare waged against them, enough drug running soldiers brandishing weapons and knives. I do not want them to ever be afraid of me."

"I understand."

She pursed her lips. "Just watch. The Yanomami know very little Portuguese and no English. Say nothing. Be respectful."

Roan accepted her orders. She quickly moved out of the rain forest and onto the hard-packed dirt paths of the village. One of the first people to spot her was an old woman. Her black-and-gray hair was cut short, the red fabric of her skirt thin and worn around her crippled body. She gave a shrill cry in her own language, and instantly, villagers came hurrying toward where the old woman sat, hovering over her black kettle of bubbling monkey stew.

Roan stayed a good twenty paces behind Inca. The Yanomami looked at him, and then their expressions turned to adoration, their dark eyes glittering with joy as they threw open their arms, raised more cries of greeting and hurried toward Inca.

Every person in the village rushed forward until they surrounded Inca. Roan was startled by the change in her. No longer was she the defensive warrior. Instead, she was smiling warmly as she reached out and touched each of them—a pat on a person's head here, a gentle caress along a child's cheek there. Surrounding her, they began to

chant, the people locking arms with one another and beginning to sway back and forth. Their faces were illuminated with unabashed joy over Inca's unexpected arrival.

Inca hailed them by name, laughed and smiled often.
The Indians then ceased their welcoming chant in her
honor, stepped away and made a large, respectful circle
around Inca. Someone hurried forward with a rough-
hewn, three-legged stool. They set it down and excitedly
ask her to sit on it. As they brought her gifts—fruit and
brightly colored parrot feathers—she complied.

A mother with a baby hurried forward. Her singsong
voice was high-pitched, and tears were running down her
tobacco brown face as she held her sickly infant toward
Inca.

Inca murmured to the mother soothingly, and took the
baby, who was no more than two months old, into her
arms. The mother fell at Inca's feet, burying her head in
her hands, bowing before her and begging her to heal her
baby.

From where he stood, Roan could see that the infant
was starving, his small rib cage pronounced. Did the
mother not have enough milk to feed him? More than
likely. Roan stood very still, knowing he was privy to
something that few people would ever see. Even thirty
feet away, he felt a shift and change in energy. It was
Inca. He watched as she closed her eyes. Tenderly, she
shifted the weak infant in her hands and gently placed
him against her breast.

The mother's wailing and sobbing continued unabated
and she gripped the hem of Inca's trousered leg. The
pleading in her voice didn't need any translation for Roan.
Narrowing his eyes, he saw darkness begin to gather

around and above Inca. Blinking, he wondered if he was seeing things. No, it was real. A dark grayish-black smoke was coming out of the ethers above Inca's head. Then, quickly, the smoky mist began to take on a shape as it eased down across Inca's form. Roan stared hard. It was the jaguar! Roan recalled seeing it seconds before he'd lost consciousness the day before.

This time he steadied himself. He saw the jaguar apparition completely engulf Inca's upper body. It was superimposed upon her and he could see both simultaneously. Instead of Inca, he saw the jaguar's massive flat head, sun-gold eyes and tiny black, constricted pupils. A wave of energy hit Roan, and it reminded him of standing out in knee-high surf in the ocean and being struck by a large, far more powerful wave. He rocked back on his heels and felt another pulsating wave of energy hit him, and then another, as if the jaguar's intense and powerful energy was causing tidal fluctuations that rocked him rhythmically.

Roan tried to keep his concentration on the baby Inca held gently to her breast. Her head was tipped forward. At one point, she turned the child on his back and blew gently into his opened mouth. The sobs of the mother continued. Her face was streaked with tears; her eyes filled with agony as she begged Inca to save her dying baby.

Blinking, unsure of what all he was perceiving, Roan saw golden light coming out of Inca's and the jaguar's mouth simultaneously. He saw the golden threads move into the infant's slack mouth and fill his tiny form, which began to sparkle and throb with life. What was once a grayish, murky cocoon around the infant suddenly became clearer and more distinct. The grayness left, replaced by the white and golden light of life that now enveloped the baby.

As Inca raised her head, her eyes still closed, Roan saw the jaguar disappear. Instantly it was gone, as was the smoky cloud the animal had come out of. All Roan saw now was Inca and the baby. Holding his breath, along with the rest of the villagers, he realized he was watching a miracle take place. As Inca slowly opened her willow-green eyes, the infant in her hands moved and gave a weak cry. And then the baby's cry no longer wavered, but was strong and lusty.

The mother breathed the infant's name, leaped to her feet and stretched out her arms. Inca smiled softly, murmured reassuring words and carefully passed the baby back to her.

The woman held her child to her breast and bowed repeatedly to Inca, thanking her through her sobs. She looked at the baby, noting his animation and the fact that he was thriving and not sickly any longer. Face wet with tears, she knelt down before Inca.

Inca stood and drew her to her feet. She embraced the mother and held her for just a moment. Then releasing her, Inca asked who was next. Who wanted to be healed?

Roan stood there for a good hour, witnessing one healing after another. First to come were babies and mothers. After they were cared for, young boys and girls came forward. Sometimes Inca would simply lay her hand on a child's head. Sometimes she would ease youngsters onto her lap and hold them for a few moments. In nearly every case there was improvement, Roan noted. When it was finally time for the elderly, Inca went to them. Some were crippled. Others were so sick that they lay on pallets inside their makeshift huts.

Roan didn't mind waiting. A part of him wished that people like Colonel Marcellino could see this side of Inca. This was not the warrior; this was the healer. He began to understand what Mike Houston had said to him earlier. It was clear now why the Indians of the Amazon basin worshipped Inca as the jaguar goddess. No wonder. She had the power to heal. The power to snatch people from death's door and bring them back.

Her spirit guide did, Roan realized, mentally correcting himself. Inca was humble and lacked any egotism about her healing skills. That was typical of Indians. His own mother was one of the humblest souls he'd ever met. She never took credit for the energy that came through her and flowed into her patient. No, she gave thanks to the Great Spirit and to her spirit guides—just as Inca did.

Roan found a log to sit down on near the edge of the village. He was in no hurry today. As a matter of fact, being able to find out more about Inca and create a bond of trust with her was far more important than hurrying downriver to Marcellino's awaiting company. Roan hoped Inca would want to stay here overnight. He still felt weak, but was getting stronger and stronger as each hour slid by.

The peacefulness of the village was infectious. The laughter of the children, the barking of the dogs, the happiness on the faces of the people relaxed Roan. Above them, the clouds parted and sunlight lanced down through the triple canopy of the rain forest surrounding the village. A squadron of blue-and-yellow macaws winged overhead. They reminded him of rainbows in flight. Looking around, he saw that Inca was emerging from the last hut at the end of the village. He heard wails and cries coming from that hut. Inca looked tired. No wonder. She must have worked on fifteen people, nonstop.

Rising to his feet, he walked across the village to meet her. Without thinking, he reached out and slid his fingers around her upper arm. He saw turmoil in her eyes. The way her lips were set, as if against pain, touched him deeply.

"Come on," he urged her quietly, "come and sit down. You need to rest...."

Chapter 6

Jaime Marcellino stifled his anger toward his son. He had had only two children, but now only one was left. Julian was just a young, shavetail lieutenant straight out of the military academy, and Jaime wished mightily that he was more like his older brother, Rafael, had been: bold, brash and confident. As Jaime sat at his makeshift aluminum desk in the canvas tent, which was open at both ends to allow the humid air to sluggishly crawl through, he gripped his black-and-gold pen tighter. Julian stood at strict attention in front of him.

Oh, how young and cherubic his son's face was! At twenty-two, he looked more like a little boy than a man. Rafael had had Jaime's own sharply etched, proud and aristocratic features. Julian took after his mother, who was soft, plump and dimpled. Scowling as he scribbled his signature on some of the orders in front of him, Jaime jammed them into his attaché's awaiting hands. Around him, he could hear the company of soldiers preparing for the coming trek. They had just disembarked from a number of tug boats, and the men were setting up camp in the muggy afternoon heat.

"Lieutenant," he muttered, "your request to lead point with that—that woman is denied."

Julian's large, cinnamon-colored eyes widened. He opened his mouth to speak. His father's face was livid with rage. He could see it as well as feel it. The colonel's attaché, Captain Humberto Braga, blanched and stood stiffly at attention next to his father's chair.

"Sir, with all due respect—"

"Enough!" Jaime smashed his closed fist down on his table. Everything on it jumped. Snapping his head up, he glared at his son. "Permission denied. Point is the most dangerous position! I will not allow you to risk your life. You have a platoon to take care of, *Tenente,* Lieutenant. I suggest you do so. You have tents to set up, food to be distributed, and make sure that the men's rifles are clean and without rust. You have *plenty* to do. *Dismissed.*"

The attaché glared at Julian and jerked his head to the left, indicating that he should get out of the tent. Julian knew his father's rage well. He'd been cuffed many times as a child growing up, though after Rafael had been murdered, his father was less inclined to deride him and not take him seriously. Rafael had been a huge, heroic figure to Julian. He'd always looked up to his older brother. He'd gone to the military academy to follow in his big brother's footsteps, which he felt he could never possibly fill. Julian had labored and struggled mightily through four years of academy training. He'd barely gotten passing marks, where Rafael had gotten straight A's. Rafael had been captain of the soccer team, while Julian couldn't even make second string.

"Yes, sir," he murmured, and he did an about-face and stepped smartly out of the tent.

"Damn youngster," Jaime muttered glumly to his attaché after his son was out of earshot. He scribbled his signature hurriedly on another set of orders. He hated the paperwork. He was a field officer, not a paper pusher. Oh, that kind of attitude had garnered him many enemies among the army ranks, that was for sure, but Jaime didn't care. He loved the outdoors. He reveled in missions such as the upcoming one. The only fly in the ointment was that the jaguar goddess was going to lead the company. And what the hell was wrong with Julian wanting, of all things, to work side-by-side with her? Had his youngest son gone *louco?* Crazy?

"I think he's trying to behave as Rafael might have in this situation, sir," the attaché ventured gently. "To do something heroic, to get your attention. My opinion, of course, sir." Humberto steeled himself for an explosion from his superior.

Grunting, Jaime looked up. He folded his hands restlessly. Looking out the side of the tent where the flap was thrown upward, he growled, "He'll *never* be Rafael. I wish he'd quit trying. Ever since he was murdered, Julian has been trying to make up for it." With a shake of his head, he muttered, "And he never will. Julian will never be what Rafael was."

"I think he knows that, sir," Humberto said, some pity in his tone.

"He's soft. Look at his hands! No calluses. His face is soft and round. I doubt he'll even be able to keep up with

his men on this mission,'' Jaime fumed in a whisper so
no one else would overhear. ''Rafael was tough—hard as
a rock. He was an incredible athlete. Julian has trouble
making the mandatory runs and hikes.'' Snorting, Jaime
looked up at the thirty-year-old career officer. Humberto
Braga was a trusted individual who had come from the
poverty of Rio de Janeiro and worked his way through
college and eventually joined the army. Jaime admired
anyone with that kind of courage and guts. Humberto was
someone he could trust and confide in, too.

''Yes, sir, he's not Rafael in those respects,'' Humberto
said, ''but his men like him. They listen to him.''

Raising his thick, black brows, Jaime nodded. ''Yes,
thank goodness for that.''

''Perhaps this mission will be good for the boy, sir. He
needs to show you he's capable.''

Leaning back in the metal chair, Jaime pondered the
younger man's reflection. ''Asking to work with Inca is
like asking to work with a bushmaster snake.''

Humberto chuckled indulgently. Bushmaster snakes
were well known to be one of the most poisonous in the
Amazon. Not only that, but when the snake was disturbed,
it would literally chase an unfortunate person down, bite
him and kill him. Not many snakes were aggressive like
the bushmaster, and it was to be feared. It had earned its
reputation by leaving bodies of people in its wake over
the centuries. The legends about the snake had grown, and
Humberto knew most of them were true. ''I hear you,
sir.''

Looking at his watch, Jaime muttered, ''Where the hell
is Storm Walker? He said they'd meet us here this morning. It's already noon.'' Again Jaime snorted and went

back to the necessary paperwork. "And Morgan Trayhern said he was punctual. Bah."

Humberto was about to speak when he saw a tall man, an Anglo dressed in cutoff pants, a burgundy polo shirt and sandals, approach the tent. He'd seen a picture of Roan Storm Walker, so he knew it was him. Surprised, he stammered, "Colonel, Senhor Storm Walker is here...."

"Eh?" Jaime glanced up. Humberto was pointing toward the tent entrance. Jaime turned his head and met Roan's narrowed eyes. Storm Walker had a two-day growth of beard on his hard face and it made him look even more dangerous.

"It's about time," Jaime snapped. "Enter!"

Roan moved into the tent. He glanced at the thirty-year-old captain, who curtly nodded a greeting in his direction. "Colonel, I'm a little late."

Jaime glared up at him. "More than a little. I'm not impressed, Storm Walker."

Roan stood more or less at ease in front of the colonel, whose face had flushed a dull red. He saw the anger banked in the officer's eyes.

"I think you know why, too."

"What? What are you talking about?"

Roan studied him. The officer seemed genuinely surprised. "That unmarked helicopter that came out of nowhere and blasted the tug we were on to pieces? Does that ring a bell, Colonel?" Roan tried to keep the sarcasm out of his voice. Who else but Marcellino knew of their plans to meet, as well as the place and the time? No one.

Chagrined, Marcellino put down the pen and gave Roan a deadly look. "I haven't the faintest of what you are talking about, Storm Walker. What helicopter? And what tug?''

"We were attacked yesterday," Roan said tightly, "first by thugs in two cars. We barely made it onto the tug before they started firing at us with military rifles. There were six of them. And an hour later we were attacked by a green, unmarked military helicopter. It rocketed the tug. We jumped off it and dove as deep as we could." Roan decided not to tell of his wounding and of Inca's healing. He wanted to stick to the point with the colonel. "We had to swim to shore. And if it weren't for Inca knowing the lay of the land, I wouldn't be here now. We were twenty miles northwest of your landing area when the attack happened."

Marcellino slowly rose. "I know nothing of this attack," he protested strongly.

"You were the only one who knew our itinerary," Roan retorted, barely hanging on to his temper. He rarely got angry, but the colonel's innocent look and remarks stung him. He'd had a restless night's sleep, and hiking through the humid rain forest for fifteen miles this morning hadn't helped his mood at all.

"Are you accusing *me* of those attacks?" Marcellino struck his chest with a fist. Then he placed his hands flat on the table, leaned forward and glared up into the *norteamericano*'s livid features. "I had *nothing* to do with either attack!"

"You hate Inca," Roan declared. "You'd do anything to kill her because you mistakenly believe she killed Rafael, your eldest son."

Rearing back, Jaime put his hands on his hips in a defiant stance, despite the fact that he wasn't anywhere near

Roan's height. "I gave my word to Senhor Trayhern that I would *not* lay a hand on her. And I have not!" His nostrils flared and quivered. "You are gravely mistaken, *senhor*."

"Inca's angry. She has a right to be. She thinks *you* were behind the attack."

Jaime laughed explosively. "Oh, how I wish I were, Senhor Storm Walker." He lost his smile and glared at him. "But if I had of been, believe me, you two would not be alive today. I'd have hung that helicopter over the water and put a hundred bullets through her body when she came up to get air." He jabbed a finger toward Storm Walker. "Captain Braga!"

Humberto snapped to attention. "Yes, sir!"

"Take Senhor Storm Walker to our quartermaster. Get him a set of army fatigues, a decent pair of boots and other gear. And loan him a razor. He needs to shave."

Roan looked at the colonel. Was he lying? Was he telling the truth? Roan wasn't sure. The colonel's response seemed genuine; he'd looked surprised when he'd learned of the attacks. "As soon as I get cleaned up, I need a copy of the map you're using. Inca will look at it with me and I'll get back to you about the route we'll take tomorrow morning at dawn."

"Fine." Marcellino looked out of the tent. "Where is she?"

"Nowhere that you or your men will ever find her," Roan growled.

Shrugging, Jaime said, "Make sure she stays out of my way. I have ordered my men *not* to fire at her, or to make any overture toward her that she may read as harm."

Turning on his heel, Roan ducked beneath the canvas

of the tent and followed Captain Braga out into the main encampment. The hundred and eighty men of Macellino's company were loosely strung out for half a mile along the shore of the Amazon. He could tell that the contingent wasn't used to rain forest conditions. Tents were going up. Men were smoking cigarettes and talking as they dug in for the evening hours ahead. The odor of food cooking caught his attention.

"Hungry?" Humberto asked with a slight smile.

Roan looked over at the officer who accompanied him. Humberto Braga sported a thin, black mustache. His face was square and he was built like a bulldog. He wasn't aristocratic in bearing or facial features; he had more of a peasant demeanor. Roan couldn't dislike the soft-voiced officer. "Yeah, just a little."

"You hiked fifteen miles this morning?"

Roan gave him a cutting smile. "Yeah." Inca had taken the lead and moved effortlessly, hour after hour, through the rain forest. He'd known she was in superb shape, but her ability to move at a continued trot without rest had stunned him. She'd only rested when he needed to take a break. As she had pointed out to him, he was wearing sandals that one of the Indians had given him, and sandals were not best for that kind of march.

Humberto pointed to the quartermaster's large tent. "Here we are. I'll help you with getting all the equipment you will need." He eyed Roan again. "Fifteen miles in how many hours?"

"Three."

Sighing, Humberto said with a grin, "And I wonder how fast we can push this company starting tomorrow morning."

Roan halted. "That's a good question, Captain, and not one I can answer right off the top of my head." He eyed the struggling company entrenching its position. A number of soldiers were heading out to predestined points several hundred yards ahead of the encampment, he saw. They would be forward observers—the eyes and ears of the company—to protect it from possible attack by drug runners.

"I think we will need two or three days to get—how do you say—the hang of it?"

Roan nodded. His mind and his heart were elsewhere—with Inca. She'd agreed to stay out of sight. Worried that the FOs might surprise her, he wanted to get done with the clothes exchange as soon as possible and get back to where she was hiding.

Julian Marcellino took off his helmet and wiped his sweaty brow with the back of his arm. He'd stumbled over some exposed roots and nearly fallen. Looking back, he grinned a silly grin. As usual, he wasn't watching where he was going. Rafael would never have tripped. He'd have seen the twisted roots sticking above the damp layer of leaves on the rain forest floor, and avoided them completely.

Halting, Julian heard the noise of the encampment far behind him. He had chosen men from each platoon to serve as forward observers, had picked out stations for them and ordered them to begin digging their foxholes, where they would remain for a four-hour watch before another two men took over for them. Then he'd made an excuse and gone off on his own.

He didn't like the cacophony of noise that was ever-present at the camp. No, in his heart he longed for the pristine silence of nature. As he looked up admiringly at the towering trees, the brightly colored orchids hanging off the darkened limbs, the sunlight sifting through the canopy, he sighed softly in appreciation. Tucking his helmet beneath his left arm, he wandered on into the rain forest, glad to be relieved of his responsibilities for just a little while. The leaves were damp and there was a wonderful musty, sweet scent from their decay. The screech of monkeys in the distance made him turn in their direction. The floor of the forest wasn't flat, but undulating. He climbed up and over a hill, and the noise from the company abated even more. That was good. He loved the silence.

Wiping his sweaty brow again, he moved quickly down the hill. At one point, he slid because of the dampness. Here in this humid country the rains would come and go, keeping the ground beneath the fallen leaves slick and muddy. Landing on his butt, he slid down to the bottom of the hill, where there was a small, clean pool of water. Laughing out loud over his lack of athleticism, Julian was very glad his father hadn't seen his awkward, unmanly descent. Or his men. Julian knew they tolerated him because his father was a colonel. He saw the amused and disdainful looks they traded when they thought he wasn't looking.

Remaining in a sitting position, Julian raised up enough to push his helmet beneath him. At least his butt would stay dry. Drawn to the beauty of the deep blue oval pool, of the orchids suspended above it on branches, he sighed again. Most of the noise of the company had faded in the distance. Here there was peace. A peace he craved. Placing his elbows on his thighs, he rested his jaw against his hands and simply drank in the beauty of the landscape. Being in Amazonia was turning out to be a wonderful, surprising gift to him.

Inca watched the soldier. She sat very still against a tree, hidden by the extended roots that stretched out like flying buttresses. When he'd appeared at the top of the hill, she had focused in on the soldier instantly. She had been eating her lunch, her back against one of the sturdy roots, when her guardian had warned her of his approach.

He was young looking. No threat to her. His face was babyish, his lips full. His eyes were wide with awe as he slowly absorbed the scene around him. The pistol he carried at his side indicated he was an officer, not an enlisted soldier. Snorting softly, she finished her mango and wiped her glistening lips with the back of her hand. Rolling over onto her hands and knees, she continued to watch the man. There was a bright red bromeliad on a dead log near where he sat. She watched as he reached out, his gesture graceful, the tips of his fingers barely grazing one of the many bright red bracts, which were really leaves and not petals. The way he touched the plant piqued Inca's interest. Most men would not even pay attention to it, much less touch it with such respect and reverence.

His hair was black, short and close cropped like Roan's. His ears were large and stuck out from the sides of his head, which was probably why he looked more like a boy growing through an awkward stage than a man. Inca smiled mirthlessly. She felt no threat from this young whelp. He looked out of place in a uniform. The way he touched the bromeliad again and again, and raptly studied it, made her decide to reveal her presence.

Julian heard a sound across the pool. It wasn't loud, just enough to snag his attention. As he lifted his chin, he gasped reflexively. There on the other side of the pond was a woman in military gear. Her willow-green eyes ruthlessly captured and held his gaze. She stood with her head high, a challenging look on her face, her hands resting arrogantly on her hips. And then, just as quickly, he realized *who* she was.

Inca laughed, the sound carrying around the pool. She felt the young man's shock when he realized who she was. Lifting her hands, she said, "I am unarmed, *Tenente.* I come in peace. Do you?"

He saw the laughter in her willow-green eyes. He heard the derision and challenge in her sultry tone. Her hair was unbound and flowed freely across her proud shoulders and the bandoliers of ammunition she wore crisscrossed on her chest. Swallowing hard, he leaped to his feet. The heel of his boot caught and he slipped hard to the ground once more. Julian felt a rush of shame and humiliation. He expected her to deride him for floundering around like a fish out of water.

But she did not. Scrambling to his feet, he spread his boots far enough apart to give him some stability on the soft, damp leaves near the lip of the pond. Breathing hard, he stared across the hundred feet that separated them.

"Y-you're Inca...the jaguar goddess...." he croaked. "Aren't you?"

Julian had seen rough sketches of the woman on Wanted posters. She was supposed to have murdered his brother. He had never believed it. In person, she was shockingly beautiful. Just looking at her Indian features, the light shining in her eyes and the way she smiled at him, he rejected even more strongly the possibility that she had murdered Rafael. She had the face of an angel. Never had he seen anyone as beautiful as her! Even his fiancée, Elizabeth, who was truly lovely, could not match Inca's wild, natural beauty.

"I am," Inca purred. She removed her hands from her hips. "So, you are from the company that I am to lead?"

Gulping, his heart pounding, Julian stammered, "Er, y-yes…we are. I mean, I am…."

Laughing, Inca watched as his face flushed crimson. "Do not worry. I will not harm you, *Tenente*." She held up her hands. "I was finishing my lunch. Would you care for a mango? I have one left."

Stunned by her pleasant demeanor, Julian found himself utterly tongue-tied. Maybe it was her beauty. Or maybe it was all the whispered legends about her filling his head in a jumble that made him cower before her obvious power and confident presence.

Inca leaned over, picked up the mango. "Here," she called, "catch!"

Julian's hands shot out. He caught the ripe mango.

"Good catch." Inca laughed. She watched the young officer roll the fruit nervously in his hands. "You are quick. That is good. We will need that kind of reaction where I am going to lead you."

"Th-thank you, Inca…or do you want to be called jaguar goddess?"

Inca felt the shame and humiliation coming from him. Why? Her heart went out to this young man, who really didn't belong in the army. He belonged in a garden tending his vegetables. Or perhaps in a greenhouse tending beautiful orchids. That would make him happy. Still, Inca respected him. "Call me Inca. And you are?"

Holding the mango gently in his hands, he said, "Y-you may call me Julian." He hooked a thumb across his shoulder. "I'm a lieutenant with this company. I have a platoon that I'm responsible for. I was really looking forward to being here. I've never been out in the rain forest and I've always wanted to come...."

She smiled and said, "You are at home here."

Julian was dumbfounded. "Why, yes...yes, I am. But—how could you know?"

"I read minds when I want to."

Gulping, Julian nodded. "I believe you. I really do." His heart was pounding hard with the thrill of getting to see this legendary woman in person.

"And the other men," Inca called, "are they as friendly and unthreatening as you are toward me?" The corners of her mouth lifted in a barely disguised smile of sarcasm.

"Oh, them...well, they are all right, Inca. I mean... most of them have heard the legends about you. They are all hoping to see you, to get a glimpse of you—"

"Why? To put a bullet through my head?"

Wincing, Julian held up his hand. "Oh, no, no...not that. There's been so much speculation, even excitement, about you...the possibility of seeing you. That's all."

She moved slowly toward the edge of the pond and said, "What about Colonel Marcellino? Does he still want to see me dead?" Her voice was flat and hard.

Gulping, Julian raised his eyes. "That...my father has mixed feelings about you. I mean, it's understandable...I never believed you did it. Not ever. But he was so full of anguish and grief that he had to blame someone. I don't believe drug runners, and that is who said you killed Rafael.''

Inca froze. Her eyes narrowed to slits. The moment she heard Julian say ''my father,'' her hand went to the pistol at her side. ''Colonel Marcellino is *your* father?'' she demanded.

''Y-yes, he is. I'm Julian Marcellino. I apologize. I should have told you my last name. It's just that…well, I'm a little shook up, afraid.…'' His voice drifted off.

Looking at him, Inca growled, ''You do not believe I killed Rafael?''

Shaking his head adamantly, Julian said, ''No…and now, seeing you in person, even more I do not believe you killed my older brother.''

Inca knew that something greater was at play here. What were the chances of the brother of Rafael showing up where she was hiding? Very slim. She understood the karma of the situation. The soldier was white-faced now, and stood stiffly, the fruit clutched in his hands. Buffeted by his tumultuous feelings, Inca ruthlessly entered his mind to see if he was, indeed, telling her the truth.

Julian winced. He took a step back, as if he'd been physically struck.

''Sorry,'' Inca called. She moved more gently into his mind. Julian staggered and sat down unceremoniously. As she moved through his psyche, she saw and felt many things. That was the problem with telepathy—it wasn't just about getting information, it meant feeling all the damnable emotions that came along with the information. It was so hard on her that she rarely read minds. She didn't want to deal with many emotions.

In her mind, she saw Julian as a baby, a youngster, a

teenager during his time spent in the military academy. As she withdrew her energy from him, he uttered a sigh of relief. Inca squatted down on her haunches and stared at him across the pond. "You are not a soldier at heart. This is not a job you love. You are doing this to please your father, not yourself."

Rubbing his head, Julian felt a slight headache. The power that Inca possessed stunned him. "Yes, well, my father wanted me to carry on in Rafael's place. How could I say no? He put such importance on me carrying on the family name and tradition. All the firstborn men went into the army and distinguished themselves. It is expected."

Laughing harshly, Inca said, "Better that you go tend a garden, my young friend." She knew now that Julian bore her no grudge. He wasn't a killer. Inca seriously wondered if he could even pull the trigger of a rifle pointed toward an enemy. No, he was a peaceful, serene person who was not faring well in the military world. At all.

"I like gardening," Julian said, slowly getting to his feet. He retrieved his helmet and settled it awkwardly on his head. "Is there anything I can do for you? Do you need supplies? Food?"

Touched by his thoughtfulness, Inca said, "No...thank you. I am waiting for Roan Storm Walker to return with the map."

"Oh, to see which direction we go tomorrow morning?" Julian smiled a little. "I'd give *anything* to be with you two as you take us into the rain forest."

The eagerness in his voice was genuine. Inca slowly relaxed. "Your father would never let you near me and you know it. Go back. Go back to your men and say nothing of our encounter. If your father finds out, he will be very upset about it.''

"Yes, he would,'' Julian admitted ruefully. He smiled a little hesitantly. ''Thank you for the fruit. That was very kind of you, Inca. And if there is anything I can do to help you, please let me know?''

She lifted her hand. ''I will, *Tenente*. Go now.''

Inca watched the soldier clamber awkwardly up the incline. Shaking her head, she realized that the entire company would struggle like that on this slick, leafy terrain. Turning, she went back to her hiding spot between the roomy wings of the tree roots, more than adequate to protect her from prying eyes. Sitting back down, she leaned against the smooth gray bark and closed her eyes.

Missing Roan, Inca wondered if he was all right. She felt a connection to him, like an umbilical cord strung invisibly between them. She sighed. The fifteen-mile hike this morning had been hard on both of them. Wanting to take a nap now, but not daring to do so, Inca felt her jaguar guardian move around. Instantly, she sat up, her eyes flying open.

There on the edge of the hill above the pool was Roan. He carried a map in his hand. She smiled and felt heat rush through her. How handsome he was in her eyes. And this time he was dressed in jungle fatigues and had a good pair of black leather boots on his feet instead of the sandals. Standing, she left the tree to meet him halfway down the hillside.

"You look different.'' She grinned and pointed to his face.

Rubbing his jaw, Roan absorbed her teasing expression. ''Yeah, the colonel wanted me clean shaven. Now I know why I got out of the Marine Corps." He chuckled. Holding up the map, he said, "We've got work to do. Are you up to it?"

Inca nodded and fell into step beside him. There was something wonderful about his height, and that feeling of warmth and protection that always surrounded her when he was near. "Of course. Are *you?*"

Giving her an intimate look, Roan said, "Of course." He saw she had some mangos for him in the small cotton knapsack tied to her web belt. It was spring in Amazonia, and far too early for such fruit to be ripe. When she'd reached into it and brought out fruit and nuts earlier, during one of the rests they had taken on their march, Roan had considered asking about them.

"Where do you get this fruit? It's out of season," he said now, sitting down against the tree with her.

Inca picked out a mango and handed it to him. "I will it into being."

Opening the map before her, he glanced up. "What do you mean?"

"We are taught how to move and use energy in the Jaguar Clan village. If I will a mango into existence, it occurs. Or nuts." With a shrug, Inca said, "Our will, our intent is pushed and ruled by our emotions. If I am in alignment with my feelings and really desire something, I can manifest it on a good day." She grinned mirthlessly. "And on a bad day, when my concentration is not good, or I am emotionally shredded, I forage on the rain forest floor like all the rest of our relations to find enough food to stop my stomach from growling."

Taking the mango, Roan bit into it. "It's real."

"Of course it is!"

The flesh was juicy and sweet. He pointed to the map. "This is the army's best attempt at defining the trails through Amazonia. We're here—" he tapped his finger on the map "—and this is where we have to go. Now, you tell me—is there a better way to get there? I don't see any trail marked between here and there."

Studying the map, Inca grimaced. "This map is wrong. I expected as much." She tapped her head. "I know how to get us there."

"At least draw it on the map for me? The colonel will want something concrete. He's not a man who can go on a wing and a prayer like you or I do."

"Humph." Inca took the map and placed it across her lap, her thin brows knitting.

Roan absorbed her thoughtful expression. The moments of silence strung gently between them. Her hair was loose, and he had the urge to thread his fingers through that thick silken mass. There was such sculpted beauty in Inca, from her long, graceful neck to her fine, delicate collarbones, prominent beneath the T-shirt she wore, to the clean lines of her face.

"You will not guess who I just ran into minutes before you came."

Frowning, Roan asked, "Who?"

Lifting her head, she met and held his dark blue gaze. "Tenente Julian Marcellino."

Eyes narrowing, Roan rasped, "What?"

Chuckling, Inca told him the entire story. When she was done, she said, "He is a sweet little boy in a man's body. He is not a warrior. He does this for his father, to try and fill in for his missing big brother."

Sucking air between his teeth, Roan said worriedly, "That was a little too synchronistic."

Shrugging, Inca said, "We got along well. He believes me to be innocent of Rafael's murder. That is good."

Saying nothing, Roan allowed her to continue to study the map. After Inca had traced a route in pencil and handed it back to him, he said, "Marcellino swears he didn't try and bushwhack us with that helicopter, or those men on shore."

Inca eyed him. She slid her long fingers through her dark hair and pushed it off her shoulders. The afternoon humidity was building and it was getting hotter. "Do you believe him?"

"I don't know," Roan murmured, studying the route she'd indicated on the map. "He seemed genuinely surprised when I told him."

"If not him, then drug runners," Inca said flatly.

"Maybe. How could they get the info on where we'd be going and the time we'd be at the dock?"

"They have their ways," Inca said. "They are part of the Dark Brotherhood, and have people who can read minds just as I can. They can travel in the other dimensions, look at information, maps, reports, and bring the information back to the drug lords."

"I didn't know that."

One corner of Inca's mouth pulled inward. "Do you think I and my kind fight a battle only on this dimension you call reality? No. The battles occur on many other levels, simultaneously. The Dark Brotherhood works to see chaos replace the goodness of the Sisterhood of Light." She waved her hand above her head. "If you think for a moment that the drug lords do not use every tool they can, think again.''

''Then...Colonel Marcellino could be telling the truth.''

She smiled a little at his thoughtful expression. The urge to reach out, slide her hand across his cleanly shaved jaw caught her by surprise. But then, Inca was finding that around Roan, she was spontaneous in ways that she'd never been with another man. Pulling her focus back from that unexpected urge, Inca whispered, ''Yes, the colonel could be telling the truth.''

Chapter 7

"**W**ell?" Marcellino snapped, as he mopped his perspiring brow with his white, linen handkerchief, "what do you have for us, Storm Walker?"

Roan stood before the colonel, who had decided to leave his stifling tent and continue to make plans at a makeshift table beneath the tangled, grotesque limbs of a rubber tree fifty feet from the bank of the Amazon.

"I've talked to Inca," Roan said, spreading the map before the colonel, his captain and lieutenants, who stood in a semicircle around the metal table. Dusk was coming and shadows had deepened. When he'd arrived back in camp, all the tents were up, in neat order. The men had eaten and were now cleaning their rifles for the coming march, which would take place at 0600 tomorrow morning.

Moving his large hands across the map of the area, Roan traced the route with his index finger for the colonel.

The lamp was suspended precariously above them on a limb and drawing its fair share of insects. "This is the route that Inca feels we should go."

Scowling, Jaime squinted his aging eyes. At fifty-three, he had to wear bifocals now. Grudgingly, he pulled them from his blouse pocket and settled them on the end of his nose. The light was poor, but he could see the penciled line on the map. Leaning down, he studied it for a number of minutes.

"This takes us through some of the worst terrain in the basin!" he muttered, as he lifted his head and straightened up. Perspiration trickled down his ribs. The long-sleeved fatigues, which everyone wore as protection from biting insects, did not breathe well. Jaime was gulping water like a camel to stay hydrated. Wiping his wrinkled brow, he saw his son, Julian, standing among the four lieutenants across the table from him. The boy's expression was eager as he studied the route.

"Sir," Julian said respectfully, "I see why Inca is doing it." He tapped his finger on the map. "We avoid the swamp to the south of us. To the north, there is a major river to cross, and we do not have the capabilities to span it. By tackling the steep terrain, we take the safest route. Swamps are well known for their diseases, piranhas, snakes and other vermin."

Many other soldiers were crowding around, at a distance, to eavesdrop. They had nothing else to do in the twilight, and Julian's soft voice made them trudge a few inches closer to hear his words.

"That's exactly why she chose the route," Roan intoned. He saw the colonel's narrow face flash with annoyance. The glare he gave his hesitant son made Roan angry. The young man was diplomatic, yet had the guts to take on his father, who everyone tiptoed around.

Captain Braga leaned down and studied the map. "The swamp is too large to try and march around, sir. But at this time of year, in spring, there is the chance of heavy rains, flooding, and that is lowland area. If we get too much rain, that swamp will rise five or ten feet in a hurry. Men could drown in such a scenario." He frowned and looked closely at the suggested route. "Yet I see why you don't like the other route, Colonel. It is very steep, hilly terrain."

"Exactly," Marcellino snapped. "It will increase our time to the valley by another week. Besides, men will fall, slip, and we'll have injuries—sprained ankles and perhaps broken legs." Marcellino looked down at the damp leaves beneath his shining boots. "This is slippery footage at best."

"Colonel, Inca strongly suggests you do not choose the swamp route," Roan said. "Even though spring signals the end of the wet season here, that doesn't guarantee it won't rain. If your men get out in the swamp and the river floods its banks, they could drown. We have no quick, sure way of rescuing a company that's stuck on one of the islands in that swamp. It's too far from any base, and helicopters, unless they refuel in flight, couldn't manage a rescue attempt."

"The swamp is the fastest route to the valley," Marcellino growled. "We can send point men ahead to test the terrain where we're going to march."

Julian compressed his lips. His father remained ramrod straight, his mouth thinned, hands resting imperiously on his hips. He was going to take the swamp route, Julian knew. He opened his mouth to say something when, from the back of the large group of men, there came a shout of surprise. And then another. And another. Because he was short, barely five foot ten inches tall, he stood on tiptoe to find out what all the excitement was about.

Roan turned on his heel when he heard a number of men calling loudly to one another and moving rapidly aside at the rear of the assemblage. It was Inca! She was striding toward them like she owned the place. Didn't she? Roan turned sharply and pinned the colonel with his eyes.

"It's Inca," he warned him tightly.

Instantly, Marcellino's hand went to the holster hanging at his right hip.

Roan nailed him with a glare. "Don't even think about it," he rasped.

Julian smiled in greeting as he saw Inca, who strode, tall and proud, up to the table. The crowd parted for her, the men's mouths hanging open in awe, their stares all trained on her. They gave Inca plenty of room. When she swung her cool, imperious gaze toward him, Julian bowed his head slightly in honor of her unexpected presence. She was, indeed, a goddess! Every man, with the exception of his father, looked up at her in admiration, respect and fear. She was afraid of no one and nothing. Marching bravely into their camp only made her more untouchable, in Julian's eyes.

Roan met and held Inca's laughter-filled eyes. The half smile on her mouth, the way she held herself as she halted at the table, opposite the frozen colonel, made him go on alert. Inca was in danger. Marcellino's face darkened like a savage thunderstorm approaching. His eyes flashed with hatred as he met and held her challenging look.

"If I were you, Colonel, I would listen to your son and your other officer, here." Inca flicked a hand lazily in Braga's direction, who stood staring at her in awe. "If you go the swamp route, you are guaranteeing the death of a number of your men. Is that what you want? A high body count before you even reach that valley where the Valentino Brothers hold my countrymen as slaves?" she demanded, her husky voice quieting the throng.

Roan moved to Inca's side, standing slightly behind her to protect her back. He trusted no one here. Marcellino had given his word that he and his men would not harm her, but he believed none of them. Cursing to himself, he wished Inca hadn't marched into camp like she owned the damn place. Keeping his eye on the men who were gawking like slobbering teenage boys at Inca, and the colonel, whose face was turning a dusky red with rage, Roan geared himself to take action.

"What you say has nothing to do with anything!" Marcellino hissed in a low, quavering tone. "You promised to stay out of my encampment."

Shrugging easily, Inca growled in return, "I am in the business of saving lives, Colonel, unlike you, who considers your soldiers nothing more than cannon fodder on the road to reaching your own objectives."

As she stared him down, beads of sweat popped out on the colonel's wrinkled brow. His hatred spilled over her, like tidal waves smashing against her. Because she was innocent, she did not connect emotionally into the colonel's rage, grief and loss. She had no compassion for the man whose fingers itched to pull the pistol at his hip out of that black, highly polished leather holster, and fire off round after round into her head and heart.

Marcellino cursed. "You bitch! You murdering bitch. Get out of here before I kill you!"

Roan stepped forward. "Colonel—"

It was too late. Marcellino unsnapped his holster, clawing at the pistol resting there.

Just as Roan moved to step in front of Inca to protect her, he felt the energy around her change drastically. It felt as if someone had sucker punched him with a lightning bolt. Roan staggered backward, off balance. Braga made a choking sound and backed away, too. Julian uttered a cry and fell back many feet. The energy sizzling around Inca was like an electric substation that had just been jolted with fifty thousand watts of electricity.

Roan heard Marcellino give a cry. Jerking his head around, he saw the colonel drop the pistol from his hand. Grabbing at his throat, he squawked and took two steps back, his face going white and then a gray-blue color. His eyeballs bulged from their sockets. His mouth contorted in a soundless scream.

"Do not presume you can kill me, Colonel," Inca snarled.

Roan blinked. Something invisible had the colonel by the throat, strangling him. He cried out and crashed to his knees, wrestling with the invisible force. He cried out again and began to choke.

Julian grabbed the tent pole to steady himself. When he saw what was happening, he leaped forward. "Papa!"

Roan turned, his back against Inca's. His narrowed gaze swept the men, who were now mesmerized and frightened by the unfolding spectacle. Automatically, he drew his

pistol and held it in readiness, should any one of them try
to shoot Inca.

Jaime choked. Slobber sputtered from the corners of his
gaping mouth. He felt as if some large, powerful animal
had gripped him by the throat with its invisible jaws. He
was dying! Unable to draw in a breath of air, he fell,
writhing, to the damp ground. All he saw were Inca's
willow-green eyes, thoughtful and concentrated upon him.
Devastated and shocked by her power, he kicked out. The
table went flying.

Julian fell to his side, sobbing for breath. "Stop! Stop!"
he begged Inca. "Don't kill him! He's my father!"

Inca lifted her chin slightly. She ordered her spirit
guardian, Topazio, to release the white-faced colonel from
his massive jaws. The army officer, now semiconscious,
fell into his son's arms. "Very well, Julian. For you, I do
this," she stated.

Marcellino gasped and then gagged. He rolled onto his
side and vomited. Julian pulled out his handkerchief and
cleaned around his father's mouth, then held him protectively in his arms.

Gripping his neck weakly, Jaime swore he could still
feel the invisible force, though the sensation was dissi-
pating rapidly. Head hanging down, he lay in his son's
arms, breathing harshly. How good it felt to have air in
his lungs again!

Julian's hand fluttered nervously over his shoulders.
"Leave me!" he ordered his son hoarsely. "I'll be fine!"
And Jaime forced himself to sit up on his own. Angrily,
he shoved his son away from him, embarrassed that his
men had seen him in such a compromising position.

Julian winced and staggered to his feet. Trying to hide

his hurt over his father's rejection, he sought out and found Inca's gaze. "T-thank you...."

"Everyone stand down," Roan ordered, his voice carrying across the assemblage. "Inca came in peace and she's going to leave that way. If I see anyone lift a weapon, I'll fire first and ask questions later." He held up the pistol as a reminder.

Rage fueled Marcellino. He staggered to his hands and knees, and sat down unceremoniously, still dizzied. Spitting out the acid taste in his mouth, he twisted his head and glared up at the cool, collected woman warrior at whose boots he sat at like a pet dog.

"You promised not to hurt me," Inca reminded him in a dark tone. "You went back on your word. You are not to be trusted. I came here to help you."

"And you will," Jaime rasped as he staggered to his feet. Gripping the edge of the table with one hand, he wiped his other hand across his mouth. "The great Green Warrior will go back on her word, eh? So now you refuse to lead us?"

Inca smiled a deadly smile. "I will lead you, Colonel. My word is my bond. The only thing that will break it is death. But I am warning you—do not go through the swamp. It is too dangerous at this time of year as we move from wet to dry season."

"Inca, you'd better leave," Roan warned over his shoulder.

She smiled laconically and slid her fingers beneath the leather strap of her rifle, which rested on her right shoulder. "I am leaving now."

Julian rushed forward. He gripped Inca's arm.

Inca froze momentarily. She looked down at the lieutenant.

"Thank you," he whispered unsteadily, giving her arm an awkward pat. "For your compassion, your understanding…"

There was something heart-wrenchingly innocent and vulnerable about Julian. Inca reached over and placed her hand across his. "I did it for you, *Tenente*. Not for *him*." And she glared at the colonel. "Your son needs you as a father. I hope you realize that someday. You treat him like a mongrel dog come late to your family, and that is wrong."

Marcellino stared in shock at Inca as she turned on her booted feet and imperiously marched off the same way she'd come. He hated her. She had murdered Rafael. In the twilight, as she reached the rain forest beyond his gaping soldiers, Inca seemed to disappear into thin air. Rubbing his eyes angrily, Marcellino told himself it was the poor light of the coming dusk that tricked him. Gently touching his aching throat, he tried to explain away the pain that still throbbed where invisible hands—or jaws—had wrapped powerfully around his throat and damn near choked him to death.

"Pick up my pistol," he ordered Braga in a scratchy voice that warbled with fear. Irritated, humiliated in front of his men, Marcellino turned on all of them. They looked as if they'd seen a ghost. "All of you!" he roared, his voice breaking. "Get back to your quarters and your posts. We rise at 0500. Get some sleep!"

The men quickly departed. Marcellino saw Roan holster his pistol and come back to the table, his black brows drawn down with displeasure. Too bad. Grabbing the map, Marcellino threw it at his attaché.

"We go through the swamp, Captain."

Braga blanched, but took the map and gently folded it up. "Yes, sir, Colonel."

Roan stood there in shock. Was the man crazy? And then it dawned on him that whatever Inca said, Marcellino was going to do the exact opposite. Fuming, he turned away.

"I'll see you at 0600, Colonel."

Nodding brusquely, Marcellino turned and hurried back to his tent.

Roan moved back into the darkening rain forest. Very little light trickled down through the canopy as, with monkeys screaming and chattering, the cape of night was drawn across Amazonia. Being careful where he walked, he allowed his eyes to adjust to the gloom. What the hell had prompted Inca to make that kind of entrance? What was going through her mind? She was a proud woman. And she probably couldn't stand not being in on the planning of the march. In some ways, Roan didn't blame her.

He moved along the trail back to their hiding place. A sound—someone crying possibly—drifted into earshot. Halting, Roan keyed his hearing. Yes…there is was again: a soft, halting sobbing. Where? He turned and slowly allowed his ears to become his eyes. Turning off the trail, he moved quietly down a slight incline. Below were six silk-cotton trees, their winged roots splaying out around them. The grove looked like a darkened fortress in the twilight. The sound was coming from there.

Scowling, Roan lightened his step. It *was* someone crying. A woman weeping. Who? Frowning, he stepped down into the clearing among the trees. As he rounded one of the huge, winglike roots, he stopped. Shock jolted through him. It was Inca! Crouched there, her head bowed upon her arms, she was crying hard. Taken aback, Roan stood, unsure of what to do. He felt embarrassed for her, for coming upon her without her knowledge. Why was she weeping? Stymied, he cleared his throat on purpose to let her know he was there. Every particle of him wanted to rush over and embrace her and hold her. He felt her pain.

Sniffing, Inca jerked up her head. Roan stood no more than five feet away from her. Shaken and surprised, she quickly wiped her face free of tears. Why hadn't her guardian warned her that he was coming? Feeling broken and distraught, Inca knew emotionally she was out of balance with herself. When she was in this state, her guardian often had a tough time trying to get her attention. She was, after all, painfully human, and when she allowed her emotions to get the better of her, she was as vulnerable as any other person.

"What do you want?" she muttered, humiliated that he'd seen her crying.

"Stay where you are," Roan urged softly. Taking a chance, a helluva big one, he moved over to her. He slowly crouched down in front of her, their knees barely touching. "I don't care if you are the jaguar goddess," he whispered as he lifted his hand and reached out to her. His fingers grazed her head, the thick braid hanging across her left shoulder. Her hair felt crinkly from the high humidity.

Inca wasn't expecting Roan's gesture and she stiffened

momentarily as his long, scarred fingers brushed the crown of her head. Warmth flowed down through Inca. She was shaken by his continued, soothing stroking of her hair. At first she wanted to jerk away, but the energy in his touch was something she desperately needed. Forcing herself to remain still, Inca leaned back against the trunk of the tree and closed her eyes. An unwilling sob rose in her. She swallowed hard and tried to ignore her tumultuous feelings.

Roan moved closer, sensing her capitulation to his grazing touches. He saw the suffering in her face, the way the corners of her mouth were pulled in with pain. "I'm glad to see you this way," he said wryly. "It's nice to know you are human, that you can cry, that you can let someone else help you...." And it was. Each time his fingers stroked her soft, thick hair, a burning fire scalded his lower body. Roan wanted to lean down and brush her parted lips with his, to soothe the trembling of her lower lip with the touch of his mouth. More tears squeezed from beneath her thick, black lashes.

"I cry for Julian," she managed to whisper hoarsely, in explanation of her tears. "I felt his pain so sharply. Julian adores his father, and yet his father does not even realize he exists." Sniffing, Inca wiped her nose with the back of her hand. She looked up at Roan's dark, heavy features. His eyes were tender as he leaned over her. She felt safe. Truly safe. It was such an unusual feeling for Inca. Her whole life was one of being on the run, being hunted, with no place to let down her guard. Yet she felt safe with Roan.

Smiling gently, Roan settled down next to Inca. It was a bold move, and yet he listened to his heart, not his head.

He eased himself behind her, placing his legs on either side of her.

"You're crying for Julian. Tears for the boy who needs a father." Roan whispered. He allowed his fingers to caress the back of Inca's neck. Her muscles were tight. As he slowly began to massage her long, slender form, he felt her relax trustingly.

Everything was so tenuous. So fragile between them. As if an internal thunderstorm was ready to let loose within him, Roan felt driven to hold her, to comfort her, to be man to her woman.

Inca trembled. Roan's fingers worked a magic all their own on her tight, tense neck muscles. She leaned forward, her head bowed, resting her arms on her drawn-up knees so that he could continue to ease the tension from her.

More tears dribbled from her tightly shut eyes as he massaged her neck. "Julian is sweet. He is innocent, like the children I try to help and heal. He tries so hard to please his father. Back there, I watched him. He was a man. More of a man than his father. And he is right about the path. I was surprised he accepted my route."

Roan could smell her sweet, musky odor and inhaled it. She was like a rare, fragrant orchid in that moment. It would be so easy to pull her into an embrace, but his heart warned him that it would be rushing Inca and could destroy her growing trust in him. No, one small step at a time.

"If Julian knew you were crying for him, I think he would cry, too."

Choking on a sob and laughter, Inca nodded. "I like him. He is a kind man. He reminds me of Father Titus, the old Catholic priest who raised me for a while."

"You don't see many of those kind of men down here, do you?" Roan moved his hand tentatively from her neck to her shoulders and began to ease the tension from them.

Inca moaned. "You have hands like no one else."

"Feel good?" He smiled a little, heartened by her unexpected response.

"Wonderful…"

"You let me know when you've had enough, okay?" Roan knew it was important for Inca to set her own emotional boundaries with him. She trusted him, if only a little. His heart soared wildly. He was close enough to press a warm, moist kiss on her exposed neck. What would her flesh feel like? Taste like? And how would she respond, being such a wild, natural woman?

Lifting her head, Inca gave him an apologetic look. "Much touches my heart."

"You just don't let others know that about you," Roan murmured as he moved his hand firmly against her shoulders. "Why?"

"Because the miners, those who steal the timber and those who put my people in bondage will think it is a sign of weakness." Inca wrinkled her nose. "What do you think Colonel Marcellino would do if he saw me crying over how he treated his devoted and loving son? He would put that pistol to my head faster than he tried to today."

"I can't argue with you," Roan said heavily. "How do your neck and shoulders feel now?" He gave her a slight smile as she turned sideways and regarded him from beneath tear-matted lashes.

"Better." Inca managed a broken, trembling smile. "Thank you…" She shyly reached out and slid her fingers across his large hand, which rested on his thigh. It was an exhilarating and bold move on her part and she could see Roan invited her touch. She'd never had the urges she felt around him. And right now her heart was crying out for his continued touch, but she felt too shamed and embarrassed to ask him to do more.

"Anytime."

"Really?"

He grinned a little. "Really."

She lifted her hand from his, her fingertips tingling pleasantly from the contact. The back of his hand was hairy. She felt the inherent strength of him, as a man, in that hand. Yet he'd been so incredibly gentle with her that she felt like melting into the earth.

"I think you are a healer and do not know it yet."

Roan lifted his hands. "My mother wished that her medicine had moved through me, my blood, but it didn't. Sorry." Giving Inca a humorous look, he told her conspiratorially, "If I can ease a little of your pain, or massage away some tight muscles, then I'm a happy man."

She snorted softly and wiped the last of her tears from her cheeks. "It takes very little to make you happy, then, Storm Walker."

"I don't consider what we share as little or unimportant," he told her seriously. "I like touching you, helping you. You carry the weight of the world on those proud shoulders of yours. If I can ease a little of that load, then it does make me happy."

Inca considered his words, which fell like a warming blanket around her. She craved Roan's continued closeness. She liked the way his bulk fit next to her. In some ways, he was like a giant tree whose limbs stretched gently overhead, protecting her. She smiled brokenly at the thought. The warmth of his body was pleasant, too, with the humidity so high and the sun gone away for the night. The night hours were always chilly to her. What would Roan think if she moved just a few inches and leaned her back against his body? Frightened and unsure, Inca did nothing. But she wanted to.

"What is it about you that makes me feel as I do?" she demanded suddenly, her voice strong and challenging.

Eyebrows raising, Roan stared down at her. The way her petulant lips were set, the spark of challenge in her eyes, made him smile a little at her boldness. "What do you mean? Do I make you feel bad? Uncomfortable?"

"No…just the opposite. I like being close to you. You remind me of a big tree with large, spreading branches— arms that reach out and protect people."

"That's my nature," Roan said in a low tone. He saw her eyes narrow with confusion for a moment. Her tentative feelings for him were genuine and his heart soared wildly with that knowledge. Roan knew instinctively that Inca was an innocent. He realized she was a virgin, in more ways than one. Her relationship skills were not honed. Yet the honest way she had reached out to him touched his heart as nothing else ever could.

"You make me feel safe in my world—and in my world there is no safety." Inca's lips twisted wryly. "How can that be?"

"Sometimes," Roan told her gravely, "certain men and women can give one another that gift. It is about trust, too."

Inca sighed. "Oh, trust…yes, that. Grandfather Adaire said until I could trust someone else with my life, that I would never grow. That I was stuck." She frowned and leaned her head back, looking up at the silhouettes of the trees in the darkness surrounding them.

"And what did Grandmother Alaria say?"

Surprised, Inca twisted to look up at him. His eyes gleamed in the darkness, rich with irony and humor. "How do you know she said anything to me?"

"She's the leader of the village, isn't she? I'd think that she'd have something positive to say to you while you're working on the emotional blocks that were created by your being abandoned at birth."

His insight was startling. Inca found herself not feeling alarmed about it as she normally would. Raising her hands, she said, "Grandmother Alaria said my heart wound was stopping me from trusting, but that, at some point when I was a little older, more mature, I would work on this blockage. She said she had faith in me to do it."

"Because you have a magnificent heart, Inca. That's why she said those words to you."

Deeply touched by his praise, she said, "I am a bad person, Roan. Grandfather Adaire has said that of me many times. A bad person trying to fulfill the Sisterhood of Light's plan to help all my relations here in Amazonia."

Reaching out, Roan captured some errant, crinkled strands of her hair and gently tucked them behind her ear. He saw her eyes mirror surprise and then pleasure. Good, she was beginning to see his touch as something positive in her life. Tonight Inca had opened her heart to him. The trust in him that inspired that made him feel like he was walking on air. The joy that thrummed through him was new and made him breathless.

"You're a good person, Inca. Don't listen to Grandfather Adaire. Good people make mistakes." He frowned and thought of how he hadn't given Sarah his medicine necklace to wear on that fateful climb. Why, oh why, hadn't he followed his instincts? "Guaranteed, they do. Sometimes really disastrous mistakes. But that doesn't make them bad." Just sorry for an eternity, but he didn't mouth those words to Inca. She was suffering enough and didn't need to know from what experience his words came.

Inca gave him a flat look, her mouth twitching. "Then what? If I am not bad, what am I?"

"Human. A terribly vulnerable and beautiful human being…just like me. Like the rest of us…."

Chapter 8

"They are going to have many of their men injured or killed going through the swamp," Inca said the next morning as she stood beside Roan on a hill that overlooked the thin, straggling column of men a good half mile away. They were well camouflaged by the rain forest. Luckily, the floor of the forest was clear of a lot of thick bushes and ferns, due to the fact that the triple canopy overhead prevented sunlight from reaching the ground. It made marching faster and easier.

"The colonel is bullheaded," he said, turning and looking at her. This morning he felt a change in Inca. Oh, it was nothing obvious, but Roan felt that she was much more at ease with him. It was because of the trust he was building with her. "I wish he'd listen to his son."

Snorting, Inca adjusted the sling of the rifle on her right shoulder. "Julian has more intelligence than his father ever will."

''You like him, don't you?''

With a shrug, Inca said, ''He is a gentle person in a machine of war. He does not fit in it. I like his energy. He is a man of peace. My heart aches for him, for all he wants from his father. The colonel is lucky to have Julian. But he does not know that.''

''You don't find many men like that,'' Roan said, partly teasing. ''The peaceful type, that is.''

''You are like that.''

''Yeah?'' He baited her with a growing grin. Just being next to her was making him feel happier than he had a right to be. Roan recalled that Sarah had made him feel that way, too. There was something magical about Inca. She was completely naive to the fact that she was a beautiful young woman. Not many of the men of the company had missed her beauty. Roan had seen them staring openmouthed at her, like wolves salivating after an innocent lamb.

Inca liked the warm smile he turned on her. ''Sometimes I think you have been trained by the Jaguar Clan. You handle yourself, your energy, carefully. You do not give it away. You conserve it. You know when to use it and when not to.'' She found herself wanting to reach out and touch Roan. That act was foreign to her, until now. He stood there in his fatigues, the shirt dampened with sweat and emphasizing his powerful chest and broad shoulders. Recalling his touch, Inca felt warmth stir in her lower body like sunlight warming the chill of the night. An ache centered in her heart as she lifted her gaze to his mouth, which was crooked with that slight, teasing smile. She liked the way Roan looked. His face was strong and uncompromising, like him. When he'd moved to her back and drawn his pistol to protect her from possible harm by the soldiers as she confronted the colonel, she'd been grateful. Not many men would stand their ground like that. Though badly outnumbered, he'd been good at his word; he had protected and cared for her when it counted. He *could* be trusted.

She smiled a little as she watched the army column below. The men were slipping and falling on the damp, leaf-strewn rain forest floor. Inca wanted the colonel to make twenty miles a day, but the men of this company were too soft. They'd be lucky to make ten miles this first day.

"With the way they are crawling along, the Valentinos will be well prepared for them when we finally make it to that valley."

Roan nodded. "The troops aren't in good shape. It will take at least five days to toughen them up. We'll lose a lot of time doing that."

Inca's eyes flashed with anger. "And Colonel Marcellino said these were his *best* troops. Bah. My people would embarrass and shame them. The Indians are tough and have the kind of endurance it takes to move quickly through the forest."

"Well," Roan sighed, his gaze brushing her upturned features, "we'll just have to be patient with them. I'm more worried about what's going to happen when we hit the edge of that swamp two days from now."

Giving the column a look of derision, Inca growled, "Marcellino is going to have many of his men injured. The swamp is nothing but predators waiting for food."

Roan reached out and briefly touched her shoulder. Instantly, he saw her features soften. It was split seconds before she rearranged her face so that he could not see her true feelings. "Do you want to move ahead of the column?"

"Humph. They are many at the pace of a snail," Inca complained as she started gingerly down the slope. "I think I will move ahead to where I think they will straggle to a stop at dusk. We need meat. I will sing a snake song and ask one of the snakes to give its life for us as a meal tonight."

Roan nodded. "You'll find us, I'm sure."

She flashed him a grin as she trotted down the last stretch of slope to the forest floor below. "I will find you," she promised, and took off at a slow jog, weaving among the trees.

Roan smiled to himself. Inca moved with a boneless-ness that defied description, her thick braid swinging between her shoulder blades. He thought he saw a black-and-gold jaguar for a moment, trotting near her side. When he blinked again, the image was gone, but Roan knew he wasn't seeing things. His mother had been clair-voyant and he'd managed to inherit some of that gift him-self.

Moving along at a brisk walk, Roan opened the blouse of his fatigues, his chest shining with sweat. The humidity was high, and the cooling breeze felt good on his flesh. Planning on moving ahead and remaining with the point guards out in front of the column, he already missed Inca's considerable presence. Yes, he liked her. A lot. More than he should. His heart blossomed with such fierce longing that it caught him by surprise. Inca was like a drug to his system, an addiction. Roan had thought his heart had died when Sarah left him. But that wasn't so, he was discovering. And for the first time in two years, he felt hope. He felt like living once more, but squashed that feeling instantly. The thought of ever falling in love again terrified Roan. The fear of losing someone he loved held him in its icy clutches. He fought his feelings for Inca. He didn't dare fall for her. She lived her life moment to moment. Hers was not a world where one was guaranteed to live to a ripe old age. And compared to Sarah's love of climbing, Inca's career was even more dangerous.

Inca squatted down in front of the open fire. She had found Roan at dusk. He was in the midst of making sure the colonel's column was getting set up for the coming night. As he left the company, she met him near one of the moundlike hills and led him to her chosen hiding spot for the night, in a grove of towering kapok trees. It was easy to hide among the huge, six-to-eight-foot tall, winglike roots. There were smaller trees nearby, and she'd already hung out two hammocks for them to sleep in.

Just seeing Roan made her heart soar. Inca had found that as she traveled the rest of the day without Roan at her side, she had missed him more than she should. His quiet, powerful presence somehow made her feel more stable. Protected. And that scared her. In her panic, she had left him with the troops instead of staying with him. She was afraid of herself more than him, of the new and uneasy feelings she was now experiencing. No man had made her feel like he did, and Inca simply didn't know what to do with that—or herself.

Inca had called a snake to give its life so that they could eat. It had come and she had killed it, and after praying for the release of the spirit, she had skinned it and placed it on a spit. As it cooked, she looked across the fire at Roan. The shadows carved out every hard line in his angular, narrow face. "I thought about you a lot today after we split up," she said. "It feels odd to me to work with someone." She squarely met his blue eyes, which were hooded and thoughtful looking after she tossed the bombastic comment his way.

"You're used to working alone," he agreed. "My job here is to be your partner." Roan lifted his chin and looked down at the clearing where the Brazilian Army continued to set up camp for the night. They could see the company, but the men there could not see them.

Snorting, Inca tried to ignore his deep, husky baritone voice. Fear ate at her. She decided to bluff him, to scare him off. "I told you before—I was abandoned to die at birth and I will die alone. I work alone. My path is one of being alone." But she knew, whether she liked it or not, she had felt a thrill race through her that Roan had chosen to be at her campsite and not remain with the colonel's company. Pursing her full lips, she concentrated on keeping the four-foot-long snake turning so it would not burn in the low flames. She liked the warmth of the fire against her body as she worked near it. "I do not need you. Go back to the company. That is where you belong, with the other men."

Roan swallowed his shock. Where was this coming from? Until now, Inca had seemed happy with his presence. What had changed? Had he said something to her this morning? Roan wasn't sure. Seeing the fear in Inca's eyes, he realized she was pushing him away. If he didn't have the directive from Morgan Trayhern, he'd respect her request, but leaving her alone was not an option. Roan had given Mike Houston his word to protect Inca, and he sure couldn't do that if he was half a mile from her campsite at night. Clearing his throat, he said softly, "Everyone needs someone at some point in their life."

Inca scowled as she continued to deftly turn the meat over the fire. Her heart thudded with fear. Her bluff was not working. "That is not my experience. Jaguars, for the most part, live alone. The only time they see one of their own kind is during mating season, and they split shortly thereafter. The female jaguar goes through her pregnancy and birthing alone, and raises her cubs—alone." She lifted her head and glared across the fire at Roan. "I do not need a partner to do what I do here in Amazonia."

"Because?"

Anger riffled through Inca. The expression on Roan's face told her he wasn't going to budge on this issue. Her black brows dipped. "You have an annoying habit of asking too many questions."

"How else am I to know how you feel?" Roan decided to meet her head-on. He found himself unwilling to give up her hard-earned trust so easily.

"I am not used to showing my feelings to anyone." She raised her voice to a low, warning growl. Usually, such an action was enough to scare off even the bravest of men. Inca recalled vividly how Roan had found her weeping yesterday and how his touch had been soothing and healing to her. When she looked up again, she saw his blue eyes had softened with interest—in her. That set her back two paces and she felt panicky inside. Roan was not scared off like the male idiots she'd had the sorry misfortune to encounter thus far in her life. And maybe that was the problem: Roan Walker was *not* the usual male she was used to dealing with. That thought was highly unsettling.

"I'm not either, so I know how you feel," Roan murmured. "Sometimes, when we're in so much pain, we need another person there just to hold us, rock us and let us know that we're loved, anyway, despite how we're feeling." *Love?* Where had that word come from? Reaching out, Roan placed two more small sticks of wood on the fire. Light and shadows danced across her pain-filled face. A flash of annoyance and then fear laced with curiosity haunted her lovely willow-green eyes. He smiled to himself. Roan felt her powerful and intense curiosity in him as a man. He sensed her uneasiness around him and also her yearning.

More than anything, Roan needed to continue to cultivate her trust of him. Unless he could keep her trust, she would do as she damned well pleased and would leave him behind in an instant—which was exactly what Mike Houston and Morgan Trayhern didn't want to happen. Especially with that trigger-happy Brazilian colonel looking for Inca's head on a platter and the multimillion dollar reward he'd collect once he had it. And then the colonel would have his revenge for his eldest son's death at Inca's hands. No, it was important Roan be able to act as her shield—another set of eyes and ears to keep danger at bay, and Inca safe.

The snake meat began to sizzle and pop as the juices leaked out. With a swipe of her index finger, Inca quickly began to catch them before they fell into the fire. Each time she put her finger into her mouth and sucked on it, making a growling sound of pleasure.

"This is good...."

Roan smiled a little, enjoying her obvious enjoyment of such small but important things in her life. "So tell me," he began conversationally as he watched her sit back on her heels and continue to expertly turn the meat, "why do you distrust men so much?"

Inca laughed harshly. "Why *should* I trust them? Many of them are pigs. Brazilian men think they *own* their wives like slaves." She glared up at him. "No man owns a woman. No man has the right to slap or strike a woman or child, and yet they do it all the time in Brazil. A woman cannot speak up. If she risks it, her husband can strike her. If she so much as looks at another man, the husband, by law, has the right to murder her on the spot. Of course, any married man is allowed to have all the affairs he wants without any reprisal. To other men, he has machismo. Pah." Her voice deepened to a snarl. "I see nothing good in that kind of man. All they can do is dominate or destroy children and women. I will not be touched by them. I will not allow one to think that he can so much as lift a hand in my direction. I will not allow any man to dictate what I should or should not say. And if I want to look at a man, that is my right to do so, for the men here stare at women all the time."

"That's called a double standard in North American."

Curling her upper lip, she rasped, "Call it what you want. Men like that mean destruction. They manipulate others, and they want power *over* someone else. I see it all the time. I walk through one of my villages, and I see what drug dealers have done to those who will not bend to their threats and violence. I see children dead. I see women shot in the head because they refuse to give these men their bodies in payment for whatever they need."

"That's not right," Roan agreed quietly. He heard her stridency, saw the rage in her eyes. It was righteous rage, he acknowledged. And while he was a stranger to Brazil, he had heard of the laws condoning the shooting of a wife who looked at another man. And he'd also heard from Mike Houston that husbands here often had a mistress on the side, as a matter of course.

"Many men are not *right*." She pointed to her breasts beneath the thin olive-green tank top she wore. Earlier, she'd taken off her bandoliers and hung them on a low branch nearby. "All they can do is stare here—" she jabbed at her breasts "—and slobber like dogs in heat. You would think they had never seen a woman's breasts before! Their tongues hang out. It is disgusting! Yesterday, the soldiers stared at me when I walked into camp to challenge Colonel Marcellino."

Raising his brows, Roan nodded. With the bandoliers of ammo set aside, he had to admit that the thin cotton did outline her small, firm breasts beautifully.

"I have watched you," Inca said, slowly rising to her full height, the skewer in hand. "And not once have you stared at my breasts like they always do. Why not?"

Chuckling to himself, Roan reveled in Inca's naive honesty. He watched as she walked over to her pack. There was an old, beat-up tin plate beside it. She squatted down and, sliding the huge knife from its scabbard at her hip, cut the meat into segments and removed them from the skewer. Putting the skewer aside, she picked up the plate and stood up.

"Well?" she demanded as she walked back to him, "why do you not stare at me like they do?"

Roan nodded his thanks as she set the tin plate between

them. Inca squatted nearby and quickly picked up a steaming hot chunk of meat with her fingers. There was such a natural grace to her. She was a wild thing, more animal than woman with that feral glint in her eyes.

Reaching for a piece of the roast white meat, he murmured, "Where I come from, it's impolite to stare at a woman like that."

"Impolite?" Inca exploded with laughter, her lips pulling away from her strong, white teeth. "Rude! Piglike! Even in nature—" she swept her arm dramatically around the jungle that enclosed them "—male pigs do not salivate like that over a female pig!"

Roan looked at her as he popped a piece of meat into his mouth. It tasted good, almost like chicken, he thought as he relaxed and watched the firelight lovingly caress her profile. Her hair was frayed and it softened the angularity of her thin, high cheekbones. She was more sinew and bone than flesh. There was no fat whatsoever on Inca. She was slender like a willow, and each hand or finger movement she made reminded him of a ballet dancer.

"So the men from your tribe do not stare at a woman's breasts?"

He shook his head and took a second chunk of snake meat from the plate. "Let's just say that men of my nation consider women their equals in every way. They aren't…" he paused, searching for the right words "…sexual objects to be stared at, abused or hurt in any way."

She gave him a sizzling sidelong look. "Pity that you cannot teach these Brazilian soldiers a thing or two! I would just as soon put a boot between their legs when they stare and slobber like that, to remind them of the manners they do not possess.''

"Try and refrain from that," Roan suggested dryly, hiding a grin desperately trying to tug at one corner of his mouth. "We need their cooperation. I can't have you injuring them like that. We wouldn't make twenty miles a day in this jungle if you did.''

Throwing back her head, Inca laughed deeply, the juice of the meat glistening along her lower lip. With the back of her hand, she wiped her mouth clean. "These men, with kicks between their legs or not, will *never* make ten miles a day. They are out of shape. Unfit weaklings.''

Roan didn't disagree. "You're right. We'll be lucky to make ten miles a day until they get their legs under them.''

With a snort, Inca wiped her long fingers across her jungle fatigues. "They are city boys. They are not hard. They cannot take this hill climbing and humidity. They pant like old dogs with weak, trembling hind legs.''

Chuckling, Roan motioned to the last piece of meat in the tin. "It's yours. Eat it.''

Inca shook her head. "You have eaten too little today. You are larger and heavier than me. If you are to keep up with me again tomorrow, this will give you strength." She jabbed with her finger. "Eat it." Rising, she stretched fitfully. "You were the only one to keep my pace." She eyed him with respect and acknowledged that although he towered over her, he was lean, tight and hard muscled. There was a litheness to him that reminded her of a jaguar fit for territorial combat. She liked the humor she saw glinting in his eyes as he took the last piece of meat and bit into it. Pleased that he would take directions from her,

Inca walked slowly around the fire as she peered out into the darkness that now surrounded them.

"So how does your tribe see women, then? I am curious."

Roan nearly choked on the meat as he looked up at her. She stood proudly, her shoulders thrown back, the thick braid lying across one shoulder, her chin lifted at an imperious, confident angle once again. Her green eyes glimmered as her gaze caught and held him captive. Her hands rested comfortably on her hips as she stared down at him waiting for him to answer. Swallowing the meat, he rasped, "We see a woman like a fruit tree filled with gifts of beauty and bounty."

"Fruit tree?" Inca saw the sudden seriousness in his eyes and knew he was not joking with her. Why was he so different? And intriguing? Allowing her hands to slip gracefully from her hips, she moved back to where he remained in a squatting position. Taking a seat on a nearby log, she held her hands out toward the fire and savored the heat from it.

Wiping his hands on his fatigues, Roan twisted to look in Inca's direction. He saw that she was genuinely interested and that made him feel good. He hungered for deep, searching conversation with her and about her. "All life comes from Mother Earth," he began, and he patted the damp, fallen leaves on the soil next to where he was crouching. "We see women as a natural extension of Mother Earth. They are the only ones who are fertile, who can carry and birth a baby. I was taught a long time ago that a fruit tree, which can bear blossoms, be impregnated by a honeybee and then bear fruit, is a good symbol for women. Women are the fruit of our earth. For me, as a man, a woman is a gift. I do not assume that a fruit tree or a woman wants to share her fruit with me. We always give a gift and then ask if the tree—or the woman—wants to share her bounty with us. If she or the tree says yes, then that's fine. If she says no, that's fine, also.''

Inca rested her chin on her closed hands. She planted her elbows on her thighs and pondered his explanation. "Women and trees being one and the same…''

"Symbolically speaking, yes.'' Roan saw the pensive expression on her face, the pouting of her lower lip as she considered his words. The firelight danced and flickered across her smooth, golden features, highlighting her cheekbones and wrinkled brow. She was part child, part wise woman, part animal. And at any given moment, any one of those facets could emerge to speak with him. He found her exciting and had to contain the thrill he felt. But, Roan also felt her hatred and distrust of the Brazilian military, and he couldn't blame her at all for her defensive stance around them. After all, they had a high bounty on her head—dead or alive.

As she stared into the fire, lost in thought, Roan tore his gaze from Inca. She was too easy to savor, as if she were a priceless, rare flower. Too easy to emotionally gorge himself. If he took too much, it would destroy her pristine, one-of-a-kind beauty. Besides, he knew Inca did not like to be stared at; but then again, he didn't like it either. He wondered if it was their Indian blood that made them feel that their energy was being stolen when someone stared. Anglos certainly didn't get it, but he understood Inca's unhappiness. Still, she was incredibly beautiful and there wasn't a man in that military contingent that wasn't smitten by her drop-dead-gorgeous looks. Inca was as natural and wild as the rain forest that surrounded them with its humid embrace. Roan had seen more than a few looks of lust in those soldiers' eyes today as they marched and talked animatedly about her dramatic entrance to their camp the night before. And he knew Inca sensed their lust and was completely disgusted by it.

Inca's husky voice intruded upon his reverie.

"Then, if you see women as fruit trees—" she turned and stared at him fully "—how do you see their breasts?"

She asked the damnedest questions. Roan understood it was innocent curiosity, her obvious naïveté of men and the world outside this rain forest. Opening his hands, he said, "I can only speak for myself on this, Inca."

"Yes?" she demanded, goading him impatiently.

"A woman's breasts remind me of warm, sun-ripe peaches."

Her brows knitted. "Peaches? What is a peach? Do they grow here in South America?"

Shrugging, he said, "I don't know. They do where I live."

"Tell me about this peach. Describe it. Does it look like a breast?"

A slight smile curved his mouth. Staring into the fire in order not to make the mistake of looking at her too long, he murmured, "A peach is about the size of my palm," and he held it up for her to look at. "It's an incredible fruit. It's round in shape and when you lean close and smell it, well, it has the sweetest fragrance. When it's ripe, it's firm and has a soft fine fuzz all over it. The colors take your breath away. It's often a clear pinkish gold, but that graduates into red-orange, and orange, or to apricot or a bright sun-gold." He closed his eyes, picturing the fruit. "When I see a ripe, sun-warmed peach on the branch of a tree, all I want to do is reach out and cup my fingers around it, feel those soft, nubby hairs sliding against my fingertips. I want to test the firmness, the roundness and the heat of it as I continue to encircle it...."

Inca felt her breasts tighten and she sat up, surprised. What was going on? She gave him a disgruntled look. Roan sat there, his hands clasped between his opened thighs, his head lifted slightly and his eyes closed. What would it be like to feel him slide those long, large-knuckled, work-worn fingers around her breasts? Instantly, her skin tingled wildly. She felt her nipples harden and pucker beneath her shirt. A wonderful, molten ache began to pool through her lower body as she continued to stare at his hard, angular profile. It was as if her body had a life of its own! And worse, it was responding on its own to his husky, melting words, which seemed to reach out and caress her like a lover.

Scowling, Inca sat there. She'd never had a lover. She couldn't describe what having one was like. Yet his deep, rumbling words continued to touch her almost physically. Her breasts felt hot, felt achy, and she wanted Roan to reach out and caress them! The thought was so foreign to her that Inca gasped.

Roan opened his eyes and slowly turned his head in Inca's direction. He saw a pink stain on her cheeks. He saw her startled expression, and the way her lips parted provocatively, looking so very, very damn kissable. What would it be like to kiss that wild, untamed mouth of hers? How would she feel beneath his mouth? Hot? Strong? Fierce? Hungry? Or starving, like he felt for her? As Inca turned to meet and hold his gaze, Roan sensed her chagrin, her embarrassment and—something else he couldn't quite put his finger on. If he wasn't mistaken, the gold flecks in her willow-green eyes hinted of desire—for him. The impression he received from her was that she wanted him to reach out with his fingers, touch the sides of her breasts, caress them and... With a shake of his head, he wondered what the hell was happening.

It was as if he was reading Inca's thoughts and feelings in her wide, vulnerable-looking eyes during that fragile moment. He saw that her nipples were pressed urgently against the material of her shirt and he could see the outline of the proud, firm breasts that he ached to encircle, tease and then suckle until she twisted with utterly, wanton pleasure in his arms. Roan wanted to be the man to introduce Inca to the realm of love. It was a molten thought. She had never been touched by any man, he knew. A virgin in her mid-twenties, she was a wild woman who would never entertain the touch of a mere mortal, that was for sure.

Inca tore her gaze from Roan's dark, hooded stare. She felt a lush, provocative heat radiating from him toward her. Because she was of the Jaguar Clan, her six senses were acutely honed. For a moment, she'd allowed her mind and heart to touch his. When it had, she'd seen the flare of surprise and then his smoldering, very male look in return. Inca understood in that split second that Roan could touch her in a way she'd never before experienced...and the sensation was galvanizing, aching, filled with promise—yet it scared her.

Heart palpitating wildly in her chest, Inca stared, disgruntled, into the fire. Suddenly breathless beneath that glittering look in his blue eyes—one that reminded her of lightning striking the earth—she was at a loss for words. Her skin tightened deliciously around her breasts. She felt needy. She felt hungry for *his* touch. A man's touch. Of all things! Inca could not reconcile that within herself. Her mind railed against it. Her heart was wide-open, crying out for the intimate touch he promised her in that one look, in that one touch with his mind and heart. Closing her eyes, she hid her face in her hands momentarily.

"I am tired," she muttered. "I must sleep now." Getting up quickly, she moved around the massive root to where she had placed her hammock.

Roan heard the turmoil in her tone. He sat very still because she appeared to be poised like a wild horse ready to spook and hightail it. What had happened? He swore he'd felt her very real presence inside his head—and even more so, in his expanding heart. For an instant, Inca had been *in* him, somehow—attached to or connected to his thoughts and feelings as if... Stymied, Roan wished he could talk to Houston about this experience.

Something had happened, because when Inca had lifted her face and her hands fell away, he'd seen the fear in her eyes. Fear and...did he dare put the name desire to it, also? Was that smoldering, banked desire in her cloudy gaze aimed at him? Very unsure, Roan muttered, "Yeah, we both need to turn in and get some sleep. Tomorrow is going to be a rough day."

In more ways than one, he thought as he rose to his feet. *In more ways than one...*

Chapter 9

Inca halted in her tracks and gulped. It was the third morning of the march into the swamp, and she had gone down a hill to wash herself before the day's activities began. Only, Roan had beat her to the enchanting place. He stood out in the middle of a shallow pool that had been created by the seasonal winter rains. Though the pool was small now, it was just large enough for a person to be able to grasp the white sand surrounding it, and scrub his flesh clean before rinsing off in the knee-deep waters. Hiding behind a tree, her hand resting tentatively against the smooth, gray bark, Inca found herself unable to resist watching Roan's magnificent nakedness as he bathed. Surprise and then pleasurable, molten heat flowed through her.

Inca was torn. She *should* leave. Oh, she knew what men looked like, but an unbidden curiosity and something else was tempting her to remain hidden and devour Roan with her eyes. His clothes were hung on the limb of a nearby rubber tree. He was sluicing the clear, cooling water across his thick, broad shoulders and well-sprung chest, which was covered with a dark carpet of black hair. Gulping unsteadily, she dropped her gaze lower...and lower...then just as quickly, Inca looked away. Disgusted with herself, she spun around and placed her back against the tree, her arms wrapped tightly across against her chest. Nostrils flaring, she told herself she shouldn't be doing this.

Heart pounding, Inca felt that warm, uncoiling sensation deep in her body. It was a wonderful, new feeling that seemed to blossom within her when she was around Roan. She had not been able to bully or scare him off. He'd stayed at her side like a faithful dog would its master, and Inca had grudgingly given up on trying to get him to go back to the company of men. The last two days had cemented their relationship to the point where Inca felt the last of her defenses toward him dissolving. Oh, it was nothing he did directly, just those smoldering looks he gave her from time to time, that crooked smile that heated her spirit and made it fly, his sense of humor and ability to laugh.

She heard him singing, his voice an engaging baritone. The forest around the pool area absorbed most of the sound as he chanted in a language that was foreign to her. Understanding it was a ceremonial song of his people, to greet the rising sun, she slowly turned around and peeked from behind the tree. Both hands on the trunk to steady herself, Inca watched as he leaned down, grabbed some sand from the bottom of the pool and briskly began to scrub his chest. There was something vulnerable and boyish about Roan in that molten moment. Gulping hard, Inca found herself wondering what it would be like to slide her fingers through that dark hair splayed out across his broad, well-developed chest. Or to allow her hands to range downward in exploration....

Making a strangled sound, Inca jerked away and dug the toe of her boot into the soft, muddy earth. She had to get out of here! Hurrying silently up the hill in a line that would hide her from his view, she wiped her lips with the back of her hand. Her whole world was crumbling because of Roan. She could not keep him at bay. She melted a little more each time he shared an intimate glance with her, or smiled at her.... So many little things were unraveling her mighty defenses!

Panicked by all that she was feeling, because she'd never felt it before, Inca had no one to turn to to ask what was going on inside her. She wished one of the Jaguar Clan mothers who had raised her were still alive. They'd been old women when they nursed her from babyhood to girlhood. They were all gone now, having long ago walked across the Threshold to the other worlds. Again the biting reminder that she was alone, abandoned by everyone, sank into her.

Back in their makeshift camp, Inca hurriedly removed her dark green nylon hammock from between two trees and stuffed it in the bag she would carry across her shoulders. If only she hadn't been banished from the Jaguar Clan village. Inca yearned to talk to Grandmother Alaria. Yes, Grandmother Alaria would understand what was going on inside her. Grandfather Adaire, however, would block her entrance to the village and tell her to leave—or else deliver the worst punishment of all: ban her forever not just from the village but from the Jaguar Clan. Inca couldn't tolerate the thought of being forced to give up the one thing that she'd been raised to do all her life—work as a healer for her people.

"Your turn."

Inca gasped. She dropped the hammock and spun around, caught off guard. Roan stood behind her, dressed in his fatigues, his upper chest naked, the towel draped over his head as he casually dried his dark hair. She saw the sparkle in his blue eyes. Gulping, she realized he knew she'd seen him bathing. Heat rolled up her neck and into her face. She avoided his tender look. There was no laughter, no censure in his eyes. Indeed, he seemed to understand what she'd done and why. Inca wished she did.

"I—it was an accident," she stammered, nervously picking up her hammock and rapidly jamming it into her small canvas pack.

"Of course," Roan murmured. The rosy flush in her cheeks made Inca unbearably beautiful to him. He saw the surprise, the shame and humiliation in her darkening eyes. "Accidents happen. I wasn't upset."

Lifting her head, she twisted to look in his direction. "You weren't?" She would be.

Wiping his brow dry, Roan hung the small, dark green towel on a branch to dry. Not that it would dry much in this humidity. Shrugging on his fatigue blouse, he rolled up the arms on each sleeve to his elbow. "No."

"I would not like someone coming upon me as I washed."

"That's different." He smiled as she straightened. Inca was not the confident warrior now. Instead she was a young woman, unsure of herself, of her relationship to him, and possibly, Roan ruminated, of what she was feeling toward him. He knew, without question, that Inca was drawn to him like a bee to sweet honey. And he was no less smitten with her even though he was trying desperately to ignore his feelings toward her. Constantly, Roan had to harshly remind himself that they had a mission to complete. He refused to fall in love with another woman. He would not indulge in his growing, powerful feelings for her. Having to cap them, sit on them and ignore them was becoming a daily hell for him. It was a sweet hell, however. Inca was precious to him in all ways—from the smallest gesture to her great unselfishness toward others who were less fortunate than her.

"Humph," Inca said as she grabbed her towel and moved quickly toward the pool. "I will return."

Buttoning his shirt, Roan grinned to himself. When he heard the snap and crackle of boots crushing small sticks that had fallen from the canopy above, he knew someone was coming. Moving out from behind a tree, he saw it was Julian. The young officer's face was flushed and he had a worried look.

"Good morning," Roan greeted him, placing the towel on top of his pack.

"*Bom dia*, good morning," Julian said, breathing hard. "I just wanted to tell Inca that she was right. Coming into this swamp is creating a disaster of unexpected proportions." He stopped, removed his cap and wiped his brow with his arm. Looking back toward where the company was preparing to march, he continued. "I tried to talk to my father this morning. We have ten men down with malaria symptoms. We have another five with dysentery. And six from yesterday that have assorted sprained ankles or knees from falling and slipping." He shook his head. "I don't know what to do...."

Roan patted the shorter man on the shoulder. "There isn't much you can do, Julian. We're halfway through the swamp." Looking up, he saw a patch of bright blue sky. It looked as if the weather was going to be sunny. That meant it would be very hot today, and with the humidity around ninety-five percent at all times, the stress on the men would be great. "How about heat exhaustion? How many cases?"

"My *médico*, Sargento Salvador, says we have fifteen men who are down. We need to get a helicopter in here, but we are too far into the jungle for them to land. One of the other officers is taking all the injured and sick back to the edge of the swamp. From there, they will march to the river, where the helicopters will fly in and take them to the nearest hospital, which is located in Manaus."

"A lot of technical problems," Roan agreed somberly. He reached down and removed his tin cup, which had coffee in it that had been warming over the last of the coals of their morning campfire. He offered some to Julian, who shook his head.

"Does Inca know any *quick* way out of this swamp? Is there any way we can get out of it now?"

Roan shrugged and sipped his coffee. "She said there is none. That was the problem. Once you committed to this route, there was no way out except back or straight ahead."

"Damn," Julian rasped. "Very well. I am lead point with my squad today. We will be working with you and Inca." He smiled a little, his eyes dark with worry. "I'm afraid we'll lose many more men today to this heat. There's no cloud cover...."

"Just keep them drinking a lot of water, with frequent rests," Roan advised solemnly.

"My father wants out of the swamp. He's pushing the men beyond their physical limits. I can try, but he's in command...."

Roan nodded grimly. "Then we will just have to do the best we can to get through this."

Inca moved silently. It was dusk and she was watching the weary soldiers of the company erect their tents and reluctantly dig in for the coming night. Perspiration covered her. It had been a hot, humid, brutal day. She saw Colonel Marcellino in the distance. He was shouting at Julian, who stood stiffly at attention. Her heart broke for the young officer. She liked Julian. Why did his father have to treat him so cruelly? Did he not realize how fragile life was? They could all die in a minute in this deadly swamp.

She felt Roan coming, and leaned against a tree trunk and waited for him. The day had been hard on everyone. Even he, with his athleticism and strength, looked fatigued tonight. She nodded to him as he saw her. When he gave her a tired smile in return, her heart opened. Crossing her arms, she leaned languidly against the tree. Roan halted about a foot away from her, his hands coming to rest on his hips.

"They look pretty exhausted," he muttered.

"They are. How many men went down today?"

"Twenty more to various things—malaria, dysentery and heat exhaustion."

"Humph." Brows knitting, Inca watched as Julian was dismissed. He disappeared quickly between the tents that were being raised. "The colonel is an old man and a fool. He will lose as many tomorrow, before we get out of this place."

Scratching his head, Roan studied her in the soft dusk light. She had discarded her bandoliers and her rifle back at their recently made camp. Tendrils of hair stuck to her temples, and her long, thick braid was badly frayed by the high humidity. The soft pout of her lips, her half-closed eyes, made Roan want her as he'd never wanted another woman. He hoped she wasn't reading his mind. Inca had told him she rarely read other people's thoughts because it took much energy and focus. Most people's thoughts were garbage anyway, she told him wryly. Roan sighed. Well, Inca was tired, there was no doubt. There were faint shadows beneath her large eyes. The heat had been brutal even on her, and she lived here year-round.

There was a sudden scream, and then a hail of gunfire within the camp. A number of men were running around, screaming, yelling and brandishing their weapons. More shots were fired.

Inca stood up, suddenly on guard. "What…?"

Roan moved protectively close, his hand on her shoulder, his eyes narrowed. The company of men looked like a disturbed beehive. There were more screams. More shouts. More gunfire. "I don't know.…"

Keying her hearing, Inca heard someone shout, *"Médico! Médico!"*

"Someone is hurt," Inca said, her voice rising with concern. "Who, I do not know. There are no drug runners around, so what is going on?"

Before Roan could speak, he saw one of the point soldiers they'd worked with today, Ramone, come racing toward them. The point patrol always knew where they had their camp for the night. The look of terror etched on his young face made Roan grip Inca a little more securely. "Let's see what's going on."

Inca agreed. She liked the touch of his hand on her shoulder. He stood like a protective guard, his body close and warm, and she hungrily absorbed his nearness.

Both of them stepped out into the path of the running, panting soldier. He cried out their names.

"Inca! We need you! Tenente Marcellino! A bushmaster snake bit him! Hurry! He will die!"

Stunned, Inca tore from beneath Roan's hand. She knew she wasn't supposed to enter the colonel's camp. She was unarmed, and risking her own life because the colonel was capable of killing her.

"Inca!" Too late. Roan cursed. He saw her sprint down the trail, heading directly for where the men were running around and shouting. *Damn.* Roan gripped the soldier by the arm. "Let's go. Show me where he's lying." Roan was a paramedic, but he didn't have antivenin in his medical pack. He wasn't even sure there was antivenin for the poison of a bushmaster. As he ran with Ramone, who was stumbling badly, he mentally went over the procedure for snakebite. This particular snake was deadly, he knew. No one survived a bite. No one. He saw Inca disappear between two tents. Digging in his toes, Roan plunged past the faltering and gasping soldier.

Julian Marcellino was lying on the ground near his tent, next to the brackish water of the swamp, and gripping his thigh. Blood oozed from between his white fingers. No

An Important Message from the Editors

Dear Reader,

Because you've chosen to read one of our fine novels, we'd like to say "thank you"! And, as a special way to thank you, we're offering you a choice of two more of the books you love so well, and a surprise gift to send you – absolutely FREE!

Please enjoy them with our compliments...

Pam Powers

Peel off Seal and Place Inside...

THE EDITOR'S "THANK YOU" FREE GIFTS INCLUDE:

▶ 2 Romance OR 2 Suspense books

▶ An exciting surprise gift

YES! I have placed my Editor's "thank you" Free Gifts seal in the space provided at right. Please send me the 2 FREE books which I have selected, and my FREE Mystery Gift. I understand that I am under no obligation to purchase anything further, as explained on the back of this card.

PLACE FREE GIFTS SEAL HERE

Check one:

	ROMANCE
	193 MDL EE3L 393 MDL EE3X

	SUSPENSE
	192 MDL EE3W 392 MDL EE4A

FIRST NAME   LAST NAME

ADDRESS

APT.#   CITY

STATE/PROV.   ZIP/POSTAL CODE

▶ DETACH AND MAIL CARD TODAY! ▶

(ED1-SS-06) © 1998 MIRA BOOKS

The Reader Service — Here's How It Works:

Accepting your 2 free books and gift places you under no obligation to buy anything. You may keep the books and gift and return the shipping statement marked "cancel." If you do not cancel, about a month later we'll send you 3 additional books and bill you just $5.24 each in the U.S., or $5.74 each in Canada, plus 25¢ shipping & handling per book and applicable taxes if any.* That's the complete price and — compared to cover prices starting from $5.99 each in the U.S. and $6.99 each in Canada — it's quite a bargain! You may cancel at any time, but if you choose to continue, every month we'll send you 3 more books, which you may either purchase at the discount price or return to us and cancel your subscription.

*Terms and prices subject to change without notice. Sales tax applicable in N.Y. Canadian residents will be charged applicable provincial taxes and GST.

more than three feet away lay a dead bushmaster snake that he'd killed with his pistol. Julian's eyes were glazing over as Inca leaned over him. The *médico*, Sargento Salvador, had tears in his eyes as he knelt on the other side of the semiconscious officer.

"I can't save him!" Salvador cried as Inca dropped to her knees opposite him.

"Be quiet!" Inca snarled. Out of the corner of her eye, she saw Roan running up to her at the same time Jaime Marcellino did. "Move away!" she shouted. "Give me room. Be quiet! All of you!"

The men quickly hushed and made a wide semicircle around Julian. All eyes riveted upon Inca, who studied the two fang punctures as she gently removed Julian's hand from his thigh.

"Uhh," Julian gasped. His eyes rolled in his head. He saw darkness approaching. Inca was watching him intently through her slitted gaze. Her mouth was compressed. "I—I'm going to die...." he told her in a rasping tone.

"Julian," Inca growled, "be still! Close your eyes. Whatever you do, do *not* cross the Threshold! Do you understand me? It is important not to walk across it."

"Stop!" Jaime screamed as he ran toward them. "Do not touch my son!" He saw Inca place one hand over Julian's heart and the other on the top of his head. His son lay prostrate and unmoving. His flesh, once golden, was now leached out like the color of bones found in the high desert of Peru.

Roan jerked the colonel's arm back as he reached out to haul Inca away from where she knelt over Julian.

"No, Colonel! Let Inca try and help him," Roan ordered tightly.

Glaring, the colonel fought to free himself from Roan's grip. "Let me go, damn you! She'll murder him, too! She's a murderer!" His voice carried in the sudden eerie calm of the camp as the men stood watching the exchange.

Breathing hard, Roan pulled the pistol from his holster and pressed the barrel against the colonel's sweaty temple. "Damn you, stand still or I'll take you down here and now. Inca isn't going to kill Julian. If anything, she's the only thing standing between him and death right now. Let her try and heal him!"

Jaime felt the cold metal pressed against his temple. He saw Storm Walker's eyes narrow with deadly earnestness. Yes, this man would shoot him. Sobbing, he looked down at Julian, who was unconscious now, his mouth slack, his eyes rolled back in his head.

Roan looked around. "No one move!" he roared. "Let Inca do her work."

Taking a deep, steadying breath, Inca leaned close to Julian. With one hand on his heart, the other on top of his head, she silently asked her guardian to come over her. She felt the incredible power of her guide as he did so. The moment he was in place, much like a glove fitting over a hand, she could see through his eyes. A powerful, whirling motion took place, and she felt herself being sucked down counterclockwise into a vortex of energy. In seconds, she stood in the tunnel of light. They were at the Threshold. Breathing hard and trying to hold her focus and not allow outside sounds to disrupt her necessary concentration, Inca saw Julian standing nearby. Two light beings, his guardians, were on the other side of the Threshold. Moving to them directly, she asked, "May I bring him back?"

Under Jaguar Clan laws, if the light beings said no, then she must allow his spirit to cross over, and he would die, physically. Inca had only once in her life made the mistake of disobeying that directive when she'd brought Michael Houston back from this place. He should have died. But she'd decided to take things into her own hands. And because she was young and only partly trained, she had died physically doing it. Only Grandmother Alaria's power and persuasion had brought her back to life that fateful day so long ago.

Inca waited patiently. She saw the light beings convene. Julian was looking at them. She saw the yearning on his face to walk across that golden area that served as the border between the dimensions.

"If you decide to bring him back to your world," one of the light beings warned, "you may die in the process. He is full of poison. You must run it quickly through your own body, or you will die. Do you understand?"

Inca nodded. "Yes, I do." In her business as a healer, she had to take on the symptoms, in this case, the deadly snake venom, and run it through her own body in order to get rid of it. She would certainly perish if not for the power of her jaguar guardian, who would assist her with his energy in the process, draining it back into Mother Earth, who could absorb it. If it was done fast enough, she might survive.

"Then ask him to return. His tasks are not yet complete."

Inca held out her hand to Julian. "Come, Julian. I will
bring you home. You have work to do, my young friend."

"I don't want to return."

Inca saw the tears in the young officer's eyes. "I
know," she quavered unsteadily. "It is because of your
father."

"He doesn't love me!" Julian cried out, the tears splattering down his face. "I am so distraught. I drew the
snake to me, to bite me. I can't stand the pain any
longer!"

Inca knew that when things in life were very tough on
a person, they sometimes drew an accident to them in
order to break the pattern, the energy block they were
wrestling with. By creating an accident, the gridlock was
released and the person was allowed to work, in a new
way, on the problem they'd chosen to learn from and
work through. "I understand," she told Julian in a soothing voice. Stretching out her fingertips, Inca moved slowly
toward him. "Come, Julian, take my hand. I will bring
you back. Your father loves you."

"No, he doesn't!" Julian sobbed. He turned toward the
light beings on the other side. "I want to go. I want to
cross. He's never loved me! He only loved Rafael. I tried
so hard, Inca...so hard to have him love me. To say he
loved me, or to show me he cares just a fraction of how
he cared for Rafael. But he treats me as if I'm not there.
That is why I want to leave."

Inca took another, deliberate step forward. "You
cannot. You *must* come back with me, Julian. Now."
Once he touched her outstretched fingers, he had committed to coming back. Julian didn't know that, but Inca
did. It was a cosmic law. Halfheartedly, he took her hand.

"I don't know..." he sobbed.

"I do." And Inca forced the darkness she saw inhabiting his body to funnel up through her hand and into her body. She was literally willing the snake venom into herself. Instantly, she groaned. She felt the deadly power of the poison. Losing sight of Julian, of the light, Inca felt as if someone had smashed into her chest with a huge fist. Gasping, she tightened her grip around Julian's hand. She knew if she lost him at this critical phase, that his spirit would wander the earth plane forever without a physical body. *Hold on!*

Roan heard Inca groan. She sagged against Julian, her head resting on his chest, her eyes tightly shut. Her mouth was contorted in a soundless cry. Worriedly, he sensed something was wrong. Marcellino moved, and Roan tightened his grip on the officer's arm. "Stay right where you are," he snarled, the pistol still cocked at his temple.

"My son!" Jaime suddenly cried, hope in his voice. He reached out toward Julian. "Look! Look! My God! Color is returning to his face! It is a *miracle!*"

Roan shot a glance toward Julian. Yes, it was true. Color was flooding back into Julian's once pasty face. The men whispered. They collectively made a sound of awe as Julian's lashes fluttered and he opened his eyes slightly.

But something else was wrong. Terribly wrong. Inca was limp against Julian. Her skin tone went from gold to an alarming white, pasty color. Roan felt a tremendous shift in energy—a wrenching sensation that was almost palpable, as if a lightning bolt had struck them. The soldiers blanched and reacted to the mighty wave of invisible energy.

As Julian weakly lifted his arm, opened up his mouth

and croaked, "Father…" Inca moaned and fell unconscious to the ground beside him.

Roan released the colonel. Jamming the pistol into the holster, he went to Inca's side. She lay with one arm above her head, the other beside her still body. Was she breathing? Anxiously, he dropped to his knees, all of his paramedic abilities coming to the forefront.

"Salvador! Get me a stethoscope! A blood pressure cuff!"

The *médico* leaped to his feet.

Jaime fell to Julian's side, crying out his name over and over again. He gripped his son by the shoulders and shook him gently.

"Julian! Julian? Are you all right? My son, speak to me! Oh, please, speak to me!" And he pulled him up and into his arms.

A sob tore from Jaime as he crushed his son against him. He looked down to see that Julian's color was almost normal. His lashes fluttered. When he opened his eyes again, Jaime saw that they were clear once more.

"Father?"

Jaime reacted as if struck by a thunderclap. A sob tore from him and he clasped his son tightly to him. "Thank God, you are alive. I could not bear losing you, too."

Roan cursed under his breath. He took Inca's blood pressure. It was dumping. She was dying. Heart pounding with anxiety, he threw the blood pressure cuff down and held her limp, clammy wrist. He could barely discern a pulse.

The men crowded closer, in awe. In terror. They all watched without a sound.

"Inca, don't die on me, dammit!" Roan rasped as he

slid his arm beneath her neck. He understood what she had done: used her own body to run the venom through. That was the nature of healing. Could she get rid of it soon enough? Could her jaguar spirit guide help her do it? Roan wasn't sure, and he felt his heart bursting with anguish so devastating that all he could do was take her in his arms and hold her.

As he pressed her limp body against his, and held her tightly, he blocked out Jaime's sobs and Julian's stammered words. He blocked out everything. Intuitively, Roan knew that if he held Inca, if he willed his life energy, his heart, his love, into her, that it would help her survive this terrible tragedy. He'd seen his mother do this countless times—gather the one who was ill into her arms. She had told him what she was doing, and he now utilized that knowledge.

The instant Roan pressed her hard against him, her heart against his heart, his world shattered. It took every ounce of strength he'd ever had to withstand the energy exploding violently through him. Eyes closed, his brow against her cheek, he felt her limpness, felt her life slipping away.

No! It can't happen! Breathing hard, Roan tried to take deep, steadying breaths of air into his lungs as he held her. Behind his eyes, he saw murky, turgid green and yellow colors. Out of the murkiness came his cougar. He'd seen her many times before in his dreams and in the vision quest he took yearly upon his mother's reservation. The cougar ran toward him full tilt in huge striding leaps. Roan didn't understand what she was doing. He thought she would slam into him. Instead, as she took a mighty leap directly at him, he felt her warm, powerful body hit and absorb into his. The effect was so surprising that Roan felt himself tremble violently from it.

The yellowish-green colors began to fade. He felt the cougar in him, around him, covering him. It was the oddest sensation he'd ever experienced. He felt the cougar's incredible endurance and energy. It was as if fifty thousand volts of electricity were coursing through him, vibrating him and flowing out of him and into Inca. Dizzy, Roan felt himself sit down unceremoniously on the damp ground with Inca in his arms. He heard the concerned murmurs of soldier's voices. But his concentration, his focus, belonged inside his head, inside this inner world where the drama between life and death was taking place.

Instinctively, Roan held Inca with all his strength. He saw and felt the cougar's energy moving vibrantly into Inca. He saw the gold color, rich and clean, moving like an energy transfusion into her body. The murky colors disappeared and in their place came darkness. But it wasn't a frightening darkness, rather, one of warmth and nurturance. Roan knew only to hold Inca. That in holding her, he was somehow helping her to live, not die.

When Inca moaned softly, Roan felt himself torn out of the drama of the inner worlds. His eyes flew open. Anxiously, he looked down at the woman in his arms. Her flesh had returning color. And when her lashes fluttered weakly to reveal drowsy willow-green eyes, his heart soared with the knowledge that she was not going to die. Hot tears funneled through him and he rapidly blinked them away.

He felt Salvador's hand on his shoulder. "How can we help?" he asked.

Slightly weakened, Roan roused himself and looked up.

"Just let me sit here with her. She's going to be okay...." he rasped to the soldiers who stood near, their faces filled with genuine concern.

Looking down at Inca, Roan gave her a broken smile. "Welcome back to the land of the living, sweetheart."

Though incredible weakness stalked Inca, she heard Roan's huskily spoken words and they touched her pounding heart. She was too tired to even try to lift her hand and touch his face. How wonderful it felt to be held by him! Inca had wanted to experience this, but not like this.

"Roan...take me home...out of here. I need rest...." Her voice was a whisper. Gone was her husky, confident tone. She felt like she was a drifting cloud, at the whim of the winds.

"I'll take you home," he promised.

Roan eased Inca into a sitting position. Many hands, the hands of the soldiers who had witnessed this drama, came to help. Inca sat with her head down on her knees. She was very weak and incapable of walking anywhere on her own. Getting to his feet, Roan felt the last of the dizziness leave him. Looking over, he saw Julian sitting up, too, his father's arm around his shoulder. And he saw Jaime's face covered with tears, his once hard eyes now soft with love for his son.

Several of the soldiers lifted Inca into Roan's awaiting arms. He reassured them all that she would be fine, that all she needed now was a little rest. Julian looked up, his eyes still dull from the event. Roan nodded to him and turned and left. Right now, all he wanted to do was get Inca to their camp to tend to her needs.

* * *

The soup tasted salty and life-giving to Inca as she sat propped up against a tree at their camp, and accepted another spoonful from Roan. He had opened up a packet of soup and made it for her and the chicken broth was revitalizing. He stood up and moved to the fire to place more wood on it, the flames dancing gaily and highlighting his hard, carved face. Inca was covered with only a thin blanket and was chilled to the bone. Though the soup warmed her, she wished, more than anything, that Roan would come and sit next to her, embrace her and warm her with his powerful body.

"More soup?" Roan asked as he came back to her and knelt down beside her.

"No…thank you…." Inca sighed deeply.

"You almost died," Roan said as he sat down.

Inca avoided his hooded look. She felt terribly vulnerable right now. "Yes. Thanks to you and your spirit guide, I will live."

His heart told him to move closer and take her into his arms. After almost losing her, he no longer tried to shield himself from Inca. Roan wasn't sure when his guard had come down, only that the crisis earlier had slammed that fact home to him. "Come here," he murmured, and eased her against him. She came without a fight, relieved that he was going to hold her. Her flesh was goose pimpled. As Roan settled his bulk against the tree with Inca at his side, her head resting wearily on his shoulder, he'd never felt happier.

"Okay?" he asked, his lips pressed to her long, flowing hair. She felt good in his arms, fitting against him perfectly, as if they had always been matched puzzle pieces just waiting to be put together.

Sighing softly, Inca nuzzled her face into the crook of his neck. "Yes..." And she closed her eyes. Risking everything, she lifted her hand and placed it on his chest. The moment was so warm, so full of life. She could hear the insects singing around them, the howl of some monkeys in the distance. All that mattered right now was Roan.

"You are so brave," she whispered unsteadily. "I needed help and you knew it. I was told before I took Julian's hand to help him return that it might kill me."

Roan frowned. "And you did it anyway?"

Barely opening her eyes, she absorbed Roan's warmth, felt his hand moving gently across her shoulders. "What choice did I have? He had not finished his life's mission on this side. He had to come back. He drew the snake to him to create a crisis that would overcome his father's reserve."

"Well," Roan muttered, "that certainly did the trick. The man was crying like a baby when Julian returned."

"Good," Inca purred. She nuzzled against his shoulder and jaw, a soft smile on her lips. She felt the caress of Roan's fingers along her neck and across her cheek and temple. How wonderful it felt to be touched by him! All these years, Inca had been missing something. She couldn't verbalize it. She hadn't known what it was until now. It was the natural intimacy that Roan had effortlessly established with her. The warmth, the love she felt pouring from him brought tears to her eyes. Was this what love felt like? Inca had no way of knowing for sure. She'd read many books by famous authors and many poems about love. To read it was one thing. To experience it was something new to her.

"Do you often get into this kind of a predicament with someone you're going to heal?"

Inca shook her head. "No."

"Good."

She smiled a little. Roan's fingers settled over the hand she had pressed to his heart. She could feel the thudding, drumlike pounding of it beneath her sensitive palm. "Someday you must go with me to the Jaguar Clan village. I would like you to meet the elders. I think you have powerful medicine. All you need is some training to understand it and work with it more clearly."

Roan nodded. He lay there in the darkness, near the dancing fire, and told her what he'd felt and seen when he'd taken her into his arms. When he was done, he felt Inca reach up, her fingertips trailing along his jaw.

"You are a very brave warrior," she told him. Lifting her head so that she could look up at him, she saw the smoldering longing in his eyes—for her. Because she was weak and feeling defenseless, or perhaps because she'd nearly died and she was more vulnerable than usual, Inca leaned up...up to press her lips to his. It wasn't something she thought about first, for she was completely instinctual, in touch with her primal urges. As her lips grazed the hard line of his mouth, she saw his eyes turn predatory. Something hot and swift moved through her, stirring her, and she yearned for a more complete union with the softening line of his mouth.

Surprised at first, Roan felt her tentative, searching lips touching his like a butterfly. Her actions were completely unexpected. It took precious seconds for him to respond—appropriately. Primally, his lower body hardened instantly. He wanted to take her savagely and mate with her and claim and brand her. But his heart cautioned him not to, and instead of devouring her with a searing kiss, Roan hauled back on his white-hot desires.

If anything, he needed to be gentle with Inca. As her lips tentatively grazed his once more, he felt the tenuousness of her exploration of him, as a man to her woman. He understood on a very deep level that people did odd things after they almost died. Making love was one of them. It confirmed life over death. All those thoughts collided within his whirling mind as her lips slid softly across his. She did not know how to kiss.

The simple reminder of her virginal innocence forced Roan to tightly control his violent male reaction. Instead, he lifted his hands and gently framed her face. He saw her eyes go wide at first, and then grow drowsy with desire—for him. That discovery just tightened the knot of pain in his lower body even more so. Swallowing a groan, Roan repositioned her face slightly, leaned over and captured her parted lips. The pleasure of just feeling her full mouth beneath his sent shock waves of heat cascading through him. He felt her gasp a little, her hands wrapping around his thick, hairy wrists. Easing back, Roan tried to read Inca and what her reaction meant.

He saw her eyes turn golden-green. The heat in them burned him. She trembled violently as he leaned down and once more tasted her lips. This time, he captured her firmly beneath his mouth. He felt her hesitantly return his kiss. Smiling to himself, he broke it off and moved his tongue slowly across her lower lip. Again, surprise and pleasure shone in her half-closed eyes. Smiling tenderly, he leaned over and moved his mouth against hers once more. This time her lips blossomed strongly beneath his. She caught on fast.

Inca purred with pleasure as Roan's mouth settled against hers. This was a kiss. The type she'd seen other people give to one another. And now she understood the beauty and sensual pleasure of it, too. Now she knew why people kissed one another so often. A flood of heat flowed through her. She felt the caresses of his mouth upon her lips, the gliding heat created by their touching one another. Her heart was skipping beats. Lightning settled in her lower body, and like a hot, uncoiling snake, she felt a burning, scalding sensation flowing through her. The feeling was startling. Intensely pleasurable.

Shocked by all that she was feeling, Inca tore her mouth from his. She blinked. Breath ragged, she whispered, "Enough... I feel as if I will explode...."

He gave her a lazy, knowing smile. Brushing several strands of hair from her cheek, he rasped, "That's good. A kiss should make you feel that way." Indeed, the flush in Inca's cheeks, the golden light dancing in her widening eyes told Roan just how much she'd enjoyed their first, tentative kiss. Exploration with her was going to be hell on earth for him. He felt tied in painful knots. Inca could not know that, however. She was a child in the adult world of hot lovemaking and boiling desire. It would be up to him to be her teacher and not a selfish pig, taking her in lust. If nothing else, today had taught Roan that he felt far more toward Inca than lust, but because of his past, he had denied it. He told himself their relationship was only temporary, that when the mission was over, their torrid longing for one another would come to an end.

Inca shyly looked up at him, and then looked away.

Her lips were throbbing in pleasure. She touched them in awe. "I did not know a kiss could do all this. Now I know why people kiss so much...."

Laughter rolled through Roan's chest. He embraced her a little more tightly and then released her. "I'm not laughing at you, Inca. I agree with your observation."

She smiled a little tentatively. Touching her lips once more, she looked up at him. "I liked it."

He grinned. "So did I."

"The feelings..." she sighed and touched her heart and her abdomen with her hand "...are so different, so wonderful...as if a fire is bursting to life within me."

"Oh," Roan said wryly, "it is. But it's a fire of a different kind."

"And it will not burn me?"

He shook his head solemnly. He would burn in the fires of hell while she explored her sensual nature, but he was more than willing to sacrifice himself for her. "No, it won't hurt you. It will feel good. Better than anything you can imagine."

Stymied, Inca lay content in his arms. "Being like this with you is natural," she whispered. "It feels good to me. Does it for you?"

"You feel good in my arms," Roan told her, pressing a small kiss to her hair. "Like you've always belonged here...." And she did as far as he was concerned. He was old enough, experienced enough to realize that Inca owed him nothing. He was her first man, and he understood that it didn't mean she would stay with him. No, he expected nothing from her in that regard. Inca was the kind of wild spirit no man could capture and keep to himself. She had to be free to come and go as her wild heart bade her.

Selfishly, he wanted to keep her forever. But Inca's life was a day-by-day affair. And in his own philosophy of life, Roan tried to live in the moment, not in the past and not trying to see what the future might bring him.

Inca nuzzled beneath his hard jaw. She closed her eyes. "You saved my life today. And you gave me life tonight. I do not know how to thank you."

Grazing her shoulder, Roan whispered, "Just keep being who you are, sweetheart. That's more than enough of a gift to me."

Chapter 10

"Inca...you've come...." Julian weakly raised up on the pallet where he lay. Shortly, two soldiers were going to carry him out of the swamp and back to the Amazon, where a helicopter would take him to a hospital in Manaus for recovery. He smiled shyly and lifted his hand to her as she drew near.

Inca ignored the soldiers who stood agape as she approached the *tenente*'s litter. There was admiration and wariness in their eyes. They didn't know what to make of her, and that was fine; she liked keeping people off balance where she was concerned. She'd known intuitively that Julian would be gone as the sun rose this morning, and she wanted to say goodbye to him. In her usual garb, she removed the rifle from her shoulder and knelt down beside the young officer, who was still looking pale. Inca knew that the colonel didn't want her in camp with weapons, but that was too bad.

"*Bom dia,* good day," she said, reaching out and gripping his fingers. "You are better, eh?"

Julian's mouth moved with emotion. His lower lip trembled. The strength in Inca's hand surprised him. He held her hand as if it were a cherished gift. "Yes, much... I owe you everything, Inca." His eyes grew soft with gratefulness. "I understand from talking to the men earlier that you risked your life to save mine. I don't recall much...just bits and pieces. I was so shocked when I walked out of my tent. The snake was waiting for me at the flap. I never saw him until it was too late. After he sank his fangs into my leg, I screamed. I remember pulling my pistol and firing off a lot of shots at it. And then...I fell. I don't remember much more." His eyes narrowed on hers. "But I do remember being in the light, and you were there." His voice lowered. "And so was your jaguar. I saw him."

Julian glanced about, wanting to make sure the men of his platoon couldn't hear his whispered words. "I felt myself on the brink, Inca. I wanted to leave, and you brought me back." He squeezed her hand gently and closed his eyes. "I'm glad you did. Don't think for a moment that I wasn't glad to open my eyes and find myself in my father's arms." He looked at her, the words filled with emotion. "He was holding me, Inca. Me. And I owe it all to you, to your strength and goodness."

She saw the tears well up in his eyes. Touched to the point of tears herself, she whispered, "Yours was a life worth saving, my friend."

Julian pressed a soft kiss to the back of her scarred hand and then reluctantly released her strong fingers. Sighing, he self-consciously wiped the tears from the corners of his eyes. "I shouldn't be crying. I feel very emotional right now."

Inca nodded. "That always happens after a near death event. Let your tears fall." She smiled a little. "I see you and your father have connected again?"

Julian's eyes grew watery. "Yes…and again, I have you to thank."

Shaking her head, Inca sensed the crush of soldiers who had begun to crowd around to get a closer look at her and to try and hear what they were talking about. "No, Julian, I had nothing to do with that. I am glad that it happened, though."

Julian kept his voice down. "Yes, we are really talking to one another for the first time since Rafael's death." Choking up, he rasped, "Last night, my father told me he loved me. It's the first time I can recall him saying that to me. It's a miracle, Inca."

Smiling tenderly, Inca nodded. "That is wonderful. And so, you go to Manaus to recover, my friend?"

Nodding, Julian said unhappily, "Yes. I want to stay…. I want to lead my men into that valley, but my father says I must go." With a wry movement of his mouth, he said, "I shouldn't complain. He cares openly for me, and he wants to see me safe. He told me that I was their only son and now it is my turn to carry the family's honor and heritage forward."

"A wise man," she murmured. Patting Julian's hand, she rose. "I wish you an uneventful journey, Julian. Because where we go, it will be dangerous and interesting."

Julian's gaze clung to hers. "I'll never forget you, Inca. The legend about you being the jaguar goddess is true.

I'll speak your name with blessings. People will know of your goodness. Your generous heart..."

She felt heat tunnel up her neck and into her face. Praise was something she could never get used to. "Just keep what you have with your father alive and well. That is all the thanks I need. Family is important. More than most people realize. Goodbye..." She lifted her hand.

The men parted automatically for her exit. Inca looked at them with disdain as she strode through the crowd toward Roan, who stood waiting for her at the rear of the crowd. Her heart pounded briefly beneath the smoldering look of welcome he gave her. When his gaze moved to her mouth, her lips parted in memory of that scorching, life-changing kiss they'd shared last night. She had left camp early this morning to bathe and then find Julian. At that time, Roan had still been asleep in his hammock as she moved silently around their camp.

The warm connection between her heart and his was so strong and beautiful. Inca felt as if she were not walking on Mother Earth but rather on air. Just the way he looked at her made her joyful. A slight smile curved her lips as she drew near.

"I see what you are thinking," she teased in a husky voice meant for his ears only.

Roan's mouth moved wryly upward. He slid his hand around her shoulder and turned her in another direction. "And feeling," he murmured. His gesture was not missed by the soldiers, for they watched Inca as if mesmerized by her presence and power. "Come on, Colonel Marcellino wants to see you—personally and privately."

Instantly, Inca was on guard. She resisted his hand.

Roan felt her go rigid. He saw the distrust in her eyes,

and the wariness. "It's not what you think, Inca. The man has changed since yesterday. What you did for Julian has made the difference. He's no longer out to kill you."

"Humph, we will see." She shouldered the rifle and moved with Roan through the stirring camp. There were a hundred and twenty men left in the company, thanks to the colonel's poor judgment in taking them through this infested swamp. Inca was angry about that. Julian would not have been bitten by the bushmaster had they gone around the swamp.

Inca tried to steady her pounding heart as they approached the opened tent, where Colonel Marcellino sat at his makeshift desk. His attaché, Captain Braga, bowed his head in greeting to Inca.

"Colonel Marcellino would speak privately with you," he said with great deference, and he lifted his hand to indicate she was to step forward. Inca looked over at Roan, a question in her eyes.

"I'm staying here."

"Coward."

Roan grinned. "This isn't what you think it is. Trust me."

Flashing a disdainful look at him, Inca muttered, "I will. And I will see where it leads me."

Chuckling, Roan touched her proud shoulder. "Sweetheart, this isn't going to be painful. It's not that bad."

Inca thrilled to the endearment that rolled off his tongue. She liked the way it made her feel, as if physically embraced. Roan was not aware of his power at all, but she was, and Inca indulged herself in allowing the wonderful feelings that came with that word to wrap around her softly beating heart.

Turning, she scowled and pushed forward. Might as well get this confrontation with the colonel out of the way so they could get out of this dreaded swamp today.

Jaime Marcellino looked up. He felt Inca's considerable presence long before she ducked beneath the open tent flaps to face him. She stood expectantly, her hands tense on her hips, her chin lifted with pride and her eyes narrowed with distrust.

"You wanted to see me?" Inca demanded in a dark voice. She steeled herself, for she knew Marcellino was her enemy.

With great deliberation, Jaime placed the gold pen aside, folded his hands in front of him and looked up at her. "Yes, I asked for you to come so that we may talk." Flexing his thin mouth, he said with great effort, "Most important, I need to thank you for saving my son's life. I saw firsthand what you did. I cannot explain *how* you saved him. I only know that you did."

Inca held herself at rigid attention. She did not trust the colonel. Yet she saw the older man's face, which was gray this morning and much older looking, lose some of its authoritarian expression. His dark brown eyes were watery with tears, and she heard him choking them back. It had to be hard for him to thank her, since he accused her of murdering his eldest son.

Her flat look of surprise cut through him. Her facial expression was one of continued distrust. Jaime wanted to reach inside that hard armor she wore. What could he expect? He'd treated her badly. Lifting his hands in a gesture of peace and understanding, he whispered, "I wish to table my earlier words to you, my earlier accusations that you murdered my eldest son. Because of what has happened here, I intend, when this mission is over, to go back to Brasilia and interrogate the drug runner who accused you of shooting Rafael. And I will use a lie detector test on him to see if indeed he is telling the truth or not.'' His brows drew downward and he held Inca's surprised gaze.

''I owe you that much,'' he said unsteadily. ''My logic says that if you saved Julian, why would you have murdered my firstborn? All that I hear about you, from the gossip of my soldiers, as well as the villagers we have passed on this march, is that you heal, you do not kill.''

Inca slid her fingers along the smooth leather sling of her rifle. ''Oh, I kill, Colonel,'' she whispered rawly. ''But I do it in self-defense. It is a law of my clan that we never attack. We only defend. Do you really think I *enjoy* killing? No. Does it make me feel good? Never. I see these men's faces in my sleep.''

''You are a warrior as I am,'' he replied. ''Killing is not a pleasure for any of us. It is a duty. A terrible, terrible duty. Our sleep is not peaceful, is it?'' He cleared his throat nervously. ''I have heard legends surrounding you, of the lives you have taken.'' Jaime rose, his fingers barely touching the table in front of him. ''And judging from what I've seen, you do *not* enjoy killing, any more than I do.''

Inca's nostrils flared. Her voice quavered. ''What sane human being would?'' She waved her hand toward the encampment. ''Do any of us *enjoy* killing another human being? Only if you are insane, Colonel. And believe me, I have paid dearly...and will continue paying for the rest of my life, for each person's life I have taken. Do you not see those you have killed in your sleep at night? Do you not hear their last, choking cries as blood rushes up their throat to suffocate them?'' Eyes turning hard, Inca felt the rage of injustice move strongly through her. ''Even the idea that I would murder anyone in cold blood is beyond my comprehension. Yet you believed it of me.'' She jabbed her finger at him. ''I told you I did not kill your other son, Rafael. Father Titus has an affidavit, which is in your possession, that tells you I was nowhere near that part of Brasil on that day.''

The colonel hung his head and moved a soiled and damp sheet of paper to the center of his desk. ''Yes...I have it here....''

''Since when did you think priests of your own faith would lie about such a thing?''

Wincing, Jaime rasped, ''You are right, Inca....'' He touched the crinkled, creased paper that held Father Titus's trembling signature. ''I have much to do to clear your name of my eldest son's death. And I give you my word, as an officer and a gentleman, that once I return home, I will do exactly that.''

Inca felt her rage dissolving. Before her stood an old man worn down by grief and years of hatred aimed wrongly at her. ''I will take your words with me. Is that all?''

Nodding, Jaime said wearily, ''Yes, that is all. And I also want to let you know that you were right about this swamp. I'm afraid my arrogance, my anger toward you, got the better of me. From now on I will listen to you. You know this land, I do not. Fair enough?''

Inca hesitated at the tent opening, her fingers clenching the strap of the rifle on her shoulder. ''Yes, Colonel. Fair enough. In five more days we will reach the valley, if we follow my route through the jungle.''

Inca lay on her belly, the dampness feeling good against her flesh in the midday heat as she studied the valley below. Roan lay beside her, and his elbow brushed hers as he took the binoculars from her and swept the narrow, steeply walled valley.

''Do you see the factory?''

Roan kept his voice low. ''Yes, I see it.''

Inca watched as the colonel's company spread out in a long, thin line along the rim of the valley. They had a hundred men ready to march against the Valentino Brothers' factory, which was half a mile away, nestled at one end of the valley. The factory was large, the tin roof painted dark green and tan so that it would not be easily spotted from the air. They had positioned it beneath the jungle canopy to further hide its whereabouts from prying satellite cameras.

Eyes narrowing, Inca watched as her Indian friends moved ceaselessly in and out of the opened doors of the huge factory. A dirt road led out of the area and down the center of the valley, more than likely to a well-hidden villa up the steep valley slopes. They carried bushel baskets of coca leaves, which would be boiled down to extract the cocaine. Other Indians were carrying large white blocks wrapped in plastic to awaiting trucks just outside the gates. That was the processed cocaine, ready for worldwide distribution. Guards would yell at any Indians who moved too slowly for them. She saw one guard lift his boot and kick out savagely at a young boy. Her rage soared at the bondage of her people.

"It looks like an airplane hangar," Roan muttered, adjusting the sights on the binoculars. "Big enough to house a C-130 Hercules cargo plane."

"I estimate there are over a hundred Indians in chains down there," she said, anger tinging her quavering tone.

"There's a lot of guards with military weapons watching every move they make," Roan stated. "A high fence, maybe ten feet tall, with concertina wire on top to discourage any of them from trying to escape."

"At night, the Indians are forced to live within the fence. Sebastian and Faro Valentino are down there. Look near that black Mercedes at the gate." She jabbed her index finger down at them. "That is them."

Roan saw two short men, one with a potbelly and the other looking like a trim, fit athlete. Both were dressed in short-sleeved white shirts and dark blue trousers, and they were talking with someone in charge of the guards, a man in military jungle fatigues. "Got 'em."

"They look pitifully harmless," Inca growled. "But they are murderers of my people—hundreds of them over the last four years. The one with the pig's belly is Sebastian. Faro is the thin one, a pilot. His helicopter is over there." She pointed to the machine sitting off in the grass near the compound. "He has a fleet of military helicopters that he bought from foreign countries, and he uses them to ferry the cocaine out of the area. He has also used his helicopters to shoot down Brazilian Air Force helicopters that have tried to penetrate this area. He is dangerous. He is here to pick up a load of cocaine and fly it to Peru. The Indians are carrying it to the machine right now."

Roan heard the grating in her voice. Faro had a military helicopter, dark green in color and without markings.

"I've read up on these two. Sebastian is the lazy one of the family. He stays put in Brazil, which is his territory. He's satisfied with doing business from here. Faro has his own military air force, with choppers in nearly every South American country. He wants to dominate not only all of South America, but eventually Central America, as well. We're lucky to catch the brothers together. I was hoping we'd get Sebastian." His voice lowered with feeling. "I'd like to take 'em both down."

"Do not be fooled by the piglike expressions on their faces. They are as smart as jaguars."

"And you think the best time to attack is at night?"

"Yes, under cover of darkness. The guards go inside the factory at night to package the cocaine into blocks and wrap them, while the Indians sleep outside. I will go down, contact the chief who leads all the people there, and they will spread the word quickly and quietly as to the coming attack. I will break open the chain around the gate and open it. They will run. That is when the colonel will attack."

Roan nodded and counted the guards. "I see twenty guards."

"There are more inside the factory. Perhaps an equal number."

"Forty men total. Against our hundred."

Snorting, Inca gave him a cutting glance. "Do not think forty men cannot kill all of us, because they can." She glared at the line of Brazilian soldiers hunkering down on their bellies along the rim to observe their coming target of attack. "While these soldiers have gotten stronger over the last ten days, no one says that they are battle hardened or can think in the middle of bullets flying around them.

The Valentinos' men are cold, ruthless killers. Nothing distracts them from the shots they want to take. Nothing.''

"I understand," Roan said. He reached out and touched Inca's cheek. Time was at a premium between them. And as much as he wanted to kiss her, he knew that she had to come to him. Inca had shyly kissed him two more times. The enjoyment was mutual. He could almost feel what she was thinking now, as if that invisible connection between them was working with amazing accuracy. Inca had told him that because a bond of trust was forged between them, he would easily pick up on her thoughts and feelings—just as she would his.

Roan watched her eyes close slightly as he touched her cheek. "I worry about you. You're the one taking all the chances. What if the guards spot you at the fence?"

Inca captured his large hand and boldly pressed a kiss into the palm of it. Smiling widely, she watched his eyes turn a dark, smoky blue, which indicated he liked what she had done. The last five days had been a wonderful exploration for her. She felt safe enough, trusting enough of Roan to experiment, to test her newfound feminine instincts. He made her happy. Deliriously so.

"Do not worry. They will not see me coming. I will use the cover of my spirit guide to reach the fence. Only then will I unveil myself." She released his hand and turned over on her back, her gaze drifting up through the canopy. Above her, a flock of red-and-yellow parrots skittered among the limbs of the trees. "You worry too much, man of my heart."

Roan gave her a careless smile in return. He lay on his back, slid his arm beneath her neck and moved closer to her. When she pressed her cheek against him, he knew she enjoyed his touch. "I like where we're going, Inca," he told her quietly as they enjoyed one of the few private moments they'd been able to steal during the march. "I don't know where that is, but it doesn't matter."

Inca laughed softly. She closed her eyes and fiercely enjoyed his closeness, the way he nurtured her with his touch, with his hard, protective body. "I do not know, either, but I want to find out."

A sweet happiness flowed through Roan. "So do I." And he did. In the last five days they had bonded so closely. Despite his fear, Inca had somehow surmounted that wall within him. Roan was scared. But he was more frightened of losing Inca to the danger of her livelihood. Did she love him? Was there hope for their love? There were many obstacles in their path. Was what she felt for him puppy love? A first love rather than a lasting love built upon a foundation of friendship and mutual respect? Roan wasn't sure, and he knew the only way to find out was to surrender his heart over to her, to the gift Inca had given to him alone.

Inca opened her eyes and looked at Roan, a playful smile on her face. "You are the first man to open my heart. I do not know how you did it, only that it has happened." She lightly touched the area between her breasts where the bandoliers of ammo met and crossed.

More serious, Roan held her softened willow-green eyes. "What we have...I hope, Inca...is something lasting. That's what I want—what I hope for out of this."

"Mmm, like Grandfather Adaire and Grandmother Alaria have? You know, there is gossip that they are a thousand years old, that they fell in love on an island off the coast of England. They were druids on the Isle of

Mona, where they were charged with keeping the knowledge of druid culture alive for the next generation. When the Romans came and set fire to the island, destroying the druid temples and thousands of scrolls that had their people's knowledge recorded on them, they fled. It is said they came by boat over here, to Peru, and helped to create the Village of the Clouds.''

"And they're husband and wife?"

Chuckling, Inca said, "Oh, yes. But Grandmother Alaria is the head elder of the village. Grandfather Adaire is one of eight other elders who comprise the counsel that makes decisions on how to teach jaguar medicine and train students from around the world.''

"A thousand years," Roan murmured. "That's a long time. How could they live so long?"

Inca shrugged and gazed up through the trees. "I do not know. It is said that when humans have a pure heart, they may live forever or until such time that they desire to leave their earthly body." She laughed sharply. "I do not have a pure heart. I will die much, much sooner!''

Roan moved onto his side, his body touching hers. He placed his hand on her waist and looked deeply into her eyes. "You have the purest heart I've ever seen," he rasped. Reaching out, he brushed several strands of hair away from her brow. "The unselfish love you have for your people, the way you share with others…if that isn't pure of heart, I don't know what is.''

Just the touch of his fingers made her skin tingle pleasantly. Reaching up, Inca caressed his unshaved jaw. "Roan Storm Walker, you hold my heart in your hands, as I hold yours. You think only good of me. Those of the

Jaguar Clan are charged with seeing us without such feelings in the way." She smiled gently.

Leaning down, he whispered, "Yes, you hold my heart in your hands, my woman—"

"Excuse me...."

Roan heard the apologetic voice just moments before he was going to kiss Inca. Instead, he lifted his head and sat up. Captain Braga stood uncertainly before them, clearly embarrassed for intruding upon their private moment. "Yes?"

Clearing his throat, Captain Braga said, "A thousand pardons to you both."

Inca felt heat in her face as she sat up. She picked several tiny leaves out of her braid. "What is it?" she demanded. More than anything, she'd wanted Roan's kiss, that commanding, wonderfully male mouth settling against her hungry lips.

"The colonel...he asks you to come and help him with the attack plans. Er, can you?"

Inca was on her feet first. She held out her hand to Roan, who took it, and she pulled him to his feet. "Yes, we will come...."

Roan tried to quell his fear for Inca's safety. He'd followed her down the steep, slippery wall of the narrow valley in the darkness, but Inca had disdained his offer of a flak jacket and headphone gear. Roan adjusted the microphone near his mouth. He was in contact with the officers of the company, who also wore communication gear. He wished Inca had agreed to the headset and protective vest. She had told him it would hamper her abilities to shape-shift and he'd reluctantly given in. The one

thing he did do, however, was take off his medicine necklace and give it to her—for protection. The urge to give
it to her had overwhelmed him, and this time he'd followed the demand.

Inca's eyes had filled with tears as he'd hung it around
her neck, the beautiful blue stone resting at the bottom of
her slender throat. She'd smiled, kissed his hand, knowing
instinctively the importance of his gesture.

The clouds were thick and a recent shower made the
leaves gleam. The rain had muffled their approach to their
target which was fortunate. The factory was less than two
hundred yards away. The road to it was deeply rutted, and
now muddy. Trees had been cleared from the edge of the
road, but otherwise the valley was thickly covered by rain
forest. Faro's helicopter sat tethered near the factory. He
and his brother had disappeared inside the main facility
hours earlier.

Roan's heart beat painfully in his chest for Inca as he
followed her, for her raw courage under such dangerous
circumstances. She didn't seem fazed by her duties, and
if she felt fear, he didn't see it in her eyes or gestures.
How brave she was in the name of her people.

Inca carefully removed her bandoliers and put her rifle
aside. She took off the web belt. There was a guard outside the gate, his military weapon on his shoulder as he
walked back and forth in front of it. Hidden in the forest
above and around the factory were the Brazilian soldiers,
who had crept carefully into position. The attack would
take place in a U-shaped area. The only escape for the
Indians would be down the road. Inca would urge them
to run and then take cover in the rain forest. There was a
squad of Brazilian soldiers half a mile from the front gate,

their machine gun set up to stop any guards from driving away from the factory once the battle began.

Roan said nothing. His heart hammered with worry and anxiety for her. What was Inca going to do? Just walk up to the guard and knock him out? The guard would see her coming. Though his mouth was dry, Roan wiped it with the back of his hand. She slowly stood up, only a foot away from him.

"It is time," she said. Looking up at him, her mouth pulled slightly upward. "Now you and all of them will see why they call me the jaguar goddess."

Roan reached out and gripped her hand. "Don't do anything foolish. I'm here. I can help you...."

She squeezed his fingers. "You just gave me the greatest gift of all, my man." She gently touched the medicine necklace. "Your heart, your care, will keep me safe." Stepping forward, she followed her wild instincts. Her mouth fitted hotly against his. She slid her fingers through his damp hair, and hungrily met and matched his returning ardor. Pulling away, her heart pounding, Inca whispered, "I will return. You have captured my heart...." Then she quickly moved down the last stretch of slope to a position near the road.

Roan's lips tingled hotly from her swift, unexpected kiss. He watched through the lazy light filtering through the clouds from the moon above them. Inca's form seemed to melt into the surrounding grayness. For a moment, Roan lost sight of her. And then his heart thudded. Farther down, something else moved. Not a human... what, then?

Eyes slitting, he lifted the light-sensitive binoculars to try and pinpoint the dark, shadowy movement. He was looking for Inca's tall, proud form. It was nowhere to be found. *There!* Roan scowled. His hands wrapped more strongly around the binoculars. He saw the shadowy outline of a jaguar moving stealthily toward the guard in the distance. His black-and-gold coat blended perfectly into the shadows and darkness surrounding him. Was that Inca? The jaguar was trotting steadily now toward his intended target—the guard walking past the gate. She had told him of her shape-shifting ability, of being able to allow her jaguar spirit guardian to envelope her so that she appeared in his shape and form. Roan didn't know how it was done, exactly, but he recalled his own experience with his cougar recently. Among his own people, there were medicine men and women who were known to change shape into a cat or wolf. In this altered form, Inca had told him, she possessed all the jaguar's powerful abilities, including sneaking up on her intended target without ever being noticed.

Roan's breath hitched. The guard had turned and was coming back toward the corner of the fence closest to the jungle. Compressing his lips, Roan hunted anxiously for the cat. Where was it? It seemed to have disappeared. Instead, he watched the guard, who was lazily smoking a cigarette, a bored look on his face. Just as the guard reached the corner and was going to turn around, something caught his attention. Startled, he dropped the cigarette from his lips, jerked his rifle off his shoulder and started to raise it to fire.

Out of the darkness of the rain forest, a jaguar leaped toward the man. In an instant, the stunned guard was knocked on his back, the rifle flying out of his hand. In seconds, the cat had strangled the soldier by grabbing hold of his neck in his jaws and suffocating him into unconsciousness, not death though that was how a jaguar killed.

Roan stood, the binoculars dropping to his chest. He picked up his rifle and moved rapidly down the hill. In the distance, he could barely see the soldier lying motionless on the ground. A number of Indians had run to that area of the fence. All hell was going to break loose in a few seconds. Running hard, Roan hit the muddy road and sprinted toward the front gate. The other guards would be making their rounds. Inca would have only moments to open that front gate and release her people.

Inca moved soundlessly. It took precious seconds for her spirit guardian to release her. Shaking off the dizziness that always occurred afterward, she blinked several times to clear her head. Then, breathing hard, she picked up the machete the soldier had strapped to his belt.

The Indian factory workers pressed their faces to the fence, clenching the wire. Their expressions were filled with joy as they whispered, "the jaguar goddess." Inca hissed to them in their language to be silent. Digging her feet into the muddy red soil, she lunged toward the gates. Gripping the handle of the deadly three-foot-long machete, Inca raced to where a chain and padlock kept the two gates locked together.

The Indians followed her, as if understanding exactly what she was going to do to free them. Men, women and children all ran toward her without a sound, without any talking. They knew the danger they were all in. Their collective gazes were fixed on the woman they called the jaguar goddess. The thin crescent moon on her left shoulder blade—the mark of the jaguar—was visible as her sleeveless top moved to reveal it. There was no question in their eyes that she was going to save them. She was going to free them!

Breathing hard, perspiration running down the sides of her face, Inca skidded to a halt in the slimy clay. She aimed the machete carefully at the thick iron links that held the Indians enslaved. Fierce, white-hot anger roared through her. She heard a sound. *There!* To her left, she saw a guard saunter lazily to the end of his prescribed beat. He'd seen her! His eyes widened in disbelief.

Lifting the machete, Inca brought it down not only with all her own strength, but with that of her guardian as well, the combined power fueled by the outrage that her people were slaves instead of free human beings. Sparks leaped skyward as the thick blade bit savagely into the chain. There was a sharp, grating sound. The chains swung apart.

Yes! Inca threw the machete down and jerked opened the gates. She saw the guard snap out of his stupor at seeing her.

"Come!" she commanded, jerking her arm toward the Indians. "Run! Run down the road! Hurry! Go into the forest and hide there!"

They needed no more urging. Inca leaped aside and allowed them to run to freedom. She jerked her head to the left and remained on the outside perimeter of the fence. The soldier was croaking out an alarm, fumbling with his rifle. Yanking at it with shaky hands, he managed to get it off his shoulder. He raised his rifle—at her. With a snarling growl, Inca spun around on her heels and ran directly at the drug runner guard. It was the last thing he would expect her to do, and she wagered on her surprising move to slow his reaction time.

The man was shocked by her attack; he had expected

her to run away. He yelped in surprise, his eyes widening enormously as Inca leaped at him. She knocked the rifle back against his jaw, and there was a loud, cracking sound. As the guard fell backward, unconscious, Inca tumbled and landed on all fours. Breathing hard, she saw the soldier crumple into a heap. Grinning savagely, she scrambled to her feet, grabbed his rifle and sprinted down the fence to find the third guard. By now there was pandemonium. Gunfire began to erupt here and there.

Breathless, Inca slid to a halt in the mud near the corner of the compound. She nearly collided with another guard, who was barreling down the fence from the opposite direction after hearing his compatriot's shout of warning. This man was big, over two hundred pounds of muscle and flab. He saw Inca and jerked to a stop. And then his lips lifted in a snarl as he pulled his rifle to his shoulder and aimed it at her. As he moved to solidify his position, one foot slipped in the mud. The first bullet whined near her head, but missed.

Firing from the hip, Inca got off two shots. The bullets tore into the legs of the guard. He screamed, dropped his rifle and crumpled like a rag doll into the mud. Writhing and screaming, he clawed wildly at his bleeding legs.

Inca leaped past him and began her hunt for the fourth and last guard outside the gate. If she could render him harmless, the colonel's men would have less to worry about. Jogging through the slippery mud, she ran down the fence line. Glancing to her left, she saw that the Indians had all escaped. *Good!* Her heart soared with elation. She heard the Brazilian soldiers coming down the slopes of the valley. They were good men, with good intent, but nowhere physically fit for such a battle.

Turning the corner, Inca spotted the last soldier outside the gate. She shouted to him and raised her rifle. He turned, surprised. Rage filled his shadowed face as he saw her. Lifting his own weapon, he fired several shots at her.

Inca knew to stand very still and draw a bead on the man who fired wildly in her direction. She heard the bullets whine and sing very close by her head. Most men in the heat of battle fired thoughtlessly and without concentration. Inca harnessed her adrenaline, took aim at the man's knee and fired. Instantly, he went down like a felled ox. His screams joined the many others. From the corner of her eye, she saw a shadow. Who?

Twisting to face the shadow that moved from behind the building inside the fence, Inca sensed trouble. When the figure emerged, his pistol aimed directly at her head, her eyes narrowed. It was Faro Valentino. His small, piggish eyes were alive with hatred—toward her. He was grinning confidently.

At the same instant, through a flash of light in the darkness, she saw Roan. He shouted a warning at her and raised his rifle at Valentino.

Her boots slipped in the mud as she spun around to get off a shot at the murderer of so many of her people. And just as she did, she saw the pistol he carried buck. She saw the flicker of the shot being fired. She heard Roan roar her name above the loud noise of gunfire. And in the next second, Inca felt her head explode. White-hot pain and a burst of light went off within her. She was knocked off her feet. Darkness swallowed her.

Chapter 11

"**S**he's down! Inca's down!" Roan cried into the microphone. Scrambling, he leaped down the slope to the muddy ground near the compound. "I need a *médico!* Now!" He slipped badly. Throwing out his hands, he caught his balance. *Run! Run!* his mind screamed, *she needs you! Inca needs you!*

No! No! This can't be happening! Roan cried out Inca's name again. He ran hard down the fence line toward her. He fired off shots in the direction of Faro Valentino, who was standing there smiling, a pleased expression on his face he eyed Inca's prone, motionless form. The drug runner scowled suddenly and jerked his attention to Roan's swift approach. He took careful aim and fired once, the pistol bucking in his hand.

Roan threw himself to the ground just in time. The bullet screamed past his head, missing him by inches. Mud splashed up, splattering him.

Faro cursed loudly. He turned on his heel and hightailed it down the fence to where his helicopter was revving up for takeoff.

Cursing, Roan realized he faced a decision: he could either go after Faro or go to Inca's side. It was an easy choice to make. Getting awkwardly to his feet, he sprinted the last hundred yards to her.

Roan sank into the mud next to where Inca lay on her back, her arms flung outward. "Inca!" His voice cracked with terror.

The gunfire was intense between drug runners and soldiers as the Brazilian army closed in around the compound. Several nearby explosions—from grenades—blew skyward and rocked him. The drug dealers were putting up a fierce fight. Faro's helicopter took off, the air vibrating heavily from the whapping blades in the high humidity. He was getting away! Hands trembling badly, Roan dropped the rifle at his side.

"Inca. Can you hear me?"

His heart pounded with dread. Automatically, because he was a paramedic, Roan began to examine her from head to toe with shaking hands. It was so dark! He needed light! Light to see with. *Where is she wounded? Where?* Gasps tore from his mouth. In the flashes of nearby explosions, he saw how pale Inca was. *Is she dead? Oh, Great Spirit, No! No, she can't be! She can't! I love her. I've just found her....* His hands moved carefully along the back of her head in careful examination.

Roan froze. His fingers encountered a mass of warm, sticky blood. After precious seconds, his worst fears were realized. Inca had taken a bullet to the back of her skull. *Oh, no. No!* He could feel where the base of her skull protruded outward slightly, indicating the bones had been broken. Lifting his fingers from beneath her neck, he screamed into the mouthpiece, "*Médico! Médico!* Dammit, I need a doctor!"

Médico Salvador came charging up to him moments later. Panting, he slid awkwardly to a halt. Mud splattered everywhere. His eyes widened in disbelief.

"*Deus!* No!" he whispered, dropping to his knees opposite Roan. "Not Inca!"

"It's a basal skull fracture," Roan rasped. Sweat stung his eyes. He crouched as gunfire whined very close to where they knelt over Inca. Automatically, he kept his body close to hers to shield her.

Salvador gasped. "Oh, *Deus...*" He tore into his medical pack like a wild man. "Here! Help me! Put a dressing on her wound. *Rápido!*"

Roan took the dressing, tore open the sterilized paper packet, pulled the thick gauze out and placed it gently beneath Inca's neck and head. He took her pulse. It was barely perceptible. Roan shut his eyes and fought back tears.

"Pulse?" Salvador demanded hoarsely, jerking out gauze with which to wrap the dressing tightly about her head.

"Thready."

"Get the blood pressure cuff...."

More bullets whined nearby. Both men cringed, but kept on working feverishly over Inca.

Roan went through the motions like a robot. He was numb with shock. Inca was badly wounded. She could die.... He knew her work was dangerous. Somehow, her larger-than-life confidence made him believe she wasn't mortal. Could he hold her as he did before? Could he heal her? Another grenade exploded nearby, and flattening himself across Inca's inert form, Roan cursed. She *was* mortal. Terribly so. The battle raged, hot and heavy around them, but his mind, his heart, centered on her. *Great Spirit, don't let Inca die…don't let her die. Oh, no… I love her. She can't die—not now. She's too precious to you…to all of us….*

Salvador cursed richly as he pumped up the blood pressure cuff. "This is bad—90 over 60. Damn! We have no way to get her to a hospital for emergency surgery." He gave Roan a sad, frustrated look.

Just then, Roan heard another noise. *No! How could it be?* Lifting his head to the dark heavens, he held his breath. Did he dare believe what he heard? "Do you hear that?" he rasped thickly to Salvador.

The Brazilian blinked, then twisted in the direction of the noise, a roaring sound coming from the end of the valley. Within moments, it turned deafening and blotted out the gunfire around them. "*Deus,* it's helicopters! But…how? They cannot travel this far without refueling. Colonel Marcellino said none were available. Is it Faro coming back with reinforcements? We saw him take off earlier. He's got a chopper loaded with ordnance. What if it's him?" Frightened, Salvador searched the ebony heavens, which seemed heavy with humidity—rain that would fall at any moment.

Out of the night sky, to Roan's surprise, at least three black, unmarked gunships sank below the low cloud cover and came racing up the narrow valley toward them. He croaked, "No, it isn't Faro. They're Apache helicopters! At least two of them are, from what I can make out from here. They must be friendlies! I'll be damned!'' Roan had no idea how they'd gotten here. Or who they were. There was still a chance they were drug runners. He knew from Morgan's top-secret files that Faro Valentino had a fleet of military helicopters stationed in Peru. And according to their best intelligence from satellites, there were no enemy helicopters in this immediate area. So who were these people? Brazilian Air Force? Roan wasn't sure. Even if they were, they would have had to have refueled midair to penetrate this deeply into the Amazon basin. Colonel Marcellino had never said anything about possible air support. Roan was positive he would have told his officers if it was an option. Besides, the Valentinos were known to have refuelling capabilities to get in and out of areas like this one.

''Captain Braga!'' Roan yelled into his microphone. ''Are these approaching Apaches ours? Over!''

Roan waited impatiently, his eyes wary slits as he watched the aircraft rapidly draw near. If the copters were the enemy, they were all dead. Apaches could wreak hell on earth in five minutes flat. Roan's heart thudded with anxiety. He jerked a look down at Inca. Her mouth was slack, her flesh white as death. Her skin felt cool to his probing touch. Looking up, he saw Salvador's awed expression, his gaze locked to the sky. Flares were fired. The sky lit up like daylight as the helicopters approached the compound area.

Roan scowled. Of the three helos, two were Apache and one was a Vietnam era Cobra gunship. Surprised, he didn't know *what* to make of that. The valley echoed and reechoed with the heavy, flat drumming of their turning blades. Who the hell were they? Friend or enemy? Roan was almost ready to yell for Braga again when Braga's winded voice came over his headset.

"We don't know *whose* they are! They're not Brazilian! They're not drug runners. Colonel Marcellino is making a call to headquarters to try and find out more. Stand by! Over."

"Roger, I copy," Roan rasped. Blinking away the perspiration, he saw the Cobra flying hell-bent-for-leather between the two heavily armed Apaches. There was a fifty-caliber machine gun located at the opened door. He saw the gunner firing—at the drug runners!

"They're friendly!" Salvador shouted. *"Amigos!"*

The gunships all had blinking red and green lights on them. The two Apache helicopters suddenly peeled off from the Cobra; one went to the right side of the valley, the other to the left side. The Cobra barreled in toward the compound, low and fast, obviously attempting to land. The valley shook beneath their combined buffeting.

Roan suddenly put it all together. Whoever they were, they were here to help turn the tide against the savagely fighting drug runners! The Cobra began hovering a hundred feet above them, an indication that it was going to land very close to the compound. Sliding his hands beneath Inca, Roan growled to Salvador, "Come on! That chopper is going to land right in front of this factory. We can get Inca outta here! She has a chance if we can get her to the hospital in Manaus. Let's move!" Inca weighed next to nothing in his arms as Roan lifted her gently and pressed her against him. He made sure her head was secure against his neck and jaw. Every second counted. Every one.

The sound of powerful Apache gunships attacking began in the distance. Hellfire missiles were released, lighting up the entire valley. The missiles arced out of the sky toward the main concentration of drug runners, many of whom began to flee down the road toward the other end of the valley. Brutal noise, like that of a violent thunderstorm, pounded savagely against Roan's eardrums.

Salvador jerked up his medical pack and ran, slipping and stumbling, after Roan as he hurried in a long, striding walk to the compound entrance. The rain forest was alive with shouts from excited Brazilian soldiers. Hand-to-hand combat ensued. Out of the corner of his eye, Roan saw Captain Braga running down the slope with a squad of men. In the flashes of light, he saw triumph etched across the captain's sweaty, strained face.

Gripping Inca more tightly, Roan rounded the corner of the compound fence, heading directly to the Cobra, which had just landed just outside the gates. Neither he nor Salvador had weapons. Salvador was a medic and they never carried armament. Roan had left his rifle behind in order to carry Inca. Out of the darkness came two drug runners, weapons up and aimed directly at them.

Roan croaked out a cry of warning. "Salvador! Look out!" He started to turn, prepared to take the bullets he knew were coming, in order to protect Inca, who sagged limply in his arms.

Just then another figure, dressed in body-fitting black flight suit and flak jacket, helmet on his head, appeared almost as if by magic behind the drug runners who had Roan in their gunsites. The black helmet and visor covered the upper half of his face, but his pursed lips and the way he halted, spread his booted feet and lifted his arms, told Roan he was there for a reason.

Roan stared in horror and amazement as whoever it was—the pilot of the landed Cobra helicopter?—lifted his pistol in both hands and coolly fired off four shots. All four hit the drug runners, who crumpled to the muddy earth. The man then gestured for Roan and Salvador to make a run for it. He stood tensely and kept looking around for more enemy fire.

"Come on!" Roan roared, and he dug his boots into the mud. He saw the pilot turn and yell at him, his voice drowned out by the machine gun fire of the nearby Cobra. The pilot lifted his arm in hard, chopping motions, urging them to hightail it.

Roan's breath came in huge, gulping sobs as he steadied himself in the mud. *Hurry! Hurry!*

Salvador slipped. He cried out and smashed headlong into the ground and onto his belly. His medical pack went flying.

Roan jerked a look in his direction.

"Go on!" Salvador screamed. "*Corra!* Run! Get to the chopper! Don't worry about me!"

Roan hesitated only fractionally. He surged forward. Barely able to see the six-foot-tall pilot except in flashes of gunfire, Roan saw him reach toward him. The grip of his hand on his arm was steadying.

"Stay close!" the pilot yelled, his voice muffled by the shelling.

Roan's only protection for Inca as he ran along the compound fence was the wary pilot, who moved like a jaguar, lithe and boneless, the gun held ready in his gloved hand. Roan followed him toward the front corner of the barbed-wire barrier.

As Roan rounded the corner, he saw the helicopter, an

antique Huey Cobra gunship from the Vietnam War, sitting on high idle waiting for them, its blades whirling. Roan followed the swiftly moving pilot back to the opening where the machine gunner was continuing to fire at drug runners. More than once, the pilot fired on the run, to the left, to the right, to protect them. Bullets whined past Roan's head like angry hornets. Slugs were smattering and striking all around them. Mud popped up in two-foot geysers around his feet. Roan saw the copilot in the aircraft making sharp gestures out the opened window, urging them to hurry up and get on board. The gunfire increased. The drug runners were going to try and kill them all so they couldn't take off.

Hurry! Roan's muscles strained. They screamed out in pain as he ran, holding Inca tightly against him. Only a hundred feet more! The pilot dived through the helicopter's open door, landed flat on his belly on the aluminum deck and quickly scrambled to his knees and lunged forward into the cockpit. The gunner at the door stopped firing. He stood crouched in the doorway, arms opened wide, yelling at Roan to hurry. All of them were dressed in black flight suits, with no insignias on their uniforms. Their helmets were black, the visors drawn down so Roan couldn't make out their faces. They looked brown skinned. Indians? Brazilians? He wasn't sure. Roan thought they must be from some secret government agency. The real military always wore patches and insignias identifying their country and squadron.

The blast of the rotor wash just about knocked him off his feet. His arms tightened around Inca. The pilot was powering up for a swift takeoff. The violent rush of air slapped and slammed Roam repeatedly as he ducked low to avoid getting hit by the whirling blades. The gunner held on to the frame of the door, the other hand stretched outward toward them. He was screaming at Roan to get on board. An explosion on the hill rocked him from behind. Fire and flame shot up a hundred feet into the air. One of the attack choppers must have found an ammo dump! Thunder rolled through the narrow valley, blotting out every other sound for moments.

By the time Roan made it to the doorway, his arms were burning weights. The gunner wrapped a strong hand under his biceps and hefted him upward, then moved aside and made a sharp gesture for Roan to place Inca on an awaiting litter right behind him in the rear of the small helicopter. Wind whipped through the craft. As Roan gently lay Inca on the stretcher and quickly shoved several protective, warm covers over her, the gunner placed a pair of earphones across Roan's head so he could have immediate contact with everyone else in the helicopter.

"Get us to the nearest hospital!" he gasped to the pilot as he knelt over Inca. "She's got a basal skull fracture. Time's something we don't have. She's gonna die if we can't get her stabilized. Let's get the hell outta here! Lift off! Lift off!"

The gunner went back to his station, and in seconds, the machine gun was firing with deep, throaty sounds once again. Red-and-yellow muzzle light flashed across the cabin with each round fired. Roan heard bullets striking the helo's thin skin as the craft wrenched off from the ground and shot skyward like a pogo stick out of control. He bracketed Inca with his own body, the gravity and power of the takeoff a surprise. This old machine had a lot more juice in it than he'd thought. The ride was violent and choppy. Everyone got bounced around. The pilot took evasive maneuvers, steering the aircraft in sharp zigzag turns until they could get out of the range of gunfire from below, moving swiftly up the valley, to gain altitude and head for Manaus.

The instant they were out of rifle range, the gunner stopped firing. He slid shut the doors on each side of the Cobra so that the wind ceased blasting through the aircraft. The helicopter shook and shuddered as it strained to gain altitude in the black abyss surrounding them. Before Roan could ask, a small, dull light illuminated the rear cabin where they were sitting on the bare metal deck, allowing him to see in order to take care of Inca. Quickly, he tied the green nylon straps of the litter snugly around her blanketed form so she couldn't be tossed about by the motion of the chopper.

"Give him the medical supplies," came the husky order from the pilot over his earphones.

Roan was in such shock over Inca's condition that it took him precious seconds to realize the ragged voice he heard was a woman's—not a man's. Surprised, he jerked a look toward the cockpit. He saw the pilot, the one who had shot the two drug runners and saved their lives, twist around in her seat and look at him for a moment. She pushed the visor up with her black glove and gazed directly at him and then down at Inca, the expression on her face one of raw emotion. Her eyes were alive with anger and worry as she stared at Inca.

His mouth dropped open. Even with the helmet and military gear, Roan swore she was nearly a carbon copy of Inca! How could that be? The light was bad and her sweaty face deeply shadowed, so he couldn't be sure. The

shape of her face was more square than Inca's, but their
nose and eyes looked the same. The pilot's expression was
fierce. Her eyes were slitted. There were tears running
down the sides of her cheeks. She was breathing heavily,
her chest heaving beneath the flak jacket she wore.

"How's Inca doing?"

Roan blinked. Clearly this woman knew Inca. His mind
tilted. He opened his mouth. "Not good. She's stable for
now, but she could dump at any time."

Nodding, the woman wiped her eyes free of the tears.
"She couldn't be in better hands right now."

Stymied, Roan saw the depth of emotion in her teary
eyes. Tears? Why? The stress of combat? Possibly.

"I know you have a lot of questions, Senhor Storm
Walker. In time, they'll be answered. Welcome aboard the
black jaguar express." She made a poor attempt to smile.
"I'm Captain Maya Stevenson. My copilot is Lieutenant
Klein. Take care of my sister, Inca, will you? We're heading for Manaus. My copilot's already in touch with the
nearest hospital. There'll be an emergency team waiting
for us once we land. We brought some help along." She
jerked a thumb in the direction of her door gunner. "Ser-
geant Angel Paredes has a lot of other skills you can use.
We call her the Angel of Death. She pulls our people from
death's door." Her lips lifted, showing strong white teeth.
"Get to work." She turned back to her duties.

"Here," the door gunner said, "IV with glucose solution." She pushed up the visor into her helmet, her
round Indian face in full view beneath the low lighting.

Stunned, Roan looked at her. Paredes grinned a little.
"This is a woman's flight, *senhor.* Tell me what else you

need for Inca.'' She gestured toward a large medical bag nearby. ''I'm a paramedic also. How may I assist you?''

Shaking his head in stunned shock, Roan had a hundred questions. But nothing mattered right now except Inca and her deteriorating condition. ''Put the IV in her right arm,'' he rasped. Leaning out, he pulled the IV bag over to him and hung it on a hook so that the fluid would drip steadily into her arm. ''You got ice on board?''

Paredes nodded as she knelt down and wiped Inca's arm with an alcohol swab. ''Yes, sir.'' She pointed to it with her black, gloved hand, then took off her gloves and dropped them to the deck. ''In there, *senhor*. In that thick plastic container.'' She skillfully prepped Inca's arm to insert the IV needle.

Roan found the containers and jammed his hand into the pack. This was no ordinary paramedic's pack, he realized. No, it was like a well-stocked ambulance pack. It had everything he could ever want to help save Inca's life. The helicopter shook around him. His ears popped. He heard constant, tense exchanges between the pilot and copilot. Both women's voices. A three-woman air crew. What country were they from? He picked up the plastic bag of ice and struck it hard against his thigh, then waited a moment before gently placing it beneath Inca's neck. It was an instant ice pack, which, when struck, mixed chemicals that created coolness. The door gunner handed him some wide, thick gauze.

''To hold the ice pack in place,'' she instructed.

Nodding his thanks, Roan began to feel his adrenaline letdown make him shaky. Inca lay beneath the warming blankets, her beautiful golden skin washed out and gray looking. Reaching for the blood pressure cuff, he took a reading on Inca. To his relief, her pressure was holding steady. Ordinarily, on a wound like this, the person dumped and died within minutes because the brain had been bruised by the broken skull plates and began to swell at a swift rate. So far, her blood pressure was remaining steady, and that was a small sign of hope.

"How's Inca doing?" Stevenson demanded.

Roan glanced forward. The captain was flying the helicopter as if the hounds of hell were on her tail. They needed all the speed this old chopper could give them. Time was of the essence, and she seemed to share his sense of haste. The aircraft shook and vibrated wildly as the pilot pushed it to maximum acceleration, tunneling through the clouds.

"Stable," he croaked. "She's remaining stable. That's a good sign."

"I could use some good news," Stevenson growled.

And then Roan noticed that the helicopter was following another one, at less than one rotor length. Stymied, Roan saw the red and green, flashing lights on the underbelly of the copter in front of them.

"What's that chopper doing so close?" he demanded, terror in his tone.

Stevenson gave a bark of laughter. "This old bag of bones doesn't have any IFR, instrument flight rules, equipment on board to get us through the clouds or for night flight, Senhor Storm Walker. The chopper ahead of us is a state-of-the-art Apache gunship. She's equipped with everything we need to get the hell out of here and get Inca to Manaus. I'm following it. If I lose visual contact with it, we're all screwed. I'll lose my sense of direction in this soup and we'll crash."

Roan's eyes narrowed. She was doing more than following it, for there was barely a hundred feet between them. One wrong move and they'd crash into one another. That kind of flying took incredible skill and bravery. No wonder the Cobra was shaking like this; it was in direct line of the rotor wash of the far more powerful Apache. Yet he knew the gunship was a two-seater and had no room for passengers.

"Shove this old crone into the redline range," the pilot ordered the copilot. "Tell them to put the pedal to the metal up there. Squeeze *every* ounce of power outta her."

"Roger."

Roan shook his head disbelievingly. He looked down at Inca. Her face was covered on one side with mud. Taking a dressing, he tried to clean her up a little. He loved her. He didn't want her to die. Moving his hand over Inca's limp one, he felt the coolness of her flesh.

"Pray for her, *senhor*. Prayer by those who love someone is the most powerful," the door gunner said as she got up and crawled forward toward the cockpit.

Roan touched Inca's unmarred brow with trembling fingertips. She looked so beautiful. So untouched. And yet a bullet had found her. Why hadn't he realized she was vulnerable just like any other human being? Why hadn't her spirit guide protected her? Squeezing his eyes shut, Roan ruthlessly berated himself. Why hadn't he shot first before Faro Valentino had fired at her? His heart ached with guilt. With unanswered questions. Again he stroked Inca's cheek and felt her softness. Gone was her bright animation. Inca's spirit hung between worlds right now. Roan didn't fool himself. She could die. The chances of it happening were almost guaranteed.

"Another hour, Senhor Walker," the pilot murmured. "We'll be there in an hour...."

How could *that* be? Roan twisted to look toward the gunner, who was crouched in a kneeling position, her hands gripping the metal beams on either side of her as she hung between the seats of the two pilots. They were a helluva lot farther from Manaus than an hour! What was going on? Roan felt dizzy. He felt out of sync with everything that was going on around him. He realized he was in shock over Inca's being wounded. He was unraveling and everything felt like a nightmare.

"An hour?" he rasped. "That can't be."

The pilot laughed. "In our business, *anything* is possible, Senhor Walker. Just keep tending Inca. Be with her. I'll take care of my part in this deal. Okay?"

Who are these women? The question begged to be asked. Roan watched through the cockpit Plexiglas as they rose higher and higher. Suddenly they broke through the soup of thick clouds. He gasped. The Apache gunship was just ahead of them, and he felt the hard, jarring movement from being in the air pockets and rotor wash behind it. Captain Stevenson was within inches of the Apache's rotors. Marveling at her flying skills, Roan turned away. He couldn't watch; he thought they'd crash into one another for sure. The woman was certifiable, in his opinion. She had to be crazy to fly like this.

His world was torn apart and tumbling out of his control. Roan felt stripped and helpless. He leaned close to Inca and placed a kiss on her cool cheek. All he could do now was monitor her blood pressure, her pulse, and simply be with her. And pray hard to the Great Spirit to save her life. She was too young to die. Too vital. Too important to Amazonia. Oh, why hadn't he taken out that drug runner first? Roan hung his head, and hot tears squeezed beneath his tightly shut lids.

He felt a hand on his shoulder. "You did all you could, *senhor,*" Paredes said gently. "Don't be hard on yourself. Some things are meant to be…and all we can do is be there to pick up the pieces afterward. Just hang in there. Manaus is nearby…."

Roan couldn't look up. All he could do was remain sitting next to Inca, his bulk buttressing the litter against the rear wall of the aircraft so that she had a somewhat stable and stationary ride. He felt Paredes remove her hand from his shoulder.

His world revolved around Inca. Never had he loved someone as he loved her. And now their collective worlds were shattered. All the secret hopes and dreams he'd begun to harbor were now smashed. Closing his eyes, Roan took Inca's hand between his and prayed as he'd never prayed before. If only they could be at Manaus right away. If only they could get her into emergency surgery. If only…

Roan sat tensely in the waiting room on the surgery floor of the hospital in Manaus. There was nothing else he could do while Inca was being operated on. Forlornly, he looked around at the red plastic sofas and chairs. The place was deserted. It was one in the morning. The antiseptic smells were familiar to him, almost soothing to his razor-blade tenseness. An emergency team had been waiting for them when the woman pilot landed the Cobra on the roof of the Angel of Mercy Hospital. And just as soon as Inca was disembarked by the swift-moving surgery team, Captain Stevenson had taken off, her Cobra absorbed into the night sky once again. He hadn't even had time to thank her or her brave crew. Instead, Roan's attention had been centered on Inca, and on the team who rushed her on a wheeled gurney into the hospital. He gave the information on Inca's condition to the woman neurosurgeon who was to do the surgery. Her team hurried Inca into the prepping room, while he was asked to go and wait in the lobby area.

Reluctantly, Roan had agreed. He'd paced for nearly two hours, alone and overwhelmed with grief and anger. Life wasn't fair, that he knew. But to take Inca's life, a woman whose energy supported so many, who held the threadbare fabric of the old Amazonia together, was too unfair. Rubbing his smarting, reddened eyes, Roan had finally sat down, feeling the fingers of exhaustion creeping through him. He was filthy with mud that had encrusted and dried on his uniform. Inca's blood was smeared across it as well. He didn't care. He stank. He could smell his own fear sweat. The fear of losing Inca.

Nothing mattered except Inca, her survival. He heard a sound at the doorway and snapped up his head. The neurosurgeon, Dr. Louisa Sanchez, appeared in her green medical garb. Her expression was serious.

"Inca?" Roan voice rang hollowly in the lobby. He stood up and held his breath as the somber surgeon approached.

"Senhor Storm Walker," she began in a low tone, "Inca is stable. I've repaired the fracture. The bullet did not impact her brain, which is the good news. It ricocheted off the skull and broke the bone, instead. What we must worry about now is her brain swelling because of the trauma of the bone fracture. It is very bad, *senhor*."

Roan blinked. He felt hot tears jam into his eyes. "You've packed her skull in ice?"

"Yes, she is ice packed right now."

"And put an anti-inflammatory in her IV to reduce the swelling of her brain tissue?"

Dr. Sanchez nodded grimly. "*Sim*. I've given her the highest amount possible, *senhor*. If I give her any more, it will kill her." The surgeon reached out. "I'm sorry. We must wait. Right now, she's being wheeled into a special room that is outside of ICU. She will be monitored by all the latest equipment, but it is not glass-enclosed. It is a private room."

Roan felt his world tilting. He understood all too well what the doctor was saying without saying it. The private room was reserved for those who were going to die, anyway. This just gave the family of the person the privacy they needed to say their goodbyes and to weep without the world watching them.

"I—see...." he croaked.

Sadly, Dr. Sanchez whispered, "She's in the hands of God, now, *senhor*. We've done all we could. I anticipate that in the next forty-eight hours her fate will be decided.... I suggest you get cleaned up. And then you can stay with her, yes?"

The doctor's kindness was more than Roan had expected. Inca was going to die. Blinking back the tears, he rasped unsteadily, "No, I want to stay with her, Doctor. Thank you...."

The beeps and sighs of ICU equipment filled the white room where Inca lay. Normally, Roan felt a sense of security with all these machines. Inca was breathing on her own, which was good. As he stood at her bedside, he saw how pale she had become. Her head was swathed in a white dressing and bandage. The ice packs were changed hourly. And every hour, her blood pressure was moving downward, a sign of impending death. Miserably, Roan stood at her bedside, her cool hand clutched within his. Dawn was peeking through the venetian blinds. The pale rose color did not even register with him, only as a reminder that Inca would enjoy seeing the beauty of the colors that washed the dawn sky. So many conversations with her played back to him. Each one twinged his aching heart. He had tried to heal her as he had once before, but it didn't work. He was too exhausted, too emotionally torn to gather the necessary amount of laser-like concentration. Never had he felt so helpless.

Leaning down, Roan pressed his lips to her forehead. Easing back a little, he studied Inca's peaceful face. She looked as if she were asleep, that was all; not fighting a losing battle for her life. Roan knew that the brain could continue to swell despite whatever efforts doctors made, and that if it swelled too much, it would block the necessary messages to the rest of the body and she'd stop breathing. Her blood pressure dropping was a bad sign that her brain was continuing to swell despite everything. A very bad sign.

"I love you, Inca. Do you hear me, sweetheart?" His voice broke the stillness of the room. His tone was deep and unsteady. Hot tears spilled from his eyes. "Do you hear me? I love you. I don't know when it happened, it just did." He brushed the soft skin of her cheek. "At first,

I was afraid to fall for you, Inca. But now I'm glad I did. I want you to fight, Inca. Fight to come back to me. To what we might have. This isn't fair. None of it. I've just found you…loved you…. Please—'' he squeezed her fingers gently "—fight back. Fight for our love, fight for yourself, because there are so many people who need you. Who rely on you…''

The door quietly opened and closed. Roan choked back a sob, straightened up and twisted to look in that direction. He'd expected the nurse, who would take Inca's vitals and replace the old ice pack for a new one. His eyes widened. It was Captain Stevenson. She was still dressed in the clinging black nylon uniform, her flak jacket open. Beneath her left arm was her helmet. His gaze ranged upward to her face. His heart pounded hard. She looked drawn and exhausted as she stepped into the room.

He met her slightly tilted emerald-green eyes as they locked on his. Blinking, Roan again saw the powerful resemblance between her and Inca. They almost looked like—twins! But how could that be? His mind spun. She had her black hair, tightly gathered in a chignon at the nape of her long neck. The pride and confidence in her square face was unmistakable. But there was grief in her eyes, and her full lips twisted slightly in greeting.

She moved soundlessly to the other side of Inca's bed. Glancing down at Inca, she quietly placed her helmet on the bedstand. "You're right, Senhor Storm Walker. I *am* her twin." She smiled tenderly down at Inca and ran her fingers along her arm. "Fraternal twin."

"But…how…? Inca never told me about you."

Maya shrugged. Her expression softened more as she leaned down and placed a kiss on Inca's damp brow.

Straightening, her voice hoarse, she said, "Inca never knew I existed. So she couldn't tell you about me. I was told of her being my sister a year ago by the elders of the Jaguar Clan. Once I knew, I was told I would meet her." She grimaced. "They didn't tell me how I would meet her until a week ago. That's why I'm here...."

Stunned into silence, Roan stared at the woman. She was a warrior, no doubt. She was as tall as Inca, and he could see the black leather holster on her thigh.

"My poor sister," Maya whispered in a choked tone as she continued to stroke Inca's hair in a gentle motion. "Our fate has been one made in darkness. I'm so sorry this happened. I wished I could've stopped it, but I couldn't. You have one more bridge to cross, my loving sister. Just one..." And Maya straightened and looked directly at Roan.

"She's going to die," Maya told him in a low tone.

Roan rocked back. He gripped Inca's hand and tried to deal with the truth.

Maya sighed as the pain moved through her heart. She held Inca's other hand in hers.

"I tried to save her like I did once before," he told Maya.

She shook her head. "You don't have the kind of training it takes to be able to heal in the middle of a battle." She gave him an understanding look. "It takes years of training to do it, so don't blame yourself."

"It worked once...I hoped...wanted it to work again...."

"You're lucky it happened once. There's a huge difference between a snake bite and a firefight. You just didn't have the emotional composure to pull it off when she got shot.''

Roan stared at her. "Earlier you said 'black jaguar express.' I thought you were kidding. But if you're Inca's sister, then you're from the Jaguar Clan, too?"

She smiled tightly. "The *Black* Jaguar Clan, *senhor*. Very few know about us. Let's just say we do the dirty work for the Sisterhood of Light. The Jaguar Clan you know of, Inca's people, work in good, positive ways. The Black Jaguar Clan…well, let's just put it this way—someone has to clean up the ugliness in life." Her mouth was grim. There was a glitter in her eyes that said she was committed to what her life was about.

"You—work for the Brazilian government, then?" His mind spun. His heart ached. Inca was going to die.

Maya shook her head and gave a low growl as she continued to devote her attention to Inca. "What an insult. We work for a much higher power than that. But enough of this. You need to listen to me carefully, *senhor*. Inca has one shot at living. That's why I'm here. I've been told that she can have her life back. There's only one possibility for her to live, however."

Eagerly, Roan listened. "How? What can I do?"

Maya studied him fiercely. "You are a credit to the human race, *senhor*. Yes, you can help." She pointed toward the ceiling. "In the laws of the Sisterhood of Light, it's said that if a person willingly gives up her or his life for another, the one who is dying may survive. But—" Maya gave him a hard, uncompromising look "—in order for that to occur, that person must *willingly* give her or his life in exchange. It must be someone who loves the dying person unselfishly."

The silence swirled between them.

Roan looked down at Inca. He would have to die in order for her to live. His hand tightened around hers. He felt Maya's stare cutting straight through him. It was clear she possessed a power equal to Inca's, and then some.

Inca's life for his own. His heart shattered with the finality of the her words.

"You know," Roan whispered in a broken tone, "I've been a lucky man. I never thought I'd know what love was in this lifetime until I met Sarah. And then she was torn from me. After that—" he looked up at Maya, tears in his eyes "—I never expected to fall in love again, until Inca crashed into my life. I'd given up hope. I was just surviving, not living life, until she came along." Gently, he brushed Inca's arm with his fingertips. "My life for hers. There's no question of who's more important here. She is."

Roan lifted his chin and met and held Maya's hard emerald gaze. Her expression was uncompromising as she stood there, the silence deepening in the room.

"Yes. Take my life for hers. Inca is far more important than me. I love her...."

Maya regarded him gravely. "In order for this exchange to occur, you must love her enough to not be afraid of dying."

Shaking his head, Roan rasped, "There's no question of my love for Inca. If you're as powerful metaphysically as she is, then you already know that. You knew the answer before coming here, didn't you?"

Giving him a mirthless smile, Maya whispered, "Yes, I knew. But you see, my brave friend, there's always free will in such matters." She glided her hand across Inca's unbound hair. "If I could give my life for hers, I'd do it in a heartbeat. But the laws state that I can't. We're twin souls, and therefore, it's unacceptable."

Roan looked at one monitor. He saw Inca's blood pressure dipping steeply. "She's dumping," he growled, and pointed at the screen. "She's dying. Just do it. Get it over with. Just tell her when she wakes up that I loved her with all my heart and soul."

Maya took a deep breath and gave him a warm, sad look. "Yes, I promise she'll know. And…thank you. You've given me my sister, whom I've never been allowed to approach or to know. Now we'll have the time we need to get to know one another…and *be* sisters…."

Roan nodded. "More than anything, she wanted a family, Maya. I'm glad she has one. I know she's going to be happy to see you when she wakes up."

Blinking hard, Maya whispered, "Place your hand over her heart and your other hand over the top of her head. Keep your knees slightly bent and flexed. It will allow the energy to run more smoothly. If you lock your knees, you'll block it and cause problems. And whatever happens, keep your eyes closed and keep a hold on her. Me and my black jaguar spirit guide will do the rest."

Roan leaned down. One last kiss. A goodbye kiss. His mouth touched and glided against Inca's, whose lips were slightly parted. Her lips were chapped and cool beneath his. He kissed her tenderly, and with all the love that he felt for her. He breathed his breath into her mouth—one last parting gift. His breath, his life entering into her body, into her soul. As he eased away, he whispered, "I'll see you on the other side, sweetheart. I love you…."

"Prepare!" Maya growled. "She's leaving us!"

Roan did exactly as Maya asked. He stood at Inca's bedside and braced himself against the metal railing for support. He had no idea what would happen next. Well, he'd had one hell of a life. He'd been privileged to love two extraordinary women—two more than he deserved. The moment his hands were in place, he felt Maya's strong, warm hands move over his. It felt like a lightning bolt had struck him. He groaned. The darkness behind his lids exploded into what could only be described as sparks and explosions of color and light. In seconds, Roan was whirling and spinning as if caught in a tornado's grip. He lost all sense of time, direction and of being in his body.

And then he lost consciousness as he spun into a darkened void. The only thing he felt, the last thing he remembered, was his undying, tender love for Inca....

Chapter 12

An intense, gutting pain ripped through Roan and made him groan out loud. His voice reverberated around him like a drum sounding. Was he dead? He felt out of breath, gasps tearing raggedly from of his mouth, as if he'd run ten miles without resting. Everything was dark. His body felt as if a steel weight was resting on him. It was impossible to move.

"Lie still, lie still, and soon the pressure will lift. Be patient, my son...."

Roan didn't know the woman, but her voice was remarkably soothing to his panicked state. Had he died? Struggling to see, he groaned.

"Shh, my son, just relax. No, you are not dead. You've just been teleported from Manaus to here. In a few moments your eyes will open."

He felt her hand on his shoulder, warm and anchoring. His head hurt like hell, a hot, throbbing sensation. What of Inca? What had happened to her? He opened his mouth to speak, but only a croak came out of it.

He heard the woman chuckle. She patted his shoulder. "Young people are so impatient. Try to take a deep breath, Roan. Just one."

Struggling to do as the woman asked, he concentrated hard on taking a breath. His mind was scattered; he felt like he was in five or six major pieces, floating out of body in a dark vacuum.

"Good," she praised. "And again…"

Roan was able to take the second breath even more deeply into his chest. He was hyperventilating, but by honing in on her voice, he was able to slow his breathing down considerably.

"Excellent. My name is Alaria. When you open your eyes, you will find yourself in a large hut here at the Village of the Clouds. You and Inca are welcome here."

Roan felt a surge of electricity move from her hand into his shoulder. The jolt was warm and mild, but he was very aware of the energy moving quickly through him. "My son, when Inca returns from the Threshold, she will want to see your face first…." He felt the gentle pat of Grandmother Alaria's hand on his shoulder.

And then, almost without effort, he lifted his lids. Bright light made him squint, and he turned his head briefly to one side to avoid it. Shafts of sunlight lanced through an open window. Blinking several times, Roan managed to roll onto his side and then slowly sit up. Dizziness assailed him. All the while, Alaria's hand remained on his arm to steady him. That electrical charge was still flowing out of her hand and into him. Shaking his head, he rubbed his face wearily.

"Take your time. You've been through a great deal," she said quietly. "Inca is fine. She is lying next to you, there." She pointed to the other side of the mat where he sat. "Inca will recover fully, so do not fret. I need you to come back, into your body, and become grounded. Then the dizziness will leave and you will no longer feel as if you're in pieces, floating around in space."

Next to him, on a soft, comfortable pallet on the hard dirt floor, was Inca, who was asleep or unconscious. She lay beneath several blankets. Her skin tone was normal and no longer washed out. Most of all, the peaceful look on her unmarred features made Roan's fast-beating heart soar with hope. Looking up, he saw the woman named Alaria for the first time. Relief flooded him that Inca was here and she was all right. He didn't know *how* she could be; but having been around Inca, he knew that miracles were everyday occurrences in the life of Jaguar Clan members.

And perhaps a miracle had just occurred for both of them. He felt better just looking into Alaria's aged but beautiful face. Her eyes sparkled with tenderness, her hand firm and steady on his shoulder. She had her silver hair plaited into two thick braids, which hung over her shoulders, and she was dressed in a pale pink blouse and a dark brown cotton skirt, her feet bare and thickly callused. His mind spun. With her parchmentlike hands, she continued to send him stabilizing energy, reassuring him that he wasn't dead.

"I know you have many questions," Alaria soothed. "Just rest. You are still coming out of the teleport state that Maya initiated with our help. All questions will be answered once Inca has returned to us." She brushed his dampened hair with aged fingers. "You are a courageous and unselfish warrior, Roan Storm Walker. We have been watching you for some time. Be at peace. There is safety here in the Village of the Clouds for you and Inca." Pouring some liquid into a carved wooden cup, she handed it to him. "Drink this warm tea. It contains a healing herb."

He was thirsty. His mouth was dry. Eagerly, he drank the contents of the mug. There was a slightly sweet and astringent taste to the tea. Roan opened his mouth to speak, then closed it. He watched Alaria slowly get to her feet. She straightened and gave him a grandmotherly smile.

"Inca will be awakening soon, and she will be disoriented and dizzy just like you for a while. Be with her. We are monitoring her energy levels at all times. Her wound has been healed. There is no more swelling of her brain." A slight smile crossed her lips. "And you are not dead. You are both alive. I'll return later. Give Inca the herbal drink when she's ready for it."

"T-thank you," Roan said, his voice sounding like sandpaper.

Alaria nodded, folded her thin hands and moved serenely out of the roomy thatched hut. Outside, thunder caromed in the distance, and he saw an arc of lightning brighten the turbulent blue-and-black sky. It was going to rain shortly. The beam of sunlight that had blinded him earlier was gone, snuffed out by the approaching cumulus clouds, which were dark and pregnant with water.

Turning his attention to Inca, Roan moved his trembling fingers along her right arm. She wasn't dead. She was alive. Her flesh was warm, not cool and deathlike as before. Dizziness assailed him once more, and he shut his eyes tightly and clung to her hand. He still felt fragmented. He felt as if pieces of him were still spinning wildly here and there in space. It was an uncomfortable sensation, one he'd never experienced before.

Opening his eyes, Roan studied Inca's soft, peaceful features. Her lips, once chapped, were now softly parted and had regained their natural pomegranate color. Her hair was combed and free flowing, an ebony halo about her head and shoulders. And his medicine piece now lay around her neck, resting on her fine, thin collarbones. The last thing he remembered was placing the amulet between their hands—a last gift, a prayer for her, for her life. Someone must have put the necklace back in place around Inca's neck, but he didn't know who had done it. Roan gently touched the opalescent blue stone which felt warm and looked as if it was glowing.

So much had happened. Roan couldn't explain any of it. One moment he was in the hospital room in Manaus, following Maya's orders to save Inca's life. And the next, it felt as if fifty thousand volts of lightning had struck him squarely. Roan remembered spinning down into a dark abyss, but that was all. And then he'd groggily regained consciousness here, in this hut.

Frowning, he felt a wave of emotion. Inca was here with him. He loved her. His heart swelled fiercely with such feeling that tears automatically wet his lashes. Not caring if anyone saw him cry, Roan didn't try to stop the tears that were now moving down his unshaved face.

"Come back, sweetheart. They said you would live...." he rasped thickly, as he moved his fingers up her arm in a comforting motion. She should have had needle imprints and a little bruising around where the IVs had been placed in her arms, but there was no sign of them on her beautiful, soft flesh. And when he examined the back of her head, the wound was gone. Gone! Her skull bone no longer protruded. There was no tissue swelling. It was as if the injury had never occurred.

How could this be? Roan couldn't stop touching Inca. His heart was wide-open and pounding with anguish one second, giddy with joy the next. Her skin was warm and firm. Her thick, black lashes rested across her golden, high cheekbones. Moving his fingers through her lush, silky hair, he marveled at her wild, untamed beauty.

The rain began, pelting softly at first on the thatched roof. Lightning shattered across the area and illuminated the rain forest at the edge of the village, its power shaking the hut. Thunder caromed like a hundred kettledrums being struck simultaneously. Cringing slightly, Roan waited tensely.

Inca stirred.

His hand tightened around hers. He held his breath. Did he dare hope? Was she coming out of the coma? Would she be whole or brain damaged? Would she have amnesia and not recognize him? Roan leaned down, his eyes narrowing, his heart pounding wildly.

"Inca? Sweetheart? It's me, Roan. You're not dying. You're alive. Open your eyes. You're here with me. You're safe. Do you hear me?" His fingers tightened again about hers. Once more her lashes fluttered. And then her parted lips compressed. One corner of her mouth pulled inward, as if she were in pain. Was she? Anxiety tunneled through him. Roan wished mightily for Alaria to be here right now. He had no idea what to expect, what to do in case Inca was in pain. It was his nature, as a paramedic, to relieve suffering, and right now he felt damned useless.

"Inca?"

Roan felt her fingers twitch, then curve around his. He smiled a little. "That's it, come on out of it. You're coming back from a long journey, my woman. You're my heart, Inca. I don't know if you can hear me or understand me, but I love you...." He choked on a sob. Roan watched in amazement as color began to flood back into her face. He felt a powerful shift of energy around her and himself. Her cheeks took on a rosy hue. Life was flowing back into her.

A second bolt of lightning slammed into the earth, far too close to the hut. Roan cringed as the power and tumult of the flash shook the ground. Rain was now slashing down, the wind howling unabated. The wide, sloping roof kept the pummeling rain from coming into the open windows. Instead, cooling and soothing breezes drifted throughout the clean, airy hut.

Inca's brows moved downward. Roan's breath caught in this throat as her lashes swept upward and he saw her drowsy looking, willow-green eyes. Anxiously, he searched them. Her pupils were huge and black as she gazed up at him. Was she seeing him? Or was she still caught in the coma? Roan knew that it took days and sometimes weeks or even months for a person who was in a coma to come out of it and be coherent. She stared up at him. Her pupils constricted and became more focused. His heart pounded with anxiety.

"Inca? It's Roan. I'm here." He lifted her hand and pressed it against his heart. Leaning down, he caressed her cheek. "I love you. Do you hear me? I'm never going to leave you. You're coming out of a coma. Everything's all right. You're safe...and you're here with me...." He managed a wobbling smile of hope for both of them.

A third bolt of lightning struck, even closer to the hut than the last one, it seemed. This strike made the hut shudder like a wounded beast. Automatically, Roan leaned forward, his body providing protection for Inca. As the thunder rolled mightily around them, Roan eased back. It was then that he recalled that Inca had been born in an eclipse of the moon and during a raging thunderstorm. Sitting up, he watched her eyes become less sleepy looking and more alive, as if her spirit were moving back inside her physical form and flooding her with life once again. The symbolism of the storm was not lost on him. Mike Houston had told him she'd been born in a storm it would make sense that her rebirth would take place during another storm.

He smiled a little, heartened by that knowledge. Indians saw the world as a latticework of symbols and cosmology that were all intertwined. As he gently pressed her hand against his heart, he saw her lashes lift even more. Inca's eyes were now clearer and far more focused. Her gaze clung to his. Roan felt her returning; with each heartbeat, he felt Inca coming home, to him, to what he prayed would be a lifetime with her if the Great Spirit so ordained it.

"Where...?" Inca croaked, her voice rough from disuse.

"You're here at the Village of the Clouds, sweetheart. With me. Alaria said we were teleported by her from the hospital in Manaus." Roan didn't care if his voice wobbled with tears. With joy. Inca was here. And she was alive! He reached down and tenderly caressed her cheek. Her pupils changed in diameter, so he knew she was seeing him and that her brain was not damaged as he feared.

"Welcome back," he rasped. "You're home, with me...where you belong...."

The words fell like a soft, warm blanket around Inca. The sensation of vertigo was slowly leaving her. She felt her spirit sliding fully and locking powerfully into her physical body. Roan's large, scarred hand held hers. She closed her eyes, took in a deep, shaky breath and whispered, "I can feel your heartbeat in my hand...." And she could. Inca opened her eyes and drowned in his dark, smoky-blue gaze. There was no question that she loved him. None. Just that little-boy smile lurking hesitantly at the corner of his mouth, and the hope and love burning in his eyes, made a powerful river of joy flow through her opening heart.

"Are you thirsty? Alaria said you should drink this herbal tea. It will help you."

As Inca became more aware of her surroundings, she frowned. Alaria? Yes, Roan had mentioned Grandmother Alaria. Inca's heart bounded with hope. She had been here with her? Could it be they were *really* at the Village of the Clouds? Her head spun. She had been banned from her real home. So why was she here now? Nothing made sense to Inca. Her hope soared. "Y-yes..."

Roan reached for a pitcher and poured some of the contents into a mug carved out of a coconut shell. "Hold on," he murmured, "and I'll help you sit up enough to drink this."

Inca heard the wind howling around them. It was a powerful storm. She felt it in her bones, felt it stirring her spirit back to life within her body. As a metaphysician, she had experienced many strange sensations, but this one was new to her. She'd teleported once or twice before and was familiar with the process. But this was different. When Roan leaned over and slid his thick arm behind her neck and shoulders and gently lifted her into his arms, Inca became alarmed at how weak she was.

"Don't fight," he soothed as he angled her carefully, cradling her against his body. He watched as Inca tried to lift her hand. It fell limply back to her side. Seeing the surprise in her eyes, he raised the mug to her lips.

"Drink all you want," he urged. "Alaria said you would be weak coming out of the teleportation journey."

He held her like he might hold a newborn infant. The sense of protection, of love, overwhelmed Inca, and she drank thirstily. The warm herbal tea tasted sweet and energizing to her. She was a lot thirstier than she'd first realized. She drank from the mug four times more before her thirst was sated.

The medicinal tea brought renewed strength to her. This time when she forced her arm to move it moved. As Roan placed the mug on the mat beside him, Inca looked up at him with pleading eyes. "Just hold me? I need you...." And she weakly placed her hand against his thick biceps. Roan was dressed in his fatigues, spattered with dried mud, with blackish-red blood stains on his left shoulder. She realized it was *her* blood. From her wound. And yet she felt whole, not wounded. So much had happened. Inca was unable to sort it out. Later, she knew, the memories would trickle back to her.

Roan smiled down at her. "Anytime you want, sweetheart, I'll hold you." And he slid his other arm around her and brought her close to him. A ragged sigh issued from her lips as she rested her head against his shoulder, her brow against his hard, sandpapery jaw.

Closing her eyes, Inca whispered, "I almost died, didn't I? I feel as if I've just returned from the Threshold. You saved me, Roan. You gave your life willingly for me—I remember that. But that's all. I recall nothing more...."

Rocking her gently in his arms, he took one of the blankets from the pallet and eased it around Inca's shoulders and back to ensure her continued warmth. The fierce thunderstorm was dropping the temperature and there was a slight chill in the hut now. He smiled, closed his eyes and gave her a very gentle squeeze.

"Between the two of us, Inca, you're the one that should've had the chance to live, not me." She felt so good in his arms—weak and in need of his protection. That was something he could give her right now, and it made him feel good and strong. Gone was the fierce woman warrior. Right now, Inca was completely vulnerable, open and accessible to him, and it was such a gift. Roan knew that when a person had a near death experience, he or she came back changed—forever. Sliding his arm across her blanketed back, he caressed her.

"I love you. I never told you that before you were shot and went into a coma."

Inca lifted her head and met his stormy blue gaze. She saw the anguish in his eyes and felt it radiating out from him. Roan's love for her was so strong and pure that it rocked her returning senses. "I did not think anyone would find me worth loving," she whispered brokenly. Lifting her hand, Inca added hoarsely, "I am not a good person. I have a dark heart. That is why I was told to leave the village and never return.''

''Well,'' Roan said in a fierce whisper, ''I think all that's changed, sweetheart.'' He caressed her loose, flowing hair. ''And your heart is one of the purest and finest I've ever seen. So stop believing that about yourself.''

A sad smile pulled at her mouth. ''I am so tired, Roan. I want to sleep....''

Roan eased Inca to the pallet. ''Go ahead. Sleep will be healing for you. I'm going to close the windows. There's too much breeze coming in on you.'' He got to his feet, groping for the wall of the hut to support himself. The dizziness was gone and his legs felt pretty solid beneath him. He shut the windows to stop the wind from filtering into the hut. Turning, he saw Inca watching him from half-closed eyes. She opened her hand.

''Will you sleep with me? I need you near....''

Touched, Roan nodded. ''There's nothing I'd like better.'' He expected nothing from Inca. He had shared his love with her. Even if she never loved him, she would know the truth of what lay in his heart. As he knelt down upon his pallet, which was next to hers, he heard the storm receding. The pounding rain was lessening now. Father Sky had loved Mother Earth. That was how Indians saw the dance of the storms that moved across the heavens— as a way of the sky people and spirits caressing and loving their mother, the earth.

Inca sighed, her lashes feeling like weights. Her heart was throbbing with so much emotion, feelings she'd never experienced before. Just the way Roan cared for her told her of his love for her, and quenched and soothed her thirsty heart. She could no longer say she did not know what love was for she had experienced it with him—on the highest and most refined level. He had given his life so that she could return and continue her work in Amazonia. And through whatever mechanism and for whatever reasons, Roan's life had been spared. Joy filtered through her sleepy state. Inca knew she was still weak from having nearly died. It would take days for her to recover fully. The fact they were here in the Village of the Clouds surprised her, but she was too exhausted, and too in need of Roan's steady and loving presence to find out why.

Inca nuzzled Roan unconsciously as she awoke from the wings of sleep. She felt his large, strong body next to hers. She had one leg woven between his, and his arms were around her, holding her close to him. The masculine odor of him drifted into her flaring nostrils. The scent was heady, like an aphrodisiac to her awakening senses as a woman. Automatically, she began to feel heat purl languidly between her legs. Her belly felt warm and soft and hungry—for him. All these sensations were new to her and she reveled in them. Around her, she heard the screech of monkeys, the sharp calls of parrots in nearby trees, and the pleasant, gurgling sound of a nearby creek behind the hut.

She was alive...and Roan loved her. Stretching like a cat, Inca gloried in the movement of her strong, firm body against his. One of her arms was trapped between them, the other wrapped behind his thick neck. Savoring their closeness, Inca sighed, leaned forward and pressed a small kiss on his roughened jaw. How good it felt to be alive! And how dizzying and glorious to know that someone loved her—despite her darkness. Roan loved her as a woman—not as a goddess to be worshipped, as her Indian friends did, but as an ordinary human being. Opening her eyes, Inca absorbed the sight of Roan's sleeping features. His breath was like a warm caress against her cheek and neck. Wondering at all the small, beautiful things that a man and woman could share, Inca welcomed this new world of love he'd opened to her. No wonder being in love was written about so much throughout literature. Now she knew why.

Roan stirred. He felt Inca move. Automatically, his arm tightened and his eyes groggily opened. He felt her pull away, to sit up. Drowsily, he watched as her dark, shining hair cascaded about her shoulders. She wore a soft cotton shift of the palest pink color. As she eased her fingers through her hair, he watched in sheer enjoyment of her femininity. Her profile, that proud nose and chin, and her soft lips, grazed his pounding heart. Today was a new day. A better day, he realized.

Rousing himself, he eased into a sitting position beside Inca. The covers fell away. Through the open doorway, Roan saw a bright patch of sunlight slanting into their hut. Moving his gaze back to Inca, he smiled tenderly at her.

"You look more like your old self. How are you feeling?"

She brushed her hair back and drowned in his sleepy blue gaze. "I feel human again." She leaned forward and placed her hand on his shoulder. He had taken off the soiled shirt and was bare chested. Moving her fingers through the dark hair there, Inca murmured, "I feel alive, Roan, and I know it is because of you...because of your heart and mine being one...." And she pressed herself against him and placed her lips against his mouth.

Pleasantly shocked by her boldness and honesty, he felt her small, ripe breasts grazing his chest, the surgery gown a thin barrier between them. Roan knew Inca's innocence of the world of love and respected it. She was reaching out to him as never before, and he gratefully accepted her bold approach as normal and primal. Sliding his hands upward, he framed her face and looked deeply into her shining willow-green eyes, which seem to absorb him to his very soul. Her pupils were huge and dark, filled with sparkling life once more. And with returning love for him. Oh, she'd never said the words, but that didn't matter to Roan as he smiled deeply into her eyes. The fierce, proud warrior woman had now shifted to her soft and vulnerable side with him. It was an unparalleled gift for Roan. He thanked the Great Spirit for her love, for her courage in reaching out boldly to him despite her own abandonment.

He wasn't about to destroy the new, tenuous love strung delicately between them. Inca needed to explore him at her own pace. As her lips grazed his curiously, he kissed her gently and warmly. She growled pleasantly over his actions, her arms moving sinuously up across his and folding behind his neck as she pressed herself more insistently against his upper body. Roan smiled to himself. He loved her boldness. She tasted sweet and innocent to him as her lips glided tentatively against his. Rocking her lips open, he took her more deeply, his hands firm against her face. He felt her purr, the sound trembling throughout her. Her fingers slid provocatively along his neck and tunneled sinuously into his hair and across his skull. Fire exploded deep within Roan. She was sharing herself with wild abandon, not realizing how powerfully her presence, her innocence, was affecting him. It didn't matter, he told

himself savagely. Inca needed the room to explore him
and what they had in her own timing. Roan wanted to
ignite the deep fires of her as a woman, passions she was
just being introduced to through his love for her.

"Ahem…excuse me, children. Might I have a moment
with you?"

Roan tore his mouth from Inca's. Grandmother Alaria
stood in the doorway of their room, her face alight with
humor. In her hands was a tray filled with steaming hot
cereal, fresh fruit, a pitcher and two glasses.

Inca gasped. "Grandmother!" She blushed deeply and
avoided the older woman's shining eyes, which were
filled with understanding and kindness.

"Welcome home, my child," Alaria murmured. With
a sprightly air, she moved into the large room and said,
"I felt you awaken. You are both weak from your experiences. I thought that a good hot cereal would bring you
back to life." She grinned as she placed the tray across
Roan's lap. "But I see that life has returned of its own
accord to both of you in another way, and I'm joyful."

Inca stared up at the old woman, who was dressed in
a long-sleeved white blouse and dark blue skirt that fell
to her thin ankles. "But—how—how did I get here?" she
stammered.

"Tut, tut, child. Come eat. Eat. Both of you. I'll just
make myself at home on this stool here in the corner.
While you eat, I'll talk. Fair enough?" Her eyes glimmered as she slowly settled herself on the rough-hewn
stool in the corner.

Shaken, Inca looked at Roan, who had a silly, pleased
smile on his face. He, too, was blushing. She touched her
cheek in embarrassment. It felt like fire. And then she

stole a look at the village elder. Alaria had the same kind of silly grin on her mouth that Roan had. What did they know that she did not? Roan handed her a bowl made of red clay pottery, and a hand-carved wooden spoon. The cereal looked nourishing and good. The tempting nutlike flavor drifted up to her nostrils.

"I took the liberty of putting some honey in it for you," Alaria told Inca. "This was always your favorite meal when you were with us."

Inca thanked Roan and held the bowl in her hands. Much of her weakness was gone, but she was still not back to her old self. "Thank you, Grandmother." As always, she prayed over her food before she consumed it. The spirits who had given their lives so that she might live needed such thanks. Lifting the wooden spoon, she dug hungrily into the fare. Her heart was still pounding with desire, her senses flooded from the swift, hot kiss Roan had given her. Her body felt like lightning, energized and unsettled. She wanted something, but could not name what it was.

Alaria nodded approvingly as they both began to eat. "Food for your spirits," she murmured, "and a gift to your physical body." She lifted her hands from her lap. "I know you both have many questions. Let me try to answer them in part. Some other answers will come later, when you are prepared properly for them."

Inca discovered she was starving, and gratefully spooned more of the thick, warm cereal into her mouth. Grandmother Alaria had doted upon her when she was at the village in training. At one time she had been a favorite of Alaria's and Adaire's. Once, Alaria had admitted that Inca was like the child they'd always wished to have, but

never did. In some ways she'd been like a daughter to
them, until she'd gravely disappointed them by breaking
the laws of the clan.

"I do not understand why you have allowed me to
come back here," Inca said, waving the spoon at the ceiling of the hut.

"I know," Alaria whispered gently, her face changing
to one of compassion. "There was a meeting of the elder
council after you were wounded and dying."

Inca frowned. "A meeting? What for?"

Roan looked at her. "You don't have a memory of Faro
Valentino shooting you, do you?"

Inca solemnly shook her head. "All I remember is that
I was dying, Roan, and you traded your life for mine.
That is all."

"She will recall it," Alaria counseled. "All things will
come back to you in time, my child, as your heart and
emotions can handle the experiences."

"I was wounded by Faro Valentino?" She looked
down at the cereal bowl in her hand, deep in thought. She
aggressively tried to recall it, but could not. Frustration
ate at her.

"In the valley..." Roan began awkwardly. He knew
that victims of brain trauma often wouldn't remember
much of anything for weeks, months or years after the
experience. "We were with Colonel Marcellino's company. You had freed the Indians who were slaves in the
cocaine compound of the Valentino Brothers. You were
working your way around the outside of the compound,
getting rid of the guards, so that Marcellino's men
wouldn't be in such danger when they attacked from the
walls of the valley." He looked to Alaria, who nodded

for him to continue the explanation. "One drug runner—"

"Faro Valentino," Alaria interjected unhappily.

Roan nodded, trying to handle his anger toward the man. "Yes, him."

Gravely, Alaria said, "He has murder in his heart. He is one of the darkest members of the Brotherhood of Darkness." She turned to Inca. "Faro shot at you before you could turn and get a shot at him. Roan was behind you, and shouted at you, but you slipped in the mud, and that is what doomed you. At the angle Roan was standing, he couldn't get a bead on Faro to stop him before he fired at you. A bullet grazed the back of your head, my child, and broke your skull, and you dropped unconscious to the ground." Alaria gestured toward Roan, tears in her eyes. "He saved you later, by giving permission to give his life so that you might return from the Threshold to us. There are few men of Roan's courage and heart on the face of Mother Earth. Without his unselfish surrendering, you would not be with us today."

Inca lost her appetite. She set the bowl aside and looked deeply into Roan's eyes. "I remember only part of being on the Threshold. I remember him calling me back.... That is when I knew I was dying."

"And you took his hand, which you had to do in order to decide to stay here instead of moving on to the other dimensions in spirit form." Alaria smiled gently and wiped the tears from the corners of her eyes. "His unselfish act of love did more than just save your life, my child."

Inca reached out and threaded her fingers through

Roan's. He squeezed gently and smiled at her. "What else did it do?" Inca asked.

Alaria looked at her for a long time, the silence thickening in the hut. She placed her hands on her thighs. Her mouth turned inward, as if in pain. "You were told not to come back to the Village of the Clouds because you broke a cardinal rule of the Jaguar Clan."

"Yes," Inca said haltingly. "I did."

"And when a clan member knowingly breaks a rule, the council must act on it. You were told to leave and never return."

Hanging her head, Inca closed her eyes. She felt all those awful feelings of the day she'd been asked to leave. Roan held her hand a little more tightly and tried to assuage some of her grief. Choking, Inca whispered, "I had been abandoned once without choice. By coming to Michael's rescue, I knowingly gave up my family, and it was my choice. I have no one to blame for my actions but me. I knew better, but I did it anyhow."

"Yes," Alaria murmured sadly. "But we, the council, have been watching you the last seven years since you left us. We have watched you grow, and become less selfish, living more in accordance with the laws of the Sisterhood of Light." She gestured toward the rain forest behind the village. "For seven years you have followed every law. We have watched and noted this, Inca. You have turned into a wonderful healer for the sick and the aging. This is part of your blood, your heritage. But it is also part of your life to protect and defend the people of Amazonia. And this you have done willingly, without any help from us at any time. You have been completely on your own. You could have gone over to the Brotherhood of Darkness, but you did not. You struggled, grew and transformed all on your own into a proud member of the Jaguar Clan.''

Inca blinked. ''But I am not of the clan. I stand in the in-between world, neither dark nor light. That is what you said at my judgment.''

''That was then.'' Alaria spoke quietly. She held Inca's unsure and fearful gaze, feeling the pain of her abandonment and loss. ''You came to us without family. Without relatives. We loved you like the daughter we never had. Adaire and I cherished you. We tried to give you what you had been denied all those years, without a true mother and father.''

Hot tears moved into Inca's eyes. She felt emotionally vulnerable because of all that she'd just experienced, and could not hide how she felt, or hold back the tears that now ran down her cheeks. ''And I hurt both of you so very much. I am sorry for that—sorrier than you will ever know. Grandfather Adaire and you loved me. You gave me so much of what I was hungry for and never had before I came here.'' Self-consciously, Inca wiped her cheeks. ''And I ruined it. I did not respect the love that you gave to me. I abused the privilege. I will be forever sorry for the hurt I have caused you, Grandmother. You *must* believe me on that.''

''We know how sorry you are, Inca. We have always loved you, child. That never changed throughout the years while you were away.'' Alaria's face grew tender. ''Inca, you could have chosen so many other ways to lead your life when you left the village. No one but Adaire and I had hope that you would turn out to be the wonderful human being you are now. You care for the poor, you protect them, you heal them when it is within the laws, and you think nothing of yourself, your pain or your suffering. You have put others before yourself. This is one of the great lessons a clan member must learn and embrace. And you have done that.''

Inca sniffed and wiped her eyes. ''Th-thank you, Grandmother.''

''You're more than welcome, child. But here is the best news yet. The council has decided, unanimously, that you are to be allowed back into the Jaguar Clan with full privileges and support.'' She smiled as she saw the shock of their community decision register fully on Inca's face. She gasped. Roan placed his arm around her and gave her a hug of joy. He was grinning broadly.

Alaria held up her hand. ''Not only that, Inca, but when you are fully recovered, the council wants to publicly commend and honor you for what you have accomplished in Amazonia, thus far. *That* is why you are here, child. Your banishment is over. You have earned the right to be among us once again.'' She smiled a little, her eyes glimmering with tears. ''And I hope this time that you honor the laws and never break any of them ever again.''

Inca sobbed. She threw her arms around Roan and clung to him as she buried her face against his shoulder.

Roan felt tears in his own eyes. He understood what this meant to Inca. Moving his hand through her thick, dark hair, he rasped against her ear, ''You have your family back, sweetheart. You're home...you're really home...''

Chapter 13

Roan found Inca wandering in a field near the village. Since it was nearly noon, he had made them lunch. Swinging the white cotton cloth that held their meal in his left hand, he stepped out into the field. It was alive with wildflowers, the colors vibrant against the soft green of the grasses, which were ankle- to knee-high. The meadow was bordered on three sides by old, magnificent kapok trees, their buttressing roots looking like welcoming arms to Roan.

Above him, as always, were the large, slowly rolling clouds that seemed to always surround the village. He'd been here seven days and he had more questions than answers about this very special place. All his focus, however, was on Inca and her continued rehabilitation from her near death experience. From the day that Grandmother Alaria had told her she was part of the Jaguar Clan once more, Inca had become more solemn, more introspective.

She was holding a lot of feelings inside her; Roan could sense it. He saw his part in her adjustment as simply being on hand if she wanted to talk about it and a needed, sympathetic ear, a shoulder to lean on. So far she hadn't, and he honored her own sense of healing. At some point, he knew, Inca would talk with him at length. All he had to do was be patient. Fortunately, his Native American heritage gave him that gift. The other good news was that the mission led by Colonel Marcellino had been successful.

As he crossed the field, the sunlight was warm and pleasant. The village seemed to be climate controlled at a balmy seventy-five degrees during the day and sixty-five degrees at night—neither too hot nor too cold. Even the temperature reflected the harmony and peace that infused the village and its transient inhabitants. The white-and-gray clouds that slowly churned in mighty, unending circles around the village had something to do with it, he suspected. He could see the steep, sharp granite peaks of the Andes in the distance. On the other side of the village the rain forest spread out in a living green blanket. They were literally living between the icy cold of the mountains and the hot, humid air arising from the rain forest below. No wonder there were always clouds present around the village, hiding it from prying, outsiders' eyes like a snug, protective blanket.

Inca was bending over a flower and smelling it, not yet aware of his presence. Since her accident, she seemed much more at ease, not jumpy and tense like before. As Grandfather Adaire had told him, this was a place of complete safety. Nothing could harm the inhabitants who lived and studied in the village. Maybe that was why he was seeing her relaxed for the first time. The change was startling and telling for Roan. Here Inca wore soft cotton, pastel shifts and went barefoot, her hair loose and free about her proud shoulders. Gone was the warrior and her military garb. There were no weapons of any kind allowed in the village. All the people Roan saw—and there were many from around the world—were dressed in loose fitting clothing made of natural fibers.

Inca lifted her head in his direction, her eyes narrowing. Roan smiled as he felt her warm welcome embrace him, an invisible "hug" he knew came from Inca. The serious look on her face changed to one of joy upon seeing him. This morning he'd gone with Grandfather Adaire on an exploratory trip around the village. The elder had shown him many of the new and interesting sites that surrounded them. No wonder Inca had loved living and studying here. Roan understood more than ever how devastating it had been when she was told to leave. The way she had sobbed that morning when Grandmother Alaria told her she was welcomed back had been telling, pulled from the depths of her hurting, wounded soul. Roan had held her, rocked her and let her cry out all her past hurt and abandonment, the relief that she was once more welcomed back to her spiritual family. And they had told him not to mention anything about Maya to her yet. Inca was still reeling emotionally and Grandmother Alaria said that at the right time, Inca would meet her sister. Roan could hardly wait for that to happen. He knew how much Inca needed her real family.

Waving his hand, he quickened his stride toward her. The breeze lifted strands of her shining ebony hair. How soft and vulnerable Inca appeared as she stood expectantly waiting for him. In her hand were several wildflowers that she'd picked. He grinned. Gone, indeed, was the warrior. In her place was the woman who had resided deeply in Inca until she could be released in the safety of such a place as the village. Roan liked the change, but he also honored her ability to use her masculine energy as a warrior. Every woman had a warrior within her, whether she knew it or not. He was at ease with a woman who could use all the strength within herself.

Every woman had to deal with the myriad of issues life threw at them. They were far stronger emotionally and mentally than men, and Roan had no problem acknowledging that fact. He'd seen too many women squash that latent primal warrior, that survival ability within themselves, never tap into it because society said it was wrong for a woman to be strong and powerful. At least Inca had not allowed that to happen to her. She had carried her warrior side to an extreme, but her life mission asked that of her. Still, it was good that she had the village to come to, to rest up. To let go of that role she played.

Lifting the cloth bag with a grin, he called out, "Lunchtime. Interested?" His heart seemed to burst open as he heard her light, lilting laughter bubbling up through her long, slender throat. The gold flecks dancing in her willow-green eyes made him ache to love Inca fully and completely.

"I'm starving!" she called, and eagerly moved toward him, the hem of her dress catching now and then on taller flowers and grass blades.

How Roan loved her! A fierce need swept through him, and as Inca leaped forward, her hair flying behind her shoulders like a dark banner, he laughed deeply and appreciatively. Suddenly, life was good. Better than he could ever recall. Sarah, his wife, would always have a part of his heart. But Inca owned the rest of it.

Every day, Inca surrendered a little more to her own curiosity and feminine instincts to touch him, kiss him. Someday, he hoped, she would ask him to love her fully and completely. Right now, Roan knew she was processing a lot of old emotions and traumas, and working through them. Her heart was shifting constantly between healing herself and reaching out to him, woman to his man. He was more than content to wait, although it was wreaking havoc on him physically.

Inca reached him and threw her arms around his neck. Laughing, Roan caught her in midair and pressed her body warmly against his. Her arms tightened around his neck. He saw the mischievous glint in her eye and dipped his head to take her offered, smiling mouth.

Her lips tasted of sunlight and warmth. Staggering backward from her spontaneous leap into his arms, he caught himself, stopped and then held her tightly against him. She had such a young, strong, supple body. Like a bow curved just right, Roan thought as he held her against him.

"Mmm...this is my dessert," Inca purred wickedly as she eased her lips from his. Looking up into Roan's eyes, she saw his hunger for her. She felt it through every yearning cell in her body, and in every beat of her giddy heart. How handsome Roan looked to her. That scowl he'd perpetually worn in Brazil was gone here in the village, which lay within Peru's border. Today he dressed in a pair of cream-colored cotton trousers, sandals on his huge feet, and a loose, pale blue shirt, the sleeves rolled up to his elbows. The warrior in both of them had been left behind when they came to the village.

Chuckling, Roan eased her to the ground. "Still hungry, or do I finish off this feast by myself?" he teased. Sliding his arm around her waist, Roan led her to the edge of the meadow. Sitting down in the shade of a towering tree, his back against one of the buttressing roots, he pulled Inca down beside him. She nestled between his legs, her back curved against him.

"No, I am hungry. Starved like a jaguar...." And Inca quickly opened the cloth bag.

Roan leaned back, content to have her within his loose embrace. He heard her gasp in delight.

"Pineapple with rice!" She grinned with triumph. "You must have begged Grandmother Alaria to make this for us. It is my favorite recipe. She used to make this for me when I was training here in the village."

Tunneling his fingers through her dark hair, Roan watched the breeze catch it as it sifted softly down upon her shoulders. "Yep, I bribed her."

"Oh!" Inca held up a container, her face alight with surprise. "Cocoa pudding!"

"Your second favorite, Grandmother said. I asked her to make you something special, and she said you used to hang around her hut every day and beg her to make it for you."

Inca gloated as she tore the lid off and grabbed a spoon. "Hah! And more times than not, Grandmother gave in to my pleadings."

"Hey, that's dessert! You're suppose to eat your other food first."

Inca twisted around and gave him a crooked grin of

triumph. "Who said so?" She pointed to her belly. "It is all going to the same place. It does not care what comes first, second or third!" And she laughed gaily.

Watching her spoon the still-warm pudding into her mouth, Roan picked up a sandwich of cheese and lettuce liberally sprinkled with hot chilies. "Now I know why you like this place so much. You can do exactly what you want to do here."

Chuckling indulgently, Inca leaned back and quickly consumed half of the pudding with gusto. When she'd finished, she set the container aside. "Your half," she instructed him primly.

"That's big of you. I thought you were going to wolf the whole thing down in one gulp."

"Jaguars do such things," she agreed wryly, meeting his smiling eyes as she picked up the other cheese sandwich. Munching on it, she announced, "Today, I feel magnanimous in spirit. I will share with you my favorite dessert."

"I like it when you can smile and tease. Here you have a sense of humor and you're playful. I never saw that side of you in Brazil. It's nice."

Inca nodded and eagerly finished off the sandwich. The bread, too, was still warm from the oven. Licking her fingers one at a time, she murmured, "Here I do not have to be anything but myself. I do not have to be a warrior constantly. I can relax."

Sobering, Roan wiped his hands on another cloth and reached for the bowl of chocolate pudding. "I'm glad you have this place to return to, Inca. You were worn down. You needed someplace to heal." He gazed around. In the distance he saw a great blue heron flying toward what he knew was the waterfall area. The day was incredibly beautiful. But every day in this village was like being in a secret, hidden Shangri-La.

Inca turned around and crossed her bare legs beneath the thin fabric of her dress. Taking one of the mangoes, she began to methodically peel it with her long, slender fingers. "I feel better today than ever before, Roan. More..." she searched for the right word "...whole."

"Yes," he murmured. "You've had a long, hard journey for seven years, sweetheart. You've more than earned this place, this down time." He looked fondly toward the village. "All of it."

"I have my family back," Inca said as she bit into the ripe mango.

Roan nodded, understanding the implications of her softly spoken, emotion-filled words. There was so much more he wanted to say, but he was under strict orders by Grandmother Alaria to say nothing of Maya, who had helped to save Inca's life. A part of him chaffed under that stern order. He wanted to share his discovery of Maya, and the fact she was Inca's twin sister, but Alaria had warned him sufficiently that he backed off from saying anything. Inca needed time and space to heal. She would know the truth when Maya chose to appear and break the news to her, Alaria had told him.

Roan watched Inca through half-closed eyes, the afternoon heat, the good food and her company all conspiring to make him feel regally satisfied in ways he'd never experienced.

Wiping her hands on the damp cloth, Inca looked at him. "You look like a fat, old happy jaguar who has just eaten more than his fill and is going to go sleep it off."

His mouth lifted. "That's exactly how I feel." Roan reached out and grazed her cheek. "Only I have my jaguar mate here with me. That's what makes this special."

"I put you to sleep?" Inca demanded archly, unmercifully teasing him.

The fire in her eyes, the indignation, wasn't real, and Roan chuckled. "You would put no man to sleep, believe me," he rasped as he eased her around so that her back fit beautifully against him once more. "Come here, wild woman. My woman…"

Sighing contentedly, Inca settled against Roan. He took her hands in his, and they rested against her slightly rounded abdomen. A small but warming thought of someday carrying his child in her belly moved through Inca's mind. As she laid her head back on his broad, capable shoulder and closed her eyes, she sighed languidly. "I have never been happier, Roan. I did not know that love could make me feel this way." She felt the warmth of the breeze gently caressing her as she lay in his arms, his massive thighs like riverbanks on either side of her slender form. "You make me feel safe when I have never felt safe before. Did you know that?" She opened her eyes slightly and looked up at him, and felt him chuckle, the sound rolling like a drumbeat through his massive chest.

"I know," he replied as he moved his fingers in a stroking motion down her slim, golden arm. He saw many old scars here and there across her firm flesh. It hurt him to think of her being in pain, for Inca had lived with not only physical pain, but the sorrowful loss of her family, from the time she was born. In a way, it had made her stronger and self-reliant. She was able to move mountains, literally, because of the strength this one event had given her in life. Roan tangled his fingers with hers. "I love you, my woman," he whispered next to her ear. Her hair was soft against his lips. "Just know that you own my heart forever."

Her fingers tightened around his. Nuzzling his jaw, she whispered huskily, "And you hold my heart in your hands. You did from the beginning, even if I was not aware of it at first."

"When I saw you," Roan said in a low, deep tone as he caressed her hair, "I fell in love with you on the spot."

"Is that possible?"

"Sure. Why not?"

Inca shrugged. "When I first saw you, I felt safe. Safe in a way I never had before. I knew you would protect me."

"That's a part of love," Roan said, smiling lazily.

"I do not know much of what all love is about," she began, frowning. "This is new to me." She touched her heart. "I see others who are married. I see them touch one another, as we touch one another now. I see them kiss." She pulled away and met his hooded eyes. "I think our kisses are more active than others I have seen. Yes?"

Grinning, Roan said, "*Passionate* is the word I think you're searching for."

"Mmm, yes… And I see married couples touch each other's hands and hold them…and we do that, too."

"Loving a person, Inca, means loving them in many ways. There's no one way to tell that special person that you love them. You love them in many, many ways every day."

"And you brought me flowers that morning after Grandmother Alaria told me I was a member of the clan once again." Inca smiled up at him. "I was deeply touched. I did not expect such a gift from you."

"I wish I could have done more. I know what it meant to you, to be allowed to come home." Roan caught several dark strands of hair that moved with the breeze across her cheek, and tucked them behind her ear.

"I must understand more of this love that we hold for one another. I try to learn by watching what others do." Her eyes lit up with laughter. "And then I try it out on you to see if it works or not."

He chuckled. "No one can accuse you of not being an astute observer," he said dryly. "I like discovering love with you. Just give yourself time and permission to explore when it feels right to you, Inca."

Sliding her hand across his dark, hairy one, she said, "My body is on fire sometimes. I ache. I want something...but I do not know what it is, how to get it, how to satisfy that burning within me."

"I do."

"Yes?"

"Yes." Roan looked down at her animated features.

"Will you show me? I feel as if I will explode at times when you kiss me, or touch me, or graze my breasts with your hand. I ache. I feel...unfulfilled, as if needing something and I do not know what it is. I feel frustrated. I know something is missing...but what?"

Roan kept his face serious. Caressing her cheek, he said, "All you have to do is ask me, Inca, and I'll show you. It's something I can teach you. Something that is beautiful and intimate, to be shared only by those who love one another."

Nodding, she sighed. "Yes. I'd like that."

"A woman should always be in control of her own body, her own feelings," he told her seriously, and pressed a kiss to her hair near her ear. "You tell me what you want, next time you feel like that—where you want me to touch you, where you want my hand placed. Making love to another person is one of the most sacred acts there is between human beings."

"It is more than the mating frenzy," Inca said. "I have watched many animals couple. It is because they want to make babies. I understand that. But…" She hesitated. "This is different, yes? Between people? Do they always want to make a baby when they couple?"

He felt her searching. Having lived her life in a rain forest, without any education about her own sexuality, about how a man and woman pursued intimacy, Inca was truly innocent. Gently, Roan took her hands into his. "Maybe we're lucky, sweetheart. Humans don't have to couple for the express purpose of having a baby. We can do it because it feels right, and it feels good for both of us. It's the ultimate way to tell the other person how you feel about them."

Inca smiled and closed her eyes. "Grandmother Alaria said I should go to the Pool of Life and bathe there. She said I need the healing water to help me. Right now I want to have a nap with you. After I wake up, it feels right for me to do that."

Roan held her gently. Closing his eyes, he murmured, "Go to sleep, my woman. When you wake, go to the pool."

Inca lay in the soft grass beside the Pool of Life, where she had bathed and swum for nearly an hour. Now she understood as never before the healing qualities of the sparkling, clear water. The glade sheltering the oval pool was filled with flowering bushes and trees. As she lay on her back, arms behind her head, watching the lazy, late afternoon clouds move across the deep blue sky, she sighed. Never had she felt so whole or so much in balance. Her errant thoughts centered on Roan and how much he meant to her. She loved him. Yes, she knew now as never before that she loved him. When she left this wonderful place, she would search him out and tell him that to his face. A tender smile pulled at her lips as she lay there, enjoying the fragrance of the wildflowers and the warmth of the sun.

Dressed once again in her pale pink shift, her skin still damp from the pool, Inca dug her toes joyfully into the grass that tickled the soles of her feet. Birds were singing, and she could hear monkeys screaming and chattering in the distance. Life had never felt as good as it did now.

Inca suddenly sat up, alert and on guard. She felt a vibration—something powerful that distinctly reminded her of someone teleporting in to see her. Who? The energy was very different, like none she was familiar with. Turning, Inca looked toward where the energy seemed to be originating. She saw a woman—a stranger—standing near the bushes, no more than twenty feet away from her. She was dressed in a black military flight suit and black, polished boots. As her gaze flew upward, Inca gasped. Instantly, she was on her feet in a crouched position, her hands opened, as if prepared for an attack by the unexpected intruder to her reverie.

Shock bolted through her, made her freeze. Her eyes widened enormously as she met and held the dark emerald gaze of the intruder. Her gasp echoed around the flowery glade. The woman looked almost exactly like her! Head spinning, Inca slowly came out of her crouched position. All her primal senses were switched on and operational—those instinctual senses that had saved her life so many times before. The woman who stood relaxed before her had black hair, just as she had. Only it was caught and tamed in a chignon at the base of her slender neck.

Breathing hard, Inca shouted, "State your name!"

The woman gave her a slight smile and lifted her hand. She took off her black flight gloves. "Be at ease, Inca. I'm Captain Maya Stevenson. And I come in peace." Her smile disappeared and she took a step forward. "I'm unarmed and I'm not an enemy. I'm here to fulfill a prophecy...." Tears glittered in her narrowed eyes.

Gulping, her heart pounding, Inca was assimilating all kinds of mixed messages from this tall, darkly clad woman warrior whose face was filled with emotion. "Y-you look like me! Almost..." She took a step back, not understanding what was going on. Her pulse continued to race wildly and she had to gasp for air. She felt like crying as a sharp, jolting joy ripped though her heart. Inca understood none of these wild, untrammeled feelings as the woman walked slowly down the slope toward her, and halted less than six feet away.

Searching her face, Inca saw that there were minute differences between them. This woman—Maya—had a square face. Though her eyes were slightly tilted like Inca's, Maya's were a different color—emerald and not willow-green. Her mouth was full and her cheekbones high, but her face was broader. Her bone structure was different, too; while Inca was slender, Maya was of a larger, heavier build, and more curved than she. Still, the woman in black warrior garb stood equally tall, with that same look of confidence, her shoulders thrown back with unconscious pride.

"I—I do not understand this. You look like me. A mirror image. What is going on? What prophecy?"

Maya wiped her eyes. She tucked the gloves, out of habit, into the belt of her flight suit. "I think you'd better sit down, Inca. What I have to tell you might make you faint, anyway." And she gestured to the ground.

"No. Whatever you have to say I will take standing."

"Okay...have it your way. You always did have one helluva stubborn streak. Me? I need to sit down to say this to you." Maya grinned a little and sat down in front of her. She pulled her knees up and placed her arms around them, hooking her fingers together. "Of course, your stubbornness also gave you the guts to survive and flourish."

Breathing hard, Inca stared down at Maya. "What do you speak of? Who *are* you?"

Maya looked up, her emerald eyes dark and thoughtful. Her voice lowered, soft and strained. "I'm your fraternal twin sister, Inca. Our mother birthed us minutes apart. I came out first, and you, followed. We're sisters, you and I. I was finally given permission by the elder counsel to come and meet you, face-to-face, to initiate contact with you." She shook her head sadly. "And I've waited a long time for this day to come...."

Inca staggered backward. Her eyes flared and her lips parted. When she felt her knees go wobbly, she dropped to the grass on her hands and knees. Staring at Maya, who sat calmly watching her, she could not believe her ears.

She saw the compassion in Maya's strong face, the tears running freely down her cheeks. In the next moment, Inca felt a shift of energy taking place between them, and she swallowed, unable to speak. Indeed, Maya was almost a carbon copy of her. Shaking her head, Inca clenched her fist.

"I do not understand!" she cried in desperation. "How can you be my sister? I was abandoned by my parents at birth! I was left for dead until a jaguar mother came and carried me back to her den to raise me." Inca's nostrils flared. Her breathing was chaotic. Her heart was bursting with pain and anguish.

Maya leaned forward, her hand extended. Gently, she said, "I'm sorry you had to suffer so much, Inca. You were so alone for so long. And for that, I'm sorry. We agreed to this plan long before we ever entered human forms. We each did," she stated with a grimace. Looking up, she took a deep breath and held Inca's anguished gaze. "I have a story to tell you. Listen to me not only with your ears, but with your heart. Sit down, close your eyes and let me show you what happened—and why. Please?"

Unable to catch her breath, Inca sat down and faced Maya. She had a sister? *She* was her sister? Maya looked so much like her. How could this be? Tears escaped from Inca's eyes. "Is this a trick? A horrible trick you have come to play on me?"

"No, my loving sister," Maya said in a choked tone, tears filling her eyes again, "it isn't. Please...try to gather yourself. Close your eyes. Take some deep breaths... that's it. Let me tell you telepathically what happened to us...."

Inca rocked slightly as she felt the energy from Maya

encircle and embrace her. It was a loving, warm sensation and it soothed some of the ragged feelings bursting out of her hurting heart. Transferring her full focus to her brow, between her eyes, Inca began to see the darkness shift and change. Like all clairvoyants, Inca could literally see or perceive with her third eye. Her brow became a movie screen, in color. What she saw now made her cry out.

She saw her mother and father for the first time. Her mother was breathing in gasps, squatting on the ground, her hands gripping two small trees on either side of her to stay upright. She saw her father, a very tall, golden-skinned man with black hair, kneeling at her side, talking in a soothing, calming tone to her. His hands opened to receive the baby that slid from his wife's swollen body. Within moments, the child was wrapped snuggly in a black blanket made of soft alpaca wool. To Inca's shock, she saw a second baby being delivered shortly thereafter. The infant was wrapped in a gold blanket with black spots woven into it. Inca knew at once that it was she—the second baby born from her mother's body. Twins...she had a twin! And she'd never known it before this moment.

Heart pounding, Inca zeroed in on her mother's gleaming face as she slowly sat down on another blanket with the help of her husband, and then reached out for her babies. She had a broad, square face and her eyes were the deep green color of tourmaline gemstones. Her hair was long, black and slightly curly as it hung around her shoulders. She was smiling through her tears as her husband knelt and placed each baby into her awaiting arms. Both parents were crying for joy over the births of their children. The exultation that enveloped Inca made her injured heart burst open with such fierceness that she cried out sharply, pressing her hand against her chest. She felt her heart breaking.

For so long she'd thought her parents did not want her, did not love her. That that was why they had abandoned her, to die alone.

But she was not alone! No, she had an older sister! Inca watched with anxious anticipation as her father, whom she most closely resembled, put his arm around his wife and his babies. He held them all, crying with joy, kissing his wife's hair, her cheek, and finally, her smiling mouth. It was a birth filled with joy, an incredible celebration. That realization flowed like a healing wave of warmth through Inca's pounding heart. She was loved! She was wanted! And she had a sister!

Staggered by all the information, Inca could no longer stand the rush of powerful emotions that overwhelmed her. She opened her eyes, her gaze fixed on Maya's serious, dark features.

"Enough!" she whispered raggedly. "It is so much... too much...." And she held up her hand in protest.

Maya nodded and stopped sending the telepathic information. She threw her shoulders back, as if to shake herself out of the trancelike state. When she looked up, she saw Inca's face contorted with so many conflicting emotions that she whispered, "I'm sorry it had to be revealed to you like this. You've been through a helluva lot...almost dying...but they said you needed this information now, not later."

Staring at Maya, Inca whispered unsteadily, "Who are 'they'?"

Smiling a little, Maya lifted her hand. "The Black Jaguar Clan. The clan I come from."

More shock thrummed through Inca. She sat there feeling dizzy, as if a bomb had exploded right next to her. She'd heard talk of this mysterious clan, and of those who volunteered their lives to work on the dark side knowingly, in the service of the Sisterhood of Light. Blinking, she looked strangely at Maya. Hundreds of memories came cascading through her mind. For several minutes, she sat there trying to absorb them all. Finally, Inca rasped, "I remember you now.... You saved my life, didn't you? I was shot in the back of the head and Roan was carrying me to your helicopter. You came around the end of the compound fence and shot two drug runners who were taking aim at us."

With a slight nod of her head, Maya said, "Your memories of that night are coming back. Yes, that's right. I couldn't let them kill my little sister, could I?"

Maya's teasing threaded through Inca's continuing shock. The rest of her rescue avalanched upon her, the memories engulfing her one after another. She saw the helicopter she was flying in, with Maya at the controls. She felt the urgency of Maya, her worry for her life as it slowly slipped away. And then she saw Maya standing at her bedside, opposite Roan. "Y-you saved me...."

Maya shook her head. "No, I can't take credit for that one, Inca. Roan saved you. I was under orders to tell him that he had to give up his life in order to save yours. Of course, that was a lie. It was really a test for him. And you know how tough our tests are." Her mouth pulled downward in a grimace. "He didn't know it was a test, of course, but in order to get you back, it had to be played that way. Those were the rules of the Sisterhood of Light. I told him the truth—that he had to love you enough to surrender his life. The elders of this village set up the conditions for him, not me or my clan. If Roan could pass this test, they knew he was worthy of being trained here, at the village. Of course, he willingly said yes. I had him place his hands on your heart and the top of your head, just as we do when we transmit a catalytic healing energy into a patient with the help of our jaguar spirit guide.''

Her smile was gentle. ''He did it. It was his love for you that brought you back. All I did was facilitate it by sending him to the Threshold to retrieve you. Then I teleported all of us here, to the Village of the Clouds. Helluva job, I gotta say. I did good work.'' She flexed her fist, pleased with her efforts. ''I don't have many metaphysical talents, unlike you. But I'm a damn good teleporter when I set my mind—and heart—to it.''

Maya shrugged, her eyes brimming with tears. ''In my business, I work in the underbelly of darkness. It was something else to see Roan's pure, undiluted love for you pull you back from the Threshold. He doesn't have memory of this—yet. He will when it's right for him to know. Right now, *you* need to know that I'm your sister and that our parents loved us—fiercely. They surrendered their lives for us, so that we could come into being, to help a lot of other people. Our destiny was ordained long before our births. We agreed to come, to fight for the light, to fight for the underdogs and protect them. And we both do this in our own way.''

Gulping back tears, Inca whispered, ''Tell me more about our parents. I *have* to know, Maya…please….''

Wiping her eyes, Maya said, ''Our parents knew who

we were, spiritually speaking, and why we were coming into a body for this lifetime. Our mother was a member of the Jaguar Clan. Our father, a member of the Black Jaguar Clan. They met, fell in love and married. The elders who married them here, at the village, twenty-seven years ago, told them of their destiny—that they were to give each of us up. To trust the Great Mother Goddess and surrender their two children over to her. They were told they would then be killed by drug runners shortly after our births.'' Maya frowned. ''They accepted their fate, as we all do as clan members. We know we're here for a reason. They knew ahead of time what those reasons were. They had two wonderful years together, before we came. They were very happy, Inca. Very. After we were born, they kissed us goodbye, and our mother took you and went east. My father took me and went off in a westerly direction. They were told where to leave each of us.''

Shaken, Inca moved a little closer. Close enough to reach out and touch Maya, if she chose. ''Who killed them?'' she rasped thickly. ''I want to know.''

''Juan Valentino. The father of the two Valentino sons, Sebastian and Faro. And Faro damn near added you to his coup belt,'' Maya said grimly. ''We're in a death spiral dance with the Valentinos, Inca. They murdered our parents. And now Sebastian has been captured and faces a life in prison in Brazil. That's one down, and one bastard to go. Faro nearly took your life.'' She flexed her fist again, her voice grim with revenge. ''And shortly, I'll move into a death spiral dance with him. He's fled to Peru in his gunship. He thinks he's safe there. But now the bastard's on *my* territory…and I promise you, dear sister of my heart, I'll find him and avenge what he did to you...."

Staring disbelievingly at Maya, Inca whispered, "This is all too much. Too much..." She dropped her head in her hands.

Gently, Maya reached out and slid her strong fingers along the curve of Inca's shaking shoulders. She was crying, too. "I know," she said in a choked voice. "You don't know how long I've waited to finally get to meet you in person. To tell you that you weren't ever alone, Inca. That you weren't really abandoned. That you were loved by our parents—and by me...." Smoothing the cotton material across Inca's shoulders, Maya inched a little closer to her. Sniffing, she whispered brokenly, "And how long I've dreamed of this day, of being here with you...with my own blood sister...."

Inca heard the pain in Maya's husky voice. Turning, she allowed her hands to drop to her sides. Tears ran freely down her cheeks as she stared into the marred darkness of Maya's gaze. "You really *are* my sister, aren't you?"

Maya nodded almost shyly. "Yes...yes, I am, Inca. We came from our mother's body. Greatly loved. Given over to a destiny that needed us for a higher calling." Reaching out, she slid her hands once more over Inca's shoulders. "And all I want to do right now is hug the hell out of you. I want to hold my sister. It's been so long a time in coming...."

Inca moved forward into her twin's arms. The moment they embraced, her heart rocked open as never before. When Maya tightened her arms around her, Inca understood for the first time in her life what family connection truly meant. She wept unashamedly on her sister's shoulder, and so did Maya. They cried together at the Pool of Life, locked in one another's embrace, saying hello for the first time since they had been separated at birth.

Chapter 14

Inca gripped Maya's hand after her tears abated. She felt that if she released her, Maya would disappear into thin air and she'd never see her again. Oh, that was foolish, Inca realized, but her heart was so raw from learning she had *real* family that she couldn't stand the thought of Maya being ripped away from her again.

Squeezing her fingers in a gesture meant to comfort Inca and allay her worries, Maya said, "Listen, from now on you'll see so much of me you'll be sick of me." And she gave a wobbly smile as she brushed the last of her tears from her cheeks. The clouds parted for just a moment and sent golden, dappling sunlight glinting upon the quiet surface of the pool at their feet.

Inca laughed a little, embarrassed by her sudden clinginess, and released Maya's hand. "I know my response is not logical. And I will *never* tire of seeing you, Maya. Not ever."

Maya reached out and patted Inca's arm. "Well, you're stuck with me, little sister. And I only found out about you and our past a year ago. Grandmother Alaria told me. I wanted to see you right then, but she said no, that you had the last of your karma to work through." Maya frowned. "She said you must experience death, but that I could be there to help save you. That's why we were waiting at a nearby secret base we use. I didn't know how your life might be threatened. When the time drew near, Grandmother Alaria told me when to go and where to fly in order to help you through all this."

"It must have been very hard for you to wait and say nothing," Inca whispered painfully.

Maya sighed and held her compassionate gaze. "I gotta tell you, Inca, it was hell. Pure torture. I wasn't sure I could abide by the rules of the clan and stay away from you."

"You are stronger than I am," Inca acknowledged.

"Not by much." And Maya smiled a little.

She turned and looked over her shoulder. "Hey, I think Grandmother Alaria and Roan are coming our way. I know Grandmother had more to tell us after we got over our introductions. Are you ready for them?"

Inca realized that she was so torn up emotionally—in shock, in fact—that she hadn't even felt their energy approaching the secluded glen. Her jaguar guardian had manifested and was lying near the pool, his head on his paws, asleep. She looked up. "Roan is coming?" Her heart beat harder. With love. With the anticipation of sharing her joy over her newfound sister. A sister!

Grinning, Maya said, "And Grandmother Alaria, too." She reached out and playfully ruffled Inca's hair. "I can tell you're head over heels in love with that hunk of man." She smiled knowingly. "Wish that I could get so lucky. All I know is Neanderthal types from the last Ice Age who are out to squash me under their thumb because I'm a woman. I envy you, but you deserve someone like Roan. I like him a *lot*. He definitely has my seal of approval." She winked wickedly. "Not that you need my okay on anything. You've got excellent taste, Inca!"

Blushing fiercely, Inca absorbed her sister's playful touch and teasing. It felt so good! Almost as good as having Roan in her life. As Inca impatiently waited for him to appear on the well-worn dirt path that led to the pool, she realized that there were different kinds of love— what she felt for her sister, what she felt for Roan. And for Grandmother Alaria. All were different, yet vitally important to her.

Grandmother Alaria appeared first. There was a soft smile on her face and tears sparkled in her eyes. Roan appeared next, an unsure expression on his face. He hung back at the entrance to the grove.

"Come on in," Maya invited with a wave of her hand. "You're supposed to be here, too, for this confab."

Roan looked over at Inca. Her eyes were red and she'd been crying. Not wanting to assume anything with her, he looked to her for permission to join them. Even though Grandmother Alaria had coaxed him into coming with her, he felt like an outsider to this group of powerful women.

"Sit by me?" Inca asked, and she stretched out her hand toward him.

Roan nodded and held her tender willow-green gaze. He felt such incredible love encircling him and knew it

was Inca's invisible embrace surrounding him. Carefully
moving around the group, he sat down next to her. She
smiled raggedly at him.

"I have a sister, Roan. A sister! Maya, meet Roan. He
holds my heart in his hands."

Maya grinned broadly. She reached across the small
circle they had made as they all sat cross-legged on the
earth. "Yes, we've met. But official introductions are in
order. Hi, Roan. It's good to meet you—again." And she
gripped his proffered hand strongly, shook it and released
it.

"Same here," he said. "I never got to thank you for
saving our lives when those two drug runners had a bead
on us. Nice shooting." He liked Maya's easygoing nature.
She was very different in personality from Inca.

Maya nodded and grimaced. "We knew there was going to be danger for you two. I'm just glad I got there in
time."

Grandmother Alaria settled her voluminous cotton skirt
across her knees. "Children," she remonstrated, "let me
pick up the threads of why you are here. Inca, I've come
to tell you all that happened, and why. I know some memories are returning to you, my child."

Inca felt Roan's arm go around her shoulders, and she
leaned against his strong, stalwart body. "I have many
questions," she said.

Inca listened as the elder told her everything, from beginning to end, about that night she'd nearly died. Alaria
smiled kindly as she finished. "It was Maya who was able
to teleport you, herself and Roan here, from that hospital
in Manaus. Members of the Black Jaguar Clan are the
most powerful spiritual beings among our kind. She had

our permission to transport." Alaria gave Roan a gentle look. "And it could not have been accomplished without Roan. His heart is large and open. Maya needed to tell him to give his life for yours, Inca, because it required that kind of surrendering of his energy, his being, in order to try and affect this transport. If the heart is not engaged in such an activity, teleportation will not work for all concerned."

Maya laughed softly. "And I've gotta tell you, folks, it wasn't easy. Oh, I've teleported when I managed to get my ducks in a row, but nothing like this...not when it was my *sister* involved. I've never had to overcome so many fears as I did that day, Inca. I was crying inside. I was afraid of losing you. Roan here helped keep the stability of the energy pattern, whether he knew it or not. His love for you was so pure, so untainted, that it held this paper bag on wheels together so I could affect the transfer."

Inca nodded and felt his arm tighten slightly around her waist. "His heart is pure," she whispered, and she gave him a tender look. "I was saved by people who love me."

"I thought I was going to die," Roan admitted quietly. "I was ready to give up my life for Inca. She was far more important than I was. The things she was doing in the Amazon far outweighed anything I'd ever done in my life."

Grandmother Alaria looked at him for a long moment, the silence warming. "My son, you are far more powerful than you know. Your mother was a great and well-known medicine woman among us."

Roan gave her a startled look. "What do you mean?"

Alaria reached out and touched his arm in a kindly manner. "She was a member of the northern clan, the

Cougar Clan, which is related to the Jaguar Clan here in South America. When she died, she sent her chief spirit guide, a female cougar, to you. What you did not know was that this cougar was in constant contact with us." She patted his arm in a motherly fashion. "We were watching, waiting and hoping that you would make the right decisions to come down here, to meet Inca and, hopefully, fall in love with her, as she is beloved by us."

Inca nodded, overwhelmed. "When I met Roan, I knew it was not an accident, Grandmother. I knew it was important. I just did not know *how* important."

"We're faced with many, many freewill choices," Alaria told them gravely. "Roan could have chosen not to come down here. He could have hardened his heart, because of the loss of his wife, and not given his love to you. You also had choices, Inca."

"I know," Inca whispered, and she looked down pensively at the green grass before her. "From the moment I met Roan I felt this powerful attraction between us. It scared me—badly. I did not know what love was then."

"You do now," Maya said gently, and she gave them a proud look. "You made all the right moves, Inca. Believe me, it was hell on me waiting, hoping, praying and watching you from afar."

Inca looked over at her. "You knew all along that if I made the right choices, I would be wounded out there in that valley that night, did you not?"

Glumly, Maya nodded, then gave Grandmother Alaria a pained look. "Yeah, I knew. And it was hell on me. I didn't want you hurt. I was told that you would have to go through a life-death crisis. I didn't know the details. I was able to get permission from both clans to fly my helos into the area and be ready to help you when it happened. I was told when I could fly into the valley, and that was shortly after you were shot by Faro Valentino. It took all my training, all my belief and trust and faith, to stand back and let it happen. It was one of those times when I seriously considered breaking a clan law. I didn't *want* to have you go through all that stuff." She managed a crooked smile. "But I was told in no uncertain terms that if I didn't abide by the laws in your karma, I'd *never* get to see you, and that's something I didn't want to happen." Maya reached out and gripped Inca's fingers briefly, tears glimmering in her eyes.

Inca gave her a sad look. "I know how you feel. I have been placed in such a position before—and failed."

Maya made a strangled sound. "Well, I damn near did, too, with you. It's different when it's someone you love. It's real easy to let a stranger go through whatever they need to experience, but it's a whole 'nother stripe of the tiger when it's your family involved." Maya shook her head and gave Grandmother Alaria a rueful look. "I hope I *never* have to go through this kind of thing again with Inca."

"You will not, my child."

Roan frowned. "What I want to know is how you got those helicopters into that valley. Did you teleport in? There's no known airport or military facility close enough to give you the fuel you needed to reach us."

Maya laughed and slapped her knee in delight. "Hey, teleporting *one* person, much less three, is a helluva big deal. But a bunch of helicopters? No way. I don't know of anyone who can facilitate that kind of energy change. No, we knew ahead of time what could possibly happen, so we flew in days earlier. Trust me, there are hundreds of small bases of operation that we've laid out all over South America. We've been fighting the drug trade in all these countries for a long, long time on our own—long before any governments got involved, or the U.S. started providing training support for the troops and air forces.''

Roan nodded. ''Colonel Marcellino mentioned that he's seen unmarked, black helicopters from time to time. And he said he didn't know where they were from, or who they represented.''

''Not the druggies, that's for sure,'' Maya chuckled derisively. Humor danced in her emerald eyes. ''Like I said before, the Black Jaguar Clan is the underbelly, the dark side of the Sisterhood of Light. We aren't constrained by certain laws and protocols that Inca and her people are. We're out there on the front lines doing battle with the bad guys—what Inca knows as the Brotherhood of Darkness—no matter what dimension they are in. To answer your question, we have a base near that valley. We were simply waiting.'' Maya lost her humor and reached out and gripped Inca's hand momentarily. ''And I'm sorry as hell it had to happen to you, but in nearly dying and being saved with Roan's love, you were able to spiritually transcend your past and move to a higher level of ability. It gave you the second chance you wanted so badly. When I was told by the elders what could happen to help you, I stood back. Before that, I was more than prepared to interfere to save you from being hurt, law or no laws.''

''I understand,'' Inca whispered. ''Sometimes it takes a near death experience to break open the door to the next level on our path.'' She gave Roan a wry look. ''And thanks to you, I made it.''

Roan shrugged, embarrassed. He looked around the circle at the three women. "I think," he told her huskily, "that this happened because of a lot of people who love you."

"Yes," Grandmother Alaria said, "you are correct. Anytime people of one mind, one heart, gather together, miracles will happen. It's inevitable." She turned her attention to Inca. "And we've got a wonderful gift to give you, my child, because of all that's happened." She smiled knowingly over at Roan and then met Inca's curious gaze. "The elders have voted to have you remain at the village for the next year for advanced spiritual training. And—" she looked at Roan, a pleased expression on her features "—we are also extending an invitation to you, Roan Storm Walker, as your mother once was invited, to come and study with us. You may stay to perfect your heritage—the abilities that pulse in your veins because of your mother's blood."

Gasping, Inca gripped Roan's hand. "Yes! Oh, yes, Grandmother, I would be honored to remain here! Roan?"

Stunned, he looked down at Inca. "Well...sure. But I'm not a trained medicine person, Grandmother. I don't know what I can offer you."

Chuckling indulgently, Alaria slowly got to her feet. Her knee joints popped and cracked as she stretched to her full height. She slowly smoothed her skirt with her wrinkled hands. "My son, people are invited to come here to the Village of the Clouds and they haven't a clue of their own heritage or traditions—or the innate skills that they may access for the betterment of all life here on Mother Earth." She gave him an amused look and gestured toward the village. "You see every nationality represented in our community, don't you?"

"Well, yes…" There were people from Africa, from Mongolia, Russia, the European countries and from North America, as well. Roan thought he was at a United Nations meeting; every skin color, every nationality seemed to be represented at the Village of the Clouds. It was one huge training facility to teach people how to use their intuition, healing and psychic abilities positively for all of humanity, as well as for Mother Earth and her other children.

"Our normal way of contacting an individual is through the dream state. We appear and offer them an invitation, and if they want to come, they are led here through a series of synchronistic circumstances. We talk to them, educate them about themselves and their potential. It is then up to them if they want to walk the path of the Jaguar Clan or not." She smiled softly. "Do you want to walk it?"

Roan felt the strong grip of Inca's fingers around his own. He looked over and saw the pleading in her eyes. "I'll give it a try, Grandmother. I still don't understand what you see in me, though.…"

Maya cackled and stood up, dusting off her black flight suit. "Men! Love or hate 'em. I don't know which I'd rather do at times. The Neanderthals I know would be telling the elders they *deserved* to be here, and then there's guys like you, who are harder to find than hen's teeth—and you wonder why you're here." Maya threw up her hands and rolled her eyes. "Great Mother Goddess, let me find a man like you, Roan!" And she chuckled.

Inca frowned. "Do not worry about this, Roan. I came

to this village when I was sixteen without knowing anything. They will teach you and show you. You will be taught certain exercises to develop what you already have within you.''

''And,'' Alaria said, ''it is always heart-centered work, Roan. The people who are invited to come here have good hearts. They are terribly human. They have made many mistakes, but above all, they have the courage to keep trying, and they treat people as they would like to be treated. Two of the biggest things we demand are that people have compassion for all life and respect for one another. You have both those qualities. That is not something you find often. You are either born with it or you are not. One's spirit must have grown into the heart, developed compassion for all our relations, in order to train here with us. And you are such a person. We'd be honored to have you stay with us.''

Roan felt heat in his cheeks and knew he was blushing. Giving the elder a humorous look, he said, ''I'll give it a go, Grandmother. Thanks for the invitation.'' He saw Inca's eyes light up with joy over his decision. She pressed her brow against his shoulder in thanks.

''I have to go, Inca,'' Maya said reluctantly as she looked at her military watch on her left wrist. She glanced apologetically over at Grandmother Alaria. ''Duty calls. My women are telling me it's time to saddle up.'' She hooked her thumb across her shoulder. ''I've got my squadron of black helicopters winding up outside the gates of the village back in real time. We've got a drug factory to bust.''

Scrambling to her feet, Inca threw her arms around her sister. ''Be safe?''

Maya hugged her fiercely and then released her. "Don't worry. I watch my six, Inca. Six is a military term that means we watch behind our backs. The bad guys are the ones who are in trouble when I and my force of women are around. In our business, I'm known to hang ten over the surfboard of life. I scare my copilots to death when I fly, but I guarantee you that drug runner is going to be out of business when I get done with him." She chuckled indulgently. Reaching over, Maya gripped Roan's hand. "Take care of my little sister? She's all the family I've got, and now that we have each other, I don't want to lose her a second time."

Roan gripped her strong hand. "That's a promise, Maya. Be safe."

Inca stood with Roan's arm around her waist as Maya hurried up the path and disappeared behind the wall of ferns and bushes. "She is so different from me in some ways, and yet so much like me."

Grandmother Alaria moved to Inca and gently embraced her. "You and Maya have twenty-five years to catch up on. She was raised very differently from you. Now you have time to explore one another's lives. Don't be in a rush, Inca. Right now, Maya is entering a death spiral dance with Faro Valentino. She will not get to see you very much until her own fate can be decided."

Roan frowned. "A death spiral dance? What's that?"

"Faro tried to kill Inca. Maya had freewill choice in this karmic situation, Roan. She promised that if Faro decided to try and kill Inca, she would take it upon herself to even out the karma of his actions toward her sister. She will be his judge and jury in this, provided all things work the way she desires." Alaria shrugged her thin shoulders and looked up at Inca. "You know from your own death spiral dance that things often do not go as planned. And many times, both parties die in the process."

"I wish she had not taken the challenge against Faro," Inca whispered. "I do not want to lose Maya."

Alaria held up her hand. "Child, your sister knew what she was getting into when she promised revenge against Faro Valentino. Right now, she and her squadron of helicopters are working to free the Indians at those five other factories that Colonel Marcellino never got to in Brazil. Be at ease. She and her women warriors know what they're doing. Maya is highly trained for military warfare. But more about that at another time. You need to trust your sister in the choices she's made. And not worry so much."

Roan squeezed Inca's tense shoulders. "I think it's only natural, Grandmother," he murmured.

"Of course it is," the elder replied as she moved up the path. "Come, it's time for siesta. I know you're both tired. You need to sleep and continue your own, individual healing processes."

As they followed her out of the glade, Roan asked, "You said Maya is going to free the Indians at those other factories we had targeted?"

"Yes." Alaria turned and stopped on the trail back to the village. "Colonel Marcellino was completely successful in his attack on the first compound. His men captured forty drug runners who worked with the Valentino Brothers. Sebastian was captured, too. They marched them back to the Amazon River, where Brazilian military helicopters took the company and the prisoners back to Brasilia. Of course, the colonel was worried about his young son, Julian, so he called off the rest of the attack. And he didn't have Inca to lead him or his men.''

"I see...." Roan murmured, relieved. At least one of the Valentino Brothers was out of commission.

"Does he know that Maya and her helicopter squadron are going to take over the assaults?''

"Of course not. In our business, Roan, we are like jaguars—you see us only when we *want* you to see us.'' She smiled mischievously. "Maya is going to continue to clean up Inca's territory for her. That way, Inca won't have to worry about drug runners putting her people into bondage during the year she's with us. By the time you're both done with your education here, you'll return to the Amazon to live out your lives. You'll be caretakers of the basin, and of its people and relations. The difference is, this time you'll have our help and intervention, when asked for. Previously, when Inca was banished, she had no support from us whatsoever.'' Alaria eyed Inca. "Now it's different, and I think the drug barons are going to find it much harder to carry on business as usual in Brazil.''

Roan moved down the path that led to the rainbow waterfalls, a small cloth in his right hand. The morning was beautiful, with cobbled apricot-colored clouds strewn like corn rows in the sky above. Inca had left much earlier to go down and wash her jaguar, Topazio, in the pool below the waterfalls. It was a particularly beautiful place, one of Roan's personal favorites. As he stepped gingerly down the well-trodden path, away from the busy village, his heart expanded with anticipation. With hope.

He knew that time at the village was not really based upon twenty-four-hour days, as it was in the rest of the world. Still, it had been three months, by his reckoning, since they'd arrived here. And today, he felt, was the day. Inca knew nothing of the surprise he had for her.

As he moved along the narrow, red clay path, he watched as a squadron of blue-yellow-and-white parrots winged above him. The lingering, honeyed fragrance of orchids filled the air. Early mornings were his favorite time because the air was pregnant with wonderful scents. What would Inca say? His heart skittered over the possibility that she'd turn him down. How could she? They had drawn even closer together over the months. And although it was a personal, daily hell for Roan, he patiently waited for Inca to ask him to love her fully. Completely. They had time, he told himself. But he had long waited for the day he could physically love her, fulfill her and please her in all ways.

More than once, Roan had talked to Grandmother Alaria about the situation, and she'd counseled time and patience.

"Don't forget," the elder would remonstrate, "that Inca was a wild, primal child without parental guidance or direction. She was loved and cared for by the priests and priestesses who raised her, but she never experienced love between a man and woman before you stepped into her life. Let her initiate. Let her curiosity overwhelm her hesitancy. I know it's challenging for you, but you are older, and therefore responsible for your actions toward her. Wait, and her heart will open to you, I promise."

Today was the day. Roan could feel it in his heart. His soul. As the path opened up and he left the ferns and bushes, he spotted Inca down at the pool. Her male jaguar was standing knee-deep in water and she was sluicing the cooling liquid lazily across his back. Her laughter, deep and husky, melted into the musical sounds of the waterfall splashing behind them. Because of the sun's angle, a rainbow formed and arced across the pool. Yes, Inca was his rainbow woman, and made his life deliriously happy.

"Roan!"

He smiled and halted at the edge of the water. "Hi. Looks like Topazio is getting a good washing."

Laughing, Inca pushed several strands of damp hair behind her shoulder. "We have been playing." She straightened and gestured to her wet clothes, which clung to her slender, straight form. "Can you tell?"

Roan grinned. Inca was dressed in an apricot-colored blouse and loose, white cotton slacks that revealed her golden skin beneath them. "Yes, I can. When you want to come out, I have something for you."

Instantly, Inca's brows lifted. "A gift? For me?" She was already turning and wading out of the clear depths of the pool.

Roan laughed heartily. "Yes, something just for you, sweetheart." Inca had changed so much in the last three months. She was no longer guarded, with that hard, warriorlike shield raised to protect herself. No, now she was part playful child, part sensuous woman and all his...he hoped.

As she hurried up the sandy bank, Roan gestured for her to join him on a flat, triangular rock. It was their favorite place to come and sit in one another's arms, and talk for hours. Often they shared a lunch at the waterfall on this rock, as their guardians leaped and played in the water. Of course, her jaguar loved the water, and Roan's cougar did not; but she would run back and forth on the bank as the jaguar leaped and played in the shallows.

Breathing hard, Inca approached and sat down next to him. She spied a red cotton cloth in his hands. Reaching out, she said, "Is that for me?"

Chuckling, Roan avoided her outstretched hand and said, "Yes, it is. But first, you have to hear me out, okay?"

Pouting playfully, Inca caressed his recently shaved cheek. Because the weather was warm and humid, all he wore was a set of dark blue cotton slacks. He went barefoot, choosing to no longer wear sandals. His feet were becoming hard and callused. Sifting her fingers through the dark hair on his powerful chest, she teased, "Can I not open it first and then hear what you say?"

As he sat on the rock, his legs spread across it, Inca sat facing him, her legs draped casually across his. "No," he chided playfully. He warded off her hand as she reached for the gift lying in his palm. "It's not a speech, so be patient, my woman."

A wonderful sense of love overwhelmed Inca as he called her "my woman." It always did when that husky endearment rolled off his tongue. Sitting back, she folded her hands in her lap. "Very well. I will behave—for a little while."

Smiling, he met and held her gaze. "I love that you are a big kid at heart. Don't ever lose that precious quality, Inca. Anyway—" Roan cleared his throat nervously "—I've been thinking...for a long time, actually...that I want to complete what we share. With your permission." He saw her eyes darken a-little. His heart skittered in terror. "Among my people, when we love another person,

Inca, we give them a gift of something to show our love for them. In my nation, if we love someone, we want to make a home with them. We want to live with them—forever. And if it's agreed on by both the man and the woman, children may follow.''

She tilted her head. ''Yes?''

Fear choked him. Roan knew she could turn him down. ''In the old days of my people, a warrior would bring horses to the family of the woman he loved. The more horses, the more he loved her. The horses were a gift to the family, to show the warrior's intent of honoring the daughter he'd fallen in love with, wanted to marry and keep a home and family with for the rest of his life.''

''I see....'' Inca murmured, feeling the seriousness of his words.

Clearing his throat again, Roan said, ''I don't have horses to give your parents, Inca. But if I could, I would. I have to shift to a white man's way of asking for your hand in marriage.'' He opened his fingers and gave her the neatly tied red cloth. ''Open it,'' he told her thickly. ''It's for you—a symbol of what I hope for between us....''

Roan held his breath as Inca gently set the cloth down between them and quickly untied it. As the folds fell away, they revealed a slender gold ring set with seven cabochon gemstones.

Gasping, Inca picked up the ring and marveled at it. ''Oh, Roan, the stones are the color of my eyes!'' She touched the ring with her fingertips, watching it sparkle in the sunlight. ''It is beautiful!'' She sent him a brilliant smile. ''And this is a gift to me?''

''Yes.'' He tried to steady his voice. He saw the surprise and pleasure in Inca's expression, the way her lips curved in joy as she held up the ring. "It symbolizes our engagement to one another. An agreement that you will marry me...become my wife and I'll be your husband...." His throat became choked. He saw Inca's eyes flare as she cradled the ring in her palm.

"You are my beloved," she whispered softly, reaching out and gently touching his cheek. "You have always held my heart...."

"Is that a yes?"

Inca looked down at the ring, her eyes welling with tears. "For so long, I thought no one loved me. That I was too dark, too bad of a person, to love," she said brokenly. "You came along—so strong and proud, so confident and caring of me that I began to think I was not as bad as I thought I was, or as others have said of me...." Sniffing, Inca wiped the tears from her eyes and looked up at Roan. She saw the anguish, the unsureness, in his eyes, but she also felt his love blanketing her just as the sun embraced Mother Earth. "I understand what love is now...and I have had these months to take it into my heart." She pressed her hand against her chest.

"You were never a bad person, Inca. Not ever. Enemies will always say you're bad—but that's to be expected. You shouldn't listen to them. And I know you thought you were bad because you were banished from the village."

Inca hung her head and closed her eyes. "Yes," she admitted hoarsely. Reaching out, she gripped his hand, which was resting on her knee. "But you showed me I was a good person. That I was worthy of care, of protection, of being loved." Opening her hand, Inca stared down at the ring through blurry eyes. Tears splashed onto her palm and across the delicately wrought ring.

"If I accept this gift from you, it means you will be my husband? That you love me enough to want me as your partner?"

Tenderly, Roan framed Inca's face with his hands, marveling in her beauty. Tears beaded on her thick, black lashes. He saw the joy and suffering in her eyes. "Yes, my woman. Yes, I want you as my partner and wife. You're my best friend, too. And if the Great Spirit blesses us, I want the children you'll grow with love in your belly."

Sniffing, Inca placed her hands over his. "I love you so much, Roan.... You have always held my heart safely in your hands. I want to be your wife. I want Grandmother Alaria to marry us."

Gently, he leaned down and placed a soft, searching kiss on her lips. He tasted the salt of her tears. He felt her hands fall away from his and glide across his shoulders. Her mouth was hot with promise, sliding slickly across his. She moved to her knees and pressed her body against his in an artless gesture that spoke of her need for him.

Slowly, Roan eased his mouth from hers. He took the ring from her hand. "Here," he whispered roughly, "let me put it on your finger to make it official." His heart soared with such joy that Roan wondered if he was going to die of a heart attack at that moment. Inca was smiling through her tears and extending her long, slender fingers toward him. How easy it was to slip that small gold ring onto her hand. She wanted to marry him! She was willing to be his partner for life....

Sighing, Inca admired the ring. "What are the stones

in the ring?'' She marveled at their yellow-green, translucent beauty.

"They're called peridot," Roan said. "And they came from a mine on an Apache reservation in North America."

Murmuring with pleasure, Inca ran her finger across them. "Indian. That is good. It comes from their land, their heart."

"You like it?"

She nodded. "I like it, yes." Lifting her head, she looked at him through her lashes. "But I love the man who gave it to me even more...."

Chapter 15

The time was ripe. Inca sighed as Roan pulled her into his arms after he'd moved off the large, flat rock.

"There's a special place I found," he rasped as he lifted her easily. "I want to share it with you. It was made for us...."

"Yes...show me?" Inca pressed a kiss to his bristly jaw. The ferns gently swatted against her bare feet and legs as he carried her away from the waterfall and deep into the rain forest. Eventually the path opened up into a small, sunlit meadow ringed with trees. Bromeliads and orchids of many colors clustered in their gnarled limbs.

There was a shaded area beneath one rubber tree, and Inca smiled as Roan set her down upon the dark green grass. Looking up into his stormy eyes, she whispered, "Teach me how to love you. I *want* to love you, Roan, in all the ways a woman can love her man."

Nodding, he squeezed her hands and released them. She

sat there, chin lifted, her innocence touching his heart as never before. "We'll teach one another," he told her as he began to unbutton his pants. "But you'll take the lead, Inca. You tell me what you want me to do. Where you want me to place my hands on you. I want you to enjoy this, not be in pain or discomfort."

Nodding, she watched as he eased out of his pants and dropped them to one side. He stood naked before her, and she thrilled at seeing him this way. There was no fat on him anywhere. His body was tightly muscled. The dark hair on his chest funneled down across his hard, flat stomach, and she gulped. Unable to tear her gaze from him, she felt her mouth go a dry. Oh, she'd seen animals mate, but this was different. This was a sacred moment, holding a promise of such beauty and wonder. Her mind dissolved and her feelings rushed like powerful ocean waves throughout her.

Just looking at Roan in the power of his nakedness as he knelt in front of her, his knee brushing hers, made her smile uncertainly. "I am shaking, Roan," she whispered. "But not from fear…"

Roan smiled in turn as he eased the buttons of her blouse open. "Yes, that's the way it should feel," he told her in a low, roughened tone. "Anticipation, wanting… needing one another."

Inca felt the material brush her sensitized breasts, her nipples hardening as the cloth was pulled away to expose them. She felt no shame in her nakedness with Roan. As he eased the blouse off her shoulders, she gloried in the primal look in his narrowed eyes as he absorbed the sight of her. His hands were trembling, too. Elated that he wanted her as badly as she wanted him, Inca stood. In moments, she'd followed his lead and divested herself of her damp cotton slacks. Standing naked in front of him, she felt a sense of her power as a woman. The darkening, hooded look in his eyes stirred her, making her bold and very sure of herself. She took his hand and knelt down opposite him. Acting on instinct, she lifted her hands and drew Roan's head down between her breasts.

Closing her eyes as their skin met and melded, Inca sighed and swayed unsurely as his hands, large and scarred, moved around her hips to draw her between his opened thighs and press her fully against him. The feel of his warm, hard flesh was exciting. The wiry hair on his chest made her breasts tingle, the nipples tighten, and she felt dampness collecting between her legs. Inca uttered another sigh of pleasure at the sensual delights assaulting her. The sounds of the rain forest were like music to her ears, the waterfall in the distance only heightening her reeling emotions, which clamored for more of Roan's touch.

As he lifted his head away, his hands ranged upward from her hips to graze the rounded curve of her breasts. A gasp of pleasure tore from her and she shut her eyes. Moaning, she guided his hands so that her breasts were resting in his large palms. Her skin tingled, grew even more tight and heated.

"Feel good?" he rasped.

Inca could not speak, she was so caught up in delicious sensations as his thumbs lazily circled her hard, expectant nipples. Oh! She wanted something...and she moaned and dug her fingers into his thick, muscular shoulders.

Understanding what she needed, Roan leaned over and licked one hardened, awaiting peak.

Uttering a cry of surprise, of pleasure, Inca dug her fingers more deeply into his flesh. She tipped her head back, her slender throat gleaming.

Seeing the deep rose flush across her cheeks, her lips parted in a soundless cry of pleasure, Roan captured the other erect nipple between his lips and suckled her. Inca moaned wildly, her hands opening and closing spasmodically against his shoulders. Trembling and breathing in ragged gasps, she moved sinuously in his embrace as he lavished the second nipple equally. A sheen of perspiration made her body gleam like gold in the dappled shade and sunlight beneath the tree where they knelt.

Inca collapsed against him, her head pressed against his, her soft, ragged breath caressing him. Roan was glad for the experience he had, so he could lead Inca to the precipice of desire. When the right moment came, she would gladly step off the ledge with him, he had no doubt. Gathering her into his arms, he moved to a grassy hummock, a few feet away from the tree and sat down, leaning his back against the firm, sloping earth. He smiled darkly up at Inca as he guided her so that she straddled him with her long, curved thighs. His hands settled on her hips and he gently positioned her above his hard, throbbing flesh.

Inca's eyes widened as she opened her legs to move across him. Never had she been close to a man like this! But she trusted Roan. Besides, her mind was so much mush that she could no longer think coherently. He lifted her into place, and her hands came to rest on his thick, massive shoulders. And as he slowly lowered her against his hard, warm length, she gasped, but it was a cry of utter surprise and growing pleasure. Her own feminine dampness connected and slid provocatively against him.

She heard and felt him groan, as if a drum thrummed deeply in his body. A tremble went through him as if a bolt of lightning had connected them invisibly to one another.

The utter pleasure of sliding against him, the delightful heat purling between her legs made her shudder and grip him more surely with her thighs. What wonderful sensations! Inca wanted more and she wasn't disappointed. As if sensing her needs, Roan tightened his grip around her hips and dragged her forward across his rigid, pressing form. A little cry escaped her. More sensations shot jaggedly up through her boiling, womanly core as he slid partially into her throbbing confines. Her belly felt like a bed of burning, glowing coals. Her hands moved spasmodically against his chest. Her breath was coming in gasps.

Lost in the building heat as he moved her slowly back and forth against him, Inca felt him tremble each time. There was something timeless, something rhythmic and wild about this, and she wanted more, much more. Leaning forward, she brushed her breasts against his chest. Capturing his mouth, she kissed him with fierce abandon. He gently teethed her lower lip in the exchange, and she felt him lift and reposition her slightly. The sensation of something hot, hard and large pressed more deeply into her feminine core. The pressure remained, and heat swirled deeply within her and between her tensed thighs.

Gasping, Inca pressed downward and drew him more deeply into herself. Instantly, she heard Roan growl. Oh, yes, she recognized that growl. She'd heard it many times when two jaguars were in the throes of mating. He felt large and throbbing as she eased herself fully down upon him. The pleasure doubled. Then tripled as she slowly sat up, her hands tentatively resting against his hard abdomen. He was guiding her, monitoring her exploratory movements. Eyes closed, Inca marveled at all the exploding feelings, the wildness pumping through her bloodstream, and her heart pounded with a fierce, singular love for the man with whom she was coupling—for the first time in her life.

Moving her hips, she moaned and eased forward, then back. The oldest rhythm in the world took over within her. She was moving with the waves that pummeled the shore of her being, a movement so pure and necessary to life that she gripped his arms and pushed more deeply against him. Again he groaned. His body was tense, like a bow drawn too tightly. She could hear him breathing raggedly. His hands were tight around her hips, guiding her, helping her to establish that harmony, that wild rhythm between them.

Somewhere deep within Inca, something primal exploded. The savagery, the vibrant, throbbing pleasure, rolled scaldingly through her. She gripped Roan hard with her thighs and pushed rhythmically against him. The moment he lifted his hips to meet and match her hot, liquid stride, another powerful explosion rocked her, catching her off guard and tearing her breath from her lungs. For a long, amazing moment Inca sat frozen upon him, her hands lifting, her fingers flexing in a pleasure she had never before experienced. She could not move, the shower of hot ecstasy was so intense within her. When Roan eased her forward, the sensation was intensified tenfold. Inca threw her head back as a growl, as deep as her unfettered spirit, rolled up and out of her parted lips.

Roan could no longer control himself. As Inca moved wildly against him, lost in the throes of pleasure pulsing through her slender, damp form, he found his own pleasure explode in turn. Thrusting his hips upward, Roan took her deeply and continuously. White-hot heat mushroomed within him, and he groaned raggedly. He gripped her hips. Tensing, he felt himself spilling into her sacred confines.

Unable to move after the intensity of his release, he lay there panting for endless moments, his eyes open barely. Instinctively, Inca moved her hips in order to prolong the incredible sensations for him. A fierce love for her overtook him, and Roan lifted his hands and placed them on her shoulders.

Drawing her down upon him, their bodies slick against one another, Roan eased Inca off him and to his side. The grass welcomed them, cool against their hot flesh as he slid one arm beneath her neck and rolled her to her back. Pushing up on one elbow, he raised himself above her, their body's touching from hip to feet. Beads of sweat trickled down the sides of his face. His heart was beating erratically in his chest as he smoothed several dark, damp strands from her brow and temple. Inca's mouth was soft and parted, her lips well kissed and her eyes closed. Breathing raggedly, Roan studied her intently. It had been wonderful for both of them and he was thankful.

Her hands were still restless, wanting to touch him, feel him and absorb him. Her flesh was like a hot iron against him as her fingers tunneled through the damp hair on his chest. Inca dragged open her eyes. Her body vibrated with such joy and pleasure that she could only stare up through her lashes at Roan in wonder. His mouth was crooked with pride. She could feel his pleasure, his love for her and she sighed, then gulped to try and steady her breathing.

"I—I never knew...never imagined it felt like *this!* Why did we wait so long if it felt like this?"

Leaning over, Roan slid his mouth against her lips. She was soft and available. Although he knew the warrior side of her was still within her, he was privileged to meet, love and hold the woman within her, too. Lifting his mouth from her wet lips, he rasped, "There's a time for all things, sweet woman of mine. And it will get better every time we do it."

Gasping, Inca whispered, "I do not know how I can stand it, then." She slid her fingers across his damp face and into his thick black hair. "I feel like I am floating! As if the storm gods have come into my body." She gestured to her belly. "I still feel small lightning bolts of pleasure within me, even now. This is wonderful to share with you."

"Good," Roan whispered raggedly. Lying down, he drew Inca against him once more. She rested her head wearily in the crook of his shoulder, her arm languidly draped across his chest. The warmth of the day, the slight breeze, all conspired to slowly cool them off. Closing his eyes, Roan murmured, "I love you, Inca. I will until the day I die, and after that...."

Touched, Inca tightened her arm around his chest. Lying next to Roan was the most natural place in the world for her to be. "Our love created this," she whispered unsteadily. "How I feel now, in my heart, is because of you—your patience and understanding of me." She lifted her head and gazed deeply into his half-opened eyes.

There was such peace in Roan's features now. Gone was that tension she'd always seen around his mouth. "I understand what love is, at last. You have shown me the way."

As her fingertips trailed across his lower lip, he smiled lazily up at her. Her hair was slightly disheveled, a beautiful ebony frame around her flushed face and widening, beautiful eyes. There was such awe and love shining in her gaze. It made him feel good and strong in ways he'd never felt before.

"Love is a two-way street, sweetheart. It takes two to make it work. We love one another and so the rest of easy." He trailed his fingers across the high slope of her cheek. "And best of all, you're going to be my partner, my wife. It doesn't get any better than that...."

Inca nodded and playfully leaned over and gave him a swift kiss, feeling bold and more confident about herself as a woman. "I never thought I would have anyone, Roan. I thought I was born into this life alone, and that I would die alone."

"No," he said thickly, catching her hand and placing a kiss into her palm, "you changed that, remember? You made a mistake, but you proved to everyone after making it that you were cut from a piece of good cloth. You worked long, hard years alone, to show the elders you were worthy of reconsideration." Using his tongue, he traced a slow, wet circle across her open palm. She moaned and shut her eyes for an instant. How easy it was going to be to give Inca all the pleasure he knew how to share with her. She was wide-open and vulnerable to him. She'd given the gift of herself to him, her innocence, and he cherished her for that. He hoped he would never hurt her in the coming weeks or months—that he would always honor the sacredness of the wild, primal woman she was.

"My jaguar woman," he teased gently. "I just hope I can keep up with you." As he moved his hand across her left shoulder, he felt the small crescent of jaguar fur that would always remind him she was uniquely different from most human beings. But that didn't mean she wasn't human, because she was.

Laughing delightedly, Inca said, "You are of the Cougar Clan! Why should you not be my equal? The cougar is the symbol of the north, just as the jaguar is of the south. One is not stronger or better than the other."

Roan sat up and took Inca into his arms. It felt damned good to be naked against one another. She threw her arms around his neck and kissed him spontaneously on the cheek.

"Let us go to the Pool of Life," she whispered excitedly. "I will wash you, my beloved. And you will wash me."

Grinning, Roan said, "I like your take-charge attitude, Inca." He helped her to her feet and then holding her hand, gathered up her clothes and his.

"Let's go, sweetheart."

Inca was standing beneath a rubber tree near their hut, at the round table where they took their meals, when she felt a disturbance in the energy around her. She was preparing lunch for her and Roan when it happened. Roan was out in the field with the rest of the men, tending their large, beautiful vegetable gardens beyond the meadow in the distance. Soon he would arrive, and she wanted to have a meal prepared for him.

Looking around, she saw that other inhabitants of the village were going about their noontime business. Shaking her head, she wondered what she'd felt. It was vaguely familiar, but nothing she could put her finger on right away. Sunlight glanced off the peridot ring on her left hand. Holding it up, she smiled happily. How had three months flown by? Grandmother Alaria had married them shortly after they had loved one another in that wonderful, private glade near the Pool of Life. Inca had never known what happiness was until now. She had been slogging through life alone, and suddenly life had taken on wonderful shades and hues of joy—ever since Roan entered her world. Yes, love made the difference. That and the fact she had family now.

Placing bowls on the table, Inca straightened. Maya, her sister…she had seen her only four times in the last three months, and only for an hour or two at the most. Maya was busier than Inca was. Yet they utilized every scrap of every moment to talk, share and search one another's separate lives, to understand how life had shaped them and made them into what they were today.

Inca always marveled at how alike they were. It was a joy to connect telepathically with her sister, to share, openly all her emotions with Maya. To have a sister was as great a gift as having Roan as her husband. And after talking it over with Roan, she had gifted Maya with the medicine necklace that Roan had bestowed on her. Somehow, Inca knew that the blue stone in the center of it was a great protection. How or why, she couldn't explain, but that didn't matter.

Roan had approved of her giving Maya the very ancient and powerful amulet. And Maya had received it with tears of thanks in her eyes. She told them that, as a pilot, she wasn't supposed to wear any jewelry when flying her daily, dangerous missions against the drug runners. Maya had tucked it gently beneath her flight suit, a grin of pride playing on her wide mouth. She thanked both of them for it, for she knew it had originally come from Roan's family and that sacred articles were always passed down through family.

Yes, Inca was truly blessed. She knew now that she had been in a dark tunnel for the last twenty-five years. She was out of that tunnel now, and in the light. It felt good. Very good. And Maya was now protected with the mysterious necklace that held that incredible blue, opalescent stone. That made Inca sleep better at night, knowing that the stone's amazing powers were supporting her sister's best interests.

"How are you today, child?"

Inca turned and saw Grandmother Alaria moving slowly toward her. She wore her hair in thick braids, her shift a dark pink color and her feet bare and thick with calluses. The gentle smile on her face made Inca smile in turn and eagerly pull out one of the rough-hewn stools for the old woman to sit upon.

"I have coffee perking. Would you like some, Grandmother?"

Sighing, Alaria nodded. "Yes, that sounds perfect, thank you." Settling down carefully on the stool beneath the shade of the rubber tree, Alaria painstakingly arranged the shift over her crossed legs. "The day is beautiful," she mused as Inca handed her a mug with steaming black coffee in it. "Thank you, child. Come, sit down near me."

Inca sensed the change in the air. Over the months, as she'd gone into training with her, she knew when Alaria had something of importance to say to her. Taking the other stool, she sat opposite her. Today she wore a sleeveless, white cotton tunic and dark red slacks that barely reached her slender ankles.

"Something is going on, is it not?" Inca asked.

Alaria sipped the coffee. "Yes. I have asked Roan to come in early from the fields. He'll be here shortly."

Frowning, Inca sensed that all was not well. She knew better than to ask, because if she was to know, Grandmother Alaria would tell her at the appropriate time.

"Did you sense a shift in the force field around the village?"

Raising her brows, Inca said, "Was that what it was? I sensed something but I could not identify it directly."

"Your sister just landed her helicopter outside the village. That is what you felt."

Gasping with joy, Inca said, "Oh! Maya's coming?"

Smiling, Alaria said, "Yes, and she's bringing Michael Houston with her."

"Really?" Inca clapped her hands in joy. She shot off the stool and craned her neck to look down the path toward where the clouds met the earth. That was one of two entrances in and out of the highly protected village. She saw no one—yet.

"Yes, you will have much of your family here in a few minutes," Alaria told her with a soft smile.

Unable to sit in her excitement, Inca saw Roan coming across the meadow. He had a rake propped on his shoulder as he walked in sure, steady strides toward the village center.

Joy thrummed briefly through Inca. She stopped her restless pacing and looked down at the elder, who sipped her coffee with obvious relish. "This is unusual, for Michael to be here, yes?"

"Yes."

"Are Ann and the baby coming, also?"

Alaria shook her head. "No, my child. I'm afraid this is a business visit."

A warning flickered though Inca's gut. She halted and scowled. Placing her hand against her stomach, where she felt the fear, she whispered, "Business?"

Setting the coffee on the table, Alaria nodded. "I'm afraid so."

Inca's heart pounded briefly with dread. She didn't want her perfect world shattered. She knew it was a childish reaction and not mature at all. Still, her love with Roan was so new, so wonderful and expanding, that she wanted nothing to taint what they had. Knowing that the grandmother could easily read her thoughts and emotions, Inca glumly sat down, all her joy snuffed out like a candle in a brisk breeze.

"I feel fear."

Reaching out, Alaria patted Inca's sloped shoulder. "Take courage, my child. You are of the Jaguar Clan. We face and work through our fears—together."

Just as Roan put his rake up against the hut and arrived at the table, Inca saw Maya and Mike Houston appear out of the gauzy, white cloud wall and walk toward them. Inca gave Roan a quick hug of hello, turned on her heel and ran through the center of the village toward them, her arms open, her hair flying behind her like a banner.

Roan chuckled, poured himself some coffee and sat down next to Alaria. "Looks like family week around here for Inca."

"It is," Alaria said, returning his smile and greeting.

Resting his elbows on the table, Roan watched with undisguised pleasure as Inca threw her arms first around her sister, who was dressed in her black flight suit, and then Mike Houston, giving him a puppylike smooch on his cheek. Then, nestled between the two, she slid her arms around their waists and walked with them. Roan couldn't hear their animated words, but the laughter and joking among the three of them made him grin. He was so happy for Inca. She had family now. People who loved her, who wanted her in their lives. He shifted a glance to Alaria, who was also watching them, with kindness in her eyes.

"She deserves this," he told the old woman in a low tone.

"Yes, she does, my son."

"All I want to do is keep that smile on her face, Grandmother. Inca's been deprived of so much for so long."

Patting his sun-darkened hand, Alaria said, "All you need do is continue to love her and allow her to grow into all of what she can become. I will warn you that Maya and Mike coming today is not good news. Inca will be distraught."

"Forewarned is forearmed. I'll take care of her afterward." Roan was grateful for the warning. At least he could hold Inca, console her, and be there for her. It was more than she'd had before, and Roan wanted to serve in that capacity. Being married meant being many things, wearing different hats at different times for his partner, and it was something he could do well. The years he'd spent with Sarah had prepared him for Inca. And he was grateful.

After everyone had shaken hands or embraced, they sat around the table. Coffee was poured and Inca brought out a dish of fresh fruit and cheese, plus a warm loaf of wheat bread and butter. Then she sat close to Roan, anxiety written in her features. Maya sat across from her. She'd placed her helmet on the table and thrown her black gloves into it. Her hair, as usual, was drawn back into a chignon at the base of her neck. Mike Houston was in military fatigues, his face grave. Inca threaded her fingers under the table nervously.

Alaria spoke quietly. "Inca, your sister is going to be working directly with Michael for the government of Peru. As you know, Maya and her band of pilots and mechanics have hidden bases in every country here in South America. When we want them to lend their considerable support in a situation, they fly in and help. Maya's main staging area is a Black Jaguar base near the Machu Pichu reserve in Peru. The Peruvian government has requested aid from Morgan Trayhern, and he's asked Michael to coordinate a plan to do so. Michael has spent most of his life in Peru, and he knows the land and its people well."

Inca nodded. She felt her mouth going dry. "This has to do with the death spiral dance between Maya and Faro Valentino, does it not?" The words came out low, filled with concern and trepidation. Seeing her sister's green eyes narrow slightly, Inca glanced back at Grandmother Alaria, for she was the authority at the table.

"It does, my child."

Inca's heart dropped, then froze with fear. She stared at Maya, who sat looking completely unconcerned about it all. Oh, perhaps there was a time in Inca's past that she'd behaved similarly, but not now. Not in the last three months. Compressing her lips, she struggled to keep quiet and let the elder do the talking. It was so hard, because Inca's love for Maya was just taking root. She'd just met her. They'd had so little time together. Inca acknowledged her selfishness, but still she wanted more. Much more. And a death spiral dance meant that only one of the two people involved would come out alive—with luck. Too many times, Inca had seen both people die as they circled one another like wary jaguars fighting over turf and territory. Fights to the death in the spiral dance were common—the death of both protagonists.

Dipping her head, Inca shut her eyes tightly, the tears feeling hot behind her lids. "I—I see...." The words came out brokenly. When Roan's hand moved gently across her drooping shoulders, Inca felt his concern and love. It stopped some of the fierce anguish and pain from assaulting her wide-open heart.

"Inca," Maya pleaded gently, "don't worry so much about me. This isn't any different from what I do out there every day. I'm always in the line of fire. And I *want* to take down Faro Valentino, more than anything."

Inca lifted her head and opened her eyes. She saw the fury burning in Maya's narrowed gaze. "I do not want you in a death spiral dance on my behalf, Maya. I want you alive. I—need you...."

Reaching across the table, Maya gripped Inca's proffered hand. "Silly goose. You have me. Don't worry, okay? I've been around this block many, many times. Mike will tell you that.''

Mike leaned forward, his voice low and cajoling. ''Inca, I've worked off and on with Maya for years. Now, I didn't know who she was, or what her relationship was to you. We called those black helicopters the 'ghosts of the rain forest.' Sometimes, during a hot firefight, when I and my men were tangling with drug runners or a drug lord, she and her colleagues would show up out of the blue. Many times, they made the difference between us living or dying, the battle moving in our favor and not the enemies. I never got to meet Maya personally to thank her. I had no idea it was a woman-run operation, or that they were part of the Black Jaguar Clan. Not until recently.''

Inca saw the challenging sparkle in Maya's eyes as she released her hand and straightened up. There was no doubt that Maya was a leader in every sense of the word. It was clear in her defiant and confident expression; in the way she walked with military precision, her shoulders thrown back; in that sense of absolute power and authority exuding from her.

''Inca,'' Maya pleaded, ''we have a chance to not only get Faro, but close down his main factories in Peru in this sweep. Mike is going to coordinate the whole thing from Lima. He'll be buying us new Boeing D model Apaches to compete with Valentino's Kamov gunships. He's our contact. Morgan Trayhern is assigning people from Fort Rucker, Alabama—Apache helicopter instructors—to teach us the characteristics of the D model. I haven't met them yet, but Mike says Morgan is borrowing the best instructors from the U.S. Army, and they're considered the cream of the crop. The best! So you see, you have nothing to worry about. I'm in the best of hands.'' She flashed a triumphant grin.

Alaria looked from one sister to the other. ''Inca can feel many possible outcomes of this death spiral dance,'' she stated quietly.

Maya lost her smile. ''I'm prepared to die, little sister, if that's what it takes.'' Shrugging, she said, ''I was born to die. We all were. My life is lived in the now, the present. That is how the Jaguar Clan operates, as you know.'' And then she eased the blue medicine piece from the neck of her flight suit. ''See? I wear it twenty-four hours a day. It keeps me safe.''

Nodding, Inca whispered brokenly, ''Yes, yes, I know all that.'' She lifted her hand, searching Maya's grave features. ''Suddenly, taking revenge on Faro does not feel right to me. Not if it puts you at risk, Maya.'' She looked pleadingly at Alaria. ''Must the Jaguar Clan always even each score against it? Is there not another, better way?''

''My child, each member of the clan must walk through this lesson. Yes, it is much better not to seek revenge for hurt against one you love. Each of us learns this truth individually, however. One day, you and Maya will come to realize that surrendering over the hurt to a higher authority is better than trying to settle the score directly. Inca, you are at that place where you can see and understand this. Maya is not.'' Alaria held up her hands. ''You can't stop Maya. Nor should you. I suggest you pray daily for her, for her life. That is all you can do. Just because you love someone does not mean that love protects them always.''

Roan slid his arm around Inca. He could feel her tensing up with fear and anxiety, see it written clearly across her face. He wished he had the words to soothe her, to quell her anxiety, but he didn't.

Mike sighed and gave Inca a half smile. "Listen to me. Maya is in the best of hands. These army instructors will be the best— They will be there to make the difference, to give her and her squadron even more of an edge. We've got some incredible technology for the gunship she flies. That will help her in finding and locating the drug runners and their facilities in northern Peru. So stop worrying so much."

"Are these other instructors members of the Jaguar Clan?"

Maya shook her head. "No…they don't know a thing about us, our skills and other talents. They're walking into this cold. I don't intend for them to know about our closet abilities, either." She flexed her hands. "Besides, compared to you, I'm nothing. The only thing I can do is teleport when I'm in a good mood." Maya grinned. "You, on the other hand, can heal, teleport, read minds…the list goes on. I'm blind, deaf and dumb compared to you." She laughed good-naturedly and reached over and gripped her sister's hand again. "Whoever these pilot instructors are, I'm not about to tell them about us, either. So far as they know, we're a spook ops comprised of women pilots who are crazy enough to fly the best damned helicopter gunships in the world where they aren't supposed to be able to go."

Inca nodded. "I see.…"

"Anyway," Maya said with a quick grin, "I'm starving to death! Inca, I'm gonna help myself to this bread you just made." And she reached for a thick slice of it. Rising from the stool, she grabbed a knife. "Mind if I dig in?"

Everyone chuckled.

"Just like a black jaguar," Mike intoned, trying not to smile. "Take no prisoners..."

Alaria cackled. "Black jaguars aren't known for their diplomacy or subtleties. Did you notice?"

Inca snapped out of her self-pity. She should savor the time she had with her family, not wallow in worry over their unknown futures. Live today for today. Expect nothing; receive everything. Those were Jaguar Clan Maxims. Well, she had to continue to learn how to do that. Rising, she reached out and gripped her sister's arm.

"Manners, please. Sit down. I will serve all of you."

Mike chuckled. He pulled a wrapped gift out of a duffel bag he'd brought with him. "Hey, Inca, this is for you—from Ann, the baby and me."

How quickly the energy shifted, Roan thought as he saw Inca rally. She snapped out of her funk and her expression brightened. How much he loved her. She was at such a precarious point in her growth. Finding her sister, being allowed back into the clan and getting married all in three months was asking a lot of anyone. But especially someone with her background.

"What is it?" Inca gasped, as she reached out for the bright red foil wrapped gift topped with a yellow ribbon.

"Open it," Mike said with a laugh. "You'll see...."

Like a child, she eagerly pulled the paper from around it. "Oh! Smoked salmon!"

Pleased, Mike winked at Roan. "In case you don't know, she's a real jaguar when it comes to fish."

Roan grinned. "Jaguars eat fish. At least, that's what she told me."

"Humph," Maya growled, sinking her teeth into the

warm, buttered bread, "they'll eat *anything* that isn't moving."

"And even if it is moving, we'll freeze it, jump it and make it our own," Mike added, grinning broadly. Jaguars killed their quarry by freezing its movement. What few knew outside of those in metaphysics was that the jaguar pulled the spirit out of the body of its victim. Without the spirit, the victim cannot move.

Again, laughter filled the air. Roan watched as Inca quickly opened up the package and placed the salmon on the table so that everyone could partake. A fierce appreciation of her natural generosity rolled through him. He saw Inca trying to release her fear about Maya's coming mission. As always, she was putting others ahead of herself.

Rising, Alaria bestowed a warm smile upon them all. "Enjoy your lunch together, my children. I've already eaten and I'm being called to a counsel meeting. Blessings upon you…" And she turned and slowly walked away.

Mike dug into his bag again. "Hey, I brought something else for us, too." He grinned and lifted a bottle of champagne up for all to see.

Maya clapped her hands. "Yes! Perfect! What else have you got in that bag of tricks of yours, Houston?"

"Oh," he crowed coyly, "some other things." And he shifted the bag to the other side of his stool, out of Maya's reach—just in case.

Laughing, Inca quickly set wooden plates on the table and passed around the large platter of fresh fruit. Roan got up and handed everyone a mug so that the champagne could be uncorked and passed around. He then went to work on slicing the cheese.

Maya took the dark green bottle and, with her thumbs, popped the cork. It made a loud sound. The cork went sailing past Roan, struck the wall of the hut and bounced harmlessly to the ground. "One of the few times I've missed my intended target!" she exclaimed.

"You have to do better than that," Roan told her dryly. "I duck fast."

Laughing deeply, Maya stood and poured champagne into each cup. As Inca placed the sliced cheese on a large plate, she passed the first cup to her.

"Here, little sister, taste this stuff. You're gonna like it. You're a greenhorn when it comes to modern society, and this is one of the nice things about it. Go on, try it."

Sniffing the champagne cautiously, Inca sat down next to Roan. As the others began to reach for the sliced bread, fruit and cheese, she pulled her cup away and rubbed her nose. "It tickles!"

"You've been out in the bush too long," Maya said with a giggle. "That's champagne. It's supposed to bubble and fizz. Here, lift your mug in a toast with us." Maya raised her mug over the center of the small, circular table. "Here's to my sister, Inca, who I'm proud as hell of. For her guts, her moxie and never giving up—this toast is to her!"

Everyone shouted and raised their mugs. Inca hesitantly lifted hers. "This is a strange custom, Sister."

Roaring with laughter, Maya said, "Just wait. You've been sequestered in a rain forest all your life. I wasn't. So, each time I visit you, from now on, I'm gonna share a little of my partying lifestyle with you."

Inca watched as everyone grinned and took a drink of

the champagne. Unsure, she sniffed it again. Lifting the mug to her lips, she tasted it. "Ugh!"

Roan smiled when Inca's upper lip curled in distaste. Brushing her cheek with a finger, he said, "Champagne is an acquired taste. The more you drink it, the more you like it over time."

"I do not think so." Inca frowned and set the mug on the table.

Giggling, Maya said, "Jungle girl! You've been too long out in the boonies, Inca. Come on, take another little sip. It will taste better the second time around. Go ahead...."

Giving Maya a dark, distrustful look, Inca did as she was bid. To her surprise, Maya was right. Staring down at the mug, Inca muttered, "It tastes sweeter this time...."

"Yep. After a couple more sips, you'll see why we like it so much." Maya reached for the champagne bottle, which sat in the middle of the table. "Come on, Houston, drink up. I'm not polishing this bottle off by myself." She wiggled her eyebrows comically. "Of course, I *have* been known to do that—but not this time."

Inca sat back and laughed, the mug between her hands. She couldn't believe that Maya could drink a whole bottle by herself! Her sister was so funny, so playful and joking compared to her. Inca looked forward to Maya's visits so she could absorb every tiny detail of her sister's life. Compared to her, Inca felt as though she had been raised in a bubble.

Inca shared a loving look with Roan. Warming beneath his tender gaze, she felt a lot of her worry dissolving. Maya was a woman of the world. She knew and understood life outside the rain forest and how it worked, while

Inca did not. Perhaps Maya *would* be safe. Inca prayed that would be true. With Michael working with her sister, Inca felt some assurance of that. However, she also knew that no Jaguar Clan member was impervious to death. They died just as quickly and easily as any other human being if the circumstances were right. She knew that from her own dire experience.

Epilogue

Inca sighed, nestling deeply into Roan's arms. They had just settled down for the night in their own hut, which to her delight was situated near the bubbling creek. Inhaling Roan's scent, she gloried in it as she moved her fingers languidly across his chest. Feeling his arms clasp her in a tender embrace, she closed her eyes.

"Each day, I become more happy," she confessed.

Smiling in the darkness, his eyes shut, Roan savored Inca's warm naked body pressed against his. He lay on his back, the pallet soft and comfortable beneath them. A cool breeze moved through the windows and brought down the temperature to a pleasant range for sleeping.

"I never thought I would have the kind of happiness I have now," he murmured near her ear. Sliding a strand of her soft, recently washed hair through his fingers, he pressed a kiss to the silky mass.

Snuggling more deeply into his arms, Inca lay there a

long time, her eyes partly open, just staring into the darkness.

"What is it?" Roan asked as he trailed his hand across her shoulder. "You're worrying. About Maya? Her mission?"

"I cannot keep my thoughts from you, can I?"

Chuckling indulgently, Roan said, "No."

"I am glad you allowed me to give her the necklace you gifted me with. Did you see Maya's eyes light up when she saw that blue stone?"

"Mmm, yes I did. She seemed to know a lot about that rock. One day, when the time's right, maybe she'll tell us about it. At least we know it comes from one seam in a copper mine north of Lima."

"And she held it as if it were precious beyond life."

Nodding, Roan continued to move his fingers down the supple curve of Inca's spine. Gradually, he felt the fine tension in her body dissolving beneath his touch. Love could do that. And he loved her with a fierceness and passion he'd never known before. "That stone has been passed down through my family for untold generations. My mother gave it to me after my vision quest at age fourteen—at the ceremony when I turned into a man. She told me then that it came from the south. I thought she might have meant the southwest—perhaps Arizona or New Mexico. Now I realize she meant South America, and specifically, Peru. It's had an amazing journey, and now it seems like it's come home to where it started so long ago."

Sliding her hand across his massive chest, Inca absorbed his warmth and strength. How wonderful it felt to be able to touch him whenever she pleased. It was a heady gift. "Maya said there is only one mine in the world that has a seam of this stone. It is so rare. She said men kill to steal it from miners who look for it."

"Yes, and that it possesses certain powers." He smiled a little. "I'd sure like to know more about what they are."

"I think Maya knows, but sometimes, because we are in the clan, information is given only when it is appropriate. Otherwise, we are not told."

Roan nodded and quirked the corner of his mouth. "Still, I'm curious. I'm beginning to think that maybe one of my ancestors was South American, but I have no way to prove it. Our people pass on traditions verbally, so nothing's written on paper to verify it one way or another."

Pressing a kiss against the thick column of his neck, Inca murmured, "I believe you are right. Why else would you have come back? Our spiritual path always makes a circle of completion. Perhaps one of your ancestors walked north and met and fell in love with one of your Lakota relatives, and remained and lived there. That would explain your twin path between the two Americas, yes?"

It made a lot of sense to Roan. "I like the idea of living in the Amazon basin with you and helping the Indian people to keep their land as the hordes flee the cities of Brazil. I'm looking forward to making a life for us there."

"I am content that our people are safe without us being there."

Roan knew Inca had worried about that. She was driven and responsible in the care and protection of the Indians in Amazonia. Maya's reassurances that they had reduced the number of cocaine-producing factories and, therefore, the ability of drug lords to enslave the Indians, lessened her anxiety about it.

"I want to use this next nine months here in the village as a well-deserved rest for you," Roan said, turning onto his side and pressing her gently against him. He felt Inca make that deep-throated purr that moved through him like promising, provocative fingers of heat. "See this as a vacation."

Laughing throatily, Inca eased back and looked up into his dark, carved features. She melted beneath his smoldering blue eyes, which regarded her through dark, spiky lashes. Mouth drawing upward, she whispered, "We are here for training. And the elders are pleased with your progress."

"I think they're pleased with both of us," he said, tracing the outline of her broad, smooth forehead with his fingertips. "And I also think they're very glad you're back home here, with them. You're a powerful person, Inca. They need warriors with hearts like yours. People like you don't grow on trees, and they know that. Best of all, Grandfather Adaire has made amends to you. He's no longer the enemy you thought he was, and I'm glad to see that rift between you healed."

She nodded, her eyes softening. "He has always been the father I did not have, and now he is that again for me." Inca caught Roan's hand and placed a soft, searching kiss into his palm. She felt him tense. Lifting her head, she said, "In our business, there are not always happy endings, Roan. I was glad to hear of Julian, and his father, Colonel Marcellino, from Michael."

"Yes," Roan murmured, "the colonel embraced Julian and finally came to realize that his second son is just as worthy of all the praise and attention his first son had received. I'm sure it's made a difference in their family dynamic.''

"So perhaps getting bitten by the bushmaster was a good thing." Inca sighed. "So often I see bad things happen to good people. At the time, I know they think they are being cursed, but it is often a blessing. They just do not realize it yet.''

"No argument there," Roan said as he leaned down and nibbled on her bare shoulder. She tasted clean, of mango soap with a glycerin base that someone in the village had made days earlier. "I had a lot of bad things happen to me, and look now. Look who is in my arms and who loves me, warts and all." And he chuckled.

Laughter filled the hut, then Inca said petulantly, "You are not a frog! You have no warts, my husband.''

"It's slang," he assured her, grinning at her impertinence. "In time, I'll have you talking just like Maya does.''

"Humph. Maya was educated in North America. She picked up all those funny words and sayings there. Many times, I do not understand what she talks about.''

"Slang is a language of its own," he agreed, absorbing Inca's pensive features. Her eyes were half closed, shining with love—for him. "But next time Maya visits us, you'll be able to understand her better. I'll teach you American slang.''

"Good, because half of what she says, I do not grasp.''

"Like?''

"Well," Inca said, frustrated, "words such as *fire bird.*''

"That's slang for an Apache helicopter gunship.

They're called fire birds because of all the firepower they pack on board. They've got rockets, machine guns and look-down, shoot-down capabilities. A fire bird is one awesome piece of machinery. And in the right hands, it's a deadly adversary.''

"Oh. I thought she meant a bird that had caught its tail on fire.''

Roan swallowed a chuckle. "What other slang?''

Rolling her eyes toward the darkened ceiling, she thought. The chirping of crickets and croaking of frogs was a musical chorus against the gurgling creek. "Herks.''

"That's a C-130 Hercules—a cargo plane. I think she's referring to the Herks that provide her helicopters with fuel in midair. The Apache can be refueled in flight to extend its range of operation. The Herk carries aviation fuel in special bladders within the cargo bay.'' He lifted his hand above her to illustrate his point. "The Herk plays out a long fuel line from its fuselage, like a rope, and the helicopter has a long, extended pipe on its nose. There's a cone at the end of the fuel line, and when the helo connects with that, gas is pumped on board, so the helo can continue to fly and do surveillance to find the bad guys.''

"I see....'' Inca sighed. "Her world is so different from mine. She was adopted and taken north and educated there. She is a pilot. She flies like a bird.'' Inca shook her head. "I am on the ground, like a four-legged, and she is the winged one.''

"Both of you carry very heavy responsibilities in the jobs you've agreed to take on,'' Roan reminded her. "Maya's role might appear more glamorous to outsiders, but the ground pounder—the person in the trenches, doing what you do every day—is of equal importance. Winning sky battles is only part of it. If people such as yourself were not on the ground doing the rest of the work, the air war would be futile.''

''She has told me of the sky fights she's had with drug lords. She said they have helicopters that can shoot her out of the air.'' Inca frowned up at him. ''Is this so?''

Groaning, Roan gathered her up and held her tightly to him. ''My little worrywart,'' he murmured, pressing small kisses against her wrinkled brow. ''Over the next few months, I'll try to outline what Maya does for a living. Mike Houston told me a lot about her background and education. I think once you know and understand more about her, you'll stop worrying so much. Maya is considered the best Apache helicopter pilot in this hemisphere. That's why the army is sending their best instructor pilots here. The army's hoping to map out a long-term strategy to eradicate drug lords from the highland villages, destroy all the little, hidden airports so that they can't ship their drugs out so easily. Maya's been trained for this, Inca. She's just as good at what she does as you are.''

Satisfied, Inca sighed and surrendered to the warmth and strength of his arms. Lifting her hand, she looked at the two rings glittering on her finger. One of the gifts Michael had brought with him in that sack of his was a plain gold wedding band. Unknown to her, Roan had asked the major to furnish him with one to compliment her peridot engagement ring. Roan had given her the second ring when they were alone in their hut that very evening. Its beauty and symbolism touched her heart and soul deeply.

"I love you, man of my heart...." she said softly near his ear.

Roan smiled tenderly and stroked her hair. "And I'll love you forever, Inca. Forever..."

* * * * *

Do you enjoy fast-paced, romantic, high-octane stories? Want to know where you're guaranteed four riveting and unpredictable reads every month?

Check out Silhouette Bombshell, the women's romantic suspense line series in which strong, sexy, savvy women save the day and get their men—good and bad!

Turn the page for a sneak peek of this upcoming Silhouette Bombshell release.

FLASHBACK
by Justine Davis

Available April 2006 at your favorite retail outlet.

"Ready for your car?" The young, red-jacketed valet was earnest and exceedingly polite, managing not to laugh at Alexandra Forsythe in a floor-length gown with bare toes sticking out and a pair of spike-heeled shoes in her hand.

She smiled at him for that. He blushed.

"Yes, thank you," she told him.

"I'll be right back, Ms. Forsythe."

He was good, too, she thought, if he remembered her name out of the hundred or so people there.

He was also, she thought after several minutes, incredibly slow. The parking lot wasn't that big, even if you included the overflow lot down the hill a few yards. Yet she hadn't even heard—

Ah, she thought as she heard an engine start from the back of the lot, there it is.

Her mood changed yet again as she heard the squeal of tires.

Leave ten thousand miles of wear on the asphalt, why don't you? she muttered inwardly.

She saw the top of her small SUV over the roofs of the shorter cars in the lot as it careened her way. And there was literally no other way to describe the racing, skidding approach. The valet nearly clipped the corner of the big limo parked at the closest end of the row.

Her annoyance grew.

He'd seemed nice, she thought, but this was ridiculous.

He made the last turn and headed toward her, still speeding.

She noticed three things at once.

The driver no longer had on the red jacket.

He was accelerating.

Right toward her.

No time to think. Her car leaped up over the curb, came after her like a hungry tiger. The driver seemed to realize he was in trouble and tried to swerve. She knew there wasn't enough room.

Alex dove to the right—behind the concrete pillar that held up the portico. Rolled. Prayed it would hold. Not sure it could.

A split second later, her car plowed into the pillar.

The pillar held.

It cracked. Leaned. Chunks fell. But it held.

Alex rolled to her feet, heedless of the damage already done to her hideously expensive dress. Her ears were ringing from the explosive grinding sound of the impact. Despite that, she heard a faint tinkling sound and realized it was bits of glass falling from the shattered windshield.

Something had clipped her left arm. She felt the sting and the wetness of blood. Instinctively she flexed it, assessed. Not impaired, she quickly decided.

She couldn't see into the crumpled car from where she was, but she could see movement in the driver's seat. He was alive.

She stepped toward the car, ignoring the stabs at the soles of her bare feet as she encountered debris from the wreckage.

The driver trying to extricate himself wasn't the parking valet, but she'd expected that. She hoped the young man was still alive.

As the car thief twisted to shove at something in the damaged cab, she moved swiftly. Came up behind him. Jammed the object in her hand into his back.

"Don't move. FBI."

He went still as commanded. The FBI announcement didn't surprise him, she noted. She could almost feel him assessing, and she wondered if he was trying to figure out where in the slinky dress she'd hidden the gun jammed into his back.

"Who sent you?"

"Don't know what the hell you're talking about, lady. Ouch!" This as she shoved harder into his back.

"You just totaled my car. I *liked* that car. Talk."

"No way."

He looked like a cousin to the man who'd tried to kill her in the desert, she thought. Whoever was behind trying to stop her from solving Athena Academy founder Marion Graulyn's decade-old murder should work on his hiring practices. He needed to get better quality in his workforce.

"When he hired you, didn't he give you a story to tell if you got caught?"

"Yeah, but—" He broke off, realizing he'd been suckered.

She exerted a little more pressure with her right hand, digging into his flesh. "Tell me who sent you, and I won't shoot you and pretend I had to do it to keep you from hitting me."

He swore, a string of words she hadn't heard in a while. "You won't. You can't. He told me you're a fed, you'd have to explain."

So he had known who—or at least what—she was.

"I'll lie," she said sweetly. "Not hard to do when someone's trying to kill you."

"Son of a bitch, he said you'd be easy," the man muttered. "Said you were just some lab rat."

I'm also part of Athena Force, she told him silently. *We're never easy.*

She heard the commotion behind them and knew the crash had been heard inside and they were about to draw a crowd. With a sigh she gave up the threat tactic.

"He was wrong. But then he usually is, didn't you know that?"

The man twisted his head to give her a sideways glare from muddy-brown eyes that were bloodshot. Hungover? she wondered. Or worse?

"Don't know anything abut him," he muttered. "Except he wants you dead. Bad."

"That," Alex said grimly, "I already figured out."

The crowd drawn from the party arrived, the clamor growing as they saw what had happened. Soon Alex and her would-be killer were surrounded by onlookers and, thankfully, the security guard for the club.

"Could somebody call 911?" Alex asked. Then, with some relish, she moved her right hand and stepped back, letting the driver see her "gun."

"Before my shoe goes off," she added, brandishing the spike heel in his face and grinning at the man's stupefied expression.

SURVIVAL INSTINCT

by Doranna Durgin

Former bad-girl Karin Sommers had distanced herself from her con-game past by assuming the identity of her deceased sister. But her sister had witnessed a terrible crime, and the perpetrators were dead set on covering their tracks. Soon Karin was back on the run... from someone else's past.

*Available April 2006
wherever books are sold.*